THE WARMTH OF
INDIAN
Summer

JACKIE BARNES

Copyright © 2023 Jackie Barnes.

All rights reserved. No part of this book may be reproduced, stored, or transmitted by any means—whether auditory, graphic, mechanical, or electronic—without written permission of both publisher and author, except in the case of brief excerpts used in critical articles and reviews. Unauthorized reproduction of any part of this work is illegal and is punishable by law.

ISBN: 979-8-89031-523-6 (sc)
ISBN: 979-8-89031-524-3 (hc)
ISBN: 979-8-89031-525-0 (e)

Because of the dynamic nature of the Internet, any web addresses or links contained in this book may have changed since publication and may no longer be valid. The views expressed in this work are solely those of the author and do not necessarily reflect the views of the publisher, and the publisher hereby disclaims any responsibility for them.

One Galleria Blvd., Suite 1900, Metairie, LA 70001
(504) 702-6708
1-888-421-2397

To my devoted wife, Elizabeth

CHAPTER

1

Weary from travel, Richard McCloud sat hunched on the wagon seat half asleep, mesmerized by the rhythmic beat of the horses' hooves. If his map held true they should be only a few day's journey from Courgat, Texas. Gambling against time and nature, he was pushing the team and his luck. Day after day marched treacherously on, revealing nothing of what might be waiting over the next hill, and their isolation became more threatening as they traveled through Indian Territory.

Inside the wagon Elizabeth lay huddled on her lumpy cotton mattress clutching the blanket that covered her swollen belly. Her dark eyes were vacant and staring, fixed on the canvas wagon sheet that swayed and fluttered above her head in the brisk May wind. The terrain was rocky and rough, jarring the wagon with every turn of the wheels, and she cringed silently in discomfort.

They had traveled along the banks of the Pecos River for many miles. Mac was never sure when they moved beyond the open range of Henry McCloud's ranch that extended from New Mexico into the Texas Plains.

Henry was a greedy, selfish man who owned miles of grass land, but wanted more, and provoked Indian aggression in order to clear his path. However, he had changed his tactics to a more advantageous conclusion, realizing it was to his advantage. Instead of killing the Indians and burning their villages, he used the young bucks for cheap labor. If they became hostile, he complained to the army, leaving the destructive intervention to their discretion. The soldiers had been trained to kill Indians, not negotiate with them. And so the slaughters continued as Henry McCloud's ranch expanded, moving further into the Indian hunting grounds.

The shroud of evening shadows had begun to move across the western sky when Mac pulled the team to a halt close to a shallow creek. They had traveled alone for the past three weeks, ever since they left the wagon train. Having water was comforting, but it was also a calculated risk in Indian Territory. They had followed the river all the way to the Texas border, then swung back south-east, heading for Courgat, Texas, a little town about 500 miles from Oklahoma City.

Before climbing down from the wagon seat, Mac parted the flap and looked in on Elizabeth. He found her sleeping. She had slept very little in the past few weeks and he crept about quietly.

He unhitched the horses and staked them about twenty yards from camp, enabling them to reach water and graze along the creek bank. After tending the horses he gathered small sticks and dry grass to start a fire. He struck two flints together until the sparks ignited the dry tinder. As the fire caught, smoke boiled up into his squinting eyes. He fanned it away with the brim of his hat until flames sprang up, and then added more wood. Taking a wooden bucket, he walked down the slippery creek bank for water before preparing their evening meal of bacon, coffee, and fried corn bread.

He poured himself a cup of coffee and settled back against the wagon wheel to rest his stiff neck and aching shoulders. The heat from the fire felt hot against his face, even through his heavy growth of beard. He looked skyward with a searching gaze, anxious to reach their destination before Elizabeth gave birth. All he could do was hope and pray the weather held, and the team withstood the long hard hours on the trail; more punishment than any animal should have to endure. The nights were cool, but the days were heating up, causing Elizabeth even more discomfort. Their supplies were running low, and there was little time to rest. Time was running out for Elizabeth. They were without the protection of the wagon train now, and he felt the weight of his responsibility. He had been told that the army was patrolling this section of Texas and driving the Indians further north, but that eventually they would began to drift back south in search of buffalo, which was one more reason he was pushing on to reach Courgat.

The night had become too still, too close, and his mind would give him no rest. He couldn't remember how long they had been on the trail. He had lost all track of time. Each day was just like the day before, the nights filled with bad dreams, flying insects, and fear. Stretching behind them lay miles and miles of prairie, hills, dry stream beds, and dust. Ahead was more of the same.

He had a painful vision of the last time he had seen his brother. It seemed impossible that it had been more than ten years since Ralph packed his gear and rode out, promising Mac that he would return. But for Ralph it had been a one-way trip. As for Mac, his brother's death was tearing his guts out. Ralph, twelve years his senior, had been more like a father to him. Mac would have gone with him had he been older.

"I'll come back for you, Mac," Ralph had said, "as soon as I get settled and get a hold of some money. I promise."

And Ralph had kept that promise, reaching out from the grave to free Mac from the clutches of his ruthless father, who was driven by greed and a mad determination for power. Mac's thoughts of his father were bitter.

Henry was a handsome man, tall and dark skinned, with arms and shoulders of great strength. His tongue was sharp, and he rarely smiled. His personality was one of cold savagery. He had the unscrupulous ways of a politician, and his function was that of a leader. He was indifferent to being hated, but demanded respect, and his wealth captured the respect of those who feared his wrath should they oppose him.

Mac did not respect Henry; however, he did fear him. In time his fear had turned to hate, for it was impossible for him to love a barbarian. A man might get by with crossing Henry once, but he dare not try for seconds, not if he valued his life.

Henry McCloud had become a widower when Mac was two years old. He saw to it that his son's immediate needs were taken care of, but as far as being a devoted father, he had been too busy building his cattle empire to take the time to get acquainted with them or show them the least bit of affection. He didn't want sons; he wanted followers, blind puppets who obeyed without questions or understanding.

In his world there existed solely his own needs, and they were satisfied by a never ending supply of cringing, obedient men and pretty house maids. He had at least two women to take care of his sexual needs at all times, plus a gourmet cook who was anything but provocative. Henry did not scrimp on his stomach. Good food and liquor came first, even before sex.

Like most men, Henry had his favorites. He kept Rebba strictly for his mistress. Just how involved he became with her, no one actually knew, but certainly not enough to propose marriage. Marriage seemed to be the only thing between Heaven and Hell that Henry feared. He had lost one wife to death, he would not lose another.

He fought his own battles with the Indians, hiring an army of cut-throats to ride herd on his cattle and push the Indians back out of his way. Henry thought no more about killing an Indian than stomping an ant. He came to have miles of the best grass land in the territory, all for the taking, bought and paid for with the blood of countless Indians. His was a risky business, but if the going got too rough, the military was always there to back him up.

Mac never got used to the killings, the raids, or the burning of Indian villages in the dead of night, even though it was as much a part of his every day life as breathing. Because Ralph felt the same way, he sacrificed his part of the empire, pulled up stakes in New Mexico, and started a new life in Texas. Freedom that ended all too soon, snuffed out by a cholera epidemic that swept through the state like a grass fire in high wind.

Now Mac was leaving for the same reason, dragging his pregnant wife hundreds of miles across Indian infested territory, wondering now if he had made a mistake. True, his brother had made a place for him. Ten years of hard work had gone into the trading post he built, but was that reason enough to risk the life of his wife and their unborn child?

Mac was roused from his thoughts by the sound of movement inside the wagon. He glanced at the horizon, frowned, and got to his feet. The sky was turning gray in the west as heavy clouds gathered, slowly blotting out the last rays of the setting sun. Humid stillness had settled over the country side. Not a breath of air seemed to stir. A dark ceiling hovered over them, closing the atmosphere down around them like a vacuum.

Mac walked to the back of the wagon and peered inside.

Elizabeth pushed herself up on one elbow and looked wearily at him.
"Are you all right?" he said, trying to smile.

"I think so."

"You look tired. Why don't you try to get a little more rest?"

"It's too stuffy in here. Help me down." She held her arms out to him, her eyes fixed on his face.

He swung her down to the ground very gently, holding her close for a moment. "How about some supper? Are you hungry?"

"No, I feel like I never want to eat another bite."

"You have to eat," he pleaded, "or you'll get sick."

"Get sick? I am sick!" she cried, clutching her stomach.

He glanced down apologetically. "I'm sorry." He walked away, too ashamed to face her. He stood with his back turned and his head bent, aimlessly poking at the fire.

Elizabeth felt a stab of guilt, moved to stand beside him and laid her hand on his arm. "Forgive me," she said softly.

"For what?" He turned to face her. "I should be asking your forgiveness. I should have waited until after you had the baby. I'm a damned fool. What difference would a few months have made?"

"No!" she cried sharply

"In your condition you should be at home," he said in a tired voice. The long miles were eating away at him, and the constant strain was wearing worry lines on his face.

"Home!" she said in anger. "That place was never my home. This is." She spread her hands out in front of her. "This is the home of an Indian." She became silent for a moment, and then laid her head against his chest and whispered, "We are both here for the same reason. We want freedom. I think that is what brought us together. Now we must forget the past. It is dead, and remembering the dead can only bring great pain."

Their eyes met and held for a moment as understanding passed between them. Her expression was a picture of innocence and trust.

There was a splendid charm about Elizabeth. She was so very beautiful and desirable, with raven black hair, dark eyes, and golden skin as smooth as satin. She appeared small and delicate in spite of the great bulk of her abdomen. He held her protectively as if he might shield her from all the ugly things in the world by simply taking her into the safety of his arms.

Here they were, free, married, and about thirty miles from their new home, standing in the middle of nowhere locked in a loving embrace. He lifted her chin and kissed her lips. "I adore you," he whispered.

There was concern in his voice, and what she thought looked like tears in his eyes. She couldn't be sure as the fire had burned down to smoldering embers and the light of day was completely gone. He moved away from her to add more wood to the fire. He placed a stool near the fire and Elizabeth sat down to accept the plate of food he offered her. She ate a few bites of corn bread and drank a cup of coffee. He helped her into the wagon and lay down beside her, with her head resting on his shoulder, her breath warm and sweet against his neck.

Mac found it impossible to sleep. He was tired in body and limb, but his mind remained alert as disturbing thoughts tumbled through his head. As soon as Elizabeth went to sleep, he climbed out of the wagon.

He kept the fire blazing and sat beside it sweating, his rifle cradled in his arm. He was not anticipating an Indian attack, for they had seen no signs of their presence, and Indian's rarely attacked after dark. But there were other dangers to be considered: the four footed vermin that roamed in the night and howled at the moon. He heard the shrill cry of night birds, and the soft pad of predators stalking the edge of the fire lit camp.

He thought about the day Elizabeth came to live in his father's house. Henry claimed that he had bought her for three ponies and two sides of bacon. Her father, a Comanche chief, had supposedly needed horses for his sons more than he needed a daughter. Knowing the Comanche, Mac was never convinced by his father's story. To even imagine that a Comanche chief would trade his daughter was like trying to swallow a mouthful of sand burrs. Henry always took what he wanted and would not hesitate to shed blood in doing so. She had been only twelve years old, a lovely young girl with all the right ingredients necessary to create a beautiful woman. It was there that she had learned to speak the white man's language and adjust to their ways.

Henry had brought her home, gave her a bath, dressed her like a lady, and changed her name from Morning Star to Elizabeth.

But the name did not change the fact that she was Comanche.

In many ways Elizabeth seemed older than her twelve years, especially her eyes, innocent yet wise and understanding. She moved through the house like a shadow, seemingly content, making no move to throw off the yoke of slavery, serving with honor and without reward.

At first Mac had not really noticed Elizabeth. He was aware of her ever presence but considered her as a child, not really aware of her as an adult. He might have never thought of her as a mature woman if he hadn't happened upon a very exasperating scene one night when he was awakened by the sound of loud voices. For a moment he thought he was dreaming, but a shrill scream jarred him to reality. He hurriedly pulled on his pants and eased his way down the dim lit hall. He passed by Reba's room and then his father's. There was no sound coming from either. At the far end of the hall he paused in front of Elizabeth's room, pressed his ear against the door panel and listened for a moment. From inside came the sound of scuffling and his father's angry voice.

"Bite me will you! You little hell cat," Henry raged, and then came the sound of a blow being delivered by an open hand, followed by the unmistakably sound of a body falling against the floor.

Seconds later the door burst open and Mac was face to face with his father. Looking past him into the room he saw Elizabeth crouched on the floor cowering like a scared animal. She looked up at him with pleading eyes, tears glistening on her cheeks like tiny lights, illuminated by the kerosene lamp. Her gown was torn away to the waist leaving her magnificent breasts exposed. She quickly wrapped her arms across her chest. Mac experienced a hot flash of rage.

"What the hell are you doing out here in the hall? Waiting your turn?" Henry yelled, pushing Mac aside with explosive rage.

Shocked beyond words, unable to believe this was actually happening, Mac stood rooted to the floor, watching as Elizabeth slowly rose to her feet and arranged her gown to cover herself. She shuddered and trembled like a frightened filly as she made her way to the door. Her eyes locked with Mac's until she closed the door between them.

Henry continued to rave. "Now I know why she gives me the ice treatment. It's you she lavishes her affection on. Huh? Boy! Well don't just stand there. Go on in! I got her all ready for you."

"Why her?" Mac shouted contemptuously. "Why that helpless girl? You have Rebba, and God only knows how many more. Why must you always be abusive? All you care about is your own depraved desires. You're completely insane."

Without warning Henry let him have the back of his hand full in the face. Mac stumbled backward, bleeding from his nose and mouth.

"You'll be sorry you did that," Mac managed, his head swimming with stars.

"Yeah? Well you'll be a hell of a lot sorrier the next time you question my actions or call me crazy. That Indian bitch belongs to me. I paid for her just like I pay for everything else around here. Who do you think buys your fancy clothes, your liquor, and your good times?" With that remark, his eyes came to rest on Elizabeth's door.

"Are you trying to say that I don't earn my keep?" Mac shot back.

"I don't try to say anything, Boy! The facts speak for themselves. You're here because I'm here. You have money because I give it to you. And that's where we differ. I take what I want. You stand around with your hand out waiting for a donation. Tending the herd ain't the only thing ranching involves, but that's where you and your cowardly brother draw the line. When it comes to killing to keep some sneaking red devils from stealing you blind or moving in on your land, you don't have the guts to handle it. A man has to protect what's his if he expects to keep it. I don't mess around with the golden rule. That Bible fairy tale: 'Thy shall not kill' is a crock of shit.

If I didn't take the defensive in this world of cut-throats, I would end up with an empty purse and no damned pride. I've never crawled on my belly. Worms do that, and the likes of you and Ralph. I'd think twice, if I was you, before I did anything rash, like lightin' out the way your brother did. Now, I'm going to bed, and you can go to hell." With that, Henry stomped down the hall, leaving Mac standing there struck dumb, staring after him, shaking his head.

Mac had many things to think about that night. His reaction to what happened between Henry and Elizabeth caused him to explore his own mind for a reason. Seeing her half naked, he felt shame, but it also caused a secret fire to blaze deep inside him.

After that, when he looked at Elizabeth he saw again the way she had looked that night, the smooth skin of her naked body glowing in the lamp light, her scared pleading expression, and he longed to hold her, make love to her, and erase the pain in her eyes. His shameful longing for her was like a boil festering to the breaking point. It was hard to believe that after living under the same roof with her for five years, that he was just now aware of his feeling for her.

Because Henry believed Mac and Elizabeth to be lovers, he stayed away from her room, but the look in his eyes when she was near plainly admitted his desire.

Mac was sure of his feeling for Elizabeth, but he had no way of knowing if she was interested in him. Several weeks later, when his hand accidentally touched hers in the dark as they scurried about closing windows against a sudden rain storm, he realized that she had feelings for him. He held her hand for a second, and her fingers tightened around his. When he pulled her close, she pressed against him. With his heart pounding excitedly he sought her lips, and they clung together in a passionate embrace that left him trembling. She slipped her hands beneath his shirt and ran her fingers up his spine. Her gesture of passion was equal to his own, leaving him no alternative. Sweeping her into his arms he carried her up the stairs to his room. He slowly undressed her beautiful body and lay down with her beneath the heavy quilt on his bed, dizzy with the feelings she aroused in him. He wrapped his arms and his heart around her and she gave her virginity to him in an unforgettable moment. Things might have been different if he had known she was a virgin, but the truth came too late.

Henry was well aware of where his son spent his nights and he was clearly jealous. Rebba no longer satisfied him. Her beauty came no where close to the budding body of Elizabeth. His anger grew along with his resentment. His son had stolen the pleasure that was rightfully his, bought and paid for. Being a man used to having his way he would not be brushed aside. In the past he had always taken what he wanted, and now, more than ever, he wanted Elizabeth.

Knowing his father's intentions, Mac did a very foolish thing. He felt very awkward, and the words sounded both silly and childish as he strung them together. "I love Elizabeth," he confessed. "We want to get married."

"You what?" Henry gave out with a short ugly laugh. "Did I hear you right? Did you say something about getting married?"

"I'm serious. It's no laughing matter. We're in love."

"Well, I'll be damned. So you really like the little Indian maid. It would be funny if it wasn't so damned ridiculous."

"I'm not trying to be funny. I intend to marry her, with or without your approval."

"Quit your dreaming, Boy! There ain't gonna be no wedding. Sleep with her all you want, but that's where it ends. No son of mine is going to marry a stinking Indian. I'll see her dead first. I don't know if you're ignorant or just plain stupid, or maybe you'd enjoy being branded a 'squaw man.' I sure as hell don't intend to be laughed at behind my back. I'll cut her damned throat. I swear. On the other hand, I'll forget the whole thing if I don't hear anymore foolish talk about a wedding."

"You can't just dismiss me like a school boy. I'm twenty-one years old and able to make my own decisions."

"As long as you're under this roof, carrying the name of McCloud, I'll do your thinking for you."

"Now what's that supposed to mean?"

"It means you're a disappointment to me, Boy! I wanted to make a man of you. Your pissant brother didn't have the balls for it, and by god neither do you. Children are supposed to be the fruit of the belly, well you and your brother have turned out to be a pain in my ass. You're old enough to be a man, but you act like a pussy, getting all sentimental over a dirty little Indian tramp."

Mac felt his temper building right along with his father's fury. "Forget it." he spat, turned abruptly and walked from the room in long angry strides. He should have had more sense than to try a fool stunt like that. He had never been able to talk to his father, much less reason with him. Why had he made a jackass of himself? He had failed before he got started, and he hadn't even gotten to the good part yet, the part about the child Elizabeth was carrying.

When the letter came informing Mac of his brother's death, he felt a renewed hate for his father. Ralph had left because of the way Henry made him feel less than a man. His hopes of finding the man who existed inside the shell he called his hide, had led him down a trail of dreams that ended in some desolate graveyard.

And now Mac was having that same dream, except he knew where he was going, his brother had made a place for him.

CHAPTER

Mac awoke with a start, jerked the wagon flap open and looked out at the dark sky. The air was stifling hot and unnaturally still, lightning darted jaggedly across the Heavens, eerie and threatening, and fear took hold of his heart like an iron fist. Elizabeth stirred beside him. "What's wrong?"

"Storm's brewing. We have to move fast and find a windbreak."

"Are you sure?" she said, panic stricken.

"Yeah, no doubt about it, you could cut the air with a knife." The gray overcast was becoming heavier and more menacing by the minute. Dark clouds boiled in their direction and thunder rumbled over their heads accompanied by sharp splintering lightening that darted toward the earth in bright veins that lit up the horizon.

"From the looks of those clouds, they might turn into a tornado. I want you in a safe place when it hits." He hurriedly pulled his boots on and jumped down from the wagon. The wind had increased and whipped at the canvas top with powerful force.

By the time he had the horses in the traces, masses of clouds beneath the dark cloud started to boil and twist.

The animals knew instinctively that a storm was approaching.

They danced nervously, whinnying, eager to run headlong from the deafening thunder and streaking lightening.

About a hundred yards to the east Mac made out some low hills. If they could make it over the ridge before the storm hit full force, they would have a margin of shelter; otherwise, they were trapped in the storm's destructive path.

Mac braced himself against the wind, snapped the reins, and the team moved out with a jerk. A strange hissing sound suddenly added to the rumble of thunder all around them. Continuous flashes of lightning ripped across the sky illuminating half the country side, giving off a sulfurous odor. The clouds were twisting and revolving as they gradually extended downward. The horses were harder to hold now. Mac stood up in the wagon box, urging them to obey his commands, yelling and cursing them, fighting the lines. His urgent cries were whipped away by the force of the howling wind as the storm gained velocity. Heavy rain came pelting down in a powerful solid wall of water, peppering his face like hail stones and filling his eyes and mouth. He couldn't see three feet in front of him and was forced to depend on the animal's instincts to guide him. He held tight to the reins, struggling to stay on his feet. The hissing sound had turned to an earsplitting roar. He saw the funnel cloud swirling closer, coming from the northeast. With their ears laid back, the horses ran hell-bent toward the dark hill that loomed before them. The wagon jarred over brush, branches, rocks and gopher holes, causing the back end to bounce sharply into the air, slinging Elizabeth in all directions.

The wind was at their backs, pushing them. The horses hit the crest of the hill in blind, churning confusion, wrenched up over the lip and plunged perilously downhill heading toward a thicket of mesquite trees that the wind was bending close to the ground. At the bottom of the hill Mac drew in the reins to slow the excited animals, and pulled the wagon up short, hugging the side of the hill under an outcropping of shelf rock. He pushed the brake down hard, jumped down from the wagon and hit the ground running. He hurriedly unhitched the frightened animals giving them free rein, dreading the possibility that in their terrified state they might run themselves to death. It would be of little use to hobble the poor critters, even if it were possible. He figured they would either break loose or kill themselves trying.

There was a tremendous roar when the funnel cloud touched the earth near the top of the hill stirring up dirt and debris. It jumped their wagon and touched ground again about twenty feet in front of them. Around the edge of the funnel, trees were being plucked from the earth like flowers while everything in the center was exploding. Giant oaks were being carried away like feathers. Charged with panic, Mac struggled back to the rain swepted wagon and crawled inside to comfort his wife.

Elizabeth was huddled on her bed screaming his name, afraid the tornado had taken him with it.

He gathered her into his arms and held her tight, but there was little safety there. He was as helpless as she was. He judged what he had done as pure insanity. He should never have left New Mexico with Elizabeth, not in her condition. His stupidity and lack of forethought had created a situation that was nothing short of a nightmare. The storm raged furiously on, the wagon rocked and creaked, while rain pounded the heaving canvas cover. Several times he thought the wagon might overturn. Elizabeth was screaming again.

"Elizabeth, it's all right," he said into the darkness, rocking her while she sobbed against his chest. "We're safe now. The tornado missed us. All we have to do is wait out the tail of the storm." She hung on to him trembling and crying hysterically. He held her close until her panic subsided, kissing her face, eyes, and mouth. She was warm and soft like a kitten.

Along with the sound of exploding thunder, rain beat down like angry drums above their heads while lightening fired the sky in blinding flashes, bright as another sun. The wagon's wood frame creaked and groaned under the terrific pressure of the gusting wind, but miraculously held through the night.

The dawn brought with it a misty, cloud encased sky under a struggling sun. Mac threw open the flap and took a deep breath of the cool damp air. The mesquite trees had taken a beating. Many had been blown up by their roots and banked like leaves. Debris, including dead animals, littered the ground as far as he could see. He had feared his team might be among them, but to his surprise and relief, the horses were grazing near by, calmly waiting to be put back into harness. Instead of running in wild panic, they had undoubtedly stayed close to the wagon, as it was the only thing they had known for the past four months. He jumped down from the wagon and picked his way over to them. "Good boys," he said, and he felt like hugging them. He hated to think of the consequences if they had been stranded this far from civilization. Shuddering at his harrowing thoughts, he tried to dismiss them from his mind, but they were still a long way from home.

After giving the horses a small portion of grain, rewarding them for their hard work, he scouted about searching for dry wood to build a fire. He was looking forward to a cup of strong, hot coffee. He had to dig deep under a dead log and layers of leaves to find anything less than soggy. Finally, in desperation, he poured kerosene over the damp tinder to get it started.

He had the fire going when Elizabeth stuck her head out the open flap and called to him. "Help me down so I can cook breakfast."

"Oh, no you don't. You stay put. I'll do the cooking. It's too muddy." He laughed and lifted a boot to display at least five pounds of mud clinging to the sole. "It's all I can do to pick my feet up."

"I don't care," she said. "Come here."

Very reluctantly he helped her down from the wagon and carried her over to the fire. "You need rest," he said, looking at her with a worried expression.

"So do you," she tossed back, bent over and picked up the skillet.

He noticed the circles under her eyes had deepened and she was moving more slowly, every movement seemingly painful. "Do you feel okay," he said, taking the skillet from her hand and pulling her to her feet.

"I'm all right."

"Well, you don't look all right, and you shouldn't be bending over that way. Let me do the cooking and you sit over there and supervise." He led her over to a stool, placed his hands on her shoulders and forced her to sit down. She frowned up at him, but didn't argue. She watched him silently where he sat on his heels beside the fire, turning two strips of bacon until they curled up crisp and brown.

"Here's your vittles, maam," he said jokingly, handing her a tin plate. She managed a thin loving smile.

It was a relief to be rolling again. By midmorning the sun had won its struggle to penetrate the clouds. Elizabeth sat beside Mac on the wagon seat basking in the warm fresh air, looking with wonder at the clear blue sky where it met the rolling green hills. The hills of home, she thought, studying the patterns of fluffy white clouds floating in a shimmering lake of brilliant color. "It will all be over soon," she said dreamily. "The journey, the waiting, the baby will come, and soon we will be able to rest."

Mac felt good as he made camp that night knowing it was for the last time. They were only a day away from starting a whole new life. Elizabeth was in high spirits as she went about preparing their evening meal.

They ate in silence, preoccupied with their own thoughts, glad to be on the last leg of their journey. All the months of eating dust, fanning mosquitoes, trying to stay warm, and dreading what might be waiting over the next hill would soon be only a memory.

Mac woke early the next morning before day break. Elizabeth stirred beside him, sighed and turned on her side.

"You awake?" he asked softly, so as not to disturb her if she was still sleeping.

Turning over again, she gave him a drowsy glance through half-closed eyes. "I'm awake," she answered almost unwillingly, and then added, "can we get started soon, I mean—we don't have to make a fire do we?"

"No," he answered. "Don't you feel well?"

She looked at him thoughtfully as though trying to decide before answering. "I'd rather not wait, that's all. We're so close. I just want to get there."

He nodded. "We won't wait. We'll get started as soon as I hitch up the team."

They traveled through a green valley that spread before them like a dream. Mac had never known such beauty existed. It was not range land but a wonderland of open country where deer and antelope trails crisscross their path, and a canapé of trees cast shadows upon the sun bathed grass.

"When we reach our new home and you have the baby, everything will be perfect," Mac said.

"Henry can never hurt us again. We will be free from worry, and with no regrets," Elizabeth said solemnly.

Except for the guilt gnawing at Mac's insides, he had no regrets. He felt gutless for not standing up to Henry and telling him the truth. At the time it seemed the best thing to do. Now, thinking back filled him with shame. He wished he could find the courage to tell Elizabeth why things happened the way they did. He wanted to apologize for the hurry up wedding on the way out of town. Explain to her that he really wasn't a coward for pulling out in the middle of the night and leaving his father only a hastily scribbled note.

When they had received the news of Ralph's death, Henry read the letter, dropped it on the hall table, and walked from the room without speaking a single word, nor could Richard read anything into his expression. Whatever he might have felt about Ralph would remain his secret. Mac would always wonder if he cared.

Elizabeth's screams cut through his chain of thoughts and he pulled the wagon up fast, terror clutching his heart.

"Oh, Mac," she sobbed, fear stamped on her pale face.

"Is it the baby?" he cried.

"Yes!"

Mac knelt beside her and took both her hands in his, fear gripping his guts. "We're almost there." he said, trying to soothe her fears and give her courage. Elizabeth looked up at him, her face drawn with panic. She gripped the covers with both hands as another pain tore through her body.

"You'll be fine. I'll have you to a doctor in no time." He kissed her and climbed back on the wagon seat. He whipped the horses into a dead run. The ground was uneven and rocky and each bump and swerve added to Elizabeth's misery.

She bit her lips to smother the screams swelling in her chest. Her pains had become close together, lasting longer. They started low in her back, crept slowly around her sides, and settled deep in her abdomen, gaining strength with every passing hour. She became helpless, lost to pain, her body trapped in the unmerciful jaws of agony, suffering she was sure she could not endure, that she would gladly die to escape. "Oh, Mac!" she screamed frantically. "Oh God! Help me!"

Her screams turned his blood cold. He felt sickness welling up in his guts, for there was nothing he could do to ease her suffering. For the next few hours he lived in terror, pushing the horses for every agonizing mile they covered, wondering if he should stop and try to help her. But he knew his limitations, he could do nothing to ease the fate of Mother Nature as Elizabeth lay trapped and screaming in pain, maybe dying. Their only hope was for him to reach a doctor as soon as possible.

As he topped the rise of the next hill, stretching out in the valley below, lay the small town of Courgat. "Thank God!" he cried. "Elizabeth, we made it! We're home!" Mac rolled into town shouting, "I need a doctor!"

A man shouted back, pointing a fore finger, "Last house on the left."

Seconds later he pulled up in front of a neat white house with a sign over the door that read, "Doctor Edward Keel."

He gathered Elizabeth into his arms and made his way quickly down the rock edged path.

The doctor heard the commotion and was on the porch holding the door open by the time Mac mounted the steps. "Bring her in here," he motioned to a bedroom. "Helen!" he yelled. "I need your help." Instantly a woman appeared in the doorway. Taking in the situation she hurriedly turned down the bed covers.

"She's in a bad way." Mac said, laying her gently on the bed. "She's been suffering for a long time."

"I'll take a look at her." The woman was already removing Elizabeth's clothes. "You can wait out there," the doctor said, jerking his head toward the door.

Mac collapsed in a chair in an adjoining room, buried his face in his hands and wept. After what seemed like an eternity, the doctor appeared, his face grim. "How is she? Will she be all right?"

"She's in the second stage of labor. It could take a long time. It usually does with the first one. And I assume it is."

"Yes."

"Would you like a cup of coffee while you wait? Mr.—" He paused.

"McCloud," he answered. "Richard McCloud."

"Mac? Ralph's brother?"

"Yes, Ralph was my brother."

"I'm glad to meet you, Mac." He pumped Mac's hand with genuine pleasure. "Your brother was the best friend I ever had. His passing was a great loss to us all. This entire town was indebted to him. After this is over we can have a good long talk."

"I look forward to it."

"May I ask you a question?" Mac shook his head. "Since your name is Richard, how did you come by the name, Mac?"

"Strange that you should ask that. I figured you knew."

"Ralph always referred to you as Mac. I never asked him why."

"Ralph gave me that name when I was two years old, and I've carried it ever since."

"Now, I had better get back to your wife. I'll keep you informed about her progress."

Mac paced the floor while Elizabeth wailed. Finally the doctor appeared, his face drawn with worry.

"How much longer will she have to suffer?" Mac said through his tears.

"From what I can tell by my examination, the baby is in a breech position."

"Breech? What does that mean?"

"The baby is coming doubled up, buttock first."

"Is that bad?"

"It can be fatal."

"Do something! Don't you let her die!"

"I'm going to try to turn the baby."

"What if you can't?"

"We won't borrow trouble."

Mac took hold of the doctor's arm in a panic grasp. "Don't let anything happen to her, please!"

"I'm doing all within my power, you can rest assured," He turned abruptly and left the room.

Mac paced the floor for hours. Never before had he felt so helpless. His whole reason for living was lying in the next room suffering to bring his baby into the world, perhaps dying, and he could do nothing to help her. He held his hands to his ears to muffle her screams. He wanted to run. He wanted to die. "Oh, God! Please help her!"

He lost track of time, not realizing how long she had suffered until the light of day broke through the windows and spilled across the room. She was calling his name over and over, begging him to help her. When he could stand it no longer he threw the door open and burst into the room. She lay on the bed wringing wet with sweat, her eyes dilated, rolling from side to side in agonizing pain, pleading, screaming, straining with every muscle she possessed to expel the child. If ever a man was to witness a sight that could make his heart stand still, this was it. He knelt beside the bed and laid his head on her heaving breast. "I'm here, darling. I'm here. Everything will be all right."

"Oh, Mac," she whispered weakly, "I'm dying. I will never hold my baby."

"No!" he sobbed, pulling her into his arms. "I won't let you die, you can't die. I can't live without you."

He felt strong hands take hold of him. He was being lifted, pulled, and pushed from the room. Outside the closed door, Doctor Keel shook him back to his senses. "You must not go to pieces. For her sake you must be strong." He had Mac by the shoulders. He released him and stepped back. "I'm going back in there to your wife. You can go or stay, that's up to you, but which ever, do it like a man."

"Is she dying?" he cried brokenly, tears dripping down his face.

"She's mighty weak and has suffered about all her heart can stand. One thing I do know, I have my hands full with your sick wife; don't you make more problems for me." He turned and walked back into the room where Elizabeth was screaming Mac's name.

He hung back for a moment, scared and unsure of himself, then followed the doctor back to his wife's bedside, his eyes riveted to her pale face.

She suffered only a few minutes longer before she was finally delivered of the child. Mac saw her body give one last heave, and then he heard the screams of his infant daughter. Elizabeth lay lifeless, her face growing ashen as the blood drained from her body. Mac put his face in the soft curve of her neck and prayed to God to let her live. She held on to him weakly for a moment while the doctor worked frantically to stop the hemorrhaging. He felt her body relax and her chest become still as she slipped quietly away from him. He cradled her limp body in his arms, rocking her back and forth, crying, kissing her pale lips and caressing her damp dark curls. At length he was led from the room by kind understanding hands, and Doctor Keel closed the door softly behind them shutting away all the hopes, dreams, and future of a grieving man.

The hours that followed were intolerable for Mac. He could feel the stillness of death inside the house. The only sounds were the ticking of the old clock on the mantel, and very hushed voices coming from the room beyond as the doctor and his wife prepared Elizabeth's body for burial.

The sun shown brightly through the thin curtains in the doctor's parlor, but for Mac there was no light, only black grief that clutched his heart. Like cold darkness, agonizing pain gathered around him, squeezing the spirit from his body, leaving him no more than an empty shell. He sat motionless, staring but not seeing. When the two men brought the pine coffin, he seemed not to notice. He was lost inside an impenetrable hell.

Time passed without his knowledge. The silence was finally broken by Doctor Keel's voice. "Mac," he said softly, "we have Elizabeth laid out. Would you like to see her before we place her in the coffin?"

Mac raised his eyes with torturous slowness to meet the doctor's, his face as expressionless as a stone statue, his eyes without light. "She's dead! Oh, God! I lost her!"

"Yes, she's gone," the doctor said, laying a soothing hand on his arm. "Elizabeth is dead, but her baby lives. Try to draw strength and comfort from that. It was a miracle that we didn't lose them both. And now we must lay Elizabeth to rest. I have done all I can for her, the rest is up to you." The doctor left Mac alone to say his good-byes to Elizabeth. He had never pitied a man more, and there was absolutely no way to ease his pain.

Mac went to his knees in soul racking sobs. He kissed her still, cold lips for the last time and whispered his ever lasting love.

At long last Doctor Keel went back into the room and laid his hand on Mac's shoulder. "I'm so very sorry, Mac. If it will help, I can take care of the services and all—" His voice trailed off as Mac stormed suddenly to his feet.

"Close the coffin; no one is to see her. Do you understand? No one!"

"But—" Doctor Keel began to protest, and Mac cut him off sharply.

"Close the coffin, I tell you!"

The doctor studied Mac for a moment before asking reluctantly, "What about a grave side service? Do you want me to arrange that?"

"Will that bring her back to me? What good are words? She can't hear them. She's gone." he sobbed brokenly. "But I have a daughter, and no one is to know that her mother was an Indian." His words were delivered as both an ultimatum and a warning. "I refuse to have my daughter branded with the stigma half-breed. Even the child is never to know."

"I can see that you have given this a lot of thought, and I agree with your decision. Some people are narrow-minded and unreasonable. It's better that they never discover the truth. You're right, words won't bring Elizabeth back, but the lack of them can shield your daughter from much prejudice suffering."

"Do I have your word?" Mac asked.

"Completely, and I can promise you that my wife will honor your wishes also. Your secret is safe with us."

CHAPTER

Evening had fallen. The sun was only a shell of pink, sinking below the horizon, dragging with it, like the tail of a kite, tentacles of darkness to enhance Mac's already bleak world of grief and emptiness. The small four room log cabin stood like a tombstone in the hazy shadows of the giant trees behind the trading post. All was silent and motionless; the only sign of life was a thin curl of gray smoke drifting lazily from the stone chimney.

Richard McCloud's grief was inconsolable. A heavy stone of devastation weighed heavily on his mind and soul. He was alone in his brother's house, leaning over the cradle near the fireplace staring down at his baby daughter, the only thing in the world he had left to live for. His grief-stricken face looked gaunt and ravaged in the flickering light, his eyes plainly revealing the terrible anguish in his heart. The secure warmth of love had vanished. His heart buried forever in the cold ground with Elizabeth. Remembering sent tremors of torment shuddering through his body, and he became choked with sobs.

He glanced toward the door and a light tapping, but made no move to answer. When the knocking grew loud and persistent, he became irritated. He crossed the floor in angry strides and flung the door open. It struck the inside wall. He was not surprised to find Doctor Edward Keel standing on his porch, especially since he and his wife were the only two people in town that he knew.

"Good evening," Edward said in a sonorous voice. "Hope you don't mind my barging in this way, but I think we have a few things to discuss."

"Come on in," he said blandly, stepping aside. He hadn't noticed the girl at first, and he felt a twang of shock when she followed the doctor into the room.

"This is Amy," Keel said, making a motion toward the young woman at his side. She lifted her head slightly at the mention of her name and smiled meekly. "And this is Mr. McCloud. Shall I address you as Mac or Richard?"

"Either."

"Then, if you don't mind, I prefer to call you by your given name. I have never been fond of nick names. They are invariably misleading or ridiculous." He cleared his throat. "I figured you might need a woman to help you look after the baby. That's the natural order of things."

He hated the intrusion and glared at his visitors for a moment while he gathered his response. The woman looked at the floor instead of him. She was small, had pleasant features, short cropped hair that curled around her face, and enormous breasts. At last he spoke, working at keeping his tone level. "Yes, I guess that would be best."

The girl smiled a little, continued to look at the floor, her hands clasp nervously. She walked slowly over to the cradle and looked down at the tiny squirming infant. The baby began to cry and she leaned down and took it up into her arms.

"Why don't we step into the kitchen and have a cup of coffee?" Keel suggested, smiling. "Amy will see after the baby."

Mac eyed the doctor suspiciously, as if trying to read his mind, perhaps in self-defense, before conceding and leading the way into the kitchen. He lifted the stove lid and laid a stick of wood on the smoldering coals, poked at it for a time, replaced the lid, and set the coffee pot on it to warm.

Keel watched him in silence, feeling a bit apprehensive about his mission. He did not speak until Mac faced him across the table. "I suppose you could call what I'm about to say, meddlesome, and you certainly have the right to tell me to mind my own business, but you need help with the baby."

"I know that."

"Have you given her a name yet?"

"Elizabeth said if she had a girl, she wanted to name her Dawn."

"So her name is Dawn. I think it's fitting. Have you made any plans?"

"I'm not in the mood to make plans."

"You had better start getting in the mood. You can't afford to stay idle and eat your heart out. Not unless you intend to go crazy."

"What do you expect? I'm sick with grief, depressed, and I don't know what to do about it. My wife just died this morning. Have you forgotten?"

"No, and I don't expect you to. God didn't create man to do woman's work. Leave that to Amy. You need to concentrate on your business. Ralph did a lot of good things for this town, and built a prosperous business. You can do the same, but not if you sit around on your back side. I sure would hate to see all Ralph's years of hard work wasted while you grieve over something you can't change."

"I loved my wife, Doctor Keel. I hurt like hell. I miss her. All my plans included her. We planned a life together."

"And now you have a daughter to plan for. I'm sure your wife would have expected no less."

"I need time."

"Time is your worst enemy right now. You have to move forward because you can't move backward. The past is over and done with, but you can do something about your future and the future of your daughter."

Mac studied the doctor thoughtfully for a time, and then he pushed back from the table and walked over to the stove. He picked up the coffee pot and two cups, retraced his steps back to the table, filled the cups and sat back down.

The expression on his face made Keel uneasy, but he had already said too much to back down. For the sake of the baby, he had to say it all. If he took it the wrong way, he couldn't help it. Even a show of anger would be an improvement, anything that might deliver him from limbo, get his senses aroused, and start him to thinking about the living instead of the dead. "I'm not saying that you have to hire Amy for the job," he began again, "but she's willing and able. You won't find a better offer."

The idea filled him with revulsion. There was an uncomfortable silence, and then he said, "I don't want another woman in my home. I loved my wife." He turned his face away as tears filled his eyes. "Anyway, she's too young."

"She's not that young, and be danged with your nit picking. This has nothing to do with your likes or dislikes. I'm thinking about that child in there. She needs a woman's care. What do you know about babies? I'm a doctor, and I'm telling you, she'll not survive with you caring for her."

"Maybe I don't know anything about babies, but I know plenty about what happens to young girls keeping house for bachelors. The reason I know is because my father started out just like this."

"Forget about your father. I know all about him. I'm talking about you. What you are and what you do has nothing to do with Henry. You're two different people."

"How come you know so much about him?"

"Ralph and I were close friends. He confided in me."

"You don't know anything about me, and Ralph hadn't seen me in ten years. Henry McCloud's blood flows in my veins. I could be just like him for all you know."

"Are you?"

"I don't know." A mask of pain filled his clear blue eyes. "Is it worth the risk?"

"I'm willing to take the gamble, because the stakes are too high not to risk it, especially after you've sweetened the pot with your baby daughter." Keel's tone changed to one of tenderness. "I know this is hard on you, but you have to pull yourself up by your boot straps, re-muster, and start over again. You have to think about Dawn. She has already lost her mother. She can't afford to lose her daddy too. If you don't start pulling yourself together you're likely to blow away like a sand hill. Look at you! When was the last time you slept or had a decent meal under your belt?"

"All this is easy for you to say. It's my wife who died, and my child who lost her mother. What do you know about my grief? You're a doctor, not God!"

The older man looked stunned at first, then his expression turned to anger. "I'll tell you what I know about grief. I was ten years old when I dug my father's grave with my own two hands. Then I got lucky. I was twelve before I lost my mother and baby sister. I lost another sister before I was fifteen. The only reason I didn't lose a brother was because I never had one. I married when I was seventeen. I lost my wife and baby before I turned nineteen. She didn't even have a doctor, because there wasn't one. All she had was an old half-blind midwife. She suffered five days and nights before the Lord finally took her to rest. I loved her like I never loved anything in my life. She was all I had, but it was a blessing when her misery finally ended and her pleading and crying stopped. I know what you're going through, what you're feeling right now, how it's tearing your guts out just thinking about her. I know about the long cold nights without her lying close beside you, and how daybreak fails to bring relief. You'll keep hearing her voice. You'll forget sometimes and expect to see her walk into a room. You'll miss her smile, the touch of her hand, even the way she could rant and rave when you did something she don't approve of. Believe me, I know, and so do a lot of other people. That's the reason I became a doctor. To end, or at least relieve, some of the suffering and dying. When you lost your wife, I lost something too. I was the one who stood by with all my medical knowledge and practice and watched her die. She was your wife, but she was my patient, and a part of me died with her because I couldn't save her. After I buried my wife, I felt I had nothing left to live for, no reason to fight God and fate, but I was able to pull myself together and get on with my life.

"At least you have a business that can give you security, and a nice standing in this town. Your brother was highly respected. You will be too. All I had was a half interest in nothing. I was share cropping on land too poor to raise healthy weeds. I didn't have two beans to rub together." Suddenly the doctor looked at Mac and a funny expression flooded his face. He blinked as if he had just awakened from a deep sleep. "I hadn't planned to run off at the mouth like this. I didn't come here to cry on your shoulder, or preach you a sermon. I came here to help you. I haven't talked this much about my personal life in forty years."

"I feel like a fool. I guess I figured I was the only person in the world to lose a loved one. I'm sorry."

"Don't go feeling sorry, but I do want you to take a good, long look at the situation and try to see it for what it is. Grief is selfish and useless. Can't you understand? It's not your wife you're grieving for, but yourself."

"I don't know what to do. I'm so damned lost."

"Work! Around the clock if need be, but work your tail off. Be so dog tired at night that you can fall asleep the minute your head touches the pillow. The nights will be the worst. I think that's the reason people wear black to show their grief."

Mac was thoughtful for a time, seeing the doctor in a new light. He wondered if it was the years or grief that had etched the lines on his face and turned his hair gray. "You're probably right," he said. "I'm just so torn up right now that I can't seem to think for myself. Work most likely is the best medicine. But can anything take my mind off what I did to Elizabeth?"

"What kind of nonsense are you talking?"

"I killed her as sure as I'm living."

"Many women die giving birth. It was not your fault."

"I'm responsible for dragging her clear across the country in her condition. If we had stayed at home, none of this would have happened."

"It would have been all the same. Elizabeth was strong and healthy. It was the will of God, or else a freak of nature. Here or there, made no difference. The baby would have been born breech regardless. It had nothing to do with your journey."

"I can't accept that."

"She would have died if she had stayed home." He laid his hand on Mac's shoulder. "You will come to understand that one day. You're angry and hurt, ready to lash out at everyone and everything, even yourself. It will get easier, but you will never forget."

"I don't know where to begin to put my life back together. Where should I start?"

"You can start by calling me Edward, and I might as well get used to calling you Mac, although I dislike the name. You're a fine looking man, and you should not have an ugly name, but it matches the name on the trading post. All this time I thought Ralph was just shortening the name, McCloud. I was mistaken. He had named his business after you. He loved you very much. Now, what about Amy?"

"I can't agree to her moving in here with me. It's not right. You know what people will think."

"You can stop the gossip by marrying her."

"Marry her!" he cried in a state of shock. "Do you actually think that I can bury one wife on Monday and marry again on Tuesday? And what makes you think she would have me in the first place?"

"Why not?"

"That's no answer."

"I'm not saying that you have to treat her as a wife right off, but at least—"

"It's out of the question. If and when I marry again, I will do the picking."

"You're sure as hell a stubborn man."

"Yeah? Well you're sure as hell a crazy one."

"I'm only trying to simplify the situation for you."

"Simplify!"

"Get off your high horse."

"You put me on it, you get me off."

"All right, you made your point. Now I'll make mine." He got slowly to his feet, took a few steps toward the adjoining room, and then turned and motioned for Mac to follow. "Come look at this."

Mac hesitated a moment, and then followed the doctor to the doorway and looked in. Amy was sitting before the fire rocking his tiny baby. Barely visible in the firelight he could see one large exposed breast and the child sucking it greedily.

"I don't understand this," he said, when he found his voice.

Doctor Keel didn't reply right away. He returned to the kitchen and helped himself to another cup of coffee, blew the steam off, and took a sip before he spoke. "It's really quite simple. Amy is a wet nurse."

"To be a wet nurse, she had to first give birth. Where is her baby?"

"Her baby, a perfect little boy, was still born three days ago."

"Are you itching to get me killed? What about her husband? Should I let him move in too?"

"There is no husband—never was."

"Somebody was damned well responsible."

"Her mother and daddy were killed in an Indian raid nine months ago. Amy was raped. The child would have been a half-breed. It's a blessing that it never took its first breath."

Mac bristled immediately. "Is that the way you feel about my baby daughter? She's a half-breed. What would you have me do? Knock her in the head?"

"You have taken all the right steps to protect her from that stigma. She won't suffer because of who her mother was. Everybody in town knew Amy was raped by an Indian, and the damned fools held it against the girl. They still do. The child would have been an outcast and hated. She's all alone, Mac. She doesn't even have a friend. She's been put through hell, though it's no fault of her own."

Mac felt sick and ashamed. "I guess she's had her share of grief too."

"We are all guaranteed our share of that; we only come up short where happiness is concerned. Needless to say, the citizens of Courgat are ready to kill every Indian on sight, and with good reason. Well, what's your answer? You have to decide today, right now. Women are like cows, if they don't get milked, they dry up. I warn you, there isn't another woman in town who can nurse your baby. You're a lucky man. It's made to order, a miracle, and you're a fool if you don't take advantage of it."

"Do I have a choice?"

"Not if you want your baby to survive. She's a part of Elizabeth—all you have left of her."

"I won't marry her."

"Have it your way."

"Will she have to live here?"

"Would be ideal if she did. She could do the cooking, washing, ironing, and cleaning. She can handle all your needs."

"Not all of them. I'll have to move out."

"You can fix up the back room at the trading post. Your brother lived there for a couple of years before he had the money to build this cabin. He survived just fine; plus, he could keep an eye on his business."

"Don't worry, Edward, it will suit my needs perfectly."

Calling the doctor by his given name made Mac feel a little uncomfortable. It sounded disrespectful. It didn't seem fitting, but if that was what the doctor wanted, who was he to complain?

When Edward left for home he was triumphant over his victory. Relieved that Mac had taken the first step toward recovery. Prolonged grief in a man's heart was as deadly as a disease in his blood. Refusing treatment for either could destroy a man in many different ways.

CHAPTER

4

Amy was all Doctor Keel proclaimed her to be. She took excellent care of the baby, and ran the house with such efficiency that Mac found it hard to believe that she was only fifteen years old.

Dawn was an energetic happy baby, with classic features, dark curls, enormous brown eyes and a very special smile that displayed two dimples at the corners of her mouth. She loved the outdoors, and had discovered ways of escaping the cabin by the time she had learned to walk. When Amy started after her she would dart ahead of her and run to the trading post located a few yards in front of the cabin, scramble up to the porch on all fours because her little legs were too short to span the steps. She would bound inside and throw herself into Mac's arms for sanctuary, squealing and laughing. Mac would grin as he looked over the top of the child's head to see Amy standing in the doorway with her hands on her hips, shaking her head in disapproval.

His daughter was his world, his reason for living. He spent his evenings with her, playing games and teaching her. If not for his continuing grief over Elizabeth, his life might have been flawless. As for Amy, she was only a shadow in his thoughts, he could not see beyond his tiny dark haired, daughter, the part of Elizabeth that he held so dear to his heart. When she put her soft arms around his neck and snuggled close she was his solace, and her love was his strength, making it possible for him to endure the pain of losing Elizabeth.

Doctor Keel had been instrumental in helping him adjust his thinking, coaxing him to concentrate on his business. He realized it was still too soon to expect a profound recovery, but he had noticed a more realistic change in his attitude. He hoped that in time his ambition might overshadow his grief.

In an attempt to shake loose from the depression that bound him like shackles, Mac occupied his mind with new ways to expand his business, and threw himself into his work whole heartedly. He had set a goal for himself, something tangible to strive toward. He did not intend to spend the rest of his life behind dusty counters, content only in buying and selling. He wanted to own land, live in a nice house, and raise cattle and horses. But most of all, he wanted security for his daughter.

One spring day Mac was having a drink with Pete Rowling at the Silver Buckle Saloon. Pete, a small man in size, made up for it in other ways. He was easy going most of the time, but commanded respect when he was riled. He had a reputation for moping up the floor with men twice his size. He was a family man, had three sons he took pride in. Ned, the eldest, was tall and lean, with Pete's easy going nature. Jack, ten years old, and second in line by two years, was almost as tall as his brother Ned, with the fiery disposition of his mother, Martha. Clay, last, but certainly not least, was big for his age and already had the grace of a bull elephant. He really couldn't be called fat; stocky would better describe his square build. He was much of a nuisance, always seemed to be under foot. Between the three boys, Pete sometimes felt like he was being pulled apart. He had gone to town early just to get away from their bickering, pretending to be taking care of business to keep them from tagging along.

"It's getting to the point that I have to explain every move I make to them boys," Pete complained.

"Don't fret too much about having to account for your whereabouts when they're young. Wait till they're older and expect you to buy their beer," Mac razzed.

"Now that's a real comforting thought. When they get old enough to drink, they'll be old enough to work. They can buy their own beer, and I might let 'um buy me one."

"If it will help keep them out of your hair, I might find something around the store one of them can do."

"Sounds like you might be cooking up some big plans for the future. You got something going I ain't heard about?"

"Maybe," he answered mysteriously. "How's the price of cattle?"

"This ain't the time to buy, unless it's calves. With the grass coming and water plentiful, the ranchers are feeding their stock at a cheap price, hanging in there, waiting for the fall market when the grass is gone."

"When's the next drive?"

"We ain't got a head count on steers yet. We're having a meeting next Saturday to decide. We want top money for every cow we drive. Everything depends on the size of the herds and if we have enough beef to make the east market worth while. We may decide to drive 'um north. It's a longer pull, but we can get a better price."

"I want to buy ten head and pay you to leave 'um where they are."

"Now hold up a minute, Mac. You better run that by me again. I think I may need to clean the wax out of my ears. You don't buy beef and leave 'um."

"You heard right. I'm opening a meat market and I intend to sell top quality beef."

"I didn't know you was a butcher."

"I'm not, but Zeek Yates is, and he needs a job."

Pete laughed. "You're joking! A drunken butcher? He's likely to turn out nothing but stew meat."

"I've made all the arrangements. All I need is the beef. I figure to butcher one a week, and sell all the meat in one day while it's fresh. Do we have a deal?"

Pete held out his hand and Mac grasp it. "What can I say? You want to pick 'um out?"

"As I need 'um. Now, let's talk price."

"Twenty dollars a head. A dollar more a month if they stay on my grass."

"Sold. Cut 'um out and meet me at the bank in the morning and we'll close the deal."

With the business at hand finished they settled back to do some serious drinking. When the two men parted Mac's hopes were at a new high. He was looking forward to a more prosperous future, but his happiness was marred because Elizabeth wasn't there to share it with him.

In spite of the rainy spring, with Zeek's help, Mac was able to complete the slaughterhouse and meat market by the middle of June. The addition was quite impressive, and drew a lot of attention.

The date of the first slaughter was posted outside the trading post in big letters, and far enough in advance for the whole town to make arrangements to be there in time to buy fresh meat. All the meat had to be sold the same day it was butchered, or else thrown to the dogs or used to bait traps.

Zeek started butchering in the middle of the night, stopping periodically to take a little nip from his jug. By sunup the counters were filled with cuts of fresh red meat, and Zeek was dead drunk.

Mac was surprised to find several women gathered outside the front door of the store when he opened for business the next morning. In less than three hours he had sold the last scrap of meat, right down to the soup bones.

Andy Holmes, the saloon keeper, was disappointed to find he had arrived too late to make a purchase. People arriving too late left empty handed and disappointed.

Mac began thinking of ways to improve his booming business. He wanted a cool place to work and store the fresh meat. It was time to move past the salt cure and dried meat preserving methods. Some cuts of meat could be preserved in jars for several months, canned under water pressure, but the procedure was risky and time consuming. Ice was the answer, but the only time there was ice was in the dead of winter. So Mac's thoughts turned to the construction of an ice house. If he dug a deep underground room, he would be able to keep the ice for months and the space cold enough to preserve fresh meat for longer periods of time. He hired several men to start digging the mammoth pit, reinforced with heavy beams on all sides.

In the mean time he decided to start selling meat by special order. He posted another notice outside the store. This time stating a dead line on all meat orders, and the date the meat would be butchered. This arrangement worked perfectly. There was no waste, and no one walked away disappointed. Mac knew exactly how much meat to butcher, and allowed Zeek ample time to fill the orders.

Mac had fallen into a gold mine. There was no doubt but that he had a gift for making money. He had prospered so in the past year that he started thinking on another idea to promote sales. With the accumulation of cow hides, he went into the saddle making business, buying all hides offered him. He was slowly branching into other fields of leather goods, included coats, belts, holsters, chaps, and boots. Richard McCloud was becoming a rich man. No one was surprised when he began to buy land and cattle. He was soon supplying his own beef to meet the town's demands for fresh meat.

Mac realized as Dawn grew older, her needs would also grow, and he intended to have enough money to meet all her demands, however expensive. His mind was brimming full of plans and projects.

As Dawn grew in years, she also grew emotionally. Her relationship with her father changed completely by the time she was nine years old. Instead of depending on him, she seemed always to seek new ways to please him and make him more dependent on her. She did more and more of the housework, cooked some of his meals over the objections of Amy, and cried when he left the cabin to go to his lonely room at the trading post. Plainly she was trying to squeeze Amy out of the picture, prove to her father they could get along without her.

Amy had changed with the years also. She fell desperately in love with Mac. Every time he walked into the cabin her heart pounded with excitement. She watched him with adoration written in every line of her pretty face. Mac never noticed her eyes dance when she looked at him, nor did he hear the note of affection in her voice when she spoke his name softly. She tried desperately to make him notice her as a woman, not just someone to look after his child. She would fuss for hours over the stove preparing his favorite dishes, and spend half the afternoon making herself attractive. For all her trouble he never so much as mentioned her new dress, nor complimented her on the way she piled her hair high on her head to show off the seeping lines of her graceful neck. So many things she did and said signified her feelings, yet he remained aloof. He could not see beyond his beautiful daughter. Anything she asked of him, he did.

In time Amy began to resent Dawn. There was certainly nothing romantic about tending a child, cooking, mending, washing, ironing, and all the other boring things that made up housekeeping. After nine years of such drudgery, she was ready for a change, anxious to make a life for herself, and have a family of her own.

She might have endured nine more years if Mac had admired something about her. Perhaps her curly hair, her slender shapely figure, even her tiny feet. But he showed no signs of recognizing her as a woman, and certainly not a woman who craved love and attention. Mac's coolness toward her became as annoying as a stone in her shoe. At times she found it hard to conceal her feelings. She longed to creep into his bed, feel his arms around her, his body pressing against hers. She liked the way he looked, moved, and talked. She adored everything about him. There wasn't another man in Courgat to equal him. She wanted him passionately.

Finally she was forced to acknowledge her pain and frustration of solid defeat. Mac didn't have the slightest interest in her romantically. Since he lived and breathed for Dawn, she decided the only way to gain his attention was through her. If she could convince him that she would make Dawn a good mother, he might want her for the child's sake. For the most part, she had very little use for Dawn, and the child seemed to be aware of it. She snapped at her frequently. Everything Dawn did and said irritated her, and it was beginning to show. She decided to change her tactics, do whatever was necessary to gain Mac's attention, and if this was the only way, it was the course she would take. She felt a little guilty that evening as she started her pretense. She was a picture of sweetness. Several times she caught herself just before speaking sharply to Dawn. If Mac noticed her new quiet attitude he certainly showed no signs.

Dawn noticed, and shot her a look of suspicion when she failed to scold her for spilling milk down the front of her dress and onto the clean white tablecloth.

After supper Mac sat in the big mahogany rocker with Dawn in his lap, listening to her read. Meanwhile Amy busied herself with the dishes, watching them resentfully from the kitchen, feeling jealous and neglected. She was no part of their world.

When the grandfather clock struck nine, Mac rose to leave. This had been his routine for nine years, and each time Amy felt resentment. Why couldn't he stay just one time after Dawn was put to bed? Immediately after tucking her in and kissing her good-night, he would leave, not returning until breakfast time the next morning. They were never alone. Dawn was always there between them, demanding all his attention and soaking up all his love.

Amy had not stayed because of the child or her needs, but a stupid dream of winning Mac's love one day. Now at twenty-four she felt life was passing her by. She wanted a home of her own, and children. She wondered how Mac could be so blind as not to see the simple truth of her feelings.

She refused to contain her feelings any longer. As Mac started to leave, she called to him from the kitchen. "Wait a minute."

He stopped halfway through the door. "Is there a problem?"

"No," she said, dropping her eyes, avoiding his inquiring gaze.

"I just thought you might like another cup of coffee. There's plenty left, and it's still hot."

"No, thank you," he said, a note of coolness in his tone. "You know I never stay past nine o'clock."

"I guess I forgot," she said quietly. "It's just that I never have anyone to talk to. I get lonely sometimes." She turned quickly away, all her courage leaving her when she needed it most.

"I'm sorry," he said, seeing the hurt in her eyes. He stepped back inside, walked over to her and laid his hand on her arm.

A little tremor moved through her body. He had never touched her before. She reached out to him and he dropped his hand and stepped back. While he stood there at a loss for words, she whirled around and ran out the back door. He waited only a moment before following her. She was standing on the back porch holding on to the rail, bending slightly over it, crying softly. He turned her to face him, his hands firm on her shoulders. "Have I done something to offend you?" She shook her head. "Then tell me what's wrong."

"Will you help me?"

"I can't unless you tell me what's wrong."

"It's hard for me to explain. I don't know how to put my feelings into words." She paused, her eyes meeting his boldly.

"I love you, Mac."

Her words struck him blunt as a blow. All he could do was stare at her. He wetted his lips and uttered lamely, "I had no idea."

"I know I'm behaving badly, but please try to understand the way I feel."

He stood above her, now he was steadying himself against the porch railing. He felt suddenly weak, alarmed in fact, and uncertain of what he should do. He even felt a spur of guilt.

While he seemed to be in shock, she continued. "I thought I might never have the courage to say this. I have wondered for a long time how I could make you love me back."

Mac swallowed hard. "What have I done to make you feel this way? To think you love me?"

"You made me love you," she said with a sob.

"How! I've never touched you, or acted in any way to make you feel this way."

"For nine years I have known only you. Don't you see? I was bound to love you. There was no one else to love."

Her words might have been chosen to hurt him, if that was what she had in mind. Or for that matter, the same statements could be used to trap a man. Her admission cut through him like a whip lash. Of course she must love him. What chance had she to love anyone else? He had been a fool, a double fool. He wondered if she was trying to trick him by playing on his sympathy. Did she want him to feel guilty? Was she using her nine years of loyal services as a weapon? Perhaps she was trying to persuade him in the name of decency to marry her? "You didn't have to stay," he said defensively. "You were free to leave anytime you felt like it. I hired you to take care of my baby, and I asked nothing more.

"You still need me," she reminded him.

"I need someone to care for Dawn, but it doesn't have to be you. I appreciate what you've done for her, make no mistake, and I paid for your services. I can never love another woman. I still love my wife."

"Your wife is dead!"

"Yes, but not forgotten."

"You still think of me as a child. Why don't you admit it? I'm a woman now, and I think and feel like a woman. I even look like a woman."

"I can't deny that," he said in almost a whisper, looking at her as though seeing her for the first time, "but I'm just not interested."

"Forget what I said. Pretend it never happened." She gestured with her hands, dismissing the subject, walked back inside with a great display of dignity and closed the door in his face.

In the days that followed, both Mac and Amy became increasingly edgy and uncomfortable. Amy was cloaked in humiliation, and Mac felt more like a rat everyday. Amy had built something out of nothing and she was making him the scapegoat. He had never displayed any affection toward her other than kindness, and certainly no romantic notions had ever crossed his mind.

It was Amy who finally broke the silence, displaying much self-control, sparing Mac the ugly task of speaking the words they both knew were inevitable. "I can't stay here now that you know how I feel about you. Besides, Dawn resents and hates me."

"No, you're wrong. She loves and respects you."

"You don't have to lie to spare my feelings."

"You have been like a mother to her. How could she possibly hate you? She has loved and needed you all her life. I know you're upset about our relationship, but don't take it out on Dawn. I'm sorry," he said with regret.

"I had no right to burden you with my feelings. I had hoped that you might love me too."

"I care about you, Amy. You know that. I wish I felt the same way about you, but I don't."

She lifted her head and displayed the tears streaming down her cheeks. "I'll have to go away soon, and it hurts me to leave you." Impetuously, she threw her arms around his neck and pressed firmly against him, daring to kiss him long and passionately, expecting he would resist. For an instant she felt his arms tighten around her, his body yielding to hers, and he returned her kiss with equal passion. Then suddenly he stiffened and pushed her away. She cried out in protest.

"Dawn's asleep, you don't have to leave. Stay with me."

In that reckless moment he came to understand his father's actions. How easy it would be to make love to this woman and satisfy the hot desire burning in his loins. If he did, he would be the same kind of animal as Henry. He felt disgust for himself. "I'll make arrangements for you just as soon as you decide where you want to go. I'll take care of your expenses until you can get settled into another position."

"It makes little difference where I go," she said, her voice filled with pain.

"I'll always be beholding to you, Amy. I want you to know and believe that." He bent low and brushed her cheek with a kiss. Their eyes met for a moment, and then he was gone from her sight. Her body still tingled, reliving the brief moment when he had forgotten to restrain himself. He had been aroused, their was no mistake about that, but had refused to let it go.

During the next few days of preparation for Amy's departure, the air seemed to have cleared somewhat. Bringing her feelings out into the open and facing them honestly had given her new understanding. The sudden power she had held over him for one exciting moment left her feeling sad, but triumphant. Richard had wanted to make love to her.

She planned to leave on the morning train, on her way to begin a new life in a new town, where no one knew about her tragic past. Mac had made all the arrangements. What he had not made arrangements for, was her return.

Mac walked her to the station feeling both relief and regret. As she stepped up into the coach, she smiled bravely. There was no sudden rush of tears. Her heartache was well concealed. As the train began to roll, Amy waved her white handkerchief from the window, still smiling.

With Amy safely gone, Mac turned his thoughts to Dawn, who was spending the day with Debbie Benson, the daughter of Joe Benson, owner of a large cattle ranch. He had driven her out in the buggy early that morning. He had picked today for a reason, because he was keeping Amy's departure a secret, dreading the questions she was bound to ask.

He picked her up before dark and drove her slowly back to town. Wondering now what the town might be thinking about Amy's sudden departure. He was sure that some of the good women would offer to undertake Dawn's care, and hated the thought of a stranger in his house.

When they arrived back at the cabin it was dark and deserted.

Mac felt a chill as they stepped inside the empty room.

"Where's Amy?" came the question he hated to answer.

"She's gone, honey. She won't be back."

Dawn threw her arms around Mac's neck and kissed him. "Oh, Daddy! She's gone? Is she really gone forever?" Her voice rang with delight. "You sent her away?"

"Hey! Why are you so happy?" He hadn't expected this.

"I hated her," she said, still hugging him.

"Why did you hate her? She was good to you."

"She was mean and she hated me. Do you want to know why? Well, I'll tell you. She wanted you to like her more than you like me."

"Hush up!" he scolded, feeling stripped naked before her eyes. She was so young, yet she saw and understood so much. Even more than Mac himself could comprehend. He refused to let her draw him into a discussion about Amy. Already he was no match for her.

Usually he could think with some degree of intelligence without losing control. He realized suddenly that his senses were seriously confused. Hearing Dawn admit that she hated Amy had thrust him into an emotional convulsion. She had been like a mother to the child, had breast fed her as an infant. Her reaction confused him, but he said no more on the subject.

Mac moved his things into the cabin, unwilling to leave Dawn alone at night for fear she might awaken and become frightened. He had seen to it that she had never been left alone day or night.

He felt strange and empty as he lay beneath the sweet smelling linens on Amy's bed. His mind was filled with feelings and thoughts that stirred him deeply. Remembering the touch of her lips, the feel of her slim, beautiful body pressing against his caused pangs of depression and loneliness to engulf him like a fever. He began to wonder if he had made a mistake by sending her away. For the first time in many years he experienced feelings of doubt, and a yearning he tried to dismiss from his mind.

CHAPTER

During the twelve years Mac had lived in Courgat, there had been no serious Indian trouble. Some of the settlers had lost stock, but they could not truthfully accuse the Indians of being responsible. Because Indian wars occurred in all parts of the country, Indians were generally thought of as savages without souls. What was not taken into consideration was the fact that they only became hostile when they were being threatened. As more and more settlers moved into the territory, they began to push the Indians off their hunting grounds, but at no time were they confident or comfortable with the situation. They were plagued with constant fear of Indian retaliation, yet nothing seemed dangerous enough to stop the steady flow of wagons.

Some of the misinformed squatters felt that the military post, being only a day's ride away, would hold the Indians in check. Little did they realize that the Indians would "take up the hatchet" for survival, going head to head with the soldiers if necessary, fighting until the last drop of Indian blood was spilled on the soil of their hunting grounds.

It was natural that Mac would turn to Indian trade if he expected to expand his business. They would both prosper. He had what the Indians needed, and they most likely had more pelts than corn, seed, salt, and cloth.

His meat market was a success, and something Zeek could manage single handed if it became necessary. Even when he was drunk, he could do as much work as any two sober men. To make sure his business continued to run efficiently, Mac hired Ned Rowling to work for him. He was honest and energetic, and he trusted him to take care of business when he needed time off. He was making plans to visit the village of Chief Brave Horse.

When he mentioned his plans to Edward Keel, he was shocked. "You can't possibly be serious about this. You know how this town feels about Indians."

"They act like a bunch of scared rabbits. The Indians aren't causing any trouble. They're peaceable."

"Only as long as they're not riled."

"I have no intentions of riling them."

"If you start trading with Indians, they will be running all over town. You may get some of them killed."

"My business is buying and selling, and I refuse to draw the line where Indians are concerned. If the town disagrees, that's their problem."

"If they have a problem, you're the source of it. I'm warning you, you're fixing to bring trouble down on your neck."

"Then so be it, because I won't change my mind."

Like the Indians, Mac was a peaceable man unless he got pushed too far, then his explosive temper took command. He didn't create quarrels because disagreements bred enemies, and that was bad for business. He was puzzled by Keel's attitude, for he had encouraged him to build up his business. He felt as if he had been doused with cold water.

The following day, just after closing, a group of men gathered outside the trading post. Some were mounted, others were standing around talking. Mac figured they were there to challenge his decision concerning Indian trade. He stepped outside to greet them, his expression one of determination. "Howdy boys," he said smoothly. "I'm closed. Come back tomorrow."

A rumble rose from the group of men. Don Willis stepped down from his horse and stood facing Mac. "Now see here McCloud," he drawled, "we know you're a reasonable man, and we expect you to take into consideration the objections of this town concerning your plans to trade with the Indians."

"Get to the point," Mac snapped.

"What we came to say is this: if you go cluttering up our town with a bunch of Indians, we're going to cram all that money you're making right down your throat."

"You aim to be the first to try, Willis? Or do you need this mob to back you up?" Mac stood over him, clenching his fists.

"I don't need no help."

A cruel light danced in Mac's eyes as he watched Don stiffen, bowing his neck like a bantam rooster. He took a step toward him and said slow and deliberately, "You got a big mouth for such a little man, now why don't you shut it before I overhaul your pucker?"

Don took three steps backward into the circle of men. Mac took three steps forward. The knot of men quickly moved out of his way. At that moment Lawrence Tompkins, the banker, separated himself from the crowd and stepped between Mac and Don.

"Now hold on, boys. I think we can settle this without violence. I hate the sight of a bloody nose. Let's all step over to the saloon for a glass of beer and discuss this like gentlemen." He looked at Mac and smiled. "Forget about what Don said, he tends to speak when he should be listening. Let it drop. What do you say?"

"Sounds sensible to me. These boys can't seem to use the head on their shoulders, maybe they will have better luck with the head on a glass of beer. I'll buy."

At his slanderous remark another rumble swept the gathering. A slick dressed cowboy stepped out of the collection and mounted his horse. "I ain't drinking with no Indian lover." He threw the words over his shoulder as he rode off in a burst of dust kicking his horse.

Mac uttered a contemptuous remark, spit on the ground, and strode toward the saloon. The remaining men followed.

The saloon was packed with the usual bunch of men who came to town on Saturday to gamble, get drunk, and visit the whores. Scattered about were those who came for other reasons. Some to escape a nagging wife, others suffering from boredom. Mac wasn't sure why he was there.

Before the bartender could draw the first round of beers, Alvin Biglo, the mayor, walked through the swinging doors. Seeing Mac, he managed a thin smile, making his way over to him. "Just the man I want to see," he said, shaking Mac's hand with the grip of a sick man.

"This does seem to be my night," Mac remarked. "I can't imagine why I'm so popular all of a sudden? Or is it because I'm so unpopular?"

"No, not at all, quite the contrary. I have a proposition to make you." He looked around for an empty table. "Let's sit down. I hate standing."

Mac's eyes fell to Biglo's sagging belly that pushed his belt so low that Mac wondered how it held his pants up. "Sorry Biglo, I can't accommodate you." He made a gesture with a sweep of his hand toward the men standing at the bar. "These gentleman asked first."

"I'm sure these boys won't mind waiting a few minutes. Do you, boys?"

"We got a little Indian business to talk about, and it won't keep," Don said with a snarl.

Mac about halfway expected him to bark.

"Well, isn't that a coincidence. That's exactly what I want to discuss with him," Biglo said smoothly.

"If you men have any ideas about changing my mind, forget it." Mac's voice rose from his usual level. "I'm not in the habit of letting other people do my thinking for me. Not all Indians are renegades. I've been here for twelve years and I haven't heard a rumble. Leave them alone, and they leave you alone. Don't you realize we're living on their land? In their eyes we're all a bunch of thieves, and they're right."

Don suddenly flew at Mac, flailing his arms wildly. "Oh, go sit down!" Mac said disgustedly, put his splayed fingers over Don's face and shoved him backwards. He crashed into a table before hitting the floor. "You runts are all the same, a big mouth, no brains, and a sparrow ass. If any of you other boys want to take it up, do it now."

Every eye in the saloon was pinned on Mac in silence. He could have heard a belly growl clear across the room. At length, two men helped Don to his feet, and the normal flow of conversation resumed.

"You men need to teach your leader some manners before he gets hurt."

"Now, Mac, take it easy," Biglo said uneasily. "No need getting all worked up like this. I'm sure these men were only doing what they thought was best."

"Yeah, best for who? You're all acting like a bunch of women. You go white at the mention of an Indian. You don't seem to understand that they only attack in self-defense, trying to protect their home. It's the same all over the country. The white men and Indians differ in the way they live.

Indians raise corn and vegetables, but they hunt wild animals for most of their food and clothing. Settlers are mostly farmers. They cut down the trees to get farm land. After they destroy the trees and the underbrush, wild animals no longer have a place to live, and the Indians lose their hunting ground, which is their survival. When that happens the Indians are forced to choose between moving to new hunting grounds or fighting to keep their old one. What happens when they have no place left to move? They are forced to "take up the hatchet."

"How come you know so much about Indians?" Biglo asked.

"I witnessed the destruction of many Indians by my father in New Mexico. They were the scapegoats, and he was the law. It was a simple thing for a man to kill his neighbor's stock and blame it on the Indians, screaming, 'hostile,' and then ask the government for help. Their villages were burned, women and children killed, whole villages were wiped out, leaving their land up for grabs. My father took advantage of the opportunity before the steady flow of settlers beat him to it."

"Then it will happen here sooner or later," Don said, his tone taking on a more human quality. "I heard the army is turning the Oklahoma Boomers back, but they keep on coming and some are crossing over into Texas, moving right into Apache territory."

"That's right, Don. And the Apache are damned hostile. They raid for the fun of it. They hate soldiers. They made lightning attacks on lonely outposts in New Mexico. I have no intentions of trading with the Apaches. They don't trade, they take. I'm talking about trading with Chief Brave Horse. The Comanches are peaceable."

"You're a strange man McCloud," Biglo said.

"How's that, Biglo?"

"I can't put my finger on it, but you run mighty deep."

"I'm a trader, and the Indians have much to trade. I have what they need: fresh meat, cornmeal, sugar, salt, tobacco, blankets, and anything else they fancy."

"And whiskey," a man yelled. "Drunk Indians go on the warpath."

"I don't sell liquor."

"Well somebody will if you give 'um a chance, and we don't want no trouble."

"If there's trouble, the squatters will bring it on themselves by squeezing the Indians into a corner, and it will eventually come to that. The Indians will soon be outnumbered. And like a simmering kettle, being pushed closer and closer to the boiling point, and then they will fight till the last one is either killed or captured. But they can't win."

"We don't want no trouble," a man spoke up.

"Neither do I," Mac said flatly. He tossed a coin on the bar, picked up his hat and pushed out through the batwings, leaving them snapping.

Mac kissed Dawn good-night and tucked her in. It was late, but he was too keyed up to sleep. Maybe he had bit off a chunk too big to chew, but he was determined not to change his plans. Trading with the Indians would be a new and exciting experience. He would be taking advantage of their many skills, especially their hunting and trapping ability. They were like children in so many ways, ignorant of the white man's ways and the way they could be cheated, trading valuable items for the white man's trinkets. He thought about his father, the Indian blood he had shed to satisfy his greed. Remembering caused him to shrink inside.

Thinking back, he saw again the expression on the faces of the men who challenged him. They were jealous because he had thought of the idea first and had the guts to go through with it. The money would be going into his pocket instead of theirs. He decided that was what really spooked them.

Mac had not yet closed his eyes when the morning sun came in through the kitchen windows. He cupped his hand over the lamp globe and blew out the flame. It was time to get on with his plans.

CHAPTER

6

"Didn't you go to bed last night?" Dawn's voice came from the doorway, thick with sleep.

"No, I had some thinking to do."

"Must be important thoughts to keep you up all night."

"Very important, for both of us. It has to do with business. I've decided to start trading with the Indians."

Dawn's eyes widened in surprise. "Oh, what a marvelous idea. When?"

"You might as well know right off, the whole town is on my back like buzzards on a dead horse."

"You're not afraid are you?"

"Not for myself, but you need friends."

"If I lose them now, they were never my friends in the first place."

"You have a point there. It's like separating the sheep from the goats," he said, getting to his feet. He stood up straight and stretched, trying to work the kinks out of his spine. "I'll have to be gone for a few days. Guess it's about time I got a woman in here to look after you."

"What far? I can take care of myself."

"It's out of the question. Don't argue with me."

"I don't want you to hire a woman, please. I'll stay with Debbie." She was looking at him with soft pleading eyes.

"All right, you win for now." He swung her high in the air, loving the sound of her laughter. Already, she ruled him completely.

Mac regretted his own stubbornness in not hiring someone to keep house for them. He had shunned the idea of anyone interfering with the relationship between him and his daughter. Taking full charge of her kept him on his toes, but he was happy. Content to be sharing the cabin with her and escape the lonely room in back of the trading post. He lapped up her attention. She seemed to understand him almost as much as Elizabeth had. She had an uncanny way of reading his thoughts. He realized with regrets that she was fast growing into an adult. The lines of her slender body were beginning to swell, transforming her into a mature woman. She looked more like her mother now than she had when she was a baby. There were times when he looked at Dawn and felt an overwhelming desire for Elizabeth wrench his insides, and the yearning he knew so well filled him with despair, driving him to drink to kill the dull ache inside him, and the liquor that burned his insides at first soon turned soothing and warm, easing the tension and dulling his memories.

His drunken homecoming was always the same. Listening for his uneven steps on the porch and the rattle of the door, Dawn would dash to his rescue. She had already guessed, even before he came home, that he was drowning his sorrows at the Silver Buckle. She would help him to bed and remove his boots, then place her cool hands on his hot face to ease the whirling in his head and the ache behind his eyes. After he fell asleep she would kiss him tenderly and tiptoe from the room. Sometimes, when she couldn't sleep, she would slip quietly from the cabin to walk in the cool night air. Looking at the small cabin, desolate in the dark, she would think about the big new house Mac promised to build one day. And a fine house it would be, made from beautiful stone with many chimneys and more rooms than they would ever need. It would have an upstairs with a wide staircase, a cellar full of good things to eat, and many bottles of whiskey for Mac and his friends.

She often wondered about her grandfather, Henry McCloud, and the great house he had built for her grandmother. She wished Mac would tell her more about his life when he lived in New Mexico. The many times she had asked him, he seemed unable to talk about it, as if it were a secret he dared not tell.

Feeling relaxed, she would slip back inside and into her own bed, lying awake for a time listening to her father toss and turn in his unnatural drunken sleep.

It was on such nights that his recurring dream returned to haunt him, the dead and painful past of his unconscious mind coming to life in a nightmare.

He was always walking through dense woods surrounded by deep, dark, shadows, and the path he followed wound endlessly in all directions. In the distance there stood a girl in the center of the path wearing a long white flowing gown trimmed in gold Indian braid, her dark hair blowing in the wind. She stood with her back to him, and he wanted to see her face. As he drew near, she began to run aimlessly down the winding path with Mac chasing after her. As they ran she would pass out of the shadows into the light. Just as they stepped into the light he would catch up to her, and taking her by the shoulders turn her to face him. The beautiful face framed in black hair was that of Elizabeth, and in her arms, pressed close to her heart, she held a baby. After Amy went away the dream became confusing, with the girl's identity changing from Elizabeth to Amy, then back again. After seeing her face, an instant later the light would disappear and the small figure of the girl with it, leaving Mac in dark confusion. He wished he could stop having the dream, it was frightening and made him uneasy, like looking into an open grave.

Mac was surprised when Charles Morgan, the town's sheriff paid him an unexpected visit.

"Hope I'm not intruding, coming by so early, but I wanted to catch you before you left the house," he said lazily.

"I'm in no hurry. Ned opens up for me, sometimes closes too. Want a cup of coffee?"

"Just a swallow. I ain't got long." He flopped his heavy bulk into the nearest chair, letting his breath out in a gasp of discomfort.

Noticing the look of pain cloud his obese face, Mac asked, "Are you ailing, Charley? You don't look too good this morning."

"I can't hardly hobble around. My rheumatism is acting up something fierce, must be a spell of wet weather on the way."

"Hope you're right. We could sure use a rain."

"I didn't come over here to talk about the weather, Mac. I got more important things to say to you," he said between slurps of coffee.

"No doubt you're referring to the fracas at the saloon last night."

"Not so much the fracas as the reason for it. Do you still aim to go through with your crazy notion?"

"If there's a law against it then you better get a cell ready, because I intend to do exactly that."

"I can't lock you up for trading with the Indians, there ain't no law against that, but I feel it's my duty as a peace officer to warn you."

"I've been warned."

"Well, let's just say that I aim to make it official."

"OK, you have, now if you're finished with your business, I can get on with mine."

Sheriff Morgan was half-lying in his chair by now, his arms folded across his swollen middle. He raised his arms in a gesture of defeat, then dropped them back on his stomach. "Even if it could work, which I doubt, how do you intend going about it?"

"Simple. I'm going to the village of Chief Brave Horse and make a deal," he stated flatly.

"Simple, you say! That's crazy. You don't know how to deal with Indians. Wouldn't surprise if you come back without your scalp."

"You deal with Indians the same way you deal with anybody else. Honest."

"Now see here, Mac, just because the Indians around here are peaceable don't mean you can sit down to dinner with 'um. They're still Indians and they still collect scalps."

"Well, if they do scalp me, you can all have a good laugh. I will have at least contributed something to amuse this town full of morons."

Morgan rose from his chair, produced one of his hideous laughs, and slapped Mac on the back in full agreement. "I have a lot of regrets about myself, and one of 'um is the fact that I ain't more like you. I respect a man who knows what he wants and then goes after it. I don't do nothing special. I just drift along with the crowd doing all the predictable things. I'm a boring man. Know what I mean?"

"I'd probably have more friends if I was a little more predictable, but I'd feel like a failure if I didn't make a few enemies."

"I always say, a man who's your enemy ain't fit to be your friend. Well, I better mosey on down to the jail, it's almost breakfast time."

"You got somebody locked up?"

"Yeah, Don Willis."

"What far?"

"For breaking up a table and chair over at the Silver Buckle last night."

"Don't seem to me like that's much of a reason for locking him up."

"Where that smart ass is concerned, I don't need much of a reason." He moved toward the door and Mac opened it and stood aside to let the great bulk of the man pass.

During the next two days Mac made the necessary preparations for his journey to the village of Brave Horse. He felt an impending crisis with the town, but refused to let their actions alter his. The only thing he was uncertain about was leaving Dawn, but there was no way to avoid that, and his worry began to threaten his decision. He didn't want to leave her with the Bensons.

Doctor Keel volunteered to look after Dawn, claiming she could earn her keep by helping him in his clinic. Mac refused at first, but reconsidered after Edward accused him of being a short witted father. "This could turn out to be more than just a short visit, Mac. You could get killed. Should that happen I want you to know that Dawn will be well cared for."

"My God, I didn't know you were having thoughts like that."

"I consider myself an intelligent man, and any man with half sense can recognize the danger you're facing. I have made up my mind. Dawn will stay at my place, and that's the end of it. Or you can forget your fool notion and stay home. I won't take no for an answer."

"I took that for granted, it's a pure waste of time to argue with you, you old goat." He spoke sharply, but was smiling.

He decided to start at sunrise on Monday. If everything went as planned he should be back by Wednesday. The anticipation of his coming adventure stimulated him like a double shot of whiskey; yet when the time came he departed reluctantly, also triumphantly, feeling he had passed every test of persuasion.

He left town trailing a pack horse loaded down with gifts for the Indians, samples of what he had to offer, just enough to get their attention, and in return he hoped his gesture would secure their business. He took the wagon road for about a mile before turning north and angling across the open grass land of the Benson ranch, the rich land at the foot of the thickly wooded hill country where the Indian hunting grounds began.

By mid-afternoon Mac was high in the hills. He traveled along the banks of a winding creek that led to the wide mouth of the river where the Indian village was located. From time to time he would stop to drink from the clear spring water where it rushed across the flat rocks. The beauty of the land here was no less then breath taking. The Indian's hunting ground was still a perfect world of virgin earth untouched by churning wagons wheels, the turn of the plow, felling of trees, and all the unsightly clutter and noise of civilization. He had become acutely aware of the sounds of nature, listening to the many different birds nesting high in the arms of the giant oak and pecan trees, blending their songs in a great and wondrous symphony. In the distance came the call of many crows as they dipped and sailed across the sky, their black wings spread wide reflecting the sun.

It was near sundown when Mac caught sight of the Indian village. It was located on the edge of the Brazos River, many miles north of Courgat. Mac was still quite a distance from the village when he was spotted. In minutes a party of warriors rode bareback out to meet him. They drew their horses up about thirty yards in front of him and waited, weapons in readiness. Two scouts swung wide in the direction from which Mac had come, making sure he was alone. One of the braves, in head dress, drew out away from the line and rode toward Mac, sitting on his horse straight and proud, watching Mac with a steady eye. Mac stared back, his heart quickening, feeling every inch of him a target. His flesh tingled at the thought of an arrow driving through his body. He clutched the saddle horn and waited helplessly, realizing just how precious his life was to him, and how easily it could be snuffed out, like blowing on a candle.

The brave questioned Mac in a demanding tone and in excellent English. "Why have you come here?"

Mac answered, seemingly calm, "I am your friend. I want to talk to your chief."

The two scouts checking the rear doubled back. They drew up a ways out and spoke in sign language, using hands, elbows, arms and head. Satisfied that he was alone and meant them no harm, they escorted him into the village and stopped before the tepee of Chief Brave Horse.

Moments later an old Indian appeared wearing the full headdress of a chief. He searched Mac's face silently for a long moment as though looking into his soul. He gestured to Mac in sign language, "Dismount." His motion, so eloquent without a spoken word that Mac was able to understand. He stepped down with caution, careful not to make any sudden moves. They stood eye to eye momentarily, and then the old chief looked him up and down, turned, and motioned Mac to follow him inside his lodge.

A small fire burned in the middle of the tepee, the smoke escaping through an open flap at the top. The air inside was thick with foul odors and wood smoke. In the shadows Mac saw an old woman squatting on a buffalo robe. When the chief motioned for Mac to sit, the woman rose slowly to her feet and left the tepee.

"You want make talk?" Brave Horse said.

"I come make trade with Brave Horse," he answered.

"Paleface cheat Indian."

"I do not cheat Indians. I bring gifts, outside on my pack horse."

"You get, bring here."

Mac brought the bundle inside and laid it at Brave Horse's feet, sat back down and crossed his legs. A slight smile pulled at the corners of the old chief's thin lips. Mac watched as Brave Horse opened the bundle and inspected its contents, his eyes glittering.

There was corn, tobacco, sugar, salt, a bright colored blanket, and a small box of beads and trinkets. It was the trinkets that got the Chief's attention. He held the box in both hands and did not put it back with the other items. It was his to treasure.

"Me keep gifts. Me like."

"My name is Mac McCloud, I run the trading post. I want make trade with you and your people."

"What you have trade Indians?"

"Cloth, blankets, beads, flour, sugar—many things." He motioned toward the bundle.

"Me like trade for whiskey, guns."

"No whiskey, no guns. Soldiers put me in jail if I trade whiskey and guns."

"You not trust Indian?"

"I trust Indians. Soldiers like squaw, they scared."

"How I know you not cheat my people."

"You can trust me."

"Indian trust no paleface."

"I bring gifts. I'm your friend."

"Paleface no friend. You bring whiskey. Me trade."

"No whiskey." Mac stood, but as he made a move to leave, Brave Horse motioned him to stay. Mac sat back down, watching Brave Horse finger the little box of trinkets.

"You bring here?"

"No, you come to trading post. We make trade there." Mac realized that his success hinged on whether or not he could persuade the Indians to come to him.

"Indian not like go to town. Paleface not like Indian. Maybe shoot, kill."

"My people won't harm your people. They will know you come in peace to make trade."

"How Brave Horse know you tell truth?" The old chief's eyes grew cold, sending a chill up Mac's backbone. Ignoring his uneasiness, Mac held his ground. "Maybe Brave Horse not so brave. He get old, weak like squaw." Mac felt his throat tighten and his lips go dry. "I not fear Indian. I come your camp to make deal. You fear come to mine?"

The old chief looked puzzled. Mac waited for his reply, watching the expression on his face slowly change. "Brave Horse make trade, come town, bring many braves, many hides. We make deal, maybe whiskey."

"White man no trade for whiskey."

The chief looked at Mac, scorn naked in his eyes. "You sleep one night here, we go with sun."

Mac agreed, without a choice, knowing the old chief didn't trust him. He hoped he still had his scalp come sunrise, wondering just how far he could trust the Indians. If he was still alive by morning, he would have gotten off to a pretty good start.

As Mac left the tepee, several braves entered. They exchanged a few words in Comanche, then began scurrying about the village. Mac guessed the chief had set the camp straight on their deal, because they gave him free run of the place. He could almost feel the staring eyes of the squaws as they huddled together talking, with the help of many gestures.

Many fires were burning about the village and the smell of roasting meat filled the late evening air. The old men, warriors, and children sat idly around the fires while the squaws hurried about waiting on them. A chunky squaw waved her arms at Mac in a motion for him to sit by her fire and eat. Reluctantly he walked over to her and sat down where she pointed a fat finger. She thrust a piece of roasted hot meat into his hands. He tossed it from one hand to the other to keep it from raising blisters, blowing on it occasionally.

Across the fire a young Comanche eyed him curiously, then laughed happily at Mac's wrestling his supper. Every time Mac looked up the boy's eyes were on his face, staring. Mac noticed right away, even at the distance between them, there was something different about the boy. After the boy finished eating, he got up and walked around the fire to where Mac sat. He was much taller than he had appeared while sitting down. He towered over Mac, eyeing him curiously.

"Sit down, boy," Mac said making a motion to the ground beside him.

The boy ignored him and kept staring. Mac stared back into the bluest eyes he had ever seen, the clearest blue he could imagine. The boy made a profound impression on him, despite the boy's age that he guessed to be around fifteen. He saw instantly an unusual quality about him, like an inner light that shown through his eyes.

"What's your name, boy?" he asked, not expecting an answer.

"Light eyes," the boy answered in a deep clear voice.

"I'll say one thing, the name sure fits."

Seemingly, his curiosity satisfied, the boy turned and walked away without a word or glance.

The Indians were beginning to disappear inside the tepees to retire. Mac rose and walked over to his horse and removed his bed roll. He rolled up in his blanket close to the fire, thinking he wouldn't be able to close his eyes all night. To his surprise, he fell asleep quickly and slept soundly.

It began to rain a little before sun up. Mac sat on a rock under a tree and pulled his blanket over his head, not being in the mood for a bath. He remembered what Charley Morgan had said about his rheumatism acting up when there was a wet spell on the way. Mac thought he was just talking a lot of hogwash, but he was forced to face the possibility that maybe Charley knew what he was talking about. Mac spent an uncomfortable hour listening to the river frogs and trying to keep his feet dry. The rain quit, leaving in its place a thin fog that dulled the beauty of the new day.

A good hour of day light was gone by the time Mac, accompanied by eight Comanche bucks, seven heavily laden pack ponies, and their chief, started the return trip to Courgat. Mac was a little surprised when he discovered Brave Horse himself was going along. He had imagined that the old chief was too old and too important to make such a long journey on horseback. They rode in silence, the seven bucks each leading a pack horse, and one buck was scouting up ahead. Mac rode a little behind the chief with the seven bucks bringing up the rear. They didn't take the same course as Mac. He had followed the tributary all the way to the river; the Indians cut across chain after chain of hills, avoiding the tributary completely until they reached the grass lands. They had cut Mac's ride by at least three hours, reaching Courgat by mid afternoon.

When Mac and the Indians topped the rise just outside of town, they came into full view of anyone who happened to be looking in that direction. Several people scurried about, voices suddenly raised, sounding the alarm. Dawn rushed to the window and peered out, sick with fear. Edward Keel stepped in her path as she started through the front door.

"It's my father," she cried.

"I'm well aware of that, but you're not leaving here until I say so." She looked at him and pouted, but left the doorway to run back to the window. Outside the town seemed to be going crazy. Men began to push out through the saloon doors and go off in all directions. Dawn gasped when she saw several men with rifles standing in the door ways. She wondered how they could become so excitable when the situation was so intently simple. She felt a flood of relief when Sheriff Charley Morgan appeared on the saloon porch.

"Put them guns away gents," he roared, holding his shot gun in readiness. "There ain't gonna be no gun play unless I take a notion to shoot one of you numb-skulls."

"Who's side are you on?" Andy Holmes, the barkeeper said, drawing a bead on one of the Indians over the top of the batwings.

"On the side of law and order. Now, you do like I say. All of you, before I throw the whole bunch of you in jail."

The men very reluctantly lowered their rifles and holstered their guns. Several of the men took refuge behind the saloon doors as the Indians drew near, a feather of dust rising behind them. Alvin Biglo ran inside his office and jerked the shades to the bottom of the windows. Lawrence Williams closed his bank in haste, with three people still inside.

Sheriff Morgan stood his ground and waited as the Indians pulled their mounts up in front of the trading post, unloaded their horses and disappeared inside. He had been looking forward to this moment ever since Mac left town. If he had backed down, Charley would have been profoundly disappointed. He took a seat in front of the saloon and waited, curious about the outcome. He realized the seriousness of the situation as regards to the town, and intended to keep the peace without interruption.

Gus Smith and Phillip Singer came out of the saloon and stood on the porch. "How you gonna stop Mac from making an Indian village out of our town?" Gus asked, his bitterness growing.

"I'm not. Why should I?" Charley's eyes challenged him.

"Because we don't like it."

"A man's supposed to be a sensible animal, maybe you'd like to explain to me why this whole town is down on one man, a man who has been a friend to all of you."

"He's still a friend of mine," Phillip said.

"I'm glad to see somebody with a little backbone. I was beginning to think all we had in this town was a bunch of snakes."

"You mean to say that you're upholding Mac too?" Gus asked Phillip in amazement.

"All the way. If you know who your friends are, you take care of 'um, because there may come a time you'll need every friend you can get." Philip swung down off the porch and mounted his horse. "If you happen to need me Charley, I'll be over at the barber shop. I could use a shave," he said, rubbing his chin, and then rode down the street feeling more like a man than usual.

In sight of an hour the Indians had loaded their pack animals with bacon, beans, salt, sugar, tobacco, blankets, corn, several bolts of colorful yard goods, and an assortment of other needs. They rode quietly back toward the hills of home and a big feast, leaving the town of Courgat to eat crow.

Mac was obliged by the way Charley had kept the peace. He had expected to have both hands full of trouble when he returned. "How did you manage to keep the lid on, Charley?"

"For a starter, I kept Don Willis locked up till you made your deal."

"You mean you kept him in jail three days for busting up a table and chair? You know I'm the one who pushed him."

"The way I figure it, he's better off in jail than running loose making trouble. Cause he'd end up right back in jail anyway, or maybe with a few holes in him. I found out a long time ago that a little man is a lot like a little dog. Since he ain't big enough to do much damage hisself, he keeps the rest of the pack excited. While they do his killing he just stands back and barks them on. I hate a dog that barks all the time. They're useless, cause they're cowards. Every time I get a dog like that I shoot it. Too bad you can't put a man out of his misery the same way. Since I can't shoot Willis, all I can do is throw him in jail. They all have a lot to say and not much to do. About the only thing they ever whip is their woman, and I've known a few that couldn't do that."

"I never realized before that he's my enemy."

"A man like Don ain't never had a friend."

Mac agreed with Charley's way of thinking, but he still felt a little guilty about the three days Don spent in jail.

Mayor Alvin Biglo finally got around to saying what he had on his mind. His first try, in the Silver Buckle, drew a blank. Now, after the damage of repercussions had passed, he made his second try. His whole idea was to weasel in on the Indian project.

"I'll keep the town in line for ten percent of your profit"

"Like hell you will. You're a joke. The only person who can keep this town in line is Charley Morgan," Mac exploded. "And another thing, don't get any cute ideas about stirring up a bunch of trouble just to change my mind. Because when the problems commence for me, a bigger headache is gonna start for you, and I'll be the one to start it."

"Now, Mac, you can't blame me if these people feel a little hard toward you. You sure don't think all this is behind you?"

Mac nodded and gave him a dry smile. "Nobody tells me what to do. When they start telling me and I start listening, I'm a dead man. I aim to stay alive in more ways than one, and you and the rest of these jellyfish won't stand in my way."

Biglo, feeling stupid and defeated, walked away empty handed, thwarted by the better man.

Because of the lightning change in the temperament of the town, Mac sometimes wondered if maybe Biglo was keeping them in line. The Indians came and went without a hitch. After a while their presence seemed natural enough, proving that they were just as human as anyone else. All the fears disappeared along with the hot summer. By winter the town was back to normal.

CHAPTER

During the next four years Mac's brilliant achievements in business had won over every man, woman, and child in Courgat. He was as generous as he was intelligent. His convictions were incontestable. He was destined to become a wealthy man.

Dawn had also grown in confidence, prompted by her irrepressible beauty, bitter sweet personality, brilliant mind, and stubborn determination that bewildered and confused all men, and it was impossible for them to resist her. At sixteen she was a mature woman, Her full breasts, like those of her mother, rose high above a trim waist and wide hips. Her innermost thoughts were hidden behind dark eyes laced with long lashes that curled slightly on the ends, and set off by dark arched brows, giving her a dreamy captivating appearance.

Mac was very much aware of his daughter's beauty and the excitement she aroused in masculine eyes. However Ned Rowling seemed to be the only young man capable of holding her interest. Mac had kept Ned on at the trading post largely because of his interest in Dawn, and vice-versa. Ned came from good stock, was honest, hard working, sensible, and morally clean. A cut above the other men she came into contact with. Even so, Mac felt comfortable keeping a close eye on him.

As their friendship ripened, so did Ned's jealousy. His thoughts were on Dawn constantly, and he wanted to fight any man who showed, what he considered, disrespectful interest. He had to restrain that part of him, knowing she would take offense at such behavior. Ned was not satisfied with seeing her in the evenings after work. He contrived ways to slip away during business hours to be with her. She scolded him for stealing away in the middle of the day, and he even liked that.

Ned was by nature a mild mannered man in every respect, except where Dawn was concerned. He was just under six feet tall, slender, with long legs. He displayed a bright smile, green eyes, good teeth, and a thick mop of blonde hair, bleached lighter by the same sun that baked his light skin to a golden tan. He had been three years old when Dawn was born, and since he had commenced working for Mac at age twelve, he and Dawn had become acquainted at a very early age.

He had been fascinated with her from the start, and very conscious of her increasing charm. Now that he was a man his interest in her had become more sensual. He wanted her for his wife and strove in that direction. However, the relationship wasn't moving fast enough to suit him. His love for her grew steadily, creating a terrible hunger inside him, and he was anxious for her to return his affection.

There wasn't a man in town he considered his competition. Dawn ignored them completely; although she showed keen interest in the unbelievable tales about an extraordinary Indian who seemed to move around like a ghost. For quite some time Ned had been hearing stories about an Indian brave known as Light Eyes. Mac was the first to mention him after he returned from his journey to the village of Brave Horse over five years ago. Since that time talk of this unusual Indian sifted into almost every conversation concerning Indians.

Thoughts of Light Eyes crowded Dawn's thoughts more and more. She wondered if such a man did actually exist, and scolded herself for thinking about a man who was little more than a myth.

There were times when Dawn felt a keen restlessness as she busied herself with the daily chores. Looking down at her small hands, red from washing dishes and scrubbing floors, she felt distressed by the monotonous tasks. She was beginning to wish that her father had hired another woman to keep house for them, but despite her feeling of boredom she would never admit that she had made a miss calculation of her feelings. After placing the last dish on the shelf and folding the dish towel, she walked indecisively to the front door and looked toward the trading post. Ned Rowling was headed her way. He smiled with a flash of nice teeth and waved his hand as he walked through the front gate, hastening his step when she smiled back. She opened the screen door and stepped out onto the porch. Ned stepped from the ground to the porch, ignoring the three steps in between.

"What are you doing over here so early?" she said in a tone of disapproval.

"I couldn't stay away from you any longer."

"Oh poof" she said happily, pulling at the knees of her tight denims as she sat down on the top step. He dropped down beside her, stretching his long, slender legs out in front of him.

"Guess who I saw today?" he said reluctantly, not really wanting to discuss the subject with her, and didn't know why he was, except he was curious to know her reaction.

She guessed by the tone of his voice that what he had to say was most likely something silly. "Probably yourself in the mirror," she teased, running her finger down the bridge of his nose.

"I'm serious. Don't you want to know?"

"I guess so, if it's interesting," she answered, minus enthusiasm.

"I saw that big Indian Zeek's been talking about."

She jerked her head up and stared at him. She felt her face grow hot and her heart beat fast. To hide her raging emotions, she spoke in a doubtful tone. "Oh, really. I doubt you would know him from any other Indian."

"It was him all right."

"How can you be sure?" she said flippantly to cover the turbulence raging inside her.

"I heard the stories enough times. I'd know him anywhere."

"I think you're just saying that to sound important. You know how people want to hear more stories about him."

"I know it was him."

"Where did you see him?"

"In that bunch of trees over by the cemetery. He was with some more braves. I figure they camped there last night."

"Why would he do that?"

"Maybe he's going to do some trading today."

"Then why aren't you over there waiting for them? Do you expect my father to do all the work while you sit on my front porch? I guess I had better hurry over there and do your job. Then I can take a look at this Indian you claim is the one all the talk is about. Indians don't have blue eyes."

"This one does."

"And I suppose he's tall, with a lot of muscles, and handsome too? What kind of horse does he ride? How was he dressed?"

"You really do want to see him don't you?"

"You act surprised because I'm curious. What's wrong with that?"

"Plenty!" His voice was shaking. "You're not just curious, you're interested."

"Is there a difference? To be curious is just another form of interest." If she wasn't careful she would make a complete fool of herself. And anyway, what she felt was none of Ned's business.

Ned was ashamed of his jealous outburst, and felt guilty because of his weakness, a fault that might drive her away from him. He did not reproach her further. He wished he had kept his mouth shut about the Indian. Truth was, he wasn't at all sure he was the Indian with blue eyes; he hadn't been close enough to make that out. Bragging to Dawn was a foolish gesture on his part, but he wanted to be the first one to tell her. Mac was certain to mention it if the tall Indian he saw was Light Eyes. He figured it was only natural for Dawn to be curious, even interested, as was every woman in town because he was excitingly different. He decided it was time to change the subject. "Are you still going to the dance with me tonight?"

"I said I would, didn't I?" she replied sarcastically.

"I just wanted to make sure that some other fellow hadn't horned in on me."

"If you keep standing around here talking, you'll be horning in on yourself. If I don't finish my chores, I won't be allowed to go to the dance with you or anybody else."

"You try to make Mac sound like a slave driver, but I know better than to swallow that. You're the slave driver. I'll see you later," he said, getting to his feet.

"Get!" she said, kicking at the seat of his pants, missing by inches. She marched inside, head high, letting the screen door slam behind her. She walked straight through the house and out the back door to the rain barrel. She skimmed the bugs and litter off the top, dipped a bucket full and carried it to the washstand on the back porch. She wished now that she hadn't promised Ned she would go to the dance with him. She had been looking forward to it all week, now she dreaded it. All she wanted to do was daydream about the magnificent red man she had never seen but could not dismiss from her mind. If it were possible to fall in love with a dream, she had indeed. At the very mention of his name she felt excited and flustered. She wished there was someplace to hide inside the store where she could see without exposing herself. Mac had warned her never to enter the trading post while the Indians were there. She was unable to stop her tenacious musing and felt disgusted with herself for the unsavory thoughts that stirred inside her.

She pictured in her mind a vision of Light Eyes, drawn from the may interpretations she had heard over the past five years. Thinking that he might be so close sent a shiver up her spine, and she wanted to be left alone with her thoughts of him. She would go to the dance with Ned because she had promised, and for no other reason. Ned bored her. He always had.

She wondered if Frost would show up at the dance. If he did, he was sure to get drunk and there was sure to be trouble. Charley would most likely end up throwing him in jail to sober up. Even behind bars he carried on something fierce. Many times Charley had threatened to shoot him the same way he shot barking dogs.

Frost had come to Courgat about a year ago with his brother Daniel, a quiet, mild tempered man, so much older than Frost that he had at first been mistaken for his father. They hit town with a good deal of money, bought several hundred acres of rich land and stocked it with good beef. Daniel's only interest was to work hard and improve his ranch. Frost's main interest seemed to be saloon brawling, women, and intoxication. He was attractive in a devilish way, and had conquered as many women's hearts as he pleased. All but one, and it was the only one he truly desired. He had gained no ground where Dawn was concerned. She nourished feelings of animosity toward him because of his loud blustering ways, too much swagger, a disgusting amount of brag, and always threatening. He had very early earned the reputation for being a trouble-maker. On Saturday nights he persistently drank too much and staggered through town with a bottle in his hand looking for a fight, and usually found it. There was always someone eager to challenge his big mouth.

Dawn would never understand why some men looked for a fight the way a thirsty horse looks for water.

She sat dreamily on a blanket spread in the sun drying her freshly washed hair. She felt lazy and languid. All the stamina she felt earlier had vanished. She lay back and gazed toward the sky, a beautiful indigo blue with fluffy white clouds moving into fascinating designs as they drifted ever so slowly toward the hills and the Indian hunting grounds. Everything around her seemed to move in slow motion, Even the birds glided lazily from branch to branch.

Her mind seemed to be in an expectant state, controlled by a mysterious force like a great waterfall that swept her thoughts with driving energy into the sea of another world. Hidden deep inside were feelings of entrapment, a growing discontentment that caused her to feel wasted and useless. There was nothing in her life to fill the emptiness, the need of something more that she could not identify. Her thoughts of Light Eyes brought her strange feelings of impatience and deep soul shaking hunger. She wanted this man, who was no more than a figment of her vivid imagination, yet she suffered an emotional need. Even as she felt self-disgust, she could not escape the passion that flamed out of control like a prairie fire, burning away every thought of Ned. Her mind was branded with lustful sensations that tormented her, an ever present thorn in her flesh stinging her imagination. The things she had heard about Light Eyes echoed in her mind like a voice in a cave. He seemed to move from place to place like a shadow. Only very few people had seen him, and each time it was an awakening in the eyes of the beholder. The men spoke of him with envy, the women with giddiness.

He had saved the life of Zeek Yates when he became lost in the hill country during a blizzard and was suffering from an injured foot he had caught in his own trap. Zeek shook violently as bitter cold penetrated his body like sharp knives, tormenting him so that he prayed to die quickly. He could already feel his senses slipping and he was becoming sleepy. As he lay barely conscious, covered in sleet and snow, an Indian suddenly appeared before him like a dream, emerging out of a wall of blinding wind swept snow. He took the blanket from his own shoulders and wrapped it around Zeek, picked him up, threw him over his shoulder like a sack of grain, and moved through the blizzard with great strength and determination, his footing sure and smooth as a panthers.

Zeek drew his face into the folds of the blanket to feel the warmth of his own breath. He was neither conscious of time nor direction. He had no idea how far the Indian had carried him before they came to a cave, its dark entrance barely visible through the falling snow. Zeek was astounded by the Indian's exceptional sense of direction, feeling certain that no ordinary man could have found his way, but would have wandered endlessly until he froze to death.

The inside of the cave was narrow, extending high above the small entrance that was covered with a buffalo hide to seal out the blowing snow and sharp wind. A fire burned near the back of the cave. The Indian laid Zeek by the fire and added more wood. In a matter of minutes the flames grew to blazing, and Zeek could feel the warmth returning to his body The smoke rose to escape through a small gap above the buffalo hide.

Zeek's eyes never left the Indian as he squatted beside the fire warming himself. Zeek saw him clearly now and marveled at his appearance. His clothes were fashioned from animal skins and he filled them out with wide shoulders and long legs. He looked down at Zeek with piercing blue eyes from his tremendous height. There was certain kindness in his gestures that made him appear pleasant, but the sharpness of his eyes and the hardness of his mouth plainly spoke of his capacities to handle any situation. His motions were smooth and exacting, but without haste. The few words he spoke were in exceptionally good English.

When Zeek asked him about himself and how he came to find him, he answered with only his name, "Light Eyes."

During the first two days they were together the oppressive weather kept Zeek close to the fire nursing his sore foot. The Indian came and went silently, busy in his pursuit of food and pelts. Slowly Zeek began to enter into a little conversation with him. At times he noticed an extraordinary sense of eagerness in the Indian's face, as though he wanted to express his thoughts, but his expression would change just as quickly, and no amount of encouragement would loosen his tongue.

Judging from the number of skins on the cave floor, Zeek surmised that the Indian had been living in the cave since the onset of winter. Zeek had been hunting and trapping since age ten, and it was his profound opinion that here before him was the greatest triumph of hunting ability, and the finest fulfillment of manhood possible. He felt privileged to be in his company.

On the third day Zeek's temperature shot up as the swelling in his foot increased. Light Eyes laid the back of his hand on Zeek's head and looked with concern at his foot. "Your head is hot and your foot is swollen with poison," he said, his eyes meeting Zeek's with an unspoken message.

"You got to cut it open, ain't you?" Zeek sucked in his breath raggedly

"If you want to live."

"Well, get it over with before I lose my nerve, cause I damned sure don't want to die after all the trouble you went to, to save me from freezing."

Light Eyes drew his knife from the sheathe and laid the blade in the coals until the point turned white hot. He knelt before Zeek on his knees and looked at his oversized foot. The skin was stretched tight and red streaks traveled up his leg. He threw one leg over Zeek and took his foot in his left hand, with his right he held the knife. His hand moved swift and sure, there came a flash of steal, a spray of pus, and blood issued forth. Zeek clenched his teeth, his face tight with pain, but he made not a sound. He knew it was important that he show the Indian his courage.

Light Eyes had done what he must. He met Zeek's eyes with understanding, saw the tortured expression on his face that spoke silently of the pain he had endured like a man. He washed the wound thoroughly and placed a poultice of fat meat over the gash, held in place with a leather thong.

Zeek looked at him, dazed with pain, his eyes feverishly bright. He managed a weak smile, then relaxed as the tension left his body. He was filled with emotion as he quietly expressed his thanks to this magnificent Indian, who was a mystery, as well as a miracle.

Zeek proudly told of his experience at the hands of Light Eyes, feeling so much emotion that his eyes would tear. There were those who passed his tale off as whiskey talk, thinking the Indian was only a figment of his imagination. Zeek would never forget the blue eyed Indian who had saved his life. A man he considered surprisingly intelligent and caring. Not like any Indian he had ever heard tell of.

Zeek left his job at the trading post for a few weeks every winter to hunt and trap in the hill country. Nothing would ever dull his desire for trapping; it was in his blood like a disease. On these hunting expeditions he searched eagerly for the Indian, but he had never seen him again, this mysterious man who lived a life of monastic simplicity; yet he was envied by all men who believed the tales they had heard.

Dawn had hung on every word the first time Zeek told her the story of his encounter with Light Eyes. Her thoughts were far away now, remembering the way Zeek had described the Indian to her. She didn't know how or when, but she was determined that one day she would meet him. What Ned had said about seeing him set her heart singing with excitement.

Dawn was folding the blanket when she heard the drumming of horse's hooves in the distance. Holding her hand over her face to shade her eyes from the bright sun, she looked in their direction, straining her eyes to see the riders. She watched as they disappeared behind a patch of trees and then came into view again as they topped the rise in the trail. The riders came thundering down the dusty road, clods flying from swift hooves. They pulled their ponies up in front of the trading post in a swirl of dust, distorting her view momentarily.

She stood like a statue watching the Indians disappear inside with their pelts. One of the Indians towered over the other four, and her heart leaped in her chest. She wanted to move closer, to see their faces. She had been watching Indians come and go with incredible interest for the past five years, always looking for the one called Light Eyes.

Today she felt something different was about to happen, something strange and wonderful. Her heart was beating wildly, and her head was spinning like a top as she hurried to the back door of the store. From inside came the sound of voices. She slipped quietly through the door, praying the hinges wouldn't squeak, as sometimes they did when the door was opened too wide. She held her breath now, for fear Mac might hear her heavy breathing or the quick pounding of her heart and send her away.

The back of the store was used to store bulky supplies: large sacks of flour, sugar and oats, leaving only a path from the back door to the far end of the counter. Dawn used the stacks of supplies as a fortress to hide herself from the eyes of the men who stood only a few feet away. She moved quietly around the sacks piled high on the wood floor. From this position she could see and hear every word without showing herself. Very cautiously she peeked anxiously over a sack of flour while fear lay in her stomach like a rock. The Indians had their backs to her and she could not see their faces, but she didn't have to. Her heart told her Light Eyes was there, sending her blood pounding through her shaking body. The brave to the right of her father was inches taller than Mac, who was over six feet. The Indian had golden skin, about the color of her own. She sank to the floor as her legs went suddenly limp, her heart beating like a thousand tom-toms in her ears. Her hand flew to her breast as though to quiet the wild pounding. Again she peered over the mound of sacks, this time she felt like crying out to him. As though mesmerized, she could not look away. He began to slowly turn toward her as if he could feel her eyes burning into his flesh. She jerked her head behind the sacks again, even as every fiber in her body cried out to see his face, but she was afraid to meet his eyes. She was suddenly aware of her appearance. She smoothed her clothes and pushed at the damp ringlets that clung to her flushed face. Losing her courage to meet the eyes of the man she had been searching for and dreaming of, she started to retreat, slipping along the wall behind the sacks like a cat, easing her way toward the back door. She suddenly stopped, hearing his voice for the first time. She couldn't see who was speaking but she knew it was Light Eyes. His voice was smooth and clear, with the substance of strength and force, and the sound released raging passion inside her. She stood frozen for a fleeing moment, and then slowly, as life returned to her limbs, moved back into the position whence she had come. She stole another glance over her precipice and looked into the face of the blue eyed Indian. Her heart gave a mighty lunge as all the breath left her body, and she trembled. She felt her face color right up to the roots of her hair, but she could not look away from the man who stood before her. She was not disappointed. He was far more than her wildest expectations. He looked exactly the way she had pictured him. His face was strong and clean cut, not sharp like the contours of most Indians. His jaw was more relaxed. His eyes were blue and clear like deep pools of water that she might drown in. She was fascinated. Light Eyes locked eyes with her as though they were being drawn together like magnets.

The sight of her ripped through him like a gunshot, and something new and mysterious began to stir inside him. He stood perfectly still, staring, unconsciously holding his breath, as if by not breathing he might control the raging desire that shook him. He sensed her passion, it was in her eyes, and he wanted her.

At long last she lowered her eyes and turned away, weak from their brief encounter. She fled through the door she had entered, rushing headlong back to the cabin. When she was safely inside, she gave way to violent weeping, letting her pent-up emotions burst forth unrestrained. Light Eyes was so close, and yet they were worlds apart. Her thoughts tormented her and she struggled to contain them.

CHAPTER

8

When Ned arrived to escort Dawn to the dance at the Town Hall, she was waiting quietly, deep in thought. She looked up when he entered the room and met his eyes, but she was not actually seeing him, her expression was without a trace of recognition. When he asked if she was ready to go, she hesitated a moment before shaking her head, devoid of eagerness.

Ned was puzzled by her remoteness, but was delighted to escort her under any circumstances. He decided to stay clear of any conversation regarding Light Eyes' presence at the trading post. The fact that he had been there was no secret. He thought that perhaps Dawn was upset because she hadn't seen him, and he knew how curious she was.

Dawn looked lovely as usual. She was even more stunning in her pale blue dress with plunging neckline and tight fitting bodice that emphasized her hour-glass figure. Ned stared at her, in awe of such perfection, feeling a bit shaken.

Dawn's restless mood continued. She felt bored, finding no pleasure in either the music or the crowd of chattering people. She was beginning to get a headache. While Ned went to get her a cup of punch she moved to the far side of the room to get away from all the excited talk about the Indian. She was absorbed in her own thoughts of him.

Ned was sick of hearing about the Indian and his seething jealousy rose to the surface. He was anxious to take Dawn and leave. He looked around for her and found her sitting alone in a corner, almost as if she was trying to hide. He realized that he had made a mistake by bringing her there.

Frost had also noticed Dawn sitting alone. He dismissed himself from the conversation he was engaged in to cast his interest in a much more delectable direction. He had been trying to court Dawn since the day he first laid eyes on her, and she had become absolutely insulting; however, there was simply nothing she might say or do that would dampen his interest.

The two men reached Dawn simultaneously. Frost sported his usual smart aleck attitude. "Well if it ain't the bell of the ball sitting one out. You need a real man to escort you. One with more wind, a man of action, full of spice," he smirked.

"You're always bragging about something," Ned said angrily, "but I never expected you to admit that you're full of wind. I'll sure drink to that." He raised his cup. "As far as I'm concerned, that's all you're full of."

Frost's expression changed rapidly. His anger flared and he took a moment to gather his repose before responding with feigned wit, "Why Ned, you should try to control that nasty jealous streak of yours."

"You need to control your mouth."

"You'll have to admit one thing, I'm more her type than you are."

"Sure you are, any fool can see that. That's why she's with me and you're by yourself," Ned shot back.

Frost looked at Dawn and laughed at his own nasty thoughts. "Did you see that big buck at the trading post today?"

"Of course I didn't."

"I don't believe you."

"I don't care what you believe. It's none of your business anyway."

"That's right. But I happened to see you run out the back door of the store as I was riding up to take a look at him."

Her temper flared. "You're blind as a bat." Ned shot her a suspicious glance that irritated her. "You need glasses."

He shrugged, "Maybe," he said, staring at her, the corners of his mouth curling into a slow smile. He was plainly gloating because he was sharing her secret. "How would you like to be married to that big buck?"

Frost was more obnoxious than usual, but Ned held his temper in check, waiting for Dawn's response. He felt ashamed when she sprang to her feet in angry defense. He should have been the one defending her.

"Shut your mouth you stupid fool. Indians don't marry white women. They marry squaws."

"I just want to point out that I come close to his size. If you like the way he looks, why not look my way?"

Dawn Laughed. "You're not even a man, big or little. You're nothing but a big mouth drunk. You talk too much, and you never say anything."

"Oh, I don't know about that. I might have something to say."

"Who would listen to you?"

"Somebody might." He looked around the room. "And don't say I'm not a man. I might have to prove it to you, I hate being falsely accused."

"That's enough, Frost!" Ned barked. "Keep your rotten mouth shut, or I'll do my best to shut it for you."

"That's mighty big talk coming from such a little man. You had better ask around, find out from some of your little friends who have tried me. Let them tell you how hard it is to shut this big mouth of mine. When do you plan to take your turn?"

"Anytime! Maybe I can't peal your head like an onion, but if you do whip me, you had better pack your lunch cause it's gonna take you all day."

"Stop it! Both of you," Dawn said. "You're acting like a couple of jackasses."

"You're right," Ned agreed. He took hold of her hand and led her toward the door. "Come on, let's get out of here."

"Gladly," she said with relief.

Outside, he gave way to his doubts. "You did see that Indian today, didn't you?"

"What difference does it make?"

"Plenty! You lied about it. Why?"

"So what? Who are you? God? You don't own me. What I do is none of your business. I'm sick of your childish probing. Now leave me alone!"

Her attitude frightened him. He tried to pull her close and she pushed him away. "I love you. Can't you understand? I don't want you even thinking about another man. It drives me out of my mind."

"That's just too bad. Maybe I should stop seeing you. Then you won't have to be jealous anymore." She wanted to be by herself and Ned's persistence irritated her. "I want to go home." He reached for her again, and she squirmed away. "Stop it," she snapped in annoyance.

Ned stared at her in confusion. "For Christ's sake, why are you mad at me?"

"Your attitude makes me sick!" She brushed him aside and ran down the empty street.

"Wait," he cried, hurrying after her. Neither of them spoke until they reached her front gate. "I don't know what you expect me to do. I love you. I'll do anything you ask."

He was pleading now, and his weakness disgusted her. She wanted him to get out of her sight. "I don't want to talk about it. I'm tired, and I have a headache."

"I can't leave things the way they are, with you mad at me, and I don't know what I've done." He took a step toward her, near enough to look into her eyes and see the tears there. "Just listen to me for a minute, please."

"I don't want to listen. I've heard enough. Stop pestering me."

"I thought you cared about me. You used to act like it. I don't understand. Tell me—"

"Why must you always question me, doubt me, and even expect the impossible?"

"What do you mean by impossible? What are you trying to tell me?"

"Go home Ned!" she said sharply, spun around and fled into the cabin. Seconds later she regretted her behavior, but he wouldn't leave her alone. Why was he so pushy? She liked him, even loved him in a brotherly way, but she could never love him the way he loved her. The thought of marrying him bored her. He was so predictable and uninteresting. She hated the thought of spending her life washing clothes, dishes, and diapers. Ned wasn't exciting, he was only dependable and hard working, and she wanted more.

While she sat in the darkness of her room, she heard Mac when he entered the house. Judging from his uneven steps she knew he had been drinking. Presently she heard his heavy breathing, then his snores. She waited for the snores to cease, but they grew louder. She felt like shaking him awake, eager to stop the nerve racking monotonous noise. Her head began to throb worse and the air inside the cabin seemed stifling hot and sticky.

She moved quietly to the front door and let herself out.

She took a deep breath of the cool fresh air as she walked along the path that wound through the woods behind the cabin. The moon was full, sending soft oblique rays through the tree branches. The oak grove stretched about two hundred yards, ending near a pond where ducks swam contentedly in the moonlight. Somewhere came the hoot of an owl, and the rustle of scurrying animals in the brush, but she felt no fear. This was her world. She was at home here, out in the open. Her head had begun to clear in the peaceful solitude of the night.

Her heart lunged in panic when she saw the dark figure of a man moving toward her in the thick shadows. She wanted to run and scream, but stood frozen in her tracks, braced against a tree trunk, while her body shook with tremors. The man moved out of the shadows and stood in the moonlight. When she saw that the man was Light Eyes a jolt of excitement shot through her. She marveled at his strong, muscular body gleaning with animal vitality, his dark hair down to his shoulders. She stared at him in paralyzing astonishment as he moved soundlessly toward her. He came close enough for her to see the reflections of light in his blue eyes as he gazed silently down at her.

Without speaking, he held out his hand and she laid her palm against his, feeling his warmth, their pulse beating as one.

Finally he spoke, still pressing her hand firmly in his. "How did you know to come here?"

"I couldn't sleep," she managed, and her body shook as with a chill.

"Today at the trading post, you were watching me."

"Yes," she admitted. "I was curious."

"Why?"

"I wanted to know if you were real or a figment of my imagination."

"Did you think I was a resurrection from the spirit world?"

"I have thought about you for five years, wondering if you were all the things I have heard."

"What things?"

"That you were so very tall, that you did not have the rough honed face of an Indian, and that your eyes were blue."

"My father calls me by Light Eyes because the sky is in my eyes and not the color of the earth.

"Why are you here in the woods?"

"Waiting for you."

"How did you know I would come?"

"Because you want me as I want you."

He dropped her hand and drew her into his strong arms. A bolt of excitement traveled up her spine and her body trembled.

Never before had she known such soul shattering bliss, and she pressed close.

"I have lived only for this moment since our eyes met from across the room. I read in your eyes your feelings for me. I came here to take you to my lodge."

"Oh, I can't. It's impossible. We need to get better acquainted. I have to speak with my father, make him understand. I'm his only daughter. He has only me."

"Do your eyes lie?"

"No! Oh, no! But I need time."

"I don't need time. I want you to come with me now, tonight, to live in my lodge, to sleep with me."

"I can't. Try to understand."

"I only understand what I feel; time will not change my mind."

"Nor mine."

"Then why must we wait?"

"I am not free as you are. I have to consider my Father."

"I am not free. I am needed by my Father also, and our people. I have decided that you will be my wife."

"Oh!" she gasped. "Right now—tonight? We don't do things so quickly. I must make plans. We have to wait."

"What is the purpose of waiting? What we feel is now. I don't want to wait."

How was she to make him understand? If she wanted him, why was she waiting? "Soon, I will go with you. I love you." He pulled her close. His mouth brushed hers lightly, and she wound her arms tight around his body, breathing him in, his manly odor. He smelled of smoke, leather, and the earth. She pressed close, her heart throbbing violently, feeling his body trembling in their embrace. Her lips waited for his, her eagerness unrestrained. But he did not kiss her, instead he pushed her away. She was hurt and shamed by his resistance. She stared up at him with tears in her eyes. Was this his ultimatum? Either she went with him now or he didn't want her? But she couldn't, she just couldn't, much as she wanted to. She would always love him and now she was afraid she had lost him already.

"I go back to my people now." His voice was thick with emotion.

"Will you come back?"

He didn't answer. He turned and disappeared back into the night. She stared after him, dumbfounded, could not perceive his reasoning. Tears streamed down her face. She heard the fading sound of hoof beats as he rode away, possibly out of her life. She did not understand the ways of an Indian. What did it all mean?

She was left in a confused state, like living in a dream where understanding is irrational and senseless. Was it his extraordinary sense of decency that caused him to push her away? She wanted him, but he had rejected her. Why? She knew the moment he touched her that she would give herself to him, and she felt certain that their love would be pure and sweet, feelings that only they could understand—them and their God.

Every detail of their meeting was vivid in her mind. She had been hasty in her love for him, allowing her heart to lead her recklessly. But his actions were mystifying, and at the same time a source of rapture. Her absorption in her own selfish desire left her little time to think about the effect her actions might have on those around her, especially Ned, whose heart she had cast aside like an empty sack. She was certain that he loved her, but there was no room for him in her heart that was filled with her love for Light Eyes. Ned's feeling for her was like a tug-of-war, with him pulling in one direction, and her another, which was a strain on each of them.

The sleepless hours of the remaining night bore down on her with increasing agony, seeming to stretch before her without end. It was impossible for her to say when her irrational love for Light Eyes began, but one thing was sure, her future happiness depended completely on his return. The thought that she might never see him again made her heart heavy. She thought about the warm touch of his hand, the soft brush of his lips, his strong embrace, and she longed for him with every fiber of her being.

Morning brought little relief. She went about the cabin in a dazed condition, doing only the essential things, her mind seemingly separated from her body.

Mac watched her thoughtfully through breakfast, trying to understand her strange behavior. She was becoming a mystery and a challenge. The closeness they had once shared was gradually slipping away. With regret he recalled the times when her concerns were laid bare before him, and together they would seek a solution. That was all in the past. They spoke two different languages. When looking at the same thing, they each saw it differently. He knew she loved him. She was still the same obedient daughter, but the restlessness that grew inside her separated them like a wall. Mac began to feel a new emptiness he had never known before. He had built his entire life around his daughter, only to find loneliness as his reward for all his sacrifices. He had certainly gained little comfort in his rejection of female companionship. Night always found him alone and filled with misery. Feelings he drowned more and more frequently with alcohol. He thought about Amy, remembering how bitterly Dawn objected to her, and how Amy had confessed her love for him. He missed her; he could not deny the truth of his feelings any longer.

Dawn found nothing of interest to relieve the monotony of her days as she waited impatiently for day to pass into evening, hoping the darkness would bring Light Eyes back to her. She slipped away night after night to wait in the woods, but Light Eyes did not return.

Ned continued his aggravating pursuit. As shabbily as she treated him, she was surprised by his perseverance, and dreaded his company more and more. He was bound to get on the same stupid, mushy, subject, and she was sick of telling him no. One evening she had hesitated before opening the door, taking a minute to decide if she should let him in or send him away.

He stepped inside acting nervous as usual; he seemed to always expect her to be obnoxious, as she had been of late.

He had been crushed by her behavior the night of the dance. "Just dropped by to pay my respects." He flashed her a dubious smile.

Dawn's attitude was anything but happy. She did not invite conversation. "I don't feel like talking to anyone."

"I was afraid you might not let me in. I promise not to say anything to upset you," he said hurriedly.

"You say that now, but what about five minutes from now?"

"I admit I get out of line sometimes. Can we just forget about it?"

"I don't know."

"What do you mean—you don't know? Of course you do. Do you forgive me or not?"

She made no reply. She looked past him, fixing her eyes on the wall behind him.

He realized she was experiencing some new qualms, and his mind worked frantically for some solution to suppress them. He felt her drifting away from him, and he didn't know why.

She looked at him now thinking it would be a relief to go into her bedroom and close the door. She longed to close him out of her thoughts and out of her life. She didn't want him there, his presence irritated her, he made her feel guilty for being so mean, and there was no way she could explain her wild disposition.

"Come on, Dawn, why are you so serious?"

"Why do you love me, Ned? I'm mean and hateful, always finding fault. I needle you, yell at you. You should hate me."

"That's a stupid question. I love you for a million reasons. How do you put your feeling into words? All I know is that I do love you. I don't know how to explain exactly why."

"I'm sorry." She couldn't look at him; he had an expression like an old hound dog. "The truth is, our feelings aren't mutual. I like you a lot, but I just don't—can't love you. What good is a one sided love to anyone?"

"I can't stand here and honestly say that I think you love me. Truth is, I want you to love me, and I think that you will in time, if you will just give yourself the chance. Come down to earth and get your mind off that blue eyed Indian." There it was, the very thing he had promised her he wouldn't do, blurted out before he realized what he was saying. "God! I'm sorry," he apologized quickly, swallowing hard.

"Get out!" she said triumphantly, pleased by his slip of the tongue. She now had a good reason to run him off.

"I can't say that I blame you for throwing me out. I got it coming."

"We can talk later if you don't keep throwing that Indian in my face." For some reason she couldn't say his name. She spoke appealingly, as though giving in to a demand he had not yet made, to prevent his pleading and her forced comments.

After a long silence, with Ned finding no way to overcome the situation, he said in a low voice as if talking to himself. "Yeah, later. We will talk later. I love you."

Dawn felt a flood of relief when he let himself out. She wanted to be left lone with her misery. She planned to be in the woods again that night, as she had been for many weeks, hoping, that by some miracle, Light Eyes might be there waiting as before.

CHAPTER

Dawn waited a few minutes after Ned left before she stepped out onto the porch. The air felt damp against her face and the smell of rain was in the wind. Lightning flickered in the distance spiking the horizon of heavy clouds that blotted out the luminary light leaving the September night in looming darkness. Because of the approaching storm she did not walk to the woods, but sat on the top step to wait, although she wasn't sure what she was waiting for. She listened attentively to every sound, and her heart lurched when she heard the whisper of moccasins against the hard ground. She sprang to her feet in wild excitement, straining her eyes into the ebony night. She saw nothing at first, and then Light Eyes moved out of the deep shadows, but did not approach closely. She rushed down the steps and ran toward him. When he saw her he turned and walked swiftly away. She understood that he meant for her to follow and fell into step behind him. He led her into the grove of trees where his horse waited. Without speaking, he lifted her effortlessly to the horse's bare back and mounted in front of her. She put her arms around his waist and settled against him. He dug his heels into the stallion flanks and it plunged forward through the darkness as if it knew its way instinctively. Dawn had no idea where he was taking her. When they passed the entrance to the cemetery, she recalled that Ned had seen him and several more braves camping near there the day he came to the trading post. She felt uneasy at the thought of being in the company of several more braves. Now that she was bound by the course of events, she could do no more than trust him. So far he had not uttered one word, and she was in doubt concerning his intentions, but more so, she doubted her own impetuous actions. Her feelings for the Indian had blinded her completely, making her vulnerable to his will.

A surge of excitement stirred her when Light Eyes pulled the stallion to a sudden halt. Throwing his right leg over the horse's left side he slid to the ground, and then reached up to lift Dawn down. She glanced around expecting to see other Indians, but no one was in sight. He had constructed a shelter under the branches of a birch tree. A few feet away a dying fire glowed in the darkness. She watched in silence as he tied his horse, and then walked over to the half spent fire and laid several sticks of wood on the red glowing coals. The flames grew quickly, throwing light across his camp site. He moved away from the fire and stood close to her, extending his hand to her in the same memorably way as he had at their first meeting. His simple gesture sent a current of pleasure through her entire body. She put her hand in his and he drew her near the fire, and stepped back to look at her in the revealing light. He gazed at her for several minutes, his eyes fixed in fascination. Entranced by his expression, she moved close to him holding out her hands in simple supplication. He drew her into the warm circle of his arms, their bodies straining together.

She looked up into his face and he saw tears sparkling like tiny stars on her flushed cheeks. She was radiantly beautiful, the purity of her heart expressed in her eyes. He took her face between his hands and examined her features with the curiosity of a blind man. He pushed her hair back and touched her ears, drew his fingers across her nose and eyes, then lowered his head and moved his lips on hers ever so gently, feeling and tasting the warmth and tenderness of her mouth.

"You are mine," he said, in a strong vibrant voice. "This is true. It is written in your eyes. I see it in your face. We belong to one another for all the days of our lives." He spoke with great sincerity, and the simplicity of his words brought fresh tears to her eyes.

"If only it were that simple. My people do things in a different way. We have laws. A man and woman cannot live together unless they are married, or it is a sin in the eyes of God."

"I know about the white man's laws, and the God of their Book. I know much about the white man, they are false, they tell many lies. They kill many buffalo and steal our land. The white man brought his law to my people. It is bad law for Indians, it takes away hunting ground and freedom. The long knives move like lions, hiding behind their laws like the wild beast crouching in the tall grass of the fields. They burn Indian villages, massacre many braves, capture women and children, make slaves of Indians. I spit on white man's law."

"I must speak with my father; make him understand that my heart is with you. If I just disappear he will send for the soldiers, and they will search for me. It would be bad for your people. We have to be careful, find a way that will not endanger your village or your hunting grounds, and bring death to your people."

"If you tell your father, he will make you stay."

She knew what he said was true. If she went with him, she realized she would have to sneak away behind her father's back. She needed time to think, to make plans, but her mind was scrambled. What she was feeling for this man smothered all rational thoughts. She wanted to spend the rest of her life with him. "If we can meet this way in secrecy it will endanger no one," she said. "I love my father as you love yours. No harm must come to them. I could not live with you and be happy if our love was to cause blood shed."

"It is not love that causes bloodshed, but hate and greed."

She was amazed by his knowledge of human nature. "Tell me how you came to be so different."

"I learn many things from pale face. I am Comanche. I live by Comanche law. I am not different."

Suddenly they realized it was raining. Neither had noticed until water broke through the tree branches and fell against them in a cool spray. Light Eyes made a sweeping gesture toward his shelter, pulled the flap back, took her hand and led her inside. She saw his bed made of buffalo hides that was barely visible in the flickering fire light coming through the open flap.

He dropped the flap into place and they stood in complete darkness. Taking her hand, he pulled her down on the buffalo robe and sat beside her. They were silent for a time, listening to the rain pelt stormily against the shelter while the wind whipped at the closed flap.

She understood now why he had walked away from her in the woods when he could have had her for the taking. He had wanted to take her to his lodge, to live with him, and to sleep with him. He undoubtedly understood that he must bring his lodge to her. If only he would talk to her, explain his feelings, why he was unlike the other Indians in character and appearance.

Presently he spoke, his lips close to her ear, sending wild passion blazing in her blood like a raging fire.

"Will you lie with me?"

"I have never been with a man before."

"Do you have fear?"

"I have no fear. I only know that I love you." She felt like melting wax when he pulled her close, his lips on her neck, caressing the soft skin of her shoulder. She trembled with desire when he laid her back gently on his bed and lay down beside her.

"You are my wife," he said.

"Yes," she whispered. She belonged to this man soulfully and completely. He had taken her to his lodge as was the custom. She understood that in his eyes they were married. In her heart she felt it was true. There had been no words spoken over them, no slip of paper bearing their names, but their union was complete and right, made in a far greater and more important way by his god. She felt no shame as he tore away their clothes until nothing remained to separate their bodies. His nearness exploded her passions, even the pain of his penetration was blanked out of her mind, all restraints breaking free. She was conscious only of his naked warmth pressing close, the feel of his manhood. She grasp him even closer, her hands exploring his hard, strong, body, eager for them to be released to the sweet rapturous sensation they could no longer hold back, the act of love that burned steadily to its conclusion.

She lay curled against him, her face pressed against his neck. "You have made me happy," he said. "I want you near me always. I will take you with me now, if you will come."

"Soon," she said, "we will find a way."

"Will you come to me here?"

"Yes."

"I do not like it this way."

"I know. I don't want to be separated from you, but we have to wait a little while."

"I will wait."

"I know that Chief Brave Horse is your father. Who is your mother?"

"My mother died three winters past. She came to my father's village to teach him about the God of your Book."

"Was she a missionary?"

"Yes. She wanted to stay with my father. She moved into his lodge and became his wife. She taught me to read and write. She had many books for me to read and study."

"Do you have any brothers or sisters?"

"I have a sister, White Swan. She is older than me. Her eyes are brown like my father's, but she is beautiful like my mother was. Her hair is golden, her nose is small, her eyes large. She has a husband, Red Elk."

"You could live in the white man's world if you wanted to. You are only half Indian."

"My people need me. My father grows old and feeble."

"Will you be their chief?"

"Yes, but I cannot save them from extinction. We will be driven to the ends of the earth, and there we will die."

"It doesn't have to be that way for you and your sister."

"I am Comanche."

"We could go away together. No one need ever know."

"You must love me for what I am, or not at all."

"You will not change your mind?"

"I cannot change the blood that flows in my veins. I know the white man's ways. My mother taught me. She wanted to change my father, make him white like herself, but he could not change the color of his skin. An Indian can only be what he is. The white one has to do the changing."

"I will need time."

"I will stay in this place while I wait two moons."

It was after midnight when they rode back to town. Light Eyes tied his horse in the grove of trees and carried Dawn through the mud and stood her on the porch. The rain had stopped sometime during the night, but the dark clouds remained, shrouding their world in darkness, but their hearts were filled with happiness beyond what their minds could conceive.

Ned stood silently in the shadows of the cabin unnoticed, watching as Light Eyes bent low, took Dawn into his arms and kissed her passionately. He felt a shaft of pain when Dawn's arms circled his neck and she stood on tip toes to return his kiss. His insides burned with intense hatred for the Indian, and he wept silently, his hand coming to rest on the pistol strapped to his hip. He trembled with rage, wanting to kill him then and there. He took a shuddering breath to contain his madness. He must not shoot him in front of Dawn; she would never forgive him, she would even hate him, although the Indian deserved to die for touching her. He knew the penalty for taking a man's life. He had never before wanted to kill a man, and the conflict he felt was tearing him apart. He reminded himself that this was an Indian, not really considered a man, but a threat, and he had killed the only chance in the world he had for happiness. He searched his conscious and found no remorse for his murderous obsession. He was resigned to what he must do.

When Light Eyes turned to walk away, Ned followed at a safe distance. When he reached his horse, Ned darted among the trees, staying out of sight until he was in close range of his target. He pulled his gun, and with a shaking hand, aimed at the Indian's back and pulled the trigger. He saw Light Eyes drop to his knees, and then on his face in the mud. Feeling a surge of panic, Ned ran. His only thought was to escape before someone saw him.

Mac heard the shot and reached the door just ahead of Dawn. He saw her behind him in the dark and yelled, "Get back! It sounds like trouble, and its close."

"Let me come with you?" she cried.

"No! Stay inside."

Mac walked out on the porch clad in his underwear, took a quick look around, and then hurried back inside.

"What's wrong? Who fired that shot?" she cried in panic.

"Soon as I get my pants and boots on I intend to find out."

Dawn paced the floor impatiently while Mac dressed, fear twisting her insides. It seemed to her that he was taking forever. Why didn't he hurry? The shot had aroused others, and there came the sound of voices and running feet. She hurried to the window and peered into the darkness.

She could make out the large bulk of Charles Morgan and the excited voice of Alvin Biglo.

Mac hurried outside to join them, and had taken the time to fetch a lantern. Dawn stood by the window watching the dark figures milling about, up and down the street. To the right of the cabin, Mac's lantern winked in and out of the trees. The men spoke to one another in raised voices. Periodically Charles Morgan's voice would rise above the others as he shouted orders.

Dawn waited in a panic for the men to complete their search. When Mac returned she ran immediately to meet him, pulling him inside. "What was it? Did you see anyone?"

"We can't tell for sure, looks like two riders rode away in different directions. One thing we do know for sure is that one of them was hurt, and from the amount of blood he's losing, it's not likely he'll get very far."

"No!" Dawn cried.

Mac was shocked by Dawn's alarm. "I don't think it was anyone from town. Some of the boys are riding out to take a look. They'll most likely find the one that got shot, but the one who did the shooting is long gone. There's a trail of blood leading from that grove of trees over yonder near the pond. Who ever was shot was able to mount and ride away."

His words cut through her like a razor. She knew Light Eyes had been shot. He carried no gun so he couldn't have been the one who fired the shot. Like a wounded animal he had rode off to some deserted place to wait for death. She had no idea how long she stood there speechless, fighting to hold back her tears of grief.

Mac studied her expression as he spoke, wondering if she was reacting from excitement as all the color had suddenly gone from her face. Then she did a very unexpected thing, she quickly left the room without asking another question.

It took all her strength to walk out of Mac's sight before her nerves snapped. She closed her bedroom door against the world, threw herself across the bed and sobbed silently, her face pressed into her pillow. Oh, God, she thought, someone shot Light Eyes. I know it; I can feel it. But who? Who would have a reason to shoot him? If they thought he was a prowler, and had shot in self-defense, why would they run away? She could find no answers to her questions, save one. Light Eyes was hurt, perhaps dying, and she was helpless to do anything about it. She felt as if she were looking at the world through the eyes of a drunkard. Nothing was in focus; everything was veiled in grief and anguish. Whirling sounds passed through her aching head, pain spun behind her eyes in dazing colors, blinding her. She huddled on her bed weeping, her face reflecting the aching sorrow in her heart. Grief closed down on her stricken mind and she wanted to die.

She knew she must face her father soon, and she wondered if she could keep up the pretense of ignorance while her whole body was screaming in anguish. She would be forced to listen to every detail of the shooting time and time again. Knowing that Light Eyes had been shot and was pouring out his soul's blood on the ground was more than she could bear. She didn't want to hear more, her shattered nerves would not withstand it.

When she entered the kitchen to cook Mac's breakfast, the exhaustion of her sleepless night showed clearly on her face.

Mac noticed, but held his tongue. He wished he could take her in his arms the way he had when she was a child and soothe her hurt feelings, kiss away her tears, but all he could do was look on in ignorance, sometimes through blurred eyes. Neither of them mentioned the shooting. Dawn served his food and he ate in silence.

Doctor Keel came by to check on Mac, as he did more often since he started drinking so heavily. Today however, his concern was for Dawn. He didn't like the empty look in her eyes. She was filled with a disturbing stillness, as though she was holding back something painful. He considered that something upsetting waxed inside her, an emotional block he had not encountered before. He studied her with probing eyes as she struggled to hold back her tears and remain calm on the surface.

"Mac, I came by to inquire about your health. But after seeing Dawn, I think I came to inquire about the wrong person."

He turned his attention back to Dawn. "What's troubling you, child? Is it something I should know about? Are you ill?"

She went rigid and said brokenly, "I didn't sleep well last night. I have a headache. I'm just tired, that's all."

"Does your head hurt now?"

"Yes," she said huskily.

"Why don't you go back to bed for a while? It will make you feel better."

She looked at Mac, her eyes asking his permission to leave the kitchen. "You go ahead," he said in a gentle tone. "You do look tired. I've been wondering about you myself ever since that shooting last night."

She tried unsuccessfully to smile as she made her way quickly from the kitchen. Before she reached her room tears were rolling down her cheeks.

"You have a lovely daughter, Mac. But I'm sure you already know that."

"Yeah, but somebody needs to give me some tips on how to understand her."

"Could be that you've forgotten one fact. She may be more like her mother than you care to admit. I'm beginning to wonder if you've forgotten who her father is too. A man needs to set a good example for his children. If you keep on drowning your sorrows in whiskey, one of these days you're going to wake up a drunk. And I'm likely to wind up a drunk myself trying to keep an eye on you, since you just about live at the Silver Buckle. Even those sociable drinks can get to be a habit."

"You don't have to worry about me Edward. I won't have time to drink for a while. I'm fixing to build that house I've been talking about."

"That's fine, Mac. I was beginning to wonder if all that talk about a house was just a pipe dream. When do you plan to get started? And where are you going to locate?"

"As soon as the builders get here, and that will be any day now. I'm not sure about the location, only that it will be near the river."

"That far from town? It could present a problem, not to speak of danger. Dawn will be alone most of the time. Have you given that any thought?"

"Yeah, and I've decided to get a woman to live in and keep her company. Dawn hates housework, so I don't think she will object as much as she did when Amy lived with her."

"I agree. She will need some help. Keeping a new house will mean a lot more work than your little cabin. I had better get going. Never can tell when somebody might happen by with a gunshot wound. I talked to Charles just before I left home. They didn't find any sign of either rider. Guess we'll know pretty soon who it was, someone around here is either going to come up missing or shot. Sure would be interesting to know what went on out there last night. Congratulations on the new house." He stood, held out his hand and shook Mac's vigorously. Their eyes met for a moment and a look passed between them, the expression of old friends, and then Keel departed.

By mid morning the rain began to fall again, leaving the atmosphere dark and grim. The wind was blowing harder, sending dry leaves flying through the air, banking against the buildings and fences.

Ned showed up for work as usual, but his mind was not exactly on what he was doing. He worked steadily, rearranging and dusting the cluttered shelves, sweeping, and trying to forget what he had done, seeing again the Indian falling to his knees and pitch forward into the mud. He had thought he had killed him, as was his intention, now he wondered if he had. It was hard for him to believe that he had mounted his horse and rode away. He felt certain that he had not seen who shot him, but he didn't feel comfortable about the way it worked out.

Mac had never seen such a burst of energy before. Ned was a long way from being lazy, but it had never been his nature to invent work. The weather had people inside and business was almost at a standstill. Ned had always gone to see Dawn in the past when business was slow, but today she seemed farthest from his mind. Many things just didn't add up. Dawn's peculiar behavior and Ned's uncommon burst of energy. He was beginning to think that they might of had a falling out. It would account for the way they were acting. And another thing was odd. Ned took no part in the discussion of the shooting that had taken place that night. He seemed to have developed a strange depth in his personality which Mac could only attribute to one hell of a fight between Ned and his daughter.

CHAPTER

10

It was a little past ten in the morning when word of the shooting reached the Benson ranch. Debbie looked at her father anxiously. "Can I go into town today? I can stay the night with Dawn and be home first thing in the morning."

For a moment Billy Joe looked annoyed. "Ask Kathryn. If she says it's all right, I'll drive you."

Debbie looked at her step-mother wistfully. It was Kathryn who made all the decisions and Debbie resented it bitterly. "Let her go! If she don't get her way, she'll pout the live long day."

Debbie felt the sting of her words, but accepted them pleasantly, delighted to be getting out of the house for a while. She hurried to her room to get ready.

Debbie was born the same year as Dawn. She was the only child of Billy Joe Benson. Her mother died when she was twelve years old, and her father had remarried shortly thereafter. Debbie hated Kathryn, fifteen years younger than her father, because she took advantage of him, flaunting her youth so that he bowed to her every wish. She made Debbie's life miserable with her constant domineering attitude. Before her mother died she had loved her home, felt safe and secure there, now she felt like a slave for her father's bed partner, as that seemed to be the only thing Billy Joe required of his wife, and the only thing Kathryn seemed enthusiastic about.

Debbie was not a classic beauty, but she possessed a genuine warm quality of love and friendliness, with an even temperament that was rarely shaken. She was thin, narrow in the hips, and small-breasted. Her hair reached to her waist and was the exact color of her soft brown eyes. She treasured Dawn's friendship; her encouragement was the only thing that saved her from crumbling because Kathryn had managed to loosen her self-confidence with her constant expression of contempt.

Billy could see no further than Kathryn's provocative side, her young shapely body. When she got that shameless, lustful, look in her eyes, he melted inside. Where his wife's faults were concerned he was absolutely blind, eager to make excuses for her when Debbie complained. The results caused a mental estrangement between Billy and his daughter.

Dawn had given Debbie the courage to stand up to her step-mother by discovering, quite by accident, the ugly side of Kathryn's secret life.

One morning while out riding, Dawn tied her horse and walked through the woods along the river looking for pecans. She became conscious of what sounded like the impatient stamping of a horse's hoof. As she made her way in that direction, she heard muffled voices. Her curiosity moved her forward. She saw a pair of breeches carelessly thrown across a bush, as apparent as a flag, and other articles of clothing on the ground. She was shocked by what she saw a few feet in front of her, partially hidden in the brush. Kathryn and Frost were twined together half naked on a blanket. She stood there watching them, close enough to see they were slick with sweat. The hot sun breaking through the tree limbs striking Frost on his shoulders and working buttock. Kathryn began to moan, lifting her hips up to meet his thrusts that were becoming faster. Her first impulse was to tell Billy Joe, but decided very quickly that keeping their secret was worth more than the telling. They were too preoccupied to notice when she strode over to them and stood looking down. "I hope I'm not interrupting anything. I wonder how understanding Billy Joe will be when I tell him about you two"

Kathryn jumped to her feet, pulling down her skirt, starting to arrange her clothes. Frost jerked his breeches off the bush and darted into the brush to hide himself, but not before his shrinking manhood was shamefully displayed.

Kathryn was trembling, her face blanched with fear. The impact of her predicament could only lead to one ultimate conclusion. "Oh! My God! Billy will kill me if he finds out."

"That's right," Dawn said, staring into Kathryn's death white face. "He'll kill Frost too."

"I have never done anything like this before. I don't know what came over me."

Dawn stood up to her with spirit and courage. "You're nothing but a slut," she said, her voice cracking like a whip. "You try to act so high and mighty, treating Debbie like dirt. Well, I know who the dirt is, and I intend to tell Debbie about her sainted stepmother."

"No, you can't. She'll tell Billy. She hates me."

"Maybe you should try to change her opinion of you. Be a mother to her instead of a tyrannical slave driver. Give her a reason to keep you alive."

"Yes, I'll make a deal with her."

"No deals, Kathryn, promises. I will make sure that your husband doesn't find out as long as you treat Debbie right."

Kathryn fell to sobbing. There were no denials, she had no defense. She shook her head up and down vigorously. "All right, you win."

"By the way," Dawn said, pointing at something on the ground. "You forgot to put your drawers back on."

"Well, ain't you the busy body," Frost said, stepping out of the brush, smoothing his hair with his hand. "I've heard about people being caught with their pants down, but I never figured I'd be one of 'um."

"You're the busy one, Frost."

Tipping his hat mockingly, his lips curling in a smile, Frost said, "Ladies, it's been a pure pleasure. Good evening." He nonchalantly mounted his horse and rode away.

Dawn remained silent about Kathryn's immoral act with Frost Jackson. She wondered if they were still having sex, thinking, they can only hang once. She even wondered if Frost might feel uncomfortable enough to watch his back.

After their first encounter, Kathryn became Dawn's bitter enemy, with Dawn holding her transgression over her head by a tiny thread of silence. It was an unforgivable thing to do, but it gave Debbie a small measure of freedom. It was unthinkable that Dawn could do otherwise. She had kept the truth from Debbie at first. Gloating when Debbie mentioned that her step-mother was treating her more kindly, Dawn told her why. A mental picture of Frost and Kathryn having sex caused Dawn to shake with anger when she looked into Billy's trusting face, thinking what a blind fool he was. She doubted Billy had the guts to leave Kathryn even if he knew the truth, and might pretend not to believe her as an excuse to avoid taking action.

Kathryn couldn't be sure what Billy's reaction would be if Dawn told him about her affair with Frost. She would deny it of course, but she couldn't take the gamble. Debbie had her over a barrel. What Billy didn't know, couldn't hurt her.

Two years had passed since the deception began. Two years of anxiety for Kathryn, and two years of justice for Debbie. There was no mistake about Kathryn's smoldering resentment. While Debbie held on to her sense of decency, never taking advantage of the situation, it was Dawn who refused to give any ground. "If you don't blackmail her, she will always treat you like a dog."

Debbie realized what Dawn had said was true as she rode toward town sitting beside her father on the wagon seat. She was only allowed to go because Kathryn was afraid to say no. She owed her new found freedom to Dawn because Kathryn gave in to her wishes out of fear; however, she was afraid there could be no happy ending to such a tragic situation.

Dawn was surprised when Debbie paid her a visit the next day. She had immediately brought up the subject regarding the baffling shooting. Dawn assumed as calm an expression as possible. "I know all about it," she said, "You don't have to tell me."

"I wonder who was shot. Have you heard anything?"

"No! I don't feel like talking about it." She had reached the limit of her composure, and slumped in a chair as an attack of weakness overcame her.

Debbie stared at her with a troubled expression. "Who was shot Dawn?"

She had not expected to be asked that question. Her head jerked up and she glared at Debbie. "How should I know?"

Debbie read the pain in her eyes. "I think you know. We've been friends all our lives, and I love you like a sister. I can feel your pain and grief. You're suffering. I can see that. Let me help you. You can't survive this tragedy if you keep holding it in."

Debbie was looking at her with warm brown eyes, and she had never needed a friend more. The control she had been struggling to maintain deserted her and she poured out all the events of the night in a burst of sobs. Debbie listened, her eyes reflecting her astonishment, then sympathy.

"Who else knows?" Debbie asked.

"No one."

"Does anyone even suspect how you feel about the Indian?"

"That's a strange question. I would have to be a mind reader to know the answer."

"I know, but you might have been watched—followed."

"I hadn't thought of that."

"Someone knows, Dawn."

"Who?"

"The one who shot him."

"Oh, God! This is all my fault. I should have gone away with him, but I was afraid my father would call on the soldiers to search for me and they would raid the Indian village and kill Light Eyes and his people."

"You did the right thing."

"I intend to find out who did this terrible thing to him. In his eyes, I'm his wife. He took me to his lodge and we slept together. Oh, I love him so—"

Debbie held her while she sobbed. "I don't want to live without him. I caused him to get killed. It's my fault."

"Listen to me, Dawn. You don't know that he's dead. He was able to mount his horse and ride. Surely he rode for help."

"If only I knew."

"If he's alive, he will come back. You belong to him."

"That's what he said." Her tears came again, unchecked, flowing down her face. She clung helplessly to her friend, her patience and understanding helping her to hang on to at least a shred of hope.

The days that followed were filled with unrest. Dawn was unable to hide her feelings of loss and grief. She was openly depressed and sad. Mac felt trapped in a situation he was at a loss to understand, and was ready to do anything to cure whatever was working on her. In a desperate attempt to break the mysterious spell that bound her, he bought the strip of land Dawn had loved all her life: the wooded acreage along the bend of the river. She had been riding over it and tramping through it since she was little more than a baby. She knew every inch of it by heart. He would have the house built in the exact spot she had loved the most, the crest of a knoll overlooking the river.

He could talk of nothing else except the new house. He had hoped Dawn would share his eagerness. However, she continued to be despondent, showing no interest in friends, food, or the plans for the new house.

Ned had purposely stayed away from her for several days after the shooting. He wanted to see her but was afraid of the consequences, that his guilt might show in his face or his attitude. When he at last found the courage to face her, it wasn't easy for him to pretend he knew nothing about the shooting. She didn't mention it right away, giving him more time to build up a thick wall of deception. When at last she did open the subject, he was amazed by his own cold, steady, calm, especially when every nerve in his body was stretched wire tight. He wouldn't have felt so guilty for deceiving her, except for the pity she roused in him. All the sparkle had faded from her eyes; she looked pale, tired, and defeated. He felt deep shame as he watching her helplessly. His mind was becoming more and more tormented. He began to loath the person he had become. He wished there was some way to make up for the sin he was guilty of.

She knew she would never love again. The fever of her first love was past, but the burden it left on her heart would forever remain. Slowly she began to do all the things she had once loved, and for a time had ignored, finding only time for grief. Her grief was pushed aside and sorted out into the proper corner of her subconscious. Although she had changed in some ways, she came to life in another way, exchanging her deadened, listless, dull personality for a strange one that by no means resembled the woman she had once been.

The hours Ned spent with Dawn brought him no relief from his flaming passion. He lived in constant fear of her discovering the truth, avoiding any mention of the Indian or the shooting, now three months past. She was still pushing him away and the reason was a sword in his flesh. He had witnessed her love for the Indian, saw the way she held him in her arms and kissed him. He would give anything to feel her in his arms and experience her passion and love in the same way. It was hard for him to accept the fact that she preferred an Indian to him.

One Sunday in December, Dawn and Ned rode to the building site of the new house, as they had done many times in the past few months. The day was bright with sun, so brilliant that it stung their eyes. The magic of the cold crisp air brought back the glow to Dawn's cheeks. Looking at her now, Ned felt happy and free, there was nothing standing in his way. With Light Eyes out of the picture he had a clear field and intended to take full advantage of it.

"I'm glad we rode out here today," Ned said, smiling happily. Dawn nodded, looking toward the river. Ned moved close to her, his back to the river, blocking her view, forcing her to look at him. She raised her eyes slowly and reached out to caress his cheek. Her fingers felt cold and soft and he caught his breath excitedly. "I love you," he said hoarsely, drawing her close. "And I need you." She became rigid, her face suddenly a dispassionate mask. Feeling her tension he quickly withdrew from her.

"Love!" she cried harshly. "Love is a waste of time."

She said no more, but the expression in her eyes disturbed him more than her words. Her scornful appraisal of him made his flesh crawl. He had no idea how to respond and stood there staring at her, feeling stupid. He turned sharply away, clenching his fists. "What are you trying to do to me?" He swung around again to face her, his eyes blazing. The words he had held back for such a long time poured from his lips with uncontrolled fury. "What do you want me to do? I've loved you as long as I can remember. You thought something of me once. I know you did. Now you won't let me near you. Why? Am I that disgusting to you?" He looked at her helplessly. "Are you afraid of me?" His voice was shaking now. "Let me love you, dammit! I want to make love to you, hold in my arms and kiss you. For the love of God! Give me a chance."

"I'm not afraid," she said. She had never seen Ned lose control before and she felt a sudden shock of amazement.

"Then prove it," he said, holding out his arms. "Come here."

She moved toward him until their bodies were almost touching.

He could no longer fight the hunger inside him. He took her face between his hands and kissed her lips eagerly, hungrily, his heart pounding wildly. His arms circled her and he strained toward her, holding her so tightly they could scarcely breathe.

Without moving out of his embrace, she said, "You will never be satisfied until you have sex with me, will you?" Her tone was cruel and calculating, but most of all accusing. "Go ahead! Take what you want. I won't fight you. Ease your pain, get it over with, and then leave me alone."

"Not like this," he said under his breath.

"What other way is there? You look at me like a sick calf. I can't stand your pleading eyes, the way you expect the impossible. You're a nagger, Ned. Do you know that?" She pulled away from him and removed her coat, then began to unbutton her shirt, her eyes glued to his face, saw naked shock in his expression and felt a spur of satisfaction.

He stood there as speechless as a rock staring at her, conscious of every inch of her body, his eyes following the perfect lines of her figure. Her shirt fell away from her shoulders, revealing the high swell of her full breasts. She was shuddering from cold, but he seemed not to notice. She reached for the buttons on her pants, her eyes still fixed on his face, as if nailing him to her like the crucifixion of a man on a cross. There was something different about her eyes. Under her spell all reasoning seemed to escape his mind. It wasn't until she undid the last button and began to slide her pants down over her hips and thighs that he found his voice. "No," he said weakly, painfully, and his eyes fell to the ground. "I won't touch you. Not like this." He felt the agony of defeat building inside him, clear to his core. "Put your clothes on before you freeze." He turned his back to her to hide his tears.

She had intentionally meant to shock him, certainly not to tantalize him, for she was angry, fed up with his irritating attempts to seduce her. His crawling, unfaltering, pursuit disgusted her. It seemed as if nothing else ever crossed his mind and the thought of him in that respect made her sick.

She made no reply as she hurriedly dressed. When he turned back to face her, he looked at her as if he was seeing her for the first time.

She glared back.

"That was a hell of a thing to do."

"Don't tell me you didn't enjoy it. Now who's afraid?" she said in cool challenge, and then laughed softly.

He found this sudden change in her shockingly cruel. She had suddenly become bold and unpredictable. She was driving him out of his mind.

"Come on!" he said sharply. "Let's get back to town."

"Still afraid?" she teased.

"Yes, damn it, but not of you, myself. Don't ever do that again and expect to get away with it. I can stand just so much. The next time I might forget that I'm a nice guy and take advantage of the invitation."

CHAPTER

11

After Ned left Dawn at her front door, he rode toward the Silver Buckle. He wasn't much on drinking, but today he felt a sharp need to escape the bitterness of reality. Dawn had left him feeling like a fool. The passion she had roused in him ached like a spur in his flesh. He stepped through the swinging doors searching for a way to quench the consuming fire she had built inside him. He picked an empty table, slouched into a chair, and ordered a shot of whiskey.

Across the room, Marcy Scott gazed at him. She had only been working at the Silver Buckle a short time, and her nice figure and pretty face had attracted a lot of admirers. She liked the looks of this cowboy. He seemed a bit displaced, and she decided he needed entertaining. His eyes followed her as she moved determinedly in his direction.

She smiled slightly, and the smile instantly disappeared. She leaned forward across the table, pressing her palms against its sticky surface. "Getting an early start, handsome?"

"You could say that," he said absently, staring down the cleft of her ample breasts.

"Like some company?"

"Not exactly."

"Can I get you another drink?"

He looked down at his empty glass and nodded. "Yeah, and I'll buy you one."

"Thanks." Her smile was more genuine this time. She moved leisurely to the bar with a swing of hip motion. She returned with a full bottle and two glasses, set them on the table and took the chair facing him. She poured. He drank.

After his third drink Marcy began to look more inviting to him. Their casual conversation began to take a more direct curve. Ned was dimly aware of people coming and going, but his primary interest was fixed on the woman who sat across the table. After a while she was sitting next to him, her arm hanging loosely around his neck.

Ned failed to notice Mac when he entered the saloon and didn't realize he was there until he spoke.

"Mind if I join you?" His question was directed to Ned. His lips were saying one thing while his expression of disgust was asking a far more serious question, wondering what had brought Ned to this outrageous exploit.

"Sure Mac. Sit down, have a drink." His speech was slow, his mind already dulled.

"What are you doing here this time of day?"

"Is there a law against getting drunk early?"

"Not that I'm aware of." His tone became more cordial.

"Have you met, Marcy?"

"No, I haven't had the pleasure." Mac looked at her more closely, noticing that she was quite attractive in a vulgar way. Her round, smooth, face was highly colored.

Marcy flashed him a contentious smile and said in a sultry voice, "I think you'll be more comfortable at another table."

He hesitated a moment, amused by her sly discourse. "You know something? I think you have a point." Marcy sneered at him, her brown eyes openly mocking him. He returned her belligerent smile, tipped his hat facetiously and walked over to the bar.

Ned lost all track of time. The room was spinning around him so fast that he was completely off balance and unable to stand. The lantern lights overhead seemed to slither across the ceiling like leaping, living, things. His eyes could no longer follow the movements around him. He squeezed them together tight and buried his face in his folded arms. As if dreaming, he heard a voice from some shadowy place calling his name. He lifted his head from the table when he felt a cool hand on his neck. Marcy was bending over him. He could faintly make out her features through the drunken haze that had dropped like a curtain before his eyes.

She pulled him to his feet, supporting him as he struggled awkwardly to put one foot in front of the other, allowing her to steer him toward the stairs. He moved slowly up the steps hanging on to her. He was in a heedless state as she maneuvered him into her room and closed the door. The green shade was drawn and the room was dark except for the wavering light of a single candle that burned beside the bed. He looking around, saw the bed, and lurched toward it.

"Wait," she said, hurriedly turning down the covers, and then began to remove her clothes indifferently. It was strictly business.

Ned stared at her with renewed pain and frustration. Seeing her this way reminded him of the way Dawn had started to strip off her clothes, taunting him, making him feel less than a man. His thoughts were tortuous.

"Undress," she said, "and get into bed," She lay down with the covers turned back and spread her legs wide, revealing what she knew he wanted. "What's the matter? Don't you like what you see? I know you want some of this."

The sight of her naked flesh roused him and he craved the pleasure she could provide. He focused his attention on the dark triangle between her thighs, the secret folds that offered him relief from the gorged heat deep in his loins, the cruel agony Dawn had branded him with. He struggled his boots off and dropped them noisily on the bare plank floor, and then began to fumble with his clothes, dropping them in a heap beside his boots. He could smell her cheap perfume as he crawled in beside her.

She felt for his manhood, stroked him, her hands slipping over his fine body, causing him to shudder violently. He was snorting and quivering. She felt his muscles tighten, nerves on edge. He was responding, anxious, rock hard. He wouldn't take long. Most of the men she dealt with were pigs, some were offensive, but it didn't matter, she knew her function, there was nothing they could ask that she couldn't do. Some were fast, some slow. Some couldn't get it up, and they were the ones that aggravated her.

She didn't get many like this one, young and inexperienced, even washed. He had a mental hang-up, it was apparent that he was looking for solace, and she would accommodate him with pleasure. She also knew he had the money.

He put his arms around her, yearning toward her. Her body felt cool and thin. Her lips were hard and cold as a statue's. The difference between this woman and Dawn amazed him. His obsession for Dawn burned out of control, stripping bare his moral decency, and he took the woman in a fit of self-reproach and anger, brutally using her in a violent explosion of pent-up lust. In the aftermath he thought about Dawn and cried.

When he awoke some hours later, he looked at the woman beside him with disgust and shame. He dressed, flung some money on the dresser and fled from the room, telling himself that it would not happen a second time. His conduct had left a scar on his conscious and a shock to his moral standards. To calm his nerves and his wounded pride, he decided to ask Dawn once more to marry him. He had already forgotten about Mac.

The following day Dawn agreed to go riding with Ned again, just to enjoy the beautiful day. Ned, on the other hand, had a special reason. He rode uneasily, dreading the possibility of her rejecting him again.

They were only a short distance from the river, but two miles from town when they saw the Indians. They came into view suddenly, seemingly from out of nowhere, crossing in front of them. Ned shaded his eyes with his hands, hoping to identify them. He counted eleven horses and nine riders, two of them were leading pack horses. He presumed them to be a small hunting party returning home with their game. When the Indians spotted them, they swung their horses directly in their path, cutting them off, catching them out in the open. Ned quickly took in the terrain. About five hundred yards to the west he spotted a bare, rocky hill that could provide them with some protection. "Head for that hill," he shouted. "That ain't no hunting party, it's a raiding party."

Dawn led off to the left, spurred her horse and headed for the hill, her mount kicking up a rain of clods. Ned followed close, glancing back over his shoulder. The Indians also cut hard to the left in hot pursuit, and then came the bloodcurdling Comanche war cry. The sudden impact of sound sent a chill up Dawn's spine, firing every nerve in her body with panic.

103

Ned whipped out his hand gun and threw two shots over his shoulder. He was surprised when he saw one of the warriors drop from his running mount.

At that moment the sky seemed to open up in a rain of arrows and gun shots, barking and echoing in the desolation.

They reached the hill about three hundred yards ahead of the Indian's. Their pack horses had slowed them considerably, but they followed steadily. Dawn sprang from her horse and ducked behind the nearest cover of rocks. Ned dragged his carbine from the saddle boot and hit the ground beside his sliding mount. The Indians boiled up about thirty yards from the hill for counsel. The Comanche war paint was now visible.

At the sight of the Indians streaked with color, Dawn was terrified. I must not go to pieces, she thought. I can't surrender to panic.

Ned too felt the full impact of the situation as he made a quick assessment of their position. The sun was to their back, and to their advantage, as it would tend to blind the Indians and spoil their aim.

"Come on!" Ned yelled. "Stay close to the rocks and climb. They ain't gonna stay put long. When they start swinging in close and firing I want to have the drop on 'um from the top of this hill."

They reached the top just in time to get a full view of the raiding party riding hard toward the base of the hill, their murderous cries carried on the wind. They were being rushed by seven warriors. One had stayed behind to hold the ropes of the two pack horses. The Indians were coming at them in a single line, firing continuously, reloading as they rode. Ned picked a target and took careful aim. He had to make every shot count. He missed the Comanche but hit his horse. The animal's front legs buckled and it went down carrying the rider with it. The fall separated the Indian from his rifle. He took cover behind his dead mount and reached out to recover his weapon. Ned squeezed off a shot as the Indian's head rose above the horse's belly. The impact pushed him backwards. His hand clawed at the rifle for an instant before he died. The remaining six Comanches drew off, preparing to make another pass. When the last shot was fired and the echo died sway, Dawn raised her head and looked over a boulder.

"They will keep coming back until they kill us," she cried. "We're trapped up here."

Ned knew she was right, but tried to reassure her. "They can't sneak up on us. If they show themselves I'll kill 'um."

"What happens when you run out of bullets?"

"I don't plan on running out. There ain't that many of 'um."

"Save one for me, Ned. Don't you let them take me." He shook his head. "I won't, I promise."

They watched helplessly as the Indians rode to the base of the hill and took cover below them. Ned dropped another one as they swarmed over the rocks. The others scattered. They could be anyplace. Ned passed his handgun to Dawn. She clasped it in shaking fingers, her expression a mask of fear. Ned knew she was scared stiff. So was he. There were five Comanches sneaking around in the rocks below, and he only had two eyes. If they were to get out of this alive, Dawn had to do a man's job, and he had to disregard the fact that she was a woman and he loved her. "Shoot anything that moves," he said, "and shoot to kill."

The next move was up to the Indians. All they could do was wait for them to attack. They didn't know what to expect, or when. They waited as the sun sank lower and lower and the chill of night crept into their bones. Ned's fear increased, also his guilt. He had only himself to blame for the spot they were in.

"Are you all right?" Ned whispered.

"I can handle a gun, don't worry," she said bravely.

Moments later they saw the dark figure of an Indian slipping silently over the rocks like a shadow. Ned was ready when the Comanche's rifle barrel snaked across a rock a few feet away. He took careful aim above the exposed barrel of the Indian's rifle. Moments later there came a brief show of feathers and head dress. At that instant Ned pulled the trigger. The slug found its target and the Indian fell forward. His rifle dropped from his hands with a clatter. A ghastly quiver racked the Indian's body, and then he lay still in a pool of blood, his head sporting a gaping hole.

Dawn screamed and Ned whirled around just in time to see the Indian behind him with drawn bow. He hit the ground and fired a snap shot, aiming point blank. The warrior let the arrow fly as he crumpled up with a slug in his gut. Ned felt the wind from the shaft as it sang past his ear. The wounded warrior moaned and rolled on the ground, both hands clasped over the bleeding hole in his belly. Ned aimed his rifle again, this time with the sights trained on the Indian's head. At that instant another brave came screaming at him with a hatchet. Ned spun around, swapping targets, putting two slugs in the second Indian. He fell at his feet. Another shot split the silence, and Ned looked around to see Dawn standing over the wounded Indian who was clutching a knife. She had blown a hole in his head the size of a tea cup. She was shaking violently, still pointing the gun at the dead Indian's head.

"You did good," Ned said.

It was quiet now, as quiet as the death that surrounded them. Night was approaching fast, and the temperature was dropping rapidly. They could see only a few feet in front of them. If the Comanches were gone, they had gone without making a sound. If they were still hiding some place in the rocks, they saw no sign of them. A crawling sickness began to form in the pit of Ned's stomach. His numbed brain could visualize one of the Indians putting a shaft through his gizzard before he could clear leather. They waited and shook and drew up like two turtles in their shells. All through the night they listened for movement and strained their eyes into the darkness. Ned even prayed a little. Dawn was silent, holding Ned's gun in readiness.

The night seemed to be six days long. Each dragging second could bring them death. If they were captured, it would not be a swift death, but a death that could take days. Indians had ways of killing the white man a thousand times before death finally took its toll. He knew he must not let them take Dawn. Before he would let that happen, he would kill her himself.

They sat huddled together for warmth as the cold night air penetrated their clothing, their backs pressed against a cold rock. As the sky began to turn gray, Ned searched the rocks for any sign of movement that might indicate that the Indians were still there. If they were it was time they made their move. Indians always attacked at dawn. As the sky lightened they could see more and more of the terrain. Overhead vultures circled and squawked, while others were already hovering over the dead bodies. The sun was thirty minutes high before Ned felt it was safe to venture out of their rocky fort.

From all indications the Indians were gone, and just as Ned had feared, they had taken their horses. So now they weren't just hungry, thirsty, and exhausted, they were miles from town and on foot. They could do one of two things: they could stay put and hope a search party would find them, or they could start walking and hope they weren't caught out in the open by the Comanches.

They decided to walk out of their situation and reluctantly headed in the direction of town. The next hour passed slowly and miserably, like waiting for a death sentence to be passed. Dawn was tired and leaning heavily on Ned. They trudged on; each step took them closer to home, or death. They had a great fear of what might be waiting for them up ahead.

Far in the distance they saw a feather of dust that could mean only one thing. Riders were approaching, and they were out in the open with no place to hide. Ned's eyes stayed fixed on the riders while his mind raced. This was not a situation they could run from or he could shoot their way out of.

Dawn gripped Ned's arm. "What if it's Indians? What can we do? There is no place to hide."

"If it's Comanches they're coming from the wrong direction."

"Do they have a certain direction?"

"I hope so." The fact that the Indians might have gone back to their village for reinforcements set his thoughts aflame. It wasn't very likely that they would stick around this long, but an Indian's actions were not laid out like blueprints. They might have pulled off to draw them out into the open.

Two riders became visible. As they approached they stood helplessly in their wake. "Don't worry," Ned said. "If they're Indians, there's only two and I can handle 'um." He handed Dawn his gun and stood in front of her with his rifle. He tried to sound reassuring even as a chill of fear traveled up his spine.

Dawn held her breath as the riders drew near. When she recognized the riders as her father and Frost Jackson, she was overcome with joy because they had just been rescued from a nightmare of horror.

A look of relief flooded Mac's face when he saw his daughter, it was self-explanatory as to the worry she had put him through. He dismounted and ran to Dawn, sweeping her into his arms. She fell against him shaking and crying. Ned stood like a dummy with his arms hanging limp at his sides, listening as Dawn sobbed out the dreadful ordeal they had experienced.

Mac looked away from his daughter, his eyes resting on Ned.

"I've been out of my mind, boy! I thought you two were dead, or worse. We've been searching all night. Charley and some more men headed back to town. They gave up, but I wasn't about to. I got a new lease on life when I spotted you two standing out here in the middle of nowhere. Come on, let's get you two back to town. You look pretty beat. We can hear the details later."

Frost had been silently watching Dawn the whole time. Ned knew what was on his mind, he could read it in his eyes. He had never made any secret of his feelings.

Frost swung down from the saddle, took Dawn's hand and drew her toward his horse. "You better ride double with me so I can take care of you. Ned might get you killed yet."

She jerked her hand free and glared at him. "I had rather walk! I'll ride with my father; I can trust him."

"Hey, that don't say much for Ned. You saying you don't trust him?"
She turned on him in renewed anger. "If I didn't trust him I sure wouldn't have come way out here with him."

"We all make mistakes," Frost said, his white teeth gleaming in a wide smile.

"Shut up, Frost," Ned warned, the muscles in his face drawn tight. "Keep your mouth shut before I strain your lips back through your teeth."

Frost's smile faded and he clenched his fists.

Mac, having had enough of Frost's smart mouth, stepped between the two men, easing their flared tempers. "That's enough," he growled angrily. "Damn you, Frost! Ned's been fighting Indians all night, he ain't in any shape to start in on you, but I am. One more word out of you and I'll kick the seat of your pants out. Let's get mounted. Ned, you and Dawn take my horse. I'll double up with Frost." Then as an after thought, added, "There's a canteen on the saddle horn."

Mac was concerned about Dawn's health, afraid she might become ill from being out in the cold all night. He wanted to have Doctor Keel take a look at her the minute they reached home, but she flatly refused.

She knew she could only put her father off for a little while, because he was bound to have his way. She stayed in bed the rest of the day as the tightness in her chest began to grow, along with her anxiety.

That evening she got up and dressed, nervously awaiting Ned's visit. It had been her suggestion that he pay her a visit after they both had an opportunity to rest.

A few minutes after Ned arrived, Mac excused himself. The Indian incident had caused quite a bit of unrest in the town, and he decided to spend some time at the saloon, talk to the men, and try to ease things before it got out of hand. He had persuaded Sheriff Morgan to put off taking action until he had a chance to talk with Chief Brave Horse. He felt sure that the Indians who attacked Ned and Dawn were most likely a bunch of renegades.

Dawn was thankful for the chance to speak to Ned alone. She sat by the fire staring into the flames, absorbed in thought. Ned stood behind her chair with his hands resting on her shoulders. "I'm glad you're feeling better," he said.

"I'm not."

"Well why in thunder don't you go to the doctor?"

"I can't. I'm afraid."

"Afraid! Afraid of what?" He walked around the chair to stand in front of her, waiting for her to explain.

She made no attempt to avoid his probing eyes. "Because," she said in a voice that was little more than a murmur. "I'm going to have a baby."

The shock of her words threw him completely off balance. "That's ridiculous," he cried. "You don't know what you're saying!"

When she remained silent, he said more sharply. His voice filled with desperation. "Are you out of your mind? You can't be! It's impossible."

She looked up at him, her face pale and tense, her body stiffly erect as she sat forward in her chair.

Ned knew she was telling him the truth. "No!" he gasped, his eyes dark with pain.

"Please, try to understand." She began to sob. "I loved him."

Ned beat his fists against the back of her chair to keep from hitting her. At this point he felt he should ask who the father was just to be on the safe side. "Light Eyes is responsible, isn't he?"

"Yes."

"How the hell could you do that? Sleep with that damned Indian? How? For God's sake, how?"

"You say you love me. If you love me then you will try to understand. Or maybe you don't love me at all."

"It's not a question of me loving you. The question is how do you feel about me?"

"You have always been like a brother to me. I love you like a brother."

"I don't want to be loved like a brother. I want to be your husband. I want to live with you, sleep with you, and make love to you. Why can't you understand how I feel?"

"I do understand. "What will I do?"

"The only thing you can do." He cleared his throat. "Marry me."

"You still want to marry me? After what I've done?"

"I love you."

"How can you still love me?"

"You act like that surprises you. I'll take you any way I can get you. Where you're concerned, I have no pride. I'll do anything to make you mine."

"What about the baby?" she said softly. "How will you explain having an Indian child?"

Her words held him speechless for a moment, gripped with sudden realization, and then he said forcefully, "I don't care what anybody thinks. I'm not concerned about other people—you're my only concern. I'll swear the child is mine, and kill any man who says different."

His wild response, the fierceness in his voice, chilled her to the bone. There was savageness about him that she had never encountered before. She had misjudged him. He was more complex than she could have imagined. For the first time she realized that he was more of a man than she had given him credit for. Her discovery came as a shock.

Mac sent for Doctor Keel the following morning. Dawn had developed a deep cough during the night and her eyes were bright with fever.

Keel finished his examination and stood with his back to her staring out the window. Dawn waited quietly for him to speak. Each second seemed to tighten a noose around her neck. He turned to face her at last, his eyes filled with concern. "You have a pretty serious chest cold," he said calmly. "But the cold is not my prime concern. You know what I'm talking about, don't you, young lady?"

She nodded, her insides suddenly cold, while the pain in her head was like fire. Trying not to cry, she bit her lower lip until her chin began to quiver.

"Have you told Ned?"

Poor Ned, she thought, he is already being blamed. She was suddenly ashamed for putting him on the spot, but realized it would be useless for him to deny it. No one would ever believe that Light Eyes was the one responsible. She met the doctor's troubled eyes. "He knows," she said.

"What about Mac?"

"No! She answered sharply.

"Do you want me to tell him? It might make it easier."

"I don't want him to know yet."

"In a little while you won't have to tell him."

"I'll tell him when I'm ready, and not before."

"Have it your way. All I can say is that I hope you know what you're doing. I sure wouldn't want to be in Ned's shoes when Mac finds out."

"By the time he finds out Ned and I will be married."

"Well, I hope so. At least that's a step in the right direction. What I can't figure out is why you haven't done something about it before now."

"The reason isn't really important is it?"

"Not to me, but the baby you're carrying might not feel that way."

"Promise me you won't say anything about this."

"I won't breathe a word," he said, moving toward the door. "I'll tell Mac that you're all right, and to keep you in bed. I'll be back in the morning to take a look at you." He paused with his hand on the doorknob. "Take a spoonful of that cough syrup every few hours."

She thanked him and smiled lamely. "I'll be fine by tomorrow."

Mac and Ned were waiting in the next room. They both came to their feet when Doctor Keel entered. "How is she?" Mac said anxiously.

"She's tough, Mac. She'll be just fine in a day or two. She has a chest cold. See that she gets plenty of rest, and make sure she takes her cough medicine."

"I'll see to it. Can I see her now?"

"Yeah, sure, Mac, but don't stay too long. She needs to stay warm and get plenty of rest."

Smiling from ear to ear, Mac entered Dawn's room and closed the door softly behind him.

Doctor Keel put his arm around Ned's shoulders and led him out to the porch. "Come up to the office so I can have a look at you."

"What for? Nothing wrong with me."

"I want to give you a going over."

"I don't need a going over. I need to get on back to the trading post."

"I'm the doctor, Ned. Now, get your hat and ride with me in the buggy. If I don't get you to go now, chances are I won't see you for a while, professionally that is. I have to make a living too you know."

Ned hesitated a moment. He had hoped to see Dawn again before he left. They hadn't really settled anything yet, and he wanted to set the date before sundown. He felt like flatly refusing, and started to do just that, but the look in the old doctor's eyes gave him a quick change of heart. Something was on his mind, that was sure. Maybe Dawn had told him the truth about herself, or maybe he had guessed. Of course he didn't have to guess, he was a doctor, he knew about such things.

"Ok," he agreed. "I'll get my hat and be right with you."

Not another word was exchanged between them until they were seated across from one another in the doctor's office.

"Well, young man, what are you waiting for? Out with it."

"It might help if you was to tell me what I'm supposed to talk about."

"Don't play dumb with me. You know damned well what I'm talking about," he snapped. "I haven't been a doctor for forty years not to recognize a pregnant woman when I examine one. Dawn is going to have a baby, and that's not good under the circumstances. Kids are supposed to have a father and a mother. I don't aim to stand by and see Dawn's baby branded a bastard. And another thing, if Mac happens to find out before you two tie the knot, he might take a notion to carve your notch in his pistol grips. Can't say that I would blame him either."

"Did she say it was mine?"

"She didn't have to. Look here, Ned, if you don't want to marry the girl and give the baby your name, that's up to you. There isn't a man in these parts that wouldn't jump at the chance, single or otherwise. And as far as it being yours, there's no doubt in my mind, and you had better watch your lip or I might take a notion to smack you myself."

"Now hold on. I'm ready to marry her anytime she says. I've been in love with her ever since I was old enough to know the difference between a man and a woman. But it takes two, and she ain't said yes yet. And don't think I ain't been working at it."

"Yeah, that's apparent."

"If you're trying to be funny, you're not. I love Dawn, and the last thing in the world I would do is to hurt her. I want to marry her more than I ever wanted anything in my life."

"When was the last time you asked her?"

"Yesterday."

"What did she say?"

"Yes, in around about way."

"What kind of a dad-blamed answer is that?"

"Well, for your information, if you hadn't been so hell bent to get me to your office to drag me over the coals, I'd have her answer by now. One way or the other."

"Sorry, son, if I sort of butted in, but this is a damned serious situation. I had to find out."

"You're telling me. Now, if you don't mind, I'll mossy on back over there and see if I can talk to her."

"I gave her a pill. She might be asleep."

"Just my luck, and I need to get on over to the trading post. Frost was supposed to open up this morning, but you know how he is. He may get drunk instead."

Ned slammed out the door, furious at himself for letting the old man get his goat. All the way back to the cabin he rehearsed what he was going to say to Dawn. Mac opened the door before he had a chance to knock.

"Come on in," he said with a big smile. "Where have you been?"

"Keel had to drag me over to his office."

"Glad to hear it. You do look a little peaked. How do you feel?"

"I felt better before I saw the doctor."

Mac laughed. "I've been telling him for years that he makes me sick." Both men laughed.

"How's Dawn feeling?"

"Hungry, and wanting to see you."

"Is she awake? Keel said he gave her a pill."

"He did, but she didn't take it."

"That sounds about right."

"Go on in," Mac urged. "I got to go make like a cook."

Ned tapped lightly on her door before opening it a crack to peek in. She was sitting up in bed drinking a cup of coffee. She looked up and smiled. "Come on in. I was hoping you would come back."

"I was having a little chat with Doctor Keel."

"I hope he didn't give you a hard time."

"No, nothing like that. From the way he acts, you'd think he was your father."

"He did give you a hard time. I'm sorry."

"It wasn't too bad. I can take anything as long as it's for you."

"I can't stand the thought of you taking the blame for my condition. It's not fair."

"It is fair." He took the cup from her hand. "It's what I want." He was in a state of mind where he did not care much what happened to him, his only concern was for Dawn. He would tell any amount of lies to protect her, leaving himself wide open to take the blame. He was willing to face the world and suffer the consequences. He felt like thanking Light Eyes. It was because of him and his misfortune that the door to Dawn's heart had finally been opened to him.

"Marry me now, today," he pleaded. Holding her small hands in his.

"I'll marry you, Ned, as soon as I'm well, but only if you're absolutely sure beyond a doubt that I'm really what you want."

"I've never been more sure of anything in my life."

"I'm grateful to you, Ned."

"I don't want you to be grateful. I want you to love me. That's all I've ever wanted."

"I know that, but you will have to be patient and give me time." She brushed his cheek with a quick kiss.

"Come here," he said, taking her into his arms. "I guess I have the right to kiss my future wife."

"You'll catch my cold."

"I don't care."

She kissed him then, a burning, lingering kiss, clinging to him, turning his blood to fire and his bones to water.

She was remembering the last time she kissed Light Eyes, and the memory stirred her deeply.

Ned never guessing that the passion she felt at that moment was not for him, but for the man whose seed she carried beneath her heart.

CHAPTER

Ned was determined to marry Dawn as soon as possible; however, Mac wanted them to wait, and approached Dawn hoping to change her mind.

"The house will be finished in less than a year," he argued. "Surely you don't intend to live with the Rowling's that long. You kids need your own place."

Dawn wished she could wait forever. She didn't love Ned. Her commitment to him was simply one of necessity. In a year she would have a baby six months old. "We don't want to wait," she said. "We plan to be married next Saturday."

"In a week?"

"Yes. It's already been decided."

The tone of her voice invited no further argument. Although Mac felt certain it wouldn't work, that Dawn would be miserable trying to live under the same roof with Martha Rowling, he held his tongue. In his estimation, Martha was a domineering old bat, and he had never liked her. She kept her three boys under her thumb, not to speak of her henpecked husband.

When Mac offered Dawn the house as soon as it was finished, she had accepted. She knew Mac would never have undertaken the construction except for her. To refuse his gift after all his carefully made plans for her future would break his heart.

He was building it on the spot she loved most: the grassy hill overlooking the river and the green valley below where she rode her horse in a swift gallop with the taste of wind in her mouth, bound by the enchantment of freedom. From the top of the hill she had a view of her own private world: the open range all the way to the tree topped hills of the Indian hunting grounds. At night she had gazed at the moon's reflection on the water and the shadow of clouds that moved across its path. Soon it would be her home to enjoy and treasure for the rest of her life.

She had never liked living in town so near the trading post, and was sick and tired of the constant parade of long nosed women with their accusing eyes and pasty smiles of resentment plastered on their ugly faces when they looked in her direction, and she would glare back unblinking and thrust her chin into the air. They acted as if it was her fault because they had broom handle figures and homely faces and couldn't catch a beau.

Ned didn't understand the way she felt, and was shocked by her attitude. "You can't accept a gift like that, not even from your father. We'll build our own house. It won't be anything fancy like the big house Mac has planned, but at least it will be ours. There are some things a man wants to do for himself."

At that moment all her tender feeling for him changed to resentment and she turned on him in blazing anger. "Since I was nine years old I have waited for this house, and my father is determined to build it for me. And now, because of my situation, you expect me to turn my back on his dream and just walk away. It would break his heart. I won't hurt him, Ned. Everything he does, he does it for me."

"I don't expect you to turn your back on him. I just thought that since were getting married you might consider my feelings."

"Well you thought wrong. I will not allow you to interfere. I have something to look forward to, something to live for. It's settled," she said in a tone of finality.

"Meaning you don't have anything with me?" His tone was composed, while his insides were churning. He had started off on the wrong foot with her from the very beginning, giving in to her the same way Mac had always let her have her way. She was spoiled rotten, and he realized it was too late to alter his behavior. If he tried, he would lose her, might lose her anyway.

"I mean that I won't settle for less with you than I had without you." She went on easily. "The house will be mine eventually anyway. He has no one else. When he dies everything will be mine. I think I owe him something, and all I have to give is my love. Don't try to change that, Ned, and don't try to change me. I may be marrying you, but I still love my father, and I'm capable of thinking for myself."

"I'm sorry, I guess I look at things a little one sided." He realized this was not the time for quarreling, but the time for patience. The waiting was almost over. Soon now, she would be his wife. He would not do or say anything at this late date that might cause her to change her mind. Whatever differences they might have, they could settle them after they were safely married.

The next few days passed slowly for Ned. He was constantly on edge, always in fear of Dawn changing her mind.

The town seethed with excitement over the news of the coming wedding. The women were jubilant because Dawn had finally decided to become Ned's wife, easing their jealousy. The men however, particularly Frost, felt regretful.

Ned felt a deep sense of triumphant, seasoned with joy, anticipation, and a hell of a lot of nervousness. When the day finally came he dressed very carefully in his best suit and new black boots. He wanted to look just right for the most important day of his life. He stepped back from the mirror to inspect himself, pleased with his reflection. He felt fit to be tied. In less than two hours Dawn would be his wife. He had thought this day would never come. Now that it had he was having a hard time realizing it. It was too good to be true, and he wondered if he had died and gone to Heaven. Deep in thought, he jumped like a prod cow when Clay burst into his room.

"Hey, Ned, ain't you ready yet?"

"How many times do I have to tell you to stop yelling at me, and don't sit on the bed."

"Why not? You ain't never cared before."

"I never been fixing to get married before either, smarty pants."

"Is Dawn really gonna sleep here tonight?" Clay said, pointing at the bed with a devilish gleam in his eyes.

"You sure ask lots of questions."

"How else will I find out? Well, is she?"

"Yes, she sure is," he said proudly.

"Wow! Boy! Just think of that."

"What are you talking about?"

"I never seen a bride up close before."

"I don't think she's ever seen a snot-nose like you up close before. Now, will you go away? Can't a man have a little privacy around here?"

"I don't see why you have to talk like that. I live here too, you know."

"Boy oh boy! You sure are ignorant. I can see right now that I need to have a talk with you."

"Well just don't act so darn smart, big brother, cause Pa's gonna have a talk with you."

"Oh yeah? Who says?"

"Ma says."

"What about?"

"How should I know? All she said was, 'Pa, you better have a little talk with Ned before the wedding.'"

Ned laughed to himself.

In spite of the cold weather, Ned thought his wedding day was beautiful. He rode to town in the buggy with Pete and Martha; Jack and Clay had gone on ahead with the buckboard so Ned could use the buggy to bring his bride home.

Pete was relaxed and happy, with a few drinks under his belt. He wasn't much of a drinking man, but he felt it was the expected thing to do when his oldest son was getting married. On the other hand, Martha was quiet and withdrawn.

Ned was puzzled by his mother's attitude, and asked right out, "What's the matter? Ain't you happy about your son getting married?"

She made a gesture with her hand as though trying to dismiss his question. "All I want is your happiness. You know that."

"Then stop looking so down in the mouth. I'm the happiest man in the world today."

"Yes, I can see that, but there will be other days."

"What's that supposed to mean?"

"Some things can seem too perfect to be true."

"Stop acting like an old mother hen. You knew your chicks were bound to leave the nest someday."

Pete spoke up. "Ned's marrying a mighty fine woman. She'll be the daughter you've always wanted."

Martha did not reply. She sat looking down at her folded hands, her mind filled with doubts.

"She'll be all right, Ned, soon as she gets used to the idea." Pete was concerned about Martha's sullen attitude also. She had certainly doused water on Ned's happiness. He was starting to look miserable.

Ned was puzzled, even a bit worried. With Dawn living in the same house with his mother, he hoped they could be friends, even love one another. All he wanted to think about right now was how much he loved Dawn, and how he ached to hold her in his arms and make love to her the whole night through. He felt as though the whole world was holding its breath, just waiting for him to claim his bride.

There was a big turnout for the wedding that was being held at the Town Hall. Most weddings were held at the church, but the building wouldn't accommodate such a large crowd. Ned had never seen so many people gathered together under one roof before.

The women folk whispered and giggled, feeling quite pleased that Dawn would no longer be a threat to the single girl's husband hunting. The young single men who had waited and hoped that they might, by some stroke of luck, marry Dawn, no longer had a reason to remain single.

Frost stood by, his face like stone, his heart filled with resentment and jealousy. He hated Ned's guts, along with a number of others who shared his feelings.

Debbie was supposed to stand up with Dawn, but for some unknown reason she had not yet arrived, and it was almost time for the ceremony to begin. Dawn waited nervously with Mac in the small dressing room at the back of the hall. "Where can she be?" she said anxiously. "Something must have happened to her. She should have been here long ago."

"Don't worry," Mac said. "Getting all upset like this will spoil your wedding. I'm sure there is a simple explanation."

"Knowing Kathryn, I can't be sure of that. Something's wrong. I know it!"

Mac had his doubts too, but held his tongue. "If she doesn't show up tonight, I'll ride out there first thing in the morning and check on her. Stop worrying. Today's your wedding day; you should be happy."

"You won't forget?"

"I promise," he said reassuringly. "After the ceremony I'll ask around. Somebody may know why she didn't show up. We had better get set. The wedding march is about to start." She took his arm and he felt her trembling.

All heads turned toward the door as Dawn entered, looking a little pale, but more beautiful than ever in her flowing white dress. Jack, standing close to Ned, saw him sway slightly and put his hand out to steady him. "Take it easy, ole man."

Ned held his breath all through the ceremony, afraid Dawn might change her mind yet. He breathed a sigh of relief when Reverend Collins pronounced them husband and wife. Ned kissed his bride, and then held her close to his trembling body for several seconds. "I love you," he said, with tears in his eyes. When he released her cheers and laughter erupted and the party began. Martha kissed her son then her daughter-in-law, blinking back her tears, and Ned wondered if she was shedding tears of joy or remorse.

Mac slapped Ned on the back a bit harder than was necessary. "Be good to her, son, she's a McCloud and we McCloud's don't take to being kicked around." He spoke in jest with a smile on his face, but Ned did not doubt the seriousness of his statement.

When the congratulations ceased, the festivities began. Mac had out done himself, planning a shin-dig in honor of his daughter's marriage such as Courgat had never seen before. Old Jess Spikes flung his hat aside, rolled up his sleeves, stood with fiddle in hand, and yelled, "Do-si-do!" There was the confusion of partner hunting and scurrying feet, and the dance began with couple after couple joining in.

"Swing your partner and do-si-do,
after a while we'll let you go,
off in the dark so you can spoon,
now everybody bow to the bride and groom."

Hand in hand, arm in arm, round and round, feet keeping time with the music, bodies swaying, hands clapping. Dawn whirled from arm to arm. The dancing went on and on, set after set. Ned began to feel that every man there had danced with his bride more than he had.

The long tables, draped in white cloths, were laden with an array of food and drink.

Frost Jackson was swigging whiskey straight from the bottle he had brought with him. An hour after the celebration commenced, Frost was already drunk. He watched Ned with cold eyes, but the looks he gave Dawn were far from cold. He had the look of a hungry man. He seemed not to hear the laughter or the music. His mind was closed to everything around him except Dawn. Admitting defeat was getting harder for him to accept all the time. Inside he felt the dead weight of jealousy.

Dawn was not aware of Doctor Keel's watchful eyes. All this exercise was not exactly what he would prescribe for a patient in her condition. A disapproving frown creased his brow as he saw her suddenly grow pale. Without hesitation he hurried to her side, and placing a guiding hand under her elbow steered her away from the crowd gathered around her. "You've ignored me just about long enough, young lady," he said jovially, taking her arm and leading her away. Out of ear shot, he whispered, "Are you all right?"

"I feel faint," she said, leaning heavily on his arm.

"You had better slow down for a while." He looked around for an empty chair. "Sit down and stay put while I get you a glass of water."

Dawn looked around, her eyes moving over the sea of faces. She wondered where Ned was, but the room was packed and she could easily overlook him. A hot sickness was welling up in her throat. Getting shakily to her feet she moved hastily toward the rear door. Once outside in the fresh cold air, away from the odor of food, whiskey, and sweat, her nausea began to subside. She stood in the shadow of the building, the darkness soothing her tangled nerves, relieved to escape the staring eyes and loud voices. Overhead the moon flickered through the bare oak limbs, casting wiry shadows on the cold ground. She felt at ease now, and leaned against the trunk of an oak tree in relief.

Inside Ned pushed his way through the crowd looking for his wife. Spotting Edward Keel, he elbowed his way over to him.

"Have you seen Dawn?"

"Yes, as a matter of fact I left her sitting right here not five minutes ago." He gestured toward the chair. "She was feeling sick, and I went to get her a glass of water. When I got back she was gone."

Ned glanced about, his eyes coming to rest on the back door. "Maybe she stepped outside for some fresh air," and then added sharply, "Where's Frost," realizing he was nowhere in sight.

"I don't know. He was standing over there by the back door a few minutes ago, looking as wooden as a cigar store Indian."

"My, God," Ned cried in alarm, heading for the rear door. "He's drunk!"

"He's always drunk."

Hearing the back door open and shut, Dawn looked up, expecting to see either Ned or Doctor Keel. Instead, Frost stood there looking at her, swaying slightly, with the same smirking smile she detested so violently playing across his face.

"What do you want?" she snapped, beginning to feel sick again.

He moved unsteadily toward her. "Just looking around."

"Well go look someplace else. I came out here to be alone."

"Now that ain't no way to act on your wedding night." He reached out and stroked her arm. "Honey, you're getting cold. Come here to ole Frost and let me warm you up."

She took a step backward. "Leave me alone before I start screaming," she warned.

'Never," he said, his hands gripping her arms. This time he held her fast.

"Let go of me!"

"How about a kiss? It's customary to kiss the bride, and I haven't had my turn yet." He pushed her back against the tree, holding her arms over her head. She twisted her head from side to side to avoid his lips. His sour breath made her stomach roll over. She kicked at him wildly. Managing to struggle one arm free, she slapped him across the face.

"You are a little wild cat, and so beautiful."

He was grinding against her, forcing her against the rough tree bark that bit into her back. She cried out, "You're hurting me!"

"I want you and, by god, I mean to have you, here and now."

Ned stepped through the door, his anger exploding. "You're going to get something, Frost, and I'm going to give it to you, here and now," he mimicked. He flung Frost away from Dawn, and he stumbled a few steps and caught himself. Before Frost could gain his balance, Ned looped his fingers together forming a double fist, pivoted a quarter turn, and swung his arms at Frost like a bat. The force of the blow lifted Frost off his feet and spun him around. He hit the ground howling, his jaw a ball of fire. He looked up, trying to focus as stars filled his head, along with a lot of pain.

He was struggling to stand when Ned hit him again. Frost went down for the second time. Ned stood over him, his breath coming in steaming bellows. "I'm going to beat you until you can't walk, and if that don't keep you away from my wife, I'll kill you." Ned was clenching his teeth when he pulled Frost up by his string tie and jabbed him in the stomach. Frost doubled over, all the wind knocked out of him. Ned brought his knee up and caught him under the chin, snapping his teeth together. Frost went down for the third time. This time he didn't try to get up. Ned straddled him where he lay, grabbed him by the neck and commenced to choke him.

"Ned!" Doctor Keel shouted. "That's enough." Ned looked up in a blinking daze, focusing on Keel's face. "You're wasting your energy. He's unconscious and beyond feeling a thing." A crowd had gathered by now, enjoying the fight more than the wedding celebration. Mac pushed his way through to his daughter. "What happened here?" he shouted. He pulled off his coat and draped it around Dawn's trembling shoulders.

"I came outside for a breath of air and Frost followed me."

"Did he put his hands on you?"

"He's drunk."

"I can see that. Did he put his hands on you?"

Dawn looked away from her father's enraged face. Mac put his big rough hand under her chin and turned her to face him. "Did he touch you?"

"Yes!"

Mac dropped his hand and turned his attention to Frost, who was now on his feet and propped up by two men. "Turn him loose, boys," Mac ordered.

The men withdrew their support and stepped back. Frost attempted to straighten up but failed. He was holding his stomach, swaying and rocking, bleeding from the nose and mouth, one eye starting to swell, and his jaw appeared to be a bit out of line.

"I got this on, Mac, and I can damned sure finish it without any help from you," Ned said, pulling away from Keel's grasping hands.

"Stop it!" Dawn screamed. "Will you just stop it?"

Ned turned around to look at her, and Frost hit him with a Sunday punch on the side of his head. Ned staggered back, his ears ringing. Frost picked up a rock and advanced toward him. Ned made a grab for Frost's arm to separate him from the rock. Frost was slowed by his injuries, and Ned was not back in focus yet, but managed to take hold of Frost's arm, and they were into a grunting tug of war.

Mac nonchalantly stepped around behind Frost, and with his hands clasped over his head, brought them down with force behind Frost's left ear. Frost hit the ground for the fourth time. "What's the matter with you, Mac?" Ned yelled. "Don't you think I can take him?"

"I know you can. There might have been some doubt once, but not anymore." Mac looked at his son-in-law with pride. "I didn't step in because I thought he might whip you. I just don't aim to see Dawn's brand new husband all skinned up on account of that vulture. Take your bride home. I think you've done enough celebrating for one night."

Ned looked down at himself, brushing at his clothes. "Damn! Frost bled all over my best suit."

"Don't worry about it, son, I'll buy you a new one."

"Better put your coat on, Dawn," Doctor Keel said, holding it for her. "You're just getting over a bad cold. I would hate to see you get another one for a wedding gift."

Dawn slipped out of Mac's coat and into her own. As she handed Mac his, he leaned down to kiss her, and held her for a moment. "He loves you, honey. Try to be good to him." She nodded and turned to Ned who was standing beside her. He put his arm around her and they walked away from the milling crowd.

"All right folks," Mac's voice boomed. "We still have some celebrating to do. There's plenty of food and liquor left, so let's make a night of it."

Ned took his wife and they headed for home. The music and laughter slowly diminished with every clop of the horse's hooves. They rode in silence with Dawn curled up beside him wrapped in a blanket.

"I'm sorry, Ned," she said softly.

"For what?"

"All the trouble I caused you with Frost."

"Trouble? The pleasure was all mine."

"Does your head hurt?"

"Not much."

"You sure?"

"As happy as I am tonight, I wouldn't feel it if somebody cut my throat."

"Are you really happy?"

"For the first time in my life." He gave her a longing look and put his arm around her.

"Did you see your folks when they left?" she said, changing the subject.

"No, I couldn't see anything but you. As far as I'm concerned that old custom of everyone dancing with the bride is for the birds."

"Do you know why they left early?"

"No, but I guess if it was something important they would have told us."

"Yeah, I guess so."

"My mother is funny about some things. She could have kept something from me just to keep from spoiling our wedding night. But I don't know how anything could spoil the way I'm feeling right now."

"Well, I guess we'll find out when we get home."

"Maybe they wanted to get to bed early so we could be alone."

"You have to be kidding."

"Yeah, you're right. I'm only joking."

"I feel bad about moving in on your folks this way."

"If you feel that way we can stay at the hotel."

"It's not that I don't want to stay with them. I had rather sleep in your room, in your bed, and in your folk's house in preference to a stuffy hotel room."

"And in my arms," he added, his eyes sparkling. "We'll have the whole upstairs to ourselves. Clay and Jack took to the bunkhouse, and mom and dad are sleeping in the granny room off the kitchen."

"Oh! That's not right, Ned. I feel bad about putting them out this way."

"They don't mind, sweetheart. Anyway, it won't be for long. After about a month we won't pay any attention to them anymore."

"And just what does that mean?"

"Damned if I know. That's what mom said. Ask her."

"I think the answer might be interesting."

Ned pulled back on the reins bringing the horse to an abrupt halt. He turned to Dawn and said softly, "Come here, Mrs. Rowling and give your brand new husband a kiss." She went into his arms, and he kissed her over and over trying to ease the fire trembling his body, but it only rose higher. He was so swept away by his own passion that he failed to notice her lack of response. "I love you," he whispered. "You drive me crazy with wanting you. If you hadn't showed up today for the wedding, I think I would have shot myself. But you did, and now you're mine. I'm not dreaming am I?'

"No, I'm your wife, and you got a pretty poor bargain."

"I got the kind of bargain Frost Jackson would cut my throat for."

"Let's not talk about Frost, if you don't mind."

"I'm sorry, he is a mighty poor subject, and I'm a pretty poor husband. I know how tired and cold you are, and here we sit. I had better get you home and into bed." He snapped the reins and the buggy moved forward with a jerk.

Yes, she thought, into bed by all means. What else is ever on his mind?

Pulling up in front of the house, they saw a light glowing in the kitchen window. "Looks like my folks are waiting up for us." Ned stepped down from the buggy and then helped Dawn down. "I'll walk you to the house before I put the buggy in the barn and unharness the horse."

"Never mind that," Jack said, coming around the corner of the house. "I'll take care of the horse. You take care of your bride."

"Thanks, Jack. Is everything all right with the folks? I noticed they left the party early."

"Everything is fine. You can pick the damnedest time to start looking for something to worry about."

"Just thought I'd ask."

"See you in the morning," Jack said, hopping in the buggy to drive it to the barn, then said as an after thought, "good-night, sister. Welcome to the family."

"Good night, Jack, and thank you." She turned to Ned smiling. "Wasn't that sweet?"

"See there, we all love you." Ned picked her up and carried her across the threshold and into the spacious parlor.

"Hi, Dawn," Clay chirped, charging into the room.

"Hello, Clay," she said in amusement. "How are you?"

"I'm fine," he said frowning, "What's wrong with your foot?"

"Nothing," she laughed.

"How come Ned's carrying you?"

Ned glared at his little brother. "It just so happens that it's the custom for a husband to carry his bride across the threshold," he said, trying not to lose his temper.

"No wonder men don't like fat wives. How much do you weigh, Dawn?"

"Clay, will you shut up. You ask too many questions about things that don't concern you. Get out of here."

Clay stuck his tongue out at him.

"Come in here, Clay," Pete roared from the kitchen.

"All I done is tell 'um good night."

"Get in here! Now!"

"OK, Dad. Good night Dawn. Good night Ned."

"Good night Clay," they said simultaneously, laughing at him as he hurried toward the kitchen.

"He's cute," Dawn said. "I've missed so much by not having any brothers or sisters."

"You can't say that now. What's mine is yours, and that includes Jack and Clay. You may change your mind about how cute Clay is. Having him around is enough to drive a person crazy sometimes."

Dawn smiled, for she knew how much Clay and Jack meant to Ned, no matter how much he complained.

"Shall we go up?"

"Yes," she said, not looking at him. "I do feel a little tired."

He carried her slowly up the stairs and down the hall, pausing in front of their room. Still holding her in his arms he kissed her on the neck. He nudged the door open with his foot, which was slightly ajar, and carried her inside. "Well, this is it," he said, not ready to put her down.

Dawn looked around the spacious room. "It's lovely, Ned."

A fire was burning in the fireplace, filling the room with pleasing warmth.

"Glad you like it. Ma worked on it for a week, putting the woman's touch on it, or something like that."

"She couldn't have pleased me more," she beamed, admiring the crisp blue curtains and matching counterpane. "Oh, Ned! We left my grip in the buggy," she cried. "Put me down before your arms break."

He stood her down gently. "Do you need your grip tonight?"

"Of course. It has my gown and underthings in it."

"Then you really don't need it," he said, with a devilish grin. She shot him a disapproving look and he quickly sobered. "OK, I'll get it."

"Seeing his hurt expression she touched his cheek and said softly, "I guess I'm being silly, but I would like to be alone for a little while, if you don't mind."

"I do mind," he said, looking at her longingly. "I'm not sure I can stand it."

"Not even for ten minutes?"

"Not even for one."

"Please."

"No way out?" She did not answer him in words, but the look in her eyes was plain enough. "Is there something wrong?" he asked, searching her face.

"Of course not."

"You won't lock me out, will you?"

She shook her head. "No, I promise."

"That's good, because the lock's broken," he laughed. He kissed her tenderly, turned, and strode slowly across the room. At the threshold he paused and looked back at her. "Ten minutes." He closed the door and moved back down the hall.

CHAPTER

13

D awn listened to Ned's foot steps until he reached the foot of the stairs. Oh! God, she thought, give me the strength to live through this night. She walked to the window, drew the curtain, and looked out into the cold night. She wanted to run away and hide someplace out there in the darkness, away from her miserable thoughts, away from Ned and the duties she was expected to perform on this night. The thought of Ned making love to her was revolting. She would never want him that way. She wasn't sure what it was she felt for him, but certainly it was not passionate love. She just wanted them to be friends, but that was impossible. She was his wife and obligated to play the disgusting role. She suddenly remembered what Mac had said to her just before she and Ned left. "He loves you, honey; try to be good to him." It was almost as if he knew the truth about her feelings for Ned. She didn't want to hurt him, but how could she pretend to love him? She knew she was indebted to him for his loyalty. She was using him, and her guilt was like a weight inside her. Putting him off would accomplish nothing.

She turned away from the window to look at herself in the mirror, turning slowly, examining her body from every angle. Her waist was only slightly swollen. Her breasts were fuller, but still held their erect shape.

She paced the floor in dread, her tension mounting as she waited for Ned to come to her. She felt like a condemned criminal awaiting punishment.

Downstairs, Ned strolled nervously into the kitchen. Pete and the boys were sitting at the big round table talking in muted voices. Pete looked up as Ned entered, an expression of disbelief on his face.

"Any coffee left?" he said.

"We just made a fresh pot," Clay answered, jumping up to get the coffee pot and another cup.

Jack shoved over on the bench to make room for his brother. "This is a hell of a time to be craving a cup of coffee," he said seriously. "Shouldn't you be upstairs?"

"That's enough," Pete barked. "Mind your manners and leave your brother be." The same question had crossed Pete's mind, but he was careful not to express his opinion.

"By the way," Jack said, "You forgot your wife's bag. I brought it in for you. I would have taken it up, but I figured you might not miss it for a while."

"She sent me after it."

"I set it to the left of the stairs."

"Thanks," he replied, taking a sip of coffee. He sighed heavily, thinking to himself that Jack was right. This was a hell of a time to be drinking coffee.

Jack cocked his head to one side and looked at Ned. "Had a spat already?"

"No, we ain't had a spat already," Ned echoed.

"From the looks of your head, you must have had more than just a spat. Looks like she knocked blazes out of you."

"Boy! Look at that knot," Clay cried. "What did she hit you with?"

"Dammit, Clay, don't you start in on him again," Pete warned, "or you'll find yourself sleeping in the woodshed, and I might run you around behind it first." Pete looked inquisitively at the knot on Ned's head that Clay and Jack were staring at. "By the way, what did happen to your head? Did you run into a rock wall?"

"No, Frost."

"Frost!" Pete exclaimed. "What did he hit you for?"

"Because I had my head turned."

Pete laughed. "That's just about what I would expect that gutless drunk to do."

"Come on, Ned, don't just sit there, tell us what happened. Did you let him lick you?" Jack said.

"Not hardly. I got in some pretty good ones myself." He held out his hands to display a beautiful pair of skinned knuckles.

"What did he do? Bump you while you was doing the do-si-do?" Clay asked, his eyes sparkling with excitement.

"He was trespassing."

"You should have expected that," Jack said. "He never could leave Dawn alone, and he never will unless he's forced. Now that you're married to her, and he's out in the cold, you had better watch your back. Next time, he might try putting a knife through you. Back to front, of course."

"Don't worry, Jack. I'll watch him, and if he ever touches my wife again, I'll kill him."

"Killing would be too good for him," Pete said.

"Where's mom? Has she gone to bed?"

"Your cousin Virginia took down sick at the dance and we had to leave early to take her home. That old stark won't wait for nothing, not even a good fight. Sorry we missed it. I've been wanting to see Frost get his tail feathers pulled for a long time. Your mother is going to spend a few days with Virginia and help out with the baby. I thought you knew."

"I had my mind on something else."

"Coffee?" Jack laughed.

"Not hardly. I was keeping an eye on my beautiful wife."

"Can't say that I blame you. About every man there had their eyes on her, especially Frost."

"He sure proved that. How's Virginia doing this time?" he asked, his mind drifting back to his cousin.

"Doctor Keel thinks the baby will make it. She's been ailing nearly eight months. The two she lost came too early. Mother Nature is a puzzling thing. I think she just forgets to count sometimes. Me and the boys would of stayed over for the night, but your mother said we would just get in the way. Doctor Keel didn't even go. He checked her before we took her home, and he said it would be many hours before she needed him. He said Martha could see after her just fine. That's female business anyhow, I reckon."

"Yeah, so I've been told." Ned glanced toward the ceiling as though he might see right through it. "Guess I'll turn in," he said quietly, feeling self-conscious, then stretched and yawned.

Clay was sitting across the table from Ned with his chin cupped in his hands, his big blue eyes staring at his brother with a fixed expression. Ned glared at him and he looked away sheepishly.

"It's late all right," Pete said, looking toward Clay and Jack. "You boys had better hit the hay too."

"I ain't sleepy," Clay said mischievously.

"Me neither," Jack added, with a bit of devilment in his tone.

"You may as well get sleepy because you're going to bed anyway. You got to jar the floor an hour earlier in the morning so you can fix breakfast and milk. Until your mother comes home, it's up to you boys."

"I'll bet Dawn's a good cook," Clay piped up.

"She might even know how to milk," Jack added.

"It ain't her place to look after us. She's Ned's wife and a guest in this house, and you will respect that fact."

"Aw, Pa, we was just teasing," Clay said.

"That's enough out of you boys. Mosey on to bed. I'll be calling you early."

Both boys got up reluctantly and dragged themselves out the back door.

"Good night, Ned," Jack called over his shoulder. "Hope all that coffee you drank don't keep you awake." They fell into each other's arms laughing hysterically.

Pete jumped to his feet, spilling his coffee, and grabbed his quirt off the peg by the back door. Still laughing, the boys ran toward the bunkhouse with Pete on their heels, snapping the quirt at the seat of their pants. Giving up the chase, he went puffing back to the house. "Never a dull moment around them two."

"They're a couple of clowns."

Pete put his arm around Ned's shoulders. "You married yourself a fine woman, Ned, and she's the prettiest creature I ever laid my eyes on. You're a lucky man."

Ned smiled at his father's praise. "I'm the happiest man in the world tonight."

Pete looked at his son seriously. "I don't know what you're doing down here, and it ain't none of my business, but you came downstairs for more reason than to fetch your wife's grip."

"You're right," he admitted. "She sent me away from her. She wanted a few minutes to herself."

"Well she's had a few minutes. Now, pick up her grip and get back up them stairs before I take this quirt to you."

"Pa, I—, well—"

"What's troubling you? Ain't that upstairs private enough? Are you uncomfortable about spending your wedding night here?"

"It's not that. I ain't sure she wants me to come back. I don't want to rush her, or anything."

"What kind of fool talk is that? She's your wife."

"I know that. I love her, and I want to be with her so damned bad it hurts."

"Did she tell you not to come back?"

"No."

"Then why in blazes are you standing around down here? Get on up them stairs! She knew what she was doing when she said 'I do', and she went right ahead and said it. I would never of took Dawn to be a shy girl, but maybe I'm wrong. Maybe she wants to be in bed with the light out before you crawl in beside her. She's your wife, so go on up there and find out if she wants you. One thing's sure, you won't be worth a damned until you do."

"You're sure right about that."

"Go on," Pete urged.

Ned picked up his wife's grip and marched up the stairs, feeling a bit more confident after talking with his father. Dawn's attitude had all but stripped him of his self-confidence.

He walked quietly down the dark hall, a nerve ticking in his stomach. He paused in front of the door, taking a moment to whip up his courage.

Dawn was sobbing softly. She was crying for Ned, Light Eyes, and herself. If by some miracle Light Eyes might have survived, her marriage to Ned ended all hope of them ever being together. While she grieved for the Indian, she was being punished ten fold by forcing herself to live with a man she could never love. She wondered where she would find the strength to pretend every day, every hour, and every minute that she cared for him. She had never been so miserable in her life. She held her hands over the tiny lump in her belly and cried for her unborn child.

When she heard Ned's footsteps, she turned her back to the door and wiped her eyes. Ned did not speak, nor did he look in her direction. He moved to stand before the fireplace with his head down, his arms hanging limply at his sides. He looked absolutely crushed.

Dawn's heart ached for him, realizing he had heard her weeping. How was she to explain? He had sacrificed for her, took the blame for her condition, and his reward was her rejection. She tried to speak, but the words froze in her throat. They were bound together by God, yet they were worlds apart. She had made a serious mistake. They were both in torment, and nothing could be worse. Not even bearing a bastard child, or being called a slut. Mac would be the one to face the disgrace and humiliation. She had to consider his feelings. She could imagine the pain and disappointment Ned was suffering. He reminded her of an old whipped dog, and she was responsible for his misery. He was standing with his back to her staring silently into the fire. She didn't know exactly what her intentions were when she crept quietly to his side. Ned sensed her presence and turned to face her. She felt tense standing so near him, conscious of what he wanted, what he had a right to expect.

She was so lovely, so desirable, that he wanted to cry. Her hair fell loosely about her shoulders and face, soft and shining, reflecting the light, her breasts rising and falling with each breath she drew. His eyes caressed her from her tiny feet to the angelic expression in her dark eyes. She did not waver under his gaze, but looked back at him with an expression that melted his bones. As they silently faced one another, she reached out and caressed his face tenderly, smiling up at him, and that small gesture was all the encouragement he needed. He took her into his arms, feeling every curve of her body as she pressed against him. He kissed her mouth, eyes, nose, and returned to her lips. "I worship you, Dawn. You're not only my wife, you're my life. I can't stand losing you. I wanted to die when I heard you crying. I tried to tell myself that you just couldn't be crying, not now, when you're finally mine. Why were you crying? Are you sorry you married me?"

She had wounded him and she had never meant to. He deserved better. She hadn't intended to lie either, but she knew she must for the sake of her baby. Once the words were spoken she would be obligated to continue her pretense. "I was crying because I had just discovered the truth about myself. I love you, Ned. I think I always have." So there it was, and she despised herself for having said it.

His arms went around her and he drew her close, feeling her breath, warm and sweet against his neck. He was stunned speechless. When he recovered his voice, his words burst forth in a rush of excitement. "I must be dreaming, or else I'm in Heaven. I can't believe this is really happening." He had never expected in his wildest dreams to hear those words come from her lips. Dawn was his wife and she loved him. He could ask for nothing more. His world was complete. He would never again feel any regrets for having killed Light Eyes. He would do it again, a million times over to gain this magic moment. He fell to his knees before her, locked his arms around her knees, pressed his face against her stomach, and wept.

"Ned, please, don't cry," she pleaded. "Please, don't."

He rose to his feet, feeling his wire tight nerves began to relax. His uphill battle was finally over. All the restraints were lifted. No more waiting and aching to make love to her. She belonged to him and he shook violently as he removed her wedding dress in a rush of rapture and laid it neatly over the back of a chair.

"Do you want your nightgown?"

"No," she said, thinking, just get it over with.

He turned the covers down and helped her into bed before removing his own clothes. She didn't want to see him naked, but forced herself to look. He was thin and muscular, his chest hairless. He was already prepared to enter her, and she felt a wave of disgust. He left the lamp burning while he removed her underthings, his hands felt hot where he touched her. She cringed inwardly, her heart like granite. She felt nothing for this man, her husband, except pity, and it was reassuring to feel anything, to learn that her emotions were not completely dead. She pitied him because his love for her was as hopeless as her love for Light Eyes.

She had heard that pity and love are so much alike that some people cannot tell the difference. She knew the difference, and even feeling pity for him made her feel less like a heartless cheat.

"Can we do this in the dark?" she asked.

A suspicious expression crossed his face for a heartbeat. Then, with out replying, he raised himself and turned the wick down.

She was thankful for the darkness, thankful he could not read the expression on her face. She wanted to turn away from his lingering kisses, his hot searching hands, his probing. His mouth was on her breasts, licking her nipples, then her stomach and belly button. She wanted to push him away, scream for him to leave her alone, but realized he had waited years to satisfy this urge. He was carrying on something fierce, trembling and snorting, telling her he loved her over and over while grinding against her, stroking and moaning. She squeezed her eyes shut and waited for it to be over. His flesh was hot as a stove, and she felt as though she might smother pinned under the weight of his body. Now he was crying a steady stream of "Ah, ah, ah." She felt his muscles tighten, and for a moment he stopped breathing. He was panting, quivering, and sweating. It will be over soon, she thought with relief.

On the verge of orgasm, he suddenly became still. He didn't want it to end. It was too good. He wanted to make it last. He waited a moment for the stimulation to subside before he resumed his stroking. When he heard her moaning he thought she was going with him, on the verge, and he became even more excited. When he couldn't hold back any longer, he cried out and hilted her, moaning deep in his chest as he gushed, crying breathlessly, "Oh! God! Oh, my God!" He flopped down on top of her, drenched in sweat, his breath coming in bellows.

He had misunderstood her moans, the shudder that racked her body. He had no idea how disgusted she was at being forced to surrender herself to him. He knew only blissful happiness and fulfillment.

When he finally rolled off, she was swept with a tangle of emotions. She had done her duty, what he had expected, and she felt like a piece of meat. She was filled with horror at the thought of having him use her time and time again. Where would it all end? Ned was her husband, he held her physically, but he would never hold her heart. As long as she lived she would belong to Light Eyes. She didn't want Ned to love her. In time, she hoped he would grow to hate her.

Ned slept peacefully and contented in the quiet coolness of the dark room. Dawn lay rigid beside him staring at the ceiling, the shame of her deception weighing heavily on her conscience. She wanted to escape Ned's arms, throw the covers off and run from the room. God help me, she thought, tears filling her eyes, I'm trapped here. She was torn between the strength of her obligation and a wild compulsion to break free. It was almost daybreak when she finally closed her eyes.

Pete rose the next morning earlier than usual, dressed quickly, and walked the short distance to the bunkhouse to wake the boys. Much to his surprise it was not quite the task he had anticipated. Before returning to the house he gathered an arm load of firewood.

There was emptiness about the house without Martha. An emptiness that even Clay and Jack couldn't fill with their constant bickering. In the twenty three years that Pete and Martha had been married, he could count the days and nights on one hand that they had been apart. He thought about Ned upstairs with his wife. It was hard for him to realize that Ned was almost twenty-one and married. Jack would be nineteen come spring. Before long he would most likely be getting married too. That would leave Martha and him with only one son at home to spoil. Thoughtfully he laid a fire in the cook stove, opened the damper, and struck a match. A warm feeling filled Pete as the wood caught and flames danced up around the oak chunks.

Jack came into the house by the back door, barefoot and shirtless, rubbing his eyes with his left hand and carrying his shoes and shirt in his right. He hurried over to the stove.

"It's a wonder to me how you boys stay alive the way you run around in the wintertime half naked. Why in blazes don't you finish dressing before you run out the door?"

"Believe me Pa, it ain't no colder outside than it is in that bunkhouse."

"Ah, come on, Jack, I think you're stretching it a little, and another thing, don't let me hear any talk like that in front of Dawn. We don't want her to get to feeling guilty about you giving up your room."

"Does seem kind of stupid to me. Me and Clay ain't gonna bother 'um."

"Just you wait, Jack, until you're married. You ain't gonna want anybody within five miles of you and your bride."

Their conversation ended abruptly when Clay slammed into the kitchen wide awake and fully dressed, ready to start the day as usual, full of devilment. He looked around the room. "Wonder why Ned ain't got up yet?"

"Little brother," Jack smirked, "wouldn't surprise me if he even skipped breakfast this morning."

"He sure will get hungry then."

"Not at all, Clay. "He'll be living on love."

"Love may be good for the soul, Clay, but it don't do a damned thing for the stomach," Pete said. "Don't let Jack pull the wool over your eyes."

"Speaking of food, Clay, get them eggs fried."

"Now look here, Jack, I ain't too handy with the pots and pans. I'll make the coffee. You fry the eggs."

"Coffee? The last time you made coffee it tasted like you boiled your drawers in it."

"Ok, wise guy, from now on you make the coffee."

"You boys stop bellyaching and get on down to the barn," Pete bellowed. "And wear a coat. I'll have breakfast ready by the time you get back. Give the calf two tits, and be sure you strip old Nelly out good. Clay, don't forget the slop bucket, it's beginning to stink."

The boys were happy with themselves for getting out of cooking. They grabbed the milk pail and the slop bucket and left the house chattering.

"Wonder if Dawn can cook?" Pete mumbled to himself. He felt sorry for Ned if she couldn't. Pete was setting the table when Clay came running into the house all out of breath. "Pa," he yelled. "Frost just rode up. He wants to know if he can hide his horse in the barn."

"Frost? Here?"

"Yeah, he's right outside. Well, can he?"

"Can he what?"

"Hide his horse?"

"What in blazes for?"

"I don't know. He ain't said, but he sure acts like the Devil's after him"

"If I know Frost, the Devil wouldn't have him. Go upstairs and fetch Ned down here." Then as an after thought, said, "Knock first."

Clay ran up the stairs tracking cow manure. Pete shook his head disgustedly, walked to the back door, and yelled, "Put your horse in the barn, Frost, and come on in the house."

Frost hadn't waited to be told, he had already put his horse in the barn and was headed to the house in a dead run. He burst into the kitchen out of breath, white as a sheet. "Thanks, Pete," he puffed.

"What the devil is after you? You look like the dead warmed over."

"Give me a cup of coffee and I'll tell you."

Pete handed him a cup of coffee and waited, eyeing him curiously. Frost took the cup in shaking fingers, flinching when he spilled some down the front of his shirt.

Clay came running back down the stairs jabbering. "Ned's mad. He said he'll be down in five minutes."

"Well I can't say as I blame him. This is a hell of a thing to happen the morning after a man gets married." Pete said, hot under the collar.

"What did you do, Frost? Rob the bank?" Clay asked. "Your face sure looks awful. Ned really did fix you. Can you see out of both eyes?"

"That's enough, Clay," Pete warned. "Get on back down to the barn and help your bother finish the chores. If there's something you need to know, I'll be the first to tell you. Now get! And don't start bitching." Clay left the house dragging his feet, looking back over his shoulder, mumbling under his breath.

"Do you think Ned will help me?"

"That's up to Ned, and you can hold off on your story telling until he gets down here. I don't want to listen to it twice."

CHAPTER

14

"What the hell do you want, Frost?" Ned growled, coming into the kitchen buttoning his shirt.

"I'm in trouble."

"What's new?"

"I'm not kidding, Ned. I'm in real big trouble this time."

"And so early too," Ned sneered.

"You two knock it off. Let's hear him out," Pete said.

"Do you promise to help me, Pete?" Frost was addressing Pete, but his eyes were locked on Ned's face.

"That all depends. If you broke the law—"

"I ain't," he said quickly.

Pete studied him for a moment before answering. "OK, let's have it, and it had better be the truth."

"What about you, Ned?" He was pointing a shaking finger.

"Personally I don't give a damn what happens to you, especially after the crap you pulled last night."

"I was drunk. I'm sorry—and I'll apologize to your wife."

"Stay away from my wife!"

"Don't worry, you about tore my head off, and my jaw ain't working right. I can't hardly chew. Will you help me?"

"If Pa thinks your sorry hide is worth it, I'll go along with him, but believe me, my heart ain't in it. Get to the point, Frost. I ain't got all day to sit here and listen to hog wash," Ned said impatiently. "I'm on my honeymoon, and I got a beautiful bride waiting for me upstairs."

Pete wanted to laugh when he saw the expression on Frost's face. Ned had not passed up the opportunity to twist the knife.

"Well, this morning I was coming back from town—" He stopped and swallowed hard. "Me and some of the boys got in a poker game after the wedding, and it lasted all night."

"Will you just tell us what happened, we ain't interested in your social life." Pete barked.

"OK, give me time. I was about a mile from home when I seen this horse standing down by the branch. I rode on down that way to see if I could place the critter, and I heard something splashing around in the creek. I rode a little closer and I seen this Indian girl taking a bath. You know me; I never turn my head when I see a pretty woman, let alone one taking a bath."

"Yeah," Ned agreed. "We know because nothing else crosses your mind. They'll be the death of you yet."

"Don't say that, man. I'm serious."

"So am I."

"What the hell happened, Frost? Stop beating around the bush," Pete said.

"I can imagine," Ned said disgustedly.

"Will you hush up Ned? Let him get on with his story before Clay gets back to the house. He never will get it told then."

"I watched her till she was done bathing and got up on the bank to dry off. I walked up within six feet of her and she didn't move a muscle, just stood there all wrapped up in a buffalo robe. I figured she'd high tail it to the brush, but she just looked at me, kind of inviting like. So hell, was I a man or a damned fool? I got me some of that stuff."

"I knew it!" Ned raved. "What did you do, Frost? Rape her?"

"It happened just like I said."

"Do you expect us to believe a story like that? Ain't nobody in their right mind takes a bath in the creek in the middle of winter. Not even an Indian!" Ned yelled.

"Hold on, Ned," Pete said, holding up his hand. "I happen to know that some Indians are clean, and they do take baths in the winter. Some of 'um act like they're half Eskimo." Pete wasn't siding with Frost, but he believed in the truth, and he figured that Frost might be telling the truth about the Indian girl taking a bath. "Go on, Frost, tell us what happened then?" Pete leaned back in his chair, crossed his arms, and waited.

"I sat around for a little while after she left, sort of resting up before I started home. I was almost to the ridge when them red devils got after me. They cut me off, so I headed in your direction, and here I am."

"You damned fool!" Pete roared. "You led 'um here. If you cause me any trouble with the Indians, I'll kill you myself. That Indian gal didn't give you no invitation. You just helped yourself, and if they decide to scalp you, I figure you got it coming. Call the boys in, Ned."

"Hold on a minute, Pete. I lost 'um down by the graveyard. They don't know for sure where I went."

"Oh, no? They can't track worth a shit, can they?" Pete stormed. "Ned, I told you to call the boys in."

Ned stepped out on the back porch and yelled for his brothers. They came on the run, sloshing milk. "What's up?" Clay said, letting the screen door slam in his brother's face.

"Never mind, and stay out of the way." Pete shoved Clay to one side. "Go sit down and keep your mouth shut."

"Jack, get the rifles and a box of shells. Ned, you go fetch Dawn down here."

"I don't want her upset again. Frost, you get that horse out of the barn, get your ass on it, and get the hell out of here!"

"You know I can't do that. They didn't get close enough to see me, but they would know my appaloosa anyplace. There ain't another one like it in these parts."

"You should have thought about that sooner. You created this problem, now you deal with it."

"You can't mean that, Ned. If I leave here now, I'm a dead man."

"The thought did cross my mind."

"I need help. I'd help you if you was in this fix."

"No you wouldn't. You would hand me over to the Indians and help yourself to my wife."

"Man! I apologized for that."

"I didn't accept it. You didn't need any help to get yourself in this fix, now why don't you get yourself out the same way?"

"I'll go if you and Jack will ride with me. I'll make it up to you, I swear." He was sweating and begging, afraid he wouldn't be able to change Ned's mind. "I ain't leaving here unless you two back me up."

"I don't know about you, Ned," Jack said, "but I ain't riding any place with him. I don't know what he's done, but from what I've heard about him, it ain't good. Why don't we just give him to the Indians and save us all a bunch of trouble?"

Clay stumbled back into the kitchen with four rifles cradled in his arms. "Here's the rifles. Who we gonna shoot?"

"I sent Jack after them rifles? It's a wonder you didn't shoot yourself."

"Yeah, but he sent me. Why don't you tell me and Jack what Frost done?"

"Why don't you tell 'um?" Ned said, glaring at Frost. "Be a shame if they got scalped and didn't know what for."

"Yeah, you're right. Frost is about to get us all scalped over a squaw he helped hisself to. They didn't get a good look at Frost, but that horse of his will identify him. They won't take the time to ask who it belongs to. They'll scalp us all to make sure they get the right one."

Clay's mouth dropped open, and he glared at Frost.

"Don't just stand there catching flies," Pete said. "That ain't no help."

"What are you worried about? Give him to the Indians."

"Jack already suggested that. You two think just alike."

"What makes you think they never got a good look at you?" Jack asked. "I think you're lying."

"They never got close enough, but they could see that horse of mine for half a mile."

"Yike!" Clay yelped. "And the critter's in our barn. We could burn the barn."

"Why don't you shut up?" Pete barked.

"I'm just trying to help."

"Well you ain't. Hush up!"

"Here they come!" Jack shouted, looking out the window.

"He's right," Ned said, standing in the open door, "but they're swinging to the south, heading away from us.

"I told you I lost 'um," Frost smarted.

"What the hell do you know?" Pete snapped. "What's to keep 'um from swinging back? They lost your trail for now, but if they pick it up again they'll come straight here."

Ned grabbed a rifle, checked the chamber, glanced around the room, and headed for the stairs.

Dawn was sleeping when he burst into the room. She raised up and looked at him, a startled expression on her face. "What's wrong?"

"You better come downstairs; we may have trouble coming."

"What are you talking about? What kind of trouble?"

"Frost has his tail in a crack again, real good."

"Frost? What does he have to do with us?"

Ned poured the story out hurriedly as he strapped on his gun belt.

"I can't go down there like this." She slid up in bed, clutching the covers, covering her breasts. "I have to get dressed unless you expect me to wear this sheet to breakfast."

"I'll wait. Go ahead and dress."

She made no move to get out of bed. Ned laughed. "What's wrong? You act like I'm a stranger. Remember me? I'm your brand new husband. Come on, honey, we have to hurry." He sat down on the bed and pulled her into his arms and held her tenderly. "God, I love you. How did I ever get this lucky?"

"I need a little more time to get used to you."

"If you want me to leave you alone, just say so."

"Do you mind?

Just like last night, he thought, and was able to smile about it. "I do mind," he said, his voice thick with passion. "I think I understand a little more about women now. They most likely feel shy in the light of day, but it's all the same. I'll wait for you downstairs." He kissed her and left the room before he changed his mind. "Damn Frost," he mumbled under his breath.

"Have you seen 'um?" Ned asked coming into the kitchen.

"No, we lost sight of 'um over the ridge. They might be headed for town," Pete said. "Where's that daughter-in-law of mine? I would like to have a few words with her before the Indian war starts."

"She's getting dressed." Ned colored slightly, but felt elated by the flash of jealousy in Frost's eyes. "I hope you're joking about an Indian war."

"So do I," Pete said. He turned his attention to Frost. "How many bucks were in that party?"

"I didn't take the time to count 'um."

"Ten? Twenty? Fifty?"

"Six or seven."

"That's a relief. We can handle a scant few like that."

Dawn moved down the stairs slowly, as if every step was taken against her will. Ned watched her proudly as she stepped into the kitchen. He put his arm around her possessively, and kissed the top of her dark head.

Pete looked at her smiling. "You're enough to brighten any man's morning no matter how far he's slipped into the grumps. Come over to the table and sit down while I pour you a cup of coffee." He pulled the chair out, set a cup in front of her and filled it. "Sorry about the commotion, but we got Frost to thank for that."

She smiled at Pete, and then glanced at Frost, her face congested with rage. "Naturally," she managed without raising her voice.

Jack was looking intently at her. As if feeling his eyes on her, she spoke to him in a sweet voice that caused him to blush.

She turned her attention to Clay then, who was busy looking at the toe of his boots. "What's the matter, Clay?" she teased. "Cat got your tongue?"

"No," Pete laughed. "He's already talked so much he wore it out."

Frost had been standing across the kitchen, but walked toward her now, clearing his throat. "Sorry about last night, Mrs. Rowling. I was a bit drunk."

Dawn looked up into his face, her eyes fixed on him nastily. "You don't have to tell me how sorry you are, Frost. I'm already well aware of that."

"I'd a never done a thing like that sober." He said, feeling a shock of alarm, seeing the murderous look on Ned's face as he crossed the room to stand next to his wife.

"Was you drunk this morning too?" Ned lashed out at him.

Frost dropped his eyes and made his way over to the window without another word. He realized it wasn't to his advantage to get Ned riled; he might throw him to the Indians.

"Anybody got any ideas?" Pete asked.

"I have," Ned said. "It's a long shot but it might work." He headed for the back door.

"What are you fixing to do?" Pete said.

"If they follow Frost's tracks this far, they might follow them further. If I turn his horse loose it might lead them away from here."

"Now you hold on, Ned. I paid two hundred dollars for that horse. There ain't another one like it in these parts."

"And that's exactly the problem."

"I don't aim to lose that horse," he declared hotly.

"Do you want the horse or your hide?" Ned barked, swinging around to face him. "You got about ten seconds to make up your mind, because one of you goes, and I don't give a damn which one."

"Okay, Ned, okay!" Frost echoed, shrugging his shoulders in defeat. "Go on and turn him loose.

Ned walked outside, took a quick look around, and ran toward the barn.

Pete handed Jack a rifle and took one for himself. "Run to the granny room and fetch my handgun, Clay, and be careful you don't shoot anybody."

Clay jumped over the bench by the table, caught his foot and fell flat on his face. He got up grinning.

From the window Jack had a good view of the south side of the house. Pete, standing in the open door, could cover the barn and north side of the house. Frost watched the activity from his safety zone, standing next to the cook stove.

He laid his rifle down, poured himself a cup of coffee, and sat down at the table facing Dawn, his thoughts stamped clearly on his face. He didn't utter a word, but the hunger in his expression was enough to make Dawn's flesh crawl. She rose abruptly and joined Pete at the door.

Frost watched every step she took, a hot flash of desire burning his insides.

"There ain't any sign of Indians this way," Jack said. "You see anything, Pa?"

"So far, so good. No, wait a minute. I see 'um. Their coming in from the north. They circled us completely. I count nine. They know for sure there ain't any tracks leading out of here. They got you cold, Frost. They know you rode in here, and they know for damn sure that you ain't left unless you're riding a flying horse. Ned's in trouble. He's in the barn with your horse."

"They'll kill him!" Dawn cried excitedly. "They'll think it's his horse. What can we do?"

"Stay put for now and hope Ned does the same." Pete tried to sound reassuring, and patted Dawn's shoulder in sympathy.

Ned heard the riders just in time. He was ready to send the horse on its way. He jerked the horse's head down, planted his foot firmly on the reins, slapped his left hand over the horse's nose, drew his gun with his right hand, and waited. The horse jerked his head wildly. "You let out one peep and you're a dead horse," Ned said close to the animal's ear.

The Indians reined in about thirty yards from the house. They had followed the tracks this far, but lost them in the confusion of tracks between the house and barn. Two braves dismounted and another Indian held the reins. They milled around, heads down, eyes glued to the ground.

"Will you take a look at the nerve of those bastards," Jack said. "We could drop 'um where they stand."

"Yeah, you got to give 'um credit. They know he's here someplace, unless he left the same way he rode in, and that ain't very likely or they would have seen him. They're moving toward the barn. If they find Ned in there with your horse, Frost, it's natural for them to think it's his horse, and that won't be good for them or you. If they touch one hair on his head your trouble making ass is mine. Get off your backside, pick up a rifle, and get ready. If it comes to a showdown and you ain't got a rifle in your hand, the first shot fired will be through your empty head. And it won't be a buck pulling the trigger."

Frost picked up a rifle and moved into position. Dawn stood motionless staring at the Indians, her heart leaped while her knees turned to water. "Light Eyes!" she cried excitedly, looking at him through her tears.

"So it is," Frost agreed under his breath, sticking his head out the door. He's a big bastard, ain't he?"

"I can talk with him," Dawn said. "He's the son of Chief Brave Horse. They trade with Father."

"He'll be trading our scalps to him if that happens to be his squaw Frost raped."

"I have to talk to him," Dawn said. "He'll listen to me."

Pete shook his head. "In a case like this, he's just one more buck. They take their women mighty serious."

Dawn made a move toward the door and Pete put a restraining hand on her arm. "Me and the boys will handle this, you don't need to worry. If they make a threatening move toward Ned, I'll drop 'um where they stand."

"No!" Dawn screamed. She lunged past Pete in a burst of panic and ran headlong out the door.

"Wait Dawn!" Jack yelled, moving toward the door to stop her, but Light Eyes had already seen her. He swung his horse around in a wide circle and rode slowly toward her. Jack brought his rifle to his shoulder and took aim, covering her from the back porch.

"Put the rifle down, Jack," Pete yelled. "That's the quickest way I know of to get her killed.

Jack lowered the rifle slowly and reluctantly.

Ned was trapped inside the barn watching helplessly, jostled by a sudden shock of panic. He had thought the Indian was dead, had prayed he was. Now he was standing before him, the only man in the world he was afraid of, for this man could easily take the woman he loved. Ned's expression changed from shock to one of blind rage.

He drew a bead on the back of the Indian's head, and was about to pull the trigger when he saw Dawn hurrying toward him, her head held high, shoulders erect. Ned watched in cold terror as his wife held her hands out to the Indian in a pleading gesture. Their eyes met in a scorching gaze, and the expression on Dawn's face revealed her feelings. Ned was shot through with jealousy because she had never looked at him that way.

Light Eyes dismounted and moved toward her, standing very near, his eyes burning into hers like two coals of fire. They stood for a moment, only inches apart, their eyes embracing. She was unable to speak, her heart was drumming hard enough to shake her, and she trembled on the verge of collapse. She longed to throw herself into his arms, hold him close, kiss his lips, make love to him, but of course it was impossible. At first the expression in his eyes was one of surprise, and then one of melting tenderness.

She noticed that he was thinner, and that his eyes had lost some of their luster, but their deep clear blue excited her no less. She could almost feel Ned's eyes watching them from the interior of the barn, and she resented him even more than she feared him. She was looking at the man she wanted, and Ned was a human wall separating them,

"Please go," she managed in a whisper.

For a moment there was no trace of expression in his eyes, and then he looked at her in puzzlement. "Why do you send me away?"

"You are not safe here. Many eyes are watching us."

"We must talk." He could not take his eyes off her. He had remembered every line of her face, every curve of her body, everything about her was sealed in his mind and heart and filled his dreams. He wanted to sweep her up and take her with him even as he sensed the danger, but his love was strong and his fear weak. His heart was pounding like the waves of the sea in a raging storm.

"Why did you not come to me?" she said with a sob. "Why did you let me believe you were dead? I needed you."

"For many moons I was filled with the spirit of pain and fire. My body grew weak. I could not mount my horse. I felt much shame. I did not want you to see me as helpless as a new born colt.

"I waited, I shed tears, I felt terrible pain. I am married now, my husband is watching us." He winced at her words, and a look of pain blanched his exquisite face.

"Who is this man you call husband?" His voice was filled with anger.

"Ned Rowling." She felt shame when she spoke his name, and her voice was little more than a weak whisper.

Light Eyes stood above her, his eyes steady, his voice choked, on the verge of tears. "Do you love this man—Ned?"

"I love only you," she said fiercely, searching his countenance. "I mourned you. I thought you were dead. I didn't know what to do." She wanted to explain but there was no time. She feared Ned's fiery jealousy might drive him to commit some insane action. Light Eyes was out in the open and vulnerable, while Ned was safely out of sight hiding in the barn.

"I came here searching for one enemy. I find two."

"No, only one."

"You hide this man?"

"No, he came here uninvited and put us all in danger. If you try to take him there will be much bloodshed. We don't care about his safety, but we want peace. Please, you must go. They have guns. I don't want you hurt, nor the people inside the house. They are my friends." She looked at him with tears in her eyes and fear in her heart, afraid of what he might do, and then her uncertainty passed. He would do nothing that might endanger her. He took a step closer and she held her breath in fear and excitement. He reached out and brushed the tears from her face. She saw love in his eyes, also pain. And then he turned away quickly and mounted his stallion, the horse she remembered so well. He raised his hand to the other Indians and the search was ended. They rode away in the direction from which they had come.

Light Eyes glanced back briefly and she knew he was in torment; she felt his pain even as she suffered her own hellish agony. She stood rigid as stone staring after him, her eyes bright with unshed tears. She would never forget the look in his eyes, the hurt tone of his voice, and the light brush of his fingers against her cheek.

She knew that by admitting to him that she was married, she had destroyed all hope of them ever being together.

As soon as the Indians departed, Ned took a long shuddering breath and holstered his gun. He tied Frost's horse and ran outside. "Dawn! My God! You could have been killed."

She gave him a cold look. "You don't really believe that."

She ran past him and into the house.

Ned hurried after her. Her words had cut him to the bone. He didn't know what to expect now, but feared the worst. He saw the curious expressions on all the faces when he looked around the room searching for her.

"She went upstairs," Jack said. "What's going on?"

Ned bounded up the stairs in hot pursuit before she could lock the door, and then he remembered that the lock was broken. He burst into the room out of breath and trembling. "Thank God you're all right!" he said.

She was lying on the bed staring at the ceiling. She turned slowly to look at him. "Why wouldn't I be?" Her voice was as cold as ice.

She was taunting him. There were many things he wanted to say but the words were stuck in his throat like a burr. Just when he thought all his dreams of having Dawn had become reality, the man he thought to be dead had risen up to sweep them away.

His anger was building along with his pain. What was she thinking and feeling? And did he dare to ask? She looked at him with the expression of a little lost child, one of helplessness and fear. He was facing the bitter truths of his situation, the battle he thought he had won, was his greatest defeat. He lay down beside her. "You most likely saved my life, along with a lot of blood shed. I love you, and the way you looked at that Indian is killing me. Talk to me, please. I'm going out of my mind. I won't give you up. You're my wife now, and you said you love me. Has seeing the Indian again caused you to change your feelings for me?"

"I thought he was dead," she sobbed.

Ned was at a loss for words. He couldn't admit that he thought the same thing; it would be like pointing an accusing finger at himself. He had to be very careful not to give himself away. If she should ever suspect the truth it would end their marriage, and it already seemed to be as shaky as a candle flame in the wind.

He rolled over and took her into his arms and kissed her, tasting the tears she was shedding over Light Eyes. While holding her close, he asked, "What did you tell him?"

"That I'm married."

"Nothing else?"

"I didn't tell him about the baby."

Ned grew silent, thinking about what she had said. He felt relieved. He wanted to know what the Indian had said to her, but was afraid of her answer.

He had to be satisfied with the small portion of hope she was giving him by admitting to Light Eyes that she was married. All he could do was wait and hope things would work out for him. One thing was sure, now that they were married, he had every right to protect their union, and he would do just that to the point of murder if Light Eyes interfered. Next time there would be no mistake. Light Eyes would not rise from the grave a second time.

CHAPTER

Mac rode out to the Rowling ranch to take Dawn her clothes and personal things since that was to be her new home. He was shocked when Pete told him about the events of that morning.

"It's a lucky thing for Frost that he hightailed it on a borrowed horse," Mac bellowed in anger. "If I could get my hands on him right now, I'd break his neck!"

"I don't like the idea of his Appaloosa being in my barn. If them Indians come back and find him they'll scalp us all, no questions asked."

Mac seemed to find trouble all around him. He had dropped by the Benson's on his way out of town to check on Debbie and found her standing in defense of her father against her step-mother, Kathryn, who had admitted to Billy that she was having an affair with a younger man and wanted a divorce. She refused to identify the other man. Because of her father's outraged state of mind, Debbie was afraid to leave him alone with Kathryn, fearing he might kill her.

When Dawn asked Mac why Debbie hadn't showed up for her wedding, he lied, not wanting to upset her. He figured she had been unnerved enough over the Indian incident, having bravely confronted them to save her husband. So he told her that Debbie had developed a bad cold and cough. He was relieved when she accepted his explanation without question.

Seeing Light Eyes had turned Dawn's world upside-down, and she struggled to overcome her depression as thoughts of Light Eyes took control of her in a violent storm of emotions. She spent her days and nights in her room, refusing to descend the stairs even at mealtime. What little she ate was served to her on a tray by her husband.

As far as Pete and the boys were concerned, they thought Dawn's reactions were justified because of the experience she had gone through. The incident would be well remembered due to Pete's boasting. He took great pride and pleasure in his spirited, courageous, daughter-in-law.

In the meantime, Ned could only watch helplessly, feeling disappointed and ill at ease in her presence. He had hoped that given enough time, she would recover from the shock of seeing Light Eyes again. After three days with no apparent change in her attitude, he faced the bitter truth. She was his wife in name only. Her heart belonged to Light Eyes.

When Martha returned home from her four day stay with Virginia, she could plainly see how her son was suffering under the strain of his wife's curious behavior. She sensed Dawn's contempt toward Ned. Underneath her weak smile and hypocritical words, Martha saw clearly her discontentment. She feared that this beautiful woman held no love for her son. She tried to quench her suspicions, but to no avail. Her son was unhappy when he should be walking on clouds.

Ned put up a strong pretense of happiness, while his true feelings were burning and tormenting him like sitting in a bed of hot coals. He felt cheated, inadequate, and miserable.

In the quiet darkness of their room he would take her gently into his arms and kiss her. Her lips were soft and warm to his touch, but there was no surrender in them. She remained passive and abstract. When he lay next to her, listening to the sound of her breathing, feeling her warmth close to him, his body would shake with passion, his flesh melting at her touch. Yet he did not exercise his rights as her husband. He did not want her to give herself to him out of duty, or perhaps pity. He would somehow manage to restrain his passion until she was willing to accept him.

The days that followed became increasingly trying for Ned. Dawn seemed to have no concern for his feelings. The only words spoken inside the room were very light, and never to the point. The situation was becoming insufferable for both of them. Ned was not satisfied to wait any longer. The yearning inside him burned like acid. The memory of her body yielding to his on their wedding night taunted him night and day. He could not pretend any longer or excuse her actions. The shameful violation of her duties as his wife was decaying his insides.

One evening after work, he made up his mind to confront her with the truth. He entered the room defensively angry, determined to bring the simmering situation to a quick boil, or cool it completely. He stood over her, his eyes glaring, tired from loss of sleep, his voice shaking with rage. Dawn suddenly became frightened when she recognized the nature of his outburst.

"How much longer do you expect me to be content with your cold shoulder? I'd like to know just what your plans are for our future, or is it none of my business? After all, I'm only your husband. I've been as patient with you as I know how, and I've had it up to here." He drew the side of his hand across his throat.

"I've never denied you your rights as my husband," she said coldly.

"Hell no, not in so many words, but I'm not so stupid that you have to draw me a picture. Can you honestly say that you want me to make love to you?"

"What do you expect me to do? Throw myself at your feet just because we're married?"

"I expect you to come out of hibernation and act like a woman instead of a spoiled brat. And don't look at me with those wide innocent eyes and pretend you don't know the hell you've put me through ever since that big buck showed up all in one piece."

"What do you mean by that!" she said in sudden bewilderment.

"You said yourself that you thought he was dead."

"And you never asked why."

"What difference does it make?"

"I don't know. I'm not sure. But I know it means something. You told me once that you would do anything to make me yours. Do you remember?"

"Yeah, sure I remember, and now that you're mine I will do anything to keep you."

"Anything?" she questioned in a suspicious tone, her eyes meeting his hotly.

He shivered, suddenly cold with terror, wondering what she was accusing him of. He knew there was danger in being too calm, she might think he was trying to appease her. If she thought him appeasing, she would think him weak. He had to remain hard and sure, otherwise there might be room for doubt.

"I'll tell you what it means. It means I don't give a damned" He was clenching his fists. "I hate the red bastard, and if I ever get him in my sights again, I'll kill him. Then you won't have to wonder if he's dead. I'll be able to tell you!"

In the back of her mind she knew she had been accusing Ned, and she was almost convinced that he would never have spoken out so boldly if he were guilty.

"You have to forget about him," Ned continued. "You have already made one mistake; don't make it worse by dwelling on something impossible. You're my wife now, and the only thing that will alter that fact, is my death. When I go to the bone orchard, then you will be free again."

She turned away with a quick movement as tears clouded her eyes. She suddenly realized that Light Eye's life depended very much on her actions.

He seized her by the shoulders and turned her to face him. "I love you, I can't live without you, I need you," he said in a rush of words. "I can't stand being near you like this and not have you."

"You don't have to," she whispered reassuringly, going into his arms, denying him nothing. What a price to pay, she thought, for one mistake. She knew she must continue giving her body to this man, whether she liked it or not. He was her husband, and this made her his slave. She felt like a common whore, selling her body in exchange for his giving her son a legitimate name. She was trapped in an impossible situation. She could never have the man she truly loved. She wondered if all men were minus their pride when it came to self-satisfaction.

When Ned failed to come down to supper that night, Martha didn't bother to take a tray up to Dawn. When they both came down to breakfast the next morning, she could tell by the contented look on Ned's face, and his calm manner, that his wife was over whatever it was bothering her. At least for the time being.

Dawn tried desperately to live up to the visual impression she had painfully produced, but as the days pushed forward, a haze of doubts and stress shook her. Each day she grew more and more restless. She tried to put Light Eyes out of her mind, but her efforts were wasted. She cherished the memory of him, his wild reckless affection from which she knew she would never recover.

Dawn became conscious of Martha's searching glances, feeling certain that she had guessed the truth about her delicate condition. She began to feel more and more self-conscious in her presence, and she took to her room again.

She was used to doing pretty well as she pleased, but now she was watched constantly. Judging from her lack of privacy, she might as well be in jail. She hated married life. She hated her mother-in-law. She wanted to go home to Mac.

Martha had been waiting patiently for her daughter-in-law to confide in her, but she only withdrew deeper into her self-made shell. Finally she confronted Ned with the disturbing situation. She waited until she found the opportunity to be alone with him before she spoke her mind.

"You're not in any hurry this morning are you, Ned?"

"No, I guess not. Why?"

"I've been wanting to have a talk with you. This seems like a good time with Pete and the boys out of the house. I'll pour us another cup of coffee just as soon as I strain the milk." She poured the foamy white liquid through a yellow milk stained flour sack draped over a heavy crock. Finished, she set two steaming cups of coffee on the table and sat down facing her son, who looked a little uneasy.

"All right, what's the problem?" he asked, eyeing his mother.

"And just what makes you think I have a problem?"

"I can read it in your eyes. When you frown like that, you have a problem."

Martha smiled, looking down at her coffee cup for a moment, and then returned her attention to her son. "Dawn didn't come downstairs all day yesterday, and when I took her dinner tray up to her she refused to eat. I'm worried about her."

"I know, Ma, so am I. I try to get her to mix with the family more, but she's just not herself lately."

"And we both know why, don't we, Ned?" Ned stared at his mother, trying to find the words to answer. Failing to do so, he remained silent.

"You two might be able to fool some people," she continued. "You should know by now that you can't fool me. I can tell when a woman is pregnant before she knows it herself. I know Dawn is going to have a baby. I also know that she was pregnant before you married her. What I would like to know is this: is the baby yours?"

Ned gasped at his mother's words and suddenly turned pale. "Don't ask such a thing! Of course it's mine. You know it is."

"I don't know any such thing, and I am asking." Martha's calmness had vanished now and her eyes were watchful upon Ned's face. She could see that he was close to tears. "Don't ever doubt that the baby she's carrying is mine."

She shook her head gravely. "All right," she said, but her suspicions remained.

Ned couldn't sleep that night. He lay beside his wife tormented by the web of lies and deceit he had spun in order to marry the woman he loved. He had thought that marrying Dawn would make his life complete. However his conception of what their life would be like together was far from reality. Their lives had been tainted by his jealousy of Light Eyes, and her love for this man. It was inconceivable for him to have thought that their problems would dissolve themselves so easily. He knew he had a battle to fight, and he was his own worst enemy.

Without warning Mac suddenly appeared the next morning with shocking news. Billy Joe Benson had killed Kathryn and then himself. Debbie had ridden into Courgat late last night to get Doctor Keel and Sheriff Morgan. Kathryn hadn't died right away, she had lived several hours with a bullet in her chest. Billy had shot himself in the head and died instantly. Debbie was in a state of shock. She had her father laid out on the kitchen table and wouldn't allow anyone to move him.

Dawn was convinced that her place was with Debbie in her time of grief, and had threatened to go on horseback if need be. Ned and Mac both objected, but she was determined and they accompanied her to the Benson ranch. Since childhood Dawn had felt a sicken terror of death. She would get cold chills looking at a still, white face. She just knew that her heart would stop beating if she touched the cold flesh of a dead person. It took all the courage she could muster to walk into the room where Billy Joe's body lay.

She felt a flood of compassion when she saw Debbie standing quietly beside her father's body holding his rigid hand, her face wet with tears. When Dawn gazed at his still ashen face, she was too horrified to cry.

"Close the door," Debbie ordered in a hushed voice, not taking her eyes off her father's face.

"Please, Debbie" Dawn pleaded, "it's too cold in here. Come into the parlor and warm yourself."

Debbie looked up when she recognized Dawn's voice, relief suddenly flooding her face. "Thank God, you came at last," she sobbed, and threw herself into Dawn's arms.

"We came as soon as we got word."

"We?"

"Yes. Ned and Father are here too. Please, come into the parlor where it's warm. It's freezing in this room."

"I can't leave him," she said through her tears. "I feel at peace when I'm near him, almost as if he were still alive."

"Just for a few minutes," Dawn pleaded. "Martha sent food along with us. She knew you hadn't eaten."

"I'm not hungry."

"Try to eat a little," she coaxed softly.

Debbie shook her head. "If you will stay with me."

"You know I will." She took Debbie's cold hand and led her from the kitchen.

Mac and Ned came quickly to their feet when they entered the room. After expressing their condolences, they went into the kitchen to view Billy Joe's body. Billy had put the gun in his mouth and the impact had exploded the back of his head. Debbie had covered it with a cup towel. Presently they joined Dawn and Debbie by the fire. They remained silent and listened to the exchange between the two women.

"Do you have any idea why your father did this?" Dawn said.

"Kathryn drove him to it!" she cried. "She called him an old man and bragged about her young lover. She raved on and on until she had him screaming and crying like a madman. It was horrible. I couldn't calm him. I pleaded with him not to pay any attention to her because she was drunk. I pleaded with her over and over to stop tormenting him, but she wouldn't listen. I even slapped her across the face. She just stood there and laughed hysterically while Daddy cried. She laughed until tears came streaming down her face. She shook with ugly, violent, screams. I hated the sound of her voice. I loathed her for what she was doing to him, what she had been doing to him for years. That's when I saw Daddy pick up his gun. His hands were trembling when he pointed it at Kathryn. I screamed for him to stop, to put the gun away, but he wasn't listening. He was beyond hearing or caring. At that moment he was completely out of his mind with hate and humiliation. I grabbed his arm and he flung me away from him. Kathryn wasn't laughing anymore. She was staring at him in stark terror. 'No, don't,' she pleaded, suddenly sober. 'Put the gun down, Billy,' she screamed, backing away from him. 'I was only fooling, really. Now put it down.' She kept backing away, her eyes dark with panic, but he followed her until she had her back to the wall. She had no place to go. She was trapped between the china cupboard and a lamp stand."

Debbie paused for a moment, shaking with sobs. When she continued, she spoke in a more calm voice. "That's when she began to throw things: cups, plates, and the oil lamp. But he didn't seem to feel the pain when she hit him over and over. He was close enough to reach out and touch her when he pulled the trigger. The blast from the gun seemed to explode inside my head. The room was filled with a loud roar. I watched as Kathryn stumbled forward off the wall and dropped at his feet. She was gasping for breath, holding her chest, blood pouring through her fingers. Daddy watched her, his face twisted in pain. I saw her lips move as she tried to speak, but no sound escaped her lips, or maybe I was deafened by the gunshot. I put my hands over my eyes when Daddy got down on his knees beside her and took her into his arms. I couldn't stand the grief stricken expression on his tear stained face. Then came the second shot. I uncovered my eyes and saw Daddy topple over on top of her, his own blood spilling with hers. Oh, why did I let him do it?" she screamed. "I should have guessed what she would do. I ran from the house, away from the horrible sight. The next thing I remember is Doctor Keel and Sheriff Morgan asking me questions. After a while we came back here. Kathryn was still breathing. I made them take her away. I couldn't stand having her in my house, not after what she had done. I knew she was going to die. I wanted her to. She deserved to die after all the terrible pain she put my daddy through. I hated her."

Debbie's words came as a complete shock to Dawn. She had never heard her speak in such a way, and had no idea that she was capable of such vindictive hate. Seeing Debbie in such a state increased her own hatred for Kathryn.

Debbie's wishes were that Billy Joe not be laid to rest until the following morning. Ned and Mac dug the grave deep in the rich soil of the peach orchard near the barn. They dug only one grave. Kathryn was not welcome to a hole in the ground on the Benson ranch. Not even her bones.

Every effort made to persuade Debbie to leave the house for the night, or to at least let some of the men sit up with Billy's body, was rejected. She wanted to spend these last few hours close to him. When night fell, Debbie drew Dawn into the miserably cold kitchen with her. Mac returned to town leaving Ned to spend the night in a chair by the fireplace in the parlor.

Dawn sat as far away from the corpse as possible, watching Debbie bend over him, her tears falling on his cold waxen face. From time to time she would bestow a kiss on his cheek. Dawn looked on in horror, her flesh crawling, and she closed her eyes. Somehow, even in the bitter cold of the dim lit kitchen, Dawn managed to doze fitfully from time to time, only to awaken to the grim scene unfolding before her intractably. It seemed to her that day light might never come. She pulled the quilt tighter about her shoulders and shifted from side to side trying to find a more comfortable position. Her neck and shoulders ached from the discomfort of the hard, straight backed, kitchen chair.

Mac had spread the word in Courgat about Billy's burial. A little after daybreak Debbie's friends began to arrive at the ranch to pay their respects. Reverend Collins conducted a brief grave side service, spoke a few comforting words to Debbie, shook her hand as if he were congratulating her for being an orphan, climbed into his buggy and quickly left. After the grave was filled in, Mac and the other assembled people moved slowly to their carriages and departed, leaving Ned and Dawn to comfort the bereaved Debbie as she stood solemnly beside the mound of damp earth that marked her father's grave.

"Come on Debbie," Ned urged. "There is nothing more we can do here. You're chilled to the bone. Let's go inside and get a cup of coffee."

Debbie nodded, and they walked toward the house. Once inside Debbie broke down completely, weeping violently, her shoulders heaving as loud sobs tore through her thin chest. She clung to Dawn, wailing, her face buried in the curve of her neck. After several minutes her sobs subsided and she regained her composure, the calm control that was so much a part of her. She behaved as though there was a set time for grief, and after that allotted time had passed, so had her grief.

Dawn wanted to spend a few days with her, or at least until she had made some sort of plans for her future, but Ned refused to allow it. Since they could not persuade Debbie to stay in town or at the Rowling ranch, they were forced to leave her alone.

Dawn was worried about Debbie and asked her father to do something to help.

Without delay, Mac called on Debbie to offer his help. Although he had known Billy for years, he knew nothing about his living relatives. Debbie told him quite frankly that she was all alone except for a few friends.

Mac realized that the death of her father had put her in a very unsatisfactory position, and he proposed to suggest certain considerations that could have a direct bearing on the lives of quite a few people.

Mac's concern did not come as a surprise to Debbie. She had been expecting his visit because Dawn would most certainly ask him to help her.

"Do you feel uneasy staying out here by yourself?"

"It will take some getting accustomed to," she said with a smile. "Dawn wanted to stay with me for a few days, but Ned wouldn't hear of it. I can't blame him, but I was disappointed."

"What are your plans? Surely you don't plan to stay on here and run this ranch by yourself."

"I really haven't given much thought to the matter," she said in a grief dulled tone.

"Want some help?"

"I know I need it."

"All you have to do is say the word, and I'll do everything I can to make life easier for you."

"You're very kind."

"Not really. To be completely honest," he said, "what I have in mind will benefit Dawn as much as it will you—maybe more. Of course it might not sound too attractive to you. However I would like to make you a proposition and see how you feel about it."

"Dawn?" she said in surprise. "I'm afraid I don't understand you at all."

"It's really quite simple. She hates living in the house with Ned's folks, and I'm looking for a way to help her. I think we might be able to turn a couple of bad situations into a blessing. By the way, has she said anything to you about her feelings where the Rowling's are concerned?"

"No, I haven't had a chance to talk to her since she married. As a matter of fact, not until she came to me after my Daddy—" She broke off, unable to continue her painful thoughts.

"This is unpleasant. I'm sorry."

"I'm all right," she said, regaining her composure.

"I figured she was making a mistake when she married Ned. It's not that I don't like the boy, I do. But I wanted them to wait a while. At least until the house was finished."

"You mean your house?"

"No, I mean Dawn's house. I'm building it for her."

"I didn't know that."

"The house won't be finished for another nine or ten months. In the mean time she needs a place to live where she can do as she pleases. She's not used to having a bunch of people under foot all the time, and some of them telling her what to do."

"Do you want Dawn and Ned to move in here?"

"Only if you and I can agree on the terms."

"Have you talked this over with them?"

"No."

"Don't you think that you should?"

"I don't need to. I already know how Dawn feels."

"What about Ned?" She raised her eyebrows in surprise.

"He already works for me, all I intend to do is change his job. I want to buy your place, put Ned in charge, and let him raise beef for half the profit. Could anything be more simple than that?"

"It sounds too simple to me."

"Now I'm the one who doesn't understand."

"Mr. McCloud, you can't continue to arrange Dawn's life for her now. She's married, and that makes her Ned's responsibility."

"In a pig's eye it does!" Mac turned red in the face as his anger flared. He realized what she said was true, but he wasn't ready to accept it.

Seeing his anger, Debbie quickly changed the subject. "What happens to me?"

"With the money you get from the sale of the ranch, you can do whatever you like."

"I don't know—" her voice trailed off. "I'll have to think about it."

"Sure, take all the time you need," then added, "I'll be back in a few days; you can give me your answer then." With a slight wave of his hand, he was gone.

The next evening, Mac decided to pay his daughter a visit. Before closing the trading post he picked out three pretty dresses he thought Dawn might fancy, folded them neatly into a box and tied it with a yellow ribbon. He tucked the package under his arm and rode out of town. Even though his daughter was married now, nothing had changed his feelings toward her. She was the only thing he had to live for, and he intended to spend his remaining years making her life pleasant, no matter how much unpleasantness he might have to suffer himself. His mouth was set in a grim line of determination when he dismounted and walked up to the door and knocked.

Pete opened the door, looking a bit surprised. "You're just in time for supper."

"Something sure smells good," Mac said, stepping into the fragrant kitchen. "Where's that daughter of mine?"

Martha was standing in front of the stove frying a pan of golden brown chicken. She turned to look at Mac disapprovingly. "She hasn't come down to supper yet," she said in a chilly voice.

"Well, tell her she has a visitor."

"Very well," Martha answered. Her mouth had an ugly curl.

She wiped her hands on her apron and left the room.

"What have you been doing with yourself these last few days?" Pete said, eyeing the package in Mac's hand.

"Same old thing. Making money and spending it. Have you seen the house I'm building?"

"I've heard about it. Must be setting you back plenty."

"You can say that again, but nothing is too good for my daughter."

"Father!" Dawn cried, following Martha into the kitchen. "What a nice surprise." She ran to him and threw her arms around his neck. "What are you doing here?"

"I came to see you. Why else? And I brought you a little present."

"What is it?" she said excitedly, taking the package from his outstretched hand.

"Why don't you open it and find out?"

She quickly untied the ribbon and opened the box. "Oh, they're beautiful," she said, holding them up for Martha to see. She hugged Mac again and ran upstairs to try them on.

"What are you celebrating?" Martha asked in a tight voice, eyeing Mac critically.

"Not a thing. I just felt like buying my daughter some new dresses."

"Don't you think that's for Ned to do?"

"She's my daughter and I'll buy her a new dress anytime I feel like it," he said a bit more sharply than he had intended, thinking that Martha needed to mind her own business.

"Martha, pour the coffee," Pete said harshly.

She glared at Pete, opened her mouth to speak, but seeing his expression, closed it again. She picked up the coffee pot and carried it over to the table, poured two cups and set the pot back on the stove. She jerked the milk bucket off the nail by the back door, mumbled something about doing the milking, and slammed out of the house.

"Sorry Pete," Mac apologized. "Guess I got a little carried away."

"Don't give it another thought. Martha never will learn to mind her own business where them boys are concerned. Ain't her place to object to you buying gifts for your daughter. She should leave the objecting to Ned, if he has a mind to."

"Sound like you agree with your wife."

"Don't matter what I think. I believe in staying clear of family squabbles. The way I do that is to keep my mouth shut and mind my own business."

"You're a sensible man. I rode out here for two reasons. I came to visit Dawn, the other reason was to make Ned a proposition. By the way, where is Ned? He left the store hours ago."

"He took Frost's horse home."

"He what?"

"That critter has been in my barn for three weeks. We got tired of cleaning up after him and feeding him."

"How come Frost didn't come back for it?"

"That coward is afraid to be seen on that horse."

"I'm not so sure that Ned ought to be out running around on it either. An Indian ain't likely to forgive a thing like Frost did. Wouldn't be too healthy for Ned if they saw him."

"Yeah, I know that. Jack and Clay rode with him."

"You better hope that they don't all three get scalped."

"They can take care of themselves."

"I hope you're right. I better be getting back to town. I can talk to Ned in the morning. I wanted to talk to both of them because this concerns them both, but it will keep."

"No need to hurry off. Why don't you stay to supper? We usually eat before now but Martha was waiting for the boys to get back home."

Thanks, Pete, but I better not. Martha's not too happy to see me, and I don't like to be where I'm not exactly welcome."

"Don't pay any attention to her. She'll be over her mad by the time she gets done milking."

"Maybe some other time," Mac said, getting up to leave. "Tell Dawn I'll see her later."

"She'll be disappointed."

"I'll make it up to her."

Pete felt sudden pity for Mac, thinking about him going home to an empty house. The extent of the sacrifices Mac had made for his daughter weighed heavily on his shoulders in the form of loneliness. Pete wished Martha could be a little more understanding. After all, the only pleasure Mac got out of life was seeing his daughter happy.

CHAPTER

16

The next morning, Mac awoke early, dressed, and walked the short distance to the trading post. He was surprised to find the meat market already open for business and began to wonder if Zeek ever slept, for he always seemed to be there.

Although the meat market was housed in the same building as the trading post, there was a thick wall separating the two with no connecting door. Mac hated the scent of blood and avoided it whenever possible.

Ned arrived for work an hour later in his usual quiet mood. "Why didn't you tell me you planned to pay us a visit yesterday? I would have stayed home."

"I'm happy to see you didn't get scalped."

"Me too. Pa said you had a proposition for me."

Mac explained his idea concerning buying the Benson ranch. He watched Ned's expression and didn't like what he saw.

After Mac finished, Ned walked across the room and stood next to the broom rack, his head lowered in thought. He had the feeling that Mac was trying to assume complete responsibility for Dawn using him as a tool, and he resented it.

Mac watched him for a moment trying to read his expression. "Don't clam up on me, Ned? Say something. What's your answer?"

Ned took a long time answering. "I don't like the idea," he said regrettably.

"What do you mean you don't like the idea? You can talk plainer than that. Where do you get the gall to stand there and say you don't like it?" Mac was becoming frustrated. "What have you got against making money?"

"Look, Mac, I appreciate the offer, believe me, but I have more to consider that just the financial side. I know I can make more money raising cattle than dusting shelves, but under the circumstances, I have to say no."

"Circumstances? What circumstances? What the devil are you talking about?"

"I don't want Dawn to be alone."

"She won't be alone. You'll be there with her."

"I'm sorry Mac, the answer is still no. Dawn stays where she is."

"You iron head!" Mac blasted, losing his patience. "I can't stand stupidity. What's the matter with you? I'm giving you a chance to stand on your own two feet, to get out from under your mother's skirt tail, and you don't have sense enough to see it. Where is your ambition, boy?"

Ned's anger came boiling up right along with his fear, and his expression became grim. "I didn't want to be the one to tell you this, Mac, but you leave me no choice. Dawn is staying right where she is until after she has the baby. Do you understand that? She's pregnant."

"You're a liar!" Mac snarled, his eyes blazing. He grabbed Ned by the shoulders with an iron grip. "Tell me you're lying!"

"I'm sorry, Mac, but it's true," he said, cringing in pain.

"You god damned snake!" Mac exploded, throwing Ned sideways into a shelf filled with can goods that clattered and rolled all over the floor.

Ned managed to catch himself before he fell and slowly straightened up. For several seconds the two men stared at one another. The hate Ned saw in Mac's eyes made his blood run cold.

"Who the hell do you think you are? You little pissant! You took advantage of my daughter, and you'll answer to me!" He was trembling, his eyes blazing with rage.

"Punishing me won't change the facts," Ned said, offering no resistance or excuses.

"It will damned sure make me feel better." He covered the space between them in two strides and took hold of Ned again.

167

JACKIE BARNES

Ned felt a sharp pain in his stomach when Mac's knee caught him dead center. He doubled over with a groan, crossing his arms over his aching belly. He reeled drunkenly, his stomach churning, his eyes tearing. Mac reached down, caught him by the hair and straightened him up. Then came the sickening sound of Mac's open hand making contact with Ned's face. He slapped him over and over until blood streamed from his nose and mouth and soaked the front of his shirt. With his head spinning, ears roaring, and his vision blurred from a gash above his left eye, he went down in a disoriented fog, a numbing pit he gladly welcomed. He stayed down.

The door flew open and Doctor Keel stood staring at the shocking scene, shaking his head in disbelief. He closed the door behind him and moved quickly to examine Ned. He was lying prone amidst a scattering of provisions. His face was covered in blood and already beginning to swell. As he bent over Ned, he spoke directly to Mac. "Suppose you tell me what insanity drove you to attack this boy?"

"He asked for it, the spineless worm." His breath was coming in bellows. "I should have killed him!"

"I can clearly see that he didn't try to defend himself. The only thing I see on you is Ned's blood How does it feel to make a punching bag out of a defenseless boy?"

"He had it coming, and more. He just congratulated me."

Keel knew immediately what had prompted Mac's show of violence, but he could not conceive of the reasoning behind Ned's confession. Why had he chosen this particular time and place to spring the truth on Mac?

Ned groaned and tried to get up. "Take it slow," Keel said, helping him to a sitting position, bracing his back against the wall.

"Thanks, Doctor," he managed through his cut and bleeding lips, pain twisting his face. He moved his hand across his injuries, feeling the damage, and brought it away bloody.

"Sit here for a few minutes until the room stops spinning, then I'll help you over to the office and put some stitches in that gash above your eye." He examined his face, a frown wrinkling his brow. When Ned regained his senses somewhat, Keel dragged him to his feet. "Can you manage to stand?"

"Yeah, I'm all right."

"You're not all right, but you will be." He glared at Mac, "And no thanks to you." For a moment they stared at one another. "How do you think Dawn will take this? Have you given that any thought? You took care of Frost to keep her brand new husband from getting all skinned up, and look what you've done to him. He might feel a bit of satisfaction if he had gotten these injuries fighting Frost, or at least in a fair fight. You knew he wouldn't resist. What did you prove?"

"He didn't get away with taking advantage of my daughter. What do you think drove me to do this?"

"Your short fuse."

"You've known about this all along, haven't you?"

"As a matter of fact, I have."

"Why didn't you tell me? What kind of a friend are you?"

"The kind that hates to see his friend make an ass of himself. Oh, come on, Mac. I had sense enough to know how you would react."

"What would you have done if Dawn was your daughter?"

"I would first stop to consider that it takes two. Ned didn't do this by himself, Mac. What do you intend to do about Dawn? Thrash the daylights out of her? If you expect to be fair, punish her too."

"Damn you Edward, don't you take sides with him."

"I don't intend to take sides with either of them, and don't you try to tell me how to run my business. Maybe you think you can knock me around the way you did Ned, and I'll agree with your way of thinking."

Mac's expression suddenly changed. "Get him out of here. I hate the sight of him."

Doctor Keel opened the door with one hand while bracing Ned with the other. Once outside he helped him into his carriage and drove him the short distance to his office. He cleaned him up and put two stitches above his eye. With each stick of the needle Ned felt a burning pain that made his eyes water. Keel ordered him to lie quietly for a while, and Ned didn't argue with him.

"Do you want to talk to me about this, Ned? Might make you feel better."

Ned blurted it out in a few words. "Mac put me on the spot. There was no way out except to tell him the truth. I really can't blame him for going a little mad."

"Well I can," Keel said.

"What do you think he will do now?"

"He's most likely on his way out to your place to confront Dawn with his knowledge, still hoping, by some miracle that you might be wrong."

"My, God! I got to get home in a hurry!" He made a move to get up.

"You will do no such thing." Keel put a restraining hand on his chest and forced him back down.

"Mac's out of his mind. No telling what he will do."

"Don't worry; he has already done all the damage he's going to."

"What makes you think that?"

"I know Dawn. Mac has been giving in to her all her life. She can handle him."

"I feel like a coward, just lying here."

"Well then, think about it this way: if you go home you will only make matters worse. Mac will have cooled off by the time he gets there, but seeing you will rekindle his rage and resentment. Let it alone."

Ned decided to give some thought to what the doctor said. He certainly did not intend to make matters worse.

Mac did exactly as Keel predicted. The minute he was left alone with his thoughts he headed for the Rowling ranch in a fit of boiling anger. By the time he reached his destination, his anger had turned into mental anguish. He realized that Keel was absolutely right about one thing, it did indeed take two.

He walked swiftly to the back door and knocked, however he did not wait for the door to be opened to him. He burst into the kitchen shouting. "Where is she? Where is that daughter of mine?"

Martha jerked her hands out of the dishpan and turned to look at him resentfully, water dripping off her fingers onto the floor. At first she thought he must be drunk, but a closer look changed her mind, his face was a mask of rage. "Richard McCloud," she snapped, "what is the meaning of this?"

"I came to see Dawn. Where is she?" He started toward the stairs.

"I want you to leave, right now!"

"Not until I see my daughter."

Dawn came running into the kitchen when she heard the commotion. She suddenly stopped in her tracks, her heart leaping with fright when she saw the expression on Mac's face. He looked killing mad.

He spun around to face her. "Is it true?" he barked. "Are you going to have a baby?" He felt as if he was choking on the words. He waited for her to answer, each second like a stabbing wound to his heart.

"Yes, I am," she whispered shamefully, turning her eyes away from his expression of shock and outrage.

Her answer hit him like a doubled up fist. He reached out and gripped the edge of the table to steady himself. He was struggling with a powerful emotion he had never experienced before. Tears streamed from his eyes.

Dawn moved to his side and laid her hand on his arm. He shook her off. "Oh," she cried. "Please don't hate me, Father. I'm so sorry. I never meant to hurt you. You have to forgive me. I love you. Please, don't be mad anymore."

"I thought Ned was lying," he said in a tight voice. "I never should have trusted him. He betrayed me."

Martha, who had witnessed the whole thing, suddenly cried out, her voice shrill with alarm. "Where is Ned? Why isn't he with you? Did you hurt him? What have you done?"

"Not what have I done! What has Ned done? I should have killed him!"

"You did hurt him! I'll have you arrested! Where is he? Is he hurt bad?"

"I knocked him around a little bit. That's all."

Martha lashed out at Mac, her bony fists flying at his face and chest, clawing for his eyes. He caught her wrists in his big, rough, hands. Dawn stared at them in disbelief, her eyes wide with panic. "No!" she screamed. "You beat Ned! How could you?" She ran headlong up the stairs.

He let go of Martha's arms, and she backed away screaming, "You bastard! Why don't you beat your daughter too?"

He went up the stairs after Dawn, and she shut the door in his face. He flung it open and stormed inside.

She turned away from him for a second, then just as swiftly turned back to face him, giving way to an uncontrolled seizure of hysterical weeping.

"Get hold of yourself," he cried. "What did you expect I would do? Pat him on the head and say, good boy? What kind of a father would I be if I didn't protect you?"

"Get out of here!" she screamed. "You had no right to punish him. Why don't you punish me? Beat me! Go on! Beat me to death if it will make you feel better. But don't you ever touch Ned again!"

"I'm going all right, and you're coming with me."

She could do no more than stare at him. He wanted to take her home. How could he know that was what she wanted?

"Don't just stand there. Get what you need and we'll be on our way."

"She's not going anyplace!" Martha was standing in the doorway holding a rifle in shaking hands, and it was aimed at Mac's heart. "Pete and the boys are riding fence. They won't be back till dark. Ned ain't here, so that leaves me. As long as you're in my house, Richard McCloud, you will do as I say. And I say she stays."

"Don't threaten me, woman. Nobody tells me what to do where my daughter is concerned."

"You're forgetting something Richard, Dawn is my son's wife. Her place is with him, and she don't leave here unless he says so, and he don't know anything about this."

"He'll know soon enough. Get your things together," he said over his shoulder, his eyes on Martha and the gun she was holding.

Dawn hesitated only a moment before she began gathering up her things, anxious to leave, ready to see the last of Martha.

Mac read the expression of relief on his daughter's face. She wanted to go with him. Mac scooped up her valise, took her firmly by the arm and steered her toward the door. "Let's go."

His words were like music to her ears.

"I'm warning you, Richard," Martha cried. "Leave her be."

"She's going with me. If you plan to stop me, you'll have to use that gun, because I'm leaving here with my daughter." With his hand on Dawn's back, he pushed her through the door. Martha stood between them and the stairs, the rifle leveled at Mac. "Either shoot me or get the hell out of my way!" he challenged.

Martha stood her ground, and for a heartbeat Mac thought she might pull the trigger, but be damned if he would back down. She would have to kill him.

Slowly she lowered the gun, stepped to one side, and they moved past her. The sound of Martha's sobs followed them out the door.

When they arrived at the cabin, Dawn went immediately to her room. Mac left her alone with her thoughts, seeing no reason to continue their disagreement. Nothing could change her condition, nor the fact that she had married Ned because of it. He would wait until she settled down emotionally before discussing the fix she was in and how he might help her.

Ned and Doctor Keel saw Mac when he returned to town with Dawn. Ned was furious. "Well, I'll be damned!" he cried. "I never thought he would go this far. He can't get away with it."

"No, he sure can't," Keel agreed. "But wait a while before you exercise your rights as Dawn's husband. Give Mac time to get used to the idea that Dawn's pregnant and you're responsible. He won't listen right now, much less understand. Tomorrow is soon enough for you to express your views. And don't forget, you have Dawn on your side. You can't lose."

"Nothing but my life. And just what is it that makes you so sure she's on my side? She came back to town with him."

"I don't think it was her idea. I think she was brought back against her will. And I don't think Mac had it in his head to kill you. If that were the case, you would already be history. I have known Richard McCloud for a good many years. I know he has a bad temper when he gets riled. But he's no killer. It takes a special kind of demon to kill a man, even if he has good reason, or what he might think is a good reason."

The doctor's words caused Ned to shrink inside. He was remembering the night he put a bullet in Light Eyes back. He was the demon the doctor had reference to. God, how he wished he could stop thinking about it. But he would do it again if that's what it took to keep his wife. "Do you expect me to just sit here and wait?"

"That's exactly what I expect you to do, only I want you to wait at home. Your folks must be half out of their minds with worry. Go home, get a good night's rest, and meet me back here in the morning. I'll go with you to face Mac."

"I appreciate your offer, but I don't need you to hold my hand. I can handle this without any help from you."

"If you change your mind, you know where to find me."

After Ned went through the embarrassing ordeal of facing his parents, and admitted the reason Mac had tried to beat him to death, he doubted that facing Mac could be any worse. Martha was all tears, tears of pain when she looked at her son's battle scars, and tears of joy because he was still alive. Pete seemed relieved, along with being disgusted because of his son's immoral act. He felt no malice toward Mac, he would have probably reacted the same way if someone had humiliated him and degraded his daughter. For once the boys, sensing the delicate situation, kept their mouths shut. Jack gave Ned a certain look and marched Clay from the house to insure peace.

The thought of sleep that night was impossible for Ned. Every nerve in his body was stretched to the snapping point. He went over and over in his mind what he would do and say the next morning when he came face to face with Mac again. He would never forget the hate in Mac's eyes, the sound of his voice raised in murderous rage, nor the sickening jolts of pain when his big hands came into contact with his flesh. He hoped he had not shown his fear, because he knew Mac would never forgive him for being weak.

By morning the storm in Mac's heart had subsided. With the first shock of the situation passed, he was in control of his senses again. He knew Ned would come looking for his wife, and he hoped he was mentally prepared for their disagreeable confrontation. However, when Ned was standing before him battered and bruised, he was taken with a sharp sense of guilt, quickly followed by a reversed attitude that he was wasting his pity. Ned got what he deserved.

Ned approached Mac eyeing him curiously, realizing the insolence was gone, and taking its place, a visible tinge of shame. He had not expected to see this expression on Mac's face, knowing he deserved the thrashing. He had misled Mac, lied about his guilt, aware of the conclusion. He would give his life for Dawn, and he had come pretty damned close. He had asked for it.

"I don't blame you, Mac. I bought it, every lick."

"Oh, I don't know," he said skeptically. "I can take part of the blame. I was so busy with my own affairs that I neglected my daughter." Mac leaped to Dawn's defense as always, placing the blame everywhere except where it belonged. He would never face the fact that his daughter wasn't perfect. Ned shuddered inside, imagining how Mac would react if he knew the truth.

"Don't blame yourself. It's not fair."

"I should have guessed something was going on between you two. She's been acting peculiar for the past few months, but I didn't have enough sense to find out what it was all about."

"Don't make it sound so sordid and filthy," Dawn said entering the room in her dressing gown. Ned turned around to face her. "My, God!"

she gasped. "What have you done to him? He didn't deserve your beating. You should be ashamed!"

"After what he's done to you, how can you say that?"

"Look what I have done to him! Blame me, not Ned. This is all my fault. I was always in control."

For a moment Ned was afraid she might confess the truth, and should that happen, he would surely lose her. The lie was all that held them together.

"You don't need to protect me, Dawn. Your father's right." Mac's confidence was rudely shaken. He felt trapped by his own stubborn attitude. The situation was much too complex, and he had been a fool to try to right it by placing the blame.

"You know why I'm here, don't you, Mac?" Ned said, bracing himself for some kind of reckless outburst from Mac, but he remained silent, shaking his head in recognition of Ned's remark. Ned felt the need of a sudden departure before his lie began to slip. "Come on, let's go home," he said, taking Dawn's arm.

"I am at home," she snapped, pulling away.

Her eyes were vague, and he could not read the meaning behind her remark. She seemed to jump from one defense to another. She had at first expressed her anger over her father's actions, and now she was leaning toward him in another sense.

"What are you trying to tell me? Have you left me on your own?"

"I have left your mother's house and I'm not going back. I cannot live under the same roof with that woman, and I don't intend to torture myself any longer."

Her ultimatum filled Mac with exaltation that was about as easy to hide as a burning bush. He had tried to tell Ned that it wouldn't work, but he refused to listen. Dawn was used to being on her own. He knew she couldn't stand being treated like a caged animal. He understood now why Dawn wouldn't wait until the new house was finished before getting married. She had been forced to marry Ned whether she wanted to or not. Maybe she didn't even love him.

For a moment Ned was at a loss for words. He had failed to see any disturbance between the two women, and her remark had caught him completely by surprise. "Why didn't you tell me you were having trouble with my mother?"

"I wasn't exactly having trouble with her."

"What was it?"

"I just don't like people hovering over me and telling me what to do. Anyway, she doesn't like me."

"Of course she likes you."

"She doesn't think I'm good enough for you."

Thinking back Ned could remember some of her remarks that had made him wonder himself. He turned to Mac, feeling defeated by the sudden turn of events. "I guess I jumped in the wrong direction about that proposition you made me yesterday."

"It's still open. I can make the arrangements if you think you might be interested."

What arrangements? What are you two hatching?"

"I offered to buy the Benson place for you and Ned to live on until the house is finished. You know I always wanted to raise cattle, but I don't have the time. If you two agree, you can move there and have a place of your own. Ned can run the ranch and pocket half the profit."

"Oh, that sounds wonderful. What about Debbie?" Her happy expression suddenly changed. "Does she want to sell her home?"

"She really doesn't have a choice unless she gets married, or hires some man to run it for her and that takes money."

"Then she hasn't agreed."

"Not in so many words, but she will."

"I will not hear of you taking advantage of her," Dawn said stubbornly. "She's my best friend. I will not stand by and see her put out of her house. Do you realize that it's the only home she knows?"

"I don't know of any way I can buy the ranch and not have her move. After all, the whole idea was to get you and Ned out of his folk's house before you clashed with Martha. The way I have it figured, things will work out to all our advantages. Ned can make a good living, I'll have the ranch I've always wanted, and Debbie will have enough money to do whatever she wants."

"I still can't stand to see her put out of her home. It's just not fair."

"She can't take care of that place by herself. It's as simple as that. If I don't help her, she's in trouble. Sooner or later she will be forced to sell. Is that what you want?"

"No, of course not, but the decision has to be hers."

"I'm not sure of what you expect me to do. I'll have another talk with her and see what can be arranged."

"You'll think of something," she said with conviction.

Ned knew that Mac was only trying to help, but he resented his superior attitude. He knew Dawn would never take his word for anything as long as Mac was around to tell them what to do. He was being denied every privilege as her husband, and he had no defense. His love for Dawn forced him to swallow his pride and turn himself into something he despised: a squeamish, mealy-mouth, excuse of a man too gutless to stand up for his rights because he was skirt whipped. Looking at the two of them with their heads together working out, not only their future, but his as well, made him furious. He might as well not be there, he had no voice in the matter, except to agree with them. He had been very comfortably forgotten.

Dawn would not allow Mac to speak to Debbie alone, fearing he might make her feel trapped because of her situation. She went herself to assure that any proposals made must be with mutual consent. The results of her conversation with Debbie convinced her that Debbie had to sell because of her financial state.

"I can't afford to keep it," Debbie confessed. "I wish I could sell the land and keep the house."

"Then just sell the land and keep the house," Dawn suggested. If it's agreeable, Ned and I can move in with you until our house is finished."

"I couldn't think of doing that. The house is the reason your father is dealing with me."

"We only need it for a few months."

"Look, your father wants to buy the ranch to give you and Ned a place of your own. If you live with me, how will that differ from the situation you're trying to get away from?"

"The difference is Martha. You aren't part of the family, and we get along together."

"I refuse to sell Richard land he doesn't want and selfishly use his generosity to my own advantage. That's cheating."

"Not quite. He really only wants the land. Can't you see what he's doing? He buys the ranch from you, that gets you out of your bind, and at the same time it gives me a place to live and he gets to raise cattle like he's always wanted."

"I don't know. I'm confused, not convinced." Debbie considered Dawn's suggestions for a moment, trying to see the situation through her eyes. "I just can't do it."

"Would you reconsider if I told you that I need you, that I want you to stay with me?"

"What would you need me for? You have a loving husband to see after you."

"I'm going to have a baby."

"A baby so soon! Are you sure?"

"I'm sure."

"That's wonderful, but it will be a long time yet. By the time the baby is born, you will be in your own house."

"No, I'm afraid not."

"What are you talking about? Of course you will."

"The baby I'm carrying doesn't belong to Ned," she whispered, sort of looking around her.

"No!" She was staring at her in disbelief. "No!" she gasped again.

Dawn had never dreamed of speaking the truth to anyone. Now that she heard the words coming from her own lips, they sounded obscene and sinful. She turned away from Debbie's sharp eyes and hid her face in her hands. "It's true," she said without raising her head. "And Ned knows it."

Debbie was too stunned to reply. She sat there staring into space. Her first reaction had been one of shock and disbelief, then instinctively she reached out and took Dawn's hands, feeling the trembling chill that rasped through her. "Of course you need me. That's what friends are for." Her words were comforting, like a blessing of peace, soothing Dawn's anxieties.

Debbie agreed to sell the ranch and keep the house and five acres. This would give her a place for a garden, cow and calf, and leave the orchard and chicken lot. Mac accepted her offer with intense eagerness, matching his daughter's enthusiasm. He even added enough money to the selling price to cover rent on the house for the next few months. Debbie did not want to accept the extra money since she would be living there herself, but Mac insisted. He was not a man to accept charity. If anyone was to be charitable, it would be he.

CHAPTER

17

It was a dark rainy day in April when Dawn and Ned moved into the Benson House. The wind had suddenly changed during the night, pushing cold air and rain ahead of it, cloaking their new home in gloom.

The house was built in a U shape with two porches. The front porch ran the entire length of the house that consisted of a parlor and two bedrooms on the south. Directly behind the three front rooms was another porch. It also ran the length of the house, and separated the front rooms from the kitchen and dining room. Actually it was more like two separate houses under the same roof. To go to the kitchen, one had to go outside and cross the porch to reach the kitchen door.

To the right of the front door was the staircase that led to three more bedrooms directly over the three rooms on the ground floor. All the windows were equipped with heavy oak shutters that could be closed from the inside. The house had been built like a fortress except for the porches. Dawn thought it was a strange way to build a house, so that you had to go outside to get to the kitchen.

Behind the house, surrounded by trees, stood a massive double log barn, beside it the cellar was located. The house had been built around the spring fed well so that it was located inside the kitchen and equipped with a hand pump. It was really a strange setup and Dawn decided it would take a little getting used to. She tried to fit herself into the pattern of ranch life, but felt out of place; however, she felt more relaxed out from under Martha's watchful eyes. She had hoped that things might get better after they were settled into their own home, but her feelings for Ned remained the same.

It was hard for Ned to realize that Dawn and Debbie were so near the same age. Dawn, with her lively tongue and quick temper, seemed sufficiently younger than Debbie, who was quiet and easy going, with an abundance of patience.

Dawn had not yet completely forgiven her father for the beating he gave Ned, and Mac, perceiving himself in a delicate position, decided the best medicine for her hangover temper was time. His past conduct would serve as a lesson to him not to make anymore rash decisions where his daughter's affairs were concerned. He had never had her turn on him with such heated anger before, and he felt crushed. He could not quench the overwhelming desire to do things to make her happy, but where her husband was concerned, it was hands off. She had warned him never to touch Ned again.

Dawn recognized her own lack of patience, feeling abandoned and miserable as she watched Ned and Debbie in the evening after supper talking quietly together while Debbie sewed delicate, small, baby clothes for her expectant child.

Ned had already begun to show an aptitude for the cattle business. He loved every minute he spent outside in the fresh air. As the days grew longer he spent more and more time away from the house. Because of her condition Dawn spent her days doing the cleaning and cooking while Debbie worked along side Ned.

When it was time for spring planting, Ned broke the ground for the garden and prepared the rows. Debbie followed close, dropping the seed. Dawn watched them work side by side, day after day. After a while she accepted it as their normal routine. Ned seemed only to speak to Debbie when the three of them were together at meal time, and in the evenings after the work was finished. They discussed things of little interest to Dawn. She listened quietly, feeling she had nothing intelligent to add to their conversation.

When they were alone in their room at night, Ned was confoundly silent. His perplexing attitude disturbed her. She felt shut out. Even though she didn't love him passionately, she was beginning to feel a tinge of jealousy as the friendship between Ned and Debbie grew. She was lonelier and more unhappy now than ever. Finally Ned's silence drove her to the offensive. One night as they were getting ready for bed, she asked quite unexpectedly, "Have you grown weary of me already?" He made no reply, and she could not see his face where he stood in the shadows. "What has changed you?" Her voice was as tense as her insides.

"I haven't changed," he answered quietly.

"Yes you have. You hardly talk to me anymore. Is it because I'm like this?" She laid her hand over her swollen belly.

"Of course not."

"Then what is it?"

He looked at her, perplexed. "What do you expect of me? If I come near, you push me away. If I don't come near, you question me. I just don't know anymore. I'm tired of being rejected. I don't know what you want me to do."

"You're like a stranger. I want you to treat me like you love me." He reached out suddenly and pulled her close. "Can I do this?" She felt a sharp pain in her back as his arms circled her body tightly.

"Please! You're hurting me," she cried. He let her go with an oath. "I'm sorry. Things will be different after the baby comes."

"In only two short months. And then how long after that," he said mockingly.

She watched him warily. "I know how you feel."

"How is that possible when you have never loved me?"

"I do love you."

"The same way I love you?"

"I don't think you love me at all anymore."

"You won't let me."

"I have let you."

"Yeah, as an obligation. How the hell do you think that makes me feel? I want you to want me, not just give in to me."

"You have to give me time. You knew from the beginning that I couldn't love you in the same way—not yet."

"Not ever!" he said in exasperation, and started toward the door.

"Where are you going?"

"What difference does it make?"

"To tell Debbie your troubles."

"I don't have to. She's not blind."

"Well neither am I," she spat.

"What's that supposed to mean?"

"Anything you want it to."

He slammed out of the room in a rage. When she heard the sound of the front door closing, she hurried to the window, saw him moving toward the barn. He stood for a moment in the moon light looking back at the house, then disappeared into the shadows. She turned away from the window, and did not watch as he rode toward town.

After that night, Ned spent most of his evenings at the Silver Buckle. Although Mac was quite concerned, he held his tongue. As long as Ned did his job he knew better than to interfere unless Dawn asked for his help. He didn't see much of Dawn; his own affairs took up most of his time. Success was beginning to have an effect on him. He was becoming convinced that one day he would be a very wealthy man. He thought about his father, the way he had criticized him for his greed, only to discover that he was cut from the same cloth. Where he had found fault with his father's ambition, he was now eating crow.

He was excited over his newly acquired possession of the Benson ranch. He enjoyed the feeling of being a land owner. He had put most of his financial resources into the building of the new house, but should another land opportunity arise, he intended to take advantage of it. His dream was to build a cattle empire. He felt he had a pretty good start with the 1,920 acres of river bottom land, and the 640 acres of highlands adjacent to the river front where the new house would soon be completed. He owned some of the best land in the State of Texas, and decided it was time he threw off the yoke completely and devote his energy to his growing interests. It was necessary for him to hire someone to take over the management of the trading post. It came as a shock to the town when he hired Darrell Holliman, a rather mysterious young man for the job, who had only recently moved to Courgat.

Mac was impressed with Darrell's intelligence at their first meeting. He appeared to be easy-going, good-natured, and eager to work. He seemed extremely mature for his twenty three years, with an outgoing personality and common sense. He was at least two inches taller than Mac, with a visible show of hard muscles beneath his shirt, and very pleasing facial features. In short, he was an exceptionally handsome man in every respect. Mac did not question him about his past, he accepted him without question, blind trust that he himself failed to understand. He knew instinctively that Darrell Holliman was no ordinary man. The only thing he knew about him was that he was an only child and both his parents were dead. He had come to Texas in search of an uncle who lived someplace in or around Courgat. He was told that his uncle had lived there for about five years, then suddenly disappeared, leaving his house standing empty and the land desolate. It was feared that he was most likely dead, or else he would have been back to dispose of his property.

"It seems a strange thing to come here like this and have a place to live waiting for me," Darrell said. "I couldn't have picked a better spot to settle down."

"I know how you feel," Mac said, "I had a similar experience when I came here." He went on to explain about his brother Ralph.

Maybe it was the loneliness the two men shared that threw them together, or the fact that they had both found a new life in a dead man's shoes. Whatever the reason, their friendship continued to grow. Darrell took on the responsibility of managing the store effortlessly. He had a good head for figures, and never fell awkwardly silent when meeting or exchanging conversation with the customers. He made friends quickly and easily, and Mac was filled with a sense of pride for having found this honest and eager young man.

Although Darrell was anxious to meet Dawn, Mac put it off because of her condition. He hoped that the town's people might somehow lose track of time and spare her the disgrace that was otherwise inevitable. He knew a great cloud of misery was persistently growing in her with each passing day, because there was no escape. The birth of the child was as sure as death. As her time drew near, Mac began to worry about her in a new way. The memory of her mother, the agonizing pain she suffered before Dawn was born, followed by her death returned to plague him.

The fact that Ned spent so much time in town at night made him furious. What if Dawn should need him? What then? Surely he didn't expect Debbie to assume all the responsibility.

Debbie had even become perturbed concerning Ned's licentious behavior. "I'm quite anxious about Dawn," she admitted to him. "I don't want to be here alone with her when it's time for the baby to come. I expect you to stay home nights, at least until after she gives birth."

"All right," he said. "I'll stay close to the house starting tomorrow."

"Tomorrow may be too late."

"I have an appointment tonight."

"An appointment to get drunk?" she said harshly.

He was shocked by the hostility in Debbie's tone. It was so out of character. "Maybe you can think of something better."

"As a matter of fact, I can. Stay home where you belong."

"When I'm ready," he stormed, stomping from the house.

That night Mac entered the Silver Buckle looking for Ned and found him drunk as usual with Marcy's arm hanging around his neck. He knew where that would lead.

"Well, I see you're having another night on the town," Mac barked with irritation.

"A man needs something."

"You're a little mixed up, boy! A man doesn't need this. If you keep this up you'll wind up on the saloon floor wallowing in your own puke."

"She hates me," he blurted. "I'm her husband, and I got fewer privileges than a damned hired hand."

"Watch your mouth," he said with an inimical tone that was quietly threatening. "Come on, I'm getting you out of here." Mac gave Marcy a hard look and she got up and walked toward the bar, swinging her hips.

"I ain't ready to go. Leave me alone!"

"You're a lost man if you keep this up, and you've chosen your own hell."

"Is that a fact? If I have, Dawn's the devil who keeps heaping them fiery coals on my back."

Mac's temper flared. "Shut your mouth!" he growled. "You're drunk."

"Yeah, I'm drunk, but I'm not blind or crazy." He raised himself a few inches off his chair, his hands splayed against the table top as if he might spring at Mac any moment.

Mac knew Ned was fighting his inner turmoil with alcohol, trying to deaden the pain. Becoming aware of the curious eyes cast in their direction, Mac pulled him to his feet and pushed him roughly ahead of him toward the saloon doors. Ned stumbled several times, and was steadied by Mac's strong supporting arm.

Mac was surprised to see a light in the parlor window when they reached the ranch. The door was bolted and he knocked lightly. Debbie peered out the window, and then hurried to open the door. She watched Mac anxiously as he helped Ned to the couch in the parlor.

"Sorry to disturb you at such a late hour. But Ned would never have found his way home in his condition."

"I know Dawn will appreciate your concern," she said softly. "She isn't feeling well, and I hate to wake her. I think it would be better if Ned slept here tonight."

"Is she all right?"

"Yes. I looked in on her a few minutes ago. She's sleeping soundly right now."

"I think you're right. He better not go in there tonight and upset her. Can you manage him?"

"Don't you worry. I can take care of everything just fine."

Mac looked at her with deep admiration. "You are the best thing that ever happened to us. I couldn't get along without you, especially after the way Ned has been acting up lately. If I were younger, you would have to look out for me. I'd come courting for sure." He gave out with a low laugh when she looked embarrassed. "I'll be getting on back to town unless you need me to help you in some way."

"I'm fine, thank you."

"Good night, and thank you."

"Good night Mac." She walked him to the door and stood for a moment with her back pressed against it after he had gone, thinking how pleasant he had been. She had never noticed that about him before.

When she re-entered the parlor Ned was sleeping, his mouth open, his breathing heavy. She spread a sheet over him and gently placed a pillow under his head. At her touch his eyes suddenly fluttered open.

He grabbed her arm. "You're an angel, and beautiful," he said in a quivery voice.

"Go back to sleep," she urged, looking at his hand that was gripping hers.

"My head hurts." He drew her toward him and placed her cool palm against his brow.

She did not remove her hand, but left it there stroking his forehead gently. "You'll feel better in the morning, after you have a good sleep."

"My head will feel better, but what about the ache inside me?" He was looking at her like a pleading child. "Why can't she love me?"

She looked away, trying to control the anxiety she felt tighten like a steel band across her heart. She could not look into his eyes as she struggled to hold back her tears. She lingered for a moment, her eyes downcast, her hand still resting on his brow, fearing any abrupt move might upset him more.

Ned suddenly sat up and pulled her down on the couch beside him. His face was close to hers and his breath was warm and sour against her cheek. "Help me," he murmured, squeezing her hand.

"I can't. I don't know how." She twisted her hand out of his grip.

His arms went around her and he forced her back on the soft cushions. She turned her face to one side as his lips searched for hers. "Please," she gasped, "don't do this. You're drunk, you don't realize what you're doing."

"You're so sweet, understanding, and loving." His voice was shaking. "I need you."

She tried to push him away, and his grip tightened. She began to struggle, but he easily overpowered her. She was about to start screaming when suddenly his face turned pale and he released her with a startled cry. "My, God! What am I doing? Did I hurt you?"

"No."

He wetted his lips, leaned back, and closed his eyes. "I'm sorry, forgive me. I guess I'm finished as a man. No one can help me."

"You're not finished. You're just tired and confused. Try to get some rest, everything will look different in the morning."

"Could we talk for a while?"

"If you want to."

"I have to. I feel ready to explode. Has she told you that I'm not responsible for her condition?"

"Dawn and I have no secrets."

"Then you know what she's doing to me." He felt ashamed of his weakness. "Being near her drives me out of my mind. Maybe I'm not man enough for her, but I'm the one who married her, and I didn't have to."

Debbie offered no comment. She had no idea what to say to this lost man. A man who had taken a beating to preserve his wife's honor, and with no rewards. Her lips were sealed. Her love and loyalty for Dawn remained the same.

"When that damned Indian showed up at the ranch the day after we were married, she took one look at him and I was forgotten completely." He shuddered with hate. "I felt like I was facing the end of the world. He came like a thief, and when he left he took her heart with him. He has destroyed my soul. Do you understand? I'm dead and in Hell." He looked at her with tears streaming down his face.

"Please, try not to think about it."

"You think this is just drunk talk, don't you? Well, I feel the same way sober, only the pain is worse. I thought I killed him. God knows, I meant to kill him."

"Ned! What are you saying?"

He looked at her, fear plain in his eyes. "I don't know why I said that."

"It's true; I can see it in your eyes."

"I saw them together, him holding her in his arms, her clinging to him, kissing him. He had taken her some place so they could make love. I was hiding in the shadows watching when he brought her back. He walked her to the cabin, then returned to his horse. I shot him in the back before he could mount. He dropped to the ground. I thought he was dead. I meant to kill him. I didn't find out until the next morning that he had been able to mount his horse and ride away. I prayed for him to die, but he had survived." He was crying now. "Why didn't he die? As long as he's alive, Dawn will never love me." He buried his face in his hands and shook with terrible helpless sobs. She left him alone and returned to her own room. She sat in the dark trying to understand how Ned was able to mask his true feelings so well before Dawn. Such a man was outside her comprehension. Dawn had always been the suspicious, cynical type, so why hadn't she seen through his incredible pretense. She wished that Ned had not confided in her, and wondered if he would remember it when he was sober. She felt certain that she was the only one to share his secret, knowledge that could become a prelude to trouble. She knew she was only a passing distraction, and that the scene between them was a warning for her to be very careful or it might happen again. She felt dirty, as though she might have invited his wild actions without realizing it. She knew he had been driven to it by his love for Dawn and her rejections of his feelings. The thing that confused her was the strange feelings she had experienced. She knew it was wrong. Being so near Ned, his forcing his attentions on her was disturbing, yet pleasant at the same time. She was aware that she sincerely pitied him, but was that the reason she had wanted him to kiss her. He was the husband of her best friend, and she had always considered herself respectable. Because of her heart felt sympathy, she was something no woman should be in relationship to a married man, and it frightened her. She would be glad when the time came for them to move into their own house, and end the false hope that someday she might be able to let go of her feelings and see where they might lead her. She covered her face with her hands as though hiding from her shameful secret feelings. I will not allow myself to think this way, she told herself. I had rather face death than shame.

When Ned awoke the next morning he felt sick at heart. He had lain awake most of the night, his mind alive with turbulent thoughts. His love for Dawn, plus his need, would give him no relief. And now he was trying to deal with his guilt for having taken advantage of Debbie's goodness. He had no fear of her telling Dawn. The last thing she would do was stir up trouble. He loathed the beast he had become, frightened by his loss of self-control, and wondered what disgusting drunken thing he might pull next. He wished he could blot out his past and start fresh, erase the streak of cruelty that grew inside him. He had been a fool to imagine that Dawn might love him. The day Light Eyes rode back into her life, she was lost to him forever. His life was moving swiftly to a dead end of confusion, robbing him of all the tenderness and compassion that had once been a part of him, leaving him hard, rude, and cowardly hiding in a whiskey bottle. He sometimes felt the need to pray, but as rotten as he had become, he refused to add hypocrisy to his list of faults. The fact that Debbie shared his worst sin did not upset him because he knew he could trust her to keep his secret. Not for him exactly, but because she was interested in Dawn's welfare. Her goodness and generosity was as much a part of her as her loving heart.

Debbie did not show any change in her attitude toward Ned. She wore the same picture of innocence, yet inside lay the knowledge that could lead to his destruction. He shuddered to think that his mask could have dropped before Dawn instead of Debbie. He had to be more careful. He might even have to give up his alcohol crutch as it appeared to make him vulnerable to telling the truth. When he confessed to Debbie that he had tried to kill the Indian, his feeling of guilt began to mend. Spiritually he was becoming whole again. When he looked at her now, a frightening sense of tenderness and compassion went out to her, and somewhere inside him a flickering flame began to burn higher. He found it comforting to give up his drinking and stay home doing decent things for a change.

Dawn appeared to wait casually for the birth of her baby, while inside she was torn to pieces, worrying about the nasty gossip and finger pointing that was inevitable.

Ned dreaded the birth of the Indian child. He would be glad for it to be over for Dawn's sake. She looked so miserable and tired. He wondered about the consequences he would suffer. He was filled with renewed doubts and jealousy. He was suffering, not for his sins, or his deeds of love, but for those of another man. The heavy hand of guilt was tearing at his insides because of his evil thoughts, but he could not stop them from pouring through his mind. Even though the helpless unborn child she carried had made it possible for him to marry her, he hated it, and he hoped it would be born dead. If it lived, it would be living proof of her love for the Indian. How was she to forget when the child would serve as a constant reminder?

He believed Satan to be in control of fate, that he had woven the disgraceful circumstances into a hangman's noose. There was no way out. He had been defeated. He suffered bouts of silent fury as he lay sleepless beside his wife, teetering on the brink of complete mental imbalance. He ached to kill the Indian with his bare hands, smash his face with his fists until it became raw meat, and stomp him to death with his heavy boots. He could think of many ways to kill him, each one slow, deliberate, and sure.

CHAPTER

The morning Dawn's labor began; Ned was awakened by her urgent plea for help. Her hand was weak on his shoulder as she shook him. He was instantly alert.

"What is it? Is it time?"

"Yes," she almost screamed.

"Take it easy. I'll wake Debbie, then ride for Doctor Keel and your father." He ran upstairs in such a state of confusion that he forgot to put his pants on.

Debbie opened her eyes when he rushed into her room without knocking. "Is it the baby?" she asked, sitting up in bed.

"Yes!" He cried excitedly.

"I'll be right down." She reached for her robe, slipping it on as she hurried out the door and disappeared down the dark stairs.

Ned stood there for a moment looking after her, breathing in ragged, quick gasps while his body shook with fear. He did not realize until he followed Debbie back to Dawn's room, that he was wearing only his drawers. His pants lay empty on a chair beside the bed. He felt his face turn red and hurriedly dressed and put his boots on. Debbie showed no signs of having noticed.

She gathered Dawn into her arms and rocked her back and forth as though soothing a fretting child. Dawn clung to her as if Debbie held life itself in her two small hands.

Ned whispered close to Dawn's ear, "I'll be back soon. Don't you worry."

Dawn nodded, her face the shade of ash as another contraction seized her.

Seeing Dawn suffer to bring Light Eyes child into the world thrust Ned's murderous rage to the apex of hate and revenge. He would know no peace until the Indian was dead. "God damn him to Hell!" he said furiously, and rushed from the room.

Debbie stayed close to Dawn, bathing her face, holding her gripping hands, and speaking words of comfort and encouragement.

"What would I do without you?" Dawn said, looking at Debbie with eyes bright with fear.

"You will never have the chance to find out."

When Doctor Keel arrived, Dawn was screaming with each contraction. She held on to Debbie with both hands, finding strength in her presence and solace in her gentle soothing voice. The night hours dragged by while Dawn's suffering increased. She slipped in and out of awareness through periods of blessed darkness. When the shimmering lamp light became visible again, agonizing pain clutched her once more.

Ned paced the floor in the adjoining bedroom shaking with fear. She might die bearing the Indian's baby and he cursed him with raging anger.

Morning came and the baby had yet to appear. Debbie fled back and forth carrying bloody sheets that she soaked in a tub of water on the back porch. If Dawn didn't deliver soon, she would bleed to death, and her strength was failing; she was too weak to push. The long hours of labor had clouded her mind and dulled her senses. She was giving up and cried out, "Please, God, let me die!"

Ned rushed into the room and dropped to his knees beside her. "You're not going to die. If you die, I'll die too because I won't have any reason to go on living." He took her hand and held it to his lips sobbing. He was on the verge of hysterics.

Doctor Keel was thankful that Mac wasn't there. He figured he was fixing to have a problem with Ned. He didn't have time for it and ordered him from the room.

Mac had not been notified of his daughter's condition. Keel had stopped on his way out of town to tell him, and was told that he had ridden to the Indian village. He realized now that it had been a blessing.

Mac would be a raving maniac because he had the memory of Elizabeth's death to strengthen his panic.

Ned heard Dawn speaking incoherently from the next room, her voice carrying quite clearly. She was begging God to spare her baby. Guilt tore at Ned's heart because he wanted the baby to die. Suddenly his world collapsed. Out of her delirium came the only words on earth that could scourge him, words more deadly than a rifle shot at ten paces. She was calling for Light Eyes. Over and over she screamed his name. Ned pounded the walls, cursing the Indian, himself, his shameful thoughts, and his weakness. He felt helpless and naked; the truth was eating him alive. His stomach was crawling and his nerves suddenly snapped. He threw the door open to the bedroom where she lay, glaring at her, his face an ugly mask. He pressed his fingers to his temples and screamed, "Make her shut up! I can't stand it!" Debbie watched him in mounting horror. She had expected the doctor to comment, express shock, but he didn't so much as lift an eyebrow. His eyes never left his patient.

At length, he spoke to Debbie in a controlled voice. "Get him out of here before I knock him in the head."

Hearing his words, Ned turned around and ran from the room.

A few minutes later came the healthy cry of Dawn's baby when the doctor picked him up by the heels and whacked his bottom. He laid the baby on Dawn's stomach and cut the cord before passing him to Debbie.

She wrapped him in a soft blanket and held him close to keep him warm. A violent shudder racked her body suddenly and she collapsed into a chair, allowing the tears she had been holding back come to the surface.

Ned was relieved when it was finally over, that Dawn's suffering had ended. He was sorry that the baby was alive. He had no idea how he would cope with its presence.

Doctor Keel left Debbie to watch over Dawn and her tiny dark haired son, who was nursing contentedly at his mother's breast. Ned sat motionless in a chair by the window, his face in his hands. He glanced up when the door opened and looked at Keel in a daze.

"You have a son," he said, then was silent, his lips wiped clean of words. The raw truth bathed his thoughts like pouring rain, washing away every single utterance of comfort. Ned's suffering was irreversible. He was walking through hell fire, and there was no water.

"I don't have a son," he sobbed. "You know that." He motioned helplessly with his hands, holding them out empty. "I don't have anything, not even a wife."

"I can imagine how hard this is for you Ned, and there is absolutely no remedy to ease your pain, except time."

"I'm afraid time ain't the answer either."

"Maybe not," he confessed. "Perhaps you two can find some way to work this thing out."

"I'll never let her go!" His face was congested with rage. He looked away for a moment, unable to continue. Then he raised his head and said menacingly, "I'll see her dead first."

"You don't mean that, Ned."

"That red bastard will never have her!"

"Try to get some rest. We can talk more later. You're tired and not thinking straight. Things won't look so dark when the sun comes up tomorrow. I could use some sleep myself. She had a hard time. Be gentle with her. She lost some blood too. She'll be weak for a few days. You're lucky you have Debbie here to see after her. It's no job for a man."

"Nothing will ever change."

"Be reasonable, Ned."

"Reasonable?" He laughed bitterly. "If I wasn't a reasonable man, I would have killed that Indian long ago."

"You went into this arrangement with your eyes wide open. You wanted her bad enough to take the gamble, now it's time to accept the price."

"You're right. I understood well enough what I was letting myself in for. I love her too much. It's killing me."

"I'll be back tomorrow to check on your wife and baby. You might as well accept the responsibility, Ned. You asked for it, and the child needs a father to love him. Just remember, he's Dawn's flesh and blood. Love her, love her child."

Ned ambled over to the bed, tired and disgusted, threw himself upon it and drew his arm across his eyes. "I have to sleep now."

Doctor Keel looked down at him with an onrush of pity, but he wasn't sure who he pitied the most, Ned or Dawn. Ned was caught in a trap of his own making, but what about Dawn? He figured she was suffering mental torture, torn between her love of one man and her duty to the other. The position was one of wretched isolation. She was separated from her true feelings and implanted into a circumstantial environment. He wondered why life had to be so cruel and complicated.

Mac got word the following day regarding the birth of his grandson, and wasted no time in paying them a visit. Looking from the baby to Dawn, his face virtually lit up with pride. She had given him a grandson, and he was proud of her. "He's a fine boy," Mac said. The baby most certainly showed his Indian blood, and he was not surprised. He had expected it. He was afraid others might see it too, and then the gossip would begin. "What are you going to name him?"

"Henry, after your father."

"I guess it will be all right. Since he'll never meet his grandfather he can't take it as an insult."

"I never realized you felt that way about your father."

Mac took the baby's tiny fist in his big hand, leaned over and kissed it. "Baby Henry," he said, testing it, then was thoughtful for a moment. "I think I like it. I haven't heard from Henry since I left New Mexico. Rarely think about him anymore, except maybe to find fault and wonder if I might pick up some of his bad habits."

"Why are you so bitter?"

"No man could scheme and push the way he did and not step on a bunch of toes. I guess my foot might have got in his way."

"I think you might have taken after your father just a little bit, except for stepping on toes." She looked at him with a soft light in her eyes.

"I suppose I should be proud of him and all his power. He built everything with his own hands, plus a lot of guts. There are some things I never understood about Henry, maybe because I never cared enough, but as a man grows older, some things in the past come back to haunt him."

"Why don't you go visit him and take me with you. I would love to meet my grandfather."

"It's perfectly normal for you to want to meet him, but I hope you never do."

"What an odd thing to say. Why?"

Mac ignored her question. He smiled, looked at his tiny grandson again, kissed Dawn, and excused himself without another word.

After the birth of the baby Ned was very careful to keep his distance from Dawn. He even went so far as to move his clothes into the adjoining bedroom, and kept the door closed between them. His cold attitude upset Dawn so profoundly that she was unable to nurse her baby. As her milk supply failed, the baby began to cry day and night. Out of desperation, Mac rode to the village of Chief Brave Horse and brought an Indian squaw back with him to nurse his grandson. Although she was nursing a child of her own, she had plenty of milk for both babies.

Ned flew into a rage when he found out about the arrangement, and threatened to send the squaw and her papoose back to the Indian village. "Just about what I could have expected," he fumed, "an Indian nursemaid to tend your Indian baby, and a little Indian sister for him to grow up with. When you see them lying there side by side, one looks as Indian as the other."

"It's a pity," she said, "that a man like you can't act a little more intelligent and thoughtful. From the way you're acting you would think that I willed my milk to dry up. The baby has to have milk if he is to live. There was no one else to turn to. She will only stay as long as the baby needs her."

"Seems funny the way those Indians are so willing to help you. You don't suppose they know, do you?"

"Know what?"

"That Light Eyes is the child's father. You know what they say about blood being thicker than water."

"And some men remain fools all their lives."

"Just what is that supposed to mean?"

"It simply means that I think you're a fool."

"For once I agree with you."

She slapped him hard across the face, felt her hand tingling, saw the finger marks on his cheek. "If you say one more word, I'll make you leave this house." He glared at her, turned, and left the room. She lay there staring at the door he slammed behind him.

The squaw moved into one of the upstairs bedrooms and took both babies with her. Dawn's baby slept on the bed. The squaw slept on the floor with her baby. The Indian, fat and happy, spoke English well enough to carry on a conversation. She was always wearing a smile and laughed like a mirthful child. Dawn and Debbie made friends with her very quickly. It turned out to be a very pleasant arrangement. Dawn named the squaw Laughing Eyes because she always had a big smile that spread across her face and made her eyes crinkle in the corners. Laughing Eyes smiled all the more because of her new name. She was inquisitive, asking many questions about their lives and ways. Dawn spent hours explaining their way of life to her.

Ned made no secret of his feelings about the squaw. Dawn resented his attitude and bit her tongue to keep from having words with him. He seemed to hang around the house more than usual, finding fault. Dawn found it nerve wrecking living under his watchful eyes. Like Debbie, she tried to talk to him in tones of composure, while feeling the time for patience was long past. She wanted to strike out at him, as wrath crept up on her like a lion on a rabbit.

When baby Henry was six weeks old his eyes began to change from brown to dark clear blue. Ned had never paid much attention to the baby, but noticed the change in his eyes right away, almost as if he were waiting for the transformation to take place. Although he didn't comment on it, the resentment he felt was written on his face and etched into the tone of his voice.

"Why don't you say what's on your mind?" she asked him one night, throwing open the door between their bedrooms.

"Since you're a mind reader, you tell me."

"It might clear the air."

"Nothing will ever clear the air now," he predicted. "Anybody with half a brain can look at that baby and figure out who his father is."

"I don't think anyone else will pay any attention to the color of a little baby's eyes. You're just looking for trouble."

"I don't have to look very far, it comes to me waving a red flag on a teepee pole."

"Why don't you leave me? Why do you stay when you hate me and my baby?" Her eyes were searing his face with rage. "I still remember all the pretty speeches you made to get me to marry you. I found out too late that they were just empty words. I think you married me to punish me for the mistake I made, not to help me. Now that the baby is here you hate the sight of him, and yet you call him your son. Why don't you just tell the world the truth? Then you will have your freedom. I'm not afraid to face the truth. I had rather suffer the consequences than take anymore of your abuse. I thought you were a man, but you're a worm squirming on the end of a hook. You're caught and you don't know what to do about it. I want out of this bargain, because it's not working. I don't intend to stay here and have you make me feel guilty all the time."

"Good or bad you will stay right where you are, and you will stay married to me. I know why you want out of this arrangement. You want to go running to that Indian Buck. I'll see you dead first."

"You talk like a crazy man. Why do you want something that we both know is over and done with? What kind of life do we have together?"

"I still love you," he said, all the fight gone out of him.

"Love? How can you speak of love when there is no trust between us?"

"I can speak of love because I love you with all my heart."

"I don't believe you. You can't love me and reject my child."

"Can't you understand? To me the child is Light Eye's flesh and blood, and no part of you."

"I suffered to bear him. That makes him mine."

"I can't live without you. You're my life, what I live for. I'll do anything to make you love me."

"You can't force me to love you."

"I know that."

"Why must you keep punishing me for my past?"

"Can you say that you never think about the past? That you only think about Light Eyes when I bring it up?"

"I'm trying to forget, but you won't let me."

"I'm sorry. You know that all married people have quarrels."

"Not like the ones we have, and not for the same reasons."

"When I'm mad I say things I don't mean. Don't we all?"

"Yes," she agreed.

"Let's try again," he said as steadily as possible. "You know I'll do anything to make you happy."

"I can't put all the blame on you. I say mean things too, and I'm sorry." Then her eyes fell and she felt her cheeks burning. "You can move back into our bedroom if you like."

His heart suddenly leaped and he moved quickly to gather up his belongings.

She watched him, sensing his weakness, his inability to stand up to her. He hurried about in a frenzy, dropping things and then was unable to pick them up with his shaking fingers. She was silent while a sudden explosion of disgust seized her. She wanted to scream.

He came toward her now, his heart pounding in his ears. He stood for a moment looking down at her where she lay slightly curled up on the bed. He reached for her, feeling the softness of her body, her familiar fragrance suffocating him. As he pressed against her, she stiffened and leaned away from him abruptly.

Her actions were like a slap in the face and he groaned in frustration. "Don't do this to me," he said morosely.

She looked at him with tears in her eyes. "I'm trying to do what you want."

For a moment there was no trace of expression in his eyes, as if his mind had left his body. He was sick of waiting, tired of aching. Giving way to the violence that had been building inside him for months, he took her unceremoniously, in haste, trembling with lust while she lay beneath him grinding her teeth, wanting to get it over with. She hated the act and she hated him. He was taking advantage of her.

When finally he lay beside her, comfortable, relaxed, and satisfied, she breathed a sigh of relief. She hated the way he expected her to appease him. He was like a little selfish boy, and she wondered if he would ever grow up to be a man.

Ned had not had Dawn the way he wanted her, the way he had dreamed of making love to her, but he was contented at present. He would find a way to win her love. Just as long as I'm married to her, he decided, there is still hope.

CHAPTER

19

Dawn decided there was more to life than being a wife and mother. She hadn't left the ranch in months. She was bored. She slipped quietly out of the house, saddled her horse and headed for town. She wasn't concerned about what the gossips might have to say about her. She had never been able to hold her tongue or control her temper when people whispered behind her back. She would shut them up quick enough. Despite all the disapproval and malediction she would face, she felt a sense of relief, like a bird out of its cage.

She went first to the trading post in hopes of finding her father there. She needed him on her side when the tongue wagging commenced. Instead of seeing her father when she opened the door, she was looking into the face of a perfect stranger. She stood on the threshold for a moment glancing about the room. Relieved at seeing no one, she stepped inside and closed the door behind her. She stared at the man across the counter, impressed by his pleasant features and warm smile.

He watched her silently as she moved toward him, admiring everything about her. "Good morning,' he said, stepping out from behind the counter, gazing into her expressive dark eyes.

She returned his greeting, also his attention. She did not look away. "I'm not usually curious by nature," he said, "but could you be, by chance, Mac's daughter?"

"I could be," she teased, a gleam in her eyes.

"All right, you win. Are you Mac McCloud's daughter?"

"As a matter-of-fact, I am."

"I'm Darrell Holliman."

"I know who you are, but how do you happen to know who I am?"

"That's easy. Your father said you were the prettiest girl in town, and you're the prettiest one I've seen."

"You're very flattering Mr. Holliman, but you can save your sales act. I never pay for a thing."

"Not flattering, truthful. Call me Darrell."

"In that case, thank you for the compliment." She had almost forgotten how pleasant it was to be noticed by the opposite sex, and felt herself blush.

"What can I do for you?" He bowed in a silly boyish manner.

"I need a new dress. I feel so shabby."

"You, my dear, could never be shabby, not even in last year's style and wearing an apron. We just got in a new shipment. If you will step right this way, I'm sure we have just the right dress for you. We have a dress for every mood, taste, and occasion, especially for a beautiful lady like you."

"With a line like that, it's no wonder father turned the store over to you."

"Are you hinting that I'm full of hot air?"

"Never," she said laughing.

"You're very kind not to say so. I love women with a sense of humor."

At that moment the door opened and Ethel Sims and her daughter, Dixie, entered. When they saw Dawn a startled look came over their faces. After a second of gaping silence, they regained their composure, eyed her coldly, and Ethel said through compressed lips. "Well, we haven't seen you in quite a while. Where have you been keeping yourself?"

"At home. Where else? I have a baby to care for."

"Oh, my yes," Dixie said spitefully. "You do already have a baby, don't you?"

"Oh, my yes," Dawn mimicked. "I most certainly do already have a baby. Isn't that the reason you're cackling like a hen that just laid an egg?"

"Well, of all the nerve!" Ethel gasped. "We haven't the faintest idea of what you're driving at, or why you're so short spoken."

"In the first place, ladies, you're the ones with the nerve, and in the second place, you're a liar when you say you don't know what I'm driving at. I'm only reading your nasty little minds." She smiled evilly. "I was married five months before my son was born, and that's what all the gossip is about. You don't have a life and so you stick your long noses in my business. Why don't you come right out with what's on your filthy little minds."

"Well!" Dixie said, in her shrill nerve racking voice. "How can you be so brazen about it? I should think you would be ashamed."

"It's a shame you busy bodies don't choke to death on your own trouble making tongues."

"Well, I never! Come, mother!"

"And you probably never will. You don't have much going for you, and a big mouth doesn't count."

The women rushed toward the door that Darrell held open for them, mumbling in low spiteful tones. When the door closed behind them, Darrell threw his head back and laughed boisterously.

"There will probably be trouble over this."

"I'll swear to anything you like, Miss McCloud."

"It's Rowling."

"I wish you wouldn't remind me of that. I'm trying hard to forget about your husband."

She looked at him with a twinkle in her eyes. "I didn't realize you knew my husband that well."

"You mean well enough to dislike him?"

"Not exactly."

"Truthfully, the only thing I dislike about him is the fact that he's married to you. When I'm around him, I get the feeling that he doesn't cotton to me too much," he said airily.

"I must say it doesn't seem to bother you very much, you're smiling."

"Am I? I didn't realize. Is this better?" he said, frowning.

"Much."

"Now that we have that settled, let me say that I think you handled those two vultures admirably."

"Some women can be mean and petty. The whole town knows about my shameful mistake. I'm in for a lot more of the same."

"I don't think you have much to worry about after the way you stood up to those two hens."

"It may not be so easy next time."

"Need a friend?"

"Yes!"

"You have one." He held out his hand and she placed her fingers in his warm palm. "Shake?"

"Shake," she echoed, looking him straight in the eyes. "I like you very much."

"I'm glad. I would be very unhappy if you didn't."

Their first meeting made an immediate impression on Darrell. He was quick to notice her unusual qualities. She was full of spirit and had an air of truthfulness about her that he found very refreshing, as well as uncommon. But the thing that struck him most was her natural beauty. He had looked her over with a critical eye, and couldn't find the tiniest flaw, except that she was already married. Looking upon such beauty as hers was like climbing out of a mine shaft into the light of a perfect day. He was in love.

Their next meeting was quite by chance. She was on her way to inspect the new house that was only weeks away from completion. She saw a rider approaching from the direction of Courgat. At first she thought it might be Mac. He rode out almost every day for one reason or another. When she recognized the rider she felt a quiver of excitement.

"Well! As I live and breathe, Dawn McCloud."

"Rowling," she corrected.

"Please, dear lady. I told you, I'm trying to forget about your husband."

"You had better stop talking like that. I might get the wrong impression and think you're serious."

"I am."

His reply astonished her. Here was a man who did not beat around the bush.

"I hope you don't let the ribbing those two old bats gave you keep you away from town, or I may never see you again."

"I don't care what they think. I do as I please."

"I presume we are both headed in the same general direction."

"If you're on your way to the new house, we are."

"I am. Mac sent me out here with a sack of doorknobs. He's tending shop for a change."

"That is a change. He's usually going around in circles."

"Just look at that!" he gasped as they came upon the magnificent structure. "I have never seen such a splendid mansion in my life."

"Oh, it is beautiful," she said proudly, her eyes glowing. "It's mine, you know. Father made me a gift of it. He intends to live in town near the trading post, but he will stay here part of the time. Do you like it?"

"To put it mildly." He whistled with delight. "I hope you will invite me to dinner sometime soon."

"Of course we will. I have watched this house built board by board, saw it start to take shape almost like magic. And now, at last, it's almost completed. Would you like to explore with me?"

"I thought you would never ask."

They wondered through each room, admiring the expert workmanship. "It's more like a palace with its broad galleries, circular stairways, and spacious rooms."

"I love the surrounding gardens," he said.

"I call it my garden of Eden. It looks like an Edenic paradise. I will spend many happy hours here."

They wondered about, avoiding the workmen, missing nothing. The portico framing the main entrance was supported by massive columns that rose three full stories high. On the south side was located a large semicircular balcony that overlooked the river.

Dawn and Ned would occupy the second floor bedrooms. The third floor would be open space until such time as it was needed.

The great drawing room, where Dawn would entertain their guests, was very impressive, and sparkled with the splendor of the Deep South, and was connected to the lavish formal dining room on the north, fenced off by the arcade of pillars supporting the upstairs balcony.

Mac was to occupy the east wing on the first floor. He would spend most of his time in town, and continue to occupy the cabin. If he should change his mind about living near the trading post, he had a place waiting for him at the ranch.

"Come on," she urged, "let's walk down to the river."

As they strolled along side by side, he was all too aware of her presence, and the fact that they were alone. He glanced at her, observing her carefully. He admired the smoothness of her skin, the sheen of her black hair, the swell of her breasts, and the narrowness of her waist. He was becoming more and more aroused by the sight of her, and wondered if she might possibly be disloyal to her husband if she so desired.

She turned to him and gazed into his eyes for a moment. "Where did you come from? What did you do before you came here?"

"My life is so dull that it isn't worth mentioning."

"I don't believe you."

"Why?"

"You're the type person who creates excitement."

"I'm not one to argue with a lady, but I'm afraid you're wrong."

"No, I'm not."

"You seem pretty sure of yourself."

"That's right."

"Are you happy now that you're about ready to move into your new house?"

"You're changing the subject."

"I had no idea how magnificent it was."

"Didn't my father tell you?"

"There are a lot of things he neglected to tell me, such as how extraordinarily beautiful and charming his daughter is. You are far beyond just pretty."

"There are some things about me that aren't quite so charming."

"Such as?"

"Such as the reason for the little scene at the store the other day."

"A bunch of old ugly crows shaking their heads in disapproval and clacking their tongues do not influence my thinking in the least. I'm not exactly a Knight on a white charger myself."

"I like you," she said a little breathlessly. "You're different."

"That's the second time you've told me that. Keep it up and I might start to believe you."

"You wouldn't dare." She laughed happily

The expression in her eyes filled him with triumph. The attraction was mutual. He found her completely irresistible, and considered taking advantage of any chance to be alone with her in the future. They continued to talk, quiet and easy, in a relaxed way. She was grateful to find an understanding ear, and had to fight her first impulse to tell him about the mess she had made of her life by marrying a man she could never love, but dismissed the idea.

"I have loved this land all my life," she said.

"Were you born here in Courgat?"

"Yes."

"How long has your mother been dead?"

"She died the day I was born."

"Why hasn't your father married again? He's a good-looking man with a hell of a lot to offer a woman." Dawn looked at him in surprise. "What's the matter? Did I say the wrong thing?"

She shook her head. "No, you didn't say anything wrong. It's just that I feel guilty."

"Guilty about what?"

"I'm not sure."

"Has your father been unhappy?"

"He has never complained. I think he just got used to being alone. Of course, he had me, and I took up most of his time. I guess he didn't have time to think about marriage."

"And now?"

"He still doesn't have time. He's too busy making money."

"Maybe he needs to stay busy to fill his lonely hours."

Dawn was shocked by what he said. She had never suspected the truth about her father, but now with it all out in the open, she was beginning to understand how her father must feel. Of course he had been lonely. Living in that room behind the trading post for years. "It's all my fault!" she cried.

"You can't blame yourself. Mac made up his own mind to stay single, but it wouldn't hurt to give him a little shove now and then toward some nice female."

"Amy!" she said, shocked by her own thoughts.

"Who is Amy?"

She told him as much as she could remember about Amy. He listened with interest, a puzzled expression on his face. When she had finished, he said bluntly, "Where is Amy now?"

"I have no idea. We never heard from her."

"You mean she just left like that? After all those years of caring for you? She never wrote a letter telling you where she was?"

"That's right."

"For a minute I was beginning to think that she might have cared for Mac, but if he hasn't heard from her since, I guess she couldn't have cared very much."

"I'm glad you feel that way, because I was feeling pretty guilty about it. Father never opposed me on anything. He agreed to send her away because I didn't like her."

"Why didn't you like her? Was she mean to you?"

"Not exactly mean, but she resented me, I think."

"Because of your father?"

"I think she might have resented the fact that he always put me first."

"That's what it sounds like to me."

"Then it's my fault that father didn't marry her."

"A child can't be blamed for a thing like that. Your father should have turned you across his knee and spanked you, married the woman, and then let her do the spanking."

"But that still doesn't answer the question as to why she never contacted us after she moved away."

"I'll bet she did."

"Then father kept it from me because he knew I would be upset if I thought she was trying to come back."

"Something like that. Why don't you ask Mac if he ever heard from her?"

"Maybe I will." She threw her arms around his neck and hugged him. "Thank you," she whispered close to his ear. Then before he could make a move, she drew away from him. She was too conscious of the wide span of his shoulders, the hard muscles beneath his shirt, but most of all, the funny feeling in the pit of her stomach. "I have to go now."

"When will I see you again?"

"You can come out with father anytime you like, but don't come alone. I have a very jealous husband." She turned then and ran up the hill to where the horses were tied, mounted, and quickly rode away.

When she reached home her cheeks were glowing with an unaccountable feeling of happiness and excitement. She had not felt such a sensation of warmth and pleasure in a very long time.

Ned was quick to notice the change in her mood, and he felt quite disturbed listening to her ramble on about the house. She had seen the house many times before, but she had not reacted in such a way, and he wondered what reason lay behind her ecstatic state.

"What have you been up to?" he questioned, trying to sound nonchalant. "I haven't seen you this happy in a long time."

"Just think, we can move into our new home any day now. Isn't it exciting?" she said happily, trying to overlook the doubt she saw in his eyes. His blooming jealousy he was trying to hide was flaring up again. She could not give him full details of her visit to the house. She was determined not to mention anything about her meeting with Darrell, knowing it would only throw him into another jealous rage.

"The next time you plan on riding out there, let me know and I'll go with you. I don't like the idea of you being around all those workmen without me or Mac there with you."

"What's the matter, don't you trust me?"

"Trust has nothing to do with it. I'm just being cautious."

"Jealous, you mean," she burst out angrily. "I'm tired of your accusations and insults. I don't have to put up with it!"

"I'm not accusing," he said in a quick, apologetic tone.

"What do you call it then?"

"Concern."

"Concern for me or for yourself?"

"For you, damn it!"

"The only thing you feel about me is my body when we go to bed at night. Your concern, as you call it, makes me sick."

While Ned stood there struck speechless with cold rage, she fled quickly through the door and was gone, leaving him with a strong feeling of disaster.

Debbie appeared moments later. She laid her hand on his arm reassuringly. "She will feel differently after she cools off," she said softly.

"You heard?"

"Yes, I couldn't help it. I was in the other room."

He nodded his head doubtfully, and then hurried after Dawn. She had locked herself in their bedroom, but when he insisted, she opened the door. She stood there looking at him with tears on her cheeks. The happiness she had felt earlier had been swallowed up by scorn. "For pity's sake, must we always quarrel?"

"I didn't mean to hurt you," he said quietly, but his tone was still harsh. He put his arms around her tenderly and kissed her. She did not return his affection.

"Don't be mad," he said, allowing her to pull away from him. She rubbed her hand across her face, wiping the tears away. "We can't go on this way."

"I know," he said calmly. "Come here." When she hesitated, he took a step toward her and she was in his arms again. With his pulse thrumming, he lifted her and carried her to the bed. She did not surrender to him, she only obeyed him silently. She had discovered it was less traumatic to give in than to resist.

CHAPTER

20

It often seemed to Dawn that the darkest spot in her life was more her relationship with Ned's mother than Ned himself. The memory of Martha's actions when baby Henry was only four days old returned frequently to reinforce her hatred for the woman. She recalled how she had been forced to submit the helpless infant to Martha's critical inspection. Her attitude had been a collection of ugly suspicions and hateful accusations. The expression on her face when she first saw the child left Dawn in a state of shock and blazing anger.

"This baby is not my grandchild," she exploded, drawing back as though the baby might contaminate her. "Who's his daddy?"

The color drained from Dawn's face. "Get out!" she screamed. Her outcry woke the baby and he began to cry. Martha instinctively reached for the child. "Don't touch him!" Dawn cried, coming to her feet, planting herself between Martha and the crib, blood pouring down her legs.

"You're bleeding," Martha said excitedly. "Get back in the bed before you pass out."

"I'm not in your house now, Martha, so stop giving me orders, and stay away from my son!"

Debbie rushed into the room. "What's all the commotion? Dawn! What are you doing out of bed? Doctor Keel gave strict orders that you are not to touch your feet on the floor for at least two weeks." She helped her back to bed.

"Get Martha out of here!" she cried.

"I'm sorry, Mrs. Rowling, you have to leave. You're upsetting Dawn. It's hard on both her and the baby."

"She's acting this way on purpose," she spat. "She doesn't want to answer my question."

"What question is that?" Debbie asked in bewilderment.

"Who the father of that child is." She pointed her finger at the baby.

"Silence!" Debbie warned. "I refuse to listen to such talk. Why don't you ask Ned the questions and leave Dawn alone? She's not well. She had a long and painful delivery. She needs rest, peace, and quiet."

"I'm asking Dawn the question because she's the only one who knows the answer. Ned will only deny the truth. She has him under her wicked spell, and he's fool enough to let her ruin his life. My concern is for my son. The child looks like an Indian, and Ned don't have a drop of Indian blood in his body. He's not Ned's baby. Are you all blind?"

"That's enough! My concern is for Dawn. I want you to leave this minute! You're no longer welcome in this house."

"I can see that she has you under her spell too. I wouldn't stay in this house another second if my life depended on it."

Debbie stepped aside and opened the door for her, watching her leave with a heavy heart. This was the first time she had ordered anyone from her home, and hoped it would be the last.

Dawn had been spared the pain of answering Martha's question, but realized the answer was apparent. There was no way to hide the child's heritage, nor did she want to. The child had Light Eyes blood flowing in his veins, and in her estimation it would make him a better man.

Several days later, Dawn answered the door and found Martha standing on the porch. "What do you want?" she snapped.

"I want to have a word with you."

"I don't have anything to say to you. You're not welcome here. Debbie told you that."

"For Ned's sake hear me out."

"What do you intend doing? Start a scandal to amuse yourself?"

"I was upset the last time I was here. I came to apologize."

Dawn smiled ruefully. "For what? I know you haven't changed your mind."

"It's quite simple. I can't explain my reason for not visiting with the baby unless I tell the truth."

"You don't know the truth."

"I know Ned's not your baby's daddy. We need to come to some sort of understanding."

"What do you have in mind?"

Martha deliberated a moment before answering. "Because I love my son, and because he loves you, I'm willing to forget that the child is not a Rowling. Ned's willing to accept the blame as long as he has you. He thinks he can't live without you. No matter what you do he'll forgive. I'm not a deceitful woman, but I promise to keep your secret as long as my silence protects Ned's happiness."

"You are a savage, Martha."

"I'm glad we understand one another."

"What would you do if you should suddenly find out that you're wrong about me?"

"I would thank God."

"You want to believe the worst. I know that, but you're guessing. The only one hurt will be Ned. You can't touch me," she said bravely.

"I don't care what people think of me. I'm shock proof."

"You're evil!" Martha said. "You married Ned to give your bastard a name. You owe him, and I expect you to make him happy. It's just that simple."

"Simple blackmail!" Dawn stormed.

"That's right."

Dawn's blood was close to the boiling point. "You've had your say, now get out!"

Martha smiled. "I'll go, but I'll be back," Martha realized she had put herself in a risky position, and it was certainly no accident. She would sacrifice her neck anytime to protect one of her sons. She realized Dawn didn't love Ned, and it was only a matter of time before she kicked him out. She knew Mac would back Dawn to the hilt. She had always been a spoiled brat, and Martha had always loathed her.

Dawn knew Martha wasn't bluffing, but she had been when she claimed to be shock proof. If she kicked Ned out, Martha would shout her transgression from the roof tops. The day was fast approaching when she would leave Ned, and she was trying to prepare herself for the shame and disgrace that was sure to follow when Martha opened her vicious mouth. Martha had promised her silence only as long as Ned got his way with her. She wondered how long Ned would protect her good name when there were no rewards. Would he keep quiet to save face? No man wants to be branded a fool. Ned was the only one who might seal his mother's lips. She had no idea what to expect. Ned had threatened to kill her if she ever left him. She didn't think he had the guts and she intended to call his bluff. She shuddered involuntarily at the prospect of what might lay ahead of her, and she was thankful for her newly acquired friend in the person of Darrell Holliman.

She had other things to crowd her mind too. Wondering what Mac had thought when he looked at his grandson. If he had recognized the child as an Indian; he had been careful to conceal his suspicions. The sudden change in the color of the baby's eyes was to her advantage, proof of his white blood. Martha was the only one who could cause her humiliation and brand her a slut. Even though Martha's lips were sealed at present, she held her secret over her like a cocked gun, ready for battle. Dawn decided the price for her silence was too great, that she had rather face disgrace as opposed to wasting her life living in misery with a man she could barely tolerate. He was too filled with suspicions and jealousy, hardly letting her out of his sight. She wanted her freedom back.

Mac came to the ranch often to see his grandson and to look his investment over. When he paid her an unexpected visit one evening, he had invited Darrell to come along with him.

Dawn was pleased, and also a little exasperated because Ned did not share her enthusiasm, becoming sulky and bad tempered.

"I hope you don't mind us barging in this way," Mac said. "I wanted Darrell to see my grandson. I feel like bragging."

"You're welcome anytime." She was delighted, looking past her father to settle her gaze on Darrell, who was looking at her in a way that caused her heart to pound. Ned remained seated, pretending to read the paper. He acknowledged them briefly, and then became silent and reserved. Dawn glared at him and frowned, but he did not show the slightest inclination for changing his mood. Mac's dark eyes reflected his disapproving observation of Ned's unfriendly attitude. Dawn was trying to find the right words to lighten the cool rift between Ned and her father. Mac would know by Ned's behavior that Darrell was not welcome there. Dawn could see her father undergoing rapid changes: from confusion to embarrassment to annoyance.

The silence of several seconds was broken when Debbie crossed the porch from the kitchen and entered the parlor, drying her hands on her apron. "I thought I heard voices." She looked from Mac to Darrell in surprise.

"You two haven't met yet," Mac said. "Debbie, this is Darrell Holliman, the new store manager.

"I haven't had the pleasure," Darrell said, holding out his hand.

She extended her hand, smiling up at him, noting his exceptional height. "So you're the store manager? I'm Debbie Benson."

"At your service, Miss."

"And a very charming lady," Mac added, beaming with pleasure.

Darrell gave Mac a pensive glance, then looked toward Dawn and smiled. She met his eyes and then quickly glanced at Ned. He was frowning over the top of the paper.

"You just can't stay away from your grandson can you?" Debbie was smiling at Mac. "He is one beautiful baby. He looks just like his mother." She took his arm. "I'll walk you up."

"Come on you two," Mac said to Dawn and Darrell over his shoulder as he moved up the stairs, ignoring Ned completely. "Is he awake?"

"Probably not. New babies sleep almost all the time. They only wake up when they're hungry."

When they entered the room where the two babies lay side by side on the bed sleeping, Darrell looked from one to the other in bewilderment. "You didn't tell me there were two of them. Did it slip your mind?"

"Only one of them is mine," Dawn said laughing, leaning over to pick her child up. She held him out for Darrell to see. He stirred slightly in her arms, stretched and frowned. When he opened his eyes, Darrell marveled at their clear blue color. He was puzzled over the presence of the other infant that he presumed to be Indian when the squaw appeared in the doorway.

"Come here," Dawn said, making a motion with her hands, and the squaw moved silently into the room, eyeing Darrell curiously. "The other baby is hers. She's caring for both babies," Dawn explained.

213

"She's a little Indian maid in more ways than one," Darrell acknowledge. "You have a fine grandson, Mac." When Mac didn't respond Darrell glanced at him, saw he was looking contentedly at Debbie, unconscious of all else. Then his mood suddenly changed as his secret thoughts deserted him.

"Why don't we stay to supper, Darrell, we could both do with a good home cooked meal."

"I believe we should be invited first," he said.

Mac looked embarrassed. "I believe you're right."

"Oh, cut it out," Debbie said happily. "You're always welcome, both of you."

Although Debbie was speaking, Darrell looked at Dawn, his words directed at her. "Thank you for your hospitality."

Dawn flushed under his gaze, not sure if she blushed from pleasure or embarrassment.

During the meal Mac kept the conversation rolling, discussing business topics and Indian affairs. "I guess you heard about the Indian trouble starting north of us."

"No," Dawn said quickly. "What kind of trouble?"

"The settlers keep moving in on the Indian hunting grounds, forcing them into the mountains. The Indians have three ways to go: fight, starve, or run. A few tribes are putting up some resistance. They'll make war if the Government doesn't step in and enforce the treaty."

"How will it affect us," Ned interrupted brusquely.

"Hard to say, but the settlers are pushing the Indians in our direction, and if they join forces with the tribes in the north territory, we may be caught in the middle of a full scale Indian war."

"You don't think they will attack us do you?" Debbie said.

"If the Indian's are starving, they will fight for survival. What other choice do they have? While we're on the subject, I might as well tell you the main reason I came out here. Since no one can predict the outcome at this point, we have to make plans accordingly and move into the new house as soon as possible." He turned his attention to Debbie. "You can't live out here alone. It's not safe."

"This is my home. I have no place else to go."

"Yes, you do. You can move into the new house with us."

"Never! I refuse to impose on you."

"We are the ones who are imposing on you. I'll hear no more about it." Mac was looking at Debbie across the table, his eyes warm. "As far as I'm concerned, it's settled."

Debbie began to tingle with a sort of gentle fear. She did not argue with Mac, but in her own mind it was far from settled.

Mac took a swallow of coffee before turning his attention to his daughter. "I'm glad you were out there the day I sent Darrell to the new house with the hardware. He had wanted to see it, so I gave him a good excuse. He was impressed by the tour you took him on."

"When was this?" Ned asked sharply.

A startled look crossed Darrell's face when he realized that Mac had just let the cat out of the bag. His eyes met Dawn's sheepishly, a half smile on his lips.

"The last time I went out there," Dawn answered, dreading the scene Ned was destined to cause.

"You didn't mention it to me." His words at first were calm enough, and then suddenly rose in anger. "Why?"

"I'm not really worth mentioning," Darrell butted in, his eyes leveled at Ned.

"I'll decide what's worth mentioning and what ain't," Ned snapped, glaring at Darrell with a hostile expression.

Darrell had been warned that Ned was a jealous husband, and he was seeing him in action. He really couldn't blame him though. If Dawn were his wife he would probably feel the same way. He knew the sensible thing to do was stay completely away from Dawn or it might prove to be a very serious mistake.

"I can't see why you're making all this fuss, Ned," Mac spoke in Dawn's defense. "After all, it's her house and she can show it to anyone she pleases."

"I'm well aware of who the house belongs to," he said hotly.

"I didn't come out here to argue with you, Ned, nor listen to an argument between you and Dawn. Now drop it!" Mac was furious, ready to knock Ned out of his chair.

"All right!" Ned exploded, transferring his belligerent expression in Darrell's direction, who was preoccupied at the moment with disliking Ned, who he had not actually detested until that moment.

"Come on, Darrell," Mac roared. "We had better be getting on back to town. If we plan to move the first of the week, we all have a lot to do."

Mac expressed his appreciation for the meal that had suddenly brought disaster by one simple statement. He knew Ned would blow up at Dawn as soon as they were out of sight, and he knew she would take just so much of his insane jealousy. Maybe he wouldn't be moving into the new house with her. He certainly wouldn't grieve about it. Ned was becoming more of a disappointment to him every day. Too bad he was baby Henry's father. The child deserved better.

As soon as the front door closed behind them Ned became obnoxious, accusing Dawn by his tone as well as with his words.

"How long has this been going on?"

"What are you referring to?" she hedged, watching him squirm. "You know what I'm talking about. What kind of fool do you take me for?"

"How many kinds are there?"

"You don't have any use for me."

"Maybe you're right! The way you act makes it easy."

"You've been slipping around behind my back—"

"I haven't been slipping around doing anything. We just happened to be going to the same place at the same time, not that I have to explain to you."

"Can you deny that you saw him?"

She laughed. "I'm not blind, Ned, nor did I squeeze my eyes shut at the sight of him. You're so filled with jealousy that you're driving yourself insane, as well as me."

"You hid it from me and—"

"I wasn't hiding anything. I just didn't mention it because I knew you would throw a childish fit. I'm sick to death of your accusations, suspicions, and temper tantrums. And be damned if I have to put up with it."

Ned stared at her, his face gone pale as a thrust of fear cut through him. "I'm sorry; it's just that I love you so much."

"You're always sorry! You keep claiming you love me, but you stay on my back with your jealous fits. You make me sick!"

"I—I promise, I won't accuse you again. Just stop hiding things from me."

"There you go again, accusing me of hiding things. I don't have anything to hide."

"You should have told me about meeting Darrell at the house."

"I did not meet him. How could I? I had no idea he was going out there to deliver doorknobs to the workmen."

"It's the same thing."

"It is not! Go to Hell!" she screamed, trembling white with rage. "Why can't you just go to Hell and leave me alone? If I ever decide to meet someone, it won't be Darrell." He started to respond, and she shook her finger in his face. "Don't say it, Ned. I'm warning you. Keep your mouth shut before I forget I'm a lady and slit your throat."

He knew he had pushed her too far this time and he was scared. He reached out to her and she struck him in the face with her fist. He was stunned, felt a sharp pain in his eye. He tried to take hold of her again and she lashed out at him with both fists.

"Don't touch me!" she screamed. "Don't ever touch me again as long as I live!"

Her anger did not pass this time, she had made up her mind not to submit her body to him again, and lay rigidly beside him, daring him to so much as lay a finger on her. She did not order him from the room; she wanted him next to her, craving her body so she could reject him. Hurting him for the way he was tormenting her had become an obsession with her. She had drawn an invisible line and she dared him to cross it.

Ned was not the least enthused over moving. The idea of living in the house Mac built only sharpened his sense of inferiority. He was unable to dismiss the thought of Dawn and Darrell meeting behind his back, wondering where her infatuation might lead. Time was against him now as he tried tentatively to draw near her again. The only thing that seemed to matter to her was her son. They had ceased to argue, but the way they spoke in quiet cruel tones was even worse. She was slipping farther and farther away from him, and he was helpless to stop her. He had resumed his old habit of spending his evenings at the Silver Buckle with Marcy. She didn't reject him, but she didn't satisfy his emotional needs either.

When Ned came home one night in a shameless drunken condition, he burst into Dawn's bedroom, confronting her boldly. "I think it's time we came to some sort of understanding."

"I thought we had already done that."

"No, you did that." He stood there weaving a bit unsteadily looking at her with his blood shot eyes. She stood with her back to the lamp, her exquisite figure revealed by the light penetrating her sheer gown. "How long do you think you can put me off?" She picked up her dressing gown that she had just laid aside and held it in front of her. He smiled cunningly. "What are you hiding from?" He jerked her shield from her hands.

She glared at him in annoyance, but made no immediate reply, nor did she challenge him. Strangely she felt no anger. He was a pitiful sight, and he had come begging again. "I'm sorry," she said in a quiet, civil, tone, "What were you saying?"

He swallowed hard, and the small glow he felt became a leaping flame of desire. He tried to speak, but the words stuck in his throat.

"What's the matter?" she said seriously. "Are you sick?"

"Sick of doing without you," he managed.

"You don't need me. I'm certain that you find what you want at the Silver Buckle. That is where you spend your free time, isn't it?"

"You're what I want, all I've ever wanted." He reached for her and she pushed him away,

"You're drunk! You need a bath and a shave."

"Yes, I've had a few drinks, and I'm surprised that you noticed. But I'm not drunk."

"You stink. You've been with a whore. I can smell her cheap perfume on you."

"I love you."

"Go to bed."

"I'm not ready to go to bed!" he yelled.

"Hush, you'll wake the babies."

"Why should I care? I don't give a shit if your little Light Eyes bastard screams his head off. He's nothing to me."

"If you have something to say, then say it, but watch out what you say about my baby."

"It's the truth."

"That's right! Henry's not yours and I thank God for that. Now get out!"

"Don't send me away," he said on the verge of tears.

"I refuse to talk to you when you're drunk. Go to bed. We can talk tomorrow." His eyes narrowed, and then he laughed, an ugly sound that made her shudder.

"You're lying; you don't intend to talk to me." He took a step toward her. "You're still my wife."

"Oh, God! Are we back to that?" she said disgustedly.

He tried to embrace her and she caught hold of the bed post, straining away from him. He tugged her arms free and held both her hands tight. She bit him on the knuckles until she tasted blood. He pushed her backward across the bed and fell on top of her. She twisted and pushed at him, struggling to free herself until she was exhausted and crying, pinned beneath him. He was breathing hard; he too was weakened by their struggle. He tore her gown off and cried, "You can't hide yourself from me. You're my wife. I have the right to look at you."

"Get off me!"

"You're a little tiger. Are you forgetting that you need me? You can't explain that little half-breed without admitting you're a slut. Think about that."

"I told you never to touch me again."

"I forgot."

"You're an idiot!"

"I'm worse. I can stand anything but doing without you."

"You had better start getting used to the idea because it's over."

"No it's not."

"I swear I will never submit to you again as long as I live."

"You don't have to submit. As long as we're married I can take what I want."

"If it makes you feel like a man then go ahead," she dared him. "I would hate to think that you went to all this trouble for nothing." Go back to your whore. You're no better than she is. You're both filth."

He despised her for the humiliation she was causing him. Then in one swift motion he sprang to his feet and fled in a state of frustration and rage, cursing her under his breath.

For days there was a sense of smoldering resentment about the house, though Dawn and Ned scarcely spoke. The situation between them seemed to engulf the entire household. Dawn tried to put Light Eyes out of her mind, for she imagined that some mysterious element had erased her from his. She wondered if he would come back if she should make herself available to him.

Ned did not make anymore demands as her husband. He had sealed his own fate by letting his jealousy take control of his senses. He was continuously filled with tension and worry, waking in the dead of night sweat-drenched and frightened, his mind clogged with memories of Dawn's sweet, tantalizing, body, and sobbed broken heartedly into his pillow. Although they shared the same house, they were indeed separated, yet Ned preferred anything to divorce. Although the word was never spoken by either of them, the threat hung there between them. His worst nightmare was his fear of losing her.

Dawn had become so absorbed in baby Henry and the new house that she had no time for outside interests, while Ned, suffering pains of loneliness, became more depressed by the day, yet determined to live in the hell of his own making. Many times the empty silence of night would drive him from his bed and he would go downstairs for a shot of whiskey to settle his nerves. On one such occasion, he opened the door to the drawing room and was surprised to find Debbie there, seated in her favorite chair with a book open in her lap. He stood for a moment trying to decided if he should join her or retreat to his room.

She looked up, saw him in the open door staring at her and said sweetly, "Come in," without waiting for him to decide. "Can't you sleep either?" He moved silently to stand beside her chair, clad in a pair of faded pants, his chest bare. Debbie felt a wave of excitement, admitting to herself that Ned was a fine looking man. He was tall with a hard lean body, nice features and a mop of sandy brown hair that needed combing at the moment.

"Thanks," he said, his voice catching in his throat. "I didn't realize you had trouble sleeping."

"I just felt like reading. Is Dawn asleep?" she said, unable to think of anything else to say.

"How should I know? I can't get as close to her as I can that Indian squaw, or haven't you noticed?"

"I suppose that just about ever one realizes you two are having trouble. I try to stay clear of family affairs. I don't consider it any of my business."

"Have you taken sides?"

"I don't think about it."

"You once told me that you and Dawn have no secrets. What's the matter, doesn't she trust you anymore?"

"Of course she does."

Then tell me, "what does she intend to do about me?"

"What do you mean?"

"It's not like you to hedge. She has turned me out to pasture like an old broken down horse, only I'm still a colt. But she forgot to put blinders on me, and every time I see a pretty little filly like you I get fence jumping on my mind."

"You must not say things like that." She was recalling the last time she was alone with him, and her thoughts made her feel uneasy.

"I'm not drunk this time, so you don't have to worry about what I might do."

For a moment she was silent, thinking about what he had just said. "I wish you wouldn't talk in riddles. You confuse me."

"I'm not trying to confuse you. All I mean is that I won't ever do anything that you don't want me to do."

She stared at him perplexed. "Do you think I want you to make advances to me?"

"Don't you?" His eyes were steady, searching her countenance.

"You must be drunk." She stared at her hands clutching the book so tightly that the pages cut into her palms.

"I know what I see in your eyes."

"You see nothing in my eyes."

"Is that what you want me to believe? That you feel nothing for me?" He waited for her to deny it, but she denied nothing.

"This is wrong. You should not be saying these things to me and I should not be listening."

"Why?"

"You have a wife."

"In name only."

"Dawn is my friend."

"Friends share."

"I can't allow you to speak about her this way."

"I never realized that you preferred lies to the truth."

"I don't, but I'm not sure you know the real truth about your feelings, or hers."

"I know she locks me out of her bedroom at night, and that is a fact. I don't want to be locked out of her bedroom, and that's another fact."

"I don't want to hear about your relations with your wife."

"I'm not talking about our relations; I'm talking about our lack of relations."

"It's all the same."

He laughed. "It's exactly the opposite and you know it."

She rose quickly from her chair, and clutching the book to her breast, excused herself. "I'm really very tired. I'm going to bed."

He took a step toward her and heard the quick catch of her breath before she moved away.

"Don't turn away from me."

"I must." She hurried from the room.

He watched her disappear, thinking how he had never really noticed how pretty she was, or how much he wanted to be near her, to be comforted by her soft arms and pale lips. He imagined that beneath her uneasiness and hesitation, she was as desperate for love as he was.

CHAPTER

21

Ned found it more and more difficult to smother his emotions where Dawn was concerned. He was miserable. The mounting tension between them had become so violent that he began to wonder if he would endure. He remained at her beck and call, but she wanted no part of him. He felt like a dog straining at the end of a short leash. He could look, but not touch. He was no more than a hired hand, ignored and taken for granted. Debbie was the only one who showed him any kindness or understanding. She was not taking sides; she was merely treating him as an equal. He watched her closely, hoping she might show him some indication of caring for him beyond simple friendship. He was reluctant to express his feelings, although he sensed that she shared his discontentment. He became tremulous when he thought about being alone with her.

It had taken much courage for him to follow her into the kitchen early one morning before Dawn was awake. He meant to confirm what he suspected she felt for him. He was conscious of his inner trembling and the sickening roll-over of his stomach, but he was determined. He took both her hands in his, and she did not pull away, though her face became blanched.

"What if Dawn should see us?"

"She's asleep," he said, trying to reassure her.

"She would misunderstand."

"Misunderstand what?"

"Our relationship."

"What is our relationship, Debbie?"

"You know we're only friends."

"Is that all you feel for me?"

"It's all I allow myself to feel. Dawn is my best friend, and your wife. There can never be more between us."

"How can you call her a wife? You're not blind. You know what the score is."

She withdrew her hands and pressed her fingers to his lips to restrain his words, looking up at him with pleading eyes. "You must not talk about Dawn to me. She's your wife."

"I'm nothing more than a hired hand. Why should we hold back because of her when she doesn't care?"

"I care, and I will never do anything to cause either of us shame."

"I know you feel something for me. At least admit it." His eyes were sad and pleading. She remained silent but he saw a soft change in her expression. "I'm falling apart Debbie. I don't have anyone to live for. I need you to care—to love me."

"I can't take Dawn's place, no one ever will. You will always love her. She's hurting you and you're looking for solace. I'm sorry, I do care about you, but it can go no further." She turned away and hurried from the room.

Her admission made him happy, he felt flattered and not quite so lonely now. She had too many scruples to let herself go, and he was forced to hold back because of the consequences.

Dawn began to sense something between Debbie and Ned. Several times she caught them looking at one another in an interesting way. Secretly she hoped that her suspicions were fact. How much easier her life would be if Ned should find another interest and voluntarily let her go. Perhaps then she might be able to shake her guilt complex. She became so engrossed in her suspicions that she made a special trip into Courgat to discuss them with Darrell, who she considered her friend and ally.

He was pleased as always to see her, so happy in fact that he closed the trading post for one hour and took her to lunch at the hotel. "I need to talk to you," she said.

"I had hoped you just wanted to see me."

She smiled, "I'm always glad to see you."

"What is it you want to talk about?"

"I think something might be going on between Ned and Debbie."

Darrell shook his head in disbelief. "You're not serious?" He looked at her closely. "You are serious."

"I have never been more serious in my life."

"Well, I must say, you're taking it rather calmly."

"I hope they are deeply in love."

"What!"

"This may be the answer to my problems."

"Then you must consider your marriage on the rocks."

"I consider my marriage a joke."

He couldn't speak for a moment, his throat was full, and he coughed slightly to clear it. "You mean to say that you want a divorce bad enough to use your best friend as bait?"

"No," she said hurriedly. "Sweet little Debbie must be dying of guilt, being the way she is, so honest and morally clean. I would never do anything to hurt her. Don't you see? If they really do care for one another, Ned will welcome a divorce."

"I doubt that."

"It makes sense to me."

"No man in his right mind would give you up for a dozen like Debbie."

"And just what's wrong with Debbie?" she said indignantly. "She's far from beautiful, and too tame to suit me. I like my women full of fire."

"We're not discussing what you like or dislike, we're talking about Ned. What he needs is someone to mother and smother him. Debbie is just that type."

"You are so right."

"You asked me once if I needed a friend. Does that offer still stand?"

"Absolutely."

"Will you do me a favor?"

"Just ask."

"I want you to court Debbie."

"Wait just a minute. I said I would do you a favor, not mix in a sticky triangle."

"If she cares for Ned, she will reject you."

"And Ned can shoot me."

"Forget it. I'm sorry I asked." She got up to leave.

"Wait a minute," he said quickly. She sat back down. "Did you expect I would jump into this without giving it some thought? I'm no monkey on a string. What if I should get something going with her I don't want? What then?"

"Don't worry, we'll think of something."

"You mean you'll think of something. I'm afraid this isn't exactly my line. And another thing, you're overlooking one very important factor."

"What's that?"

"Your father."

"I fail to see how my father fits into this."

"It beats me how you can notice an attraction between Ned and Debbie and not notice the way Mac looks at her."

"You're kidding! He's old enough to be her father."

"And a very lonely man. My grandfather was twenty-seven years older than my grandmother, and they had a beautiful relationship."

"How many years was she a widow after your grandfather died of old age?"

Darrell looked a bit surprised, and then grinned. "I see what you mean."

Dawn shook her head in disgust. "Why is it we always get on the subject of my father? You have already pointed out that he's lonely and needs a wife, but I don't agree that he's interested in Debbie. The thought is disgusting, not to speak of disgraceful."

His eyes sparkled and he laughed in a low throaty tone. "Have you ever been in love?"

His question suddenly filled her with rage. "I'm married," she snapped.

"That doesn't answer my question. It's common knowledge as to the reason you married Ned Rowling, and it wasn't for money."

"You think you have it all figured out, and in so short a time. I suppose you think I'm a tramp."

"I think you are a very beautiful, exciting, desirable lady, and I would fight any man who said different."

"There are many things to be considered, things that are none of your business."

"I probably understand far more than you give me credit for. Such as the fact that you no longer share your husband's bed."

"How dare you bring that up?"

He smiled. "I'm right."

"If we weren't in a public place, I would slap your face."

"Don't let that stop you. You would be better off if you did. Are you aware of what the old bats in this town are saying about us? In case you haven't noticed, there have been raised eyebrows ever since we stepped through the door."

"Since you knew what to expect, why did you ask me to lunch?"

"For the same reason you accepted. We're two of a kind. I don't give a damned what people say."

"Are you aware of the repercussions?"

"You're referring to Ned of course."

"Yes. He will hear about this."

He was smiling. "I'm brave enough to ask you again."

"You're crazy."

"I'm in love, and that's most definitely a form of insanity. You didn't answer my question. Have you ever been in love?"

"Yes." Her answer sounded bitter.

"Yet you married Ned." He looked at her soberly for a moment, admiring everything about her. "You're quite a woman. I envy your mysterious lover, who is most likely the father of your child, I would imagine."

"Too much imagination can be unhealthy," she said dryly.

"Even between friends?"

She laughed in a chilling way. "How good a friend you are still remains to be seen."

"I'll do it, but for one reason."

"And what is that?"

"To be near you," he said, devilment dancing in his eyes. "It gives me a good excuse to get past Ned."

"You really don't care do you?"

"I care about you."

She sat very still, her eyes downcast, her cheeks flaming. When she raised her head, her eyes met his in a moment of naked surrender. "I don't want to hear this. I have been unhappy for a long time. I could be a great danger to you."

He trembled as her words unleashed a violent storm of emotions. "I cut my teeth on danger, and for a good cause, I welcome it."

She understood perfectly. "We had better go."

He came quickly around the table to take her arm. "You're right, we had better go. I wouldn't feel comfortable kissing you in front of all these people," he whispered.

"I wouldn't feel comfortable kissing you anyplace."

"You're a poor liar."

"You seem pretty sure of yourself."

"You should know."

She did not go back inside when they returned to the trading post, because he had been right, she did want to kiss him. Thinking about it caused a funny feeling in her stomach. They said good-bye on the hotel porch.

Dawn had not expected Darrell to call on Debbie so soon, and was surprised when he showed up the next evening.

His sudden appearance caused Debbie's eyes to widen in perplexity. She sensed there was something mysterious about his sudden interest, wondering if it was due to loneliness.

Ned pretended to be in perfect accord when Darrell asked Debbie if she cared to take a stroll with him in the moonlight. While Darrell and Dawn waited for her to refuse, she hesitated only a moment before accepting his invitation.

As they walked along, Darrell was only mildly aware of the woman by his side. Her friendly, wide eyed innocence reminded him of a child, and he felt deeply ashamed to be deceiving her in such a low way. He chose his words carefully, not wanting to give her the wrong impression, and yet that was exactly what Dawn expected him to do. He made it clear that he was only interested in her in a moderate way.

Three days in a row, Darrell came to supper, then he and Debbie would sit in the parlor talking quietly. If Mac was there, he would join them. His resentment was apparent to Darrell, although Debbie seemed not to notice. Mac managed to smile when Darrell looked in his direction, while underneath bloomed an unreasoning jealousy that caused his insides to crunch. He realized he was too old for Debbie, but suddenly that didn't matter anymore. He was in love with her, and had waited too long to admit it.

Things were not working out the way Dawn had planned. Had she misjudged Darrell? Was it possible that he was getting serious about Debbie? She began to resent Debbie, snapping at her for no apparent reason, other than jealousy.

Darrell was beginning to believe that Dawn's suspicions about Ned and Debbie was a figment of her imagination, because Debbie enjoyed his company very much, and gave no hint of wanting him to stop calling on her. This could go on forever he thought bitterly. The whole idea was getting out of hand. He was involved in a situation where there seemed no end, other than marriage. He had a gut feeling from the start that he was making a mistake when he agreed to such a ridiculous scheme.

He went over it in his mind, but could not come to a logical conclusion. If Debbie cared for Ned, why did she continue to see him? And how long would she continue to grace him with her company? On the other hand, why had Ned accepted his intrusion without so much as a challenge? And then there was always the chance that Debbie was clinging to him in desperation to get Ned out of her system, and if she succeeded, he would become hopelessly trapped.

He had not had one moment alone with Dawn since he started the ridiculous courtship with Debbie. She had made no attempt to speak with him, or to free him from his foolish predicament. She merely watched him suffer from her safety zone. He was beginning to feel betrayed. He decided to face the problem courageously, to bring the farce to a head, and then bow out as gracefully as possible.

The following Wednesday he deliberately skipped his standard dinner date with Debbie, figuring that so doing would get Dawn's attention. Thursday morning when she entered the trading post he greeted her triumphantly. There were several customers in the store at the time and he approached her as casually as he would any other customer. She browsed about for a while, waiting for his customers to make their purchase and leave, trying to ignore their disapproving expressions and whispers. When they were alone in the store at last, she asked abruptly, "Where were you last night?"

He grinned. "You sound like my mother, and since you aren't, I don't like it." His smile faded. "Nobody tells me what to do. Not even you."

Realizing she had antagonized him, she quickly made an attempt to restore her good standing with him. "I'm sorry. I don't mean to sound so bossy. It's just that I was depending on you last night, and you let me down."

"You're beginning to exercise undue authority. When I agreed to your scheme I didn't realize I might be expected to marry the woman."

"What are you saying? Surely you don't mean that she's becoming interested in you?"

"Does that seem so strange?"

"I didn't mean it that way. It's just that I'm so sure she's interested in Ned."

"I warned you that this might happen."

"Yes, you did," she said emphatically.

"You also said you would think of something. So start thinking because I want out of this mess, and soon!"

She began to pace the floor nervously, then suddenly stopped. "What is it she likes most about you?"

"How should I know, for God's sake? Maybe nothing."

"It's really simple. If you change your image, it will destroy the mental picture she has of you and she will lose interest."

"What if it's my good looks," he teased. "Would you suggest I let a horse drag me?"

"Will you be serious?"

"I am serious. You're the one playing games."

"What do you suggest I do?"

"Forget about Ned, Debbie, and everybody else. Go after what you want. To hell with all those weak, miserable excuses for human beings. Ned is a damned fool and a weakling. Why does he keep hanging on to you when he knows you hate his guts? You're more of a man than he is, and believe me, you're all woman."

"You make it sound so easy."

"It is. Walk away from it. Never postpone an unpleasant chore. It becomes harder to tackle with delay. Your reputation is shot to hell in

Courgat anyway. Give those vultures something to talk about that benefits you. Let 'um all go to hell. Come play with me."

Like a striking snake, her hand shot out and caught him full in the face. "Should I turn the other cheek? Or would you prefer I apologize like a gentleman?"

"You're no gentleman!"

"You would hold it against me if I was."

"Stop it!" she burst into angry tears, and suddenly she was in his arms, sobbing against his chest.

"I'm sorry; I never meant to hurt you. Don't cry, it will make your beautiful eyes red. Dry your tears while I lock up, then I'll take you over to the hotel for a drink. It will make us both feel better."

She looked up at him and he wiped the tears from her cheeks with his finger tips, then leaned down and brushed her lips with a quick kiss. "Are you game?"

"People will talk."

"They're already talking."

"Give me a few minutes to pull myself together."

He moved quickly to the front door, locked it, and pulled the shade down. "I'm all set," he said happily. "We can go out the back door as soon as you feel like facing the world. That way we don't have to face unwanted customers standing on the porch wanting in."

She suddenly realized that they were all alone for the first time and felt a spur of nervousness. "I'm all right now. We can go."

"Are you sure you want to?" he asked, and his eyes were asking another question. He saw the answer written on her face. She had become very pale and quiet, he could see the pulse throbbing in her throat. His eyes held hers, beholding a strange insistence in them as the tension began to build. With shaking hands he reached for her, pulling her against him, feeling an awkwardness he had never realized he possessed.

He was actually frightened, and wondered where his self-confidence was hiding. "See how easy it is," he whispered. "Let yourself go—trust me."

Dawn broke away in quick excitement. "Don't come near me!"

He ignored her plea, and pulled her roughly into his arms again.

"You don't mean that." This time she did not pull away but settled against him, pressing her body close, allowing him to kiss her, their lips fused together in flaming passion, and he moaned helplessly.

For an instant she lost control completely, tremors shaking her, and she was in her own mind remembering Light Eyes and the way she had felt when he kissed her. She was confused, wanting one man while on the verge of accepting another. She was weak and shaken, her body feeling his hardness, and tears came to her eyes. Suddenly she didn't want this man at all, but he was closest to the passion she had felt for the Indian.

Darrell was loosening the buttons on her dress, pulling up her skirt, his hands on her caressing her body while she trembled in his arms.

Their madness was extinguished by the sudden rattling of the front door. They quickly drew apart and began to arrange their clothes.

"Who the hell can that be?" Darrell barked disgustedly, trying to bring his breathing under control.

"Don't answer it," Dawn said nervously, afraid of being discovered in an unexplainable predicament, quickly doing up her buttons.

"I have no intentions of answering it. Come on, let's slip out the back door." Before they could make a move they heard a key in the lock, then the door opened and Mac strode into the room with a stricken expression.

He was shocked to find Dawn there with Darrell behind the locked door with the shade drawn. He quickly closed the door and locked it. "I hope you two can explain the meaning behind this."

Dawn met her father's accusing statement easily, without hesitation, and so seemingly innocent in manner, that no man could deny her explanation, one Darrell would never forget. "I'm so glad you're here," she said happily, "now you can take me for a drink at the hotel. I came by to see you and had to settle for Darrell. We were just about to leave by the back door."

"I would like nothing better, but from the looks of the sky we're in for some bad weather, and you need to be on your way home."

Dawn stepped to the back door and looked out at the rain clouds sweeping across the sky, dark and threatening. The bright day had suddenly turned gray with a chill in the air. She shook her head and sighed. "I guess you're right. I had better head for home before the rain catches me."

"I don't want you riding out alone in this weather, and I can't leave yet. Why don't you take her home, Darrell? I'll take over here while I wait for my appointment."

"My pleasure," he said, feeling happy and a little amused by the way things had turned out.

"Since Dawn is in her carriage, you can ride back to town on one of my horses. I'll pick it up tomorrow."

Dawn was startled by her own stupidity, and shivered when she realized what might have happened between her and Darrell if her father hadn't surprised them with his presence. And all the time her carriage was parked in front, big as life, with them locked inside with the shade down. She realized with sudden shock that it was conceivable that Mac knew exactly what was about to take place, and since he was sending them off together alone, maybe he wanted it to happen. Her face flamed with shame as she hurried toward her carriage.

Darrell handed her up then climbed in beside her and gathered up the reins. "I appreciate the way you talked us out of that predicament. You think fast. If I ever decide to rob a bank, will you be my accomplice?"

"Impossible, I would be robbing my own father. He has his account with the Courgat bank."

"I suppose you're right. Your father is the most important man in town. He knows a lot of people."

"It's not only the people he knows, he knows about the people, and I think he figured us out today."

"I have the same feeling. I wonder why he didn't slap me around or shoot me?"

"He likes you."

"Well enough to have me in the family," he said in a joking way. "He likes cats too," she answered, her forehead puckered in disapproval. "He even liked Ned at first."

"What made him change his mind?"

"It's hard to say, but I rather think it's because he hates Ned's mother, Martha, and the hostility finally covered Ned too."

"She's been in the store several times. She seems a little curt. I thought maybe it was just me, but if Mac dislikes her, I'm sure the fault lies with her. Mac is the sort of man who likes everyone."

"Almost everyone," she corrected him.

"Jack helps out at the store sometimes, he seems friendly."

"And will probably turn out to be another mama's boy."

They had gone about a mile when the sky was split open by a flash of lightning. In a matter of seconds the cold rain began. Dawn huddled close to Darrell for protection from the rain blowing inside through the front of the carriage. By the time they reached the ranch she was shivering and cold, wishing she had never left from home.

Ned was standing in the gloom of the large columned porch, his eyes fixed on the stormy sky. When Dawn ran up the steps, dripping wet, he gave her a hard look. "You sure picked a bad time to go shopping. Where are your packages?"

"There aren't any, The weather was fine when I left home this morning." She brushed past him and walked through the wide door into the entrance hall.

Darrell drove the carriage around the house to the barn and unharnessed the horse. He picked a horse for himself from Mac's saddle stock, led him into the barn out of the rain to saddle him. He was just tightening the cinch when he saw Debbie running through the rain with a shawl over her head and shoulders.

"Wait," she cried, coming into the barn. "Come inside and get into some dry clothes before you catch your death."

"I'll only get wet again."

"Maybe the rain will stop before then. Anyway you can take time for a cup of coffee."

"With an offer like that, how can I refuse?"

"I don't understand why Dawn didn't ask you in." She looked puzzled.

"I guess she was too wet and miserable to give me a second thought."

"She should be ashamed, and after you were nice enough to drive her home." She smiled sweetly and took his arm. Her gentle unselfishness touched something inside him, and he felt ashamed for the dirty trick he was playing on her. He was troubled, wondering how he could free himself from the situation without hurting this kind and caring woman.

He spent the next hour in front of the fireplace in a pair of Mac's pants and one of his shirts, sipping coffee and talking with Debbie, trying to find a way to end the strange scheme of deception without causing pain.

"You're a very charming person," he said sincerely.

"Thank you, you're very kind."

He studied her, the way she looked, so soft and pure, her expression reminded him of a small child, wide eyed and trusting. "I have never known anyone like you before."

"Do you mean that as a compliment?" she teased.

"Yes, and with deep respect. Can we speak frankly? What I mean to say is—you won't be offended will you?"

"Not in the least," she said cheerfully.

He leaned toward her slightly, looking across the small table that separated their chairs. "What do you think of Ned?"

"What?" She forgot to breathe for a moment. "I'm very fond of him." She was nervously brushing at a loose wisp of hair and could not meet his eyes.

He hesitated, then continued. "I guess you probably think I'm a little strange for asking you a thing like that. I learned a long time ago, if you want to know the answer to a question, you first have to ask it."

"I agree with you."

"What do you think of me?"

"I think you're a very nice person."

"But you're not particularly fond of me, are you?"

"I—I like you," she stammered.

"Come on! We can level with each other? We're friends, aren't we?"

"Yes, of course. What are you driving at?"

"Are you in love with Ned Rowling?" There it was, it was said, he had put all his cards on the table. He watched her expression turn from shock to loathing.

"How dare you speak to me like this."

"I'm sorry, I thought the best way to ask a question was with honesty."

"Do you honestly think that I could be in love with the husband of my best friend?"

"I don't know why not. I've heard of worse things. Anyway we both know their marriage is on the rocks. It's never been more than a shell."

"How do you know?"

"Dawn and I are very close. She told me."

"I understand now."

"I'm glad."

"The state of their marriage does not change the facts. Dawn is Ned's wife and he is her husband—a holy estate."

"No, it's a disaster. If they can't love one another, then they need to be set free to find the person they can love. And if you're in love with Ned, I would be the last to know, isn't that right?"

"Maybe if I knew what business it is of yours, I might answer that question." There was a trace of bitterness in her voice.

"I asked for that." He admired her courage for standing up to him. He got up, walked around the table, and stood in front of her. He looked into her eyes and she stared back at him inquisitively. He took her hands and pulled her to her feet and held her against him. "Are you in love with Ned Rowling? When she didn't answer, he kissed her. She responded at first, then suddenly stiffened and pushed him away.

"I'm sorry. Have I offended you?"

"I have known you long enough that I should not be offended by your kiss. It is your question that offends me."

"Because it is a question you refuse to answer truthfully, and so you refuse to answer it at all?"

"Yes," she said quietly, turning away from him. "I'm ashamed to admit the truth even to myself."

"I know the answer now. You wouldn't have pushed Ned away. I hope we can still be friends."

"I would like that. I understand why you needed to know how I feel about Ned. I don't blame you for not wanting to waste your time on me."

"Being near you is a joy, even if you are in love with another man. You are the most understanding woman I have ever known. Don't ever change. There are so few like you."

"Be careful, Darrell. I'm in love with Ned, but Ned is in love with his wife. He cares for me as much as he will ever care for another woman, but his heart will belong to Dawn as long as he lives."

"How long have you known?"

"Since the first time I saw you look at her."

Darrell rode back to town that night after the rain stopped, feeling much lighter and happier, minus the burden of responsibility that he had been carrying for weeks. Dawn had been right in her suspicions, and he hoped things would work out for all of them. There was still one very important question that plagued him: the name of the man Dawn was in love with, her son's father. He had considered every man in town, and came up empty handed. It would take one hell of a man to satisfy a woman like Dawn. He wondered if perhaps the man had died. One day he would find the answer. He couldn't rest until he did.

CHAPTER

22

The west was giving way to growing pains under the stress of lawlessness and bloodshed. The frontier was becoming more and more unsettled as gunslingers and double-dealing opportunist moved in on every town in the territory, causing much conflict between the settlers and the lawless. Courgat was certainly no exception. Sheriff Charles Morgan was getting on in years and becoming slow and inadequate in keeping law and order in the fast growing town, finally forcing him to hire a deputy to help him keep the peace. As a result of this, Morgan had begun to realize that his job was a desperate and hard way to make a living and becoming more dangerous by the day. As violence spread like a lowland flood, and after due consideration, he asked the town council to replace him, explaining to them that he was getting too old for the job and his eye sight was fast failing him. A notice was quickly posted at the town hall asking for volunteers for his job, but it failed to rouse any interested parties. Courgat was in trouble. Morgan had given them thirty days to replace him. Unless the right man stepped forward to accept the position, Courgat would be at the mercy of every trigger happy saddle tramp and drover in the State. Since Courgat was a hundred miles from the nearest army post, it had become the playground of every saddle sore cowpuncher who happened to be driving a herd through.

According to the code of Western chivalry, Mac had proven himself a friend, not only to his neighbors, but also the Indians. He was known as a man who could take it as well as dish it out; however, when he was offered the job of sheriff he flatly refused. He knew his limitations; he was sure he was not the right man for the job, a job that required a man of considerable reputation as a gunfighter, maybe even a publicity seeking gunslinger. But at any rate, it was not the kind of job for a common man.

When the town council called an emergency meeting, the hall was crowded with concerned citizens. Mac, a member of the council, sat among them listening to the false assurances made by the Mayor, Alvin Biglo. He spoke in his usual whiny voice, "I must say, I certainly expected a man to step forward before now and accept the job of sheriff.

But have no fear, I'm sure that Charles Morgan's fine example as a lawman will insight each man here tonight to search his own conscious until someone steps forward."

Mac stood up and moved to the podium where he spoke in an enlightening tone, if not a spiteful one. "I consider this to be a fitting time to bring to mind a few of the negative aspects concerning the job of sheriff that Biglo neglected to mention, and the reasons no one has rushed to accept it." He moved out from behind the lectern and stood with his feet wide apart, looking into the faces of the crowd. "First of all, justice is not the responsibility of one man, or a few men, but must be shouldered by every individual in this room. We are all aware of the changing conditions. Our town has had a taste of lawlessness, but keep this in mind, what we have seen taking place here so far is mild to what it will be later. You can bank on it getting much worse, to the point a woman won't be safe walking down the street. No sooner will one outlaw's career end, before another takes his place. The survivors of one gang will join forces with another. The six shooter will rule the land, and the law is only as good as the man behind the gun. I've watched Charles Morgan work every day since I came to Courgat, and he's a fine peace officer, but like us all, age begins to creep up on us and we start to slow down. So we may as well face the facts, we need a younger man, a more alert and fast hand for the job, and there's not a man among us who qualifies. Some of you asked me to take the job, and I don't mind telling you, I wouldn't be much protection against a bunch of gun-happy fools out to make a reputation for themselves. I'm no fast gun. I wouldn't last three days, if I lasted that long. I can't draw fast, although I can shoot straight, but I'd be cut down before I got my gun out of my holster."

The crowd was silent and troubled; Mac's words had roused their fear.

"That's a mighty pretty speech, McCloud," Biglo said, "but it still don't answer the question as to what we do for a sheriff."

"I think it does, at least we can agree on one thing, the man we need will have to come from some place other than Courgat. What we need is a man with plenty of guts, a fast gun hand, and a reputation."

"Now maybe you can tell us where we can get such a man," said Biglo."

"He'll come through here one of these days and kill somebody. When this happens, we had better make him a good offer to stay on as sheriff." Mac's suggestion evoked many angry voices, and several men came to their feet in protest.

"You're crazy!" one man yelled.

"Yeah!" another voice agreed. "How will hiring some killer off the street to run our town protect us?"

Mac held up his hand to quiet the excited crowd. "Hold on a minute and use a little common sense to reason this thing out. Have you ever heard of fighting fire with fire? Maybe you think some Sunday school teacher can keep law and order here in Courgat. When a parade of drunken gunslingers start shooting up your town, making themselves both judge and executioner, picking who dies and who doesn't, what do you intend doing then? Do you think you can walk up to one of 'um and ask him real polite like to put his gun away? Hell no! I'll tell you what you'll have to do. Somebody is gonna have to face these gunslingers with a gun, not empty words. Some of you men don't seem to know the difference between a gunfighter and a killer."

"And you think one will just happen by?" Biglo said with a smirk. "It's not likely."

"Sooner or later—yes."

"What do we do in the meantime?"

"We don't have a choice. We continue the way we have been, only with the help of every man in Courgat. You would be surprised how much persuasion a few men with shotguns carry. Morgan will stay in office to make our action legal."

"Morgan is quitting next week," Biglo said.

"I can see that you don't know Charles Morgan the way I do. He won't walk out in the middle of a crisis. He has to live here too. After twenty five years, I feel certain that he will stay a little longer. How about it, Charles?" Mac said in a loud voice.

Charley rose to his feet and turned to face the people. "I ain't never been no quitter and I don't reckon I'll start now."

After the meeting was adjourned, the town seemed a little more at ease with the present situation, knowing that a solution was at least possible.

When daylight came the following morning, Morgan, who had been up most of the night keeping watch over the town, walked into the hotel for breakfast leaving his three deputies in charge of the jail. Before he had finished his second cup of coffee George Haslet, a rider from Burell, a town about twenty miles west of Courgat, came rushing into the hotel looking for Morgan. He had been riding all night and was on the verge of collapse when he dropped into the chair across the table from the sheriff and related his reason for being there.

"We got bad trouble in Burell," he cried excitedly. "Buck Femmer took over the town yesterday. He killed the sheriff in a shoot out and wounded seven more men. There ain't a man in town who will stand up to him. They're all scared to death. Buck and his gang is hole up at the Bull Horn Saloon making plans to rob the bank here. They tried to stop me from warning you and chased me for a long ways before they give up. I pert near rode my horse to death."

"How do you know what they plan to do?" Morgan said.

"Oh, they was bragging and laughing about it."

"Do you know when they plan to hit us?"

"No, I never heard 'um say that, but I think soon. They got all they want from our town."

"Since we may not have much time, I reckon we better get started making plans to stop 'um. You did good, boy. You eat you some breakfast and rest." He patted him on the back, got up, and left his breakfast untouched.

The name Buck Femmer was a name well known and dreaded by every peace officer in New Mexico. Now he was destined to terrorize Texas. His move into Texas was not altogether voluntary. He had robbed and killed so many people in New Mexico that his face was plastered on wanted posters all over the state. He was afraid to walk down the street for fear of being shot in the back by someone itching to put an end to his overwhelming success. He had even heard that women were gunning for him, carrying guns stuck in their garters. So far he had killed just about everything but a woman. He raped them.

Even though he had, quite by accident, made a name for himself by out-drawing Cliff Day, one of the fastest guns in the territory, he had succeeded in making himself famous. He was referred to as "The man who brought Day down." At the time of the shoot-out, Buck was drunk and had no idea who he was going up against, nor did he really care. Had he known he would have turned tail and run. His quick draw even surprised him, because he had never been in a position to test it. Every jealous gunman in the state came looking for him, eager to prove they were faster. He was still top gun. His famous encounters with one gunslinger after another finally went to his head. Thinking he could never be outdrawn, he started a life of crime, killing just to watch men die.

He had plagued the territory for several years, robbing killing, and bragging. His pistol grips were notched with many credits, and it had been said that no man would ever get the drop on him.

When Sheriff Morgan learned that he had a dozen men riding with him, he knew he had big trouble. He was astounded by Buck's audacity to approach within thirty miles of the new army post to rob their bank. Morgan immediately sent Glenn Allen, one of his deputies, to Fort Daily with an urgent message requesting help, hoping they would be able to hold out in the meantime.

"Ride that mount into the ground if you have to, just get that message to Captain Rush as quick as possible," Morgan ordered.

Glenn picked a good horse, saddled him, and was on his way in less than thirty minutes from the time word reached them. He had ridden about a mile when he realized he was being pursued.

Robbery had become an art to Buck. He enjoyed his work and went about it in a business manner. He had been successful because he figured in advance the best way to get a job done. He also figured all the angles of what might go wrong. He knew that the man from Burell had hightailed it to Courgat to warn them, and he was also aware that the army post was less than a day's ride away. The rider had made it to Courgat to sound the alarm, and he knew the sheriff in Courgat would immediately send a rider to the army post requesting their help. They would reach Courgat about an hour behind the rider from Burell, and they had to intercept the Courgat rider before he reached the army post.

However Buck had overlooked one very important fact, and he cursed himself. Their horses would be tired from the journey between Burell and Courgat, and the rider coming out of Courgat would be on a fresh mount. They spotted the rider and raced their horses to over take him, but he drew out away from them further and further. Suddenly going down a steep hill the deputy's horse stumbled and fell, throwing Glenn end over end clear to the bottom. He picked himself up, torn and bleeding, recovered his horse, remounted and dashed on. His mishap had given Buck and his boys the time they needed to put him within rifle range. One of the slugs hit his steed in the neck and he buckled beneath him and went down. Glenn jumped clear and took off on foot like a scared rabbit. They continued after him, firing as they rode. Two bullets pierced his body and he fell face down in the dirt, blood spreading over the back of his faded shirt. He groaned once then lay still as his pursuers rode over his body trampling him before they turned their horses in the direction of Courgat. They had nipped in the bud the move that could have caused them to be apprehended or killed.

Sheriff Morgan knew he had very little time to make defense plans, and he was disgusted to find that most of the men in town were afraid to stand up to Buck and his gang. They had rather give the town to him as opposed to a gun fight.

By three o'clock in the afternoon the few volunteers had gathered at the jail awaiting instructions. The town was in hiding, cowering behind locked doors and drawn shades.

Morgan knew he could depend on the four men he had just pinned badges on: Mac McCloud, Darrell Holliman, Frost Jackson, and Robert James, his deputy, who had all stepped forward, laying their lives on the line.

Buck waited until almost sundown to ride into Courgat. He had been camped just outside town watching the trail in all directions, making sure they had sent only one rider to the fort. No one else had ridden either in or out of town. He had Courgat isolated. He could take his time.

Sheriff Morgan and his men were armed and waiting when Buck and his gang rode slowly down the main street. "That's far enough, Buck!" Morgan said, stepping into the middle of the street. "We know why you're here, and we don't aim for you to stay. Now turn them horses around and head out the way you came in."

"Now Sheriff," Buck drawled, "that ain't very friendly talk. We been on the trail a long time. The least you can do is let me and my boys have a drink at the saloon."

"I know you didn't ride in here for a drink. We don't want your kind of trouble, so you better leave before it starts."

"Did you hear that, boys?" Buck sneered. "We ain't welcome in this here town. Ain't that big talk coming from an old fat fart?"

"It ain't just talk," Morgan said. "We aim to back it up."

"We come to town to stay a while, and that's just what we aim on doing. If you don't get your fat ass off the street, we're fix'n to ride through you or over you. Don't matter."

Morgan looked at Buck hard and long, then raised his left hand and made a motion to his deputies, while pointing his shotgun at Buck's barrel chest. His four deputies stepped out into the open armed with scatter guns that were aimed at the thirteen mounted men. Morgan grinned stiffly. "Don't see no way we can hardly miss, and we're aiming for your eyes. A face full of buckshot will damned sure spoil your aim. We'll die if need be, cause we aim to stop you." Morgan held his ground without so much as the flicker of an eyelash, waiting for Buck to make his move.

Buck reached for his gun, but half way there his hand froze in midair, then he reluctantly relaxed. "You win for now, Morgan," Buck shouted furiously. He wrenched his horse around, waved to his men, and they rode out of town as leisurely as they had ridden in. Morgan watched after them as the swirl of dust raised by the many hooves faded from sight.

"They'll be back," Darrell said, joining Morgan in the street.

"Yeah, I expect they will."

"We should have blasted them while we had the chance. They won't give us another one."

"Sounds like you might know something I should."

"Just common-sense. Buck won't make the same mistake twice. The next time you look down a barrel, he'll be the one holding it."

Under cover of darkness, Buck's men slipped back into town one at a time on foot, figuring that a single man on foot would be hardly noticeable. When the last man was in position, Buck gathered up the reins of the twelve horses, and trailing them on lead ropes, moved them quietly into position at the edge of town.

Morgan and his deputies were making ready to defend their town a second time. Morgan was surprisingly cool as he waited in the street for Buck's return. Mac was backing him up from behind the saloon doors. Darrell and Frost were stationed on the roof of the bank located across the street from the saloon. Robert James was hanging out a second story window above the saloon. Morgan had placed them in positions to catch Buck and his men in a cross fire.

All their attention was suddenly focused on the sound of thundering hooves moving steadily toward town. Buck had turned the horses loose to stampede down the dark street, kicking up clods, clearing a path. Morgan, in a disconcerted rage, fired blindly into the running horses, dropping several in whinnying pain.

By the time Morgan realized the horses were minus riders, it was already too late to stop Buck's attack. A sudden volley of rifle shots rang out and they took cover. Robert James cried out in pain and plunged headlong out the upstairs window above the saloon and fell with a puff of dust in the street below. For a moment Morgan and his deputies were in complete confusion. Buck's men were all over town and had them covered from every angle. Slugs were coming at them from out of the darkness, and they couldn't find a target to return their fire.

"Hold your fire, Morgan," Buck yelled, "unless you're ready to die. We got your town surrounded. You're all sewed up."

"You're bluffing," Morgan yelled back.

"Then why don't you try us, old man?"

Morgan knew he was telling the truth and called out to his men. "Hold your fire. They got us!" His pulse raced with anger and insult at the thought of being taken. He knew his men were no match for Buck and his blood thirsty killers. They were on the outside protected by darkness with their sights trained on his deputies, and would not hesitate to shoot.

Morgan allowed himself and his men to be disarmed without a fight, and were ushered into the saloon at gunpoint.

Within minutes Buck had his gang organized; they obeyed him without question. To disobey would mean quick death. It was no secret that he had killed a few of his own men when they rubbed him the wrong way.

He stationed five of his men at different vantage points around town, giving them orders to shoot anyone who so much as poked their head out a window, The town was isolated by two men posted at either end of the street to make sure no one came or went. Buck and the other three men stood guard over Morgan and his deputies.

"I got a man wounded out there. Let me go out and bring him in," Morgan pleaded.

Buck clacked his tongue and poured himself another shot of whiskey. "Now, ain't that just too bad. You went and got one of your boys all shot up."

"If you won't let the doctor treat him, at least let me pick him up out of the street."

"Sure thing," Buck said. "I'll see to it that he's taken care of. Hey, Otto!"

Otto downed a shot of whiskey, then swaggered over to Buck. "Yeah, Boss," he said in an odd way, pulling his lips back over his teeth so that he looked as if he only had a bottom lip.

"Go out there and take care of that wounded man."

"Oh, I'll do that. I love to play doctor," he said through a wet belch, smiling in the same one lipped way.

"Tell Otto to take him to the doctor," Mac said.

"Now we don't want to hurt Otto's feelings by telling him every move to make. He might get the idea that you don't really trust him."

"When I get through fixing him up he won't need no doctor," Otto said. He reached down with his gun hand and lifted his gun an inch, letting it back down into his holster very lightly.

"Wait a minute," Darrell yelled. "You can't turn that lunatic loose on a helpless man!"

Otto spun around to glare at Darrell, his smile gone from his one lipped face. "I don't take that kind of talk off nobody." With one quick sweep of his hand, he drew his gun and held it under Darrell's nose.

"Hold on, Otto," Buck said sharply. "I still give the orders here and I'll tell you when I'm ready to have a man shot."

For a moment it looked as if Otto might pull the trigger anyway. Then he cackled like a laying hen and dropped his gun back into his holster. He walked out through the swinging doors still laughing, his pleasure a brazen outrage. He stopped laughing when he stumbled over Robert James' bleeding body a few feet from the saloon doors. James cried out in pain.

"Does it hurt?" Otto said, bending over him.

"It's my arm," he cried, "I think it's near shot off. Help me, please."

"Which one is it?"

"My left."

"You men this one?" Otto drew back his foot and kicked the spot James indicated.

"Oh!" screamed the wounded wretch. "My, God! Have pity."

"I'm not your god, and I ain't got no pity."

"Help me, I'm bleeding to death." James was rolling around in agony, sobbing.

"Sure I'll help you." Otto drew his gun and cocked the hammer.

"Now you be still, or you'll spoil my aim."

James' eyes were glazed with fear. "No!" he screamed.

"Please, don't kill me. I don't want to die. No! Stop!"

When the shot split the silence the men inside the saloon knew what had taken place. Buck looked at Morgan, gloating. "Otto just cured your wounded deputy. Ain't that nice of him?"

"You're all yellow," Darrell yelled, coming to his feet. "Why don't you stand up to a healthy man instead of one who can't defend himself? You have some real brave men riding with you, Buck. Without their guns their spineless. You're all just a bunch of wild animals."

Buck looked at him in surprise, shocked in fact, and then he grinned. "Maybe you think you can tame me, big man."

"Fat chance. You bunch of cowards won't give me a gun." Buck threw his head back and roared with laughter. Then raised his glass to Darrell. "I toast a dead man."

"Are you plum out of your mind, Holliman?" Morgan said. "That blood thirsty bastard will blow your head off."

"Maybe."

"No damned maybe about it." Mac said. " He ain't exactly a cull you know."

"There is always somebody just a little better than what's thought to be the best."

Mac was thinking how different Darrell seemed. He saw a glimmer of madness in his eyes. He was actually taunting Buck. He had thrown caution to the wind and there was only one way Buck would go. He would kill him.

Buck stood up, his eyes traveling about the room. "You are a sorry looking lot, ain't got much to say either. But I guess this smart aleck has said enough for all of you." He jerked his thumb toward Darrell. "So you want to slap leather with me? That right?"

"I'm not crazy, Buck."

"You got a mean mouth." He looked at Darrell, scratching his head thoughtfully. "Now let me see—I better allow you some odds, after all, I believe in fair play. Ask my boys, they'll tell you." His eyes glittered as he spoke, and a cruel smile pulled at the corners of his mouth. "I have it. Just to be sportsmanlike, tell you what I'll do. I'll let you have a gun." He roared with laughter again. "Who knows? I might even let you load it."

"You're a damned comic," Darrell said furiously. He barely got the words out before Buck hit him a severe blow in his face. Darrell sprang at Buck swinging, punching him hard below the belt. Buck doubled over moaning, then sank to his knees. Instantly two of Buck's men grabbed Darrell and twisted his arms behind his back while the third man hit him over and over until he slumped unconscious, and they let him fall.

"When he comes to," Buck raved, his voice unsteady, "I'm going to kill him. I want him awake to enjoy it." For a moment he hesitated, looking down at Darrell's prone figure, and then turned his attention to Morgan. "Now suppose you tell me where I can find the banker."

"I'm not telling you a damned thing."

Turning to Frost, Buck said sharply, "Where does the banker live?"

"Go to Hell!" Frost shot back.

"Oh, another one." Buck drew his revolver and cocked it. He held it against Frost's temple. "Now, maybe you will have something nice to say, because if you don't, I'm going to blow your stinking head off, and I won't stop there. I'll kill every man in this room."

Frost tossed his head scornfully, his eyes blazing. "The big white house on the corner."

"Go fetch him Otto, and you better fetch his wife too, just in case he needs a little persuasion."

Otto returned with the banker, Lawrence Williams, and his wife, Florence.

"Well look at you," Buck said playfully. "You look like a banker, fat and soft. Leroy is gonna keep your pretty little wife company while we take a stroll over to the bank and I make a withdrawal."

Florence, overcome with panic, threw her arms around her husband and sobbed. Leroy grabbed her by the arm in an attempt to break her hold, and she screamed and kicked at him, calling him a nasty string of names. When Leroy slapped her Lawrence lunged at him, and Buck hit him with his pistol barrel. Lawrence stayed on his feet, blood pouring down the side of his face.

"Let my wife go and I'll do anything you ask."

"You'll do as I say or I'll shoot the bitch. Now you tell her to behave herself if she wants to keep on breathing."

Florence realized what she had to do. She shut her mouth, watching in terror as Buck pushed her husband ahead of him out the swinging doors, leaving them slapping. As soon as they disappeared, she began to scream hysterically.

"Shut up, old woman," Leroy ordered and hit her in the mouth. She buried her face in her hands, her shoulders shaking violently, but she made not a sound.

Morgan wanted to help her, and he was moved to do so, but the risk was too great. She was not the only one involved. A stirring sound overhead brought the three outlaws to quick attention. Otto's eyes roved about the room, then he headed for the stairs. "Better take a look. You and Gabe keep an eye on these brave deputies."

Otto drew his gun and slowly made his way up the stairs. Moments later came the sound of a door slamming and the shrill voice of a woman.

"Sounds like Marcy," Frost said.

Darrell began to regain awareness. He opened his eyes slowly, trying them out. He felt his stomach roll-over as he raised himself on one elbow.

"Did you have a nice nap, Deputy?" Leroy grinned. "Buck aims to put you back to sleep permanently."

"Why wait for Buck? Why don't you do it?" Darrell said.

"Good God! Holliman!" Morgan barked. "Are you itching to die? What the hell is wrong with you?"

"I'm a little dizzy," he answered.

"You're a little crazy. Settle down."

"Leroy wants to shoot me, but he don't have the nerve."

"Oh I got the nerve and I'd like nothing better, but Buck wants the pleasure."

"I'll make it easy for you." Darrell turned his back to Leroy. "I had rather look down a toilet hole than your face. You're too damned ugly, gutless, and stupid."

"God, damn it!" Morgan swore.

"Shit!" Frost said. "That beating he took warped his brain."

"Leroy," Darrell said, "you got a face like a horse's ass turned wrong side out. Have you got feet or hooves?"

"Turn around!" Leroy stormed. "Don't you turn your back on me."

"Kill him!" Gabe said.

"Turn around!" Leroy shouted again.

"You can't tell me what to do. Buck gives the orders." Darrell reminded him. "You're just a little pissant."

"I'm saying for you to turn around. Now, turn around!"

"You turn me around, big shot. Come on, I got nothing to lose."

Leroy walked over to Darrell, not really knowing his own intentions, and Buck wasn't there to tell him what to do. He put his hand on Darrell's shoulder. "Turn around!" he screamed.

"You're going to have to kill me, Leroy, because I'm going to do my best to take your gun away from you."

"I'll kill him for you," Gabe said.

"No, you ain't."

Gabe stepped back in confusion, his hand hovering over his .45, waiting for Leroy to make his move, whatever that might be. He was lost himself. Buck was the boss, and he was afraid of him.

Leroy let his hand drop from Darrell's shoulder. "Turn him around, Gabe," Leroy shouted. "I ain't taking anymore of his insults."

CHAPTER

23

Morgan was aware of the dangerous game Darrell was playing. While Buck was occupied at the bank, he seized the opportunity to rile his boys because they were afraid to make a move without Buck's permission. They weren't very smart either, and that was the reason they took orders like obedient children.

"Holliman's going to get us killed!" Frost bellowed. "Shut up!" Morgan grated. "He knows what he's doing."

"He's got a lot of nerve," Mac said. "I'll give him that. He took a hell of a beating to rile 'um. It's a wonder they didn't kill him."

"They will before they ride out of here," Morgan assured him. "He's a dead man as soon as Buck gets back, and that goes for the rest of us. He ain't got a damned thing to lose. This is the only chance we have to stay alive. If Gabe makes a move toward Darrell, and drops his guard for a split second, I'm going to jump him. Darrell will take care of Leroy. You watch them stairs for Otto, Frost, and you back him up, Mac."

"I'm ready," Frost said.

Leroy continued to scream in exasperation. "I said, turn him around!"

"I got my hands full," Gabe said. "You turn him around yourself, or else wait for Buck."

"Otto!" Leroy shouted impatiently. "Come down here!"

Otto was busy with the woman and paid him no mind. He was lying naked in one of the upstairs rooms taking his time with Marcy, and he wasn't finished yet. It had been a while since he had a woman, and he didn't have to hurry, this one was free.

"What's the matter, Leroy?" Darrell taunted. "What are you afraid of? You're a yellow coward, even with a gun in your hand." Darrell heard Leroy's breathing pick up, anger fluttering in his lungs. His hard shell was finally ready to crack. And now the hard part, he thought.

Infuriated to the point of insensibility, his fear of Buck had slipped his mind for one depraved moment. He grabbed Darrell and spun him around, determined to kill him. In the space of a heartbeat, Darrell's hand closed on Leroy's wrist, challenging him for control of the gun.

Shocked by what was happening, Gabe turned his attention to the struggling men, leaving himself wide open. Morgan grabbed the chair he had been sitting in and hit Gabe in the back of the head. Gabe pulled the trigger on his cocked gun as he went down; the shot went wild. Morgan picked Gabe up, and holding him over his head in a fit of insane rage, threw him down on the floor with such force that his back was broken.

A sickening flush of pain claimed Gabe's body and he screamed in shock, nerves worming in his face, his legs jerking. He quivered a few seconds as he was dying.

Frost jerked up the gun that tumbled from Gabe's hand and fired at Otto as he came bounding shirtless down the stairs. A stricken look flashed across his face. He reeled forward, going down the stairs making contact with each step, clutching for his pistol. Before he stopped rolling, Frost fired another slug into him. He died with his eyes wide open.

The struggle between Darrell and Leroy ended with Darrell holding the outlaws own gun under his nose. Leroy's arms moved up until they were high above his head.

"Now, you turn around!" Darrell barked, shoving him face first against the wall. Mac pointed to a bulge under his shirt.

"He's got another gun." He ran his hands over Leroy and found another weapon he had stuck in his belt. They tied him to one of the beams that held up the saloon roof.

"Put them lights out," Morgan ordered as he pushed Florence up the stairs. "Hurry up, woman," he growled in irritation. "Get up them stairs and stay out of sight. Buck and his boys will be pouring in here any minute like syrup over hot cakes" After he had Florence safely upstairs he began to gather up their weapons while Mac bolted the back door. Darrell and Frost buckled on their gun belts and checked their weapons. Mac and Morgan did the same.

When the first shot was fired, Buck was busy cleaning out the bank's safe. He grabbed the money and rushed outside, pushing the banker ahead of him. Four of his men were running toward the saloon. "Something went wrong," Buck shouted. "Rush 'um."

Obeying Buck's orders without hesitation, they pushed through the saloon doors with drawn guns. Morgan and his three deputies were waiting for them and opened fire. Two were dropped at the threshold. The other two were hit, but managed to struggle back outside.

Buck was shouting and cursing, calling out to his two companions who lay dead or dying just inside the door. When there was no answer they opened fire, pouring lead into the building from every direction. The four men inside were flat on their stomachs behind overturned tables, covering their faces with their arms to escape the shattering glass and splintering wood. They were pinned down helplessly, daring not to raise their heads.

Buck decided to kill the banker since his usefulness had been exhausted. He pulled his gun and shot Williams in the chest as he backed away, pleading for his life. He lay bleeding in the street, while his wife hid under a bed in an upstairs room over the saloon.

"I'm out of shells," Frost said.

"So am I," Mac admitted.

"We don't stand a chance in here," Darrell said. "We're outnumbered two to one. They'll roost out there until we run out of ammunition, then walk right through the door and blast us like caged chickens."

"They have the money," Mac stated. "Why don't they just take it and ride out of here?"

"Buck wants revenge," Darrell said. "We killed four of his men, wounded two, and captured one.

"Maybe if we give him Leroy he'll take him and leave," Frost suggested.

"I haven't felt his pulse lately, but with all the lead they threw at us, they most likely killed him," Darrell said, and the thought amused him.

"They got us nailed down all right," Mac said, "and I had planned on dying of old age."

"Maybe I can make it out the back door," Darrell suggested.

"And then what?" Morgan said. "There's seven men out there watching us. I fail to see how your getting yourself killed will help the situation."

Mac shook his head. "That's suicide. They got a man around back just waiting for that door to open."

"A man," Darrell echoed. "If my figures are correct, Buck has only six or seven healthy men left. It's reasonable that he can't spare more than one, maybe two at most, to cover us from the rear. There are four sides to this building."

Mac smiled, "Good thinking. He's got four sides and the roof to watch."

"You're right," Morgan said. "Even if you do manage to sneak out the back, how is that going to help us? Mac and Frost are out of bullets, and I only got two left. What about you, Darrell?"

"I've got a full load. Maybe I can get the drop on 'um in the dark. The most logical thing would be for me to ride for help. They'll be watching the street. They won't be expecting me to stick around."

"I can't allow you to run out there and get yourself killed," Morgan said.

"If we don't do something, we're as good as dead already."

"I see your point, but I'm still the sheriff, and I'm paid to take the risks." He stepped between Darrell and the door.

"I'll go."

"Sorry, Morgan, but in all due respect, you wouldn't stand a chance. You're too slow on your feet. You throw the door open when I give the signal, and I think I might be able to even things up a little."

Morgan stepped aside, looking at Darrell with a worried frown. "I only got two shots left to cover you."

"Save 'um. As soon as you open the door, hit the floor. You make too big a target. I'll draw the fire long enough for you to close it after I step out into the open."

"Don't be a damned fool, Darrell," Morgan said. "They'll cut you in half the minute you poke your nose out."

"Anybody ever tell you that you worry too much, Sheriff?"

One look into Darrell's eyes was enough to convince Morgan that he had made up his mind. Morgan lifted the latch quietly, waiting for Darrell to give him the signal. He saw him check his weapon, then smile slightly. "I can't afford to miss."

"I heard that!" Morgan said.

Mac shook Darrell's hand. "If this don't work out to our advantage, Holliman, it's been a pure pleasure knowing you."

"Same here." He gave Morgan a nod. "Now!" Darrell dove through the open door and landed hard on his left shoulder. A gun discharged six rounds at close range, kicking up clods into Darrell's face as he rolled to his side and fired two shots into the darkness, one high and one low where he saw the flash from the outlaw's gun. He heard the man gasp and hit the ground. Darrell scrambled to his feet and moved toward the body lying a few feet away. He edged him over on his back with his foot to make sure he was dead. He didn't want to be surprised by a slug in the back. Satisfied, he moved close to the building and eased his way down the alley. "Six more," he said to himself.

When he reached the corner of the building he saw Buck's men scrambling around like a pack of rats. Buck ordered one of them to investigate the shots they had heard coming from the back of the saloon. The man took two strides down the alley and was looking down the long barrel of Darrell's Colt.

"Make one move and it will be your last," Darrell warned. The outlaw threw his hands up.

"Who the hell are you?"

"A store keeper."

"Bullshit!"

Pistol shots sounded all around them. Buck and his men were firing into the saloon repeatedly from every angle. The sharp tinkle of shattering glass penetrated the air as they continued to riddle the saloon, their guns spitting fire into the darkness.

Darrell disarmed his prisoner, reversed his weapon and clubbed him on the side of the head. He fell at his feet unconscious. He dropped to one knee, cocked his .45 and took careful aim at one of the men across the street who had made the mistake of showing himself. He squeezed the trigger and the man fell without a sound. Someone shouted a warning and a slug splintered the wood just above Darrell's head.

"Kill that bastard in the alley!" Buck screamed, and they began to fire in Darrell's direction.

Darrell hit the ground, flat on his belly. When they ceased fire, he slowly straightened up, looking through the fog of spent powder that hung in the air.

Buck yelled, "Go see if we got him, Rusty."

Holding his cocked gun out in front of him, Rusty moved into the mouth of the alley, and there Darrell stopped him dead in his tracks.

"You son of a bitch!" Buck screamed, firing toward the flash of Darrell's gun.

Darrell took the slug in his right arm. He leaped toward a doorway and braced himself, struggling to recover from the sudden shock of pain.

"Come on out!" Buck roared.

"Come and get me," Darrell answered.

"I know you're hit."

"It's only a scratch. You're a lousy shot."

"Stay where you are," Darrell," Morgan shouted from where he stood behind the batwings. "I got the bastard in my sights."

"Stay out of this, Morgan."

"You're hit."

"He almost missed me."

"Don't try to be a hero. We got 'um outnumbered. They ain't got a chance." Morgan was bluffing. He had one round left, and if he was counting right, Darrell had two.

Another one of Bucks men suddenly rushed toward the saloon and Morgan was forced to spend his last round to drop him. Buck realized they were outnumbered and decided to make a run for it. "Get the horses," he yelled. We got what we came for. Let's ride.

The last man knew Buck had miscalculated this time, and he was done taking orders. "Don't shoot," he cried, running into the street with his hands high above his head. Buck fired at him as he ran, dropping him before he took a dozen steps.

"How about it big mouth?" he yelled at Darrell. Are you scared? You want to run too. I can plug you where you stand. I got you in my sights and this .45 has a hair trigger. Call your sheriff off or I'll blast you."

"What's your deal?"

Buck roared with laughter. "I walk with the money, and I let you live."

"No deal. Go ahead, Morgan. Drill him."

Morgan had his finger on the trigger when Buck yelled.

"You still want to slap leather with me, boy?"

Darrell pulled himself up, felt blood streaming down his arm and dripping off his hand. He flexed his fingers. He could already feel the swelling commence. In another hour his arm would be useless for anything other than hiding in a sling. Oh, well, he thought miserably, we all die from one damned thing or another. At least I wasn't shot in the back. He smiled to himself. I never dreamed it would end like this. He thought about Dawn as he stepped out of the doorway and into the street. "Any time you're ready."

"Wait just a damned minute," Morgan yelled. "You're bleeding all over the place, Darrell."

"I told you to stay out of this."

"I know what you told me, but I don't aim to stand here and let that worthless sonofabitch cut you down."

"I got my reasons for wanting to stand up to him. He's mine. Stay out of my way"

"Let him be," Mac said. "Darrell accepted his challenge. We all heard it."

"He'll kill him. Are you all crazy?"

"Buck is the only crazy one here, Morgan. Now step back and let's get this over with." Mac addressed Darrell then, "How bad are you hit?"

Darrell actually laughed. "I'm just fine. Stop worrying."

Buck felt a flutter of curiosity; wondering what the hell was wrong with Darrell. He was hit, bleeding like a stuck hog, and actually begging to be shot down. He was sure he could take him, be like shooting a dog. With his smart barking ceased, the rest would be child's play. He had shot his way out of worse messes. Morgan was fat, slow, and old, no challenge at all. He only had one problem and he was fixing to kill him. He was looking forward to it. He strutted to the middle of the street and waited for Darrell, who walked slowly to meet him. The sun was just coming up and it would be in Darrell's face, another stroke of his good luck, not that he needed an edge.

Every nerve in Darrell's body tensed as he kept his eyes on Buck in an unfaltering gaze, watching and waiting for him to make his play, barely seeing in the early morning light that streaked the horizon.

They stood motionless, facing one another, two determined men, full of fury and desperation. Only one would walk away. Darrell waited until Buck's hand flashed toward his gun, then like a striking snake, drew and fired. For a breathless instant a glimmer of surprise and shock showed in Buck's eyes as his hand clawed for his pistol grip, still holstered. He was shamed, even as he drew his last breaths, acknowledging that he had not so much as cleared leather. Blood streamed from his heart as he sank to the ground, staring with an empty expression.

"God Almighty," Morgan cried. "Did you see that?"

Mac grew so weak that he leaned against a post to steady his legs.

Frost ran into the street and actually threw his arms around Darrell.

"Come on, I'm getting you over to Keel's office before you bleed to death.

A crowd began to gather and Morgan barked, "Get the undertaker and help him with the bodies. I got a wounded deputy to take care off before I attend to the other problems. Florence is upstairs above the saloon. You women go up there and get her. Williams was killed."

The money was recovered, but the banker was dead, which was another problem for Morgan to unravel. Since most of the money belonged to McCloud, it was decided that he should assume William's position until other arrangements could be made to replace him. When Florence was dragged from beneath the bed, she collapsed.

Morgan followed the parade to Doctor Keel's house. Keel had been expecting somebody to get shot or killed. Mac and Frost sat in the parlor and waited respectfully for a report on Darrell's condition. Morgan stayed with Darrell through it all, just in case he might need some holding steady. He didn't act up, but neither did he refuse the laudanum.

"Looks like I done a lot of worrying needlessly," Morgan said, standing out of Keel's way while he probed for the slug.

"I told you that you worry too much," Darrell said, mumbling around the stick that Keel had stuck between his teeth.

"I hope you got a good reason for what you done."

"You know the reason."

"I know you took care of the situation single handed, but I had the bastard in my sights."

"But your gun wasn't loaded."

"He didn't know that."

"It wouldn't have made any difference. He would have shot you before you pulled the trigger, then spun around and took me out. He needed to be taught a lesson, even if it was of very short duration, like ten seconds."

"I don't know much 'bout you, Holliman, and I'm damned curious. Suppose you explain to me how a nice quiet, easy going, gentleman like yourself, find cause to handle a gun like that? You just made yourself a reputation that will draw more gunslingers than a dead horse draws flies. In short, you committed suicide out there. Who are you, Holliman?"

"I'm nobody, Sheriff. I came here to live a nice quiet life, fall in love, get married, and have kids. I'm just a simple guy."

"The hell, you say? What about outdrawing Buck Femmer? How do you intend to hide from that?"

"If I made a mistake today, then I have to live with it. This is my town too, and like Mac said, protecting it is our collective responsibility. Actually, Sheriff, I couldn't have done any less."

"Where did you learn to handle a gun like that?"

"I won't lie, it took a bit of practice."

"How many men have you killed?"

"What difference does it make? The only one that counts is Buck Femmer."

"Have you ever worked as a hired gun?"

"Maybe you better run over to your office and flip through your wanted posters."

"I'll get to the bottom of this."

"Bottom of what?"

"Who you really are. You're no store keeper. You know what will happen next, don't you?"

"What's that?"

"Courgat needs a man to take my place. The job is yours if you want it. You proved today that you're the man for the star. After you outdraw a couple dozen gunslingers, things will settle down for you, but you'll kill some men long before that happens."

"I don't want the job."

"As long as you live in this town, it will be yours no matter who wears the badge. Every time a problem pops us that the sheriff can't neutralize, you'll do the same thing you done today. Get you a good deputy, then all you'll have to do is the hard stuff. You can go about your business, you know, like fall in love—"."

"I've already done that."

"You can get married and still be the town's hero."

"Yeah, you got a point. I think you need to drop down to the deputy position, Charles. You know, sort of take the lead from the back seat. You're a smart, capable man. Be a shame to let all that knowledge wind up in a rocking chair."

Morgan smiled. "Thank you for saying that. It means something coming from you. Where are you from, Darrell?"

"I move around. Spent some time in the Army."

Charles gave him a look of respect, then said to Keel, "How long before he can go to work?"

"When he's ready, and that may be never."

"Never! Is he messed up that bad?"

"No, not yet, but he'll be a target as long as he lives."

"He's fast. He'll be around for a long time."

"Yeah, that's possible, if he has eyes in the back of his head."

CHAPTER

24

Because of Darrell's wound, he spent the next two weeks under the watchful eyes of Doctor Keel. The incredible story of Darrell's fast draw was the topic of every conversation. He had single handedly saved the bank from being robbed and killed the most dangerous outlaw in two states at the risk of his own life. Keel had a hard time keeping people from barging in to shake his hand and congratulate him. The newspapers were quick to print every detail of the gunfight, especially the part about Darrell out-drawing Buck Femmer. Holliman had suddenly become a celebrated figure in Western journalism.

Dawn listened in rapt fascination as Mac explained in detail how Darrell had outsmarted Buck and his gang of cut-throats.

"I knew there was something different about that man. He has nerve, and he even took one hell of a beating to make his plan work. He's exactly the man we need to take over as Sheriff."

"Has he agreed?" Dawn asked excitedly.

"He's got to get that arm healed first. It's his right, but it didn't stop him from out-drawing Buck. He's really amazing. He's wasting his talent managing the trading post. I don't understand why he accepted the job."

"Will his arm be all right?" she asked with concern.

"In a few days. Keel's keeping him at his house just to be on the safe side. The gunslingers will start drifting in here to challenge him soon enough."

"He's hiding?"

"More or less, just until he's able to protect himself."

"That's horrible. I'm going to town. I want to see him."

"I don't think Keel is allowing him to have visitors."

"He will allow me."

Mac grinned. "Yeah, you're the exception."

Ned had also been listening to Mac's version of the gunfight, and spoke up for the first time, "I want you to stay away from Holliman."

She turned on him in exasperation. "What! The man is wounded, saved the bank's money, killed that terrible outlaw and you order me to stay away from him?"

"It doesn't look proper the way you two are always hanging around together."

"Only to a nasty little mind like yours. Would you like to come along?"

"I can't stand the man."

"What has he ever done to you?"

"He's chasing my wife."

"Oh! You're driving me crazy with your suspicions and jealousy. I refuse to listen to it." She whipped around in anger and fled up the stairs.

Mac crossed the room and sat down in a chair facing Ned. He was seeing that look on Ned's face more and more, shrewd and sharp like a hawk circling over its nest. "You can't keep her in a cage, boy."

"She's my wife and I expect her to act like it. She's seeing Holliman behind my back."

Mac couldn't honesty deny Ned's observation, neither would he take sides against his daughter. "Sometimes people are thrown together by accident; it's nothing for you to worry about."

"She can barely tolerate me, Mac. If it wasn't for the baby she would never have married me. She can't stand the sight of me." He passed his palm across his face and wiped away the sweat. "I won't give her up. I told her that."

"I hope you ain't made any dangerous threats. I've stayed clear of your problems because it's none of my business, but by God, if you ever lay a hand on her or threaten to harm her, I'll kill you, Ned. You can't force your will on her. You should know her better than that. She's got a wild streak in her and she will spread her wings one of these days and take to the sky. Leave her be and she will most likely find her way back, but if you continue to dictate your will, you'll lose her. Back off, give her some space."

"I won't do that, Mac. I don't have to. I know my rights. If it comes right down to it I'll take care of Holliman."

"Surely you don't think you can outdraw him."

"I won't even try."

Mac didn't bother to question his last statement; he was talking like a crazy man. He picked up his hat and headed for the door, anxious to escape Ned's long face and rotten mood.

He couldn't blame Dawn for being sick of him. Just as he reached the door he heard Dawn running down the stairs yelling for him to wait. He held the door open and she breezed through it. "I'm going with you."

Darrell brightened the moment Keel ushered her into his room. "You have a visitor, if you feel up to it."

"I've never felt better in my life. This is a rare treat." He followed her with his eyes as she stepped into the room. She looked small, delicate, and very beautiful, with an air of dignity that caused his heart to quicken.

"I heard what happened." He made a move to stand up and she shook her head and laid her hand on his shoulder. "Lie still, you're pale as a sheet."

"He has good reason," Keel said, "he lost about half his blood. Don't stay too long now; he needs to get some rest."

Dawn nodded and sat down on the bed instead of the chair that Keel had moved close. She boldly took the hand that protruded out the end of the sling that was tied around his neck. "Is this the hand that pulled the trigger on Buck?"

Her remark shocked him. "Why do you ask?"

"You could have been killed. You used your wounded arm? I'm amazed."

"I had to, I'm right handed." He studied her for a moment. "Would you have cared?"

"I would miss you if you should die."

"That's encouraging."

"It wasn't meant to be."

"And I already had my hopes up. How did you manage to slip away?"

"I rode to town with my father."

"And, Ned?"

"Must we talk about him?"

"You're very beautiful. You take my breath every time I look at you. I'm in love with you."

"Not only are you a hero, you are very bold, and less than a gentleman for saying such wild things to a married woman. Your name is on the lips of every one in town."

"Is that why you came here? To tell me how the people in town feel about me?"

"No, I came here to thank you. What you did for this town and the people will never be forgotten."

Her evasiveness made him suddenly angry. "You're lying," he said quietly, with the hint of a smile. "You didn't come here to make pretty speeches in behalf of this lousy town full of gutless men and whining women. You're not interested in the town anymore than I am. You know me better than that, and I know you. I killed Buck because I wanted to teach him a lesson, and you came here because you wanted to see me." His anger was gone now and he watched her affectionately. "Truth?"

She resented his attitude and the fact that he knew the truth made her furious. She looked away from his steady gaze to hide her feelings. "You are a conceited ass." He smiled and she felt like slapping his face again.

He was reading her mind. "Shall I turn the other cheek? Or take you into my arms and kiss you?"

"You are ridiculous. You have no right to—"

"I have every right. If not, then call me a fool for thinking so."

"Do I have the same right?"

"You can have anything your heart desires."

"Then tell me why you keep secrets? Where did you learn to handle a gun like that?"

"I used to be a gunsmith."

"And you're still a liar."

He laughed. "You're no angel." He slipped his good arm around her waist. She drew back and looked at him. He was smiling again.

"Are you forgetting that I have a husband?"

"You're still calling him your husband?"

"I am married to him."

"I can forget it, if you can."

She looked amused. "I would like nothing better. I'm sick to death of his whining, weaknesses, and crawling."

"Get rid of him. You don't love him."

"We have a child."

"You have a child."

"What's that supposed to mean."

"It means that I don't think Ned is the father."

"Why don't you just come right out and call me a slut?"

"Because it would be a lie."

"You leave my baby out of this. He's no concern of yours."

"He could be."

"Would you like to take the blame?"

"I wish I could. What do you feel for me?"

"I'm not sure."

"Maybe I can help you decide," he said drawing her close again. She didn't push him away this time, but she was unyielding. "Are you afraid?" he whispered. "I won't hurt you."

"Doctor Keel may walk in any second and catch us."

"Are you afraid of a scandal?" His lips were moving lightly over hers, his tone a challenge.

"A scandal, I already have."

"Then to Hell with them."

Her arms went quickly around his neck and she allowed him to kiss her hungrily. His lips were intoxicating, and she trembled at his touch when he caressed her. He pulled her down on the bed beside him, pressing against her until the entire length of their bodies were touching. Shaken by her own wild behavior, she sudden sprang to her feet. "We can't do this! Not here! Not with Keel in the other room."

"If he pokes his head in I'll shoot him."

"I shouldn't have come here. This is wrong."

"How can it be wrong when it feels so right?" He reached for her again.

"You'll hurt your arm."

"What arm? Stop fighting it."

"One of us has to."

"Why? It's too late. We can't ignore what we feel for each other. We have to settle it."

"Not here."

"Then where?"

"When your arm has healed."

"Where?"

"I don't know. We have to be careful. Ned will kill us."

"What! That worm?"

"We're married. That gives him certain rights."

"You're making it hard, but I'll find a way."

"I have to go." She saw disappointment in his expression, a burning need that she could easily satisfy if the circumstances were different. She looked at him, her eyes speaking an apology, and then she hurried from the room.

Darrell stared at the door she had closed behind her, tense and frustrated. He had never eaten his heart out over a woman before, and he made up his mind that he wouldn't start now. He knew she was not holding back because of Ned, she was sick to death of him. The same question came back to haunt him again, and he could think of no way to tactfully seek an answer, yet he could feel the chasm between them, the ghost of a man that filled her mind and heart. He was sure of one thing; the man in question was the father of her child.

While Darrell recovered from his wound, Biglo used the time to approach him with the offer of accepting the sheriff's job. Although he was mystified by Darrell's fearless action and fast gun, he knew he must curb his eagerness and not trouble him for details about his past. He saw no reason to confuse the issue with questions that might cause a maze of complications. The only thing that mattered was that he accept the job.

Since Darrell was working for Mac, Biglo made him the offer in the presence of Mac, knowing he would not stand in the way; after all it had been Mac who predicted that a man of Darrell's caliber would show up quite miraculously and solve their dilemma.

The entire town was backing Biglo's decision to offer Darrell the job; being aware of their precarious position should Morgan suddenly quit or get killed.

Darrell considered the offer for a moment, and then laughed.

"No thank you. I've been a lot of things, but I don't fancy wearing a badge. I never did like jewelry. I have yet to meet a man with a badge who didn't think he was some kind of god. No reflection on Morgan, of course."

"Maybe you better give it some thought," Mac said.

"Are you trying to get rid of me?"

"I'm thinking about what's best for you. You would be a lot safer behind a badge with your new reputation then anyplace else I know of."

"That badge isn't big enough to be a shield, and wearing it wouldn't make my hide a bit thicker."

"It takes a damned stupid man to draw on a lawman. You're going to be drawing down on a bunch of glory hunting fools in the future. When you're forced to kill, do it on the side of law and order, or you might find yourself dancing from the end of a rope after standing in front of a crooked judge."

"Well taken, but I don't want to be nailed down. When I get ready to move on, I don't want to feel obligated to change my plans because of a piece of tin."

"Any job at all ties a man down," Biglo said, pulling nervously at his gray beard.

Darrell was quiet for a moment. He was thinking that after all his struggling to avoid living by his gun, that it might be actually happening, and it wasn't so bad. In fact it felt almost good, except for the slight twinge in the pit of his stomach.

"I have to agree that this town is wide open. I don't like feeling like a sitting duck, and at the moment, that's exactly what I am." There was an edge to his voice. "I'll take the job, but only until you find someone else."

Biglo's face lit up with delight. "Good, good," he blurted. "That certainly takes a load off my mind"

"I realize the decision you made was a difficult one," Mac said. "There is much involved here. I think you need the protection of this town as much as the town needs you. I hope you never regret your decision. We're indebted to you, Holliman." He extended his hand and Darrell grasp it firmly.

"I hope you're right. By the way, what do you intend doing about a store clerk?"

Mac laughed. "It will be a sight easier than finding a man who can handle a gun the way you do. You're goddamned amazing. You have a talent most men only dream about."

"I'll try to live up to all your praise."

There was something about Darrell that puzzled Mac. He felt a sense of deep admiration and affection for the man, but he also felt a tinge of fear he could not identify. He possessed a mysterious inner strength that belied his warm, friendly, exterior. Mac sensed a cold, calculating, cutting, quality in Holliman that left him deeply perplexed.

The night after the Mayor pinned the star on Darrell's shirt, he celebrated his new position as a guest at Mac's house for supper where he drank too much and his eyes rarely strayed from Dawn's direction. Although he was acutely aware of Ned's watchful eyes, he was more aware of his wife's nearness. He could think no further than the moment he had held her in his arms. She was looking at him, her eyes meeting his steadily, and he read them perfectly.

"You will make a wonderful sheriff," she said in a clear voice. "I feel safe already."

"I'll do my best to live up to your expectations," he said reluctantly, and a bit embarrassed by her comment.

"I'm a little curious," Ned spoke up for the first time. He had been sitting there in some sort of silent stupor.

"About what?" Darrell said, feeling his challenge.

"As to why you took a chance on out-drawing Buck. It's my understanding that Morgan had the drop on him and could have taken him with ease."

Darrell regarded him suspiciously. "My reason is a personal one."

"Yeah, I'll bet. You were pretty sure of yourself." Ned's jealousy was becoming more obvious. "Some people are saying that you had no doubts about out-drawing him."

"There has never been a gunfight without doubt. Most gunmen are sneaking, pushed by fear and ambition, and will take every possible advantage of their opponent, even to shooting him in the back if he gets the drop on him," Darrell said with a flare of anger.

"So, why did you take the gamble?"

"I told you it was personal. Why all the interest?"

"I think you wanted to build a reputation for yourself."

"I don't have to prove myself, Rowling. If that was my aim, I could have gunned him down long ago. I just never had a reason before. He stepped on my toes."

An intense silence followed Darrell's words, which seemed to hang in the air like smoke. Ned's expression turned to bitterness as Darrell faced him squarely. His hatred for him growing steadily until it was impossible for him to remain civil. He wanted to destroy him, feeling the threat of this man filled him with violence. "I'm afraid you have me at a disadvantage," Ned said mockingly. "I'm a peaceable family man. I know nothing about gun-fighting."

"You may get the chance to find out," Darrell said all too quickly, and was immediately sorry he had uttered the untimely remark. There was a ghastly silence, and then Darrell said while getting to his feet. "I had better get on back to town while I can still sit my horse. My compliments to the cook. The meal was delicious."

"Stay the night," Mac offered. "You don't officially start to work for a couple of days."

He was almost ready to accept when he noticed Ned's face set in grim lines of disapproval, glaring at Mac. "Better not." He looked at Ned in disgust. "Thanks for the invitation anyway. It was a hard one to turn down."

Debbie had been unusually quiet all through the meal, hardly looking up from her plate. Suddenly she stood up. "I'll walk you to your horse," she said softly.

"You don't have to do that."

"I want to."

He took her arm and they headed for the door talking companionably. Ned shot them a disapproving look before turning toward the stairs in a flash of anger. Darrell felt both exasperation and amusement as he watched him. He was a shallow, selfish man, hanging on to Dawn when he knew she had no use for him. And to make matters worse, he was leaning on Debbie like a hurt child clutching his mother's skirt when he didn't get his way.

"I'm sorry Ned was so unfriendly tonight," Debbie said in calm understanding.

"If he acted any other way, I might think I was in the wrong house."

"Are you in love with Dawn?" she said, looking up at him with great innocent eyes.

Her bluntness surprised him. "Love Dawn? She's a married woman! Have you forgotten?"

"I haven't forgotten. The question is, have you?"

He had no defense. "So what if I am? They don't have a marriage!" His voice rose in anger. "Why don't he leave like a man? The way he has lost all his self-respect is enough to make me sick. He reminds me of a fat tick the way he hangs on to her. He's a damned parasite."

"Your love for her is as hopeless as Ned's."

"What are you talking about?"

"Only that you're making a mistake."

"Don't confuse me; just say what's on your mind. You came out here because you have something to say. What is it?"

"How much do you really know about her?"

"Enough."

"Do you know about her child?"

"I know Ned isn't the father."

"Did she tell you that?"

"No, I figured it out for myself, and don't try to convince me that I'm wrong. I'm not as stupid as you might think."

"I have never thought you stupid, quite the contrary, and you're right. Ned isn't the father of little Henry."

"Who is?"

"I can't tell you that."

"But you know."

"Yes."

He stared at her in puzzlement. Was she deliberately trying to shake him up? Maybe she wasn't as sweet and innocent as she appeared. "Why are you telling me this?"

"Because I like you and I don't want to see you hurt."

"What makes you so sure that I'll be hurt?"

"Because I'm sure of Dawn's feelings."

"Where is this guy she's so crazy about? Why doesn't she go to him? Or better still, why doesn't he show himself? Are you sure he exists?"

"Her son is proof that he did exist. I have no idea where he is, or if he's still alive."

"I feel certain that she's not in love with a dead man. Why don't you tell me what you know about this guy?"

"I have told you all I know."

He had thought at first that she might be protecting Ned; however that line of thought made little sense. If Ned and Dawn were to split she would have a clear field.

"If you want Ned, why are you trying to save a marriage that's doomed? You admitted you were in love with him."

"I was."

"Meaning you're not anymore?"

"Meaning exactly that."

"Too bad. I guess he missed the boat in both ports."

"You're wrong about one thing; he's not hanging on any longer."

"From where I sit I would say he is."

"Mac is getting ready to drive a herd of cattle to Oklahoma. Ned is going along on the drive. He doesn't plan to come back."

"Do you believe him?"

"Yes, why shouldn't I?"

"He's lying."

"What makes you so sure?"

"Does Dawn know about this?"

"No."

"Has he asked you to go with him?"

"Yes, how did you guess?"

"It's not hard to figure a guy like him. You refused him, of course."

"Of course."

"He'll be back, don't worry. Does Mac plan to go along?"

"Yes, unless you can think of a way to get him to stay."

"Who needs him? I can make arrangements to stay out here and protect you ladies."

"Mac has already made arrangements for Ned's brother, Jack to stay here and take care of the place."

"He's a lucky cuss."

"And also a gentleman."

"There's a fool born every minute."

"So I've heard." She looked at him keenly.

"Sounds like a pointed accusation. I might feel the same way if I knew who my competition was. Are you certain that you know?"

"I can only tell you this much, Dawn's still in love with him, so don't be too quick to judge Ned. He's aware of her feelings and helpless to do anything to change them. Knowing this has made him desperate."

"But he cares for you."

"Not really. I'm only his crutch. If I were to go away with Ned, I wouldn't be any better than him. I would know that he would always love Dawn, and that I was only the straw he grasped for. In time I would become as bitter and vindictive as Ned."

"Looks like we're in the same boat, except that you no longer care for Ned. Maybe we should stick together."

"We tried that. It didn't work."

"We were looking for something that wasn't there. People are attracted to one another for different reasons."

She understood what he was saying. Suddenly her thoughts were like fire running through her veins as his words let loose a violent storm inside her. She was seeing him in an exciting new way. He was a hero, an important man, brave, handsome, a gentleman of sorts. "Will you kiss me?"

He pulled her into his arms and she responded, pressing against him, asking no more than just this moment of happiness. But she knew that at some later date she would yield to him completely. Even as she felt ashamed of her thoughts she would deny him nothing.

Dawn stood in front of an upstairs window looking down at them. Tears sudden sprang to her eyes as anger enveloped her. Debbie was taking advantage of Darrell's besotted condition and she wondered if he was about to take her to the bushes. When he moved away from her and mounted his horse, she felt a surge of relief.

CHAPTER 25

Mac made plans to start the cattle drive immediately after round-up. The round-up, for the purpose of branding calves and cutting out the fat steers, was started in early spring by all the ranchers in the territory. Since the cattle wandered free without fences, branding was the only way they had of identifying their stock. During the winter the large ranches would line drive the cattle to keep them from drifting, but as a rule nothing was done other than keep hay scattered to keep the animals bunched. They naturally stayed close to their source of food, especially in winter after the grass was gone.

A general round-up by all outfits was started at the same time. Neighboring cattleman would cut out all brands that were not their own and put them into corrals awaiting the representatives of each outfit to claim their stock. The practice was routine. When a cow of a certain brand was followed by an unmarked calf, the calf automatically went to the owner of the cow.

Mac had his first chance to watch Ned work and was well pleased with his performance. He had a good cutting horse and he knew how to handle him. After he selected the steer to be cut-out, Ned would work it gently to the edge of the herd, and then his horse went to work. There was much hard riding, twisting and turning, until the animal was driven to join the other steers selected for the drive.

Frost Jackson hired on as a 'calf wrangler' for the round-up, and would stay on as one of the drovers for the drive. Mac was surprised by his ability since he had been branded as a drunk and a trouble maker. He was assisted by several mounted ropers.

All the animals chosen for the drive were held in a separate herd, and left in charge of the cattle guards until the herd was ready to move out. The complete operation took several weeks and involved at least two dozen cowboys taken collectively from the ranches involved.

The thought of the coming adventure stimulated Mac with happy anticipation, bringing back memories of his childhood, as the son of one of the biggest ranchers in New Mexico.

Charles Morgan was left in charge of the trading post, and Sheriff Darrell Holliman volunteered to guide him through the operation to keep from getting bored.

During the time of round-up and preparations for the drive, Ned spent very little time at the house. Being near Dawn was a source of torment to him, yet the thought of being separated from her filled him with fear.

The night before the drive was to start at daybreak, Ned drank too much in a futile attempt to drown his misery. He blamed Dawn for the mess he had made of his life. He wondered at times if she had ice water flowing in her veins. In his own mind he could think of no justification for her frigid hostility, even though there were some discrepancies on his part. He blamed her for that too.

Mac laughed and talked with happy urgency about the coming morning, and Debbie hung on every word. However Dawn was quite unimpressed. Her eyes strayed from time to time to rest on Ned, noting his tired face and shaking hands. They had little to say to one another anymore, they were like strangers.

Ned was a different person now, all the zest and eagerness that had once been so much a part of his personality was gone. There was a weakness in him that washed away all the respect Dawn had once felt for him. He had not weakened in one respect, and that was his hatred for the innocent child, although he had not rejected him as being his son, for the child was the only link that held them together. Dawn hoped as the child grew older that he might come to accept him, not just for outward appearances, but in his heart. Looking at Ned she realized he was of her own making.

She wondered how she must look in his eyes; how he must hate her for the monster she was making him into. She felt a sick contempt for her own treacherous actions and swore to herself that in the future she would try to make things right between them. If she couldn't have the man she loved, she really had no life, so what did it matter who she lived with. After all, she was Ned's wife and she owed him something, much more than turning him into a weak drunkard. And what of Darrell Holliman? It was impossible for her to forget the passionate moments they had spent together. She knew she must stay away from him or she would one day be helplessly lost to temptation.

When at last everyone had gone to their rooms, Ned was left alone in the drawing room searching his mind to find an excuse to stay behind with Dawn. His thoughts made him feel ashamed and he slammed his hand hard against the table as a feeble release for the growing rage inside him. The table rocked violently and the half empty whiskey bottle fell over and began to spill out on the table top and run onto the floor. He cursed under his breath, jerked his shirt off and began to dab at the puddle on the carpet.

When at last he became weary, he extinguished the lamp and crossed the room in the darkness, stumbling awkwardly, almost falling, losing his balance several times. When he reached the bottom of the stairs he saw a thread of light cast by a single candle on the lamp stand at the head of the stairs. It lit his way as he moved slowly up the steps that waved in front of him. When he reached the top of the stairs he heard the light pad of footsteps. He stood very still, held his breath and waited as a figure came toward him. When he recognized his wife his breath caught in his throat.

"I came to say good-bye," she said softly. "I know you will be gone before I wake in the morning, and I want to wish you a safe journey tonight."

They stood a few feet apart, her small figure between him and the light. Except for the faint candle beam the house was in complete darkness, and an eerie silence surrounded them.

"Come," she said in a whisper, "we can talk in my room."

He followed her, his heart throbbing in his chest, his hands perspiring. The sight of her there in the darkness stimulated every nerve in his body and he trembled with excitement. Presently she closed the door quietly behind them. She crossed over to her bed and sat down with a great show of poise, spreading her gown neatly about her.

"Come, sit down," she purred, pointing to a chair.

He brought the chair near and sat down facing her. The room felt stifling hot and seemed to move hellishly about him. He cursed himself silently for being intoxicated. He drew his hand across his brow nervously as he waited for her to speak. She was looking at him in an odd way, and he read the tension in her expression that was barely visible in the dim lit room.

"I hardly know where to begin," she said, turning in profile to escape the pitiful look in his eyes. "I feel so ashamed."

She fell silent, rose from the bed and walked across the room. His eyes followed her as she moved gracefully on small feet, her waist slender, and her breasts firm and full beneath the thin gown where she stood near an open window bathed in moonlight.

He leaned forward in his chair as if she were a magnet pulling him toward her, his hands braced on his knees for support.

"What are you ashamed of?" he asked hoarsely, the words struggling to escape his throat.

"All the hell I have put you through." She felt uncomfortable, and stood with her back to him and the light.

He could not see her face, but he was aware of the pain in her tone.

"You're sorry?" he said in bewilderment, not trusting his hearing.

"Does it surprise you?"

He drew his hand across his eyes in an attempt to clear his vision. "I must be dreaming. You're sorry?"

"I can imagine how you must loath me." She was feeling great pity for this pitiful, weak, man she had married, the man who had taken a beating for her, who had lied to save her reputation from further degradation by accepting the blame for her sin. She felt on the verge of tears and was trying hard not to break down. "I have been everything but a wife to you. I had even hoped that you might fall madly in love with Debbie, that you might run away together." She saw a look of shock on his face, heard the quick catch of his breath as the full impact of her words stunned him. After a moment she said with shame, "I have known for a long time how she feels about you. I can see it in her eyes when she looks at you. Sweet, gentle, loving, Debbie. She could love you for a million years and never make a move to do anything about it. She's such a great lady. I know how much you have come to depend on her. I have noticed how you steal glances at her, your eyes full of hunger and loneliness. I also realize that I'm responsible, that I drove you to it."

"And you never accused me—never said a word," he exclaimed in disbelief. "Not once did you even hint that you knew what was going on between us. I tried to make love to her because I wanted you so damned bad. How could you do this to me? to Debbie—to us?"

"Because I didn't care," she admitted dispassionately. "All I ever thought about was myself, my disappointments. I have been completely selfish, disagreeable, and disgusting, a poor excuse for a human being. My love for Light Eyes has separated us like an ocean. I realize now that I can't just stand in one place and let life pass me by. I must remove or go around my obsession if I am to become a whole person. I have become an empty shell inside. Can you forgive me?"

"I know I'm a little drunk, and maybe a whole lot stupid, but if I understand any of what you're saying, you're telling me that you want us to try again."

"Yes, if you still want me."

"Want you? I have never wanted anything else. I love you, only you."

"What about Debbie?"

"She means nothing to me. Just my friend."

"You're sure?"

"Positive! What about you and Holliman? I have thought for quite some time that something was going on between you two." As soon as the words left his mouth he hated himself for saying them. He turned away from her and his heart skipped a beat. "I'm sorry," he said quickly. "I know you would never do anything morally wrong. I'm still jealous, and now more than ever. He's something special now—"

"Please," she said turning to face him again. "You don't have to apologize. I gave you a reason to feel the way you do. I did see Darrell several times alone, but there was nothing between us. You must believe that."

"I do," he said, rising from his chair unsteadily and crossing the space separating them. "If you mean what you said, about giving us another chance, don't send me away tonight. I need you to hold me, I need to hold you. I've missed you. I've been completely lost and miserable."

"I have no intentions of sending you away," she smiled teasingly. A lamp burned low on the table beside her bed. She cupped her hand over the globe and blew out the flame. Then she leaned toward him in the darkness, her hand resting on his arm.

"What are you doing?" he said breathlessly.

"Waiting for you to come to bed with me."

An instant later, in a rush of sudden madness, he crushed her in his arms.

When Ned awoke early the next morning he felt spent but happy. Dawn lay beside him, her face close to his, her dark hair curled about her cheeks, giving her the look of young innocence that he loved so much. He rose on one elbow and looked at her beautiful face for a long time, soft and glowing in the early morning light. As he stared at her in deep wonderment, she slowly opened her eyes.

"Good morning," she said, smiling up at him.

"I'm sorry; I didn't mean to wake you."

"You didn't wake me, but since I am awake I may as well make your breakfast," she said, throwing the covers aside.

"What's your hurry? I can eat anytime, but I can't hold you in my arms anytime."

"I'm in no hurry," she said, pulling the covers back over her as he slid down beside her. She felt the same old helpless, trapped, feeling when he drew her close and took possession of her body. She had the urge to push him away as the disgust she suffered at his touch reached the marrow of her bones. Suddenly he released her at the sound of foot steps in the hall that stopped directly in front of their door. Seconds later came a light, almost restrained, tap.

"Dawn," came Debbie's voice, and then she opened the door and stepped inside. Finding Ned in bed with Dawn threw her into a state of shock. "Oh!" she cried, and turned her back to them. "I'm sorry, I—" She groped helplessly for the right words to express her shame and embarrassment. "I didn't know—I mean since—" She reached timidly for the doorknob to leave.

"Wait," Dawn said. "What do you want?"

"Mac asked me to wake you. Mrs. Rowling is here."

"At this hour?" Ned burst out. "You go back down there and tell them we'll be down in about thirty minutes. We're not ready to get up yet."

Debbie felt her face color. She couldn't find her voice so she just shook her head vigorously. She was trembling from head to toe as she hurried back downstairs with Ned's message.

Ned was amused by the whole thing. "From the look on her face you would think it was a crime for a man to spend the night with his wife."

"What did you expect?"

He looked at her anxiously. "What's the matter? Are you going to let her upset you? You look a little pale." He held her close and started to kiss her on the lips but she quickly turned her cheek to him, and was on her feet in another second. "We can't keep your mother waiting. You should spend some time with her before you leave."

"Right now I'm wishing I could fall down the stairs and break my leg so I would have a good excuse to stay here with you."

"You wouldn't dare."

"Don't bet on it." He made another grab for her. "I'm not leaving this room until I make love to you. I was drunk last night and did a sloppy job. Let me make it up to you this morning."

She let him kiss her then and gave over to his demanding hands, thinking, just get it over with. She felt like a piece of meat again.

When they went downstairs they found a small crowd collected in the drawing room. Martha Rowling looked up as they entered the room and smiled when she saw the happy glow on her son's face and the way his arm was looped around Dawn's small waist. She was pleased by her observation.

Mac and Pete were engaged in conversation, they only nodded their greeting. Jack was standing by the marble mantle drinking a cup of coffee, he smiled as they entered the room. "Just like old times," he said. "You two missed breakfast again, as usual."

"Nothing like catching a little extra sleep," Ned teased.

Jack gave Ned a little nudge in the ribs. "I still say you can't live on love. You two go on out to the kitchen and eat, Debbie has your eggs fried, I can smell burning grease."

"If you insist," Ned said happily.

"You go ahead," Dawn said, "I'll not hungry yet. I'm not used to eating this early."

"Come have a cup of coffee with me."

"I'll be there in a minute. I want to have a few words with your mother."

"All right, but hurry." He strode toward the kitchen, not too eager to face Debbie.

She was standing in front of the stove and did not turn around for a moment. She picked up the coffee pot and carried it over to the table and filled Ned's cup. He mumbled his thanks without meeting her eyes. An awkward silence followed.

Debbie tried to feel happy for Ned, and was ashamed of her resentment. She had been aware from the beginning that she was nothing more than a crutch, yet a flood of bitterness took possession of her senses. He no longer needed her because he had regained the affection of his wife; at least temporarily, and would always be in mortal terror of losing her, satisfied to exist under her thumb just to remain under the same roof with her.

When they finally looked at one another, his eyes held a certain element of tenderness. She felt sudden pity for this man, who needed her friendship so desperately, a fact they each silently recognized.

The silence was at last broken by Debbie. "I'm glad you and Dawn have ironed out your problems."

"I'm the happiest man on earth right now, and probably the biggest fool."

"You must not say that."

"You and I both know this will never last." He leaned forward and put his face in his hands. "It's too much to ask for," he muttered through his fingers. When he looked up there were tears in his eyes. "She has never once said she loved me, and she never will."

Debbie realized that nothing had really changed, that Ned's hopes were like the frail cry of a child in the night, soon to fade.

When it came time for Mac and Ned to depart there was a round of quick good-byes and hand shaking. Ned kissed Dawn lightly and started down the steps. Suddenly he stopped, turned around, and hurried back to her. He took her into his arms with tears in his eyes and kissed her over and over in a moving scene that Martha Rowling did not realize was prompted by their reconciliation.

Mac looked on patiently, amazed by the sudden change in their relationship. He was glad that Ned's forbearance had finally paid off.

He had endured much misery and heartache that might have destroyed a lesser man. He felt a flood of new found respect for the boy. He had misjudged him.

Martha laughed with a merry note. "I'm not too sure that my son wants to go."

Mac swallowed the contemptuous remark on the end of his tongue and spoke with as little rudeness as he could muster. "Well, he better make up his mind fast, because I got a dozen drovers waiting to move a hundred tons of beef."

Ned looked into Dawn's eyes for a moment longer and said softly so that no one else could hear his words, "Leaving you is almost beyond my power. I will live on the memory of last night until we're together again. I love you." He turned away and strode toward his horse and stepped up into the saddle.

Dawn's eyes followed him with unsmiling interest as he rode away. Inside she felt the removal of an unpleasant and painful liability.

All hands had reached the starting point by the time Mac and Ned arrived. Zeek was there with the chuck wagon loaded with supplies and bedrolls, drawn by four stout horses. Mac had agreed to pay Zeek top money to entice him to take the job. Wranglers and ropers were a dime a dozen, but a good cook was hard to come by, and as welcome as a rain in July.

"Gather 'round men," Mac said with a predominant note of authority. "I got a few things I want to say before we move out. This ain't a picnic were going on. As you all well know, we will be driving this herd through hostile Indian territory, and they might be hungry. For some of you who have never fought Indians, it can mean big trouble if you lose your heads. When you lose your head, your hair is most likely to go with it." A chuckle rose from the men. Glancing about, Mac continued. "I see that most of you are armed to the teeth, and that's good, if you know how to shoot straight. I want one thing understood right now, no one fires a shot unless I give the order. I've dealt with some of the Indians in this territory, and I can speak their language good enough to make myself understood. As a-matter-of-fact, some people seem to think I might have a little influence with them, and I like to think so myself. Talk is better than killing, so let me do the talking. If I fail, then, you can do the killing. And another thing, a little horse-play is acceptable, but don't make it too rough, we ain't got time for personal quarrels. If any of you start looking for a fight, you come to me, and you'll have one. We got no privileged characters on this drive. We all have a job to do, so let's work together. Don't let me see any of you shirking your responsibility. You do your job to the best of your ability. That's all I ask."

"Any man who feels like this outfit needs more than one boss, better roll his ass toward the house, because I can't use him. Right or wrong, I still give the orders. Between here and our destination I'm the law, and I'll break the first man's back who disobeys my orders."

"We'll pick up every stray we run across on this drive, and you boys can share what ever they bring." Mac's last statement brought smiles to the drover's faces—all but one.

Ned looked at Mac, his eyes showing disapproval. "You're talking about days of extra riding. It ain't no easy chore riding down strays in brush country. We'll be on the trail weeks longer."

"It's good business for the men, makes them more a part of things. They have more to look forward to at the end of the drive than sore asses and small wages. Every drive loses stock, and ours won't be any different, and we'll not ride past a single stray that crosses our path. In case of a stampede, cows can scatter for miles, some too damned tired to wander. Eventually these cows will drift back together. Some will join another herd of their own free will."

"I think we should put it to a vote," Ned suggested.

"I said there would be no privileged characters on this drive, and that includes you. If you're figuring on rushing this herd through just so you can get back to the house, you might as well head home right now."

Ned shrugged his shoulders in defeat. "You're the boss."

Mac was aware of Ned's emotional involvement, and he hoped he wouldn't let it interfere with his common sense. It could cause a conflict, and that they didn't need.

Shorty Nolan, an old wrangler, was hired on to herd the extra cutting horses. Good horse flesh Mac respected, and he didn't intend to ride any horse into the ground. The wide loopers rode the hell out of their mounts, switching off as needed to give them a rest.

The first day out the herd moved slow, winding across rocky prairie and brush country, seeing few trees and not much water. It took a day to get strung out good, with the men working together in harmony.

The drovers urged the herd forward keeping them in a tight bunch, pushing them to close gaps, swinging wide to catch the drifters, keeping the stragglers moving forward in the drag.

Mac sat straight as a soldier in his double-cinch saddle, watching and enjoying the sight of the men working. They were all seasoned and didn't need any orders from him, and he didn't insult their intelligence by looking for fault. He wore good high-heeled boots, strapped with steel Spanish spurs. For protection from the sun during the long hours in the saddle, he wore a new top-cover, held on by a buckskin string at the back of his neck.

Ned and Travis Asher took the point, while Keith Hulcy, Harvy Lerner, Frost Jackson, Tracy Weaver, Ron Troy, Grady Jensen, and Marve Oats took their positions as flankers and swing men. Edgar Long and Dale Parish were assigned to ride drag because they were young and less experienced. They wore leather flaps over their faces to protect their nose and throat from the boiling dust.

The first few days were the hardest for both man and beast. By the time the herd was trail broke, the men were too tired to eat or sleep properly. After the herd was bedded down, the night riders took over, working in shifts. Each man was in charge of his own bedroll. If he failed to roll and cord his bedding, the cook would leave it behind and he would do without it the rest of the trip. There was no nurse maid to pick up after them.

Zeek kept the fire going, and food and coffee ready at all times of the night while he snored beneath the wagon. The men were obliged to help themselves to the biscuits and whatever grub they could find, and to drink the reboiled coffee as long as their stomachs could tolerate it. It was not unusual to see the hands drying the dishes. From time to time Mac would grab a flour sack and help get the dishes out of the way.

They all depended on Zeek, he was not only the cook, but the doctor in case one of the men got hurt. He had even set a few bones in his time, including his own leg. For all he was worth, the men didn't mind coddling him to keep him in his good-natured mood. It was a well known fact among punchers that if the cook went sour, so did the food. And nothing could be worse that having a cook quit a few hundred miles from the nearest town with a bunch of hungry men on hand.

CHAPTER

26

There was very little enjoyment on the cattle drive, so when Dale Parish, the youngest, tallest, and by far the skinniest drover in the outfit, took a rope in his unskilled hand to catch a fresh horse, the men would gather around for a good laugh. He always managed to rope the wrong horse, or the right horse in the wrong place. Several times he came close to starting a stampede.

Mac hated to put the damper down on the men's sport, but he decided it was safer for them all to have Tracy Weaver, who hurled out a more accurate coil, rope the horse Dale pointed out, and save wear and tear on both Dale and the animals. Some of the horses were a little green, but to a seasoned puncher it made little difference. They could ride any horse and stay in the saddle. However in Dale's case, it did make a difference, and he almost always had the misfortune of choosing one of the more lively mounts. Then the bucking would bring laughter and a lot of shouted advice, especially appeals to Dale not to grab the saddle-horn, and he would usually wind up on the ground with a handful of mane and a face full of dirt.

Their day started when Zeek yelled, "Chow," and that was before the sun came up. They would gather around the fire for bacon, biscuits, and mush, eaten out of tin plates while they either stood, squatted, or sat on their heels. They drank boiling hot coffee out of tin cups that blistered their hands if they held it without gloves, and the handle was no exception. After breakfast, it was another day in the saddle. They began by prodding the cattle to their feet, circling them, and moving them into position. By first light the herd would be on its move, fanning out behind the lead steers, heading north.

By the end of the second week the herd was trail wise and easier to handle, with enough grass and water to survive. They were moved slowly when the grass was good, giving them time to graze at least an hour a day, and allowed to drink when water was available. The strays were not as plentiful as Mac had hoped, so they lost very little time chasing them down.

They came upon their first Indian village three weeks from the starting time. A band of warriors rode out to pow-wow with Mac, and departed in good spirits taking three steers with them.

"Do you think they're satisfied?" Ned asked, a note of doubt in his tone.

"If they wanted more they would have took 'um."

"You mean you would have let 'um take more?"

"Three steers is a pretty cheap price in exchange for fourteen lives, wouldn't you say?"

"If it works. They may come back tonight and collect fourteen scalps while we lay sleeping in our blankets."

"You got the wrong idea about Indians, boy. They only kill when they're threatened. They'll remain peaceable as long as the white men leave 'um be. This is their hunting ground. They don't like being pushed and stepped on any better than we do."

"What right do they have to demand cows? In exchange for what? They know we're just passing through."

"In the first place, they didn't demand a thing. I gave them the beef in exchange for scaring off their game, trampling down their buffalo grass land, and feeding them dust and flies. Anytime a herd this size crosses country it's bound to shake up Mother Nature some." Ned said no more but his face held an expression of disapproval.

Frost Jackson had pretty well walked the straight and narrow since the Indian incident the day after Ned and Dawn were married. He knew he owed Ned his life, and the only way he could show his appreciation was to keep his mouth shut about Dawn. But as appreciative as he was, he still hated Ned's guts.

Mac had felt apprehensive when he hired Frost on for the drive. He feared that the bad blood between them might cause trouble. Although their attitude toward one another was cool and evasive, they were able to work together as though nothing disagreeable had gone between them. Mac's main reason for taking Frost along was to get him away from Dawn. With both him and Ned out of the way, Frost was apt to get a little flagrant, especially with a few drinks under his belt. Because of his reputation for causing trouble, Mac marveled at his behavior thus far. However, before the drive was halfway to Muskogee, Frost managed to trigger their cold war into one of flaming hostility.

One night the bone weary, red eyed, drovers lounged around the chuck wagon engrossed in one of Shorty Nolen's yarns while they ate their evening meal. Frost pulled a bottle from beneath his shirt, poured a good measure into a cup and swigged it down.

"Better go easy on that stuff," Ned warned.

"Who left you in charge?" Frost returned, already feeling the affects because of his previous nips.

"You know Mac's orders."

"Mac ain't here. By the time he gets back from checking the herd I'll be feeling no pain." He held the bottle out to Ned. "Why don't you take a pull?"

"You must be crazy," Travis Asher spoke up. "Cattle drives and whiskey don't mix. Mac will have your hide for this."

"A little drink never hurt nobody. Ain't that right, Ned?" He laughed and took another mouthful. "I don't think you boys know much about ole Ned here. Why, he's an expert on drowning his sorrows at the Silver Buckle."

"Shut your mouth, Frost," Ned warned.

"What's the matter? Don't you like to talk about your happy home life? Come on, have a little drink with me. Might help you forget about that beautiful wife of yours." He held the bottle out to Ned again, a spiteful smile playing across his face.

Ned came to his feet, fire dancing in his eyes. He stood over Frost, his fists clenched in anger.

Frost stood also, smiling at Ned. "You are a lucky man. You married the cream of the crop. Makes me wonder why a man with a wife like Dawn, would wallow with a whore like Marcy."

Ned belted him in the face, sending him sprawling into the dirt.

"Get up, you son of a bitch!" Ned roared.

Frost suddenly lost his head in a moment of drunken crazed anger and went for his gun. Travis, guessing Frost's next move, brought his big foot down hard on his arm just as he snapped his .45 from the holster.

"I wouldn't do that if I was you," Travis said in a threatening tone, his hand resting on the butt of his own gun. "You just don't make comments about a man's wife and live to tell about it."

There was a moment of uneasy silence while the only sound was the crackling of the fire. All eyes were on Frost. He made no comment, nor did his hand relax on his pistol grips. Ned's hand rested on his own iron, still holstered, his eyes wild, the veins standing out on the side of his neck in pulsing cords.

"Butt out Travis," Frost barked. "It's time me and Ned settled this."

"Not a chance," Travis snorted, his gray eyes not leaving Frost's face. "You crazy sonovabitch! One gun shot and we got a stampede." He stepped down harder on Frost's wrist. "Drop it or I'll break your arm."

Frost cried out in pain, relaxed his fingers and let the gun drop back into his holster. "That's better. Now stand up."

"We'll finish this later," Ned barked, "as soon as we deliver this herd. Mac's counting on every man here to do his job, and I don't intend to let him down."

"The time for playing games is over," Frost said.

"You say when," Ned challenged coolly.

"When we reach Muskogee, unless you want to make your wife a widow sooner."

"I ain't figuring on her being a widow."

"Then you better start, 'cause you ain't got much time left to get used to the idea." Frost picked up his bedroll and stomped away in the darkness, brushing dirt from the seat of his pants.

Ned turned his attention to Travis. "Why did you step in?"

"I wasn't gonna just stand there and watch him blow your head off."

"Do you think he can take me?"

"I've seen him draw. I know damned well he can."

"I figure the same way."

"Then why did you challenge him?"

"I had to. The bastard is challenging me for my wife. I have to kill him. That's the only way I can stop him."

"Your wife won't give him a second look."

"He already tried to force himself on her. What's to keep him from doing it again?"

"I think you better start practicing."

"Maybe I should take some lessons from Holliman."

"Frost was drunk; chances are that by morning he'll be willing to forget about the whole thing."

"No he won't," Ned said sullenly.

When Zeek told Mac about the clash between Ned and Frost, he erupted like a volcano, kicked Frost out of his bedroll and collared him. "You start anymore trouble on this drive, and by God, I'll kill you! I don't want my daughter's name on the lips of any man in this camp." His eyes were cold and his words blunt.

"Your motherly instinct is very touching Mac, but when this drive ends you stay the hell out of my way. I got a score to settle with Ned, and I aim to do it."

"I'm not going to warn you again. If you cause the least rumble, I'll cut you loose from this drive in the middle of nowhere. We'll see what a big man you are trying to snake your way past the Indians. Your hair might look mighty pretty hanging from some Comanche tent pole. If you got any whiskey hid out, you fetch it and give it to Zeek. He'll keep it for you until this drive is finished, and if you got any ideas contrary to mine, get your gear together and clear out. And another thing, don't go threatening me with a gun. I'll take the damned thing away from you and feed it to you. I don't need a gun to handle you. Just one more word about my daughter and I'll cut your damned tongue out."

"I figured Ned would go running to you for protection."

"Ned ain't said a damned word. Zeek told me I had better keep you in line before you start a stampede or cause a killing."

"Well now, that does surprise me."

"He don't need me to protect him. What's it going to be?"

"You're a hard man, McCloud. You don't give me much choice."

"I don't give you any choice. When you signed on for this drive you were well aware of the rules."

"I signed on to help drive your herd to Oklahoma, and that I'll do, but when we reach the end of the line don't give me any more orders."

"Walk easy, Frost, or I'll give you something you'll dislike a hell of a lot more than orders." Mac gave him an unmistakable look before he swung into the saddle. "When I play, I play for keeps. Remember that." He gave the brim of his hat a determined yank and rode away in the direction of the herd.

The weeks that followed were hot and dry. They found themselves in the middle of a vast parched plain that hadn't seen a drop of rain in months. They had passed the last water hole a day and a half back, and from the looks of the situation they might not find another drop of moisture until they reached the Canadian River. They drove the herd across three dry creek beds where the grass had become sparse dry patches, not tall enough to hide a jack rabbit. The herd was walking the fat off their bones and threatening dehydration. Mac was worried, and the drovers could certainly sympathize with him. By the end of the second day the animals were bawling their heads off and had slowed to a snail's pace. More and more steers dropped into the drag, moving in straggling gaps, falling behind, magnifying the dusty job of the two drag men who prodded them to keep them moving.

Mac sat staring into the flickering embers of the night fire. He had just come back from circling the herd and spotted seven dead steers.

"Looks bad don't it, boss?" Zeek said, handing him a cup of coffee. "We're down to the last barrel of water. It won't last more than a day even if we ration it out."

Mac wiped sweat from his eyes and said mournfully, "It's a helpless feeling to stand by and watch two thousand head of beef start laying down and dying, and there ain't a damned thing we can do about it. We must have lost close to twenty head today, tomorrow will be worse, the day after we'll lose 'um all."

By day light the prairie was a sweltering dust bowl. The drovers were ashamed for having to push the suffering, fading, animals to their death, watching them walk off and sweat out the precious moisture that was keeping them alive.

Mac was the first to spot what he believed to be a war party following the herd. They trailed along at a steady pace about a thousand yards behind.

Mac looked ahead at the rolling prairie that offered little protection, save a few rocks and mesquite trees. If the Indians attacked, they would be caught out in the open. When they stopped for the noon meal and to rest the herd and horses, Mac gave them a quick run-down on the dangerous situation they faced.

"We got company men, and I think they plan on having beef for supper."

"What's it mean? Them following the herd like that?" Dale asked, feeling a weakness in the middle of his belly.

"One thing is sure, they ain't following us for the fun of eating dust. My guess is that they are hungry for something a little tastier. You don't find game where there is no grass, trees, or water. I think we got a bunch of starving Indians breathing down our necks."

"How many do you think there is?" asked Shorty.

"They're too far off to count. My guess is they'll start to increase in number very shortly."

"What you aim for us to do?" Zeek said, spurting tobacco juice into the fire.

"We could give them a few head," Ned suggested. "They're dying anyway. It worked the last time."

"It won't work this time."

The tone of Mac's voice turned Ned cold. There was no longer any question about it. They were in trouble.

"What you're saying is that we got to fight." Ned asked the question with a statement of fact.

"If they were friendly, they would ride in and make their wishes known. The fact that they haven't, and are trailing at such a safe distance, pretty well tells the story. All we can do is keep the herd moving and wait 'um out. There is one consolation. They got water someplace. The very fact that they're alive out here in the middle of hell speaks for that."

"Hey, you're right!" Frost agreed, "but they ain't about to lead us to it."

Mac smiled for the first time in four days. "I've got a hunch that we're headed in the right direction. We didn't find water behind us, so it stands to reason that we ain't reached it yet. If we were going in the wrong direction they wouldn't be trailing along behind us to watch the cattle drop dead. They're smart enough to realize that the herd needs water, and they also know that we know more about driving the herd than they do. I think they're trailing us while we drive their beef. It makes sense to me."

"So when we reach water, they kill us and take the beef. Is that what you think?" Ned asked.

"I think they will try to kill us."

"You know damned well they'll have us outnumbered."

"That they will, but we will have time to take cover and defend ourselves before they swarm all over us."

"Take cover where?" Ned asked.

"Behind our mounts if need be."

"What's your plan?" Ron said.

"I want you to take point with Ned and Travis until we get up a good cloud of dust, then I want you to ride out a ways and see what you can find. Stay far enough ahead so if you spot water you can warn us before the herd smells it. We won't have to drive them then, they'll stampede toward it. In the mean time we'll mix with the herd and fire on the Indians before they get close enough to scalp us."

"But we don't know how many we'll be fighting." Ned said. "What difference does it make. We don't have a choice. We fight or we die, might die anyway, but at least we'll stand a chance. All right, boys, let's get this herd moving."

CHAPTER

27

The men not only had the heat and thirst clutching them with claws of death, now they rode helplessly toward the threat of being attacked and killed by Indians.

Mac rode past the swing toward the drag, keeping up wind of the dust, watching the Indians. They were closing the gap slowly, and they had increased in number to what looked like a hundred

Tracy Weaver, one of the swing men, sat a little to one side in his saddle looking over his shoulder, watching as the Indians moved up, and he felt panic blooming in his guts. Mac whipped by him headed for the point.

"See any sign of Ron yet?" he yelled, drawing his horse in line with Ned's.

"Not yet. What's going on back there? We can't make out a thing in all this dust."

"The little band of Indians has grown since last count. We got plenty of trouble. They're moving in for the kill. I want you to pass the word, when I fire two shots we'll turn the herd. We'll do it slow, and then stampede 'um right down those bastard's throats. If our timing is right, we'll have the herd pouring over them before they know what hit 'um. Ron may be back anytime. I hope he finds water, because as weak as they are, we'll lose every head after we push them into a stampede. We'll turn them nine o'clock and run 'um right down the middle. If any of them red devils get out of our path, use your rifles. Now spread the word, and don't drag your feet."

"Here comes Ron!" Travis yelled. As he spoke, Mac dug his spurs into his mount's flanks and shot forward to meet him.

"Water!" he cried.

How much?" Mac asked excitedly.

"Enough."

"When I give the signal we'll turn the herd back on the Indians. We can't whip about a hundred warriors, so we'll let the herd run 'um down."

"Those cows will kill themselves. They're suffering already." Ron said grimly.

"It's our only chance to come out of this with our scalps. I'll sacrifice my herd gladly to save even one man."

Minutes later Ned rode back into the lead. "We're set!"

"Good!" Mac swung to the edge of the herd and rode east until he had a clear view of the Indians. They were near enough for him to see their war paint, and were closing rapidly. Mac raised his Colt and squeezed off two rounds. The men swung into action. Ned, Travis, and Harvy commenced crowding the lead steers, while the swing men worked nine o'clock from the edge, turning them back toward the drag. The rest of the herd followed suit. When the point passed the drag in retreat, the drovers spurred their mounts for every last ounce of energy left in their thirst starved hides. They rode hard and fast, pointing the poor tired critters at the Indians like a gun, yipping, hollering, and screaming, saving their lead.

"Fan 'um out!" Mac yelled, waving his arms at the flankers to give way. The herd began to spread out as they swept directly into the path of the astounded war party that began to race in all directions panic stricken, trying to escape the rampaging mass of destruction that bore down on them with the force of a tidal wave.

The herd fanned out more, covering the Indians riding wide to avoid the rushing tangle of hooves and horns. The thundering herd split as the fan widened, and a flow of Indian ponies made for the hole. Mac saw the break and pulled his rifle from the saddle boot, locked his knees against his mount for balance, and fired into the pack. Frost, Keith, and Asher dropped back to give him a hand. About thirty bucks went down, their mounts breaking free.

Ned, Harvy, and Grady were riding hard to overtake the lead steers. Now that they had done their job, it was time to start the turn once more and head them in the direction of water. This time they had a more difficult chore, they were turning them on the run. All the drovers joined forces, their horses stretched to the breaking point, and the circle became complete The wild eyed excited animals were losing momentum and were finally brought to a trembling halt, with some falling to their knees, others ambling in circles looking for direction, their sides heaving, bawling, exhausted, wanting to lay down and die. The men sat slumped in their saddles on lathered mounts, bone tired, covered in dirt and sweat from head to boots, looking back at the trail of dead Indians, steers, and painted ponies strung out for more than a mile. Mac took a quick count and was relieved to find all thirteen of his men accounted for.

"Men," Mac said hoarsely, his throat raw from yelling. "You're a damned good bunch of drovers. I take my hat off to you. Unfortunately we don't have time to rest. We still have our work cut out for us. We've got to recover the scattered beef. Dead beef if we don't get them to water soon. Ron found water north east of here. I want him to take some of you boys and drive what's left of the herd toward the creek. As soon as you get them settled, leave two men to guard the herd, then double back here to give us a hand. We'll start rounding up strays. We'll drive the Indian ponies up too. What we get out of them will off-set some of our loss. I won't know how many we lost until we get 'um bunched. We'll spend a couple of days by the water hole to allow the stock time to recover, not to speak of ourselves. Zeek, you go with the herd and scare up some grub."

Once the herd was on the move again they drove like kittens, too tired to do otherwise. Several tried to lie down and were prodded to their feet and kept moving. They were pushed for every step they took until they got the scent of water, and then they were on the run again, thundering over the dry, hard, ground. The drovers let them go. They didn't stop until they reached the banks of the low running creek where they stood in water up to their knees, drinking.

By night-fall both man and beast was exhausted. They had rounded up over a hundred cows and thirty-eight Indian ponies. Shorty put them on lead lines and drove them to the creek to wash the war paint off their hides. Nine of the horses wore the U.S. brand. They had either been stolen or taken after they killed the riders. Some of the other horses were marked with brands or ear notches. They would decide what to do with them when they reached the stockyards.

Zeek stretched out on his blanket with a contented sigh, although his face was red and swollen from the heat of the fire he had cooked over. He laughed softly, and Mac turned to look at him curiously.

"I'll never forget this day as long as I live," Zeek said. "I wish I could of seen them buck's faces when they seen that herd coming straight at 'um. I been riding the range for forty years, and I ain't never had so much fun in my life. Anytime in the future, Mac, if you decide to make another drive, you can sure count on me."

Finding water had brought life saving relief to the men and animals, but it also brought gnats and mosquitoes. The tired drovers made night camp by the creek, upstream from the lowing, milling, cattle. It took a while before the cattle bedded down. They were still nibbling at anything green they could find, even chewing the low hanging branches of the trees that grew near the water.

The night was still thick with dust caused by the stampede. The men lay on their blankets sweating. The heat from the sun scorched earth penetrating their beds like a warming pan. The wind passing through the branches of the spiny mesquite trees that lined the sides of the slimy cattle trodden banks, brought no relief. It blew in warm gusts, shooting hot sand across the faces of the sleeping men.

Ned spent a sleepless night listening to the eerie wail of a screech owl, fanning mosquitoes, scratching, and worrying about the show-down with Frost that awaited him at the end of the drive, a showdown that would likely cost him his life. A senseless, foolish shedding of blood that would prove nothing.

The men bathed, shaved, and relaxed while the animals recuperated. They needed grass as well as water, and there was at least two day's grazing along the banks of the creek.

On the second day the sun rose in a glowing red blaze, shooting through the trees, glaring into the sullen faces of the saddle sore trail hands.

Rested now, and eager to finish what they had started, the drive moved out once more, a hundred and fifty-three head shorter than when they started, but Mac felt lucky to have salvaged a single steer. They trailed through rough, gopher infested, prairie, moved along the edge of ravines, over rock jutted hills, and brush thickets.

Mac began to worry when a low line of clouds blackened the horizon ahead of them. The dark mass of boiling clouds moved across the sky very quickly. A sudden crash of thunder sounded close, followed by ragged flashes of lightning that zigzagged toward the ground. The horses sensed the storm and danced nervously, rearing and whinnying.

"Looks like we're in for a blow," Mac cried, riding along side Ned and Travis in the lead. "Better make camp and wait this one out."

They bedded the herd down on the south side of a hill that was the first wind break they came to. The wind was gradually gaining force, and with it came the smell of rain.

"Looks like the drought's over," Mac said. "Time to break out our slickers."

"That figures," Travis commented. "We should be making the Canadian River crossing tomorrow. I've made that crossing a half-dozen times and it ain't never been running low."

"Stay saddled and tie up," Mac ordered. "We'll have plenty of riding to do before this night ends."

Around midnight the storm hit full force; the sky was lit up like a torch inside a cave as electrical jolts and thunder shook the ground. Rain was pouring down in blinding torrents.

The animals hovered together for protection. Several of the Indian ponies broke loose and made a run for freedom.

All hands struck for the herd in horrifying expectancy, but were able to hold them together in bawling, protesting, bunches. Morning came and the rain continued to fall in wind swept sheets, blowing across the cattle where they stood churning in hoof deep mud. The drovers circled the herd continuously, while the pelting rain beat down on their hats, the brims dumping a steady stream of water.

By mid-morning the rain had tamed to a steady drizzle, cloaking the sky with a gray misty veil. Mac resumed the drive, pushing the reluctant steers over the slippery rocks and boggy ground. They moved slow and steady, splashing through puddles, over gopher holes, and lunging across rocky terrain. The drovers kept them moving, pushing them toward the Canadian River, not taking the time to rest or eat. They munched biscuits as they rode.

Night found a wet, weary, miserable, bunch of men huddled around the cook's fire, grumbling and complaining, trying to dry out.

Early the following morning they reached the river. Mac stood on the bank watching the brown, boiling, water rushing past, carrying with it a wall of debris. The flooding had spread beyond the brush infested banks, cutting a trail into every small creek and branch, sweeping a clean path as it rolled bubbling dark and frothy with incredible speed.

"It's out of banks," Travis said, turning to look at Mac with a troubled expression. "I never seen it this high. It's three times above normal, and still rising."

"We cross now," Mac said, realizing that to wait would mean an even more treacherous crossing. Mac and Travis rode along the bank looking for the safest place to cross. They chose the spot carefully, and Travis rode out into the water to check the current.

"Mighty swift!" he yelled over his shoulder. He turned his mount and rode back to Mac where he waited on the shoal.

"Can we make it?" Mac questioned with a note of doubt, watching as Travis' horse struggled awkwardly up the river bank.

"It's deep and swift, but I think we can make it if we bunch the herd and keep them moving. They'll have to swim most all the way."

"All right!" Mac shouted. "Push the lead steers out in front, get the point started and keep 'um moving. Keep 'um bunched so they don't drift. Move 'um out!"

The lead steers balked momentarily, and Ned stung them with the sharp snap of his quirt. They leaped forward and splashed into the pounding flood of dirty water.

"Keep 'um moving!" Mac shouted as he rode into the treacherous path of the river, staying clear of the wild thrashing horns of the struggling steers. The current became even more hazardous as they neared the middle. The cows were swimming, pushed by the current they were fighting to overcome.

"They're drifting!" Ned yelled. Ron, Travis, Dale, and Shorty quickly joined him, plunging their mounts into the break attempting to push them back. Some of the weaker cows had been overpowered by the force of the turbulence that carried them down stream, tossed and battered, thrashing helplessly as they lost their sense of direction.

Ned felt his horse begin to drift with the steers. In a burst of panic he jerked him around and started toward the bank for safety. Suddenly a ton of long horns and muscle struck his mount a disabling blow and the animal crumbled beneath him in bleeding agony, his guts protruding through a gash in his side. Ned was thrown into the dark churning water beside his horse and they were swept helplessly down stream like two feathers in the wind.

Mac spurred his horse viciously, moving toward Ned who was screaming in shameless hysteria. "Hang on!" Mac cried, watching in a state of panic as the swift current pulled Ned under, filling his nose and mouth with water. Flailing and pumping his arms, he fought his way back to the surface amidst the struggling cows. A steer rolled past him carried by the awesome strength of the speeding water, its long horns tearing at the flesh on Ned's back. Mac saw Ned's face dimly through the swirling black torrent, his hands clawing in wild panic as the tide pulled him under and swept him away before Mac could reach him.

"Ned!" Mac screamed, spurring his horse forward in panic flight in an attempt to save his son-in-law. Travis, realizing Mac was in danger of reaping the same fate as Ned, rode along side of him, forcing his horse to a narrow sandbar on the opposite side of the river.

"You fool!" Mac screamed. "Ned's out there! Get out of my way!"

"You can't help him, Mac," Travis said forcefully. "He's gone."

Mac shuddered in horror as he realized Travis was right. "Oh, my God!" he cried, staring helplessly at the surging water, then he gave way to a convulsion of sobs.

The drovers continued to work while Mac walked up and down the wet river bank, gravely searching the dark water for some sign of Ned. He paced the bank until the last steer made it across.

Camp was pitched for the night about a half mile down river. When everything was under control, Travis rode back to the crossing in search of Mac. He found him sitting on a boulder near the water's edge in a state of utter devastation.

"We got a fire going and a pot of coffee made. Come on, you can't help Ned by sitting here."

"Take some of the men and ride downstream," he said in a disconsolate tone. "See if you can recover Ned's body."

"It's no use, Mac. His body is most likely miles from here by now. If it was right under our noses we couldn't see it. The water's too muddy. His body won't surface for several days."

"I can't just leave him here! Do like I say!"

"You're the boss." Travis turned his horse and rode gloomily back to camp to deliver Mac's order. Travis and six of the drovers, already fagged from the long hard hours in the saddle, searched until it was too dark to see, while Mac sat hunched in grief on the boulder, his face in his hands, his mind replaying the pitiful scene of Ned's clutching hands reaching out to him from his foaming grave. God help me, he thought. How will I tell Dawn. She will blame me as long as I live.

"Mac," Travis called cautiously approaching him. "We had better get back to camp. It's too dark to search anymore tonight. We can start again at first Light."

"He was so close. If only I had tried harder to reach him."

"You did all that was humanly possible to save him."

"I should have done more. His hand was only inches from mine when he went under for the last time."

"It wouldn't have made any difference if you had pulled him out."

"What the hell are you saying?"

"I saw that steer plunge into Ned's back. It sliced him open like a ripe watermelon." Seeing the shock on Mac's face made Travis ashamed of what he had just said. "I'm sorry Mac, but I thought you should know. He went under because that steer cut the life out of him. The hand that clutched out to you was the hand of a dead man."

"I didn't know. God! I didn't know."

Travis had thought at first not to tell Mac what he had seen, but it had been impossible for him to remain silent. The shock of knowing the truth would wear off, where as the guilt he felt at first would have haunted him the rest of his life.

Mac returned to camp with Travis and sat silently by the fire drinking coffee, unable to touch a bite of food. The drovers glanced at him sympathetically, pitying him for what they knew he was suffering.

After a long silence, Mac looked at Frost with staring eyes, his hate for him obvious. "This saves you the trouble of having to shoot him down, don't it?"

"Now wait a minute, Mac, I hate this as much as anybody."

"You're a liar! You've been looking for an excuse to kill Ned for a long time. How does it feel to get cheated out of the pleasure?"

"Who knows, he might have killed me."

"If you had thought that way for one minute, you would never have challenged him. I'm going to tell you something, Frost, the only thing that saved you was the fact that he did drown, because I planned on killing you the minute you stood up to him. I was looking forward to blowing a hole in your back the size of a dinner plate. And I'll still kill you if I ever see you hanging around my daughter. So you see, you lose anyway. I'm still here to see to that. Maybe you would like to challenge me next."

Frost became suddenly mute and stalked away from the circle of firelight, leaving behind him an unpleasant silence.

After the drovers turned in for the night, Mac sat alone by the fire, his thoughts drifting ahead to the moment when he would come face to face with his daughter and the heart-rending task of breaking the bad news of her husband's death.

CHAPTER

During Ned's absence Dawn spent her days at the trading post helping Charles Morgan. Charles had agreed to take over while Mac was away. When he returned Charles would pin a star on his shirt and go back to work, but not as sheriff this time, as Darrell's deputy. He had not asked for Dawn's help, but feeling the unfamiliarity of his new position made him reluctant to refuse. He was not a business man and didn't pretend to be. The job was made easy because of his association with all the customers. Having been their sheriff for so many years they naturally trusted him.

Although Dawn insisted on working at the store, she did not do so with the good of the business at heart. She had come to regard the trading post as her sanctuary, leaving the care of the house and baby Henry more and more in Debbie's most capable hands. She loved her son but hated the responsibility. She was beginning to feel trapped. Her happiness depended on a total lack of constraint, and her quest for freedom was a growing fever in her blood.

As the weeks and months passed even her enthusiasm over the new house began to fade. All the things she had once wanted so much were becoming meaningless.

Having Jack around was even beginning to get on her nerves. She would catch him staring at her in a way that made her uncomfortable. His happy, care-free attitude could become quite serious at times, admitting that he admired her and thought her beautiful. He went so far as to call his brother a fool for going off and leaving her, that she should never have to be lonely. Statements like that put her on guard and she was careful to avoid any personal contact. Working at the trading post had eased the tension because she was rarely around him anymore. On the few occasions when she was, she treated him kindly, also indifferently.

Making up with Ned had given her a peculiar sense of purification, prompting her to purge her mind of wicked thoughts. However the tedious restraints and ethical rules she assumed were becoming increasingly hard for her to maintain.

Darrell Holliman popped in at least three times a day to see how they were getting along, offering his assistance if needed. Although Dawn used a considerable amount of self-discipline when he was there, she could not deny that the sight of him excited her. She was impressed by his new image. He was the town's hero and the badge he wore fit him perfectly.

Dawn's chilly attitude disturbed Darrell but failed to alter his actions. As the challenge grew, so did his determination. He wondered if her elusiveness had anything to do with Ned's absence. Could she possibly miss him? Was she lonely and spending her time at the store as an antidote? And then he had another thought. Could her secret lover be back in the picture?

Dawn remained cool and poised during Darrell's visits at the store, but she was finding it hard to ignore the flame his presence fired inside her when he was near. She recalled with shame the exciting moments she had spent in his arms. No matter how hard she tried, she was losing control of her pure thoughts, and Darrell was the reason.

He paid them a visit one morning as soon as the door was unlocked for business.

"Don't you have enough to do as the sheriff of our town?" Dawn asked. He looked at her and smiled and she suddenly felt warm all over, admitting to herself that she always looked forward to his visits.

"Been pretty slow around town lately," he replied.

"I hadn't noticed." Their eyes met and held for a long moment before she looked away.

Morgan paid no attention to the looks that passed between them, nor did he find anything unusual about the sheriff hanging around the store.

He had a lot of respect for Darrell, and was anxious to work with him. "I think I'll go to breakfast while Darrell's here to help you look after the store—unless you two want to go eat first."

"I'm not hungry," Dawn answered, disregarding Darrell.

Charles pulled his apron off and hung it on a nail behind the counter. "I won't be gone long."

"Take your time," Darrell said happily, watching him move heavily toward the door. As soon as the door closed behind him, Darrell's attention swung in Dawn's direction. "Will you have dinner with me after the store closes?"

"I can't. I'm a married woman."

"You never let that stop you before."

She stood motionless behind the counter that she felt was her island of safety because she couldn't trust herself. "Ned will be gone for a long time. People will get the wrong idea. I can't."

"So what? Would you have dinner with me if he was home?"

"No."

"Then you really don't have an excuse. Why don't you tell me the real reason you're avoiding me?"

She looked away. "I made up with my husband before he left."

"What are you telling me?" he asked sharply. He took her by the shoulders and turned her to face him.

She felt a strange sense of guilt and struggled free of his hands. "Is there a law against a woman trying to save her marriage?"

"You don't have a marriage. What you're doing is the same as feeding a dead man. What about all the negative feelings you have for him? Were you lying?"

"No."

"Then why?"

"I have a son to consider."

"In what respect? And I don't want to hear that hog-wash about a boy needing a father."

"It's not hog-wash!"

"Ned isn't the boy's father."

"How can you say—"

Midway through her statement, Alma Fry walked in and looked around. "Where is Mr. Morgan?" She glared first at Dawn, then Darrell.

"Gone to breakfast. May I help you?" Dawn offered.

Alma looked Dawn up and down, her face pinched with disapproval. "No, thank you. I'll come back later, when Mr. Morgan is here. Good-day."

"Good-day," Dawn mimicked.

"Is that the kind of people you're trying to impress with your purity act? By all means don't give the old bitch a reason to look down on you."

"She always looks down on me. The jealous old bitch!"

"Since you won't have dinner with me, I'll drive you home."

"I shouldn't."

"Why not?"

"Have you forgotten that Ned left his brother Jack to spy on me?"

"Is that what he's doing?"

"He watches me constantly."

"For Ned's benefit? Or his own?"

"What do you mean?"

"He's not a kid, and he thinks like a man. Be careful."

"I ignore him to the point of rudeness."

"That's good, but why are you giving me the ice treatment? I promise to be a perfect gentleman."

She hesitated. "I've turned over a new leaf."

Darrell laughed. "And you're bored."

"Maybe."

"I'll be back later. Wait for me."

"You're not worth waiting for."

"I can entertain you."

"I think you're looking to be entertained."

He laughed again. "I think it's mutual."

That evening Morgan closed the trading post late because customers kept dropping in. Business had been slow all day and he didn't want to pass up a sale, even though he was tired and his feet hurt.

"You go on home, Dawn," he said. "I'll finish up here and lock the door."

"I'm in no hurry," she said, wondering where Darrell was.

After Charles closed up, bid Dawn good-evening, and hobbled toward the hotel for supper, she lingered a few minutes in front of the store looking toward the sheriff's office because Darrell had asked her to wait for him. He's too sure of himself, she thought spitefully, turned around and headed toward the livery stable to get her buggy.

"What's your hurry?" Darrell said, walking up behind her unexpectedly.

"Oh!" she cried, and spun around to face him.

"I didn't mean to startle you."

"Don't you know better than to sneak up behind a person like that?"

"Sorry," he said, his hand on her arm. "I guess it's the Indian coming out in me."

"You're not Indian," she snapped, her cheeks burning. "Why did you say that?"

"Hey! What's wrong with you? I was only joking."

"Well, don't joke about a thing like that."

He was surprised, wondering how such an innocent jest could provoke her to anger. "Come on," he said after a moment. "Walk over to the office with me. I have a get something, then I'll drive you home."

"Maybe you had better forget about driving me home."

"Don't start backing out on me."

"You still have work to do—"

"It won't take five minutes. All right?"

She shook her head, and he took her arm and walked her to the jail. She waited patiently as he opened the top desk drawer and took out an envelope. He held it out to her.

"What is it?"

"A letter to Mac. Doctor Keel asked me to give it to you. It's from Mac's father."

Dawn accepted the letter with trembling hands. "I can't believe it. He wrote! And after all these years? I wonder why!"

"Why don't you open it and find out?"

"I can't do that. It's addressed to Father."

"It may be important, and Mac won't be back for a long time." She turned the letter over in her hands, studying the handwriting carefully, then placed it unopened inside her handbag.

They looked up as Darrell's deputy, Ray Thompson, entered the office.

"I'm sorry, Sheriff," he said apologetically. "I didn't know you had company."

"Don't apologize, I'm glad you're here. Look after the office for me. I'm going to see that Mrs. Rowling gets home safely."

"Sure thing, glad to."

"With your permission," Darrell said politely, and held the door open for her. She made no reply, lifted her skirt slightly and stepped out on the porch. Ray's eye's followed them with a curious expression.

She moved quickly ahead of him, and he hurried to catch up. "What's your rush?"

"I can get home just fine by myself."

"I believe you," he said easily, and continued to walk beside her to the livery stable. Wes Hawkins, who ran the livery, saw them enter and hurried to hitch up Dawn's horse while Darrell dropped the saddle on his mount and tied him to the back of the carriage.

Dawn glanced at him, feeling a surge of excitement. Darrell Holliman was a handsome man, and she admired him for what he stood for. She had let her guard down, deciding to give the old long tongued bats something else to gossip about.

Darrell helped her into the carriage and climbed in beside her. She felt the brush of his hip as he settled himself close to her, and a hot flash traveling up her spine. He snapped the reins and the stout gray mare moved effortlessly down the street. They were neither one surprised when they drew quite a bit of attention.

Leaving the town behind, Dawn relaxed, glad to be away from the staring eyes and whispered insults. She felt safe with Darrell, and was glad she could depend on him. She didn't want to think about the rush of her heart or the tingle traveling up her spine. She had no right to feel as she did, but did not object when he drew the horse to a halt and took her into his arms. She had secretly wanted it to happen, and she returned every kiss. He drew apart from her and looked into her eyes.

"You don't really believe you can make a go of your marriage do you?"

"He loves me so much, and I have treated him mean and selfish. I feel ashamed for hurting him. I should never have married him. It wasn't fair. He deserved better."

"Then why did you?"

"I was going to have a baby."

"What did it matter?"

"I guess I was ashamed."

"Marrying him didn't change the way people feel about you. Why would you care?"

"I didn't want to hurt and humiliate my father."

"What it all boils down to is this: are you willing to sacrifice your happiness by staying with a man you don't love just to pacify your father? You can't be in love with Ned and kiss me the way you do."

"I don't love you either," she said frankly.

"You feel something for me." He kissed her again. "What is it?"

She pulled away. "I don't know." She answered without looking at him.

"Go away with me, now."

"I can't do that."

"Yes you can. You want me just as much as I want you."

"I'm afraid you misunderstood me. I like your company, I even like you, but I'm not in love with you. I have no desire to run away with you, now or ever."

"I may have misunderstood a lot of things, but not the way you kiss me. I have never had a friend kiss me like that." He watched her closely for a moment, then said thoughtfully, "I'm a patient man, but don't expect me to make a damned fool of myself. We're two of a kind. When we see something we want, we go after it, but we neither one want to be tied down. I will never tie you down. We need to spend some time together, away from here, without hypercritical bitches like Alma breathing down our collar. I want you completely, no restraints, no fear. Just the two of us doing what we feel. I'll take you to my place where we can have complete privacy."

"I'm not a whore, Mr. Holliman. Don't you ever try to proposition me again."

"If I thought you were a whore I wouldn't be seen with you on the street. What I'm trying to say is this: When two people find pleasure with one another, why wait?"

"Take me home."

"You really are a coward. I'm surprised."

"I don't intend to make Debbie and Jack suspicious."

"You mean they don't trust you?" he said, setting the horse in motion.

"Probably not."

"Don't you get a bit tired of looking over your shoulder and feeling you have to hide your behavior from a bunch of jerks who need to mind their own business?"

"It's not that bad."

"Then why are you in such a hurry?"

"Need you ask?"

"So you're still afraid of me."

"It's not you I'm afraid of. It's me. I feel different when I'm with you, and I like the way you make me feel, but I can't let myself go. I'm a married woman."

"How far would you go if you weren't married?"

"Not as far as you would like."

"You're as warm as a summer breeze one minute, and like a snow storm the next. Maybe one of these days I'll discover the secret to your hot and cold nature."

"You probably understand me as well as I understand myself." There was a slight tremor in her voice and he took her hand. Her fingers felt cold to his touch and he tightened his grip protectively.

"I have never met anyone like you," he said, his eyes taking in every adorable feature she possessed. She had a face like an angel, clear, smooth skin, classic features, perfectly formed neck and forehead. Her raven black hair curled softly about her pink cheeks, and the intoxicating cleavage of her full breasts fired his imagination. He wondered if he would be as jealous as Ned, if placed in a like position. How could any man walk away from such an exquisite woman? He was mystified by the mixture of her frankness and cunning, blended with mirth and a soft innocence. She was a woman who left nothing more to be desired, always the perfect lady—except for one mistake that came back to haunt her in the body of her child.

CHAPTER

By the time Dawn reached home the sun was almost down and evening shadows cloaked the country side. Debbie and Jack had finished their supper and Debbie was keeping the food warm for Dawn. This was the first time she had missed supper since she started working at the trading post. Although Debbie did not mention her anxieties to Jack, she could tell by his sullen attitude that he too was disturbed.

When Dawn entered the house with Darrell, looking quite happy and a bit flushed, Debbie cried in relief, "Thank goodness you're home! I was becoming concerned." She looked at Darrell and smiled. "If I had known you were seeing her home, Sheriff, I wouldn't have worried for one moment."

Jack rose slowly from his chair. "I'm going to have a look around before I go to bed."

"You need to put the buggy in the barn and unharness the horse," Darrell said.

Jack nodded. He resented Darrell's bossy attitude and the way he was squiring Dawn around. He was anxious for him to leave. "Do you need a mount, Sheriff?"

"No, I trailed mine. You can tie him at the hitching rail."

"Do you plan on staying a while?"

"I came to deliver Dawn safely, not to visit."

Jack nodded, more agreeably this time, and left the house.

"Thank you for seeing me home," Dawn said.

"My pleasure."

"How do you like your job?" Debbie said. "Is it exciting?"

"It's just a job, and it's far from exciting. Boring is more like it. I liked store keeping better."

"I always looked forward to having you wait on me, but of course Mr. Morgan is quite efficient. Now that Dawn works there she can pick up the supplies we need. That way I don't have to take the baby out."

"That sounds like a good arrangement. Of course you will have to do your own shopping for personal things. I noticed Mac got a new shipment of dresses."

"I'm surprised that you notice such things."

"I guess I'm still a store keeper at heart."

"Then I must come in and choose one. Oh, where are my manners? Have you had supper? I thought that perhaps you had taken Dawn to supper at the hotel and that's why she was late."

"I offered, but she turned me down. She's late because Charles closed late. He had a last minute run of business." She's fishing, he thought, and his irritation was apparent.

"You don't have to explain." Dawn said in a piqued voice. "I sorry," Debbie said, "I didn't mean to sound nosy."

"You sound like a mother hen," Dawn snapped.

Dawn's right, Darrell thought, she is being watched. "Since we have the mystery solved, and my services are no longer needed, I'll get on back to the office. "Good-night, ladies." He moved quickly out the door.

Jack was standing next to the hitching rail waiting for Darrell, holding the reins to his horse.

"Thanks," Darrell said, taking the reins from his hand. He had one foot in the stirrup when Jack said rather curtly.

"Not so fast, Holliman. I want a word with you."

Darrell stepped back down and looked at Jack rather humorously. "Go ahead. Get it off your chest. I hope you're not planning to challenge me."

"I am in a way. I hope you don't misunderstand what I'm about to say because I don't want to offend you, but I think you should stay clear of Dawn before people start to have some ugly thoughts."

"Does that include you?"

"It doesn't look right and I know Ned would object."

"Then let Ned do the objecting and you tend to your own business and keep your nose out of mine."

"It is my business. Mac put me in charge while he's gone."

"In charge of the cattle," Darrell said, wagging his finger in Jack's face, "not his daughter."

"Ned's my brother and I just thought—"

"Those thoughts can become unhealthy. Protecting people is my job, and I'll be the judge of whom or how I choose to do it. Your job is to take care of Mac's cows. I'll take care of Dawn." With that, he swung into the saddle, leaving Jack staring after his trail of dust.

When Jack returned to the parlor he was confronted by an angry sister-in-law.

"Have you appointed yourself my keeper?"

"All I'm trying to do is save you from starting a scandal."

"I have been gossiped about since I was nine years old," she said reproachfully. "The old nosy crows look down their noses at me like I stink. They will never accept me, no matter how sainted I am. Because I don't look like a fish in the face they all hate me. I could take my pick of the men in this town, and they hate me for that too. They would find fault with me if I were the virgin Mary. One ounce of wrong still outweighs a ton of right. Don't you judge me, Jack! I don't answer to you or this town!"

Jack was shocked by what she said. He had misjudged her and he was ashamed. He suddenly realized how much back biting she had endured because of Ned. He was responsible too, but no one was talking about him. Maybe they figured that the beating Mac gave Ned was punishment enough, and they had decided to punish Dawn in their own way. It wasn't fair.

"I'm real sorry," he said. "I had no idea."

"That's no excuse! You're just like all the rest, you want to believe the worst. Alma Fry came to the trading post today and refused to have me wait on her while Charles was at breakfast."

A swift show of anger appeared in Jack's eyes. "You don't have to stay there and put up with their insults."

"That's right. I can get insulted in my own home. I heard what you said to Darrell, and from the expression on his face, you had better watch your mouth around him. Sheriff Holliman is my friend, also a gentleman."

Jack nodded. "I'll apologize to him."

"You do that."

His eyes met hers squarely. "I promise to mind my own business from now on." He quickly left the room, deeply ashamed for having doubted her. Now that he understood, he was convinced that she could do no wrong.

After Jack went to bed, Debbie decided to air her views.

"Are you sure you know what you're doing?"

"About what?"

"Darrell Holliman. He considers himself more than just your friend"

Dawn stiffened. "I suppose you must be agreeing with the nasty gossip."

"You know I'm not. I'm only trying to protect you. Be careful that you don't get something started that you can't break away from after Ned comes home. Please stay away from Sheriff Holliman."

Dawn laughed, glaring at Debbie, her eyes flashing. "I do believe you're jealous."

"Don't be ridiculous. I had my chance with Darrell."

"Is that what you think?"

Debbie looked surprised. "Of course. Have you forgotten how many times he came to call on me?"

"Because I asked him to," she said spitefully.

"That's not true!"

"Ask him."

"Why would he do a thing like that?"

"It's very simple. I wanted to know if you could become interested in him. Do you think I'm stupid? I have known for quite some time that you sympathize with Ned."

"What are you implying?" she cried.

"Oh, stop your innocent act; it's getting a little stale. Ned has admitted that he tried to make love to you."

"No!" she cried breathlessly, covering her face with her hands.

"Don't get upset. I know you did nothing wrong. Some people just can't help feeling sorry for lost kittens, stray dogs, and cowardly men."

Debbie looked into Dawn's face, tears streaming down her cheeks. "I do feel sorry for him, I won't deny it. You don't love him and you never will. Why don't you let him go and stop holding hope out to him like a bread crumb to a starving man?"

"He's free to go anytime, but he thinks he can't live without me. He admitted that he would put up with anything just to be near me. I felt sorry for him, and guilty too, I suppose. I made up with him the night before he left. He was happy, he got what he wanted. He hated to leave me. He wanted to break a leg so he would have an excuse to stay."

"See, you did hold out hope to him."

"If he had an ounce of pride he would have left me long ago. He knows how I feel, yet he hangs on like a leech. I really wanted you and Ned to be attracted to one another, but you can't stand his crawling anymore than I can. You find Darrell Holliman every bit as exciting as I do."

"I—I do like him," she admitted. "But I will never forgive him for making a fool of me. I was cheated into believing that he was interested in me when all the time he was only acting out a part to please you. How can you be so cruel and selfish?"

"I saw no harm in it. I felt certain that you were in love with Ned. It's impossible to be hurt by one person when you're in love with another. I was just testing you to make sure."

"Are you satisfied?"

"Satisfied that you don't know what you want. I think you really did love Ned at first, or maybe it was pity. I'm certain now that whatever you might have felt for him in the beginning was erased by Darrell Holliman."

"There might have developed something between Ned and me if he hadn't been married to you. I know Ned will never love anyone else, and I'm truly sorry for him. As soon as he returns, I'm leaving this house. I made a mistake when I came here."

"You're not going anyplace. I want you to stay. I need you. What will baby Henry do without you? He loves you, we both do. You're more of a mother to him than I am."

"I have to live my life too. Surely you can see that. I can't exist forever in your shadow. You're like a sponge, absorbing everything and every one in your path. I have to get away from you."

"I thought we were friends."

"Don't you understand? It's because I love you that I must break away. You will never accept your responsibilities as long as you have me to depend on."

"Where will you go?"

"Where I go doesn't matter. The important thing is that I make a new life for myself on a firm foundation."

"I'm sorry, Debbie. I never realized how unhappy you were living here."

"It's my own fault."

"That's not true. Father all but twisted your arm to persuade you to live here. Maybe Darrell was right about his feelings for you."

"Mac, caring for me? For mercy's sake! What kind of foolish talk is that?"

"I thought so too when Darrell first mentioned it to me."

"Mentioned what to you?"

"The way Father looks at you; the way he acts when the two of you are together."

"How does he act?"

"I don't know. Darrell is the one who seems to read so much meaning into Father's actions."

Debbie paced the floor nervously, remembering many little things Mac had said that seemed to have had no apparent meaning at the time. Now, thinking back, she experienced a warm glow of hope. The idea that there might have been some hidden meaning behind his unselfish gestures tortured her. If only she had known.

"Don't worry about it," Dawn said, seeing how upset she had suddenly become. "The whole thing is utterly ridiculous. I never should have mentioned it. I feel certain that his only interest in you is a fatherly one."

"You're right of course." She knew Dawn must be right, yet she could not overcome the violent storm in her heart, or explain the physical weakness she was experiencing. "I must go to my room," she cried suddenly, spun around, and ran toward the stairs. She needed time to collect her wits.

Dawn watched her go, feeling a bit puzzled herself.

During the weeks that followed, Dawn was careful not to be alone with Darrell. She made excuses for rejecting all his invitations, none of which he believed.

"I hope your actions are as disagreeable to you as they are to me," he said.

"I told you once that I can't trust myself to be alone with you. You're wasting your time on me."

"All I have is time. When you love a person, you love them for what they are, not for what you wish they were. So, you're married, so what? He's gone. Make the most of it."

"Do you realize what you just said?"

He looked at her curiously. "Yeah, I propositioned you again."

"That's not what I'm talking about. I think you just said you love me."

He tried to recover his words. Exactly what had he said? "I don't remember saying that."

"Forget it."

"No! Tell me."

"'When you love a person, you love them for what they are, not what you wish they were. So, you're married, so what?'"

"Can I take it back?"

"Yes, if you didn't mean it."

"Does it matter?"

"I don't know. I think it might."

"I know I could love you. It would be so easy, but I will never be a rug. That's not my nature."

"If you love me, I'm sorry I can't feel the same way about you."

"Are you worried about what your brother-in-law might say? If you are, I'll shut his mouth."

"I've convinced him that you're only my friend."

"Now that you have him convinced, how do you intend convincing yourself?"

"You're the one who needs convincing."

"What have you got in mind?"

"All my ideas have been exhausted."

"Then that leaves it up to me. I plan to take a ride out to the old Benson place tomorrow around sundown and take advantage of this perfect weather. I want you to ride with me. We need to get something settled."

"Now that I'm working, I don't have time to go riding."

"Will you meet me there?"

"I don't dare!"

"These beautiful days and nights won't last."

"Of course not. It's already winter time."

"Have you noticed how mild the weather is? The days are warmer, but the nights are chilly, perfect for making love."

"I don't want to hear this."

"This happens to be a very special time of the year for Indians. They look forward to it, anticipate it, and enjoy it as long as it lasts."

"What are they celebrating?"

"Haven't you ever heard of Indian Summer?"

"Yes, but I thought their summer was the same as ours."

"It's the most perfect time of the year, but it only lasts a few days. It comes in late October or early November.

"Every year?"

"Yes, but it's not a separate season, its part of autumn. It has no definite date to begin or end. It follows autumn's first cold spell. I want to celebrate Indian summer with you."

"How come you know so much about it?"

"When I was in the army I spent some time in an Indian village during their celebration of Indian summer. It was like living in another world. It only lasted ten days. I had never paid any attention to it before, and now I look forward to it. We're into the second day of it, and I want you to share it with me. The sky turns a rich blue and appears gentle and hazy near the horizon. The air remains smoky and still, with almost no wind, and the moon has a soft orange hue. It's very romantic and ends far too soon, and then winter begins. The Indians call it the special gift from a favorite god, Cautantowwit, the god of the Southwest."

Dawn stared at him in rapt interest. "Do all Indians celebrate Indian Summer?"

"Absolutely."

She visualized Light Eyes celebrating Indian summer, gazing up at the blue sky and orange circled moon with a fat squaw snuggled up to him. The thought sent quakes rasping through her body. If she hadn't married Ned, she would be with Light Eyes, lying in his arms, making love with him.

"It sounds beautiful, but I can't share it with you."

"It will be nice and private. I'm tired of holding my feelings in a vacuum. We need some time alone to get to know one another."

"I didn't know you had been in the army."

"There are a lot of things you don't know about me."

"I'm beginning to realize that. "Why did you quit?"

"I didn't."

"Then why—"

"Spend some time with me and I'll tell you all about myself."

"What did you do in the army?"

"As little as possible."

"I'm serious."

"I was a lieutenant, now I'm a sheriff, and I don't want to discuss it. Meet me tomorrow night and we'll talk then."

"I have no intentions of meeting you. You take a lot for granted. I don't want to be alone with you."

"Yes you do."

In spite of her resolve not to meet Darrell the following day, she saddled her horse a little before sundown and rode toward the Benson house. She rode some distance before she saw the gray outline of the house and barn and fruit trees reaching high above the wood shingled roof. This was the first time she had returned since she moved away, and she felt a twinge of cold loneliness as she recalled many sad episodes of the past.

She had looked forward to seeing Darrell with as much uneasiness as anticipation at first. Now she felt a charge of excitement at the sight of his tall, lean figure. He was waiting for her in back of the house. His horse was nibbled at the grass surrounding the porch.

"You are a beautiful sight," he said, walking toward her smiling.

"You're early," she replied

"Impatient," he corrected her, swinging her down from the saddle. "If we decide to spend the night I'll unsaddle our horses and put 'um in the barn."

"I know you're kidding. How would I explain staying out all night? I told Debbie I was going riding. She would have Jack out looking for me, because they wouldn't be able to find the sheriff."

"That makes sense." He pointed toward the sky. "Look at the Indian summer moon. Isn't it beautiful?"

"It really does have a soft orange hue."

"It's getting cold. Are you ready to go inside?"

"No!"

"Ahh, come on. I have always wanted to explore a haunted house."

"You're joking of course, but did you know that Billy Joe killed his wife, Kathryn, and himself right in the parlor?"

"Why did he do it?"

"She was much younger than him and he was jealous of her."

"Doesn't seem like reason enough to kill her. Most husbands are jealous of their wives, to a degree."

"Billy had good reason to be jealous. She was playing around with Frost Jackson."

"Why didn't he kill Frost?"

"He didn't know who she was playing with, or he might have."

"How do you happen to know she was seeing Jackson?"

"I saw them together, lying on a blanket in the thickets." Darrell looked at her in surprise. "You're serious."

"Yes."

"That must have been a shock, stumbling onto a scene like that."

"I used my knowledge to blackmail Kathryn. She was mean to Debbie, and I told her I would keep her secret as long as she treated Debbie right. It worked for a while. Then out of the blue she told Billy she had a young lover and she was leaving him. She never told who it was."

"I can't believe Frost was ready to take that on."

"We will never know."

"Come on, show me where it happened."

A keen look of suspicion showed in her eyes, then she took his arm and he led her into the house through the back door. He followed her down the hall to the parlor. She pushed on the door and it swung open with a rusty grind.

"Right in there." she whispered.

"Why are you whispering?"

"I don't want to wake the dead."

"What a morbid thought. You're crazy," he laughed stepping into the dark, damp room. The windows were covered with heavy dark curtains, hanging in loose folds down to the floor. "It's sure dark in here," he said. "I should have brought a lantern."

"Light the lamp. I think it still has oil in it."

He struck a match, fumbled for the lamp, and the room was bathed in soft light. He looked around the room in astonishment. "Why did Debbie leave all the furniture?"

"It's still her house. Where else would she keep her furniture?"

Darrell carried the lamp, and they explored the remaining three rooms downstairs. "Where did you sleep?" he asked, looking from one bedroom to the other.

"In there." she pointed toward her old bedroom.

"What's upstairs?"

"Three more rooms. Don't you remember? You visited baby Henry up there when he was only a few months old."

"I remember there were two babies and one belonged to an Indian squaw."

"She had to nurse my baby because I was so unhappy that my milk dried up. Ned's jealous of you and he accuses me of meeting you behind his back."

"He knows how I feel about you."

"How do you feel?" she asked, smiling up at him.

"Don't you know?" He set the lamp down, picked her up, and swung her in the air, then held her close to his heart. "Why did you meet me?"

"You knew I would. I know I shouldn't have anything to do with you, yet here I am."

"Then why did you?" He continued to hold her against his trembling body.

"I guess I'm too easily influenced by you."

"Are you sure there's not another reason?"

"I know what you want to hear, but I can't say it. I like you very much, you make me feel alive and happy, but I don't love you."

"You don't have to love me," he said kissing her tenderly. "Just want me the way I want you."

She yearned toward him, and then her lips became burning embers, melting him, transforming him into quivering jelly. "Divorce him," he said. "You don't love him." He lifted her into his arms and carried her into her old bedroom. The light from the lamp in the next room threw pale light across the bed.

"No!" she cried. "Put me down." She struggled to free herself, caught between her burning desire and her wounded virtue. She understood now why he had asked her which room had been hers. He wanted her to be comfortable with her surroundings when he made love to her. He had thought of everything.

He held her tight, his heart pounding, his body burning where she touched him. He was only seconds away from paradise.

"I can't do this," she said weakly, her body trembling against him.

"We've waited a long time to be together like this. I know you want me. Don't fight it. Let me finish it."

What she was feeling at that moment she had never experienced before. The touch of his lips and his caressing hands were melting her insides. Her restraint suddenly flew free, she uttered a cry of surrender, and her arms went around his neck. She buried her face against his chest and her tears fell against him warm and sweet. As he removed her clothes slowly and meticulously, she said in a choked voice, "I deserve to be shot, in this house, just like Kathryn."

"No, my darling. Not you. Never you." And they came together at last and he finished what he had started. She lay in his arms in the aftermath, thinking about Light Eyes, and the memory of him suddenly grew dim and confusing.

She was very quiet, and he asked in a concerned voice, "What are you thinking and feeling?"

"I'm not sure, only that I liked what you just did to me. I like the way you make me feel."

"How was it with Ned?"

"I hated it."

He was tempted to ask her about the other man, but at the moment he didn't feel strong enough to accept her answer because he knew she would tell him the truth. What he had just experienced with her was far beyond his expectations. He had thought her perfect in every respect, and now he knew that she was more than perfect. She had sealed his fate. He could never love another woman. He held her tight, never wanting to let her go. His thoughts were painful, but he was facing the bitter truth. She was the wife of one man and in love with another. So what chance did he have? He pitied Ned even as he detested him. He had held heaven in his arms, and then lost it. And what about the other man? The one who held her heart? How was he to fight a ghost? He held her even closer. For one day he would lose her completely.

CHAPTER

30

Mac returned to Courgat an emotionally beaten man, having spent the past two months of near sleepless nights with the recurring nightmare of Ned's catastrophic death pounding through his mind. He felt tense, his hands shook, and his head ached. He was smothered in guilt, dreading the ordeal that lay ahead of him worse than death. It had been a terrible accident, for which he would be blamed and condemned. His rampant thoughts had driven him to near madness.

He reached his front door long after everyone had retired, much to his relief, granted one last reprieve before facing Dawn with the shocking account of Ned's death. The house was dark and quiet when he let himself inside. Knowing that Jack had taken over his bed, as well as his duties during his absence, he decided to stretch out on the couch in the parlor. Exhausted from the long journey and his mental anguish, his body was a knot of nerves. He closed his eyes and tried to fall asleep, but was unable to erase the vivid picture of Ned's death from his mind. After half an hour of sleeplessness he got up and made his way across the moonlit room to the cabinet near the hearth where he kept a bottle of whiskey. He poured himself a shot and belted it down, then poured another. The second drink went down smoother than the first. A warming glow spread over him and he felt his wire tight nerves begin to loosen. He was retracing his steps back to the couch when the room suddenly began to turn drunkenly while the floor seemed to buckle beneath his feet. He lost his balance and went down. Once on the floor he decided to stay there until his dizziness passed. He was struggling to get up when Debbie, wearing a blue dressing gown, appeared in the open doorway holding a candle.

She moved forward cautiously until the candle's small flame picked Mac out of the darkness where he lay prone a few feet in front of her.

"Mac!" she cried. "What on earth are you doing down there on the floor?"

"I'm all right," he said hoarsely. "Give me a hand. I can't get up with the room spinning so fast around my ears."

"When did you get back?" she asked, extending him a helping hand.

"About an hour ago."

She put her arm around his waist and guided him back to the couch. "You're drunk," she said in a shocked voice, catching the faint smell of whiskey.

"Not yet, but I plan to be shortly."

"Why? What's wrong?" She placed the candle on the low table in front of the couch and turned to face him, a frown on her pretty soft face. "Where is Ned? Has he gone up to Dawn?"

"No," he answered painfully. "He won't be going anyplace anymore."

"You mean to say he didn't come back with you?" She was frankly surprised that he had carried out his threat to stay in Oklahoma, especially after Dawn had made up with him.

"He stayed because he couldn't come back." Mac looked away from Debbie's curious gaze. "He's dead," he said with a choking sob.

"No!" she wailed. "How! Oh! Mac! What happened?"

He leaned back against the pillows and threw his arm across his eyes. Debbie seated herself close beside him and listened in silence as he wretched up the horrifying details while tears streamed down her face. At length he broke off, overcome with grief, unable to speak another word.

"Poor Mac," she said in a whisper, leaning close to take his hand, crying with him in grief, sympathy and understanding.

"I feel so helpless," he said with a shudder. "If only I could have saved him."

"You did all you could. It was God's will. Hush now," she said calmly and sweetly, her own weeping ceased. Seeing his suffering filled her with both pity and deep emotion. She tried desperately to conceal her own grief in an attempt to comfort him. She laid her head upon his chest and heard the quickening beat of his heart.

"Dear, sweet Debbie. I'm so glad to be home. Being near you is such a comfort." His hand moved to rest on the back of her neck.

She felt a slight pressure, the trembling of his caressing fingers, and then he breathed a deep sigh and relaxed.

"I missed you!" she said softly, feeling a strange flood of emotion.

"I never realized until this moment, just how much."

Taking her by the shoulder he held her away from him, looking deep into her eyes that were wet and bright in the candle light. He bit his lip to smother the words that he knew he had no right to speak, but his feelings for her were plainly stamped on his face.

Her eyes met his boldly, and she was swept with excitement and wonder. Here before her was the man she had once considered methodical and dispassionate, while inside there beat the heart of a tender, deep-feeling, gentleman. She had sensed his gentleness once before but had not considered him weak, nor did she think of him in that respect now. He was a strong willed man, possessing deep feelings that he had ignored for many years, allowing Dawn to become the soul purpose for his existence while ignoring the natural order of life, his emotional needs for companionship and the love of a good woman. Many obstacles had stood between him and total happiness. Mainly the fear of displeasing his daughter. Finding new courage, prompted by the alcohol and the gentle presence of Debbie, broke down the barriers that had silenced him for so many years and unleashed his true emotions. An instant later, he groaned and gathered her tenderly to him, kissing her passionately, feeling her response like an answering prayer.

When they drew apart she was too amazed and confounded to speak. She knew he wanted her completely and she shook with a burning physical weakness. Merciful God! I want him as much as he wants me, she thought. She resisted him only a fleeting moment, then slowly her rigid body relaxed, and trembling with passion her arms crept around his neck. Mac strained closer, becoming suddenly cold sober. He no longer felt like a man old enough to be her father, but a vibrant male animal hungry for love and fulfillment. He had been too many years without the affection of a woman. He held his breath listening to the violent throbbing of his heart, aching to discover all the secrets of her young body while he painfully remained a gentleman.

At length she drew away from him, pale and shaken. "What do you feel for me?" he asked, wanting to know the truth, yet afraid of her answer.

The moment had arrived for her when all pretenses must end, and she searched her heart for the answer. "I love you, Mac, I have for a long time, but I never dreamed that you could care for me. You're an important man, and I'm nobody." She spoke without the slightest stumbling of words, shocked by her own admission.

He embraced her again, kissing the lips that had uttered the words that touched his very soul.

"Would you consider marrying an old man like me?"

"You are not an old man. And yes, I will be happy to marry a young man like you."

He drew her into his arms. "You won't change your mind, will you? I hope I'm not just dreaming, that I'll wake up and find all this has been a figment of my imagination."

"It's hard for me to believe too. I never dreamed that Richard McCloud would ask me to marry him. Every woman in town will envy me."

Mac laughed for the first time in months. "They will most likely think you've lost your mind for tying yourself to an old man."

She studied him for a moment, his full head of dark hair, smooth face, tall, lean, muscular body, and eyes so light blue that they appeared transparent. How could anyone ever consider him old? He was a big success, the most influential man in town, and he was only thirty-nine years old.

"You are the most attractive man I have ever known," she said, "and I have always thought that the name Mac does you an injustice. You will always be Richard to me."

"That's really strange, your saying that. Dr. Keel told me the same thing years ago."

"He was right. And now I must leave you. Try to get some rest. Tomorrow will be a trying day for you, but I will be here to see you through it." She kissed him tenderly, and then fled through the darkness to her room before she changed her mind.

Mac slept spasmodically the remaining hours of the night. Daylight brought a cold chill of dread to his heart. The thought of facing Dawn as terrible as it was inevitable. He roamed about the parlor in the gray morning light, listening to the tic of the clock and the crow of the roosters. His foreboding had increased by the time he heard the light fall of footsteps on the stairs. His first impulse was to run in the opposite direction, but realized the utter foolishness of such a notion and stood untenable and silent, waiting. In a moment Dawn appeared in the doorway wearing a dark blue dress trimmed with tiny white lace, her hair falling loosely about her shoulders, looking more beautiful than ever, facing the morning light as it streamed through the windows. The look on her face was quite astounding when she saw her father standing there before her.

"Father," she cried, and rushed into his waiting arms. "When did you get home?"

"Last night," he answered, kissing the top of her head.

She released him and stepped back, looking at him with inquiring eyes. "Did you say last night?"

"Yes."

Her eyes darted quickly about the room. "Where is Ned?"

Mac turned away, reluctant to answer, searching for his courage.

"Where is he?" she repeated in a panic outcry.

"Dead," he murmured so quietly he could scarcely hear his own voice. "He drowned."

"No!" she screamed, her face blanched with horror and shock. "No! No! No!" She shrieked in disbelief. "He's not! Oh! He can't be!" She collapsed into Mac's arms crying hysterically.

Jack heard her screams and came bounding into the parlor clad only in his pants, his eyes swollen from sleep. "What's wrong?" he cried, looking from Dawn to Mac in surprise. The expressions on their faces told him the ugly story even before he heard the words.

"He's dead! Your brother is dead! Drowned!" Dawn shrieked.

Jack sank into the nearest chair, overcome with shock and grief. "Oh, God!" he cried, "How can I tell mother? It will kill her." His face was a mask of dark despair while a flood of tears streamed down his face.

Seeing his grief, Dawn rushed to him with open arms. They embraced, his tears mingling with her own. Mac stood in the center of the room watching them helplessly, his arms hanging loosely by his sides, completely at a loss for words of consolation, for so great a grief was lost to all else.

Debbie, wearing a yellow dressing gown, looking pale, her eyes red from crying, came into the parlor like a shadow carrying a large tray. She poured coffee and offered it with trembling hands. Mac watched her every move until her gaze came at last to rest on him. The expression in her eyes revealed to him her deep felt emotions.

"Thank you," he said, taking the cup she offered from her shaking hand.

She smiled slightly and patted his arm. The touch of her hand erupted in him a strange new sensation. He was beginning to feel like a whole man again for the first time since he lost Elizabeth. He watched her lovingly as she murmured soothingly to Dawn and Jack, saying all the comforting things he could not being himself to say. Her face was soft and lovely, her eyes moist.

Before Dawn's coffee was cool enough to drink, she excused herself and left the room quickly. Seeing the worried look on Mac's face because of his daughter's sudden departure, Debbie excused herself also and followed Dawn up the stairs a few seconds later. She caught up to her in the hall outside her bedroom door.

"I'll stay with you, if you like."

Dawn did not reply, but held the door open and they stepped into the spacious room. Dawn threw herself upon the bed. "I just can't believe he's gone," she sobbed.

"I know. It's such a shock. I've known him all my life. He was a good person, honest, hard working. It's such a waste."

"Oh, Debbie! I didn't tell him I loved him before he left. I did, but I just now realized it. Oh, I miss him. Why was I so mean to him? He loved me with all his heart." She broke into a fresh torrent of tears.

"He was happy when he left here. You had made up with him and he was walking on clouds."

"He didn't want to leave me—but I didn't want him to stay. I never wanted him to touch me. I'm so ashamed, now that it's too late to make it up to him. God! He even took a beating that he didn't deserve. Oh, I hurt him in so many ways."

"You have to stop this. You're making yourself sick. It's fate, Dawn, and you can't change what happened or bring him back. He's gone, you have to accept that and get on with your life. He would want you to do that."

"No he wouldn't. He would have rather seen me dead than in the arms of another man."

"But that was different. He had no idea he was going to die so young. You made him happy. It was his choice."

"I keep thinking I will wake up and find it was all a nightmare. How long have you known?"

"Since last night."

"Why didn't you wake me?"

"It was awfully late." She looked away, her face coloring slightly.

"Did Father wake you?"

"Well—not exactly. I heard a strange noise downstairs and went down to investigate. I found Mac alone in the dark parlor. He had been drinking, and I knew something was wrong. I asked him where Ned was, and he told me what happened. I was shocked beyond belief."

"Why didn't Father tell me?" She continued to look steadily at Debbie.

"It was late. I didn't see any reason to wake you. You will have the rest of your life to grieve. What difference could a few hours make?" Debbie spoke in a whisper of embarrassment. Recalling the passionate moments she and Mac had shared made her feel guilty in the presence of all the grief and unrest surrounding them.

Dawn, satisfied with Debbie's explanation, asked to be left alone.

Debbie was only too happy for an excuse to escape her questions and probing eyes. Once outside the room she felt her stretched nerves begin to relax. When she returned to the parlor she learned that Jack had left for home to tell the family about Ned's death.

Mac made plans to go later in the day to pay his respects to Pete and Martha, and to explain to them how it had happened. But his first concern was for his daughter.

The sight of Debbie, combined with the new and exciting sensation of being alone with her, made Mac's face shine star bright as a smile played across his sunburned face.

"How is she?"

"She's feeling guilty. She regrets the way she treated him now that it's too late to make it up to him."

"Will she be all right?"

"In time. She will mourn for a while."

"She has Ned's son to love. She hasn't lost him completely." He doesn't know, she thought with a measure of shock. The fact that the child had Indian blood was too apparent. Of course Dawn appeared to be part Indian herself. She had wondered for years what her mother looked like. Mac didn't even have a picture of her. It was all so strange. Mac had never questioned who the child's father was. That was apparent by the way he beat Ned for taking advantage of his daughter.

Mac was silent for a moment, then taking her hand, said in a gentle voice. "About last night—you're not sorry are you?"

"No, I most certainly am not. A little guilty maybe for being so happy while Dawn is grieving her heart out. I think I have known for a long time that we belong together."

"Even though I'm old enough to be your father?"

She was well aware of Mac's fears and doubts, and said reassuringly to restore his confidence, "I could never be happy with a younger man. I'm not young myself, at least not in thoughts or actions. Haven't you noticed?"

"You're all the things any man could want in a woman, and you please me completely."

"I warn you, I am inexperienced as a wife. You will need to be patient with me."

He squeezed her hand. "I'm not an experienced husband either. I have lived for many years without the companionship of a woman. Dawn's mother has been gone since the day Dawn was born, and we were married only a short time."

"Will you tell me about her sometime? In all the years I have known you and Dawn, you have never mentioned her. Is it because it's too painful to talk about?"

"That is one of the reasons I never talk about Elizabeth, but not the only reason. After we're married, I'll tell you a story, but it's something you must promise never to repeat. I know I can trust you, that's one of the many reasons I love you. Once you're my wife, I won't hold back anything from you."

"Thank you." She raised herself on tip toes and kissed him on the lips.

"When will you marry me? I don't want to wait long."

"We must wait until Dawn has recovered from the shock of Ned's death. This is a bad time for us all. I feel that the shock of our engagement might be too much for her to accept at present."

"You're right of course. I'll leave it up to you. If I should get a little out of hand, you just call me down."

"You can be sure that I will."

"There is one thing you must consider and be ready for."

"What's that?" she asked with concern.

"When people find out that we have been living under the same roof together, it will create some nasty gossip."

"Let them talk, we will have done nothing to be ashamed of."

"You may have to slap my hands."

"I can do that."

CHAPTER

31

News of Ned's accidental drowning spread through town the following day, leaving most of Courgat's citizens dumbfounded. However there was no mistaking the nature of Darrell Holliman's feelings when word of Ned's death reached him. He had wanted Ned out of the picture, but he hadn't expected it to happen in such a thorough way. He tried to hide his prevailing happiness, and was ashamed for having given way to such repugnant indifference in the face of great human suffering and grief. Ned's death had put an end to his battle for Dawn, but there was no reason for him to crow, because he had not actually won, not when his competition was a dead man.

He had seen Dawn only briefly since the day they had met at the Benson ranch house, that memorial day she had given herself to him completely, and without a single uttered word of love. He had many disturbing thoughts that seemed to end in a box canyon. And what about Ned? Hadn't she given herself to him completely too, and without the slightest bit of affection. He was suddenly hit with many doubts as he wondered about the mysterious man who had fathered her son, a man she must love very deeply. There could be no lasting happiness or pleasure in possessing a woman whose heart belonged to another man. He could not fight this unknown person anymore than he could fight a dead man. He was forced to face the truth, to admit to himself that the death of Ned

Rowling had changed nothing, that he was rendered powerless to remove the obstacle so imperative to his success if Dawn was to ever belong to him heart and soul. He felt like a man caught in quicksand, the more he struggled to free himself, the deeper he sank, numbed and helpless, with a heavy weight crushing his chest, smothering him, drowning in her rapturous beauty and exquisite flesh.

Mac's visit to the Rowling's ranch proved to be one of the most painful undertakings of his life. He felt a sliver of fear travel down his spine when he came face to face with Martha. A look of pure venom passed across her face like a cloud before the face of the moon. For a moment she just stood there looking at him, then sprang at him flailing and screaming. "You killed my son!" Mac made no move to defend himself as her bony fists beat at his chest. It was Pete who caught her arms and held her tight against him while she continued to kick, scream, and weep. She resisted him until her strength was spent.

"I don't know what to say," Mac uttered with a great deal of emotion. "I would gladly give my life in exchange if it was possible. I did all I could to save him."

Pete had not said a word thus far. Mac had never seen a man age ten years in a few short days.

"I know you tried, Mac. Ned was a good swimmer. I don't understand how this happened to him."

Mac felt it was time to tell them what really killed Ned.

"We were driving the cattle across the swollen Canadian River. It had rained all night and the river was out of the banks and still rising. We had to get the herd across before it rose any higher. We drove them in bunches when suddenly one bunch began to drift with the current. Ned's horse got hooked by a steer and went down, Ned went down with him. I was only a few feet from Ned when he surfaced. Beef was churning in the water all around. He didn't actually drown, Pete, he got ripped in the back by a steer rolling past him. He was dead when he went under the second time. We searched till dark trying to recover his body, but it was no use. The water was too deep, swift, and dirty."

Martha was screaming again. "My sweet, precious, son. I can't even bury him. Oh! God! I want to die too. He didn't want to go. He hung back, kissing Dawn over and over like he knew he was telling her good-bye for the last time. He knew!"

"This is killing Dawn. She won't let the baby out of her sight. He's all she has left of Ned."

"Then she has nothing," Martha screamed. "That child is no kin of Ned's, but he took the blame and a beating for something he didn't do. Your daughter cast some sort of spell over him. He said he couldn't live without her, and now he don't have to."

Mac instantly bristled. "I'm sorry for your loss, it's a great shock to all of us, but don't you take it out on Dawn. She doesn't need anything else to grieve over." He turned to address Pete. "If I can do anything, Pete, you know I will. I'm sorry for getting Martha so upset, but I wanted to pay my respects, see if you needed anything."

"You've done enough!" Martha screamed. "You killed Ned as sure as if you had shot him. I hope your daughter lives to regret her sins. Now leave my house and don't you ever darken my door again. And don't expect me to pay any visits to Dawn and her bastard son. She's a slut, and that baby is a damned Indian."

"So help me, God, if you were a man, I would kill you," Mac blasted. "No one is going to say my daughter is a slut. You lost your son, and baby Henry lost his father."

"Liar!" Martha screamed. "You blind son of a bitch! You know that child has Indian blood."

"Yes!" Mac bellowed.

Both Martha and Pete looked at Mac in shock. Mac McCloud had just eaten his own words, by finally admitting the truth. "I never intended to tell anyone what I am about to tell you, and if you repeat it, woman or not, I will kill you!"

"Just a damned minute, Mac!" Pete barked. "One more threat and I'll forget we're friends."

"There are some things better left buried, Pete. Silence can save heartache, and prevent innocent children from growing up shunned and abused. When I came to Courgat my wife was already in labor. She had been suffering for many hours, and her agony lasted many more hours before Dawn was born. Elizabeth hemorrhaged and died. I had her coffin sealed, and she was buried without a funeral. No one ever saw her except for Doctor Keel and his wife. You're wrong about Dawn, and you're wrong about baby Henry, but most of all, you're wrong about Ned. He's gone, but his son lives, and you have disowned the little baby because he has Indian blood, and it shows. He will be shunned and hated all his life, because you're the type to spread it around to punish Dawn for what you think she's done. The truth is, Dawn's mother, Elizabeth, was a Comanche Indian. My daughter is a half-breed. If you doubt what I just told you, then ask Doctor Keel. He too has kept my secret all these years to protect Dawn, and now, her son."

"God, help me!" Martha screamed. "What have I done? I've misjudged Dawn, said terrible things to her, threatened and blackmailed her. Oh! What have I done? Why wasn't I told?"

"I haven't even told Dawn. I never intended for her to know the truth. I didn't want her hurt. It's not her fault that I fell in love with an Indian and married her. Elizabeth was the most beautiful creature I had ever laid eyes on. She was absolutely perfect from head to toe. Dawn looks just like her. Ned couldn't resist her. She was all he ever wanted, and I believe he meant it when he said he couldn't live without her. After Elizabeth died, I would have died too, if not for my daughter. She's all I have of Elizabeth, and Baby Henry is all you have left of Ned. His blood flows in the child's veins. You still have a part of your son, but you're rejecting him."

Martha threw her arms around Mac and sobbed against him. "Please, Mac, you have to forgive me. I'll make things right between me and Dawn. I'm so sorry."

"That's the one thing you can never do, Martha. Don't you understand? Dawn doesn't know about her mother, and you must never tell her."

"What about the baby? Can't she recognize the color of his skin and hair?"

"He's her son, and she loves him. To her he's just beautiful, and he has blue eyes. Indians don't have blue eyes."

"What can I do? I don't want to lose him too."

"Wait, see if Dawn's feelings toward you mellows. God knows, she has good reason for her bitterness. Right now she hates the sight of you. I came here because I share your grief. Ned was your son, and he was the father of my grandchild. I have felt guilty because I couldn't save him, but I know now that he could have saved himself if the steer hadn't hooked the life out of him. I'm sorry." He shook Pete's hand, and without another word strode from the house. Once outside, he took a long shuddering breath of relief.

For several days after news of Ned's death, Darrell tried to see Dawn, but she refused to leave her room, staying completely out of sight of all persons except Mac and Debbie.

During those weary days she began to build a close relationship with her small son. Although she took complete charge of her baby herself, she did not send Laughing Eyes back to her people. She liked the white man's way of life and begged to stay. Debbie taught her to cook, clean, wash and iron. She had her own money, and went with Dawn to the trading post on occasions to buy the things she wanted. She was like another member of the family, and they all loved her.

Dawn had Henry's crib moved into her room, along with the tiny chest containing his clothes. A great change was taking place inside her, a spiritual change, filling her with uncommon tenderness and compassion. She seemed to thrive on the time she spent feeding, dressing and rocking her baby.

Debbie urged her to leave the house, to at least ride along the river the way she had done in the past. She had ignored her gentle coaxing, and continued to cling only to her son.

One day, quite by accident, Dawn discovered the letter Henry McCloud had written to her father, and she wondered how she could have forgotten about it so completely.

"We must take this letter to your grandfather," she said, lifting her baby into her arms. He gurgled delightfully, showing his two bottom teeth. She carried him down the hall to the stairs. From the landing she could see into the parlor through the open door. She stopped short, her eyes widened in shock by the scene before her. Mac was holding Debbie in his arms, with her straining toward him, standing on tip toes to reach his lips. Dawn gripped the banister to steady herself, her legs suddenly trembling. For a moment she stood frozen above them, transfixed in horror, then continued unsteadily the rest of the way down the stairs. When they saw her standing in the open door they broke apart spontaneously.

"Dawn!" Mac said in a croaked voice.

"How long has this been going on?" she asked vindictively.

"It's not what you think." Debbie said calmly. "We can explain."

"You don't have to explain a thing," Mac said in Debbie's defense.

Dawn stared at Mac, baffled by his belligerent attitude, feeling hurt and shocked. He had never spoken to her so antagonistically before.

"Mac, please, leave us alone."

He looked at Debbie curiously, doubting her decision, but left the room quietly.

Debbie waited until Mac left the house before she turned her attention to Dawn. "We need to have a serious talk."

"This should be interesting, as well as entertaining," Dawn said spitefully.

"I can guess what you're thinking. You think that your father and I are having a cheap affair, but you're wrong. We wanted to tell you how we feel about each other, but we didn't think we should, not just yet, so soon after Ned's death. Your father and I plan to be married."

Dawn laughed, amused by the thought. "Why would you agree to marry a man old enough to be your father?"

"I love your father very much."

"Like Kathryn loved Billy Joe?"

"You're not being fair."

"I guess you think you are, marrying my father when he's almost twice your age. You can't possibly love him."

"You're wrong, but I don't know how to convince you of that."

"You can't!"

"In time you will see."

"I will see you turn my father against me, that's all I will see. He has never before talked to me the way he did today."

"He meant no harm, he was just upset. After all, he is your father, and due the respect of a father. You haven't the right to question his actions, nor make him feel he must ask your permission to fall in love, or to be married. It all happened a bit too fast for me to understand. Actually we have been attracted to one another for quite some time."

"How can that be? As I recall it has been only a short time since you were attracted to my husband, and then, following that, you very quickly became attracted to Darrell Holliman. Since none of that worked out in your favor, now you are suddenly attracted to my father. I'm surprised you didn't get attracted to Jack. You might just as well rob the cradle as the wheel chair. Any old port in the storm. What shall I call you after you marry my father? Mother? I'll leave this house first!"

"I wish you would just accept the fact and be as happy as we are. Nothing has changed between us. We can still be friends, just like always."

"How can you say that nothing has changed? You are literally crowding me out of my own house."

"This is Mac's house too, and as his wife I am entitled to share it with him. We have lived here together for many months in perfect harmony, and we can continue to, if you will just be reasonable."

"That's it, Debbie, make me the scapegoat, accuse me of being unreasonable. After all, it is the most normal thing in the world for a young woman to marry a granddaddy. Have you forgotten that he has a grandson?"

"No, I haven't forgotten for one moment."

"Well I can say one thing for you, not too many women become a grandmother before they become a mother. Father is too old to start raising a family. He would never live to see them grown."

"Stop it!" Debbie cried out in anger. "Your father is not an old man. Many men have families after they reach forty."

"Don't expect me to come to the wedding. I would be too ashamed."

"Ashamed of what?" Debbie said proudly.

Dawn ignored her question, and said, "I'm going for a ride. I need time to think. Will you watch the baby for me?"

"Of course." She held out her arms to take the child.

"I think you should get out of the house for a while." She smiled pleasantly, their differences seemingly forgotten for the moment.

"I have to change my clothes first." She kissed baby Henry and hurried up the stairs, still clutching the letter in her hand. She changed into a pair of jeans and a red plaid shirt. She thrust the letter into her hip pocket, not sure of what she intended doing with it, but she refused to face her father at the moment.

She heard voices coming from below when she reached the head of the stairs. She advanced to the landing and stood there for a moment listening. Debbie was talking to Darrell at the front door. She continued to make her way down the stairs, feeling nervous, not sure how she should receive him. The memory of their last meeting caused her to flush. When Darrell saw her approaching, he stepped past Debbie to greet her.

"How are you?" He stood in front of her and took both her hands in his. "I've been concerned about you. I'm glad to see you're all right. I hope I'm not imposing."

"I'm glad you came," she said, feeling a bit jittery, reading the look in his eyes. "Want to take a ride with me?"

"I would love to."

"Take good care of her," Debbie said to Darrell while keeping her eyes fixed on Dawn. Dawn gave her a chilly look.

"Yes, indeed. She's in good hands with the Sheriff," he said lightheartedly, sliding his arm around Dawn's waist.

Debbie watched them walk out the door, noting with alarm that Dawn did not make a move to thwart his familiarity.

"Why don't we walk for a while?" he suggested. "It's a lovely day, and frankly, I'm a little saddle sore."

They walked in the direction of the river, staying in the shade of the great oaks towering over the well worn path that led to the water's edge.

"How do you feel," he said presently. "About Ned's death, I mean."

"You, of all people, shouldn't have to ask."

"I was afraid you might be feeling guilty because of our last meeting. I don't want you to ever regret what you feel for me. Just let nature take its course."

She had expected him to shower her with platitudes and sympathetic words to soothe her, but he did neither. "You seem to always read my thoughts. I did have a bad time at first, feeling sorry for him, ashamed because so many times I had wished him dead. Now that he really is gone, and I know he won't be back, I hate myself for treating him so cruel."

"Don't be so noble. Ned took advantage of a bad situation. He wanted you anyway he could get you. He deserved everything you dished out. You don't owe him a thing, not even grief."

"Does that give me an excuse for being unfaithful?"

"You weren't unfaithful to him. He was already dead by the time you and I—"

"Stop it! Can't you see that it makes little difference. I didn't know he was dead."

"Well we know it now." He looked at her with a growing hunger, aching to hold her in his arms and make love to her. Her eyes met his and in their depth he read a promise. "Will you run away with me? We can leave the state."

"I will never marry again."

"I didn't ask you to marry me, just come away with me. I told you once that I would never tie you down. That's a promise. You will be free to go anytime you so desire."

Her heart and mind responded to his promise. "I do need you. Things are getting a bit sticky at home."

"I thought you and Debbie acted a little strained. What's the problem?"

"Do you remember telling me that you thought Father might be interested in Debbie?" He nodded. "You were right."

"So, what's the problem?"

"They plan to get married."

"Ordinary people usually do when they fall in love."

"I must say, you certainly don't seem very surprised."

"I'm not. I think those two belong together."

"How can you say such a stupid thing? Don't you realize that he's old enough to be her father?"

"And she acts old enough to be his mother. You should be happy about it. Now you won't have to take care of him in his old age."

"You're terrible." She smiled at his diverting remark. "Truthful," he challenged. "The trouble with you is you borrow headaches. Now, if you had me around, you would have one of your very own, and never have to borrow again. What do you say?"

"Can I move into your house?"

Her sudden question sent him into pandemonium, he threw his hat into the air, yelled, and pulled her into his arms. "Want to know something?" he said breathlessly. "You have more nerve than I gave you credit for, and I never did think you were short on guts."

While he held her close, she kissed him in a new way. "You're good for me," she whispered. "We had better get back so I can start packing—unless you want to wait a while."

"I'll tell you how much I want to wait. We'll get a room at the hotel, and you can pack tomorrow, or the next day, or next year."

"I want to stay at your house."

"My house, dear lady, is a holy mess. I haven't lived there since I took the sheriff's job. I've been camping in back of the jail. For all I know it may have rats running through it."

"I can assure you, I have a rat running through mine."

"I think your Father just caught it in his trap."

"I think you're right. I guess it wasn't such a good idea for me to move into your house. I didn't realize that you weren't staying there any longer."

"No trouble to move back. As a matter of fact, it will be a pleasure, having you to come home to."

"Oh!"

"What's wrong?"

"The baby. I forgot about the baby."

"That's no problem? Bring him along. I like kids."

"I can't take him to a hotel. I'm sorry, Darrell, but we will have to wait until we can move into your house all proper like."

He knew she was right, and he left her regretfully, looking forward to the near future when he would have her all to himself. How long, he had no idea, but he would cherish every moment.

CHAPTER

32

Dawn had made her commitment to Darrell in haste, deeply hurt by what she considered a betrayal by her father. The thought of Debbie becoming his wife was like a slap in the face. She would become the queen, and run the house from their bedroom, with her father bowing and grinning before her like a silly old fool. She couldn't stay there and witness it. They were forcing her out of her own house. Oh! They made her sick!

Darrell's charming, devil-may-care attitude had made light of what she considered a heavy problem. That was his nature, and she always felt happy around him. He made her feel good, and he wouldn't reject baby Henry. He was her only friend.

She told Debbie her plans just to watch the stricken look on her father snatching face. She was seeing the real Debbie now. Little Miss Goody-Goody had her dark side just like everyone else.

"Foolish, silly girl!" she cried. "How can you just throw yourself away like this? Where is your self-respect? What do you think Mac will do when he finds out?"

"Why should he care? He can't see past you."

Debbie studied Dawn critically for a moment before speaking her mind. "You're still the same little spoiled brat I first met when we were kids." Seeing the anger blazing in Dawn's eyes, she rushed on before she had a chance to interrupt. "I remember Amy, and the way you fought against her and her feelings for Mac. You wanted your father all to yourself, and that was natural and understandable when you were five years old, but you're not a child anymore. You're a grown woman with a life of your own, yet you hang on to Mac, squeezing all the life out of him. He has a chance to be happy, but you'll spoil it even if you have to destroy yourself to do it. You and I know that Mac will stop you, no matter what the cost."

"He can do nothing to stop me. He's not fighting Ned or anyone like him. Darrell will not be bullied or pushed around like the rest of those jelly-fish who call themselves men!"

"If you love each other, why don't you just get married?"

"I don't want to marry him. I don't love him."

"Does he claim to love you?"

"I think so. Yes!"

"He's lying. No man who loves a woman will put her through what he's about to do to you."

"It was my idea, not his."

"For Heaven's sake," Debbie cried. "If you're doing this to punish your father for loving me, please don't. I'll go away and neither of you will ever see me again. I couldn't stand living here knowing that my presence had driven you to your own destruction."

Dawn's stubborn resolve began to weaken at the sight of Debbie's tearful grief. Doubt and regrets pushed her anger and emotional confusion aside that she was tenaciously holding on to and her tears began to fall.

Debbie put her arms around her in a comforting embrace. "We will never let you do this thing," she said with an air of indisputable authority.

Dawn wrenched roughly out of her arms, her eyes black as a storm. "You are assuming too much. You are not yet the mistress of this house. Don't push me, Debbie. I'm warning you."

"I'm only trying to make you understand what a terrible mistake you will be making. I want to help you."

"You're only interested in helping yourself to my father. I'll do as I please. Leave me alone."

Debbie did not sleep well that night, she was so overwhelmed by Dawn's nefarious scheme that her mind was left in shock. She did not want to believe that Dawn might actually carry out her plan to live with Darrell unwed. Surely she must be bluffing, she thought. But her threat carried the ring of truth. She knew well enough the fury Mac was capable of; he would not hesitate to kill Darrell, or be killed, in an attempt to save his daughter from demeaning herself and ruining her life.

Next morning, before anyone else was awake, Debbie saddled her horse and rode to town with only one thought in mind, to appeal to Darrell's sense of decency.

When she entered his office she found him seated behind his desk, his chair leaning back against the wall, balanced on its two back legs, his hands were folded behind his head for a pillow, his hat over his eyes blocking out the early morning light. Hearing the sound of the door, he pulled one hand from behind his head, and raised his hat only far enough to peer from beneath the brim. At the sight of Debbie he let the chair drop forward with a loud thud as the front legs hit the oak floor.

"My God!" he cried in surprise, "what are you doing here so early? I'm still half asleep myself. What's wrong? Is Dawn all right?"

"For the present, yes. That's what I came to talk to you about."

He stared blankly at her. "I don't follow you."

"I know about your plans." She looked at him keenly.

"What plans are you talking about?"

"Your plan to make Dawn a kept woman, your plan to destroy her reputation before God and man, your plan to ruin her life!" She was yelling at him now, taking a step closer to his desk, leaning over him, her face so near that her countenance became a blur.

"Now you just hold on a minute," he said, coming to his feet. "You got the picture hanging a little one-sided. Not my plans, our plans. She came up with the whole idea herself."

"You don't really expect me to believe that do you? I know you put the thought into her head, encouraged her, otherwise she would never have dreamed of going along with such a fool notion. Don't you have enough sense to see that she's all mixed up right now? I know that she must have told you that Mac and I are planning to be married."

"Yeah, she told me."

"She has had her father all to herself since birth, and now that he is thinking of getting married she feels like she is losing him. She's grasping at straws, running away from a situation she doesn't want to face. But she will face it in time, if someone doesn't come along and ruin that chance."

"Meaning me, of course."

"Yes, meaning you."

"Don't you think I'd marry her in a minute if she would have me?"

"I'm sure you would, and her husband not yet cold in his grave. What kind of a man are you?"

"A man in love."

"We don't hurt the people we love, Sheriff Holliman."

"Will you come off it. We both know she hated the sight of Ned."

"If you allow her to go through with this foolish idea, she will hate the sight of you."

"I'll take her anyway, anytime!"

"And regret it the rest of your life. You could get killed, or be forced to kill Mac over this situation. Is that a happy prospect for you?" Tears stood in her eyes and she turned away from his steady, outraged gaze.

Darrell nervously smoothed his hair with his hand as he walked around the side of his desk.

"Do you realize what you're asking me to do?" He paused for a moment, looking down at the floor, his expression grave. When he looked up again his eyes were filled with pain. "I love her, and I need and want her. She's coming to me of her own free will, and you expect me to turn my back on her, just walk away?"

"It would be only for a short time if she comes to you. You're forgetting, I know Dawn. I know her almost as well as I know myself. Since we were children we have kept no secrets from one another. It will be much easier for both of you, and for Mac, if you just let her go. She would only leave you a little later on down the line. You told me a minute ago that you would marry her if she would have you. Have you given any thought as to the reason she refuses to marry you?"

"I know the reason. If I knew his name, and where to find him, I'd kill him."

Debbie backed away from him, her eyes blazing. "You're just like Ned, exactly like him. On the outside you look different, you dress different, you talk different, but you think just the way he thought. If he hadn't been so selfish and blind to her feelings, she would have never gotten her life into such a complicated mess—" Her voice trailed off.

"Are you saying what I think you're saying?"

She made no comment, realizing she had already said too much in her burst of anger.

"Don't clam up on me now. Tell me. Did Ned kill him?"

"I can't tell you anymore than I already have."

"Can't? or won't?"

"OK, then, I won't."

"Can't you see that I'm grasping at straws too. If I thought I had a chance with her, I'd wait forever. But as long as this guy is in the picture, I have about as much chance as a dying calf in a sink hole."

"I refuse to tell you anything as long as you plan to go through with this sordid affair." Darrell began to walk the floor again, his mind racing. "I'll answer your question, only if you promise not to move her out of her father's house." She was bargaining now, knowing this was her last hope to break the ties that held Dawn to her senseless notion.

Darrell continued to pace the floor, listening without comment to the words he wanted to reject. It would be easier for him to cut off his right arm than lose Dawn. He was only hours away from claiming her in all the ways a man claims a wife. He realized with a gnawing ache in his heart that the decision he was about to make would change the course of his entire life. He felt a spur of anger.

"It's for the best," she said, her pleading eyes studying him. "If you love her, you will not bring anymore shame upon her. Can't you see what this will do to her? Like slow poison, it will creep through her until it destroys her completely."

"Why the hell couldn't you mind your own business? She will consider me one of those slimy things that crawl around on their bellies. She will never trust me or respect me again. I had sooner die than have her think I'm gutless."

"If you go through with this madness you will lose her completely. You're wrong about her losing respect for you. If you refuse to take advantage of her, it will take more strength than an ordinary man could muster. You are about to prove how strong you are, and how much you really love Dawn."

"All right, you win," he said, feeling he was about to choke on the words. His despair was equal to that of a dying man, for at that moment he felt a part of him pass out of existence. "You have my word. Now tell me what has become of her lover."

Reluctantly she sat down to relate the tedious details of events in Dawn's past that still had a very decisive bearing on her future, and that of Darrell Holliman.

"Ned had loved Dawn for many years," she began, "I think since they were children, and she always seemed to think quite a lot of him. But what she felt for him was not the same as his feelings for her. Later she fell in love very deeply with the man in question, but they could not show their feelings openly, so they were forced to meet secretly. One night after such a meeting he brought her home, planning to come back for her the following night so they could run away together. They weren't aware that Ned was hiding nearby watching them. After Dawn went inside, Ned followed him into the clump of trees where his horse was tied. He shot him in the back, then rode quickly away, leaving him for dead. Half the town heard the shot and rushed outside to investigate. They found evidence that a badly wounded man had managed to mount his horse and ride away, and signs that another rider had left the scene headed in the opposite direction. Since everyone in town was alive and accounted for, the person who was wounded remained a mystery. To everyone, except Dawn."

"And the man who pulled the trigger," Darrell added.

"Dawn waited many weeks for him to return for her. After a while she gave up, deciding that he must have been killed. In the meantime she found out that she was carrying his child. When she told Ned, he begged her to marry him. She tried to change his mind, but he swore that he wanted to accept the blame, that he would love the child as his own no matter who the father was. After the baby was born he broke his word. It pained him to even look at the child. He only served as a constant reminder of the man who stood between them, and who always would. He became bitter and so did Dawn. The day after they were married she saw the man she loved and had thought to be dead. But by then it was too late. The die was cast."

"Why didn't she run away with him then?"

"I think she would have if he had asked her."

"You mean to sit there and tell me that he didn't even try to get her back?"

"Yes."

"Are you sure Ned shot him in the back? Sounds more like a head wound to me."

"He never saw the man who shot him."

"How come you know so much about the shooting? Dawn couldn't have told you. If she had found out, my guess is that she would have killed Ned."

"Ned told me himself. Oh, he didn't mean to. It just sort of slipped out during one of his weaker moments."

"When he was well oiled?"

"He used to drink quite a lot to get his mind off Dawn, but it only served to make him a bigger fool. I have often wondered why Dawn never suspected Ned as being the one who shot Li—" She stopped short.

Darrell laughed. "One of these days, if I can keep you on the subject long enough, you might let the guy's name slip. As for as her suspecting Ned, maybe she did."

"She never accused him."

"Not in so many words, but in every action. That's most likely the reason they never had any kind of marriage."

"You know something?" she said softly, looking into his eyes, "you never cease to amaze me."

"How's that?"

"For a hard shelled man, even a little cruel at times, you seem to have quite an understanding of human nature."

"Maybe it's because I'm a little more human than people give me credit for."

For a moment she felt a great urge to speak up about the part he played during the time he was calling on her. But seeing no gain in embarrassing him pushed the thought from her mind.

"And now you will go to Dawn and tell her that you can't allow her to go through with her plan. Won't you?"

"I made a deal with you and I won't side-step. I'll take care of it, but my heart won't be in it."

"That's where you are very mistaken, Darrell. Your heart is most certainly in it. And please don't tell her anything about my visit. She might think I'm meddling."

"Aren't you?"

"Yes," she laughed, "but it's for her own good."

"And Mac's too, don't forget?" He smiled back at her.

"If you want to get technical, yours too."

"Do you think that there is a chance in the world that things might work for Dawn and me?"

"You have a better chance than anyone else she knows, except for the one whose name I dare not mention. Remember that the thing that came between Dawn and Ned was jealousy, more than anything else. During the course of their days under the same roof, she knew no relief from his maddening accusations. No relationship can survive that. Jealousy is a vicious animal, it's sharp fangs leave no room for happiness or contentment. Stop hating this man, or you will destroy any hope you may have of winning her for yourself. Never mention him to her, or bring up the past. How can she be expected to forget the man, if she is constantly reminded of him?"

"Are you on my side."

"I'm on Dawn's side, and if you're on her side too, we are allies fighting for the same cause, Dawn's happiness."

He was silent but she could see in his eyes the inward struggle pulling him apart. When he spoke to her at last, there was no doubt in his decision.

"Ok, we will do it your way, but if it doesn't work, then I'll do things my way, and let the chips fall where they may."

They separated then, Darrell on his way to breakfast at the hotel, and Debbie returning to the ranch, her stomach minus the knot of nerves that had felt like a clenched fist.

Debbie passed the day without having to explain her early morning ride. For this she was thankful, because if asked, she had no idea how she would answer.

Dawn was making special efforts to avoid both Debbie and her father, affording them little opportunity to express their feelings.

During dinner that evening, the general conversation was marked with a coolness of unexpressed emotions, which seemed to hover near like a wild beast.

"We may as well talk about this," Mac said, addressing Dawn.

"There is nothing to say," she said contrarily.

He met her gaze with one of his own. "If you think we are wrong for feeling as we do, explain your reason."

"I can't forget what happened between Billy Joe and Kathryn."

"What you're forgetting is that I'm not Billy Joe and Debbie is not Kathryn."

"That doesn't change the fact that you're still old enough to be Debbie's father, and words won't change that. You think you love each other, but how will you feel ten or twenty years from now?"

"I will always love your father exactly the way I do now," Debbie said, meeting her eyes without wavering. "I will be a good and loving wife, and never give him any reason for regret or grief, but I will not marry him if you object, because Mac would be pulled apart, and I love him too much to see him suffer. I want very much to marry your father, but the decision rests with you." She looked at Mac, and felt pity for him because of his stricken expression. Before he could speak, she said quietly, "I'm sorry, Mac, but we will have to be patient and hope that things will work out. The very use of the words are displeasing to me, because in my heart I know we belong together. I hope Dawn can come to feel the same way." She rose from her chair and clasp his hand in hers, he kissed her on the fingers, and then she went toward her room, her heart heavy as lead.

The room became very quiet. It was Dawn who finally broke the silence. "A letter came for you while you were away on the cattle drive. With so much on my mind I almost forgot." She pulled the letter from her skirt pocket. "It's from Henry."

Mac stared at the envelope as his mind leaped into the past, bewilderment cast in his expression. "After all these years," he said heavily.

He took the letter and walked across the room to stand before the dining room window, but he was not looking out at the scenery, he was staring down at the letter.

"Aren't you going to open it?" she cried anxiously.

"I don't know if I want to."

"Go ahead," she coaxed. "It's only a letter. It can't bite you."

He reluctantly tore the envelope across the end and removed the single, folded sheet of paper. He glanced at Dawn helplessly, then began to read the poorly written words:

"On this day of May 17, 1870
Son—

I don't know if you will ever get this letter or not. After all these years I doubt if you will read it anyway. I know you left here with Elizabeth to go take over your brother's business. I hope you stayed put so this letter can catch up to you. How are you and Elizabeth? I guess you have guessed by now that I ain't just writing this to ask about your health. I'm asking you to come home, Richard. I need you. Time ain't been kind to an old devil like me. I ain't even able to sit a horse anymore, and these Jake-legs I got riding for me that calls themselves cowboys, ain't too sure which end of a cow eats. What time they ain't drunk they're stealing me blind. They stay in jail half the time. All I got to say is to come on back home, and when I'm dead the whole shoot'n' match is yours. All you got to do is just reach out and fill your purse.

About Elizabeth, I never told you this, but I guess my tongue is getting loose in my old age, but I loved her and wanted her for myself, but I didn't want the name squaw-man that went with her. She was the most beautiful thing I ever looked at. You got more guts that your old man. I lost her and I lost you, now I got nothing. I'm all alone just waiting to take that last breath. Forgive me, Richard, and come home to me. I want to see you and Elizabeth before I die. I feel so cold inside, and lonely. Sometimes I feel like I already died. I was never happy. All I ever thought about was money and power. I was wrong. Forgive me if you can, and I don't blame you for leaving. You know that I ain't never asked anybody for anything. I was always too proud. Now I'm pleading. I found out too late that my sons were my real treasure, and I threw you both away. If you can find it in your heart to forgive me, I can die in peace. I know this comes too late, and

you most likely won't believe me, but I'm telling you from
my heart, I love you.

Your daddy,

Henry Randolf McCloud

Mac finished reading the letter and thanked God that Dawn hadn't let
her curiosity get the better of her and read the letter herself before giving
it to him. He breathed a sigh of relief, crumpled the letter in his hand and
threw it into the fireplace. He watched as it flamed, curled, and turned to
a black heap of ashes.

Dawn looked at him angrily. "Why did you do that?"

"You wouldn't understand," he said gruffly. "He's part of my past, the
part that is dead and buried. I never want to hear from him again."

"Why do you hate him so much?"

"I don't really hate him. Oh, what's the use. You would never
understand a man like Henry."

"Tell me about him. What sort of man he is, and why you left home
to get away from him. He's my grandfather, I have a right to know," she
insisted.

"He had the misfortune of having too much power that comes with
having too much money and not enough love. He has depended on one
thing all his life, himself, never giving God credit for anything. Now that
it's too late, he wants to change his course, but the race has already run,
and even though he has won the material prize, he has lost sight of the real
prize, the love of God and for his fellow man. With all his land, cattle and
money, he doesn't even have one friend. He's alone, old and sick."

"How awful!"

"True enough, but it was his choice. He has lived his whole life in vain,
and it's too late to change the outcome."

"Does he want you to come home?"

"I wouldn't go back to him if he was as close to me as you are this
minute. Maybe one of the reasons I feel this way is because in some ways
I've become just like him. I can see myself as he used to be, without even
the love of a woman."

"Don't say that," she said sharply. "Don't ever talk that way. You do have the love of a woman. Debbie loves you very much."

"And as you pointed out, she is young enough to be my daughter. I don't have any defense. What you say is true. I just hate to admit it."

"I've been blind and selfish," she said, slowly raising her eyes to look at him. "Debbie is not just any young girl, she's old in her ways, as old as you. She's kind and understanding, but she can be strong too. She's much too good for either of us."

Mac took her hand in his. "Do you mean you approve?"

"I approve of what ever makes you happy, and I have always approved of Debbie. She will always be my best friend."

She thought about Darrell, and the way he had opened her eyes to her father's needs. If he had been around sooner she wouldn't have made near as many mistakes. She would always need him.

CHAPTER

33

Darrell pulled his horse up short on a long rise about a mile from the McCloud ranch. He saw a faint glow in the northern sky growing steadily brighter, and felt a sharp uneasiness creep up his spine. He knew what it could mean and dreaded the thought. He swung his mount sharply in the direction of what he feared was a fire, moving away from his previous destination.

The sun was just setting, and on the darkening horizon his fears suddenly become reality when sparks of fire drifted skyward riding on the night breeze. He kicked his horse to urge more speed, and the animal leaped into a dead run. As he got his bearings, he realized that the Singer's place was on fire. As he neared the site of destruction, his stomach crawled at the prospect of what he would probably find. The house was still burning, only the west wall still stood, the wall with the chimney; the rest was charred, gutted and smoking. He dismounted and walked toward the ruins, glancing about as he moved forward, feeling a spur of hopelessness and grave concern. He kicked around in the smoldering coals, lifted a burning plank and swore at the blister it raised on his hand. Finding no sign of life or burned bodies, he strode quickly toward the barn located behind the house, surprised because they hadn't torched it. He pushed the door open and stepped into the dark interior. On the right wall, close to the door, he found an oil lantern. He lifted it from the peg and lit the wick

JACKIE BARNES

with shaking hands. The light cast a circle of yellow around him. There on the dirt floor, only inches from his feet, Phil Singer lay in a pool of his own blood, his eyes staring with an expression of horror. Darrell turned away from the gory sight. His guts rolling-over and he was violently sick. Phil had been scalped and mutilated. His penis and testicles had been chopped off, and from the way he had bled he figured he had still been alive when they cut him.

He took a moment to recover before searching every inch of the barn and the surrounding corral and yard. There was no sign of Phil's wife, Nancy, or their baby daughter, Pearl.

He searched until the lantern ran low of oil and the flame flickered and disappeared. He spread a horse blanket over Phil; there was nothing more he could do. He mounted his horse and made a mad dash for the McCloud ranch while fear clawed at his insides. He didn't see any smoke in that direction, but that didn't prove they were safe.

It was late by the time he reached the house, and only then did he feel his tension relax a notch. He stepped upon the porch and found Mac standing in the open doorway.

"From the way you rode in here, looks like you were pushing your animal pretty hard for some reason. What's going on?"

"Plenty! Phil Singer's dead, mutilated and scalped by Indians. No sign of Nancy or baby Pearl. The house was burned and all the stock driven off. The Indians might have taken Nancy and the baby prisoners, or they may be laying out there in the brush dead, or worse. I searched until I couldn't see any longer. I spotted the fire, but by the time I got there it was all over. I'll pick up their trail at first light."

Mac was staring at him in mute astonishment. "My God!"

"What's wrong?" Dawn said, coming into the room with Debbie.

Darrell turned to face her. "Phil Singer was killed by Indians and Nancy and the baby are missing."

Debbie's hand flew to her mouth and she bit her fist to keep from screaming.

"What can we do?" Dawn said in whispered shock. "Poor Nancy. The baby is only two years old. We have to do something."

"We can't do anything until morning," Darrell answered. "Maybe we can pick up their trail come daybreak, if I can get a posse together by then."

354

"I don't mean to tell you your business, since you're the sheriff, and a damned good one, but I think that might be a very foolish move."

"Thanks! It's not every day that I get such a nice compliment."

"No offense meant."

"What's your idea of what a sheriff is supposed to do? Close his eyes to murder and kidnapping."

"Not at all, but if you take all the able bodied men and string 'um out miles from town, you'll leave Courgat wide open and at the mercy of the renegades who are apparently on the rampage. As you know, this sort of thing has been going on for quite some time all over Texas and New Mexico. Nothing very serious yet, but enough to keep the people stirred up. This hit and miss pattern is being done by a few renegade Indian misfits. Most of the Indian aggression is going on in the Northern states."

"What are you saying? That I should forget about Nancy and the baby?"

"You have no other choice. You know what they do to women. Nancy is already dead, and everyone in this room is aware of it. Why lie to ourselves? As for the baby, if they haven't already killed it, she will be safe enough. The Indians seem to take some special kind of pleasure in adopting white children to raise as their own. Even if you did start a search for the child, it might be years before you find her. By then she would be as much an Indian as the rest of them. She wouldn't want to come home."

Darrell gave Mac his undivided attention, considering with deep respect every word the older man had to say.

"I take it that you believe your friend Brave Horse is completely innocent of this attack."

"I'd stake my life on it."

"You may have to before this mess is over. You realize, of course, that the town won't be as quick to trust him. They will demand some kind of action, and since Brave Horse is practically camping on your door steps, things may become a little uncomfortable."

"If you allow those stupid idiots in town to influence your thinking on this matter, they'll be in for a lot more than discomfort, they'll put us smack in the middle of a an Indian uprising. As sheriff of Courgat, it's your duty to keep them in line, and I'm ready to back you up if need be."

"And just how do you suggest I keep a town full of idiots, as you so ably put it, from getting excited and pulling some fool stunt?" Darrell said in a frustrated tone. "Put 'um all in jail? Or shoot 'um?"

"Too bad the jail won't hold 'um all."

"That just leaves shootin' 'um."

"Don't you think this is a poor time to be joking," Debbie said.

"Sorry," Mac said, then turned his attention back to Darrell. "Cheer up. I happen to know that General Mendle is taking steps to bring the Indian problems under control."

"And just how do you happen to know that?"

"He paid Brave Horse a visit not too long ago to make sure that his feelings toward the Great White Father are friendly. I can tell you for certain that Brave Horse is no threat to anyone. He will only take up the hatchet if his people are threatened."

"Now all I have to do is convince the idiots of that."

"That's right."

"Tell you what, I'll call the meeting, and you do the convincing."

"You got a deal."

Following the burial of Phil Singer, the settlers and the citizens of Courgat were considering an attack on the village of Brave Horse. Darrell immediately called an emergency meeting to discuss the problem, threatening to arrest any man who made an aggressive move without consulting him first. In a state of near panic, the entire town gathered at the church. Some of the women were sobbing and clinging to their children.

"As you all know," Darrell began, "we have a problem on our hands, and the best way to solve a problem is to ask the most qualified man among us to give us his views on the situation. So I have asked Mac McCloud to speak to you. He's been dealing with the Indians for years. He knows more about the way they think than anyone of us. So let's give him our kind attention for a few minutes, and see if he can shed a bit of light on the problem."

Mac stood before the crowded room of nervous men, women, and children, his eyes moving slowly over their faces. "Sheriff Holliman is right, we do have a problem, no question about that, but how big the problem becomes depends on the actions of you men here in this room."

"Seems to me like the Indians already started the action!" An angry voice rose from the back of the room.

"The worst possible thing we can do is panic. When people get scared they run wild and leave their heads home behind the door. The good Lord gave us a head to think with, and there's no substitute for brains. Sure, a family has been burned out, a man is dead because of it, and God only knows where his wife and baby are. Killing more families will not bring the Singers back. If you start attacking the Indians, you may get the whole town burned to the ground, and most of the citizens will go up in smoke right along with the buildings. The Indians from Brave Horse's village have not broken their peace treaty."

"That's crazy talk." A man shouted. "They broke their treaty the minute they killed a white man."

"This isn't the first time this sort of thing has happened, but it's the first time it has happened to us. The government doesn't view these happenings as a breaking of treaties. They realize that a very small band of Indians are doing the killing. A few are terrorizing the small unprotected ranchers and farmers. But the entire Comanche Nation is not up in arms. It isn't fair to blame them all for what a few are doing. They hate these killings as much as we do, because they realize they may get blamed."

"What do you expect us to do? Sit around and wait for them to wipe us all out at one time?"

"I expect you to put the blame where it belongs. From the talk around town, some of you have the idea that Brave Horse is the one doing the burning and killing. I would like to point out to you that he has no reason. He is at peace with the Great White Father, and he is at peace with us. What if some fool went out and shot every Indian in sight. Would it be right for the Indians to take his crime out on the whole town and come riding in here and kill every thing that walks? Are you responsible for every holdup and killing committed by white men? If your answer is yes, then by all means go right out to Brave Horse's camp and start killing his people. But if your answer is no, you had better stop and think about what you're fixing to do."

"Sounds like good advice to me," Biglo said. "We don't want to start an Indian war. You know the old saying: 'don't jump out of the frying pan into the fire', so let's think before we jump."

357

"I agree with Biglo," Darrell commented, his eyes sweeping the room. "And another thing to consider. If you men decide to go after Brave Horse, who will protect this town while you're gone? If things should get rough here, the army will step in and take up our fight."

It was decided that Mac was right, and as Biglo had suggested, they would wait before jumping. Darrell Holliman felt a measure of relief, and a bit ineffectual for depending on McCloud's power of persuasion and seasoned logic to deal with the idiots, as Mac had so accurately put it.

After the meeting Darrell detained Dawn, drawing her aside from the crowd. He hated himself for what he was about to do.

"I have to talk to you. Will you come over to the office with me for a few minutes while Mac has a drink with the men?"

"Only for a moment. I have a few things I want to say to you too. I'll tell Father where he can find me when he's ready to leave."

Mac watched them walk away together and smiled to himself. He was thinking that Dawn might not have married Ned if she had met Holliman first. If he could choose a son-in-law, Holliman was more to his liking. He was a well educated man, and he definitely had a past, but he wasn't giving any hints as to what it might have been. He was tough, but soft spoken, and he hadn't learned to draw like lightning without a reason. He would like to know what that reason might be.

Neither of them spoke until they reached Darrell's office. Dawn was the first to break the silence. "About last night, what I said about moving in with you, I can't."

Darrell stared at her in disbelief, and then relief, trying to cover his feelings. "What made you change your mind?"

"I'm going away."

"What?"

"I've made up my mind."

He clasped her in an embrace. "You're not going anyplace. I won't let you."

"You can't stop me."

"Why? What are you running from? Where will you go?"

"I have to get away from here. I feel like I'm in jail."

"We can go away together, anyplace you choose."

"No!"

Darrell looked hurt and she was ashamed of her careless attitude toward him. "I'm sorry, I didn't mean to sound mean. Where I'm going, I have to go alone."

His heart suddenly skipped a beat. Was she going to her lover, to live with him? "Can you at least tell me where you're going?"

"I'm going to New Mexico to visit my grandfather."

"You don't know what you're saying. It's too dangerous. Mac will never allow you to travel across country, not with all the Indian trouble."

"For some reason, that I intend to find out, he doesn't want me to know anything about my grandfather.

"What was in the letter?"

"I don't know. He read it, and then burned it."

"I told you to read it."

"I should have listened to you."

"It would have been very enlightening, I'm sure. That's why he destroyed it."

"Exactly! He's treating me like a child."

"When are you going?"

"I don't know exactly. I have a lot of plans to make."

"One of which is getting past Mac."

"I'll find a way, even if I have to sneak out in the middle of the night."

"What about us?"

"We will always be friends."

"Thanks! You sure know how to make a man feel good.

Why do you think you have to go alone? I won't get in your way. You need me, remember?"

"I need you to be my friend."

"I want to take care of you."

"I know, but I can't allow you to do that. You have a position in this town. You can't just walk away from it. I'll be back."

"And in the meantime, I'll go out of my mind with worry. I don't care about this town, my job, or the damned Indians. I care about you. It will take days for you to reach New Mexico, even if you take the train. And you had better check with the station manager to make sure you can go all the way by rail. I understand that over a thousand miles of track has been laid, but I'm not sure how far it extends. I haven't looked at the map lately."

"I'll take my horse along. I'll ride the rest of the way if the track ends before I get there."

"That could take six months if you get lost, not to speak of getting scalped."

"I'll find a way."

"You can't just strike out on your own. Give me a chance. I'll get you there all in one piece, and back home safely. I promise. Let me take care of you."

"You're my best friend, but—"

The door suddenly burst open and Dale Parish rushed inside.

"Sheriff! Lance Sage is in town; he's looking for you."

"Who's Lance Sage?"

"He's a gunslinger."

"That a fact? Tell him I'm busy."

Dale turned around and ran back out the door, jabbering to himself.

Darrell looked back at Dawn. "Now where were we? Oh, yes, you were saying something about us being friends. I don't know why I get this feeling, but I think we're a little beyond that."

Dale ran back inside. "He said he's fixing to kill you."

"Damn! Tell him he can kill me later. I don't have time for it right now."

Dawn looked at Darrell, her eyes wide with shock. "What are you saying? Are you so upset with me that you're going to let some maniac kill you to punish me?"

"Punish you? Nobody is going to kill me. It's just some fool showing off?"

"What are you going to do?"

"As I damned well please."

Dale came back again. "He's over at the saloon bragging about how he's going to shoot you down with ease. He's calling you a coward. Says he'll wait for you in the street."

"He may have a long wait."

"Are you afraid of him?" Dale said, a note of disappointment in his tone.

"I don't even know who he is, but I'm tired of these interruptions."

"Are you coming out? He says he ain't leaving town 'till he kills you. Mac told him to shut his mouth and he threatened to kill him too."

"Well, that does it! Wait here," he said to Dawn. "I'll be right back."

"Don't go out there. He wants to kill you."

"If I don't go out, he'll come in here. His mind is made up, he's tired of living."

"I'm going with you."

"No, you're not. Wait for me here. Look out the window, but don't set foot outside."

"What if he kills you?"

"Then I'll be dead. Would you care?"

"Yes! Of course I would care."

He smiled. "Then I can't allow him to do that."

Darrell drew his gun, checked the chamber, and twirled it back into his holster.

Mac was trying to reason with Lance, he hated the thought of Darrell having to prove himself, one way or another. "The sheriff has all the trouble he needs. We got Indian trouble, and a woman and child missing."

"You know what I think? I think he's hiding from me. He knows I'll take him."

"How would he know that? You don't even know him."

"Who the hell are you?"

"A man who can't stand the sight of blood."

Lance laughed. "It sure won't be my blood."

"You're a fool if you believe that."

"Nobody calls me a fool. Step outside big mouth and show me how brave you are."

"Is that a challenge?"

"Yeah!"

Mac smiled. "I've never been challenged before. I'm not even armed."

"I'll loan you a gun," Lance said, "and take care of you right after I blow a hole in your sheriff."

Darrell strode into the street, and Dawn ran to the window to watch, her heart pounding with fear. Dale ran into the saloon yelling, "He's waiting for you in the street, Mr. Lance."

"Ain't that just fine." He set his hat on his head, loosened his gun a tad, flexed his fingers, cracked his knuckles, spit, and stepped out through the swinging doors. Twenty men crowded in behind him.

361

"I was beginning to think I might have to pull you out of there. I know you took Buck, but I outdrew him about six months ago."

"That a fact? Then why didn't you kill him?"

"I almost did."

"You missed?" Darrell said with a snort of laughter. "What were you aiming at?"

"I wasn't aiming. Makes no difference. I outdrew him."

"If you miss me, Lance, you're a dead man, because I'll shoot back. Anytime you're ready—make your play, but I suggest that you climb back on your pony and go back to where you came from."

Lance was flexing his fingers again, and then wind milled his arms to loosen up.

Holliman stifled a yawn, and waited. Lance's hand moved a fraction toward his gun, but got no further. Darrell blasted him in the chest and the slug drove him backward. He fell with his arms spread out as if he expected to fly, his legs splayed. He looked like a spider. The crowd of men walked into the street to see where he was hit. A few seconds later the undertaker put in an appearance, rubbing his greedy hands together.

Darrell very nonchalantly holstered his .45, turned around, saw Dawn running toward him and into his waiting arms. She was trembling and he held her close, speaking softly. "You really do care if I get shot. Stay with me tonight. I'll see you home in the morning."

Before she had time to answer, Mac approached. "Nice work," he said, reaching around Dawn to shake his hand. "That fool even challenged me."

"He was begging to get killed." Darrell looked disgustedly toward the knot of men gathered around Lance's bleeding body and yelled, "Don't just stand there and look at him, help the undertaker get him off the street."

Dawn wiggled out of his embrace and looked up at him. "How can you be so—so calm about killing a man?"

"Well, I sure didn't intend for him to kill me. It was his call. What would you have me do? I had to stop him. It's my job."

She suddenly rushed into his arms again. "Oh, you were so brave!" He was smiling now; she had paid him a complement.

Mac said, "I'll wait for you in the carriage," turned and walked back across the street.

Darrell waved a hand at him, and then gave Dawn his full attention. "Will you stay with me? I'll make very tender love to you."

"You know I can't. Father would never approve, and I hate to hurt him and make him ashamed."

"Would you stay with me if it were possible?"

"Yes."

"When can I see you again?"

"I'll be coming to town in the next few days. I'll come here. We can talk then. I have to go before father comes in here looking for me."

"I don't think he minds if you visit with me."

"He has always liked you."

"I wish I could get his daughter to like me a little more. I can't get you out of my mind. I want to hold you, kiss you and make love to you."

"I can't make you any promises."

"I know, and I understand."

"I don't think you do."

"Why don't you explain it to me then?"

"One day I will."

"Is that a promise?"

"Yes."

"Thanks, you know how to make me feel good."

"I'm not the only one who knows how to make a person feel good." She looked at him and smiled, then kissed him lightly on the lips.

"Can we do that again?"

She kissed him again, and he walked her to the carriage where Mac was waiting.

"You made a name for yourself tonight," Mac said.

"I made trouble for myself tonight."

"It all goes with the star."

"Yeah, it is a pretty target."

They shook hands. Mac snapped the reins and drove his daughter toward home.

Darrell had just gotten settled at his desk when Biglo came rushing inside. "I want to congratulate you for killing Lance Sage. You certainly did this town a service." He had Sage's gun belt in his hand. "I brought this over to you; the undertaker said you should have it as a souvenir."

Darrell frowned, thinking that was a damned strange thing for him to say. "Why would I want it?"

"You just killed the fastest gun in the state."

"Who says?"

"Everybody knows about Sage. You mean you didn't?"

"No, I'm a little slow."

"Not on the draw. He has twenty-seven notches on his grips."

"He was just the type to brag."

"Sage was the only man Buck refused to challenge. Sage said Buck made it a point never to cross his path. So you see, you now own the reputation for having the fastest gun in three states."

"A reputation is like having a hump on your back, you're forced to carry it as long as you live."

"I figured you would treasure Sage's gun."

"Yeah, it not a bad gun. I might be able to get forty dollars for it."

CHAPTER 34

The next few weeks passed without incident, but there remained much fear and unrest in Courgat concerning the Indian attack on the Singer's. Little did people realize that the worst was yet to come. In the spring the settlers came in droves, moving ever closer to the fringe of the Indian reservation in the eastern part of Texas. But they did not stop there, they continued to move forward, thus causing a break in the peace treaty when they moved into the fertile valley, pushing the Indians off their hunting ground and driving them further east into the mountains and away from water. They were being forced ever closer to a revolt for survival. They had put their mark on a piece of paper that said they agreed to stay clear of the white man's land, and hunt no more in the settler's fields, and to keep to their reservation. But there were no rules regarding the white settlers who knew no bounds. They took what they wanted and dared the Indians to stop them as they rolled forward, greedy for the land they had no right to claim. Land that had belonged to the Indians for thousands of years. Like the stars in the heavens, they kept coming until the Indians had no space. To the ends of the earth they were being driven. They must either fight or starve, and they were so greatly outnumbered that any revolt was a useless waste of lives. They could not win.

This led the hitherto peaceable tribes to become hostile, killing any white man who entered the last shred of their hunting grounds. They attacked their wagon trains, killed the men, raped the women, and carried off their children. They took many scalps.

To counteract these attacks upon the settlers, General Mendle was sent by the government with a large force of men to bring the situation under control. Not by enforcing the treaty upon the white man, but by slaughtering the Indians.

The army made bloody sweep after bloody sweep through the Indian camps mowing down everything that moved, including women and children. Many of the Indian women were raped by the outraged soldiers. Some of the soldiers began to collect scalps to show their bravery and to brag.

Following the massacre of the Indians by Mendle and his soldiers, the Indians formed an army of their own with many tribes joining forces against their common enemy. Bloody Bow, a great warrior selected from the Apache tribe of Chief Gray Eagle, was chosen to lead them. The fearless warrior was a fanatic where the cause of his people was concerned. He soon became a cunning and successful leader and hero to the many warriors who fought under his command. The sunrise attacks that the Indians were famous for suddenly ceased. Changing his strategy, Bloody Bow led his men in night raids, catching the soldiers in their tents sleeping while the night guards nodded in their saddles. They were quickly silenced before they could give the alarm. Whole army posts were at Bloody Bow's disposal for a short time, until they became aware of his tactics.

When General Mendle discovered that Bloody Bow's warriors outnumbered his army five to one he feared defeat, and abandoned his original plan. He shrewdly devised a scheme to seek help from the peaceful tribe of Comanche Chief, Brave Horse. He had heard of a grudge existing between Chief Gray Eagle and Chief Brave Horse, and was quick to recognize that this antagonism could be very valuable if used to enlist Brave Horse to join their fight against Bloody Bow.

A few days later Mendle proceeded to the village of Brave Horse, along with his staff of more than a dozen good men to request a council. General Mendle asked Brave Horse to fight Bloody Bow for the Government, explaining to him that the war was spreading in his direction, and that fighting was inevitable. When this happened, Brave Horse would then have to make up his mind as to which side he would fight on. Mendle made his offer sound as attractive as possible, swearing that he wanted to help his people, and that was his main reason for coming.

"When the war spreads to your territory," he explained, "the Government will fight to stop it, and it will be for your own good to join forces with us, as it is better for your people to have the protection of the military. If you remain neutral, you will have the army and Bloody Bow against you."

"We do not want war," Brave Horse said. "We want peace. We have treaty with the Great White Father. If the white man remains at peace with us, and Bloody Bow attacks in our territory, we will fight against him to keep peace with the Great White Father."

To make sure of Brave Horse's friendship and allegiance, the General appointed Brave Horse as head chief over the Southern Comanche Nation. He realized that the chief did not ask for tolerance, sufferance, or protection from the army, and this made his job easier, but of course he did offer protection, knowing he could not make a one sided deal with the Indians.

News of open Indian war in the northern states soon spread to the south, drenching the settlers with fear and hate. Sudden panic infected the citizens of Courgat, so sudden that they did not know which way to turn. The mayor called an emergency meeting in the Town Hall to consider what action should be taken in view of the coming danger, and the town agreed whole heartedly to ask the government for military protection.

The answer they received was brought to the council's attention. The military could not interfere. Due to the Indian uprising in the North, the army had its hands full. However they promised to send an Indian agent to check on the matter.

The growing pressure for action against all Indians put a curb on Mac's ambition where Indian trade was concerned. The town's alarm at the sight of an Indian forced Mac to stop trading with Brave Horse despite his sharp disagreement with the town's decision. The curtain was beginning to come down on the good will and trust Mac had built over the years with Brave Horse and his people. To prove his own trust and friendship, Mac agreed to transport supplies to the village of Brave Horse by wagon on each full moon. He did not intend to quarrel with the Indians just to please the edgy people of Courgat. Matters would only be complicated further by such actions on his part. Mac, a past master in dealing with the Indians, was neither a diplomat nor a politician. He had earned the name, friend, and he intended to protect that friendship with his life if need be.

Dawn's plan to journey to New Mexico was suddenly drenched cold by the change of events, and she resented the interference.

She had not given up her plans to visit her grandfather and stubbornly continued in the same course of thought, caught up in a new and exciting spell of adventure, thinking of what might be in store for her. Recurring memories of the letter from Henry filled her head with suspicions. The fact that Mac refused to share the letter with her, burning it as though it contained some sinful secret, made her more determined than ever to solve the mystery. All her unanswered questions swarmed together in a collection of suspicions and intrigue, sharpening her curiosity.

Meanwhile Darrell tried to talk her out of her foolish notion by reminding her of the Indian uprising. The situation was becoming more dangerous by the day, but she refused to acknowledge it.

In due time the army sent Robert Cooper to Courgat, instructing him to settle all Indian problems collectively, and to make it clear to the citizens that where the Indians were concerned, they would follow his instructions to the letter, as he had been appointed by the government as chief of Indian affairs.

A few days later Robert Cooper sent for Mac to come to his office that had been set up temporarily in the annex of the Town Hall. When he reached the agents office he discovered Light Eyes and another young brave, Gray Bull, being questioned by Cooper.

"You wanted to see me?" Mac said, entering Cooper's office.

"Do you know these Indians?" Cooper motioned toward the two braves.

"Yes, they're from the village of Brave Horse."

"Are you absolutely certain? Look at them closely."

"I know these braves personally, as a matter of fact, since they were children. The blue eyed one is the chief's son, Light Eyes, the other is Gray Bull."

At Mac's remark the agent became greatly excited and began walking the floor. "I can't understand how this could have happened," he said nervously, rubbing his hands together.

"If something is wrong, maybe you had better tell me. I might be able to help."

"These Indians have just brought terrible news of a slaughter in the village of Brave Horse, old men and women, even babies were torn from their mother's arms and slain. They claim this was done by the soldiers, the very ones who were sent to protect these people. They were attacked during the night, giving them no chance to defend themselves.

Mac had not yet learned of the meeting between Brave Horse and General Mendle, and his blood began to boil when the Indian agent told him of the agreement made by Brave Horse to fight on the side of the Government against Bloody Bow should he attack in the southern part of the state.

"Brave Horse has done his best to teach his people the ways of the white man and to seek peace, only to find that his reward is the massacre of his people," Mac burst out in anger.

But the worst was yet to come. Brave Horse lay critically wounded. If the chief died the Indians would go on the war path.

Mac requested that Doctor Keel be permitted to treat the ailing chief. Light Eyes consented, as chief in line, but only if Mac accompanied him. Cooper refused to accept the responsibility for Keel's safety. He left the decision solely up to the doctor's good judgment. Mac talked the situation over with Keel and he decided in favor of going, but not until Light Eyes agreed not to harm him or the town in the event of the old chief's death. Light Eyes was quick to agree.

When the party of men arrived at the village all the bodies had not been removed yet. Tepee poles lay scattered about, burned and broken, the contents strewn over the ground. Two old women, stooped and weeping, were preparing the dead Indians for the ceremony before they would be removed to the sacred burial ground.

From the appearance of the camp Mac realized that the braves had put up one hell of a fight. There was no question concerning who was responsible for the raid; he saw about thirty army mounts secured by lead lines stretched between two poles buried deep in the ground. There were several dead horses, and the bodies of many soldiers lay in a heap near the center of the camp, stripped of their uniforms and scalped, their bodies covered in dried blood. Several braves were stacking wood around them getting ready for the funeral fire.

Already the stench of death filled the air, and small Indian children waved tree branches over their dead to keep the circling buzzards from lighting on the fly infested bodies. Mac and Keel stood in silence staring at the scene of useless death and destruction. They followed Light Eyes into his father's lodge where the medicine man hovered over him. Light Eyes waved his hand and the Medicine man left the tepee.

Almost all the warriors who escaped with their lives had rushed after the soldiers as they fled, determined to kill as many of their enemy as possible, leaving the camp almost deserted except for the old people, children and a few braves who were clearing away the bodies. Light Eye's first concern was for his wounded father, and had ridden to Courgat to bring the white doctor back to treat him. It was good that the doctor agreed, because he would have taken him by force had he refused.

In the event of the chief's death, they would flee into the mountains, and Light Eyes would lead the remaining warriors and join forces with Bloody Bow to fight the army. If Brave Horse survived they would remain peaceful long enough to give the Great White Father time enough to find and punish the soldiers responsible for the great wrong the Indians had suffered. If no action was taken, the Comanches would deal with them in the same manner as they dealt with all enemies.

For four days the chief's life hung in the balance. During those four days the warriors returned with many scalps and guns.

They were better armed now than before the massacre. One warrior with a gun was equal to many warriors with bows and arrows. Everyone in the camp felt safer with many guns and much ammunition. Scouts were posted around the camp day and night. They would not be taken by surprise a second time.

News of the massacre traveled fast. When the army commander received word of the incident, sent by wire from Cooper, he immediately sent a detail of soldiers, led by General Mendle, to the Indian camp to investigate.

Mendle, knowing nothing about the attack by his soldiers was certain the message had to be a mistake, and felt sure that when they reached the village they would find nothing had been disturbed. As the detail neared the camp they heard the drums and saw dust drifting into the sky from the many dancing feet. When they moved close enough to both hear and see the Indians, they found themselves completely surrounded by warriors ornamented with eagle feathers and war paint. Mendle and the party of sixteen soldiers were escorted into the hostile village and held prisoners to await the outcome of Chief Brave Horse's condition.

Early the next morning the chief regained consciousness, and Doctor Keel was relieved to tell Light Eyes that his father was out of danger and would live. Mac remained as the chief's guest to see what the outcome might be concerning possible Indian aggression.

General Mendle realized what a dangerous mission he had undertaken, and racked his brain for a plan for reconciliation. The Indians had declared they would be peaceable as long as the white men remained so. Since it was the army that started the fight, how was he to convince the chief that the whole bloody attack had been a mistake? Especially since scouts had already been sent out to all tribes in Southern Texas with a message urging their chief's to come together for council. For several weeks the Comanche chiefs, accompanied by many warriors, began to arrive for the long council. They made their bivouacs near the river under the large pecan trees. Mac did not sense any hostility among them, although they appeared reserved and curious. Only Light Eyes appeared silent and troubled.

"Will they want peace?" asked Mac.

Light Eyes shook his head. "I don't know."

When Mac spread his blanket and stretched out near the camp fire, two little Comanche children came and slept at his feet.

After the morning meal, preparations were started for the council. A blazing fire was built by the squaws, and the Indians sat around it in a wide circle smoking. Chief Brave Horse spoke to them in their language, in a slow quiet way, still weak from his wound. They listened attentively to him in silence.

"What has happened to my people brings great pain and much sadness. The Indians in the north are at war with the white man, and many Indians have died. Many soldiers have died, but more will come to take their place, like the sand at your feet there will be no end. We live off the ground, and the white man is taking it little by little. They will push us to the end of the earth, where we will die. They are many, we are few. We can fight, but we can't win. We can only die. Before we wage war with the Great White Father, we must first listen to the words of General Mendle, he has promised to punish the soldiers who caused this great injustice. You must hear with your own ears, and then decide with me what is best for our people."

As soon as Brave Horse became silent, Mendle was brought before the council. He spoke in tones as brave and friendly as he could muster. "The white soldiers have done a great injustice to Brave Horse and his people, but they did this bad thing without the knowledge or permission of the Great White Father. They are enemies of the Indians, and they are enemies of the Great White Father. The army did not give that order. I am as puzzled as you. I came here hoping that what I was told was not true, but I know that this terrible thing did come to pass. I would gladly give my life if it would undo the terrible thing that has been done here. I will not rest until all the soldiers are caught and punished for their crimes against the Indians."

"Your talk is good, but how do we know that you do not speak with forked tongue?" one chief said, and many more gave a solemn grunt.

"The Great White Father sent me to make peace with you and the white men."

"No one wants peace more than my people," Chief Brave Horse said. "We are poor people, but we do not have to remain so. We can raid and kill and take many horses, much food, but we do not, we want peace more. Will the settlers also take our land as they do in the north? Will we have to fight to keep what is ours? The Indian was on this land many moons before the white man came. Since that time, white man's greed is pushing the Indians to the edge of the world. Will the General tell the Indian what more they can do?"

"In this land," Mendle said, "there are two parties of white men. One is friendly to the Indians, the other is hostile, and have a love of war and death. I am one who hates pain and killing. I came here to make peace, and I will stay as long as necessary to do this."

Brave Horse made no reply for a minute, thinking on the words of the general. After the painful pause ended, he said, "I believe you speak the truth, but you cannot speak for all white men. I can believe that you want peace—"

Before the chief could continue his voice was drowned in a loud burst of angry voices as many warriors rushed upon the general with tomahawks raised for attack. Light Eyes threw himself between Mendle and the warriors, giving his father time to interpose. Quickly Brave Horse raised the peace pipe high above his head. One of the angry warriors, Running Fox, stood before the chief's of the council and spoke in a loud angry voice. "The soldiers kill our people without mercy, now they must die also. There can be no peace as long as one long knife remains on Indian's land. We want war, and you hold out the peace pipe to us and our enemy. We do not smoke with this killer of our people."

"There will be no war as long as I am chief of the Comanche Nation."

"You are becoming like squaw," Running Fox shouted. "You are afraid of dying."

"I am old man, my days are short. I do not fear death for myself. It is my people I am afraid for. Fighting cannot bring peace for the Indian. It can only bring death."

Light Eyes took the pipe from his father's hand, put it between his lips and puffed. Running Fox became killing mad at his gesture and spit on the ground at his feet.

Light Eyes did not flinch, but passed the pipe back to his father. He picked up his rifle and pointed it at the wet spot where Running Fox had spit, pulled the trigger sending a spray of dirt into the face of Running Fox. "If you do not wish to obey your chief, then ride out of this camp. If you decide to leave, never return, or you will die by my hand."

"The white man's blood that flows in your veins has made you a traitor to your own people." He turned away from Light Eyes and spoke to the large circle of men. "All those who wish to fight the soldiers, come leave with me. I am riding to join forces with Bloody Bow."

When Running Fox departed he took many braves with him. Brave Horse looked very sad and puzzled at the swift turn of events. "These," Brave Horse said, spreading his arms, indicating the circle of remaining chiefs, "are at peace with the Great White Father." He then held the pipe to his lips and smoked, then passed it to the man next to him. As each chief smoked, he then took out his own pipe, filled it, lighted it and passed it around after the first.

Mac stayed for several days watching many Comanches come and go, the chief's war bonnets towering above the head-dress of the warriors. With Running Fox and his friends on the war path, Mac wondered how long it would be before they attacked some settler, or perhaps a town, maybe Courgat. If this should happen, peace would be hopelessly broken forever.

He though about what Running Fox had said about Light Eyes having the white man's blood running in his veins. He had suspected that to be the case for quite some time. The fact that he had blue eyes was no freak of nature, and he was curious, wondering about the young man's mother. He was a handsome man, bigger than the other braves, much taller than his father. He was also an educated man. He had little to say, but his English was perfect.

A few days later when Mac returned to Courgat, a curious crowd quickly gathered outside the Indian Agent's office. Inside Mac related to Cooper the happenings that had taken place during the council meeting.

"I'm sorry, but things don't look too good. Running Fox is gushing with hate for the chief, the soldiers, and all white men in general. He will stop at nothing, and he has quite a following. Frankly I'm worried about what might happen right here in our town." Mac confessed. "He was driven from the village by the chief's son, Light Eyes, who threatened to kill him if he ever returned. He was disgraced and may decide to commit some vengeful act to ease the hate and resentment building inside him. He plans to join Bloody Bow as soon as possible, but it's my guess that he has no idea where to find him at present."

"We are forced to hunt him down and put a stop to his offensive actions. We have no choice," Cooper said.

"And do what with him?"

"Kill him, of course."

"So far all he has done is talk, and you don't have a law on your books against that."

"He's a damned Indian, that's all the reason I need."

"For you, maybe."

"You just said that you expect he will commit an act of vengeance."

"That's right, I do, but until he does, you can't touch him. And I'll tell you something else, there isn't a soldier alive who can track him if he heads for the mountains, and I suspect that's where he will make his camp."

"The only time we use soldiers for scouts is when we can't find a trustworthy Indian. Either we can't trust them or they refuse to trust us. I purpose to hire the best Indian scout available."

"Mind telling me how you intend to do that?"

"That's where you come in. You know the Indians and they trust you. Now if you were to go to Brave Horse and explain the reasons I need a scout, I feel certain that he would not refuse."

"I know exactly the scout you're looking for, but since he happens to be the chief's son, I don't think he would go along with the idea, and the rest of the braves are afraid of Running Fox and Bloody Bow."

"We have nothing to lose by asking."

"I think we had better get one thing straight right now. You're the Indian Agent, sent here by the government to manage Indian affairs, not me. Agreed?"

"Well, yes."

"OK then, maybe you best remember that I don't get paid a fancy salary to ride back and forth carrying messages between you and Brave Horse. I have a family to take care of, a ranch to run, and a business to see after. Now if you want to hire yourself a scout, you hire yourself a scout. As for me, I'm going home and make plans for a wedding. Mine!"

Cooper looked startled. "Congratulations! I'm sorry. I didn't know you were getting married. When is the happy event?"

"I may never find out myself, if I don't go home. I've been gone for three weeks. For all I know she may have called the whole thing off."

"I suppose there is no real hurry about getting that scout."

"I'm going to give you a little more advise, Cooper. I realize you're the Indian agent, and you must know your job or you wouldn't be sitting behind that desk, but if I were you, I'd ride out to that village and talk to the chief in person. For after all, you should get acquainted with the people you're supposed to be representing. What kind of an Indian Agent is it that conducts his business from an easy chair? You had better get used to a little saddle service, because you have plenty of that up and coming. Those Indians won't come running in here with their problems, they will settle them their own way unless you show some kind of interest, and I don't mean through me. They know I'm on their side, but where you stand is still a question to be answered. I can't answer it for you. Frankly, I don't know the answer either."

"I don't like your attitude, McCloud." Cooper raised his voice in anger.

"Now that really grieves me," Mac said, with a good measure of sarcasm, "because your attitude doesn't do much for me either. Just be careful that you don't bite the only helping hand you have, because you will need a friend before this mess is wound up." Cooper stared at him, his mouth at half-mast.

Mac stepped through the door and into the circle of men waiting outside.

"What's up?" one of them asked.

"I'd be obliged if you would all talk to Cooper concerning the Indian affairs. He gets paid for talking." With a spiteful smile, he passed through the crowd, leaving them with startled expressions.

CHAPTER 35

Walking up to his front door Mac felt ten feet tall. He was greeted by two beautiful young ladies who were overjoyed by his return. The change that had taken place inside him because of his and Debbie's betrothal had transformed him into the happiest man on earth. He suddenly found that he had a future to look forward to and a past to forget. He couldn't live on memories any longer; he needed the warmth and comfort of a woman's love, to have her beside him at night and awaken to look into her face every morning.

"I'm certainly glad Brave Horse called off the war," he laughed. "Right now I love the world. I don't think I could kill a snake."

"That's wonderful," Debbie beamed. "I know how worried you must have been to think you might have to fight against the people who have been your friends for so many years."

"I will never raise a weapon to Brave Horse," he said firmly, "nor would he raise one to me."

Debbie knew what he said was true. His truth and honor was one of the many reasons she loved him.

"If Cooper had his way, I would already be on my way back to the Indian village to do his job."

"Why you?" Dawn asked. "Can't that man take care of his own responsibilities?"

"We'll soon find out, because I refused to go. I told him I had more important things to do, like getting married." He reached for Debbie's slender fingers, a lump rising in his throat. "Dawn agrees. Did she tell you?"

"Yes, and she has made me the happiest woman on earth. Her eyes were suddenly bright with tears."

Dawn gave a deep sigh and looked away blushing. "I'm going to make us a pot of coffee."

"No, please, let me. I'm so happy, if I don't do something to keep busy, I'll burst." Debbie hurried from the room with a light step.

"She really loves you," Dawn exclaimed. "How soon will you be getting married?"

"That I leave entirely up to the bride. If the decision was left to me, we would be married today."

"Don't put it off too long, or I might not be around to attend."

"What? Not attend!" His enthusiasm was visibly shaken.

"What are you talking about?"

"I have decided to take a long vacation."

"Just where do you think you can go in the middle of an Indian up-rising?"

"You just said that Brave Horse called off the war."

"That's right, he did, but there are quite a few Comanches who don't exactly share his views."

"Brave Horse will handle them. He's their chief, they must listen to him."

"Running Fox has opposed Brave Horse, and left in anger to join up with Bloody Bow. When he left he took a bunch of warriors with him. Who do you suppose will control them?"

"That's Cooper's problem, isn't it?"

"So he claims, but I don't believe he can do anything to stop Running Fox. I doubt he can even find him."

"Can't he get help from the army?"

"Not until Running Fox attacks."

"Do you think he will?"

"I know damned well he will. That's the main reason you do not leave here, even to go to town by yourself. By the way, you never did tell me where had intended to go for a vacation.

"To New Mexico."

"Why?" He looked stunned.

"To visit my grandfather, of course."

"No! I won't allow it. It's out of the question, the craziest notion I ever heard in my life."

"Why? It sounds reasonable to me. Surely you can't blame me for wanting to know my only other living relative."

"You have a son!" he reminded her, and the fear in his voice was confirmed by the look in his eyes.

"Yes, I have a son, and Henry McCloud has the right to know that he has a great grandson."

"It's not very likely that he would take much interest in his great grandchild when he took no interest at all in his own sons."

"He wrote you!"

"He wrote a little late."

"As long as he's alive, it's never too late." Dawn's mind was swarming with many questions she wanted to ask, but she knew the answers would be evasive, manipulating, hog-wash that said nothing, distorting the truth and reality. He had been avoiding the subject of Henry McCloud all her life simply because he refused to face the truth, and she was anxious to know why.

"What are you two yelling about?" Debbie said, entering the room with a tray containing three cups of coffee.

"Dawn has some fool notion of visiting her grandfather." His words came out sharp; he was unable to keep his anger under control.

"Wouldn't that be terribly dangerous? No telling what the Indians might do," Debbie said excitedly.

"It could prove dangerous in more ways than one." Mac said, still nettled by Dawn's rejection of his argument.

"And just what does that mean?" Dawn snapped, annoyed by his mysterious attitude.

"Forget it!" he barked. "Just forget the whole thing!" Mac settled into sullen silence. Debbie realized at once that some uncontrollable factor had unnerved him, and whatever it might be, it had turned the situation into one of mutual resistance without either of them actually committing themselves to a direct course of action. Mac's behavior had also brought emphasis to many unanswered questions. His deeply expressed disapproval of Dawn's desire to meet her grandfather had conveyed some of Dawn's questions and doubts to Debbie's mind, but she was careful not to express any opinions of her own. It seemed a most natural feeling for Dawn to want to get to know her grandfather; yet Mac acted as though some crime was involved in her simple interest.

"I'm sorry you're angry. I want you to be happy, but I will not let you talk me out of going to New Mexico. I may not go for a while, but I will go," she said positively. "There are some things I have to prove for myself."

"A Journey that far, at this time, could cost you your life."

"I'm not afraid."

"You haven't got sense enough to be afraid. Running Fox is seeking revenge, and he won't recover from his sickness the way you get over a bad cold. This trouble can go on for years."

"Well, let it—I can't wait that long. I don't intend to wait until Henry McCloud is dead before I pay him a visit."

"How will you make arrangements?"

"Don't worry, I'll find a way," she said stubbornly.

"Running Fox is on the warpath because Chief Brave Horse stopped him from killing General Mendle. He could be anyplace; he may be close enough to spit on right now. Cooper wants to hunt him down, but we can't until he commits a crime. It's like sitting on a keg of black powder with the fuse lit waiting for the explosion. Cooper wants to hire a scout from the camp of Brave Horse. He expected me to return to the village fifteen minutes after I got back into Courgat to try to persuade Light Eyes to go to work scouting for the government."

"Light Eyes!" Dawn gasped in surprise, her tone high pitched.

Debbie could feel the tension building inside the room. She glanced at Dawn, who was suddenly pale and trembling.

"He's the chief's son," Mac said, watching his daughter curiously, at a loss to explain her strange behavior.

Debbie's mind raced, searching for a way to help Dawn through the crisis, to free Mac's mind from the slightest suspicions that Dawn might be involved with the Indian. She hesitated only a moment before speaking to Mac in feigned excitement to support her stricken friend.

"Oh, my goodness! Isn't that the same as being in the army?

Light Eyes! A soldier?" She tried to sound as shocked as Dawn looked. "Do they actually take Indians into the military? I can't believe it! It's shocking!"

"They can take orders just like a white man," Mac said matter-of-factly, his attention focused on Debbie now.

"Do you think Light Eyes will help track down one of his own kind? After all, Running Fox is from the same tribe. They could be blood kin."

"Light Eyes will not bat an eye at killing him, let alone tracking him down. Running Fox showed much dishonor before the chief. I'm surprised he didn't kill him right then and there. I feel he should have, but I don't make the Indian laws."

"If he kills Running Fox, will he kill the others as well?"

"Hard to say what he might do, especially after the comment Running Fox made."

"What did he say?" Dawn asked as steadily as possible.

"When Light Eyes stood up in defense of General Mendle and his father, Running Fox said to him, "The white man's blood that flows in your veins has made you a traitor to your own people."

Debbie caught her breath in paralyzing astonishment. She was beginning to understand many things that Dawn had neglected to confide in her. Is Light Eyes half white?"

"He must be or Running Fox would never have made such a statement. I had already suspected as much. There is no other explanation for his appearance."

"Why didn't you ask him?" Debbie asked impatiently.

"You don't ask a man a question like that."

"Why? Does he hate his white blood?" Dawn asked.

"How would I know what he likes and dislikes? What difference does it make?"

Quite a lot to him I would imagine," Dawn shot back. He might want to live in the white man's world."

Seeing the angry spark in Dawn's eyes and the doubt in Mac's, Debbie changed the subject. "Enough of Indian talk. We have more important things to discuss, like setting the date for our wedding."

Dawn thanked Debbie without uttering a sound as their eyes met in complete understanding. Dawn excused herself, making some excuse about being tired, and left the room.

Mac looked at his bride to be with a twinkle in his eyes. "Say when."

"Just like that? No plans or anything?"

"Plans for what? We don't need any plans. All we need is a preacher."

"You make it sound so simple."

"Only because I'm so sure it's right."

"What about Dawn?" she said thoughtfully. "She has made up her mind to visit her grandfather, and nothing you say or do will change her plans."

"She must never see or speak to Henry. It will destroy her."

"What a curious thing to say."

"I can imagine how stupid I must sound to you, but believe me; I know what's best for her. I told you once that there were some things I have never told anyone."

"You also told me that once we were married there would be no secrets."

"I have to tell you something now, and I hope it won't change your feelings about me. After you hear what I have to say, you might decide not to marry me."

"Nothing you can say will change the way I feel about you."

"You had better save all your comments until after you hear me out." He paused, took a deep breath and continued. "You know of course that Dawn's mother died when Dawn was born."

"Yes," she said softly, and with an expression of pity in her warm blue eyes.

"There is something I have kept a secret all these years, and now, when I want to tell you, I'm not sure I have the courage."

"You don't have to tell me."

"Yes I do." For a moment the lump in his throat choked off his words. "Dawn's mother was an Indian, and she was the most beautiful creature I had ever seen in my life."

The look in Debbie's eyes was total shock, and she wanted to reject his words. "No, I don't believe you. I don't want to believe that you could hide the truth from Dawn all these years, a truth she has every right to know."

"You don't understand. You have no idea what it's like to be called a half-breed, and have people look down on you."

"And how would you know what it's like? Are you a half-breed also? Is that why you are such an authority on how they must feel? And what they must suffer? Well, let me tell you something, I believe a person can suffer more because they don't know who they are, what they are, and wonder why they do and say things they don't understand."

For one brief moment he thought he saw a flicker of hatred in her eyes as she came face to face with him.

Then she said in a burst of enlightenment, "Now I understand why she has coal black hair and dark eyes. Surely others can see it, if I can. And what about baby Henry?"

He turned his head, trying to hide the tears forming in his eyes. "I'm sorry I told you. I thought you might understand."

"You are the one who fails to understand. You have told me something almost impossible to believe. Not the fact that Dawn is half Indian, but the fact that you have kept the truth from her. You have lied to her and yourself."

"You're talking in riddles."

"Maybe you're right, riddles to you, but reality to me." Her voice grew more expressive. "Do you really think your silence about her mother has benefited her? It could very easily destroy her."

"Not if she never finds out. How can she be hurt over something she knows nothing about?"

"I can't tell you that, but I beg you, tell her the truth, now! Don't wait for her to find out from someone else."

"You're the only person in the world who knows except for my father and Doctor Keel. My secret is safe with Keel, he will never breathe a word to her." He thought about his confession to Martha Rowling, but lacked the courage to tell Debbie. She would never understand how he could tell Martha and not tell Dawn.

"And you know I never will, or else you wouldn't have told me."

"I know I can trust you, even before we're married."

"All I can say is this: I hope and pray you will change your mind. Her happiness may depend on the truth you're withholding from her."

"I will never believe that."

"If her mother had lived, how would you have dealt with it? Would she have been called a squaw and you a squaw-man? Would all of you been looked down on?"

"I loved Elizabeth enough to face anything the world had to dish out."

"What you're saying is that your strength died with Elizabeth."

The expression on Mac's face underwent a strange transfiguration, an expression of surprise and grief. He turned away. "When I lost Elizabeth, I lost everything, all that mattered was that I spare her child some of the hell she had been forced to endure. My father took her from her people and made her his slave. I figured our child deserved better."

Debbie took his hand. "I'm so sorry."

"Then you agree that what I've done is for the best?"

"I will never agree with that. I still think she should be told. I'm not asking that you tell the world, just Dawn."

"No, she would hate herself."

"What was in the letter you received from your father?"

"Nothing of any importance."

"That's hard to believe. After all these years you finally hear from him and he has nothing to say. Or is it just that it's unimportant to you?"

"He mentioned Elizabeth—asked how she was."

"That was natural under the circumstances, don't you think? After all, how was he to know she died? Does he know he has a granddaughter?"

"I left him a note when I ran away with Elizabeth. In the note I told him about Ralph's death and that I was coming here to take over his business. He knows nothing more."

"After all this time you're still bitter. Don't you believe that people can change?"

"People, yes. Henry McCloud is an animal. Please, I don't want to talk about this anymore right now." He took her arm, "May I walk you to your room? You look tired, and I have upset you with the story of my life."

"You have told me very little."

"We have the rest of our lives to discuss the past. Right now I'm only interested in the future, my future with you beside me. Will you give some thought as to when you will marry me, and please, make it soon."

"I will dream about it tonight. I will give you an answer tomorrow."

"Is that a promise?"

"Cross my heart."

When they kissed good-night in front of her door. Mac held her a little tighter than usual, and kissed her a little longer. She was certain of one thing, if she didn't marry him soon, she would have a very physical problem on her hands.

Debbie was awakened by a tapping on her door. She climbed out of bed, blinking at the dullness in her eyes. She opened the door cautiously, not knowing what to expect, her pulse drumming, holding her breath in expectancy. Dawn was standing there with tears pouring down her cheeks, holding a candle.

"What on earth is the matter?"

"I have to talk to you," she whispered. "I can't sleep. I'm going out of my mind."

"You look terrible." She noticed that Dawn was fully dressed. "You haven't even been to bed yet."

"I've been walking the floor. "May I come in?"

"Yes, of course."

"I hope you're not angry because I woke you. I just have to talk to someone."

"Angry? With you? Never!"

"You helped me through a bad time tonight. I want to thank you."

"No need for thanks. That's what friends are for."

"There was a time when I almost forgot that," she admitted. "I have treated you pretty rotten lately."

"I understand. I know what you have suffered, and I know you're still suffering. I wish there was something I could do or say to soften the hurt and bitterness in your heart."

"I almost fainted when Father told me about Light Eyes. Oh! I love him so, and I can never have him now. I told him I was married that day at the Rowling's ranch after he followed Frost there, and I will never forget the hurt look in his eyes. I didn't have a chance to explain. Ned was watching us from the barn, and he was so jealous. I'm all mixed up about everything. I don't know what to do. I feel that I must meet my grandfather. I don't know why I feel this way, or what I hope to gain by meeting him, but I will never rest until I do, until I find out what Father is hiding."

"Mac is so opposed. He will do everything in his power to stop you."

"Why, Debbie? What is he afraid of?"

"What makes you think he's afraid?"

"I don't know, but I get the same impression every time we talk about Henry McCloud. The more he objects, the more determined I am to go through with my plans to visit him."

"Yes, I guessed that and I agree with you."

Dawn was astonished. "You really do agree with me?"

"Wholeheartedly."

"I never dreamed I would hear words like that coming from your mouth."

"I'm saying what I feel in my heart. I can tell you how I feel now, before I marry Mac, but as his wife I will lose that privilege."

"That's nonsense. Just because you're getting married you don't have to turn into a jelly-fish."

"No, of course not, but the husband is head of the house, and has the authority to make the final decision. This is the law of God. I will abide by that law."

"After you're married I guess you'll turn against me too."

"I will never turn against you, and I cannot bring myself to share your father's views where your grandfather is concerned. However I will be compelled to remain silent, so I will tell you now. Go see your grandfather, find all the answers locked inside your heart and mind, or else you will never be free."

"You sound so sure," Dawn said, "that all the answers will come from my grandfather. Why?"

"Let's just say that I'm hoping."

"You're hedging."

"Only because I don't know the answer to the way I feel anymore than you can find the reason for the way you feel. For all we know, Mac may be right."

"But you don't think so."

"No!"

"Thanks you Debbie, for backing me up. I need your trust." Debbie became very serious and calm in manner as she changed the subject. "I have a great deal of respect for the things that have happened to you in the past, and hope that your future is more rewarding than your past." Dawn sighed and looked at the floor. "What, if anything, do you intend doing about Light Eyes? You can't go on this way."

"What happens between us now depends on him. He must have heard by now that my husband is dead, yet he has not come to me. He will never forgive me for marrying Ned. I thought he had left this part of the country, gone far away, when he has been close all the time. How he must hate me."

"He has no reason to hate you. You thought he had been killed."

"I married Ned when I was already married to Light Eyes."

"What?"

"He took me to his lodge, that is the sign of marriage, and I went willingly. I wanted him so badly, and he did not disappoint me. The one and only time I ever made love, real love, was with him. I hated for Ned to touch me. I didn't belong to him, I belonged to Light Eyes, and Ned took advantage of me because I was pregnant. It made me hate him.

"That day at the ranch I didn't have the courage to tell him I was carrying his child." Dawn's face gave way to an expression of sorrow. "I may never see him again. Oh! Why did I have to fall in love with an Indian? Why couldn't we be equal in the eyes of the world?"

"Why do you worry so about the eyes of the world? In the eyes of God, you are equal, and that's all that matters."

"I want to love him openly and freely! Oh, Debbie! I do love him so much. I can't explain it; I don't even want to, all I know is that I can never love another man."

"I believe that you will see him again."

"Do you really think so?"

Looking at Dawn with tears streaming down her face, she reminded her of a little child. "Yes and very soon."

"Oh, I hope you're right. I'll just die if you're not. Oh, what's the good of it? He's an Indian and I'm white?"

Debbie fought against the strong urge to tell Dawn the truth, the truth that would set her free. She put her head down to hide her guilt, blaming Mac for the injustice, for the pain he was causing his daughter by not telling her the truth about her mother. Mac had sealed his lips against the truth, and she could see herself as being no better.

"There is no chasm too wide for love to bridge. Your father and I are a good example of that. Love asks no questions, makes no excuses, only the mind can do that, so lead with your heart.

"You really do think there is hope, don't you?"

"There is always hope as long as there is life. I truly feel that after Mac and I are married, that he will come to see things a little differently. When the time is right you must tell him the truth about yourself and Light Eyes and the baby."

"He will never forgive me—and he might try to kill Light Eyes."

"I have good reason to think that he will understand completely.

Now stop your worrying and run along to bed and get some sleep. Everything will be fine. You'll see."

Dawn started to leave and Debbie called her back. "By the way, I have decided to marry your father this Saturday. I hope you don't think I'm being hasty."

"Heavens, no. I'm glad that you finally have it settled."

"I haven't told Mac yet."

"Don't worry about him, just keep an eye on him, or he'll be turning the calendar up on you." Dawn became serious again. "Thanks for listening to my troubles. You helped a lot."

"I'm glad. See you in the morning."

"Good-night," Dawn said in a very agreeable voice.

CHAPTER

36

Mac preferred a quiet wedding; however his wishes were not made known to Debbie. He was very careful to leave all the planning to her. In regards to celebrating observances, her views matched those of Mac's completely. She asked only that the ceremony be a religious one.

The following Saturday the wedding took place as planned, a simple ceremony in the McCloud parlor, with few in attendance.

When they were at last united, Mac turned to kiss his wife and there were tears of joy in her eyes and a beautiful smile on her lips. He gathered her close in a moment of deep passion, and they embraced one another.

Soon after the refreshments were served, the guests, bubbling with well wishes and congratulations, began to leave. Mac, wearing a triumphant expression, mixed with impatience, whispered lovingly to his wife, "Let's get out of here."

"Yes," she replied, with a quick glance in the direction of the door they were to make their exit through. They slipped away quickly and quietly to the privacy of Mac's room in the west wing of the great house.

"It's all over," he said, pulling her into his arms. "I have you all to myself at last."

"I love you," she cried, pressing close.

"Are you ready to go to bed with your husband, Mrs. McCloud?"

"I have thought of nothing else all day."

"That sound's exciting."

There were many things he wanted to say, but the words hung in his throat, and he felt close to tears. He was in no way prepared to cope with such great emotion. He felt like a school boy on his first date. He was actually trembling, wondering if he might disappoint her. He wasn't as confident as he had been the first time he made love to Elizabeth. He was twice his wife's age, and he was actually scared. What if he couldn't perform? She came to him eagerly with all the innocence of a child, lavishing her tender love upon him, exalting him into a state of ecstasy. He made beautiful, passionate love to his virgin bride, conscious of all else but the intensity of their union, and the rapture of her nearness.

Soon after Mac and Debbie retired to their room, Dawn found herself alone with Darrell.

"How do you feel about the marriage?" he asked gravely. "Surely you can't doubt that they love one another."

"I'm glad you were able to come," Dawn said with a feeling of loneliness, ignoring his question.

"I hope you're over your objections," he said, pursuing the subject.

"Only a fool could object to Debbie. She's too good for him."

"Say, you have changed your mind."

"I just woke up, that's all."

"If you can change your mind about them so easily, maybe you will change your mind about something else."

Dawn felt a spur of uneasiness. She knew what he was about to say and she didn't want to hear it. She looked at him defenseless, for there was no way to stop his grilling. He was forcing her to hurt him.

"Will you marry me?"

"So now it's marriage you want?" she said in anger and disappointment. "Why so noble all of a sudden?"

"That's what I've wanted from the beginning."

"But you knew the answer would be no, so you just saved your breath. Well the answer is still no."

"There was a little thing like a husband in the way before, or have you forgotten?"

"You have always known that it was not my husband that stood between us."

"What have you got against me, or shouldn't I ask?"

"Nothing, but I don't have anything going for you either. I like you; can't we just leave it at that?"

"Gladly," he replied, "I can't complain about the way you like me." Her face turned flaming red at the meaning of his statement. "Do you mean that as a compliment or contempt?"

"It means I enjoy you."

"You're very truthful about some things"

"Debbie and Mac are happy, now what about you? What are your plans for the future?" He spoke now with sincerity.

"My life is pleasant enough."

"Liar! You're about as happy as a blind horse, and I would have to be blind not to notice it."

"If you really want to know the truth, I have no future here. I'm frightened at what lies ahead for me and my son."

"Tell me," Darrell urged, "who's the father of your child?"

She turned on him in a blast of cold rage. "Don't you ever ask me that again! It's none of your business! And telling you won't change the facts."

Darrell felt troubled by his inability to reach her, to explain his feelings, and to gain her confidence completely. "I'm sorry," he said, "I always seem to start an argument when I never intend to."

"You know I don't like to talk about this. It shouldn't come as a surprise."

Darrell said no more and changed the subject. "Are you still planning to go to New Mexico?"

"Yes, just as soon as possible."

"Why? Give me one good reason why you're willing to risk your life to visit a man who is a complete stranger to you?" His tone was stern and with a note of distress.

"There is a void in my life. I sometimes feel I don't know who I am or what I am. I don't really understand my own feelings, but I know I have to go there if I ever expect to find myself."

"Mac will stop you—"

"No!" she cried. "He may try, but he will not stop me. There is some mysterious reason for his not wanting me to meet my grandfather, and I intend to find out what it is. And Debbie has encouraged me to go."

"You're kidding! I can't believe that Debbie, of all people, would actually encourage you to go against Mac. I guess I don't understand her after all."

"It's really quite simple. She knows something that I don't, but she's not at liberty to tell me."

"Like what?"

"I have no idea. But I'll find the answer in New Mexico on the lips of Henry McCloud."

Darrell was in the dark about what she was saying, and thought she might be making a river out of a mud hole. Nevertheless, he offered quickly, "When you get ready to go I'll take you. I want to know you make it safely."

"You can't do that!"

"I'll take you anyplace, anytime you're ready."

"What about your job? You can't just walk away and leave Courgat without a sheriff."

"Why not?"

"Well—, they depend on you."

"So do you, whether you realize it or not. When it comes to making a choice between you and this town, I'll take you."

"You're crazy."

"Why? Because I don't care which tree I light in? One tree is as good as the next. All towns are the same to me. You're what makes the difference in Courgat, or I wouldn't be sticking around."

"You're not a bird though," she said

"How do you know? Ever hear of a jailbird?"

She laughed. "Jailer, not jailbird."

"Care to bet?"

She stared at him with a puzzled expression. "Are you serious?"

"You'll never know," he said, smiling in an odd way. "We all have our little secrets, don't we?"

She recognized his answer as a challenge; he was trying to entice her into swapping secrets. "I think you're trying to trap me."

"I've noticed that you have an incredible curiosity."

"And you don't?"

He laughed. "We're all entitled to have a few secrets. Especially if they happen to be the kind uttered behind closed doors in hushed voices."

The next hour passed cheerfully enough, with all personal problems and feelings relaxed. When it came time for Darrell to leave he kissed Dawn good-night, and he felt a change in her, as though she were free from all emotional involvement where he was concerned. He had the feeling that his competition was very near and threatening. He cursed Ned under his breath, deciding the bastard had either been a piss poor shot or the man he shot was super human. How does a man shot in the back manage to mount a horse and ride away?

Long after he left her, his new impression of her attitude continued to plague him. There was a growing restlessness about her, something pushing her, taking complete control of her mind, and this strange mental element threatened every aspect of her present life. He had always considered himself a sensible man, now he doubted his own sanity. If he had good sense, he would walk away and not look back, because he was facing an impossible challenge. The longer he hung on, the more it would hurt when she ended it.

CHAPTER

37

By the end of the week Running Fox began his bloody vendetta. He struck with all the fury and force of a hurricane. His violent outbreak was terrorizing a hundred square miles of Texas farms and ranch lands, moving swiftly and unexpectedly, bringing death and destruction upon wagon trains, cattle drives, and poor unprotected settlers, burning them out and looting, giving them no chance to protect themselves. Running Fox had not joined Bloody Bow as he had originally planned, but gathered an army of braves of his own, reaching out to make a celebrated name for himself first. It seemed as though he struck in two places simultaneously, being careful never to be caught out in the open. He was not yet ready to fight the long knives or a posse of well armed men. His prime target being that of isolated settlers and ranchers, burning their homes and crops, stealing their stock. He did not take any prisoners; they would only slow him down. When he took women into captivity, after killing the men, he kept them in his camp for only a few hours before killing them, just long enough for his warriors to rape them repeatedly. Pursuit by the army was in vain. Before they could reach one location of destruction, Running Fox would strike in another. There was no pattern to his rampage; his movements were completely unpredictable.

As promised, Brave Horse and his people joined forces with General Mendle to fight for the common cause: peace between the Indians and the Great White Father.

Light Eyes volunteered to scout for the Army before Mendle found it necessary to make the request.

"It is suicide for your soldiers to search for Running Fox's stronghold," Light Eyes said. "They will creep up on your men, kill them in one bloody sweep, and then disappear into the mountains before you even see them."

"Can you help us?" Mendle asked.

"I know every trail, hole, and canyon in all directions for many miles. He can go no place that I cannot find. The answer lies in the message of his smoke signals; they will tell us where he is and where he will strike next. He has split his army of warriors to confuse you. He does strike in two places at once, but with fewer braves and less force, but his army grows with each passing day along with his success. He must be killed to change the pattern. He is now great hero to the Comanche and Apache. They have joined forces, as is true of many tribes who now follow the destructive trail with Bloody Bow."

"What can we do?" Mendle asked.

"If you are to stop Running Fox, then you must know his destination and be there waiting. This is the only way to kill him quickly."

However, before a plan could be put into operation, Bloody Bow cut another murderous swath across eastern Texas, forcing Mendle to put Captain Racer in charge of Fort Daily, the newly constructed outpost near Courgat. Then Mendle rode out with well over half the soldiers to off-set the terrible slaughter before the situation got completely out of hand. He joined forces with the eastern Calvary, headed by Captain Prince, a young Lieutenant from Fort Trible, located on the border of Texas and New Mexico.

When Cooper heard of Mendle's actions he made no secret of his disapproval. He had a job to do, but without adequate military strength, and he felt sure he might lose the support and respect of Brave Horse, who he was supposed to protect. The question to be answered was: would Brave Horse still fight when the odds were in Running Fox's favor? In desperation, knowing the army had his back to the wall, Cooper turned once again to Richard McCloud for help.

It was after dark when Cooper reached the McCloud ranch. He walked onto the porch and into the light shining through the stained glass window of the door. From inside came the sound of voices. They ceased when he pounded impatiently with the brass knocker.

Mac greeted him solemnly, a hint of anger in his expression. "I've been expecting you. Come in."

Cooper stepped inside feeling a shade displaced. "From the look on your face I would say that you have already heard the bad news."

"I'm not sure which bad news you're referring to. I certainly haven't heard anything good."

"I'm talking about Mendle pulling out with half the troops and stripping us of military protection."

"I have heard, and I think your use of the word strip is a little strong. He did the only thing he could."

Cooper looked at Mac in surprise. "I don't agree! I think our problem with Running Fox is just as important to us as Bloody Bow is to the western section."

"True enough, but right now Bloody Bow is doing more damage than Running Fox. The bigger the fire the more water it takes to quench it, and Bloody Bow is burning mighty bright. Now, how about a drink? It might calm you down a little."

"No thank you. This isn't exactly a social call."

"Your concern is very touching, but if you don't mind, I'll have one." Mac looked at Cooper indifferently as he poured a shot of whiskey into a crystal glass. He moved to a chair and sat down, took a sip from the glass, then said calmly, "Just what is it you want from me?"

"Advice." uttered Cooper. "I don't know anything about this Captain Racer that Mendle left in charge. I met him and all that I can say is that he is still wet behind the ears."

"Age doesn't make too much difference as long as he has sense enough to carry out orders. I don't think you have any reason to worry."

"It's the orders that worry me. My position in this affair has become ineffective." Cooper was visibly agitated.

Mac looked uneasily at the other man. "Maybe you had better tell me what Captain Racer's orders are."

"Now that Bloody Bow is gaining strength, his efficiency for attack has become more daring. Mendle figures Running Fox will join him soon, but not until he has gotten his revenge on Brave Horse. He has ordered

Captain Racer to wait in hiding until Running Fox attacks the village of Brave Horse before he makes his move. My orders are to see that the Indians stay put and make sure they don't get wind of Running Fox's plan. Mendle is afraid they might panic. I tell you, McCloud, Brave Horse's people are sitting ducks, and I'm beginning to feel more like an executioner than an Indian agent."

Mac's expression changed and he barked angrily, "Bait! Brave Horse is nothing more than a decoy to draw Running Fox out into the open. By the time the army makes their counter attack, half the village will be wiped out. An Indian in the eyes of the government is less than nothing. They sure have used that old adage: 'Fight fire with fire' to their own advantage."

"My sentiments exactly, and I just can't stand by and do nothing. My duty is to follow orders, but my heart is rejecting that order. Brave Horse has put his trust in us and we are leading him to slaughter."

"I think I misjudged you, Cooper," Mac confessed.

"I still have to look at myself in the mirror every time I shave. I won't be able to do that if I allow this disgraceful thing to happen. I have come begging again, McCloud."

Mac wasted no time; he left within the hour, journeying to the village to warn Brave Horse of the possible attack on his people by Running Fox, and the army's plan to trap him during the attack.

Mac's sudden departure left Debbie in a state of dispassionate optimism on the outside, while inside her nerves were tied in knots. She had to be strong for Dawn's sake, refusing to be shaken in the face of danger. Dawn marveled at her self-controlled attitude, while she was panic stricken, fearing not only for her father's life, but for the life of Light Eyes. Running Fox would be sure to kill him above all others.

"How can you be so calm?" she questioned Debbie. "Don't you realize that Father may be caught in the middle? He could be killed!" She lowered her head, and then continued in a tone little more than a whisper, "I may lose both the men in my life."

Debbie knew she was not speaking of Ned, realizing that she had not given up on the Indian, hoping that one day they might be together.

"Stop talking like that. Where is your faith?"

She laughed mockingly. "Faith! What has faith to do with dying?"

"Without faith and prayer, we have nothing."

"Without Light Eyes, I have nothing. Where do you get all your information? You don't even go to church."

"All the answers I need are in the Bible, and I make a practice of examining the Scriptures daily."

Dawn laughed again. "Do you believe that stuff?"

"You mean you don't?"

"I don't even know what the Bible says."

"You should make a point to find out. If we can't hope in God. we have no hope."

"Father says that the Bible teaches us right from wrong, and I know he's right about that. All I know is what my father has taught me, and Amy taught me things. I guess I'm not ready to know about all the mistakes I've made. I do what I want, and I answer to no one."

"I know that you love Light Eyes, what I don't understand is what you feel for Darrell Holliman. I know you care for him, and I know he's in love with you. You will have to hurt him, when he knows there is no hope for him to ever be a part of your life."

"He knows I don't love him. I have told him that more than once."

"How does he respond?"

"He has to accept it. What else can he do? He knows I like him, and he said he likes the way I like him."

Debbie's mouth dropped open. "What did he mean by that?"

"Just what he said."

"Dawn you haven't—I mean you wouldn't—"

"Sleep with him?

"I'm sorry; I shouldn't even think such a thing."

"I did—once."

"No! He took advantage of you!"

"No, he didn't! I went to him. I wanted him to make love to me. Only it wasn't love, because I don't love him, but I liked being close to him. I like what he does to me. He makes me feel safe. I need him, Debbie. He's the best friend I will ever have."

CHAPTER

38

The sun was just rising when Mac came within visible distance of the Indian village. It was a calm morning, silent and clear, interrupted by the distant barking of dogs and the call of crows. Presently he caught sight of two riders heading his way from the camp. As they drew near Mac pulled on the reins bringing his mount to a short halt. He was received with honor by two warriors and escorted to the lodge of Brave Horse, who stood proudly in front of the open tepee flap, his hand raised to Mac in a sign of welcome.

Mac dismounted and stood before him. "I have just come from the Indian Agent, Cooper," he began. "I have a message of great importance from him."

Brave Horse made a motion with his right hand and Light Eyes came to stand at his elbow. "Call the council together, our friend wishes to pow-wow."

The Indians sat with Mac in a small circle in the council lodge, not a word was uttered until the chief gave the motion. "We will listen while our friend McCloud tells us why he has come here."

Mac looked around the circle of men as he spoke: "I have just heard the plans of General Mendle, told to me by our good friend Cooper. He told me the General's plans at the risk of being punished. As you well know, Bloody Bow is on the move again, taking much riches and many scalps.

General Mendle must stop him, this is his job, but to do this he will need many soldiers. That is why he rode out of Fort Daily taking a large cavalry troop with him. The soldiers remaining are no match for Running Fox who has many braves fighting with him. Mendle gave orders to Captain Racer to follow a plan he thinks will bring Running Fox to his knees. This plan you know nothing about, yet you must play a very big part in the outcome."

"Who is this Captain Racer you speak about?" Light Eyes asked.

"He was appointed to take Mendle's place."

"We do not know this man."

"Nor do I."

"Mendle broke his word to my father."

"It seems that way, but Cooper has not."

"What is this plan that we must play a part in?"

The Indians listened intently while Mac related the plan feeling much shame, using as few words as possible, emphasizing the dangerous part the Indians were to play in the hazardous conspiracy.

For a long moment all was quiet. All eyes were focused on Brave Horse, waiting for him to speak. He looked into Mac's eyes as he said, "Why were we not told of this plan by General Mendle?"

"Mendle was afraid you might refuse, or panic and run. He felt he couldn't take the chance."

"If we are to die then we should have a choice!" The chief's voice rose in anger. "Mendle have forked tongue. He lie."

"I know, and that's the reason I have taken it upon myself to tell you the truth while there is still time for you to decide what you will do."

"We have no place to run," Black Hawk said, and the other three Indians grunted and shook their heads.

Brave Horse said, "Then it is agreed, we must stand and fight."

"I was sure you would," Mac said. "You will not be taken by surprise this time, you will be ready." Mac was filled with anxiety as he waited with his friends for Running Fox to put in an appearance.

Throughout the parley Light Eyes remained agitated, but he quickly regained his composure as he gave the warriors unequivocal orders to make ready for the attack.

Inside the tepees deep pits were dug for the warriors to kneel in, giving them maximum protection from Running Fox while they fired from beneath the loosely stretched skins at the base of the tepees, loosened for that purpose. The women and children also had dugouts for their protection, even if the lodges were burned away from over their heads.

All that day the Indians worked frantically, women and children working right along side the young braves and older men, carrying the dirt away and spreading it upon the ground.

The following morning they saw smoke ascending into the sky from the side of a hill to the south. From the north came the answer. Light Eyes read their message and informed his father that their camp was surrounded by Running Fox's army, that they would come pouring over them very soon to wipe out the source of Running Fox's disgrace.

The day commenced warm and cloudless, but by mid-morning heavy clouds began to gather, and by early afternoon a steady rain was falling. Mac felt certain that they would attack during the rain because all the Indians would be inside their shelters and less apt to spot them from a distance. Also the steady drumming of rain upon the tight stretched hides would smother the sound of hoof beats.

Light Eyes stationed himself as lookout, staying out of sight behind the lodges, sometimes kneeling beside the brick ovens. He moved silently and swiftly through the camp, drenched from rain and spattered with mud, his magnificent body alert and ready for action.

Only a couple hours of daylight remained when Light Eyes called out to them through a terrific downpour, "Get ready, here they come!"

Mac seized his rifle and stood beside Brave Horse inside the dugout beneath the old chief's lodge. Running Fox and his braves came charging into the village with much confidence, discovering too late that a hot reception committee awaited them. They held their fire until they were almost on top of them. When they cut loose on Running Fox and his warriors, they were dropped from their running mounts like leaves blown from a tree by the autumn wind.

The battle only lasted minutes. When it was over Light Eyes was the first to step into the open, walking among the fallen enemy. Presently he lifted his arm and signaled for the others to come out. The braves began to disarm the dead and wounded, placing their weapons in a neat stack before the chief's lodge.

Light Eyes rolled Running Fox over on his back and he screamed in agony from his wound, a bloody hole through his left chest just above his heart. His glazed eyes stared into the clear blue eyes of the Indian who stood above him, his face a mask of rage.

"I warned you never to return to this village or you would die," Light Eyes said, his jaw set tautly.

Suddenly Running Fox rolled to one side, and like lightning a flash of steel left his hand. Light Eyes groaned as the knife blade disappeared into his stomach. He reeled slightly, his hand grasping the handle of the knife, and with a sudden jerk, he pulled the blade from his bleeding wound and threw it on the ground. With an oath he dropped to his knees and seized Running Fox by the throat, pressing his thumbs into his windpipe. Running Fox struggled to free himself, but Light Eye's grip only tightened all the more. Running Fox's face turned an odd shade of blue, his eyes bulged, and his tongue protruded from his thin lips. When he ceased to struggle Light Eyes relaxed his grip.

Running Fox lay silent and still before him, his eyes staring in horror.

Light Eyes got to his feet slowly, enfeebled by his wound, took three steps toward his father and slumped to the ground. There came a sudden shrill scream of a woman. Two braves lifted Light Eyes and carried him into the lodge of the medicine man. Brave Horse entered the lodge behind them, a terror-stricken expression on his face. Mac paced back and forth in front of the tepee, glancing frequently toward the near hills, hoping to catch sight of the garrison. A young Indian woman came to stand beside the tepee, her eyes were wet with tears and she bit her lower lip to control her sobs. As Mac watched the young woman he wondered if she was the warrior's wife, but somehow he just could not picture Light Eyes as a family man. Wife or not, her love for the Indian was revealed in her grief-stricken face.

A short time later, Captain Racer and his men came thundering into camp. Racer rode right up to the Chief's lodge and dismounted.

"You're a little late," Mac said bitterly. "The battle is over."

Racer looked around him, astonished by the sight of the dead enemy lying on the muddy ground. "How did they do it?" He asked in complete surprise.

"I told them Running Fox was going to attack, so they set their own trap. You men think that just because you wear a uniform, you're smart. Maybe you would like to tell me what you think the outcome of this attack would have been if Brave Horse had waited for your protection?"

"You admitted that you warned Brave Horse about the army's plan. How did you find out? My orders were to have been kept secret."

"I'm well aware of that, and if they had been, Brave Horse wouldn't be around right now, nor anybody else for that matter."

"You didn't answer my question! How did you find out about our attack plan?"

"I don't have to answer your questions. It's none of your business where I got my information. I'm not one of your flunkies, so don't try to order me around. I don't have to respect your uniform. As a matter of fact, right now your uniform looks very much like a hangman's cape. You held back, willing to let Brave Horse's entire village be wiped out."

"I'm sorry you feel that way Mr.—"

"McCloud! But my friends call me, Mac."

Racer looked very uncomfortable. He turned and spoke to one of his men. "Get the burial detail started."

"I think you had better worry about the living before you start planting the dead. We have a wounded brave inside the medicine man's lodge. He was knifed in the gut by Running Fox."

"We have a surgeon with us. I'll get him to have a look at the brave."

"You will first need permission from Brave Horse. The wounded brave is his son."

"Will he make trouble?"

"If his son dies, he might. He was setup. He knows that now. You were ready to sacrifice this whole camp to trap Running Fox, and you were too damned far away to make any difference."

"I was only following orders."

"I don't think so. You want to know what I think? I think you were scared and saved the mix, because some of your men would have died if not for the Indians doing your job."

Brave Horse did not give his permission right away to have the white soldier treat his son. Mac convinced him that the white man made good medicine. Captain Oliver was allowed to enter the tepee and examine

Light Eyes, while the medicine man and Brave Horse watched every move he made. Mac was asked to wait outside to give the surgeon more room. After a quick examination of the knife wound the doctor stepped back outside, his face set in grave lines.

"What do you think?" Mac asked.

"His condition is extremely critical. He needs surgery at once; he's bleeding internally. Can you make the chief understand?"

Mac spoke to Brave Horse, who was looking to him for direction. "Your son is bleeding inside. The doctor must operate or he will bleed to death."

"I can't perform surgery here. Even if the bleeding is stopped, he will need expert care for a long time. He will die if we don't move him to Courgat at once."

"If his condition is critical, how can you take the chance of moving him?"

"It's his only chance. I have stopped the bleeding somewhat, it is only temporary treatment. but Do you think you can convince the chief to that effect?"

"Brave Horse is a reasonable man. I feel certain that he will give his approval." He spoke to Brave Horse again. "We must move your son at once. He will die if he stays here. The doctor needs his tools, his medicine, and proper care for Light Eyes after the operation. The sooner he is moved, the better his chances for survival. Will you give your permission?"

"If McCloud goes with him and watches over him for his people. I understand and I place my son in your hands." As he spoke he laid his hand firmly on Mac's shoulder.

As soon as the doctor completed his emergency treatment, Light Eyes was placed in the back of one of the supply wagons and made as comfortable as possible. Captain Oliver took his place at his side.

A small detail of soldiers, accompanied by Mac, pulled out just before dark, picking their way over the rough ground headed in the direction of Courgat.

During most of the journey Light Eyes was unconscious and growing weaker. Because of his weakened condition the operation would be even more risky, and Captain Oliver accepted his responsibility as a challenge.

The small party of men journeyed throughout the night and well into the next day. By the time they reached Courgat and Doctor Keel's office, Light Eyes was burning with fever and suffering great pain.

When they entered the house Mac hurriedly introduced the two doctors. Keel pointed to his treatment room and three soldiers carried the wounded warrior inside.

"First the father and now the son," Keel said, glancing at the unconscious Indian.

"I'll need your help," Oliver said, feeling guilty at taking over under the other doctor's roof.

"I feel honored," Keel said, making Oliver feel much more at ease.

"You will be more comfortable waiting in the next room," Keel said to Mac. "This may take a while."

Mac headed for the adjoining room, looking back briefly as Keel closed the door. He saw that Oliver was already bending over his patient removing the bloody bandages while he gave the other doctor instructions.

Once outside the room, Mac felt depressed as old memories began to ferment in his mind. Memories of the day Elizabeth died giving birth to their daughter. He shook his head to clear away the web of grief and turned his thoughts to Debbie and his new life with her.

Inside the treatment room the operation had commenced. Oliver took a scalpel from the hand of Doctor Keel and made a deep incision into the abdominal cavity, seething blood, black and clotted filled the incision.

"From the looks of this we couldn't have waited a minute longer."

"What are his chances?" Keel said, watching the feeble rise and fall of the Indian's chest as he labored to breathe.

"Slim," he answered, his fingers moving fast and confidently. He had treated many gut wounds, and this one was no different.

Doctor Keel swabbed the scarlet stream of blood while Oliver carefully closed the torn membranes around the stomach muscles one by one with a methodical motion of the needle. At last the blood ceased to flow. Oliver stepped back, wiping his perspiring brow.

"Close for me Doctor, and do it very neatly, this man wears very little clothes. If I had a body like his I might be tempted to wear a loin cloth myself, just to show-off. He looks like a breed to me."

"He is," Keel answered. He felt a deep sense of joy as he undertook the final steps of the operation. Captain Oliver was a brilliant young surgeon. He could learn from him.

"What about his mother?" Oliver said. "Do you know if she lives?"

"I would think not, but I have no way of knowing. When Light Eyes wakes up and feels like talking, why don't you ask him. I'm curious too."

"I doubt he would answer, but I might just do that. He intrigues me."

Mac leaped to his feet when the door to the treatment room swung open. "How's he doing?"

"He came through the operation just fine," Keel said patting Oliver on the shoulder. "Doctor Oliver did a beautiful job."

"I've had a lot of practice. But you had better save the praise; he's not out of the woods yet, not by a long shot. He has an infection to fight now, and he's lost a lot of blood. He's damned weak and that's bad company to share with an infection. The next seventy two hours will tell the story."

"Are you telling me that he might die?"

"I'm sorry, but I can't make any promises. He has a fighting chance."

"Is there anything I can do to help?" Mac asked, his face reflecting his worry.

"I'm afraid about all anyone can do at present is pray," Oliver answered. "Why don't you go home and get some rest. You look bushed. I'll stay with him until I'm sure the danger is past, or until he dies." Oliver looked at Mac sympathetically. "I'm sorry, but that's the best I can do. All the damage has been repaired. The rest is up to him."

"I understand but I'm not sure Brave Horse will. That man in there is his only son, next in line to be chief."

Before starting home Mac stopped by the sheriff's office to have a word with Darrell, and was surprised to learn that he already knew most of the details of Running Fox's attack.

"You really set that bastard on his ear. Congratulations!"

"Actually I had very little to do with it. It was the chief's son who planned all the tactics."

"This Light Eyes character must be quite a boy."

Mac laughed. "I know from your remark that you have never seen him or you wouldn't use the word 'boy' to describe him."

"Well, no matter how big the man is," Darrell corrected his statement with witticism, "you saved their hides by getting the message to them, or they might be history."

"Maybe," Mac said smiling. "By the way, how come you know so much about this?"

"I just happened to be in Cooper's office when one of the soldiers came in to make his report."

"Just happened to be there, huh?"

"Ok, so I'm a bit nosy, but as sheriff of this town I have to stay abreast of things. What the soldier couldn't tell us was how the chief's son is coming along. You got any ideas on that?"

"It looks pretty bad. He may die."

"That's tough, but I don't see how he can lose with two doctors treating him."

"Yeah, well they don't share your enthusiasm."

"Are you planning to stay in town?" he inquired. "If you are, I'll ride out to your place and tell your wife and daughter the news."

"Thanks, but there is nothing more I can do here, and I could do with some sleep. Last night was the second night I've spent in the saddle."

"You do look like a wilted flower. Are you sure you can make it home without falling out of your saddle? You're welcome to sleep in the jail if you like. I'll even serve you breakfast in bed in the morning."

"Bars, I don't like. The only way I'll ever sleep in a jail cell is to be locked in."

"Well I can manage that it if will make you feel more at home," he said grinning.

"You are a joy, Holliman. I'll see you later."

CHAPTER

39

The day had worn well into the afternoon by the time Mac reached home. Dawn was not there; he noticed her horse was not in the corral when he penned his own.

Debbie heard Mac's steps as he mounted the porch and she ran to the front door to greet him. "Darling, you're back," she cried throwing her arms around his neck. "Thank God, you're safe!"

He held her tight for a moment. "Running Fox and his warriors were wiped out."

"That's wonderful!"

"Almost," he said dully.

Seeing the pain in her husband's eyes, Debbie said softly, "Something has happened. What?"

"I'll tell you all about it in a minute. Right now I need a drink. I'm dead on my feet."

"Of course you are. Come into the parlor and sit down," she urged. "I'll pour you a drink."

Mac sank down on the couch with a sigh, leaned his head against the soft cushioned back, and closed his eyes. Debbie splashed some brandy into a snifter and handed it to him. Mac raised his head and gulped a swallow.

"I haven't slept since I left here."

"My poor darling, you must go to bed at once," she insisted. "We can talk in the morning after you've rested."

He submitted to her, and they walked quietly to their bedroom in the east wing. She helped him undress, and covered him with a cool white sheet. After kissing him good-night, she turned toward the door. Suddenly he said in an outburst of torment, and he was not speaking to Debbie, but more to himself. "He must live!"

Debbie spun around, took his hand and held it to her breast. "Who, darling. Who must live?"

"Brave Horse's son, Light Eyes."

"Light Eyes? Has something happened to him? No!" she gasped.

"He may die. Running Fox knifed him in the gut. He's at Doctor Keel's office."

"He's here! You brought him all the way back to Courgat?"

"I didn't have anything to do with it. Captain Oliver, the army's young surgeon had him brought here. He needs lots of care, and this is the only place he can get it."

"Then he's in good hands," she said, trying to ease his anxiety.

"Captain Oliver operated and repaired the damage, but he lost a lot of blood, and on top of that, he has an infection. Brave Horse doesn't deserve this Hell on earth. Light Eyes is his only son, and Brave Horse is getting old. Light Eyes is next in line to be chief of the Comanche Nation."

"We must have faith. Now you must rest. We can talk later." She kissed him again, darkened the room by drawing the heavy drapes, went out, and closed the door softly behind her. Once outside the door she let her tears fall, tears of pity for Dawn, feeling the moment draw near when she would tell her the tragic news, and the prospect was frightening. She had already been through this once, and now it had happened again, and he might die right before her eyes this time. I must pray, she thought, and went to her knees.

Debbie was waiting for Dawn with a troubled heart when she returned from her ride. She had no idea what to expect, and the painful knot in her stomach was almost unbearable.

"Dawn," she called out from the parlor. "Come in here for a minute."

Dawn entered the parlor with a frightened look on her face. She glanced about the room. "Where's Father? I know he's home. His horse is in the corral."

"He's sleeping."

"Sleeping? This time of day?"

"Yes, he was very tired after riding all night."

"Why did he have to ride all night?" she asked uneasily. "Has something happened? Did Running Fox attack the village?"

"Yes, and Brave Horse and his braves wiped them out."

"Thank goodness! Now we can all relax."

"Come sit down." Debbie patted the space beside her on the couch.

A look of suspicion flashed across Dawn's face as she slowly sank down on the couch beside her. "Is Father all right?"

"Your father is fine," Debbie said quickly.

"Then what is it?" A look of panic burned in her eyes. "It's Light Eyes! Something has happened to him! Tell me!" she sobbed. "Has he been killed?"

"He's been badly wounded."

Tears welled up in her eyes and her heart lunged with alarm. "He's dead! I know it. Oh!"

"No, he is not dead. You must believe that."

"Was he shot?"

"Running Fox knifed him. He's seriously injured."

Dawn began to scream and Debbie put her hand across her mouth. "You will wake Richard. Please, stay calm. If he comes in here, how will you explain your hysteria unless you tell him the truth?"

Dawn went into her arms, sobbing against her breast. "Oh, Debbie, I must go to him, ride to Brave Horse's village. He will die if he doesn't have Doctor Keel to treat his wound. I'll take the doctor with me." She scrambled to her feet and started toward the door.

"Wait!" Debbie's voice rose urgently. Dawn stopped abruptly and spun around to face her. "He's here in Courgat, at Doctor Keel's office. That's why your father rode all night, to help the soldiers bring him here. You know how he always sticks up for the Indians. He wouldn't leave Light Eyes out there to die."

Dawn uttered a husky cry and went to her knees weeping with relief. For a long time she could not speak, and then she slowly stood and wiped her eyes. "I have to go to him."

"Of course," Debbie agreed tenderly. "I'll go with you."

"You will?" Dawn was surprised. "I thought you might try to stop me."

"I never have attempted to do the impossible, and I won't start now. Come, we had better hurry. I must return before your father wakes up."

When they entered the doctor's office, they found him seated at his desk. He was not in the least surprised to see Dawn, he had been expecting her. However he had not expected Debbie to sanction what she was doing, but he realized she was there to buffer the gossip, and perhaps keep Dawn in tow, if it were possible. He expected that Mac didn't know they were there, or he might have stopped them.

She did not speak at once. She was trembling and on the verge of tears, her hand resting on the edge of his desk to steady her. "Will he live?" she said, smothering a sob.

"He's holding his own so far." He tried to sound reassuring.

"What does that mean?"

"We don't know. He's lost a lot of blood."

"I have to see him."

"That's impossible, he's too—"

"Please," Debbie said, "You can't refuse her. What harm can it do?"

"The army surgeon is with him. This doesn't look good, Dawn. There's no way I can explain your behavior. We don't need trouble."

"I don't care how it looks. I won't interrupt the doctor. I'll wait."

Doctor Keel glanced at the clock. "It's about time Doctor Oliver got a bit to eat." He was thoughtful for a moment. "I'll see what I can do. You two wait right here."

Keel opened the door to the treatment room and went inside.

Debbie took Dawn's cold, trembling hand as they waited. "You have to control your emotions for his safety, as well as your own. You know how prejudice people are about white women and Indians. He's been hurt enough. Please, be careful."

"I will! I'll do anything it takes to keep him safe. I have to see him. I have to explain about Ned."

"He's a very sick man. He may be too sick to listen or understand. He may not even be conscious."

"Oh, why doesn't Keel hurry up?" Dawn said impatiently, her eyes glued to the door.

Presently the door opened and both doctors appeared. "Doctor Oliver," Keel said, "This is Debbie McCloud, Mac's wife, and his daughter Dawn. They're here to help out."

"That's good," he said in a tired voice, eyeing both young ladies. "Mr. McCloud is a very lucky man to have so much beauty in his family. My pleasure ladies."

Debbie smiled sweetly. "You look tired Captain, may we watch over your patient while you get some rest?"

"That's very kind of you. I would appreciate it. Someone has to be with him at all times. I'm going over to the hotel for supper. One of you ladies may sit with him until I get back."

"I will," Dawn said quickly.

"That's fine. Doctor Keel will give you instructions."

Dawn followed the old doctor into the room where Light Eyes lay on a wide flat table covered with a blood stained sheet. "Oh," she sobbed, her heart pounding painfully at the sight of his pale still face. She took his hand to her lips and kissed his cold fingers. Memories of their last meeting burned across her mind and she gripped his hand more tightly, as if she might transfer the warmth from her body into his. She would never forget the look in his eyes when she confessed to him that she was married. How was she to make him understand that it was him she loved? She gazed intently into the strong, pleasant features of the man she loved with all her heart and soul. She caressed his cool face and smoothed his dark hair that was as black as her own. She anguished over his helplessness, feeling an urgency to pray, but not knowing how. She knelt beside him, his hand clasped to her breast, and cried into the pillow he laid his head on, her cheek next to his.

Doctor Keel did not attempt to restrain her. He stood by silently watching the pathetic scene, his heart filled with poignant sorrow. He had tried to imagine these two people in love, and together. Until this moment it had been beyond him. Seeing them now, he wondered if perhaps they belonged together, that the Indian blood that flowed in their veins might have bonded them spiritually. There appeared gentleness in Dawn he had never realized she possessed, and he feared for her emotional stability should this man die. But he had even greater concern for her if he lived. What would be the outcome? What kind of a future could she have living on a reservation? And what about Mac? He could not predict his actions, and his thoughts frightened him.

"I'll be just outside the door if you need me," he said quietly. "Call me if there is any change."

She looked up, blinked away the tears in her eyes and nodded her head, her lips wiped clean of words. He patted her shoulder, then joined Debbie in the other room.

"How did she take it?" Debbie asked.

"Pretty hard. She really loves that Indian."

"Yes, I know, and if he should die I'm afraid she might die right along with him."

"Do you think there is any chance of her going home for the night?"

"No!"

"That's what I was afraid of. Why don't you go over to the hotel and get her a room. I could let her stay here, but since the Captain will be staying here tonight, it might not look too good. You know how people stretch things, especially where Dawn is concerned."

"Are you sure you won't need me?" She glanced toward the room where Dawn was watching over Light Eyes.

"I can handle Dawn. Don't you worry. Now run along home to your husband. Why don't you ask Holliman to see you home?"

"I'll be fine."

Darrell had noticed Debbie and Dawn when they rode into town, but had given no thought to their visit until he saw Debbie enter the hotel. She walked up to the desk and signed the registry. He walked in through the front door just as the man behind the desk handed Debbie a key.

"Hey, what's going on here? Did you and Mac have a fight? As tired as he was, I know who got the upper hand."

"Of course not." she said smiling.

"Why the room?"

"The room is for Dawn."

"Dawn?"

"That's right. She's staying in town to help Doctor Keel look after his patient."

"You don't say? And just what is Captain Oliver supposed to be doing?"

"Doctors, same as everyone else, need rest. Captain Oliver was up all night; Doctor Keel is an old man, and he needs someone to take part of the strain off him."

"So Dawn volunteered. That's very interesting."

"Charitable, I believe is a more appropriate word."

"That's one way of putting it, and a bit out of character."

Debbie grasped a slight note of suspicion in his tone, and a lot of jealousy. "You men are all alike!" she scolded, and then quickly brushed past him, dismissing herself.

Got to watch my mouth, he thought, disgusted by his lack of restraint.

The thought of Dawn spending the night in the hotel caused his pulse to quicken with anticipation. He was bound by the thought and could think of little else. The blissful moments they had shared in the past plagued his memory. He strode aimlessly through the town, his mind in a fog. After he finished his rounds he strode toward the hotel, saw a man coming toward him in the late shadows of dust. Darrell stood still and watched curiously as the figure moved in his direction. When he noticed the uniform he spoke. "Captain Oliver?"

"Yes," he answered, stopping a few paces in front of him. "What can I do for you, Sheriff?"

"Not a thing," Darrell said, examining the doctor with extraordinary interest. "I was wondering if I might be of service to you."

"That's very kind indeed, but I think we have all the help we need at present."

"I think you're doing a fine thing, treating that Indian. Not many people care one way or the other what happens to them. He must be special."

"It's the least the army can do after the brave battle they fought in our behalf, wouldn't you say?"

"Sure thing."

"That Indian lying in there happens to be the chief's son, and he engineered the defense that defeated Running Fox and his entire army without losing a single warrior under his command. He's an intelligent man. If he should die it would be a great loss."

"I see your point. Well, if you need anything, feel free to call on me."

"Thank you Sheriff. I believe your name is Holliman, is that correct?"

"Yeah."

"I understand that you outdrew Buck Femmer."

"All in a day's work."

"I think it amounted to quite a bit more than that. I was told that at the time, you were working as a store clerk. I believe that badge you're wearing is more suitable to your nature than an apron. Thank you for your support."

"I'll be dropping by the Doctor's office from time to time to see how your famous patient is coming along. If you don't mind?" Darrell said as an after thought.

"I would appreciate it," Oliver said as he walked away. Darrell stood looking after the Captain, a thousand questions running through his mind, but he knew the questions must wait. The biggest being Captain Oliver himself. Just how well did he know Dawn? Was she spending the night in town to help Doctor Keel? Or was she there to spend the night with Oliver? After all, Darrell had known from the beginning that there was another man in Dawn's life, a man who did not live in Courgat, and the Captain might just fill the bill. He was about the right age, well educated, handsome, and probably married. That could account for all the secrecy. He had promised himself that one day he would find the answer. This was his first lead, and he intended to follow up on it.

He decided to wait around until Dawn left the doctor's office, hoping to buy her supper at the hotel before she retired to her room. In the meantime, Debbie rode out of town, escorted by two of the soldiers, headed for the ranch. The horses were strung out in a line with Debbie riding in the middle. She waved her arm as they rode past the sheriff's office.

That's one obstacle less, he thought, as he waved back.

CHAPTER

40

"Doctor Oliver wants to have a look at his patient," said Keel, taking Dawn's arm and leading her from the room. "You will have to wait out here."

She looked through the front window and suddenly realized it was dark outside. Across the street three soldiers were sitting together on the hotel porch. One of them lit a cigarette; the flair from the match cast a dim red glow on his face and then quickly disappeared. She frowned at the sound of music coming from the saloon mingled with laughter; their brazen joy was a mockery to her ears because of the pain in her heart. She turned away from the window, tears stinging her eyes.

"You can't go on this way," Doctor Keel said, breaking the silence. "I had Debbie get you a room at the hotel before she left. Why don't you go over there and rest for a while? You have been watching over him for hours. Making yourself sick is not going to help him." He held the key out to her. "I'll let you know the moment there is any change."

"Thank you, but I won't leave him until I know he's out of danger." She took the key from his hand and dropped it into her pocket. "I'll rest later."

"His condition may not change for days."

"Then I'll stay for days. I have to talk to him."

"How will you explain all this to Mac? He will ask questions."

"I know, but I can't worry about that right now."

"Why don't you just tell him the truth?"

"I can't! I have no idea what he might do to Light Eyes. He thinks Baby Henry is Ned's son. How do you think he will feel when he discovers that he gave Ned a beating for nothing? He will most likely take it out on Light Eyes, and he's helpless. Why can't you understand that I have to be near him, see him, and touch him? I love him."

"I understand more than you give me credit for. If you're hell bent on staying all night, at least do it on a full stomach."

"That sounds like a sensible suggestion," Captain Oliver said, entering the room, smiling slightly.

"How is he?" she said, and her voice broke.

"No change," Oliver eyed her dubiously. "We will be able to tell more about his condition by morning. As for you," he said, still watching Dawn closely, "If you want to play nurse all night, then I insist you take an hour's break."

"No, really, I'm not hungry."

"Doctor's orders. Come on, I'll walk you over. I could do with another cup of coffee myself."

Dawn allowed him to lead her from the house. Darrell watched from his office across the street as they left together and disappeared inside the hotel. He waited about thirty minutes, then followed. He was relieved to find them seated at a table in the hotel dining room, just finishing their meal. "Mind if I join you?" he said, finding it hard to appear unconcerned.

"Not at all," Oliver answered smoothly, "but I'm afraid we were just about to leave."

"I just wanted to ask how your patient is doing."

"About the same. The next twelve hours will be the most critical, if he survives that long his chances for recovery will increase every hour thereafter."

"I was just about to ask Dawn to join me for supper myself," Darrell said, changing the subject, "but you beat me to it."

"Well, I didn't exactly ask her to supper," Oliver said with a smile, "I'm afraid, I ordered her to eat, but I must admit her company is most pleasurable indeed. Since she insists on sitting up with my patient all night, she must eat to keep her strength up."

"I agree," Darrell remarked, watching Dawn apprehensively, "and I think her gesture is a very considerate one."

Dawn raised her eyes very slowly to meet Darrell's steady gaze. She lifted her coffee cup to her lips and drank the last swallow, and then rose to her feet. The Captain came swiftly to his. "Thank you Captain, for supper. Now if you both will excuse me, I'll get back to the office." The Captain threw some coins on the table, excused himself to Darrell, and hurried after her. "Are you all right?" he said, catching up to her.

"Yes, of course. Why do you ask?"

"You seem a little tense for some reason."

"I do? Sorry." She glanced over her shoulder and saw Darrell standing on the hotel steps, leaning against the railing watching them. She looped her arm through the Captain's with a smirk on her face. This should give the jealous fool something to sharpen his teeth on, she thought.

"Do you dislike Sheriff Holliman?" Oliver asked.

"I guess I just don't like sheriffs. They all seem to have nose trouble."

"Perhaps he's just interested."

"Maybe," she replied after a moment.

"Do you entertain the same dislike for Captains?"

"I don't know yet, you're the first one I ever met."

"You're forgiven," he said jokingly.

When they returned to the office Doctor Keel was waiting anxiously. "I'm glad you're back. Your patient was conscious for a few minutes."

"Turn your back and that's when things start to happen," Oliver said.

Dawn sprang toward the door and Doctor Keel took a firm grip on her arm. "Wait," he whispered. "Let Doctor Oliver examine him before you go in. It's going to be a long night. No need to hurry."

"But he's conscious!"

"Was conscious. I don't think he is now. If he is, finding himself in a strange place surrounded by strangers won't be exactly comforting to him. Seeing you might throw him into shock."

"I'm not a stranger!"

"Don't wait for Captain Oliver to order you from his room, and he will if you upset him."

Dawn decided the doctor knew best and felt ashamed of herself for being so selfish and awkward. She could tell that Keel was becoming annoyed with her, and she tried extra hard to remain calm. She waited for what seemed hours before the door opened and Doctor Oliver came out. "Amazing," he said. "That Indian has the will of an elephant."

"Does that mean he's better?" Dawn cried excitedly.

"His fever is down and he's resting easy at the moment."

"That's good news," Keel said. "I think it's time you got some rest yourself. Take my room, and I'll bed down out here on the couch in case Dawn needs me."

"You sure don't have to twist my arm. Wake me up in a few hours if I over sleep." He addressed Dawn then, "I'll take over then and let you get some sleep."

Dawn nodded thoughtfully. She knew she must hide her feelings and keep her emotions under control. She must not make the slightest move that might put Light Eyes life in jeopardy. She sensed a sort of hushed anxiety as she opened the door and crept into the room, her legs trembling, her heart pounding, experiencing a strange feeling of dread and discord for some frightening reason.

She moved cautiously toward him, the lamp beside the hard table he lay on cast a circle of light about him, picking out his profile and the shape of his body beneath the clean white sheet that covered his nakedness. The sight of him was a new awakening for her and tears suddenly brightened her eyes. Leaning over him, she touched his face with trembling fingers and brushed his lips with hers.

His eyes opened and looked up at her sharply. She thought at first in surprise, and then she became aware of the scorn in them, a definite glare of anger. "Please don't look at me that way," she cried without thinking. Realizing that her apprehension had been well founded.

Light Eyes had not expected to ever open his eyes again after he collapsed in his father's lodge, and he had never expected to see Dawn again, that was certain. She had given herself to another man. His mind seemed to melt into something dark, too sensitive to be definable. He felt the lance of pain in his guts again, not from the blade of Running Fox, but from the sight of the woman he had loved and lost. "Go away from me," he said in a rush of perfect English, his voice as hard as granite.

She looked at him, her mind clicking, he doesn't know me, but she could not hide from the truth when he turned his face away from the light and her. "No!" she cried. "Don't send me away. Please, I love you. You must let me explain."

"You betrayed me!" he lashed out.

His words touched her heart with a hot slice of anguish. "You must listen. I thought you were dead."

"You are dead to me. I never want to see your face again," he said, and they were the hardest words he would ever say because he had never lied before in his life. He stared into the dark depths of her eyes and saw something there like a bright streak into her past, a dull splash of truth that pulled at him, struck out at him like a blow. But he could not forgive her. She had turned to another man after she had given herself to him.

He started to raise himself, feeling an intense stab of pain and weakness, his movements sapping the last fraction of strength so completely that sweat streamed down his face and the sides of his neck.

"Please, don't do this," she begged hoarsely, while tears ran down her cheeks. "I love you, I will always love you."

He looked at her now and his eyes met hers. "Go away!"

"No! You can't mean that." Her face was twisted in disbelief, but she saw in his eyes an emptiness that she could not deny.

"You say you loved me, yet you married another man."

"I only married him because I thought you were dead."

A swift show of anger crossed his face. "You lie. If what you say is true, how could you fall into the arms of another man so fast?"

His words were like a slap in her face. She clenched her fists in anger. "No matter what you believe about me, never doubt that I love you."

He raised himself on one elbow. "I must leave this place, and you."

"You don't have to leave because of me. You need care. You must not leave here until you are well. I'm sorry for everything. Perhaps one day you might realize that you're wrong about me. "Good-by, Light Eyes."

He made another attempt to get up and she yelled for Doctor Keel.

The disturbance woke both doctors, and they rushed into the room.

"What's going on in here?" Oliver asked.

"He's trying to leave."

"Try is all he can do," Oliver said. "He couldn't get ten feet on his own." He pushed the Indian back down and tucked the sheet around him. "You have to lie still. You're a wounded man."

"Then get her out of here."

Oliver was astonished by his request, taking a few seconds to absorb them. "I'm afraid I don't understand," he said, his eyes following Dawn as she sank into the nearest chair, her head down, her back to the Indian. "But I can see that your presence is disturbing him. Come on, you have to leave the room."

She looked up at him with a scared expression. "I must talk to him. I have to explain something."

"Not now. Wait until he's calmed down."

"Just give me five minutes."

"No!" he said sharply. Then in a moderate tone, "Trust me. I have to do what's best for the patient."

She hesitated, and then let herself be ushered from the room. Doctor Keel had remained silent through the whole thing, at a loss to explain Dawn's behavior, wondering what might be going through Captain Oliver's head.

"Take care of him, Keel. I won't be long."

"Take your time."

Oliver closed the door before turning his attention to Dawn. "Mind telling me what went on in there?"

She laughed scornfully. "Why, he thinks I'm the one who stabbed him."

"Be serious. This could be very important."

"I am serious," she sobbed. "I'm the one who really hurt him. Can't you see that?"

"No, I can't. Suppose you tell me about it."

"What difference does it make?"

"I dare say, quite a lot to him and to you. How long have you known that Indian?"

"Long enough to love him," she admitted without shame.

"You can't be serious?" he said reprovingly. "You must not admit to loving an Indian."

"If I have the guts to admit my feelings, why can't you have the common decency to believe I'm telling the truth?"

"Perhaps it's because it's dangerous for you as well as him, and the relationship has no future. Why does your presence upset him? Doesn't he share your feelings?"

"It's a long and complicated story, and I don't feel like going into it, if you don't mind."

"Does your father approve?"

"My father doesn't know," she said in quiet desperation. "And that's the reason he doesn't know, he wouldn't approve."

Oliver seemed to have forgotten Dawn for a minute, and paced back and forth silently, deep in thought. Finally he turned to her and said, "I think you had best go on home."

"I don't want to go home."

"I can't allow you to see my patient, so if you're sticking around for that purpose you're wasting your time."

"I won't make trouble for him. I have something else to take care of."

"I'm glad to hear that. We will only have a bigger problem on our hands if you try to see him. A situation like this cannot be kept secret."

"You're right," she said flatly, "All my problems stem from keeping my love for him a secret. Well, no more!"

"You must keep up your pretense for a while longer for the Indian's sake. You have already admitted that your father would object. What do you think will happen to the Indian if you tell your father the truth?"

"As you can plainly see, it's very one sided."

"Yes, and that's the big mystery, but it's of no protection to him in the least. You have to keep quiet about it."

She made a slight nod of her head to signify her acceptance of his negative reply. "You're right."

"Does that mean you'll keep your secret until we get the Indian on his feet and send him home? After he leaves here we'll make sure he's well enough to take care of himself."

"You have my word."

"Good! I can't see any reason for either you or the Indian to suffer unduly. And from the sound of it he wants no reconciliation anyway."

"He just doesn't understand why I married another man. If he would only listen, I could explain."

"Indians are curious people. They have their own code of ethics, and abide by them to the letter. White men, on the other hand, tend to bend their laws to suit the majority. I don't know what your misunderstanding is, if I did, I might be able to help. If you have broken one of their moral standards, I'm afraid you will not be forgiven easily, if ever."

"Will you let me see him again later?"

"That depends on him. If he wants to see you, yes."

"You saw the way he acted just now. He won't see me on his own. I have to make him listen."

"He's too weak, he can't stand the exertion."

"When he's stronger? Can I see him then?"

"If he seems up to it, I suppose I might yield."

"Thank you. I might as well go to the hotel and get some rest." She picked up her skirt slightly and walked out the door and across the street, throwing Darrell a swift glance as he looked at her through the front glass of his office window. He'll follow me, she thought, and quickened her steps.

"What's your hurry?" Darrell said, coming up behind her.

"I'm tired," she said with vexation and hurried on.

He whistled a low whistle and followed at her heels. "What are you sore at me about, or did you and the Captain get in a fight?"

She stopped short, turned and eyed him mockingly. "Look! I've been up all night. I'm tired and sleepy. All I want is to be left alone. Do you mind?"

"I'm missing something here. I had thought we were friends. You don't have to worry about me detaining you." He turned and walked away in long angry strides.

She was immediately ashamed for being so short with him, and started to call him back but didn't have the energy to explain her short fuse. Later, she thought, I'll apologize.

Her actions had already begun to corrupt his imagination.

She had not so much as given him a kind look since Captain Oliver hit town. He decided to pay the Captain a visit and become better acquainted. He had a few direct questions he intended to have the answers to. He burned with disgust because he had fallen so hopelessly in love with Dawn, and was very close to making a complete fool of himself. As he walked past the saloon he had a strong impulse to step inside and drink his mind into oblivion, thinking he had rather be a drunk than a fool.

Dawn had changed toward him too abruptly and too completely. He figured that Oliver must be the key. He shook his head, angry with himself. What he had in mind was not only counter productive but insane. This kind of discipline was not like him, but he was a man of action, no holds barred.

The front room of the doctor's house was deserted when Darrell let himself in. He sat down and rolled himself a cigarette and smoked in silence, his mind going over the questions in his mind, waiting for the chance to satisfy the reason he was there.

Presently Doctor Keel entered the room carrying two cups and a pot of coffee on a tray. "Well, good-morning, Sheriff," he said in surprise. "I didn't hear you come in. I'll fetch another cup."

"Never mind, I've had my coffee."

"What brings you out so early?"

"I want to talk to Captain Oliver."

"There isn't a law against talking over a cup of coffee is there? Besides, he's busy right now. He hovers over that Indian like a mother hen."

Both men looked up as the door opened. "The sheriff is here to see you Captain," Keel said vigorously, handing him a cup of coffee.

Oliver took a sip of coffee, eyeing Darrell curiously. "What can I do for you?"

Darrell looked at Keel, and said reluctantly, "What I have to say is of a personal nature. Can we step outside?"

"That's not necessary," Keel assured him. "I'm going back to the kitchen to cook me some breakfast. I'll fix you something when you're ready," he addressed Oliver. He marched out of the room and closed the door behind him.

"Why all the mystery?" Oliver said in a curious tone, taking a chair across from Darrell, making himself comfortable.

"That's what I'm here to find out."

"I'm afraid I don't follow you, Holliman."

"Keep stringing along, Captain, and you will." He was silent for a moment, studying the doctor. "How long have you known Dawn?"

Now it was Oliver who studied Darrell. He smiled slightly before answering. "Only a few days, not that it's any of your business."

Darrell had expected his emphatic denial and said in an angry tone, "I'm making it my business, and further more, I don't believe you."

"Are you calling me a liar?" Oliver said briskly.

"I think you're her lover," he announced straightforwardly.

Oliver colored slightly. "You flatter me. I'm sorry to say that you are wrong, although the idea is intriguing. I wish it were true."

"Maybe you can explain the sudden cold shoulder she's turned on me ever since you came to town?"

"Your jealousy is wasted on me I assure you. My presence has no bearing whatsoever on her treatment of you. I can appreciate your concern. If I were in your shoes I might react in much the same way. She is a very desirable woman."

Darrell looked at Oliver with a puzzled expression. "There has to be a reason."

"I quite agree, but you will have to look elsewhere for the answer."

Darrell had a strange feeling that Oliver had all the answers, and he was convinced that he was not the mysterious man Dawn was in love with. He thought about Debbie and his anger grew. Damn her, he thought, she knows and refuses to tell me. Now he was more puzzled than ever as he sank deeper into an entanglement of absurd illusions. Feeling the complete fool, ashamed of his blundering indignity, he made his way to the nearest exit.

Oliver pitied the man for his loss, the embarrassing position he had placed himself in, and for making a fool of himself over a woman who cared less than zero about his feelings. But as big a fool as Darrell Holliman might be, was no comparison to the stupidity of the Indian. How could any man turn that down?

Oliver was tempted to tell Holliman the truth, but that would lead to murder, for he had no doubt but that Holliman would kill Light Eyes.

CHAPTER

For a long time Dawn lay awake, her heart aching from the never to heal wounds Light Eyes had inflicted deep upon her soul. When her body finally relaxed and she slept from exhaustion, her subconscious raced on in a maze of dreadful dreams filled with terror.

In a maddening sequel, her dream brought her to the edge of a slippery river bank where she could see Light Eyes caught in a swift, dark current of muddy water that was pulling him under. He was reaching out to her from the frothy deep, and she was watching helplessly from the bank, her hands tied behind her back. She struggled her hands free, stepped into the swirling water and swam toward Light Eyes' outstretched hands. She was near enough to grasp him when her legs became entangled as cold skeletal fingers appeared in the black rushing water. The face that belonged to the hands was that of Ned Rowling.

He was pulling her away in the opposite direction, his face hideous as he dragged her further and further away from Light Eyes' grasping hands. She saw Ned's hands, and they were covered in blood, and blood rolled and bubbled on the muddy current. It was Light Eyes' blood, his back was awash, and then he was gone. As Ned forced her to the center of the raging river, she held on to him helplessly to keep from drowning. She wanted to be free of his painful grip, to push him away, but without his support she would slide into oblivion. Suddenly another pair of hands took hold of her.

And it was Darrell Holliman who rescued her from Ned's iron grip. Ned screamed obscenities in a jealous rage until he sank out of sight into his bottomless grave, and she knew he was gone forever. She was safe, clasped in the arms of Darrell as he carried her in his arms from the angry river of blood and death. She saw pain in his expression when she pushed him away, and he was swept away into the gathering darkness. Now she was all alone and frightened but she could not call him back. Overhead, in a turbulence of sinister clouds, came the loud echo of her name, and then the dark cloud came down upon her, blinding her so that she could not see her way. Great confusion confounded her and she ran to and fro in a frenzy, listening to the sound of her name coming out of the darkness louder and louder until her ears were filled with nothing else.

She awoke with a start, staring up at the shabby ceiling of the hotel room. She shuddered with fear, clutched her pillow, and wept. The nightmare had been so real and shocking. Was it an omen? An awakening? If only she understood. She went over and over the dream in her mind. The river and the rushing water had to mean death, because Ned had died in the Canadian River. Light Eyes had been stabbed, and he was not dead, but perhaps dead to her. She felt the pain of losing him deep down inside her. She was not ashamed of her love for him, but the Captain had been right about the danger if she should let down her guard, and what was the point if Light Eyes was finished with her, and apparently he was.

She had treated Darrell cruelly because she was upset over Light Eyes, and she had treated him even worse because she had been upset with herself. He was her friend, always there for her, but in her shocked mind she had almost forgotten.

She had to get away, separate herself from the existing situation that was breaking her heart. She decided to leave for New Mexico as soon as she could make the arrangements. If Mac wouldn't tell her about her mother, or explain why he was so bitter about her grandfather, then she would take it upon herself to learn the truth. The answers were in New Mexico, and as Debbie had pointed out, she would not be free until she knew the truth, until all her questions had been answered. She couldn't bear to stay in the same town with Light Eyes and not profess her love for him, even though he had rejected her. If only she could make him listen. She wanted to tell him about their son, Henry. Perhaps he would understand then why she had married Ned. Not because she loved him but because she loved their son and he needed a father's love, and especially his name. She would try one last time to see Light Eyes before she left for New Mexico, but she would not plead with him this time. Either he would listen, or he would not.

When Debbie rode back to town the following day, she was shocked to find Dawn in such a hideous state of mind. "What on earth happened?" she asked, taking a handkerchief from her purse to wipe away her tears. "Have you gotten any sleep?"

"How can I sleep with this broken heart inside me? Light Eyes told them to get me out of there. He was trying to leave to get away from me. He hates me because I married Ned. I could have explained but he refused to listen. Oliver warned me to keep my love for him a secret for his safety. He says that I can't love an Indian, that it will destroy us both. He may be right. Father might kill us both."

"I won't have you say a terrible thing like that about Richard. He loves you beyond all else, and you know how he feels about Brave Horse. Surely you don't believe that he would harm his son?"

"Oh, I don't know what to think. I'm too upset to think. I'm going to New Mexico if I can make arrangements for baby Henry."

"You know I will care of the baby, but he will miss you."

"If I go by train I won't be gone long enough for him to forget me. I can't take him."

"What will you tell your father?"

"I don't intend to tell him anything. After I'm gone will be time enough for him to know. I know he will try to stop me, and I refuse to be stopped."

"What about Light Eyes, do you intend to give up on him?"

"He leaves me no choice. I can't force him to accept me, or even talk to me for that matter. I'm doing what I must. I want to meet my grandfather before it's too late. Father admitted that he's old and sick and doesn't even have a friend. I know he must have asked Father to come home in his letter, but that wasn't all that was in the letter, there were things Father doesn't want me to know. I can't even imagine what horrible secrets he's hiding from me."

"What he is keeping a secret might not be horrible at all, except in his own mind."

"I know that I can't cope with all these secrets at the same time. Father is keeping secrets from me, and I am keeping secrets from him, but there is nothing bad about my love for an Indian. It's not fair to judge him a lesser man just because he's not white. Perhaps he's ashamed of having loved me. Oh, why won't he talk to me?"

There is one way to get Light Eyes attention."

"How, I'm listening."

"Take the baby to see him. He can't deny that he's his son. Seeing Henry will convince him beyond words."

"Then he will be exposed. Do you want him killed?"

"Go at night. Slip in and out of town. No one need ever know."

"If Light Eyes is convinced, then he will exercise his right as the boy's father. He has to accept me first. I will never give up my child."

"Go visit your grandfather. I have a feeling that things will change drastically when you return."

"Oh, Debbie, I love you! You are still my very best friend."

"And you're mine. Tell me something."

"What?"

"What about Darrell Holliman. He loves you."

"Yes, I know, and I love him, but it's not the same as how I feel about Light Eyes. Darrell is my friend. He's always there for me, and I've treated him shamefully."

"He knows how you feel about him doesn't he?"

"I have never led him to believe otherwise."

"That's good. He's a special breed of man, strong, loyal and I would imagine affectionate by nature."

"He's gentle and kind, but he's strong. I respect him for that."

"I'm going over to Doctor Keel's office and inquire about Light Eyes condition. Richard will be in later. He's resting at the moment, and I wanted to talk to you before he had a chance. Don't mention your involvement with the Indian. It's not a good time. He has a lot on his mind and he doesn't need to worry about you right now. So just keep him happy. Make your plans and let me know when you plan to leave. In the meantime, I'll see after Henry for you. Laughing Eyes is looking after him at the moment. Soon the two little boys will be playmates. They will grow to love one another like brothers. I think keeping the squaw was a very happy arrangement."

"So do I. If you don't mind, ask Doctor Oliver if he thinks Light Eyes might talk to me today?"

"I had already intended to do that. What are you're immediate plans?"

"To apologize to Darrell. He has offered to take me to New Mexico to make sure I'm safe."

"And—will he expect more?"

"He might, but that's up to me."

"Be careful, Dawn. Darrell Holliman runs deeper than you might imagine."

"I know. He's said a few things that leave me wondering. He has a past that he doesn't care to discuss. He wants to trade secrets with me."

"What sort of secrets."

"About our pasts. He hinted that he was a jailbird."

"He was probably joking."

"Maybe."

"What's he want from you?"

"The name of my lover."

"Never tell him."

"I have no intentions of telling him. But he has a way of figuring things out."

"Pray he doesn't."

CHAPTER

42

Darrell was sitting at his desk when Dawn entered his office. He looked up in surprise and came quickly to his feet. "This is an unexpected pleasure," he said, moving toward her. "I hope this is a social call."

"It is."

"Sit down. I just made fresh coffee. Care for a cup?"

"I came to apologize."

He searched her face for a moment, his expression serious. "For what?"

"The way I've been treating you."

"I'm sure you had a good reason. I have been under foot lately. I don't get to see enough of you, and when you're around I act like a school boy. I'm the one who should be apologizing."

"Still friends?" she said, holding out both her hands to him. He took her hands and his grip was warm and comforting. "As long as I live," and then he pulled her into his arms. "I've been a fool. I know you're not in love with me, that someone else has taken up that little niche in your heart. Some crazy notions have taken over my good senses of late. I'm curious and I'm searching for answers, but of course you're aware of that."

"You don't have to explain."

"I feel like I do. I don't want to be another Ned, but I'm drifting in that direction." He smiled, "Sorry."

She hugged him tight. "I will never think of you in that respect. I'm sorry I took my bad mood out on you. I'm all right now, and you're right."

"About what?"

"I do need you. I think I would be lost without you."

He kissed her then and she returned his affection. Then, feeling embarrassed for showing her emotions in a public place, stepped away from him. "I should be ashamed."

"For liking me?"

"For leading you on?"

"I know where I stand with you. And I still say, I like the way you like me."

They both laughed.

"I have to tell you something," she said. "I've decided to go to New Mexico as soon as possible. Debbie is going to take care of Henry for me. I checked with the station manager, and I can go all the way to Carlsbad. From there I will have to travel horseback to reach Grandfather's ranch. He's on the map. I think he must own half the state. My father neglected to tell me that."

"I wonder what else he forgot to tell you."

"That my grandfather refused to give the railroad right of way through his land."

"It's my guess that when you step off the train you can take ten steps and be standing on McCloud range land. Your grandfather is a very powerful man."

"He's also all alone and sick."

Darrell smiled slightly. "He can buy everything but love and health. He's a poor man in all the ways that matter."

"I should have listened to you and read the letter."

"The letter wouldn't have answered all your questions, it would have made you more determined than ever to meet him face to face."

"You know me so well."

"Not well enough. Not yet."

"I would like to know which tree you flew from. Where are you from, Darrell?"

"The last tree was in Colorado. A state I can never go back to."

"Why?"

"I fouled my nest. Let's talk about something more productive. So, when you reach the end of the line, you will be out in the middle of nowhere."

"Yes, I know."

"You do need me."

"It's not fair for me to burden you with my problems."

"You're the furthest thing from a burden. We will need our horses to fill in the gap. I'll have a look at the map. We could wander for days looking for his ranch house unless we know which direction to go. Don't worry, I'll get you there."

"You mean you really are serious about going with me?"

"You know I am. When do we leave?"

"How soon can you get away?"

"Right this minute, if you're ready to travel."

"I thought I might be able to slip away in a couple of days. I have to pack a bag."

"So you don't intend to tell Mac?"

"No, he'll try to stop me—lock me in the cellar or something".

"He'll worry."

"Not if he knows you're with me."

"That might add to his worry."

"Does he have anything to worry about?"

"Not a thing, but I do."

"What?"

"That Mac might shoot me on sight."

"Only if there are strings attached. Are there?"

"That's up to you. I'm a willing partner," he said, smiling, then added, "all the way, but only if it pleases you."

"I'm not in love with you."

"I'll settle for like."

"Did you know that you're hard to resist?"

"That's very encouraging."

"What about your job?"

"There are a few things I haven't told you, concerning my job. It seems that the government has faith in my ability as a peace officer. I've been offered a marshal's appointment. It will mean traveling to some of the boom towns where there are more outlaws and crooks than citizens. Crime has become a popular sport, along with gold and silver fever and get rich schemes. Miners who celebrate their good fortune by getting drunk and bragging are being robbed at gunpoint or cheated in poker games by card sharps who use a marked deck of cards."

"Can you arrest card sharps?"

"Crooked card games, poor losers, or a card up a sleeve will generally produce a shooting, and an arrest can lead to a hanging. As the West grows, crime grows right along with it. Some men want to get rich fast without sweating, so they turn into bandits and rob gold shipments. They pick deserted spots and hold up stage coaches and trains."

"That's terrible. Oh, you can't leave now."

"I have accepted the appointment. I can take some time off. If they object, they can take my badge and stick it."

"I can't let you do that."

"You can't stop me. I told you, it doesn't matter which tree I land in. Do you object to being in the company of U.S. Marshal?"

"I would be very pleased and proud."

"I don't deserve the appointment, and that's a fact. I have a past, and well—it's not exactly a subject I care to discuss. One day I might dredge up enough courage to tell you about myself, and then you might not even like me."

"Now you have my curiosity aroused. Please, can't you tell me now?"

"You have a few secrets of your own, and I'm curious too, wondering who the lucky man is who has put a lock on your heart. Don't you trust me?"

"With my life, but not his."

"I promise not to arrest him."

"Please, don't ask me."

"Can you at least tell me if he's alive?"

"What do you mean?" she said with alarm.

He looked at her curiously. "It's just a simple question."

"Can we change the subject?"

He shook his head. "Tell me about your mother. Was she as beautiful as you?"

"I have no idea what she looked like. Father refuses to talk about her."

"Why do you think that is?"

"I wish I knew. He refuses to talk about my grandfather too. He becomes angry when I question him. He never wants me to meet him. Don't you see? There is something mysterious about my mother, and I have to know the truth."

"Whatever your grandfather wrote in that letter was something enlightening. Mac didn't start a fire with it to heat the coffee. He's forcing you to do this, and he may live to regret it. Look, I have accepted the Marshal's appointment, but on the condition that I get a thirty day leave of absence to tie up some loose ends before I tie myself down."

"Do you intend to come back here?"

"I hope to come back here." He laughed. "I could run into a little trouble if I don't watch my back."

"Because you outdrew Buck?"

"No, that's no problem. I'll tell you all about it when we get back from New Mexico. If I tell you now, you might decide you don't want me along."

"I think you're joking."

"Hedging," he corrected. "By the way, how is your patient coming along?"

"I don't know. I haven't checked on him this morning. After I do that I'm going home and tell Debbie my plans. She knows I'm going, but I hadn't set the date last time we talked. I'm going in two days. The train leaves on Saturday at four o'clock in the morning. I'll come early so I can load my horse and make the necessary arrangements."

"You just come early, I'll take care of the arrangements. You know something? I'm looking forward to this. I'll have you all to myself for days."

"Do you promise to tell me all about your dark past?"

"Can you keep secrets?"

"Definitely."

"Then I'll put my life in your hands."

"Don't joke, Darrell."

"Sweetheart, I would never joke about my life. I've had one hell of a time hanging on to it."

Dawn entered Doctor Keel's office a bit hesitantly, fearing Light Eyes had not changed his mind about talking to her. The room was empty and quiet. She sat down to wait, looking toward the adjoining door where Light Eyes lay wounded.

When the door opened it was Keel who came out. He greeted Dawn with a grim expression. "I had hoped you might go home."

"I intend to just as soon as I talk to Light Eyes. How is he this morning?"

"His fever broke and he's a bit stronger."

"Strong enough to have a visitor?"

"I don't want him upset. He may try to get up again and tear his stitches loose. Why don't you wait a few days. He's not thinking straight right now."

"I have a fresh point of view where he's concerned. I came to tell him good-bye."

"Are you going someplace? Or just staying away from him?"

"I'm going to visit my grandfather, but don't tell Father."

"Why don't you want him to know?"

"He'll try to stop me. He refuses to tell me anything about my mother or grandfather. He received a letter from grandfather, read it and burned it. He wouldn't let me read it, or even tell me what the letter said. I intend to get the answers from Grandfather."

"This is no time for you to be traveling to New Mexico. The Indians are in an uproar there. You could be killed."

"I'm not going alone. Darrell Holliman is going along to take care of me."

Keel was taken aback for a moment. "He can't just pick up and leave this town unprotected. Who will—"

"He'll be back. Surely this wretched town can get along without him for a few days."

"What about his Marshal's appointment? He's needed right here. We have claim jumpers killing miners and taking over their claims illegally. Confidence men are selling worthless stock, while others are salting mines with small amounts of good ore to whet the interest of unsuspecting miners. The farmers and ranchers are losing cattle, horses, and sheep to thieves, and Holliman is taking a vacation. Has he lost his mind?"

"He can deal with all that when he gets back. He's taking some time off before he settles down to business. Is that a crime too?"

"I see. The town's not going to like this."

"That's too bad."

"Does Mac know about this?"

"Of course not. I have to slip out of here before he finds a way to stop me."

"What about Debbie? Does she know?"

"She has encouraged me to go. She knows Father is keeping secrets and she has admitted that she disagrees with him. I don't even know what my mother looked like. You saw her Doctor Keel. Tell me about her, please."

"It's been many years, Dawn. I only saw her long enough to deliver you, and then she died."

"Do I look like her?"

He looked at her thoughtfully, wanting to tell her the truth, that she looked almost exactly like Elizabeth, and that her mother was an Indian, but he had given Mac his word and he wouldn't go back on it. "I think you might," he said at last. "She had dark hair and eyes."

"Why won't Father talk about her?"

"He loved her with his whole being. When she died I saw something die in him right along with her. I thank the Lord that he has Debbie. He's been grieving for a long time. I think it hurts him to talk about Elizabeth."

"Since he has Debbie why must he keep grieving? And does it grieve him to talk about Grandfather too?"

"I know exactly nothing about your grandfather, except that he's a very wealthy man. When do you plan to leave?"

"Saturday."

"And Holliman's going with you? Watch your step, Dawn. He's not like Ned."

"If he were I couldn't respect him. He's my friend." She stood up, shifting from one foot to the other. "Now, are you going to let me see your patient?"

Reluctantly he nodded his approval "You can't stay long. Doctor Oliver is due back anytime and he will expect to examine him."

"Is he still refusing to see me?"

"I haven't discussed the subject with him. He has very little to say about anything, although he speaks excellent English. It's always been a wonder to me how some Indians speak our language better than some of us when we can't utter a word of their language."

"Thank you. If I upset him, I'll leave immediately." She opened the door and stepped inside. Light Eyes looked toward her, his blue eyes steady

437

on her face. He watched her silently as she moved toward him. "Are you still upset with me?" she said in a soft voice.

"Why have you come back? You said you would not."

"I lied."

"You make jokes."

"I had rather make love," she said spontaneously, her remark sounded like something Darrell would say. She saw Light Eyes wince. She smiled at him. "I came back because I love you, but I've already told you that, and you called me a liar. I tried to explain to you why I married Ned Rowling. It wasn't what I wanted. I couldn't have what I wanted. I knew you had been shot, and when you didn't come back, I thought you were dead."

"And you gave yourself to another man."

"It was hell for me because I was in love with you. I still am. I married Ned because I was—"

"I don't won't to hear it! I don't want you now!"

"Damn you!" she cried, and she turned away from his startled expression for a heartbeat, then came back in mounting anger. "I will not beg. What I did, you forced me to do, but you don't want to face it. I only came here to say good-bye. I'm leaving in two days to go to New Mexico to see my grandfather, and I won't trouble you anymore. I thought you were different, but you're just a dumb Indian I had the misfortune of falling in love with. I came here to tell you something else, but not now. You don't deserve to know. So lick your wounds and feel like I betrayed you, but it was you who betrayed me. You let me go on thinking you were dead. I waited four months to hear from you, but you were silent, staying out of sight. You didn't even come back to the trading post with your friends. It was the day after I married that I accidentally saw you at the Rowling's ranch. You were able to chase after the man who raped your squaw, but you were too weak to come to me. I would have run away with you that day, if you had come back for me. Why didn't you? I needed you. You broke my heart over and over, and now you're doing it again."

Light Eyes was amazed by her show of spirit, he saw in her eyes the courage of he Comanche, the hard line of her lips, the fearlessness of the eagle. What had he done to her. She was angry, there were leaping flames of rage in her eyes. He moved, trying to sit up. He searched for words to tell her how he felt. He was ready to listen. He wanted to listen. He hated the weakness that ravaged his body, he was less than a man. He was helpless in the face of her fury and he could do nothing about it. She was turning to leave.

"Wait!" he cried. "Wait!" And he raised himself, his body trembling, and he was ashamed. He was ready to touch his bare feet to the floor when she swung around to face him.

"For what? I won't bother you anymore. No more whimpering and crying. I'll leave you alone. You probably have a fat squaw waiting for you in your lodge, lying on the same bed you made love to me on."

"I have no squaw!" he said vehemently, finding his voice. "Comanche brave have only one wife."

"Meaning me," she said, then laughed. "You left me! And don't bother to get up! I'm leaving. You don't have any reason to. You're wounded. If you leave here you'll die, and your people need you—your father needs you. And your fat squaw is probably lonely. You don't want me because I've been replaced. What's your excuse? You knew I wasn't dead. You knew where to find me. Lay down!"

His jaw tightened. He glared at her. He felt like hitting her. She was two-faced, she lied, she needed beating. "I will come to you, very soon now."

She took a step toward him. "What does very soon mean? Days? Weeks? Months? Years?"

"I will come to you at McCloud's big house when the moon becomes full. I will be strong then, and I will take you with me."

"Now you speak with forked tongue. You don't want me. Remember?"

"I was hasty, I may have made a mistake."

He had weakened. Now he was crawling. She couldn't believe that her nasty temper had gotten his attention when he had rejected her whining and pleading. She crossed the room and pushed him back on his pillow, leaned down over him, and his arms encircled her. She felt his warmth, and she searched and found his lips, and they were locked in an embrace when the door opened and Doctor Oliver stood on the threshold staring at them in shock. She turned to look at him. "I was just leaving."

"I see you got your problems all worked out. I must warn both of you, here and now, keep it under control or there might be a lynching."

"You have nothing to worry about. I'm leaving for New Mexico very early on Saturday morning."

"When will you return?"

"At least by the full moon."

"I'm afraid you're confusing me."

"I'm confusing myself."

At the time Dawn first met Darrell Holliman she had been grieving over Light Eyes, and Darrell had been her lifeline, taking up the lonely nagging emptiness chewing her insides. Their friendship had been light and uncomplicated until he fell in love with her. She didn't want to hurt him, and she had been completely honest with him from the start. She needed him now, and she felt ashamed for using him with no promises or rewards, yet he accepted the arrangement without complaint. She was comfortable with him, she liked the way he kissed her, the way he made her feel when he made love to her, and she trembled at the thought of losing him, as one day she must if she wanted to share her life with Light Eyes. She was drawn to each of them for different reasons. Darrell understood her, as if he could almost read her mind. He made her happy with his dry wit and genuine concern. He was strong and brave, and she noticed how the women liked the way he looked. Light Eyes was different, with smooth chiseled features, perfect body, black wavy hair that reached his broad shoulders, and expressive eyes as blue as the sky on a clear summer's day. She could not deny the strong magnetism between them. She admired and respected his untamed nature, yet he seemed refined in a way that puzzled her. And she had his son, a part of him. A perfect baby boy that Ned had hated and rejected. Henry needed the love of his father. He had experienced no such affection, and it wasn't fair. She had almost confessed to him the existence of the baby. She was thankful now that she had not. She would not trap him. He must want her for herself, or not at all. There was always the chance that he might decide to take the child from her if he found out. She would not risk losing her baby. She had heard it said that a half-breed had just enough white blood in their veins to confuse them, but that the primitive half was more prevalent.

Dawn did not return to Keel's office the following day. She had made her peace with Light Eyes by speaking her mind, and he had accepted it. He would either come to her, or he would not. She would have the answer to another question, come the next full moon. His attitude toward her was still guarded, and he had not changed his opinion regarding what he considered her betrayal. At one point she had sensed a change in him. He had seemed less withdrawn and suspicious. And there was no mistaking the fire in his blood when he kissed her, even though he was still weak from his wound.

She and Darrell made plans for their journey to New Mexico. Darrell was wearing the badge of a United States Marshal, and it fit him perfectly. He looked and acted the part as naturally as if he had been born with the badge pinned to his diaper. He took his new responsibility in stride. In less than twelve hours he had jailed two card sharps, a horse thief, and shot and killed a drunk who threw a whore down the stairs. When he attempted to arrest him, he drew down on Darrell and he shot him.

Charles Morgan accepted his new badge with pride. He had stepped up a notch, from a deputy sheriff to a deputy United States Marshal. Courgat would be left in good hands until Darrell returned. The town was comfortable with the new arrangement. Having a United States Marshal assigned to their town made them feel safe, even when the marshal was on vacation.

CHAPTER

43

"After I've gone you can tell Father, but wait as long as possible because he will try to stop me. Once the train leaves there won't be anything he can do. You can also tell him that Darrell is traveling with me to make sure I have a safe journey. He likes Darrell so he should feel relieved."

"He may not like him after he shelters you through your plan to visit Henry McCloud. You can expect him to be angry."

"He won't intimidate Darrell. He's a United States Marshal now."

"And his being a marshal won't intimidate your father either. I hope Marshal Holliman remains a gentleman."

"He has never been less than a gentleman. I'm not a lady like you, Debbie, and I like Darrell very much."

"I'm aware of that. Sometimes I wonder if you like him more than you love the Indian."

"Like and love are two different feelings. I know the difference."

"Perhaps," Debbie said thoughtfully. Time will tell, she thought. Darrell Holliman possessed a very charismatic personality. He was an exciting man, and she wondered how exciting the Indian was.

Dawn thought she might sleep a few hours before leaving town, but she was too excited and left the house two hours before train time. She decided to wake Darrell if he was still sleeping. She knew he wouldn't mind.

Debbie was awakened by the sound of hoof beats and knew Dawn was riding out. She got out of bed, careful not to disturb her husband, and went downstairs. The house seemed strangely empty and she experienced a disturbing feeling of loss. She missed Dawn already. She dreaded Richard's reaction when he discovered Dawn was gone, and more pointedly, where she had gone. She braced herself for his storm of anger that she knew would follow. Would he blame her? In a way she had betrayed him because she had been aware of Dawn's plans and kept it from him. She felt that Richard had betrayed his daughter. It was his silence that prompted her to run away like a thief in the night seeking answers that had plagued her all her life.

Darrell was dressed and waiting for Dawn. He had expected she would arrive early, and she hadn't disappointed him.

"I thought I might have to wake you," she admitted.

"I couldn't sleep. This town is beginning to bore me."

"How does Charles Morgan feel about being a deputy marshal?"

"He feels important. It's a step up for him, not to speak of more money."

"Are you trying to get him killed?"

"He's not a target. The gunslingers will be looking for me. I gave him his instructions. He'll be all right, and Mac is always around someplace. He'll back him up."

"Maybe you should have left Father in charge."

"He's been in charge of this town for years without the benefit of a tin star. Too bad he can't draw fast. He would make one hell of a lawman."

"I don't think he has time to work it in."

He shook his head. "You're right. I made a pot of coffee. If you intend to stay awake, I'll pour you a cup. Are you sleepy?"

"Yes. I was too keyed up to sleep."

"You can take a nap on my bunk if you like. We have about two hours to kill. I'll wake you in plenty of time to board the train."

"Will you lie down with me?"

"As soon as I lock the door," he said happily.

He took her hand and led her to the small sleeping quarters in back of the office. His bed was made neatly with a folded blanket at the foot. He helped her off with her boots, and then pulled his own boots off. He removed his gun belt and badge and laid them on the lamp table. They lay down together and he covered their feet with the blanket. He took her into his arms and held her tenderly. "How's this? Are you comfortable?"

"Perfect. She snuggled up to him. Now I can sleep. I feel safe."

"I want to ask you something."

She nestled closer. "What?"

"If you had moved in my house to live with me, would you have slept in my bed?"

She raised up and looked at him curiously. Wouldn't you have expected it?"

"No, I would have wanted it that way, but I wouldn't have expected it."

"I don't know if I would have at first, but eventually I would have given in."

"You make it sound like an obligation."

"I didn't mean it that way. Eventually I would have given in to my feelings and crept into your bed in the middle of the night."

"Because you wanted to be near me?"

"Because I like the way you make me feel."

"Thanks for telling me. Now maybe I can sleep."

She settled back into his arms, her head on his shoulder and one leg thrown over him. He breathed in her fresh, sweet scent, felt her warmth, her dark hair whispering against his cheek, and he closed his eyes in contentment. He wanted time to stand still, but the hands on the clock moved ever so steadily forward, ticking his treasured moments into the past. Soon they were both sleeping peacefully.

He was awakened by the train's whistle when it was about five miles from the station. "Train's coming," he said close to her ear. "It's time we put our boots on."

She raised up, looked at him and smiled. "You are the most understanding man I have ever known" She leaned down and kissed his lips softly. He pulled her against him and kissed her with all the emotion he was feeling. When they drew apart, she looked at him with tears in her eyes. "I never want to hurt you; you mean so much to me. You're good, kind, and loving, and it grieves me to think that one day I will break your heart."

"I know," he said sadly. "I have accepted the consequences. Just keep liking me, and never feel sorry for me—I don't want that. I want your love in any degree that you care to share it. It took a lot of courage for you to kiss me with so much passion, and then tell me in the same breath that one day you will break my heart. Faint-heartedness is not a quality to be proud of, and I thank God that it's a flaw I have never been afflicted with. The truth I can accept, it's the lies that stumble me. I believe in right or wrong, black or white, it's the gray area that leaves one in a quandary."

"What is the gray area, Darrell?"

"Confusion, naturally. I think it's an island somewhere between Heaven and Hell where the Devil stands splay-legged with a bloody whip of division in his greedy sweaty hands, laughing with confidence, snapping it over people's heads, striping their backs and driving them with gratification and delight in the wrong direction. We all face uncertainty at some time in our lives, the monumental struggle to understand and escape the gray area."

Dawn was amazed by what he was saying. "You do run deep."

"What makes you think that?"

"Something Debbie said."

"I should have guessed. I think you're in the gray area of confusion."

"Concerning you?"

"Concerning a lot of things. Me included."

"Please tell me."

"There will be plenty of time for that later. We will be on the train for many hours. We had better get moving or the train will leave without us. Wait here while I make the arrangements for our horses. I'll be back for you in ten minutes. Don't be surprised if you see a few raised eyebrows."

"I've been seeing raised eyebrows most of my life."

He buckled on his gun belt, pinned the badge on his shirt, opened the door and stepped into the damp darkness.

Seeing Dawn and Darrell together so much had started the usual tongues wagging. Darrell took it in stride, and no one dared to affront him concerning his interest in the widow of Ned Rowling. It was common knowledge that he had been seeing Dawn long before Ned died. So when they boarded the train together no one was actually surprised.

They had been flaunting their incredibly tight relationship for months.

There were quite a few soldiers on the train, grouped together in one of the coaches. They were loud and obnoxious, passing a bottle between them. Darrell glanced around as he moved Dawn ahead of him down the narrow isle. He did not spot an officer. It would seem that a sloppy fat sergeant was the highest ranking among them, and undoubtedly in charge. He led Dawn straight through, guiding her around the feet extending into the isle, trying to ignore the cat calls and disrespectful comments that were typical when a good-looking woman crossed the path of drunken soldiers.

"Hey Marshal!" one yelled. "Where did you get that sexy doll?" He made a move to stand up and Darrell put his hand in his face and shoved him back down. A disquieting rumble rose from the other men.

Darrell turned to face them. "Hold it down, boys and you'll stay healthy."

"Who the hell do you think you are?" the sergeant barked. "I give the orders here."

"Then I suggest you order these soldiers to act like men instead of animals." He pushed Dawn ahead of him through the door and was about to close it when the sergeant struggled to his feet.

"I'm fixing to shove that star up your ass."

Darrell whipped around, his gun already in his hand. The sergeant stopped cold, his eyes wide with shock. "Who are you?"

"The name's Holliman."

The sergeant backed up a few steps. "You're the man that killed Buck."

"Was he a good friend of yours?"

"I heard about him."

"You keep these men in line. Don't force me to do it for you. If that should happen, you'll have a long walk to wherever you're headed because I'll put the whole bunch of you off this train."

"We're headed to New Mexico to kill us some Indians. We ain't got no time for walking."

"Then I wouldn't do anything to provoke me if I were you. One more disrespectful comment or motion regarding this young lady I'm traveling with and I'll throw you off the train and I won't wait for it to stop."

"You don't respect the army much do you?"

"The army has never given me cause for respect."

Darrell took Dawn's arm and led her to the last car in front of the caboose. It was as far as they could get from the carload of soldiers.

Dawn looked around at the collection of men they would be traveling with. Several men focused on Darrell's badge and headed for the exit. "I think those men might be in the gray area," she said thoughtfully.

"They most likely belong in jail."

Dawn sat down in the seat next to the window and Darrell took the isle seat beside her.

"I'm glad you came with me. I would be afraid if you weren't here to take care of me."

"Maybe you realize now why I didn't want you traveling alone."

"Do all soldiers act like the ones on the train?"

"They need supervision. There should be an officer traveling with them. That stupid sergeant has absolutely no control over them, nor does he care. Stick close to me. As far as the soldiers are concerned, and I'm speaking collectively, they have been turned loose by the government like wild dogs to massacre Indians. They generate more danger than protection."

"Why do you say that?"

"I spent some time in the army. I know firsthand what they're capable of."

"Do they all get drunk and abusive?"

"Any man who gets drunk is either abusive, disgusting, or both."

"How long were you in the army?"

"Five years. From 1859 until 1864."

"Why did you quit?"

"I didn't. I was court-martialled and sentenced to hang."

"No! I don't believe you! It's impossible!"

"I would never lie to you about a thing like that."

"Then you really were a jailbird?" He shook his head. "And now you're a United States Marshal. How did that happen?"

"I have a few rough edges I haven't mentioned to you. A little thing called insubordination-revolt, or sedation, take your pick. I killed my commanding officer."

She stared at him in open-mouth shock. "You didn't! Surely you knew the penalty. Were you insane?"

"No, the captain was. He needed killing."

"Did you shoot him?"

"No, I beat him to death. He was a bastard. He gave me orders I refused to carry out. He struck me in the face with the back of his hand. Needless to say that I did not turn the other cheek."

"He hit you first. You had the right to defend yourself."

"He didn't die right then and there. Several men restrained me before I was finished with him. They knew it was a fair fight. I was court-martialed for insubordination. I was already looking at a rope, so when the bastard died from the injuries I inflicted on his puny body it didn't change anything. He was dead, I had killed him, and I was glad, it made the sentencing easier to live with, or to die for."

"What did he order you to do?"

"It happened in 1864. I was a lieutenant colonel in command of 128 men. My regiment was ordered to attack and slaughter over 400 peaceable Arapaho and Cheyenne Indians near Sand Creek, Colorado. I refused to give my men that order. I was mad enough to kill Captain Wheeler, and when he struck me it gave me a damned good reason. I was replaced by another officer who thought that only dead Indians were good Indians. Those orders were carried out but not by me.

"They would have hanged me but I managed to escape when a small party of Indians set fire to the jail. That's why I showed up in Courgat. It took me five months to work my way to Texas. The Western frontier seemed like the perfect place for a wanted man to get lost in. I shaved off my beard and mustache, changed my name, and presto, I went from a wanted man to a United States Marshal."

"Oh! Darrell! I'm so glad you got away."

"My name isn't Darrell Holliman, it's Chris Roman, and that's the man they're looking to hang."

"What happens if they find you?"

"He smiled. Then I'll hang. The way the soldiers are moving around I'm bound to be recognized sooner or later."

"Surely they won't hunt you forever."

"You don't know the army if you think that. They will see me hanged if it's twenty years from now. I recognized one of the soldiers on this train. He was under my command at Sand Creek. I had a problem with him then. He was a trouble maker, and his kind never change."

"Did he recognize you?"

"He might have. I caught him staring at me."

"Let's get off this train right now before he figures out who you are."

"It's already too late to worry. There are several hundred soldiers roaming around out there who might recognize me."

"What can we do?"

"If he tries to stop me before I see you safely to New Mexico and back home again, I'll be forced to kill him."

CHAPTER

44

It was after mid-night on the second day of their journey when the train pulled into Carlsbad, New Mexico. Darrell pointed out there horses to Flip Groom, owner of the livery stable, and paid him to unload their saddles and stable their horses for the night. Flip was proud to be of service to a United States Marshal, and happy to give him directions to the McCloud Ranch. According to Flip, the station was about five miles south of the first fence that marked the north boundary of the McCloud ranch. From that point he wasn't sure how far they would travel before reaching McCloud's ranch house. At any rate, it was too late to travel on horseback, and it was misting rain. "Locating his range land from the other direction," Flip said, "can be a mite confusing. McCloud's grass land splits at the New Mexico and Texas border and extends into the Llano Estacado Plain. Some people think he's trying to buy up the world. He's a powerful man, but he's getting on in years. I been told that he can't sit a horse no more. Last time I seen him in town he was riding in a buggy driven by a tough looking woman. I think she might be his nurse."

"Thanks, Flip. We'll ride out in the morning right after breakfast."

"Are you here on official business?"

"Not that I'm aware of."

"You're needed here, that's a fact. We got a mighty nervous sheriff 'cause the last two got shot."

"Do you have a judge in this town?"

"We depend on the circuit judge when there's a case to try. Without an arrest, there's no call for him to pay us a visit."

"What about the army? Are they any help?"

"Yeah, they help make matters worse. They shoot Indians on sight. They been driving them all the way to the Guadalupe Mountains. No matter where they move to, the settlers move in and take their hunting grounds. If the Indians take a stand, the army wipes 'um out."

"That's happening all over the country. It's the white men who keep breaking the treaties."

"You got that right." Flip said. "Whether you stay or go, Marshal, it's been a pure pleasure to meet you."

Darrell nodded, took Dawn's arm, and walked her toward the hotel. They were both hungry, and the only place serving food that time of night was the saloon.

"I'll get you settled in a hotel room, then go over to the saloon and see what I can find in the way of food. They probably have meat and bread."

"I'm going with you."

"That's no place for you. The only women in there are whores. The soldiers will make that their first stop. I don't want you subjected to their filthy mouths."

"I don't want to be by myself in a hotel room."

"It will only be for a few minutes. You can lock the door."

"If I can't go with you, I won't eat." She looked up at him with a pouty expression.

"You drive a hard bargain. What about sleeping arrangements?" She knew what he was asking and a shiver traveled up her spine.

"I want to sleep in your arms."

"For the rest of my life, if it pleases you?"

"You always please me."

Loud talk and laughter came from the direction of the saloon, the tiny tinkle of a piano in the background, and two men arguing over a card game. "Just another boom town," Darrell said. "People come here to get rich, and most of them will go back where they came from broke. Very few stick it out."

Every eye was cast in their direction when they stepped through the bat wings. The piano music seemed to grow louder as the chatter of voices ebbed. The two men who had been arguing got up and pushed out through the swinging doors. Darrell looked after them and laughed. "They're badge shy. One of them was cheating."

"How do you know that?"

"Experience."

They moved toward the table the two men had vacated. "That was thoughtful of them." He pulled a chair out for Dawn and took the one beside her.

A painted woman in a low cut red dress strolled toward their table. She studied Dawn with a quizzical eye as she approached, then settled her eyes on Darrell with riotous interest. He returned her gaze indifferently. "This is an unexpected pleasure, Marshal. If you're here to clean up this rotten town, better late than never."

"We're just passing through."

"Where are you headed?"

"The McCloud ranch."

"Henry McCloud don't need no help keeping his men in line. I hear he just ups and shoots 'um."

"I don't believe you," Dawn shot back.

The whore met her outraged eyes nonchalantly. "I wouldn't know, little Miss, it's just a rumor. Maybe you ought to arrest the old goat."

Dawn started to her feet in anger and Darrell took hold of her arm and sat her back down. "Let it go."

"I meant no offense," the whore said. "I didn't realize you were a friend of his. I didn't know he had any friends. What can I do for you?"

"What have you got cooking in the kitchen?"

"How hungry are you?"

"We're past the peanut and popcorn stage."

"We got beef steak, potatoes, and black-eyed peas. Take a while to fry the steak."

"Will we be able to chew it?"

"Yeah, if you got good teeth. And from the looks of you, I'd say everything about you is good." Dawn gasped at her remark, and the woman gave her a foxy smile. "We don't get many men in here that I enjoy looking at, and none wearing a marshal's badge. The sheriffs don't last long. They either quit or get shot. The one we got now is hiding someplace. We have a shoot-out at least once a week. The miners get drunk, throw their money around, and end up getting robbed or killed for their poke." Darrell looked at her with a bored expression and she flushed and grinned. "I can see I'm straying from the subject of growling bellies. What about them steaks?"

He looked at Dawn and she shook her head. "Sounds good to us, and bring a pot of coffee."

"I'll see to it. By the way Marshal, you got a name?"

"Holliman."

She nodded her head toward Dawn. "That your wife?"

He ignored her question. "Would it be too much trouble for you to wash this table?"

She cocked her head and looked at him obliquely. "We don't get many gentlemen in here either. I'll take care of it." She walked to the bar and picked up a rag, returned and mopped the table. Minutes later she brought them a pot of fresh brewed coffee and two cups. "Steak's cooking. Where you from Marshal Holliman?"

"Texas."

"I thought so. You got a lot of curious men eyeing that badge on your shirt. I heard 'um talking, and they're wondering if you can back it up."

"It's my job to back it up."

"You may be asked to prove it."

Darrell glanced about the room. There were several soldiers lined up at the bar. The soldier he had recognized on the train was among them. Darrell felt a flick of nerves in his stomach when he saw the way he was looking at him. He knew there were bells ringing in his head. He was openly staring at him now, scratching his jaw thoughtfully, trying to place him.

All through their meal, a cowboy sitting at a card table across the room watched every forkful they put in their mouths. He kept up a steady flow of conversation with the other three men at the table. Darrell couldn't hear what he was saying, but he could guess it was foul by the responsive grins he generated from his buddies.

Cretin Fringe stayed drunk more often than sober. He rode for Henry McCloud and was about as useless as the rest of his hands. He wanted the marshal's woman and was bragging about how he intended to kill the marshal and take her. The thought excited him, and he rubbed his crotch beneath the table. He was conscious of every male eye in the room staring in the woman's direction. "They all want a sample of that snatch," he said, and the other three men nodded in agreement. "I got a plan. I know how old Henry likes women, but he's run a bit short on 'um. What he's got working for him look like they crawled out from under the shit-house. If I take that woman home for him to play with, he'll make me top hand. And I aim to cut a bargain with him. I'll turn her over to him if he agree to let me have all of that stuff I want."

"You're dreaming, Cretin," Lee said. "I don't think he's interested in that anymore. He's a sick man, the exertion would likely stop his feeble heart."

"That little peach could just set in front of him with her legs spread and get the old fart off. He ain't too damned old to look and feel."

"That lawman will kill your ass. He's cold sober, Cretin, and I seen a look in his eyes that made my flesh crawl."

"You're a bunch of girls. I can take him, and I aim to be real considerate, and let him finish his last meal 'for I blast him."

Their meal finished, Darrell stood, flipped a coin on the table, and pulled the chair out for Dawn. They had taken about three steps when Cretin yelled at them.

"Have a drink with us, Marshal, and introduce us to that good-looking woman you got with you. Is she your prisoner? What did she do? Me and the boys will be happy to pay her fine. We want to take her to the hotel with us. We got pure gold. How much will it cost?"

Darrell swung around to face the four men. His blood was just about to the boiling point. "You're drunk, and I hate killing a drunk. It always makes me feel like a bully. But sometimes that seems to be the only remedy that cures a mouth like yours. Now, you can shut it, or I'll shut it for you, free of charge."

"You talk big, Buster!"

"You must have me confused with somebody else. The name's Holliman."

"That badge don't impress me none. It's cowards that hide behind badges. You ain't got the guts to stand up to me."

"I invariably have the misfortune of being underestimated." He spoke to Dawn without taking his eyes off the four men "Step away from me. Give me room to work."

"Oh, I should have listened to you. I'm sorry. I shouldn't have come in here. I'm going to get you killed."

"I don't have time to get killed. I haven't fulfilled my promise to you yet. I intend to take you to your grandfather, and then get you back home, even if I have to shoot my way out of this town to do it." He handed Dawn his rifle and saddle bags, set her valise on the floor at her feet, and took a defensive stance.

Somebody yelled, "Get the sheriff."

"He rode out of town," somebody yelled back.

"You have a choice, cowboy," Darrell said, "you can walk over to the jail with me and step into a cell to sober up, or you can sober up where you stand."

Cretin came to his feet, weaving slightly. "I draw faster drunk than sober."

"I can see that you're tired of living, and I'll be happy to shoot you, if that's your choice. I'm not here on official business, but I can squeeze in a little side work if you push me."

"All I want is the woman. I ride for Henry McCloud and I aim to take her to him. He likes pretty women. He'll reward me for a woman like her."

"I had no idea you rode for McCloud. I hate like hell to make him short handed."

"Do you know him?"

"Never met the man."

"Then why all the concern?"

"This lady I'm escorting happens to be his granddaughter."

The room suddenly became as quiet as a tomb. "You're lying," Cretin croaked. "He ain't got no kin."

"That's your opinion, and I won't waste my breath trying to convince you otherwise."

"Draw!" Cretin barked.

"Guns or cards?" Holliman said, grinning.

455

"Guns of course." And he reached.

Darrell's slug ripped through his right hand as it hovered just above his pistol grips. Cretin let out a blood curdling scream, looked with shock at the bleeding thing that was his hand and slung it up and down, spraying the three men at the table with a shower of blood.

Howling, cursing, threatening, jumping up and down, holding his right hand with his left, he forced his three companions to restrain him, maneuver him out the door, and struggle him toward the doctor's office.

"Let's get out of here." Darrell said, "before I wind up working all night. I can see why their sheriff is hiding."

Dawn was trembling inside, angry at herself for being so stubborn and thoughtless. She could have gotten Darrell killed because she wanted to have her way. "I was so scared," she sobbed.

"It's all right. You're safe now. Tomorrow is your big day. You will meet your grandfather and he will answer all your questions."

"I'm ashamed for making so much trouble."

"You didn't make the trouble. The trouble came from the gray zone. The Devil snapped his whip and that idiot cowboy leaped in the wrong direction. I could have killed him, probably should have, but not in front of you. You might get the wrong impression of me. I'm no killer."

"I know that. You're kind and thoughtful—and I'm acting like a child. Debbie accused me of being a spoiled brat."

"Forget about what Debbie said. You're tired. You'll feel better after a good night's sleep."

Back at the saloon, the group of soldiers were discussing Marshal Holliman's skill at handling a gun. "He's accurate as hell to be so damned fast," one said. "Yeah," another commented. "He's a cake of ice, just like a sniper." Lynch Young, the soldier Darrell had recognized on the train, knew of only one man who could draw and shoot like that, but he didn't comment. If he could take him into custody it would put bars on his shoulders, and he didn't want the others horning in on his discovery. He had him placed. He was a gentleman, well educated, cool and confident, yet he had run his head in a noose to save some dirty Indians, and all for nothing. They had been slaughtered anyway. He considered Chris Roman a stupid man. It didn't make sense that a United States Marshal would be traveling with Henry McCloud's granddaughter. He didn't intend to take him into custody in New Mexico. Henry McCloud was a powerful man in New Mexico, and he might intercede on behalf of his granddaughter. He had heard him tell the whore that he was from Texas, so he would be returning to Texas. He would take him there when he least expected it. He had some leave coming. He would take it when it benefited him most. There was no doubt in his mind but that Roman was involved with the woman. He hadn't forgotten how he affected women. He was smooth, he'd give him that. All he had to do was relax and bide his time. He would know where to find him in Texas as soon as he bought his ticket home.

The desk clerk was awake, having been aroused by the gunshot.

"What's going on over there?" he asked excitedly. "Who got shot?"

"It's nothing for you to worry about," Darrell said in a tone that seemed to calm him. "We need a couple of rooms, two tubs of bath water, towels and soap. Put it on my bill."

"Right away, sir." He turned the registry around, dipped the pen in the ink-well and handed it to Darrell. He noticed his badge and was taken aback for a moment. "Welcome to Carlsbad, Marshal. It's about time they sent some law and order here."

Darrell didn't bother to explain his reasons for being there. He signed both their names and held out his hand for the keys.

"Will you be staying long, Marshal Holliman?" the clerk asked, reading his signature.

"One night."

The clerks face fell into confusion as he watched them mount the stairs with Holliman supporting the woman with every step she took. He wondered who she was, noting that she was indeed a beautiful creature.

Darrell unlocked the door to one of the rooms and helped Dawn inside. "I'll get you settled before I go to my room."

"Why did you get two rooms? I don't want you to leave me."

"I'm not about to leave you. I'll be right next door. You need to have some time to yourself to bathe and get ready for bed. I'll come back as soon as I take a bath and shave. I think you might like me better, if I'm clean."

"Will you sleep with me?"

"Wild horses couldn't drag me away." He knew his presence was all the protection she had. The sheriff was hiding and the town was wide open, to the point of killing a U.S. Marshal to take his woman. And the soldiers were just an added threat. They were drunk and without supervision. New Mexico had a few problems, and the soldiers had undoubtedly been sent there to establish law and order. He wondered exactly what their orders were. Since Henry McCloud was referred to as a powerful man, perhaps he could answer that question.

After they had their baths and the water was carried away, he went back to Dawn's room. She was all rosy and sweet smelling, wearing a white nightgown that reached the floor.

He closed the door behind him and turned the key. "You're beautiful. Every time I look at you I wonder if I'm dreaming."

She threw her arms around him and held him fiercely. "Are you going to sleep with me?"

"Yes, if you're sure that's what you want. You know I'll want to make love to you. I can't lie down next to you and not want you that way. I'm in love with you, Dawn, helplessly, and as you've made clear, hopelessly."

I want you too. I want to feel you against me, your hands on me, kissing me, making everything right and beautiful."

"What are you thinking about when I'm making love to you?"

"What do you mean?"

"Who do you think I am?"

"I know who your are."

"Do you think about your secret lover? Do you pretend I'm him?" She stared at him in shock. "Is that what you think? How can

you think that?"

"It easy, believe me. You're in the gray area, Dawn. You love him, but you like me, and yet you make love to me like no other woman ever has. You say you need me, that I make you feel safe, you like the way I make you feel, you want me now, all the way, yet you have promised to break my heart. What I want to know is this: what would it take? on my part? to make you love me? I want you to answer that question for me, if you can."

"I—I don't know. You make me happy, I like the way you look and feel, the way you talk and act. Please, don't ask me to explain."

"I just don't measure up. Something is missing. Where do I fail you. Why can't you love me?"

"I just can't, because I love someone else."

"Is it because you gave birth to his son?"

"I loved him before that, before I knew I was carrying his baby. I don't want to talk about it anymore. Are you going to nag me?"

"No, I'm just trying to understand. I'm sorry. I won't mention it again."

"Promise?"

"I promise, not another word." He hung his gun belt on the bed post. "Do you want the lamp on or off?"

"On, I want to look at you."

He unbuttoned her gown and slipped it down over her hips, and she stood before him naked and unashamed. He wondered how any woman could be that perfect. His hands were trembling as he traced every inch of her body.

She let him do as he pleased, loving the exciting way he touched her, breathing in quick fluttery gasps. She reached for the buttons on his jeans and drew them down, her dark eyes inspecting him, touching him. "Make love to me." She lay down and pulled the covers over her. He lay down with her under the quilt, and took her into his arms. She plastered herself against him, and he felt every curve of her body, and he shook with emotion, wondering how he could be lucky enough to hold heaven in his arms. She did not hold back, she was a willing partner, fired with passion, and he knew how to please her, knew how she liked to be kissed, where she liked to be kissed. He didn't want to think past this magic moment, but painful thoughts tumbled through his head like stones. One day he would lose her, she would leave him and go to her lover. She would break his heart, that was sure, and when it happened he didn't give a damned if they did hang him. If he lost her, and apparently she had made up her mind to that, he had no reason to go on living.

She said in a breathless voice while he caressed her and kissed her and made her tremble with pleasure, "You do a very ungentlemanly thing so very gentlemanly." When his mouth was on her breast she moaned, her fingers in his hair. She clutched his buttocks, guiding him where she wanted him and clamped down on him with a little cry of elation. She kissed him with her mouth open, drinking him in, meeting his every thrust, and all thought was dissolved as he rode her beautiful, smooth thighs into paradise. "Oh!" she cried. "Oh! You make me feel so—Oh!" And then she said three little words that shot through him like a white hot sword, words that gave him hope, even though they were words she had never meant to utter, but in her moment of ecstasy, cried out, "I love you!"

He felt his tears surfacing, and made no attempt to stop them. She had finally slipped from the gray area, but he would never tell her. It was his secret. In the aftermath he held her against his pounding heart, kissed her soft, full lips, and she curled against him the way she had on his bunk at the jail. Her head was on his shoulder, one leg thrown over him, her arm across his chest. He didn't want to sleep, he wanted to savor her warmth and think about what she had said. How could she not love him if he pleased her in every way? And she had confessed that he did. He was tired of fighting a ghost. The other man had him at a disadvantage, yet he was the man holding Dawn in his arms. He realized now, and it was a sudden awakening, he had the edge.

Lynch Young was having second thoughts about waiting to take Chris Roman after he reached Texas. He had him placed and he would get the credit as long as no one else became aware of his identity. He feared Roman and the way he handled a gun. He was wearing a badge and that added up to another problem. Once Roman left New Mexico he might lose the opportunity to turn him over to Burman. If McCloud should find out he was responsible for Roman's arrest his life wouldn't be worth a plug nickel. McCloud would have him killed, and he couldn't run far enough to escape his reach. He was forced to have him arrested in New Mexico or risk losing his advantage. He walked over to the telegraph office and sent a wire to Burman. He intended to ask for Burman's protection in exchange for Lieutenant Colonel Chris Roman.

CHAPTER

It was barely daylight when they rode out of town down the rough north road, cut with wagon wheels and hoof prints. It had rained just enough during the night to settle the dust, leaving the air fresh and slightly chilly. The landscape was barren for miles. Fog hovered in the distant valley, moisture the sun would soon burn away. About five miles from town they came to a fork in the road. A well worn trail led to the right. A sign shaped like an arrow was nailed to a cedar post, bearing the name McCloud Ranch in bold black letters. A skull and cross-bones was scrawled beneath the name.

Darrell turned to look at Dawn. "How's that for a friendly welcome?"

"What's it mean?"

"As a rule, it means death or poison."

"Will he shoot us?"

"I hope to hell he's not serious."

"What will we do?"

"Find out if he's bluffing."

They rode on for another mile. The trail rose and fell over the ribs of uneven ground as the horses picked their way through a rocky uphill grade. At the top they saw the main entrance to the ranch. "That's the first fence," Darrell said, "and he didn't scrimp on barbed wire."

The arched entrance embraced a sign with the MC brand, and was guarded by a high iron gate secured with a heavy chain and lock. "Looks like this is as far as we ride unless our horses can clear a fence strung six strands high."

"What now?"

"I can try firing three shots in the air. He could have at least hung a bell, but I guess that would depend on how many miles it is to his house. I don't expect you to walk, and I damned sure can't leave you here by yourself while I climb the fence in search of civilization."

"I can walk."

"This is ridiculous! If that guy I shot in the saloon is an example of his hands, he sure as hell wouldn't trust them with the keys to his kingdom. So how do they get in and out?"

"Maybe they walk."

"Five miles? They either have keys or there's a gate keeper around here someplace. I'm for firing the three shots. Go stand over there behind that tree and I'll give it a try."

"Why do I have to stand behind a tree?"

"Darling, they may shoot back."

She looked at him and smiled. "That's the first time you ever called me, darling."

"This isn't a good time for me to mention this, and I had decided to keep it a secret, but you told me something last night that set my heart on fire. You weren't aware of it, but I want to think that you meant it. I'm afraid you will deny saying it because it was your subconscious speaking."

"If it's a secret, why are you telling me now?"

"Because I might get shot, I guess."

"Don't tease me, Darrell."

"I would sooner die that tease you about this."

"What did I tell you? Not the name—"

"You said you love me."

She looked at him in shock, her eyes starting to tear. "Oh, I'm sorry. I keep on misleading you."

"Slip of the tongue?"

Before she could answer they heard the sound of an approaching horse. A cowboy rode up to the gate, and from his expression looked ready to shoot them when he noticed the badge pinned to Darrell's shirt. "What's your business, Marshal?"

"We're here to see Henry McCloud."

"What about?"

"We'll tell McCloud that. I hope you have the key to this gate."

"If you're here to make an arrest, you might as well turn tail and leave. McCloud don't tolerate lawmen on his land. He takes care of his own problems. He's the judge and hangmen when punishment is called for."

"That's very commendable. I'm not here in that capacity. I'm escorting his granddaughter."

The rider looked shocked and stared at Dawn in open admiration. "You know, it's a funny thing, when a man is ailing, might die any day, how the vultures come to pick the bones, claiming to be his next of kin. I happen to know that McCloud ain't got a granddaughter. He has one son that deserted him years ago, and he ain't heard from him since. She's a fine looking woman. If she's looking for a home, she don't need to look no further. But she might as well drop the granddaughter scheme. It won't cut no ice with Henry McCloud."

"You're overstepping your authority, cowboy. If he hasn't heard from his son since he walked out on him, how can you be sure she's not his granddaughter?"

"I see you got it all worked out. That makes sense all right, but you can't fool McCloud. He'll figure this out before you can sit your ass down in a chair."

"I suggest you leave the figuring to McCloud, since it's none of your business. Do you have the key to this gate?"

"Yeah, but that don't mean I'll use it."

"You'll use it or I'll find another way in, and I promise you, gate keeper, you won't like it."

"Is that a threat?"

"Yeah, you want to call me."

"Who the hell are you?"

"Marshal Holliman."

The rider's expression changed suddenly. "Darrell Holliman?"

"I see you know me. Who might you be?"

463

"Pine Skimp. I'm McCloud's top hand, and you're the man who killed Lance Sage. He used to ride for the MC."

"I didn't know that."

He climbed down off his mount, took a key from his pocket, unlocked the gate and threw it open. "Come on through." As soon as they were clear he locked it again. "McCloud don't give way to uninvited people. I'll ride along with you. When you're ready to leave I'll let you back out."

They followed him up a gentle rise that looked down on a vivid green valley studded with giant pecan trees that grew along the Pecos River bottom. The three story house and yard covered two acres. It was solid brick with a wide wrap-around porch. The rolling lawn was neat, bordered with shrubs and flower beds. The brick drive made a circle in front of the house, with a rock garden in the center.

At first sight of the house, Dawn caught her breath in shock. She had expected Henry McCloud to have a grand home that would reflect his wealth, but what she was looking at was more splendor in every direction than her mind could immediately grasp.

Darrell was equally shocked. "Did you expect this?"

"I'm speechless. I had no idea. It's wonderful!"

Pine watched them with a smirk. If she was McCloud's granddaughter, like she claimed, how come she didn't know about his fine house? He figured she was lying.

After they dismounted, Pine said, "I'll take your horses to the corral. McCloud don't want horse droppings on his drive."

"How many riders does he have?" Darrell asked.

"Enough to do the job. He has about a hundred Indians working for him. They're cheap labor, and we don't have much trouble with 'um. Some of the squaws work in the house. He has a white nurse, ugly as mud, but she takes good care of him. Her names, Princess Lake, but her face don't match her name. I'll see you inside before I tend your mounts, just in case he orders you to leave. He does that sometimes. He gets real fed up with them missionaries that keep pestering him. He has no use for religion or preachers or church houses."

He led them through the great house to a room of windows that overlooked the river. There was a chill in the air and there were fires in every fireplace they passed on their journey.

He pointed to double doors that led off the glass walled room, referring to it as "McCloud's thrown room" because it was from there he ruled his kingdom with an iron hand.

"Wait here. I'll find out if he wants to see you." He tapped lightly before entering the room. "Excuse me, Mr. McCloud, you have two visitors."

"Who?" he barked.

"A young lady and a United States Marshal."

"Marshal? What's he want?"

"He came with the young lady. She's the one that wants to see you."

"Well find out what she wants. If she's one of them damned missionaries, send her away. I don't know any young women who would bother to visit me. What's she look like?" he said as an after thought.

"Very beautiful."

McCloud straightened his shoulders and pulled at his waist coat to straighten it. Pine waited for another order, as it would seem that McCloud hadn't made up his mind yet.

"Don't just stand there! Go get her!"

Pine turned and moved out the door in long strides.

Dawn looked up when Pine came back. She felt a knot forming in her stomach and reached for Darrell's hand.

"He'll see you. I hope this ain't a hoax. He'll be mad as hell if you're lying to him. He's a sick man and he don't like being disturbed."

"You're welcome to your opinions," Darrell said, "but if you call this woman a liar, I'll rearrange your mouth."

He held his hands up defensively. "No need to get riled."

"That's where you're wrong."

"I'm scared," she said. "What if he thinks I'm lying?"

"You can prove who you are. You've waited a long time to meet him. What you're feeling is excitement, not fear."

"I'm thankful I have you. You give me courage."

"You don't need me, but I feel flattered."

Pine opened the door and Dawn moved cautiously across the threshold, her fingers laced through Darrell's, dragging him with her.

He felt her trembling. "I'm right here if you need me, but I should stay in the background." He released her hand and stepped back. "You're doing just fine."

McCloud was standing with his back to the door looking out the tall window made of many diamond shaped panes of glass. He felt a little surge of nerves as he turned slowly to meet his visitors.

His heart leaped inside his chest and he gasped, catching his breath sharply. He staggered a few steps and caught hold of the bedpost to steady himself. "My God!" he cried. "You look exactly like Elizabeth. I had no idea. God damn Richard! He should have told me. Why didn't he write? Why didn't Elizabeth write? How could he hate me so much? Why?" he sobbed.

He swayed and clutched at his chest. Dawn ran to him crying, "Grandfather, I'm so sorry." He held out his hands and she flew into his arms. "Please, let me help you to lie down. It's all so strange and shocking. Are you all right?"

"Oh! I have a granddaughter. Another Elizabeth. So very beautiful—the same hair and eyes, the smooth brown skin. And they kept it from me."

She moved with him, supporting him, and he sat down heavily on the bed. "Lie down," she urged, "I'll put pillows behind you."

"Just let me look at you. You are even more beautiful than your mother. Why did Richard wait so long to come to me? Where is Elizabeth? I want to see her."

"I came by myself, Grandfather. Marshal Holliman came with me to keep me safe. Father didn't want me to ever meet you. I had to slip away."

"Elizabeth? Did she object too?"

Dawn took his trembling hand. "My mother died the day I was born. I never knew her, and Father refused to even talk about her. I had no idea that I looked like her. He never told me."

She felt him stiffen, his body trembling. "Elizabeth died? All these years I have longed to see her again, and all the time she was dead and buried." He shook with sobs. "Richard took her from me in every way possible. He even took her life."

"No, Grandfather, it wasn't his fault."

"He took her away to that terrible place so many miles away. It's a wonder she lived long enough to give birth. She would still be alive if he had left her here with me."

Darrell, who had been standing near the door taking it all in, suddenly snapped to attention. The conversation was getting down to brass tacks now. The mystery was about to unravel for both of them. Neither of them were conscious of him even being in the room. McCloud had yet to look in his direction. After his first glimpse of Dawn, the old man had lost it. Darrell moved to a chair near the bed, sat down, crossed his legs, and made himself comfortable. All he needed do was wait for Dawn to ask the right questions.

"My mother was with you? I don't understand."

"Of course you don't. Richard made sure of that. I thought he was stronger than me, that he loved Elizabeth enough to take the bitter with the sweet. I misjudged him. He was a coward. Running away in the middle of the night, leaving me with no more than a farewell note."

"Why did he run away? Tell me about my mother."

"He took her with him. Stole her away from me."

"But—they were married—"

"Oh, yes, and I'm wondering how he managed that."

"Didn't she want to go?"

"Yes, but she made a fatal mistake. He caused her death.

Darrell sat forward a bit, his mind on fire, he was beginning to get the picture, and he didn't like it.

"I found Elizabeth. She was the most beautiful little thing I had ever seen in my life. She was so very young. I moved her into my house. She worked as one of my servants. She was perfect, without one flaw, and I loved her."

"Where did you find her? Was she lost? Did the Indians take her?"

He waved her questions away, taking a minute to gather his thoughts. "The army had been called in to clean up the trouble making Indians who ignored the peace treaty. The government put them on a reservation, but they were not satisfied with the boundaries and continued to hunt on my land. They moved their village away for a while, and then moved it back onto their old hunting grounds. When they were ordered to move back to their reservation they became hostile. The army was called in to settle the dispute. Many Indians were killed; some of the braves were captured and put to work building the railroad. The squaws were used for other dirty jobs. All but one."

Darrell uncrossed his legs and sat forward in his chair. He saw Dawn's expression change. It was getting through to her. She was going to need him after all.

"My mother," she cried. "My mother was an Indian!"

McCloud looked shocked. "He didn't even have the guts to tell you that. He didn't deserve Elizabeth. She was too good for him. She was too good for any man. I would have made her a queen. I worshiped her."

"Oh, I knew he was hiding something. How could he have done this to me? All my life he has lied to me. Why? I hate him! Hate him! Hate him!" She was screaming.

Darrell was on his feet now, and in the next instant she was in his arms, clutching him, sobbing against his chest.

"It's all right. You know the truth now. You just escaped the gray zone."

And in her mind she was set free. She knew the ultimate truth at last. Tremors surged through her body, the force of her revelation. She had come face to face with the building blocks of her heritage. Henry's words flared in her mind. It was such an obvious answer. It explained her restlessness, her love of the land, the seclusion, the silence of a still night. Her blood ran as wild as a Comanche warrior's. She was like Light Eyes. They belonged together. She was now able to piece together the puzzle of her life, to understand that Mac was trying to protect her from herself, to make her totally and wholly white, when she wanted only to be what she was, a half-breed like the Indian she loved. Perhaps Darrell would stop loving her now. He was a white man, and she was a half-breed. She would not break his heart now, because he would want no part of her. She would lose him, and the thought chilled her to the bone. She held him a little tighter.

McCloud watched them, reading between the lines. She was the marshal's woman, and he was taking care of her. "What's your name, Marshal? I don't believe we've met."

"Darrell Holliman."

"Oh, yes, you're the man with the fast gun. You outdrew Buck Femmer and Lance Sage."

"How do you happen to know that?"

"I make it a point to know things like that."

"My life seems to be an open book."

"And that seems to bother you. Are you worried about it?"

"I have cause to be."

"You have a past?"

"We all do."

"Yes indeed. I've crossed some bridges I'm not too proud of. You brought my granddaughter to me safely. I thank you for that." He held out his hand to Dawn and she took it. "Come over here and sit by me. What's your name?"

"Dawn."

"I would imagine that Elizabeth had the name all picked out before you were born. It's an Indian name, and it suits you. You're as beautiful as the dawn of time, the beginning of the world. The first perfect woman."

"I'm far from perfect, Grandfather. I tell lies, have temper fits, commit immoral sins, and break hearts. I'm not a very nice person."

McCloud was smiling. "You're a chip off the old block, and very human. I love you, Dawn McCloud."

"Even with all my faults."

"Especially with all your faults. You're strong, you admit your faults, and that, in my eyes, washes you clean."

"I love you too."

"The way I see it, the morals of the world are beyond redemption. Indians have no place in this world. Their rights have been stolen by people like me. Every time an Indian dies it puts an end to more suffering." He stood, took a moment to steady himself. "Marshal Holliman would you like a drink?"

"I would appreciate one. Thank you, sir."

He held out his hand. "I would like to shake the hand of a gentleman."

Darrell shook his hand and was surprised by the strength of his grasp. "If you knew me better, you might change your opinion."

"I doubt that." He moved a little unsteadily toward the liquor cabinet. "Indians rely on spirits for all their problems, and they haven't figured out yet that all that bone shaking, blowing smoke, and mumbling fails them completely. I believe in spirits myself, the kind that comes out of a liquor bottle. Many times it has solved my problems by letting me forget for short periods of time. I need that spirit in my blood at the moment, but not to solve a problem or forget my pain. I want to drink to the resurrection of Elizabeth, and know that her spirit is in the body of my granddaughter." He poured two drinks, handed one to Darrell and took the other for himself. He held his glass high. "I drink to my granddaughter, the light of my life."

"She's the light of my life also," Darrell said. "I love her." Dawn looked from one to the other, tears slipping down her cheeks.

McCloud cleared his throat and said grimly, "Richard was ashamed of the fact that he was married to an Indian squaw. What other reason could there be for him keeping Elizabeth's identity a secret? I confessed to him in my letter that I had wanted Elizabeth for myself. But she didn't love me, she loved Richard. They ran away to get married. I wanted her, but I would never have married her because I had no love for being called a 'squaw man'. I realize now that Richard was ashamed too. And I wonder how any man could feel shame for marrying the most beautiful woman on earth. I was a fool!"

"I bought her from an army General, whose name I will not divulge. I stopped the war of passion and dreams when I brought her here after she was captured. She was a child, but anyone with half sense and one good eye knew she would grow into perfection. Men were ready to kill for her, ready to wait for her to grow to womanhood, as I was willing to do. For years Richard paid no attention to her. He still considered her a child and a servant, but I did not. I was ready to make her mine completely and he stepped between us. Later he was sharing her bed. She became pregnant under my roof, by my son.

"Richard made his choice and he stuck by it, and now I must change all my plans to fit the situation. I pleaded to him in my letter to come home. I begged his forgiveness, and he ignored me. You, Dawn McCloud, are my only living relative."

"Not quite, Grandfather. You have a great grandson almost a year old. His name is Henry, after you."

McCloud was shocked again. "I'm surprised that Richard would allow that."

"He didn't mind. He doesn't hate you; he just doesn't like the things you do."

"What things?"

"I don't know. He has never talked to me about you."

"Does the boy have a last name?"

"I was married. The child's name is Henry Rowling."

"Where is the boy's father? I was thinking that perhaps Holliman might have—"

"No, I hadn't met Darrell yet, or it might have been a different story. Ned was killed on a cattle drive to Oklahoma. He drown in the Canadian River."

"So the boy has no father."

"Ned took the blame, but he was not responsible."

"Will you tell me who was responsible? Since he's my great grandson, I have a right to know."

"No one knows except for the doctor who delivered him, and Debbie, my stepmother."

"Richard doesn't know."

"No, as a matter of fact, Ned took a beating from Father and he wasn't guilty."

"Why did he take the blame?"

"He wanted me to marry him."

"So he decided to settle for your body minus your heart."

"I never loved him—I think I might have hated him because of his weakness."

"Why do you keep the man's name secret?"

"For his safety."

"I don't understand that. Is he married?"

"Yes, to me." The words were out and she couldn't call them back. She glanced at Darrell; saw him pale, his eyes fill with shock and pain. He had guessed the truth.

Suddenly his eyes were opened; the truth came rushing at him like a tidal wave. How could he have been so blind? It was the Indian. She had never cared for Ned, Captain Oliver, nor him. She was in love with Light Eyes, the half-breed, the man he had heard so many stories about. Why had she left Courgat to visit her grandfather while he lay wounded at Keel's office? He was within her reach. Why did she leave him? He felt like a prime fool. He should have paid him a visit while he was there and satisfied his curiosity. He wondered how they managed to get together. She claimed they were married. Of course it was Indian style, and didn't mean a thing in the white man's book. He tried to hide his feelings, to blink away the tears in his eyes, but his startled expression spoke the truth. He was shocked into silence.

McCloud understood immediately, but decided not to press her for answers while under Holliman's watchful eyes. It saw plain enough, by

Holliman's reaction, that he had not known the truth until this moment. He would let it drop for now. Later, she would tell him. She had admitted that she lied and broke hearts. He didn't need to ask who's heart she was breaking. He would not hear of her saddling herself with an Indian, nor would his grandson live in a tepee. As soon as he found out who the Indian was, he would have him eliminated and save her from a fate worse than death. There were a few things about Darrell Holliman he needed to know too. He was a gentleman, well educated, handsome and with a past. One day Dawn would inherit the McCloud kingdom, and she needed a strong, honest man by her side. Darrell Holliman seemed to measure up on the surface, but he had to be absolutely certain that he could be trusted. Things were becoming complicated.

He insisted that they spend a few days with him getting acquainted. He needed to watch Holliman operate. He understood that they would be sharing the same bed, which didn't bother him. He had two rooms made ready, although only one was needed. He invited them to explore the house and grounds, that they would talk again at dinner. "This is your home, Dawn," he said proudly. "I want you to enjoy it. Stay as long as you like."

"Darrell has a job waiting for him, and I have a son waiting for me. We can only stay a day or two, but I promise to come back to see you often."

"We can discuss this later. As you must realize, I'm not a well man. Meeting my granddaughter for the first time has been a great shock, but one I welcome. I must rest for a while. You and the Marshal might like to take a nap before dinner. You look tired."

"We were up late, and got up early. We are tired."

"Then you must rest."

"Can I do anything for you?"

"You two run along. I have a nurse living here. She takes care of all my needs."

Dawn kissed him on the cheek, hugged him, took Darrell's hand, and they left the room.

She knew Darrell would ask questions about Light Eyes, and she tried to brace herself for his reaction to her answers. She had warned him several times that she would one day break his heart, but that would not shield him from the pain. Her greatest fear was that Light Eyes' life was in danger once more.

CHAPTER 46

Henry was informed by one of his riders that Cretin had been wounded in a shoot-out in the saloon during the night, and that his hand was one hell of a mess. The cowboy telling the story had been one of Cretin's drinking companions that night, but was being careful not to incriminate himself. He had seen the kind of punishment McCloud could dish out.

"What's the fool done this time?" Henry said, with a generous amount of anger and disgust.

"He popped off to a marshal by the name of Holliman. Cretin was drunk, talking crazy. Seems he took a fancy to the marshal's woman and challenged him for her."

Henry's face turned beet red and he looked as if he might explode. "The woman you're talking about is my granddaughter. Holliman should have killed the sonofabitch!"

"He could of done that real easy. I never seen a man draw like that, nor shoot that straight. Cretin was just reaching when Holliman put a slug in his hand."

"Where is Cretin at the moment?"

"In the bunkhouse suffering. He's left handed now, that's for sure. He won't be of much use for a spell. What do you want us to do with him?"

"Shoot him," he said, with the absence of emotion.

"Yes, sir."

"Now get out of my sight. I would like to take a nap before dinner. Tell that damned squaw out there, if she lets another person in here to disturb me, I'll have her shot."

The cowboy shook his head vigorously, went out, and closed the door very softly.

Dinner was served in the large dining room that overlooked the river. The table was set with silver, porcelain china, crystal, and two silver candelabra, one at either end of the table. The table cloth was snow white with matching napkins. The setting was very elaborate. Two squaws served them in silence, watchful to keep their cups and glasses filled, and to offer more food before there was need to ask.

"The table is lovely," Dawn said, "and the food delicious."

"My compliments to the cook," Darrell added to her praise. "Nothing is too good for my granddaughter," Henry said, beaming with pride. "Now that you've had a chance to look around, what do you think about my ranch?"

"This is the most beautiful house I have ever seen Grandfather. I think it's wonderful. I love being so near the river, it's peaceful and refreshing."

Henry smiled with satisfaction. "And what do you think, Holliman?"

"I see the results of a lot of planning, sweat and time devoted to a dream that has become reality. And when it's all said and done, an equal amount of tears."

Henry was astonished by his appraisal, and puzzled by his conclusion. "I'm impressed, Marshal. I assure you, there are no tears shed over success. You have a theory, no less. May I inquire as to what it might be?"

Dawn was impressed too, and set a little on the edge of her seat, for she was seeing another side of Darrell. What she understood was not praise on his part, but perhaps demeaning.

"I assure you, sir, I have no theory. I merely lean toward reasoning and the end results of any action. It seems to me that at the termination of all hopes, dreams, work, sweat and prayers, that the end results are actually pointless, for what is the actual personal gain, other than satisfaction."

Henry was shocked anew. "In other words, it's your observation, or belief, that I have been wasting my time all these years. That I have accomplished nothing." His face was suddenly dark, his brows drawn together in a scowl.

"You have accomplished much."

"That's a very contradictory statement."

"To have and to hold are not one and the same."

"I have never been modest about the thundering success I have made of this ranch and of my life. I must admit, I haven't been admired for some of the ways I worked out the wrinkles. I had more gumption than to toil my life away with no prospect of power or money. I have both, and it took, as you say, a lot of planning, sweat and time. I don't pray. It's pointless. I have known men who prayed for everything they wanted, and got nothing in return. I have never asked God for a damned thing. I refused to crawl. A man walks tall, takes what he wants, and pays the price in blood, if necessary. My belief is this: a man of guts and gumption helpeth himself. Many men look up to me, Holliman."

"Yes, sir, I'm sure they do. I'm also certain that an equal amount look down on you. Your son is a good example of that."

"Have you ever thought about going into politics?"

"No honest man entertains that thought."

"I haven't made up my mind about you yet, Holliman. You keep me guessing. You're very intelligent, but you're wasting a good mind standing behind that badge. You are your own man, and I respect you for that. You run as deep as that river out there. Men agree with me verbally, although I'm sure they differ with me mentally. That's what power does. It controls. I find myself surrounded by yes people. I control a lot of men in high places. Wealth does that. For the love of money, there is no greater god."

"And you look down on the yes men," Darrell stated, meeting Henry's eyes unabashed. "You own acres of land, and that's where the control comes in. Wars are fought over land. The Indians have fought a losing battle to keep the land that has been their homes for thousands of years, and they will fight on in an attempt to hold on to the last scrap of their hunting grounds. I pity them."

"I think you would make an excellent missionary. You seem to tend toward moralizing. Perhaps that's why you chose to wear a badge. That's control too. I think most lawmen are a bit sanctimonious by nature. The good guys against the bad guys, craving to see them punished for their sins."

"I live by my own rules. I follow no one unless I agree. Indians are human beings. I love them for their courage, and I pity them because they are being robbed and slaughtered."

Dawn was listening with great interest to their exchange, which was beginning to sound more like a moral disagreement. Darrell's courage to stand up to her grandfather amazed her. Darrell sounded as though he might have some Indian blood in his background. She thought about her mother, Light Eyes, and herself. Darrell was plainly on her side. She had no idea where her grandfather stood.

"I don't own acres, I own miles of land in every direction. I have land in Texas. I did not stop at the border. I draw no lines or limits. Land is land, no matter what the state."

"I bought land cheap from the emigrants, paying one dollar an acre more than they paid for it. I paid three dollars an acre, and would have paid more, but they were satisfied. I own land in Kansas, Oklahoma and Arkansas. All I'm doing is paying the taxes and waiting for the right price before I sell.

"Settlers come here, find out it takes guts and sweat to make a living, and turn tail and run back home. Damned fools can't think past getting something for nothing, and end up with growling bellies. They want to eat but they don't want to sweat for it."

"No one ever really owns land, McCloud, they only use it. You have spent your life climbing to the top, and now you're enjoying the power that comes with wealth. You have used Indians and emigrants as stepping stones. You have your dream, and you spent your life achieving it. Now that you can enjoy your success, you're running out of time. And in the final analysis, come the tears. We all die, we all have dreams. The bigger the dream, the more time consuming. Someone else will enjoy your hard work, and the cycle starts all over again. So who does the land really belong to? Quite simply, no one."

"You paint a gloomy picture."

"Only because it is gloomy."

"What is it you want out of life, Holliman?"

"Human comforts, and I'm willing to work and sweat to achieve it. I have no need of wealth or power. I want the love of a good woman, a family and a clear conscious."

"If you have a clear conscious, then you have achieved the impossible."

"I'm not without my share of faults. I'm as far from perfect as a man can get, but my love for your granddaughter is pure, and for life, and I'm sorry she can't feel the same way about me. She likes me, and I have accepted her decision, but it does not alter my feeling for her in the least."

"I see." He looked at Dawn, studying her for a moment. "So you like him, and that's it. Then for his sake, why don't you cut him loose? He's an honest man, also a fool. And you, Dawn McCloud, are about to make a big mistake."

She looked down at her plate in embarrassment, feeling confused and a little frightened by her grandfather's assertion. He was finding fault with her, and her personal life was none of his business. She needed her father. She wanted to know what Henry had done that was so terrible that he had kept it a secret all these years. It was not just the fact that her mother had been an Indian. It had to be much more, for Henry could not take the blame for Mac marrying an Indian. So what had he done? She suddenly wanted to go home. It would seem that Darrell was at odds with Henry, and Henry was at odds with both of then. "How can you say that I'm about to make a mistake" You don't know what my plans are?"

"I know more than you can even imagine. You have to think with your head, not your heart."

She raised her head and looked at him with tears in her eyes. "If you will excuse me, I'm going upstairs to think." She stood and turned toward the door.

Darrell was on his feet. "If you will excuse me? I'll go upstairs with her."

"Sit down, Holliman, I want to talk to you."

"It's all right," Dawn said. "You stay and talk to him."

"I'll be up in a few minutes," he said.

Dawn nodded and hurried from the room. She ran up the stairs sobbing, anxiously seeking the silent sanctuary of her bedroom. Her tears came hot and furiously, and she didn't know why she was crying. She needed Darrell to hold her, to make her feel safe, but most of all she wanted to feel loved.

"She's all right," Henry said, "Give her time to think about what I said. I have a few questions to ask you that directly concerns Dawn, and your answers are important to me."

He sat back down. "None of this concerns me. I have no intentions of mixing in family matters. Dawn's a grown woman. She knows what she wants."

"That's true, of course, but she doesn't seem to know what's best for her. You must realize that she stands to inherit every grain of sand on this ranch and every dollar. I must make sure that she has the right man to guide her steps carefully. An honest, educated man of honor and principle. I think you also know what her plans are for the future. It's important that I know what she intends doing so I can intercede."

"I would change those plans if I could. The simple truth is, she is not in love with me. I have no choice but to accept her decision."

"None of this makes any sense to me. How can she be in love with an Indian? I have figured out that much. She does not identify him by name. Why is that?"

"I can think of a few reasons. She hasn't told me his name either."

"I suspect you know his identity by the look on your face when she said they were married. I will not allow her to ruin her life and that of baby Henry. I will not have my great grandson living in a tepee in a hostile environment, eating dogs and snakes. I'm ready to do whatever it takes to prevent that from happening."

So he's figured it out, Darrell thought. Not good. "You can't rearrange other peoples' lives, McCloud."

"I'll be the one to decide that. You may be satisfied to stand back and let her ruin her life, the child's and break your heart, but I refuse to settle for that."

"I can do no less."

"Then you're a fool. I can turn this around for you. I just found her, and I don't intend to lose her to some damned stinking Indian."

"There are worse things."

"I can't think of anything worse than two wasted lives. I can and will do something about it."

"I hadn't intended telling you this, but you leave me no choice. I'm a wanted man. When, or if, I'm caught, I'll be facing a rope."

Henry was taken aback. "That's hard to believe. You're not the criminal type. I'm not that far off in my judge of character. What have you been charged with?"

THE WARMTH OF INDIAN SUMMER

"Insubordination. I also killed my commanding officer."

"You refused to take his order to kill four hundred peaceable Indians. He struck you in anger and you beat him to death." Henry was actually smiling. "I understand he died later. It's a pleasure to meet you, Lieutenant Colonel Chris Roman."

"How—"

"I told you, I make it my business to know things like that. I knew you were no ordinary man. Did you know the Indians who burned the jail so you could escape?"

"I have no idea who they were. They knew what happened, that I refused to order my men to slaughter and burn their village. They decided to cancel the order to hang me."

"Why did you do it? You knew the consequences."

"I couldn't live with it. The Indians were peaceful. I want a clear conscience, to be able to look at myself in the mirror, sleep peacefully, and love Dawn without a black mark against my soul."

"Tomorrow I need some time to talk with her alone. She hangs on to you like the raft of life, but she's holding back. Evidently she's afraid you might try to stop her from throwing herself away on a damned Indian."

"Her feeling are quite normal under the circumstances. She's afraid for his life."

"You have her at the moment, and with the Indian out of the way, you can keep her."

"I don't want her like that. Ned thought that way."

"How do you know that?"

"He admitted it to Debbie McCloud while he was drunk, but he wasn't aware of it. He shot the Indian in the back and left him for dead, but the Indian recovered."

"He had the right idea, but went about it in haste. Now his loss turned out to be yours. I won't make his mistake. All I need to know is the Indian's name and where his village is located, and I will take care of the problem."

"I still feel the same way about killing peaceful Indians. I refuse to tell you anything."

"Even to protect the woman you claim to love."

"Exactly."

"You deserve to hang, Roman."

"That's what I expected you to say. If the Indian was out of the picture, my presence would be of no benefit to her if I'm caught and hanged. I don't have the right to marry her. My days may be shorter than yours."

"Your point is well taken. You will never be safe. For the rest of your life you'll be looking over your shoulder."

"I wouldn't put Dawn through that even if she agreed to marry me. I have already been recognized by a soldier on the train coming here. It's only a matter of time before he makes trouble for me."

"I agree with that. You have to kill him before he shoots his mouth off, or perhaps he already has."

Darrell was beginning to understand why Mac ran away in the middle of the night and took Elizabeth with him.

"I admire your honor and courage, Roman, but I still consider you a fool. If you refused to give an order that would cost the lives of Indians, then I feel certain that you would not kill a white man to keep your neck out of the noose you voluntarily stuck your head in. You have way too many morals, Chris. Survival is what it's all about. What's the soldier's name?"

"Lynch Young. If he points me out, I'm finished. No one will be able to help me then."

"And as long as that rope is hanging over your head, you don't have a life."

"I think Dawn realizes that."

"The Indian's days are even shorter. I will do whatever it takes to save Dawn from herself."

"Is it Dawn you want to save, or your land and money?"

"She will not do the things I've done to hold on to my fortune, but the right man will."

"What do you expect the 'right man' to do?"

"Are you asking for a confession?"

"You seem to be leaning in my direction as Dawn's keeper. I'm just curious as to what the limits might be for survival."

"There are no limits. Whatever it takes. Tell me something, Roman, would you turn down ten million dollars?"

"I'm not insane, McCloud."

"Thank you. That all I need to know."

Darrell rose to his feet, and this time he didn't intend to be stopped from going to Dawn. She needed him to comfort her. Henry had hurt her feelings. "Good-night, sir."

"Good-night, Lieutenant Roman."

"I don't answer to that name anymore, if you please."

"Your secret is safe with me. Now go about your business of comforting my granddaughter. I'm going to bed."1/

CHAPTER

47

Darrell tapped lightly on the door before stepping inside. The moment he crossed the threshold Dawn flew into his arms. He held her and kissed her.

"I missed you," she cried.

"Are you all right?"

"I am now. Grandfather had no right to talk to me that way. I thought he was kind and loving, but he's not. I feel sorry for him because he's sick, but he's mean."

"Don't let it bother you. Your personal life is your own business. He's an old man and used to having his way."

"What did he talk to you about?"

"You mostly, and what he expects."

"What does he expect?"

"It's time we talked about Light Eyes."

"You know!" she cried, turning away from him.

"Henry guessed that the man you're in love with is an Indian at the same time I realized it was Light Eyes. I should have figured it out long ago. You should have told me."

"Why, so you can hurt him?"

"I'm no threat. I would be a fool if I thought killing him would be any advantage to me. You made your decision, and I'm forced to live with it. I'm not like Ned."

"Why did you say that?"

"I think you always suspected that it was Ned who shot Light Eyes in the back."

"Oh! No! I don't want to believe that! Ned was timid and weak. He couldn't—"

"You're right. He wasn't man enough to face the Indian. He hid like a mouse and shot him in the back. He thought he had killed him."

"You don't know that! How could you? That happened before you came to Courgat."

"I'm surprised that Ned was able to conceal the truth from you. I think you suspected and that's the reason you hated him. He didn't marry you to protect your reputation. He proved himself a liar when he promised you he would accept your son as his own. He wanted you and that was the only way he could have you. He used your unfortunate condition to trap you. Taking a beating from Mac was a small price for him to pay in exchange for you. He was the worst kind of coward."

"I did hate him and deep down I never trusted him. He guessed the truth about Light Eyes and me."

"He didn't guess, he knew. He saw the Indian bring you home that night. He hid in the trees and waited for him. He told Debbie what he had done one night while he was drunk. He never remembered telling her."

"She knew! Why didn't she tell me?"

"That's the way she is. You had a son to consider and she didn't want to make anymore trouble for you."

"I'm glad he's dead. I would have killed him if I had known the truth. I hate him still! He was jealous of every man I looked at."

"Was he jealous of me?"

"Yes, and he had good reason to be."

"I guess I'm lucky he didn't shoot me in the back. Tomorrow Henry intends to talk to you alone. He wants to make sure that I don't influence you."

"About what?"

"He will attempt to pressure you for the Indian's name."

"What difference can it make to him?"

"He doesn't have any respect for Indians."

"I'm half Indian, so he can't care about me either!"

"It's not the same thing. You're Elizabeth's daughter, and he was in love with her. You heard what he said. He would have made her a queen. You're his queen now, and the way he thinks no man is good enough for you, especially an Indian. If you tell him about Light Eyes it could cost him his life. Henry thinks he'll be saving you from yourself."

"Oh! He wants to hurt him too."

"He plans to eliminate him. He has the idea that with the Indian out of the way you might turn to me. He doesn't seem to realize that I have nothing to offer you. It's just a matter of time before the army catches up to me."

"This is all my fault. If you hadn't been traveling with me to New Mexico that soldier wouldn't have seen you."

"Traveling with you was my idea, and you didn't know anything about my past, that I'm a wanted man. Being with you is the only pure joy I have ever known. At least I won't be going to the gallows without having loved a good woman."

"Please! Don't talk about dying. I can't stand it. I will always need you in my life."

"You will soon be with the man you want and love. He will fulfill all your needs and dreams; you won't have room for me in your life. You won't need me any longer. Forget about me and make a new life for you and your son. You could never depend on me, because one day, I won't be here. For your sake it's better that you never loved me. You can skip the grief."

"I don't want anything to happen to you. I want you safe no matter where you are. It's not fair! And I will grieve."

"I knew what I was letting myself in for when I disobeyed that order, and I'm not going to fret over it now. What's done is done. As for Light Eyes, never tell Henry who he is or where he can find him. He's a determined man, and he has the power to make things go his way. He can have Light Eyes killed, or his whole village wiped out if it's the only way to get at him."

"I don't understand what Grandfather hopes to gain."

"He will explain it all to you tomorrow."

Dawn held Darrell in her arms all night, her heart heavy with grief, thinking about what he was facing. She felt sorry for her grandfather, but she didn't understand him at all. Why would he want to eliminate the man she loved and the father of his grandson? He was old and sick, ready to die, so why all the concern?

All through breakfast she was nervous and withdrawn, conscious of Henry's eyes never leaving her face. Her hand trembled when she lifted her coffee cup to her lips.

Darrell excused himself from the table, leaving Dawn alone with her grandfather. She had dreaded this moment and wanted to get it behind her and go home. He had found fault with her, and the spark of reproach she had felt for him last night still burned bright.

Henry's eyes were steady on her face examining every exquisite line, thinking how remarkable it was that she could look so much like Elizabeth.

Dawn returned his gaze silently, waiting for him to speak. He smiled and leaned back in his chair. "You're very quiet. I'm afraid I offended you last night. I'm concerned about your future. You have so much to offer the right man. Not just yourself, and that's more than any man deserves, but as my granddaughter you stand to inherit my kingdom, and I don't cotton to having a stinking Indian living in this house, perched on my thrown, spending your money."

Dawn glared at him. "I didn't come begging Grandfather. I don't want your house and money. My father built me a house just as grand as this one. Your son is a very successful business man. He has land and cattle and money. He's rich!"

Henry was taken aback. He admired Dawn's quick spirit, the way she flew to Richard's defense. "I'm pleased to hear that. Maybe I had him figured a little wrong. The difference between Richard and me is that I started from scratch. Ralph gave Richard a hand up. He didn't have to dig for it; all he had to do was make it grow."

"All he got from Uncle Ralph was the trading post and his little cabin. He started trading with the Indians, and that's what made him rich."

"You said something about a step-mother. Is she an Indian?"

"No, she's my best friend. We grew up together."

Henry smiled. "I see he likes them young. He may not approve of me, but we certainly think alike in many ways."

"It's not what you think."

He smiled again. "Of course it is."

Dawn decided not to argue with him. It seemed to make him happy to find fault with his son. "I'm going back home today, Grandfather. I miss my baby."

"Before you go we have a few things to settle. First of all, I want to know the identity of my grandson's father, and how you happened to become involved with him in the first place."

"I can't tell you that. I'm sorry."

"Then am I to believe that you plan to sneak away with him in the middle of the night, just as Richard did when he took Elizabeth away from me?"

"If that's what I have to do to keep him safe, then the answer is yes."

"I refuse to have an Indian walk across my grave. As far as I'm concerned you're as white as I am, and for your sake let it be thought so. You will inherit my estate, that's the way I want it, but up until the day they shovel dirt in my face, I will guide you along the right course."

"What does that mean?"

"You'll know when the time comes. Stay here with me and keep me company. I don't want to die all alone and lonely. I know Holliman is facing a rope; he told me about his misfortune. I had no idea that Holliman was Chris Roman until he told me, although I knew he was no ordinary man. I was well aware of what Roman did, and I had wondered what sort of man he was. Now I know. He's a man of honor, but he's also a fool. I can keep him safe if he stays here, and he will stay, if you do. Forget about the Indian. You have no future with him. Your future is here with me as long as I live, and beyond that. Tell me you will stay."

"I can't. I have a life with my son and my father."

"You will lose that life if you go to that Indian. I'm giving you a chance to correct that mistake before you ruin your life and your son's."

"I only have one life, one chance for happiness, and that's with the Indian I love. I plan to leave immediately."

"What about my plans?"

"I'll be back."

"When?"

"As soon as I settle things at home. I have a lot to think about." She stood and walked around the table to stand next to Henry's chair. "I do love you, Grandfather. You have answered all the questions that Father refused to even talk about. I thank you for that. Now I know who I am." She kissed him on the cheek and walked from the room.

Darrell was waiting for her in the adjoining room. He stood when she entered and held out his hands to her. She grasped his fingers. "How did it go?"

"You were right. He wanted me to identify the Indian. I refused of course, but I'm afraid he might find out some other way. He's so determined. He's leaving this house and all his land to me. I don't want it. The thought scares me."

"Did you tell him that?"

"Yes, but he just seemed to ignore my feelings."

"He intends to have his way, that's certain."

"Do you think there is any chance that he might accept Light Eyes into the family?"

"About as much chance as a snowball lasting in Hell."

"He's old. He'll die soon and then I can do what I please.

Do you think Light Eyes would be happy living in this house?"

"Why wouldn't he? He's as much white as he is Indian. He can jump either way and so can you. Would you be happy living in a tepee? wearing skins? taking a bath in the river, eating wild game, and growing old before your time? And you wouldn't have all those pretty dresses either. One of you will have to change."

"I'm well aware of that and I'm ready to face it. Things are different now. If Grandfather leaves me his ranch, I can give Brave Horse and his people their own land. The Army won't have any reason to kill them and burn their village."

"Indians can't own land."

"Why not?"

"Because the government doesn't recognize them as human beings. They consider the land belongs to the white men. If the truth of your heritage becomes known, you won't be allowed to own land either."

"No! That's not fair."

"The government is prejudice. That's why Mac kept his secret about your mother being an Indian. He was trying to protect you. He wasn't ashamed of Elizabeth. He loved her, but you would have paid the penalty."

"Do you hate me now? I'm just one more Indian. If you had known, would you have asked me to marry you?"

"I would live with you in a tepee, under a tree, or in a cave. What you are and who you are makes no difference to me. I'm not prejudice. I think I proved that point when I put my head in a noose trying to stop the slaughter at Sand Creek. For your own sake, and for the Indian's sake, you have to keep your heritage a secret or you can't help Light Eyes and his people. Henry said that he offered Mac his ranch and land in his letter. But of course Mac's silence is the same as a rejection. If Mac could bring himself to patch things up between them, he would inherit the land and be in a position to give Brave Horse and his people a home. You'll always be in danger of being found out." He smiled ironically. "Seems we are in the same boat in that respect. The only difference being, I'll be hanged when I'm caught, and you'll only lose all your rights as a human being."

"I had rather be hanged."

"No you wouldn't. You'll have your lover. All I'll have is a pine box. When you go to Light Eyes it will serve as proof positive that you're an Indian. You will have him, but you will have lost everything else. And what about baby Henry? What will his future be?"

"He's Light Eyes' son. He should be with his father."

"He will be one hundred percent Indian if he's raised on a reservation, or wherever the Indians wind up. But he will never be free. He is at the moment, but you can change all that. If you love Light Eyes enough to become a Comanche squaw for the remainder of your life, if that's what you want, it's the price you must pay unless you can persuade the Indian to change his life. And that brings us back to the only sensible solution. Mac holds the keys to Henry's kingdom, but will he reach out to accept them. Mac is the only one who can make your dreams come true. But you must bare your soul to do that."

"Oh! I never thought about that. He will never forgive me! He beat Ned and he wasn't guilty."

"Ned deserved every lick he gave him."

"I lied to him over and over. He'll hate me!"

"You have to think with your mind instead of your heart. Nothing comes easy if it's worthwhile."

"He never wanted me to meet Grandfather. Can you imagine how angry he must be?"

"You did what you felt you must, and actually a lot of good has come of it. Perhaps you can understand now why Mac didn't tell you about your mother, why it has been a closely guarded secret."

"I want to go home."

"Anytime you're ready."

"What about that soldier who recognized you?"

"The fact that he hasn't made a move against me so far tells me something. He wants to take all the credit."

CHAPTER

48

Mac anguished over the knowledge that Dawn had defied his wishes and gone to New Mexico to visit Henry McCloud. He had only himself to blame, and couldn't expunge the guilt flaming inside him. He had resisted her curiosity and avoided her questions all her life, and he had faith in his convictions.

He knew in his heart that he had done the right thing when he confessed the truth to Martha Rowling. She had spitefully accused Dawn of a transgression when Dawn was innocent. He felt no danger of her divulging the truth. She was bound to protect her grandson and Ned's memory. He was comfortable with what he had done. He had felt responsible for Ned's death, and the truth about the baby being Ned's had helped to ease Martha's suffering. He feared now that what had eased Martha's suffering would be devastating for Dawn.

She was now facing the bitter truths that would change her life to one of despair. The truth of her Indian blood was now absolute, there were no contradictions. He was afraid she might consider his silence a betrayal and refuse to accept his explanation. He must make her understand that she would remain safe and secure only as long as she believed in her own mind and heart that she was white. Pretense would bring her no relief. Soon she would know every thing about her mother. Henry would put the last piece of the puzzle into its proper place.

Debbie watched Mac's suffering helplessly. His contentment had suddenly disappeared, taking with it his happy disposition that had become so much a part of him since they were married.

"You should have realized that this was bound to happen." she said. "Dawn is no longer a trusting child, but a grown woman who realized you were keeping secrets from her, and she wanted some answers."

"If I had known she was actually serious about visiting Henry, I would have found a way to stop her. She may never reach New Mexico. There is danger every way she turns. Hostile Indians roaming in all directions, outlaws, and soldiers who use women as brutally as an Indian on the war path. I may never see her again. She's facing a thousand dangers and I'm responsible. I'm leaving for New Mexico immediately. I can't sit here and do nothing. Worrying is useless. If something should happen to her, you can blame yourself for not telling me her plans. I thought I could trust you."

"You can! I could have told her the truth myself and saved her the trouble of going to New Mexico to get the answers from Henry."

"I'm surprised you didn't!"

"Don't you dare try to make me the scapegoat? You made me promise to keep your secret, and I kept that promise. Put the blame where it belongs, Richard. You should have told her the truth years ago. You were unfair. Elizabeth was her mother, but she never knew her, and you refused to tell her what her mother even looked like. Elizabeth gave her life in exchange for Dawn's. All I'm saying is that Dawn deserves to know."

"You betrayed me when you shared her secret and kept the truth from me. She's my daughter, and I have a right to know when she plans to endanger her life. I would have stopped her."

"Now you listen to me, Richard McCloud. It was you who caused her all the confusion. You side-stepped every question she asked about her mother and grandfather. Didn't you ever stop to consider that she would be, not only curious, but suspicious? Because you were vague and secretive, so was Dawn. She was afraid to come to you with her problems and feelings. She came to me because she couldn't go to you. She held everything inside, her confusion and her emotions. She learned to sneak because she was afraid of displeasing you. If you had been open with her, all these complications could have been avoided."

Her anger shocked him. He had never heard her raise her voice, and she was raising it at him. "Why are you talking to me in that tone?"

"Because you do not know any of what's going on here. Dawn has suffered because she has held it all in, afraid to ask you for help, so she turned to Ned because he was anxious to help her. But his help turned out to be a trap."

"What are you talking about?"

God help me, she thought. He has to be told, but I hate to be the one to tell him. He may throw me out of his house.

He was looking at her, waiting for her to answer him. Tears were forming in her eyes, her insides trembling. "Promise me one thing, Richard, before I say another word."

"What?"

"That you will not blow up, make threats, and lose control of your emotions. That you will stop and consider what I am about to say, and above all, make an effort to understand Dawn's side of the situation."

"Is that all?" he said in exasperation.

"Yes, for now. I hope I never regret this."

They had both been sitting down; suddenly Mac was on his feet. "For God's sake! What is it?"

"Sit back down, Richard. I won't talk to you if you stand over me." She waited for him to take his seat. Her eyes met his boldly, while her insides churned. "First, Ned Rowling was not little Henry's father."

The air left Mac's lungs in a rush, he became rigid, unable to move or speak for several seconds. He heard the amplified beating of his own heart. "You're lying!" he yelled, and he was on his feet again.

"I don't lie! And I will not be called a liar by you or anyone else. Rejecting the truth does not change the facts."

"If not Ned, then who?"

She crossed her arms, as if seeking shelter behind them, and turned her face away from him. He realized very quickly that she would say no more if he didn't get a hold on himself. He paced up and down, then sat back down. She turned to look at him.

"Well, what did you expect?" he said. "Do you realize what a shock this is?"

"I expect you to stay calm, like you promised. Getting emotional solves nothing."

"Holliman wasn't responsible. He hadn't arrived in town yet. She was seeing no one."

"No one that you knew of."

"Who?"

"Because she didn't know the truth about her mother, that she was a half-breed, she didn't have the courage to tell you the truth, that she was in love with the Indian, Light Eyes. They were married Indian style. He's the child's father."

"Oh! God! And Ned took the blame. Is there no chance that Ned could have been the father?"

"None what-so-ever. She was never with Ned until they were married. Don't you see? That was the only way Ned could have her. The man who was shot in the woods, who had managed to mount his horse and ride away, was Light Eyes. Ned had seen them when Light Eyes brought her back home. He hid in the dark and shot the Indian in the back. Dawn knew Light Eyes was the one who was shot, but she didn't realize it was Ned who shot him. Ned told me about it one night after he came home drunk. When Dawn found out she was pregnant with the Indian's child, and believed him to be dead, she told Ned about it. He asked her to marry him. She had a fear of shaming you, and she was afraid to tell you. Otherwise she would never have married Ned. She didn't love him and he knew it. He took advantage of her condition. She hated him for it. He had promised her that he would accept Henry as his own, while in his heart he despised the child because he was a constant reminder of the man Dawn really loved. She hated him for that too."

"I have made a terrible mistake. I told Martha Rowling about Elizabeth."

"How could you? You had no right. You should have told Dawn. Why did you tell her?"

"She was so grieved over Ned, and I told her that she hadn't lost her son completely, that she had a grandson by him. She laughed in my face. I had to tell her. She called Dawn a slut."

"Dawn is no slut!"

"But Martha was right about Ned not being responsible. It eased her grief, but it's a lie."

"She need never know."

"I beat Ned because I thought he took advantage of Dawn, and he was innocent."

"Innocent! He meant to kill the Indian so he could have her. He took advantage of her in the most despicable way imaginable. A beating was too good for him."

"You knew all this and you never said a word."

"It would have caused Dawn enough grief to drive her over the edge."

"You should have told me."

"I was concerned about Dawn. She didn't have you to confide in, and she needed me. We have been best friends since we were small children. I have kept her secrets. And now I have broken my promise to her. I have told you."

"Don't you trust me?"

"I trust you to do what you think is best for you, but I can't trust you to do what is right for Dawn because you can only see in one direction. Yours."

"Don't you care that she might get killed or captured on her way to New Mexico?"

"I care, but I'm not worried. Marshal Holliman went with her to make sure she has a safe journey. He won't let any harm come to her. She will be under his protective wing. He's in love with her."

"I had that figured out long ago. It's too bad that Light Eyes is in the picture. I don't approve."

"I hope you don't plan to beat him. He would never survive. He's much too weak and sick."

"Light Eyes is an honorable man. In his heart and mind Dawn is his wife. I can't even imagine how he must have felt when he found out she was married to Ned."

"I think you are beginning to understand."

"What I understand is that Holliman is going to be hurt.

I know he'll do his job, that he will deliver Dawn safely to her grandfather and then bring her back to us in good health."

"She loves the Indian. What will happen to them?"

"Light Eyes will expect to take her with him when he's well enough to go back to his people."

"And you object?"

"I don't want to lose her. But if she's made up her mind, there is no way on earth I can stop her."

"Would you stop her if you could?"

"I fell in love with an Indian. No power on earth could have kept me away from her. And now I have you, and I had sooner die than lose you. I won't even attempt to stop her. She has to make up her own mind about her future."

"You will have to make your peace with Dawn when she comes home. She will need your understanding and your help."

"I will do whatever it takes. But I can tell you this, she will not be happy living in a wigwam. If she's looking for freedom, what she'll discover is just the opposite. Indian squaws spend their lives catering to their husbands and they don't take vacations."

"But she loves the Indian, and they have a son together."

"Whatever she decides, I'll accept and do as much for them as Light Eyes will allow. Comanches are a proud people. He will take care of his wife in his own way."

"And now I must tell you this. Light Eyes will come here when the moon is full and take Dawn with him. She told me just before she left for New Mexico."

"So it's settled then. I'm losing my daughter and grandson. Why did I build this house?"

"Because you and your daughter had a dream and you made it come true."

"I would have built you a house, Debbie, if we had married sooner. I suppose it's yours now."

"Ours, darling. Until Dawn comes back home."

"Do you think that's possible?"

"Anything is possible."

CHAPTER

49

Henry McCloud had tears in his eyes when it came time for Dawn and Darrell to leave. "I hate to see you leave like this Chris."

"I don't answer to that name anymore, sir. It has brought me nothing but rotten luck."

Henry looked grave. "I can protect you as long as you're on my ranch."

"I appreciate your concern. But hiding is a bit out of my line. It's not my nature."

"I hope my suggestion didn't offend you." Darrell smiled slightly. "Actually, it sounded more like an offer."

"As a matter-of-fact I could use a good man to ride herd on these worthless damned men I got laying around here."

"I can understand that. I ran into one of your hands in town. He was drunk and lost control of his manners, if he ever had any."

"So I've been informed. Why didn't you kill him?"

"A lady was present. How's his hand?"

"He's feeling no pain."

So the whore was right. Henry did take care of his own problems. Darrell nodded his understanding.

"I sent Pine on ahead to open the gate. I wish you a safe journey. Now that I know I have a granddaughter I'll stay in touch."

"Please do, Grandfather."

"Will you come back when I need you?"

Dawn understood what he was asking her. "I promise I will."

"Tell Richard my offer still stands if he's interested. I need him." He kissed his granddaughter good-bye and shook hands with Darrell.

As they mounted and rode toward the gate Dawn wiped tears from her eyes. She was afraid she would never see her grandfather again. He was a very sick old man and he was going to die all alone. The thought grieved her.

Darrell felt a surge of adrenalin when he saw the crowd of men hanging around the depot. He had not expected to find so many soldiers roaming through the town like a bunch of tourists. He had been on guard for two years, expecting any day that he would be recognized. He had changed his appearance as best he could, from a mustache and short beard to clean shaven. As a rule most men paid little attention to other men, but having Dawn by his side turned every male eye they approached in their direction. Maybe he should wear glasses, let his hair grow, and stuff a pillow under his shirt. That might help, but there was no way he could shrink his height, other than walk stooped, and that would give him a backache. He was afraid it was a little too late to worry about that now.

He kept Dawn close beside him, his arm looped through hers. They were being watched closely by a group of soldiers standing near the ticket window. Darrell knew immediately what was about to happen when he saw an officer break away from the group and approach them. Darrell glanced at the other men. Lynch Young was among them. The expression on his face was self-explanatory. He didn't want to be arrested in front of Dawn, but there was no escape. He still had a job to do and a promise to keep. He had to see Dawn safely back home.

"Don't panic," he said in a low voice. "I'm about to be arrested." He felt her stiffen and let go of her arm as he turned to face the captain, stepping in front of Dawn to shield her.

She was trembling and grabbed hold of the back of his shirt. "No!" she cried. "Oh, please, this can't be happening to you."

"Stand easy," the captain said, addressing Darrell. "This is an official arrest. I'm Captain Lee Rush, acting under the orders of General Stanley Burman. You have been identified as Lieutenant Colonel Chris Roman. I have with me the official court-martial charges and a warrant to place you in custody. You will be taken to Fort Daily where the sentencing will be carried out."

"You've made a mistake, Captain Rush. My name is Darrell Holliman, a United States Marshal out of Courgat Texas."

Lynch stepped forward. "He's lying. I served under him at Sand Creek. He killed Captain Wheeler."

Darrell shoved Dawn out of his way, stepped back and drew his gun. "I have a job to finish, Captain, and this woman's safety depends on whether or not you allow me to escort her back to Texas. If you try to stop me, I'll kill you."

"Don't be a fool, Roman. You're surrounded by a dozen armed men. You can't escape this time."

"I'm not trying to escape. Allow me to escort this woman safely back to Courgat, Texas and I'll surrender myself voluntarily and peaceably."

"If you pull that trigger, you're a dead man."

"I'm a dead man anyway. I can only hang once. I don't have a damned thing to lose and not much to live for either."

Dawn's legs were trembling and she could feel the hammering of her heart. She looked around her in a daze. It was a nightmare, one she would never awaken from. She moved to stand next to Darrell even as he motioned her to stay clear. She was sobbing as she wedged herself between Darrell and the officer. "Leave him alone!" she screamed. "All he did was try to save the lives of four hundred peaceable Indians, and you want to hang him for that?"

"He killed a man!" Lynch yelled.

"It was a fair fight," Darrell reminded him. "Wheeler struck the first blow."

The officer withdrew a document from his jacket pocket and scanned it quickly. "You have not been charged with the death of Wheeler. The charge is insubordination. You refused to carry out a direct order to attack the Indian village at Sand Creek."

"That's right, sir. I refused to slaughter helpless women and children. There was absolutely no threat involved. More land was needed to accommodate the flood of greedy squatters. General Burman decided to eliminate the Indian village in order to make more room. He made a grave mistake. I knew the penalty for refusing to take that order, but it was easier to accept the consequences for saving lives than being responsible for the slaughter of four hundred helpless human beings."

"Don't listen to him," Lynch yelled. "He's a tricky bastard."

"He's wearing the badge of a United States Marshal," Rush said.

"And that's no trick. It speaks loud of this man's credibility."

"The last time he was arrested we had to put him in leg irons. It took five men to shackle him and he about crippled two of 'um."

"I wasn't resisting arrest," Darrell said. "They were forcing me to go to the Indian village. I would never have gone voluntarily. They were determined to have me witness the aftermath of their raid to prove to me that the village had been wiped out regardless of my objections. They put a chain around my neck and dragged me through the carnage. The sand was stained with blood, the bodies covered in flies, and overhead the vultures were circling, drawn by the stench of death. The old chief had been scalped, his hair taken for a trophy. It was hanging from a flag pole beside the American flag. The village was strewn with the bodies of women and children. The women had been stripped naked, their legs spread obscenely. It was apparent that they had been raped. One squaw, clutching a small baby, had been stripped, raped and her throat cut. The baby, not more than a few weeks old, had its head bashed in. Its tiny mouth open in a scream of horror." Darrell fell silent for a moment, his mind filled with the hideous image of death and destruction the army had wrought. "I cried from grief and shame, and I wondered why God had allowed this to happen. One of the soldiers who had assisted in putting me in leg irons, said, 'I have never seen an officer cry before. I didn't think they had hearts.'"

Dawn was weeping softly. She was feeling Darrell's pain, saw tears fill his eyes, brought by the memory of the horror he had witnessed.

Rush was also touched deeply by Darrell's vivid account of the massacre. In his own mind he knew Chris Roman did not deserve to be punished, but honored for what he tried to prevent. Chris Roman was an intelligent man. He figured that he might have been a general by now if he had obeyed that order at Sand Creek.

"What happened at Sand Creek shames us all." Rush said. "I'm sorry lieutenant Roman, it's a damned shame what the army did to those poor people. That order was a terrible mistake, but once given by a general, it's impossible to change. The action you took only stalled the inevitable.

Holster your weapon, Lieutenant. There will be no leg irons." Rush turned to face his men who were standing in readiness for his next order. "At ease men. Lieutenant Roman has agreed to surrender peacefully when we reach Courgat, Texas. He asked only to escort this young woman safely home. He has given me his word."

"You're a fool," Lynch yelled. "You won't be able to find Roman by the time we reach Courgat. He's facing a rope and you're crazy if you think he's about to stick around long enough to swing."

"Place Private Lynch under arrest," Rush ordered, "and make sure you shackle him."

"What! You can't arrest me! I deserve the credit for finding Roman. You're as stupid as he is. You're both damned Indian lovers. I'll see you court-martialed for this!"

"Gag him!" Rush said.

Lynch fought and screamed until they had the leg irons secured and a gag stuffed in his mouth.

"I'm going to trust you Roman, as a gentleman and an officer. Do I have your word?"

"You have it."

"When we reach Courgat I will take you into official custody. I hope you realize that I'm staking my reputation on your word. I understand that what you did was in your eyes right and just, and I sympathize with you."

"Thank you, I appreciate your trust. I won't let you down."

"By the way, mind telling me who the young lady is?"

"Henry McCloud's granddaughter, Dawn."

"My God! You should have told me. Does he know who you are?"

"He knows everything."

"What does he have to say about it?"

"You'll have to ask him that."

"He controls New Mexico from his bedroom, I understand. He will know about your arrest immediately. He may cause trouble if he objects. He's a very powerful man."

"And also a very sick one."

"Who's his successor?"

"His next of kin, naturally."

"And who might that be."

"At this point, his granddaughter."

"What about you? What's your position in all this?"

Darrell laughed. "That's pretty obvious, isn't it?"

"Damned shame."

"Are you going to sit in the seat beside me on the train?"

"No, but we will occupy the same car. I'll not infringe on your privacy. You don't have much time, so make the most of it."

"I appreciate this, Captain."

"I appreciate your cooperation. You had me worried for a moment."

"Sorry about that."

"A man condemned to die has nothing to lose, as you pointed out."

"You were about to force me to break a promise, and my word has always been important to me."

"I have wondered about something, Roman. Did you know the Indians who burned the jail so you could escape?"

"No. Why do you ask?"

"I was just wondering if your arrest might cause another incident."

"You needn't worry."

Darrell knew that the time he spent with Dawn on the train would be the last hours he would ever spend with her. She crawled into his lap and held on to him like a frightened child.

He tried to comfort her, but she was beyond that. Darrell felt ready to fall apart. It seemed to him that his relationship with Dawn was a figment of his imagination, only a hopeful dream that he might have a future with her. For he was now living a nightmare. The train was taking him on a collision course. His life would end at the end of the tracks.

He thought about Light Eyes, how she would have him to love, and that love would help her forget that he ever existed. He would soon be just a memory.

"Tell me about your Indian," he said. "Have you made any plans?"

"Yes. He will come for me when the moon is full. He will be strong again by then.

"And take you where?"

"To his village, to live in his lodge with him."

"And you will take baby Henry with you of course."

"He doesn't know about his son."

"Why haven't you told him?"

"I tried to, but he refused to listen to anything I had to say. He was angry because I married Ned after I had already given myself to him. I thought he was dead. If he had come to me, let me know that he was alive, I would never have married Ned because I didn't love him, could never love him."

"Why did you leave Courgat to visit your grandfather while Light Eyes was so close? He was finally at your disposal and you walked away from him. I don't understand that."

"He sent me away because he didn't understand that I was forced to marry Ned to protect our son. He said he didn't want me anymore. I was mad too, and I didn't tell him he had a son. I decided not to because I wanted him to want me for myself, not just because of the child. Later, after I screamed at him and told him I would never see him again, as I started to leave he called me back. He had changed his mind. He said he would be strong by the time of the full moon and he would come to me at the big house and take me with him."

"And you will live happily ever after."

"That's the way it should be."

"So your new life will begin with the full moon. Kind of poetic, don't you think?"

"Oh, Darrell, how can I be happy if I lose you? You're the only friend I have. I trust you. When will they—" She burst into tears. "Oh! I can't talk about it. Why does it have to be this way?"

"I'm sorry I won't be around to keep you company. At least I was able to keep my promise to you. You will soon be safely back at home so you can plan your future."

"I did this to you. I wish now that I had listened to Father. If I hadn't gone to New Mexico you would be safe. Oh! I'm so sorry."

"Stop blaming yourself. It was my idea. Now or later, it was bound to happen."

"Maybe Grandfather can do something to help you. I'll send him a wire as soon as we get home."

"There's no time. They will hang me within forty-eight hours after the arrest."

"So soon? No!"

"I've had two years of freedom, purely by accident. I'm thankful for that."

"Are you scared?"

"The waiting is the worst part. Thinking about it prolongs the misery. It's best to get it over with fast. At least I won't have to look over my shoulder any longer. I have no regrets, except for one. I don't want to leave you. I had dreams about you, impossible dreams because I had two strikes against me from the beginning. Light Eyes and a rope. It's for the best that you have someone to love, because it wouldn't have worked out for us. I'm thankful for the part you played in my life. I have been a very lucky man because you like me. I have never been in love before. You're the first, and you have fulfilled all my dreams of what loving a woman should be like, but I never dreamed that I might find a woman as beautiful and perfect as you are."

"I have never had a friend like you before. I don't think I can manage without you. I will always need you."

She moved against him, put her arms around his neck, and when he kissed her he tasted her tears. He held her in his arms, tight against his aching heart. The heart she had said she would have to break one day.

The sun had set and it was dark inside the coach. The soldiers were sleeping. It was Rush you kept the vigil, feeling the awesome weight of responsibility. He was damning Lynch Young to Hell for recognizing Roman. It was a rotten shame that a useless man like Lynch could bring to ruin a man like Roman. Chris Roman was worth a dozen men, and soon this extraordinary man would be silenced. He wished there was some way to protect him, but he didn't have the authority. He thought about Henry McCloud, wondering if he might take action when he received word of Roman's arrest. He heard Dawn sobbing softly and he could imagine the agonies Roman must be suffering. Rush has never seen a woman as beautiful as McCloud's granddaughter. He had no choice but to allow Roman to escort her back home. Without protection she would have been in a world of danger. If anything should happen to her, Henry McCloud would have his head on a platter.

Before the train reached Courgat, Rush explained to Darrell what he expected. "I don't want any trouble, Roman. I allowed you your freedom to escort the young woman, but when this train stops, you will be officially under arrest. How far does Miss McCloud live from town?"

"About two miles. I would appreciate your letting me speak to my deputy, Charles Morgan, to explain about my arrest. He will see Dawn home safely."

"I will allow you that, but I'll have to accompany you. I'll turn your gun over to him if you like. And you won't need that badge where you're going."

Dawn was clutching Darrell's arm and staring up into his face as if she might be drawing a picture of him in her mind because he would soon be gone from her sight. Her tears came again. "This is wrong!" she sobbed.

"When we get off the train, Miss McCloud, I want you to stand away from Lieutenant Roman. He's no longer a free man. I know how hard this is for you, and I don't want to put him in restraints, but I can't control the situation if you interfere. You can go with us to the marshal's office, but no further. Do you understand?"

She shook her head. "Please, I want to kiss him good-bye."

Rush swallowed the lump in his throat. "I can't allow it. I'm sorry. You will have to say your good-byes before we leave the train. I'll have both your horses unloaded. Roman will ride his to the fort. I'll have yours taken to the livery."

"Please don't put restraints on him," she cried. "He's no criminal. He's the most gentle person I have ever known. He's good and kind—"

"If you can control your emotions it will make it a lot easier for him."

"I'll do anything you say, just don't shackle him."

"I have no intentions of shackling him."

Darrell would never forget the look on Morgan's face when he and Dawn walked into the office flanked by Rush and two soldiers. Rush had agreed to let him tie up his loose ends, and the first order was for him to turn over his marshal's badge. Dawn looked on with tears in her eyes as Darrell unpinned his badge and dropped it on the desk.

Morgan looked thunderstruck. "What the hell is the meaning of this? Put that badge back on, Holliman."

"I'm sorry about this Morgan. These soldiers have me mixed up with a man called Chris Roman. They think I look like him."

Morgan was fighting mad. He looked the three soldiers over, then spoke to Rush. "I see you're the big chief, so I'll talk straight to you. This man is Marshal Darrell Holliman."

"He's an Army lieutenant colonel, his real name is Chris Roman. He has been charged with insubordination and sentenced to hang."

"Bullshit!" Morgan roared. "What are you trying to pull? Holliman saved this town when he went up against Buck Femmer and his gang of cutthroats, and you want to hang him for disobeying an order. Don't you have anything better to do? I can vouch for this man. The whole town can."

"Save your breath Charles," Darrell said. "It's not Captain Rush's fault. General Burman gave the order."

"Mac ain't gonna like this."

"I don't like it either," Rush confessed, "but there is nothing I can do to change it. We will be leaving immediately for Fort Daily. Please see Miss McCloud home safely."

"No!" Dawn screamed. "Charlie, stop them. Please don't let them take Darrell. They will hang him!"

Morgan picked up his scatter gun and held it on the three men. "You say the word Marshal, and I'll shoot these bastards."

"Put the gun down, Charles. You'll get yourself killed." Charles lowered the gun. "This ain't right."

"Take care of Dawn, and tell Mac I'm sorry. I never meant for this to happen."

"Let's go," Rush ordered, and marched Darrell outside where his horse was saddled and waiting with the other mounted soldiers. Rush joined them and they rode out.

Dawn was standing in the street looking after them, screaming.

For an instant Darrell had a wild notion to make a run for it. Knowing they would shoot him in the back, and he wanted to die, to end the suffering, to erase the memory of Dawn's helpless screams and his agony for not being free to comfort her.

Rush was watching him. "Don't even think about it, Roman."

"Are you a mind reader?"

"I saw it in your eyes."

"What have I got to lose?"

"The point is, you have nothing to gain. I won't shoot you in the back, if that's what you're banking on. I'll have your horse shot out from under you. I intend to take you to Fort Daily one way or another, but alive, even if you have to walk."

"I appreciate your understanding," he said mockingly. "It's not over for you until that trap door springs open."

"Well now, that's a real comfort."

CHAPTER 50

Henry McCloud stepped down from the train in Daily, Texas, which was a small settlement two miles outside Fort Daily. He was accompanied by his nurse, Princess Lake, a tall, robust woman who looked more like a man than most men. Her expression was grim and fixed. She supported Henry easily with one strong, muscular, arm as they made their way to the livery stable where they rented a buggy. She lifted Henry onto the padded seat, covered his legs with a blanket, and drove him to the military post without delay.

Princess assisted him inside as far as the noncom's desk where Henry dismissed her with a slight flick of his hand and resorted to his cane for support.

The soldier looked up, squinting at Henry through his wire rimmed glasses. "May I help you, sir?"

"I'm here to see Captain Rush."

"If you will state your name and business, I'll tell the captain you're here."

"Don't dally with me, boy! I'm Henry McCloud and he'll damned sure see me. Which office is his?"

The young man swallowed hard, pointing toward an office located directly behind him. Henry made a move toward it. "You can't go in there, sir." He rose quickly, took a few steps and planted himself between Henry and the door.

Princess Lake was on her feet also, moving quickly to Henry's side. She brushed the soldier aside with a determined forearm. When he opened his mouth to object, she wagged her finger in his face. He moved back, looking up helplessly into the hulking woman's ugly face. She threw the door open and stood guard as Henry stepped inside. She moved like a puppet, with Henry the master of the strings.

Rush glanced up in surprise, then smiled. He stood briskly and walked around the desk to greet Henry McCloud. "Welcome to Fort Daily, Mr. McCloud. I've been expecting you." He held his hand out. Henry frowned at it for a moment before he reached to shake it. "Please, sir, sit down." He saw how Henry was trembling and pushed a chair toward him. "Are you all right, sir? May I offer you a drink?"

Henry eyed him thoughtfully, noting his military stance. Lee Rush, forty-six, was trim and neat, his dark hair beginning to gray at his temples. He had a pleasant, clean shaven face and a genuine friendly smile. "Brandy," Henry replied.

Rush moved toward his liquor cabinet and took out a bottle of brandy. He poured a good measure into a snifter and handed it to Henry.

Henry swirled the golden liquid for a moment before taking a swallow. "Since you have been expecting me, Captain, I must assume that you're aware of my reason for being here."

"What is your interest in Lieutenant Colonel Chris Roman?"

"I assure you, I am not here to witness his execution, sir. I'm here to stop it!"

"You certainly didn't waste any time. I only just arrived myself with the prisoner. How did you find out so quickly?"

"I outguessed you Rush. Roman knew he had been recognized. The damned army is so predictable that it was absurdly easy to figure your moves. I had a man posted at the station. He saw the setup at a glance. I was a passenger on that same train."

"I shouldn't be surprised, but I am. You have gone to a lot of trouble. I'm truly sorry that I can't help you. I wish I could, but it's out of my hands. General Burman was Roman's commanding officer. He brought the charges against him, not I. I was ordered to arrest Roman. I had nothing to do with his punishment."

"I don't want to hear your excuses for letting an innocent man hang! I happen to know that you will give the final order that will end his life."

"If I refuse the order to carry out the execution, I'll be hanged right along with Roman, and that's certainly no help to him."

"Then turn him loose!"

"He's ready to get it over with. He's tired of looking over his shoulder. He doesn't have a life as long as he's a wanted man. I've learned quite a lot about Roman since we met. He surrendered voluntarily. He actually had me in his gun sights, and he would have killed me if I hadn't agreed to let him escort your granddaughter safely back home. Even if I opened the cell door, he wouldn't walk through it."

"No man is that stupid!" Henry stormed.

"He's tired of running, McCloud, and he's not afraid to die."

"Burman is a crooked bastard. I've had dealings with him."

"What sort of dealings?"

"He's done some things for me that involved killing. I know he ordered the Sand Creek massacre, but it was not to my advantage."

"Are you saying that he has wiped out Indian villages for the soul purpose of vacating the land so you could claim it?"

"Many times."

"My God! I had no idea."

"Of course I can't prove it, and I wouldn't want to."

"Then you're not concerned about the four hundred Indians that were slaughtered at Sand Creek?"

"Not in the least. That massacre didn't benefit anyone, and it put Roman's head in a noose."

"I don't understand what you expect me to do."

"Bluff Burman. Tell him I'm ready to blow the lid off if he allows Roman to hang."

"But you just admitted that you have no proof."

"He doesn't know that. He's not the kind of man to gamble with his own life. He has already proved that Roman's life means less than nothing to him. If Burman has a reason to worry about his own neck, he can be brought to his knees."

"And if he doesn't buy it?"

"I'm a sick man, so you can figure that I didn't come all this way for my health. I have enough money and power to take care of Burman anyway I choose. If Chris Roman hangs, Stanley Burman will die a slow, painful death. I guarantee."

"Do you realize what you're suggesting?"

"What have I got to lose?"

"You still haven't answered my question. What is your personal interest in Lieutenant Roman?"

"I'm not concerned with my own interest. I'm concerned with my granddaughter's interest."

"I understand now."

"You think you understand, but you don't."

"You're a curious man, McCloud."

"I want you to have a message delivered to General Burman. Tell him what his choices are. Either Roman goes free, or I'll take steps to see him behind bars."

"Evidently you're not aware that Roman will hang tomorrow morning at daybreak. It's too late McCloud."

"You can delay it a few days. Stall until you hear from Burman."

"That can be a problem. I have my orders."

"Have you been ordered to witness the execution?"

"Of course."

"What if you're sick?"

"It would depend on how sick."

"Then claim your horse threw you. You'll think of something. It's worth a thousand dollars to you."

"You can't bribe me, McCloud."

"It's no bribe. It's a gift."

"There is no guarantee that Burman will cooperate."

"Is there a hotel in this town?"

"If you plan to stay, we have guest quarters."

"I have a woman with me."

Rush looked surprised. "I didn't realize."

"She's my nurse."

"Then we don't have a problem. I'll have a cot brought in for your nurse."

"I'm not leaving here until I know the hanging has been delayed."

"I'll think about it."

"You don't have time to think about it. You are the deciding factor."

"I'm very aware of that fact."

"Now that we understand one another, I'll take you up on your offer to use the guest quarters. I'm tired. I need rest."

"I'll have my clerk show you the way. He will also arrange for your meals while you're my guest."

Rush gave some serious thought to McCloud's offer. He could use the money, but he didn't need the complications. He decided it was worth being thrown by a horse if he could help Roman. Becoming suddenly ill seemed a bit too pat under the circumstances, but no one would question an accident.

When Rush saddled his horse later that day, he put a tack under the blanket. The horse instantly began to pitch and buck. There were several soldiers tidying up the parade ground and they stopped to watch him. Because Rush was expecting to be thrown, he braced himself for the landing. But since he was not a seasoned bronc rider, he had little control over how he hit the ground. He felt the fall in every part of his body, it even jarred his teeth. He struggled to his feet holding his back and wiping dirt from his eyes. He allowed two soldiers to assist him back to his quarters. He didn't have to pretend, he was in pain. No one questioned his condition when he took to his bed. Postponing the hanging had now become necessary, and he did it with a clear conscience.

Darrell had prepared himself for the big event as best a man could. His life span was down to less than an hour. He had expected a clergyman to say a few words of comfort to him before they put the black sack over his head. He had never been a very religious man; however he had found spiritual peace. He was lost in the labyrinth of the past that came rushing back, a nightmare he was never to forget. In his mind he was back at Sand Creek once more, manacled and dragged by the chain around his neck, stumbling again over the tortured corpses of women and children, leaving his boot tracks stamped upon the blood soaked sand. The charred lodges still smoldered. And above it all, snapping in the wind flew the American Flag, raised under the direction of General Burman to signify his victory. And now he was very close to celebrating another victory. To end the life of an officer who disagreed with him to the point of his own death. Roman's thoughts consumed his mind with hatred.

Doom's day came and went. He wasn't anxious to die, but he felt the waiting was going to kill him quicker than the rope. His first awareness came when one of the cooks brought him a breakfast tray.

"I didn't think I would still be around for breakfast," he said. "Did the hangman misplace his rope?"

"Captain Rush had an accident late yesterday. He's laid up with a bad back."

"What happened?"

"His horse threw him."

"What? How the hell can a cavalry soldier get thrown by his own horse?"

"Spooked by a rattler."

"I suppose the army will send a replacement to carry out my execution."

"I wouldn't know about that, sir. All I do is cook. But I do have the privilege of disagreeing. You don't belong in here. What would you like for dinner?"

"Why? Is it supposed to be my last meal?"

"Not as far as I know."

"Anything you cook will suit me just fine."

"Thank you, sir." He turned on his heel and walked away. Rush had admitted sympathizing with Darrell, and he wondered if he had actually been thrown by his horse, or perhaps he had something else in mind. What, he had no idea. At any rate, he was back to waiting. He pushed the breakfast tray aside. He had lost his appetite.

He lay down on his cot and closed his eyes. He thought about Dawn and the Indian Summer night they had spent together at the old Benson house. He had been awed by the perfect curves of her body, her luscious lips that sought his frantically in her deeper moments of passion. The innocence in her eyes when she gazed up at him and confessed that she liked the way he made her feel. God, it hurt! He remembered the one and only time she had uttered the words that would have made his life complete, if she had meant them. She had apologized for misleading him.

He looked out at the moon through the small barred window of his cell. For an instant Dawn's face seemed to float across its misty yellow surface, and then he was looking at it through a blur of tears.

Charles Morgan was left in shock over the startling events that had just transpired. Dawn was clinging to him crying helplessly.

"He's on his way to die," she sobbed. "If not for me none of this would have happened. He went with me to keep me from harm, and I'm sending him to the gallows. Oh! This is killing me. I don't know what to do."

"You have to stop blaming yourself."

"How can I? It's my fault."

"Did you ask him to go with you?"

"No, I tried to stop him."

"Then it was Holliman's decision. He knew the risk he was taking. I'll ride out to the ranch with you and tell Mac about this."

"Maybe father can do something to help him." Morgan knew there was absolutely nothing Mac could do, but he didn't have the heart to tell Dawn.

Mac looked up in surprise when Dawn rushed into the house with Morgan following her. He had expected to see Darrell Holliman. He wanted to thank him for bringing his daughter safely home.

"Oh, Father!" she cried. "You have to help Darrell. He's been arrested! They're going to hang him!"

"What are you talking about? Who arrested him? Where? Is he still in New Mexico?"

"No. Captain Rush is taking him to Fort Daily to hang him for insubordination. You have to do something!"

Mac looked at Morgan. "What's this all about, Morgan."

"Those damned idiots have him confused with some other guy. I told them they were wrong but you know how them cock-sure army officers are. They think they know it all."

"Well, who do they think he is?"

"Some Lieutenant Colonel by the name of Chris Roman."

Mac suddenly turned pale. He recognized the name at once. He had heard the story about the young lieutenant, but he had no idea that Darrell Holliman and Chris Roman were one and the same. "Oh, my God. I knew there was something about that young man that was way above the ordinary. I know all about Lieutenant Roman. He was the officer at Sand Creek who refused to carry out the order to massacre four hundred peaceable Indians. So they finally caught up to him. Oh, hell!" Mac slumped into a chair and put his face in his hands.

"Please, Father!" Dawn cried. "You have to do something! We can't let them hang him. It's not fair when a man like Darrell is punished for doing the right things, and a man like Frost Jackson can get away with just about anything. He raped that Indian girl."

He looked up at her with moist eyes. When she saw the expression on his face she broke into hysterics.

Debbie rushed into the room. She stopped short when she saw Morgan instead of Darrell. "What's happened?" she said, taking Dawn into her arms in an attempt to console her. She asked the question again. "What's happened? Has something happened to Darrell?"

Mac rose to his feet slowly, as if his movements were painful. He paced a few feet before turning to face her. "Yes, something very serious has happened. The man we know as Darrell Holliman is actually Lieutenant Colonel Chris Roman. He's been arrested and taken to Fort Daily to be hanged."

"No!" Debbie screamed. She tightened her hold on Dawn. Now they were both crying. "We should have guessed that he was more then he admitted to. You thought so yourself, Mac. But you never bothered to ask him about his past."

"I didn't want to put him on the spot. His past didn't matter to me. I liked him. He was trustworthy and honest, but above all, he was a gentleman."

Dawn's head jerked up. "Stop it! You're talking about him as if he were already dead."

"We can't help him, Dawn. You have to understand that and accept it. Lieutenant Roman was found guilty of insubordination. I can't change the ruling of the court. No one can. Don't you know I would if I could? I liked that young man the first time I met him. I was impressed by his high intelligence and the fact that he was a gentleman. I didn't bother to ask any questions about his past, but I knew he was above being a store clerk. Now that I know who he really is, I know the entire story. Chris Roman is well known because he tried to save the lives of four hundred peaceable Indians at Sand Creek Colorado."

Debbie burst into a renewed torrent of tears. "Poor Darrell! He's being punished because of his love and compassion for human life, no matter what the color of their skin. Surely there must be something we can do to help him. I can't stand the thought of his young life ended so suddenly and senselessly."

"Maybe Grandfather can help him," Dawn cried.

At the mention of Henry's name Mac reeled under the force of his memories. He had to discuss his past with Dawn, drudge up all the things he had hoped to forget and had kept secret for the past eighteen years. It would not be easy, but he knew it had to be done. Debbie had been right. He should have told Dawn years ago, before she heard it from someone else. And he wondered how Henry might have twisted the truth to his own advantage. He would like to wait until the shock of Darrell's arrest eased somewhat before opening old wounds. But if Dawn should question him about what she heard from her grandfather, then he would tell her everything, no holds barred. He had hurt Dawn badly, driving her into the arms of an Indian as she reached blindly to understand herself. He wondered what sort of foolishness Henry had put into her head. "We have to talk about this. I need to know what Henry told you. You will need me to shield you. It must never be known that—"

"That I'm a half-breed? I'm not ashamed of my Indian blood, even if you are."

"I'm not ashamed, but the knowledge can do you harm where others are concerned. You should realize by now that Indians have no rights whatsoever."

"I'm aware of that fact. Both Darrell and Grandfather explained it to me. I understand why you kept the truth from me."

Mac had not expected to hear these words coming from Dawn's mouth. He was thankful that Darrell had been on his side. He had saved him a world of grief. Darrell was a miracle, and he was on the verge of dying for it. Her decision to meet her grandfather, and Darrell's love for her, his decision to keep her safe, had led to Holliman's arrest, and his subsequent death.

Debbie was not surprised when Mac decided to go to Fort Daily to visit Darrell. "I don't know how to face the man. This is indirectly my fault. My stubbornness forced Dawn to hunt the answers to the questions she had been asking me all her life."

"You couldn't have possibly known things would turn out this way."

"I don't want Dawn to know I'm going to see Darrell. She would want to go with me. She would fall apart right in front of him, and he doesn't need anymore grief."

"She will never see him again. Please, Richard, take her with you. She needs to hold him one last time." Debbie was sobbing, her face in her hands.

"She doesn't need to remember him like that, waiting behind bars for his execution. It's killing me. Can't you imagine how Dawn would feel? That picture would remain in her mind the rest of her life."

Mac arrived at Fort Daily before sunrise the next morning, hoping to see Darrell before he was executed. It was the least he could do. He was all alone waiting to die and Mac was grieved to the point of tears. His heart felt like a rock in his chest. He was told that the hanging would not take place as scheduled, that the officer in charge had been injured and the sentencing postponed until a later date. He was granted permission by Rush to see Darrell, and his throat almost closed at the thought of what he would say to him. There were no words of comfort that could ease his suffering. All he had left was his own courage. Mac was escorted to the guardhouse. Darrell was in a cell by himself. He was standing with his back to the barred door staring out the small window that overlooked a bland strip of dried fall landscape.

He looked taller than Mac remembered. He was a fine looking man. His ears lay close to his head and his features were well chiseled. Mac swallowed the lump in his throat.

Hearing footsteps, Darrell turned toward him. A look of surprise crossed his face, and then he smiled. He took the few steps necessary to reach the bars and hold his hand out to Mac. Mac gripped it with both of his. "Darrell, my God!" he managed in a choked voice, and he could say no more.

"I know this is a shock, and I'm sorry, Mac. I guess I should have told you, but I had a foolish notion that I might get lucky. I stuck around too long. I should have kept moving, but I fell in love with your daughter, and the fact that she was married made no difference. I had hoped she might love me, but it didn't happen. I feel the need to get this off my chest, to be honest at least, if not honorable."

"I understand. You don't need to confess to me. I've made a mess of my own life. It's my fault Dawn went to Henry for the truth. I want to thank you for seeing after her. I knew you would keep her safe."

"I had a bit of a problem, but Captain Rush trusted me enough to let me escort Dawn back home."

"I heard about that. Would you have shot Rush?"

"You can be certain of it."

"You are quite amazing. A gentleman, a hero, and a man who will commit murder over the woman he loves. That's quite a combination. I know about the Indian, Light Eyes. Debbie told me everything."

"She would never tell me, and I practically got on my knees. I knew Dawn couldn't love me, and I wanted to know who the lucky man was who held the key to her heart."

"I don't approve."

"Neither does your father."

"Henry knows."

"He sent me with a verbal message for you."

"I can imagine."

"He said that his offer still stands. He needs you."

"I suppose he poisoned Dawn's mind against me."

"No, but he did explain it all to her, of course it was his version. He made her understand why you kept the truth about Elizabeth from her."

"She will never forgive me for that."

"You're wrong about that. She understands the pitfalls for having Indian blood. She can never own property if the truth is known. He encouraged her to keep it a secret, for her sake and baby Henry's. I'm going to tell you something now that may be a big mistake, but since I won't be around to suffer the consequences, I feel you should know. Henry plans to kill Light Eyes, if he can learn his identity. He does not want him for a grandson-in-law, living in his house, spending his money. He has a real big problem. If he leaves Dawn his kingdom, and it's discovered that she's a half-breed, the government will take the land away from her. She can't give Brave Horse a home because he's an Indian and so is she. What it all boils down to is this: either he leaves it to you, and that's his first choice, or Dawn gets it, and if her heritage should happen to be discovered, it's all over. You lose, Dawn loses, and Brave Horse won't have a place to live when the settlers crowd him off his hunting grounds. In an effort to survive, he will 'pick up the hatchet' and fight a war he can't win. If they don't starve, the army will slaughter them. You can turn that around, but if you wait too long, you will miss your chance. Henry McCloud's time is down to single digits. He's a sick man. I think he's dying. He wants forgiveness. I actually feel sorry for the old man. I don't know all he's done, evidently you do. And now I'm going to shut up and mind my own business, and I don't have much business left."

Mac was silent and thoughtful for a long time, tears glistening in his eyes. Finally he said in little more than a whisper, "I took Elizabeth away from him. He bought her when she was a child, and waited patiently for her to grow into a woman. When he went to her, to claim her the way a man wants to claim the woman he loves, she rejected him. He became irate. He tore her clothes off and struck her. She turned to me, and I took advantage of her. She was perfect; every line of her face and body was flawless."

"Just like Dawn," Darrell said.

Mac's head snapped up and he looked Darrell straight in the eyes. "There is only one way you could know that."

"She wanted me, Mac. I never forced her. She was a willing partner."

Mac's face was filled with pain and disbelief. "Then I don't understand about the Indian."

"She met him first. They were married Indian style. She had his son, and that sealed her love for him. She only likes me. She told me from the beginning that one day she would break my heart. So you see, Mac, I can never have her. It grieves me. I really don't have any reason to live."

"Your frivolous attitude betrays you, Holliman. You run mighty deep. You made one hell of a lawman. It was short, and that was our loss. You had already made a name for yourself as Darrell Holliman, and Chris Roman will never be forgotten. You're a hero, no matter what you call yourself."

"I intended to make a career in the military. I spent four years of my life preparing for it at West Point. My grades were exceptional, and I proved psychologically sound. I threw it all away because I had one very big flaw: compassion. When the Indians broke me out of jail I decided to get lost in the new frontier. I didn't have any plans for the future, and then I met your daughter. She was my dream come true. I fell in love with her on sight. All I wanted was to marry her and live happily ever after. I didn't mind being a store clerk, dusting shelves and moping floors. I had learned how to be neat at West Point. I can make a fair bed. It was an accident that

I became your sheriff. I was forced to take a stand against Buck to protect the woman I loved, and friends like you and Keel and Morgan. A man can change his appearance, but he can never change what he is inside."

"It's hard for me to live with this injustice." Mac said. "I wish there was something I could do. I would give all I own to save you from this miscarriage of justice if it were possible."

"I appreciate your coming to see me, Mac. I wrote Dawn a letter. I hope you will see that she gets it."

"I'll give it to her personally."

"She plans to join the Indian when the moon is full. That's only two days away. She may not want the letter after she's with him. I was staring at these four walls thinking about her and I wanted her to know that she is, or was, the light of my life. That she gave herself to me, I never expected, but it was an awakening I will never forget. Actually Mac, I haven't accomplished very much in my twenty-three and a half years, except to fall in love. I asked Dawn to marry me, and that tells you how selfish I am. I was a wanted man, anxious to get married, but she would affect any man that way."

"I'm sorry things didn't work out."

"If I had been the man responsible for giving her baby Henry, would you have handled me the way you did Ned?"

"I can't answer that."

"Why not?"

"Because I would have been proud to have you in the family. I think my daughter deserves the best."

When Mac left Darrell he was experiencing a new kind of grief. It was like saying good-bye to a dead man, yet he wasn't through dying. It was a horrible waste to snuff out the life of this extraordinary man. Mac felt like screaming his protests, and he would have, if it would alter the outcome. He had shaken his hand for the last time, and his strong grip would haunt him the rest of his life. It was a grip of strength and life that would very soon cease to exist.

CHAPTER

51

Mac gave a lot of thought to what Darrell had told him about Henry. He had certainly impressed Darrell. He couldn't be sure if it was adversely, but there was the presence of pity in the tone of his voice when he talked about Henry.

Losing Darrell had put the town right back where it was before they had miraculously discovered him. They were down to Charles Morgan again, and Mac didn't feel like playing nurse maid for the town a second time. He had enough to worry about. What should he do about Light Eyes? He had to walk easy where he was concerned, or he might start a war. For after all, Light Eyes would be the chief of the Comanche Nation in the near future. He wondered how Dawn would cope with the hard life the Indians lived. As the son of the chief, Light Eyes was bound to stay with his people, to guide and protect them. If there was any changing to be done, then Dawn had to be the one to submit.

And what about Henry? He had threatened to have the Indian killed to eliminate the problem. While curing one problem, Mac knew he would be creating a far greater one. He was beginning to think there were no answers or cures for the jumble of trouble that lay at his feet. Love was indeed a complicated emotion. But greed was a more destructive state of mind. Henry had revolved around his greed for more land, money, cattle, and power. And what did he have in the final analysis? Exactly nothing. All he used the land for was to make more money. Mac saw the opportunity to give some of the land back to the Indians. They were fewer in number now, and they needed hunting grounds if they were to survive.

Mac had never wanted to see his father again, his pain and resentment had gone too deep, and now he was experiencing doubt. If Henry was actually serious about leaving him his estate, then he could not refuse for Dawn's sake. It didn't sound like something Henry would do. Perhaps he realized that he couldn't take it with him. Dawn could never own land, as was true for Light Eyes as well. Mac felt his whole world was changing. His goals in life were being absorbed by other people's problems. He cursed under his breath. He had dreams of spending the remainder of his days with Debbie in a peaceful atmosphere, watching his grandson grow up. But what about Dawn? She was still unsettled. If she went with Light Eyes, he would lose both his daughter and his grandson. Little Henry would grow up to be just one more buck, hated and feared, forced to fight or starve. Henry's kingdom seemed to be the answer. A haven for the Indians that no one could take from them as long as he held title to their land. He knew what he must do, and the realization caused his stomach to roll over. Facing Henry after so many silent years was frightening. As ridiculous as it might seem, he feared Henry as much today as he had twenty years ago. Henry had that effect on people. He had thought his tortured feelings were dead and buried, that he was beyond caring. He felt his dread returning, stirring the same old emotions. Henry would find fault with him, ridicule, blame him for Elizabeth's death, and shame him for keeping secrets from Dawn. What really upset him was the fact that he had no defense. Could he have been wrong all these years? He had lost respect for his father soon after his mother passed away. In his grief over Virginia, Henry had gathered around him a harem of shameless women. They paraded through his house half naked, and shared his bed, doing things no decent woman would dare. His life had been shattered over the loss of his wife, rocking him with storms of loneliness and grief, always searching for, but not finding, love. His future held only one consolation. He drew relief from amassing material things, replacing love with power in an attempt to ease his suffering. He became cold and dispassionate. Even his sons had become victims of his suffering and scorn. Henry McCloud had died inside.

When Henry found Elizabeth, he had been moved to his core by the sight of her. Wanting her, waiting impatiently for her to grow to maturity. His last shred of happiness had been swept away by his son, a deed that had resulted in Elizabeth's death when she gave birth to Mac's baby daughter. And Mac had even withheld his granddaughter from him.

Mac's thoughts caused him to shudder inside, certain that Henry would remind him of all his mistakes, that he had been a weak, sniveling, coward, running off with Elizabeth in the middle of the night, leaving him only a hastily scribbled note.

Darrell had seemed certain that Henry's days were short in number, reminding Mac that he had little time to set the McCloud house in order. As it stood, as Holliman had stated, unless Mac accepted Henry's offer, they would all be the losers.

His most urgent concern was for his daughter. She was in a state of devastation. She had undoubtedly considered Darrell Holliman a permanent fixture in her life, and now he was doomed. She had expected that he would be hanged this day at sunrise, as they all had. Since he had not, they were all back to facing the inevitable. He couldn't even imagine how Darrell must be feeling; however, he seemed to be accepting his fate remarkably well. There was no training that could prepare a man to face death casually and composed. He realized it was Darrell's own strength that held him together. He admired Chris Roman more than any man he had ever known, and he had earned his respect the hard way.

Mac had one less worry. While Dawn was gone to New Mexico, Light Eyes had been taken back to his people. He would do his mending there.

As soon as he had been strong enough to stand on his own two feet, he was threatening to leave the white man's house, even if he had to walk back to his village. The army took charge of delivering him to his father safely. He was hauled in one of their supply wagons, bedded down on blankets. He was given every consideration.

Mac was worried about how Dawn would react when she found out about his visiting Darrell. He had the letter Darrell had written her in his saddle bag, and he wondered how she would handle that. He had many trying situations facing him. How would he explain to Dawn that the execution had been delayed, but that Darrell must still die? He wished now that he had told Debbie not to mention where he had gone. He decided to stop at the Silver Buckle and have a few drinks before he went home. He needed to pad his nerves.

Debbie was having a few worries of her own. She had broken her promise to Dawn when she told Richard about Dawn's love for Light Eyes, and that baby Henry was the Indian's son. Now she must confess her betrayal to Dawn. She only hoped she would understand that she had Dawn's best interest at heart, that she had not meant to cause dissension between her and her father. Dawn had been spared the agony of confessing her involvement with the Indian. She realized that Dawn had kept her secret out of fear for the Indian's safety.

"He had to be told," Debbie said with tears in her eyes. "It was the only thing I could do after you left here to visit your grandfather. He realized that Henry would answer all your questions, and to his own advantage, he imagined. I wanted to save you the burden of confession, and give Mac time to absorb it all."

"Was he angry?"

"He was shocked, of course. He did not blame Light Eyes, because he knows him to be an honorable man. He understood it all. Why you had been forced to marry Ned. Martha Rowling knows about your mother. Mac told her to ease her suffering. She still has a part of her son in little Henry. She must never be told the truth. Let her go on thinking that he's Ned's son."

"I still hate her!" Dawn cried.

"You must learn to forgive. All your hate only hurts you."

"When I go with Light Eyes, she will know the truth then."

"Then it won't matter anymore."

There was an eerie silence inside the house as if the great structure was holding its breath. Dawn was treading lightly up and down in front of the tall east windows in the parlor, twisting her fingers together, a dull sickness spreading and swelling in her stomach. The room was in darkness except for one lamp that cast a small circle of light into the gauzy predawn shadows. She stopped pacing and stood staring toward the eastern hills beyond the valley that rimmed the banks of the Brazos River. "Oh, Darrell," she cried, her cheeks awash with tears. In the distance, like a flower opening its pedals, a sliver of pink tinged the gray horizon. "Oh, God!" she cried hysterically. "They're hanging Darrell at this very moment." She began to scream. She couldn't stop.

Debbie watched her helplessly. She understood that she needed to grieve, to get it out of her system, that there were no words or gestures to reach her pain.

When Dawn's tears had been exhausted, she sat with her face in her hands, trembling. Debbie sat beside her and took her into her arms, rocking her gently.

"I can't believe he's gone," she sobbed. "He was so full of life, always cheerful and humorous. But he had a serious side too. He loved me, Debbie. He loved me so much. I miss him. I will miss him as long as I live."

"I know how your heart is breaking. Darrell was a very special person. The entire town will miss him."

Debbie was trying to console Dawn when her own heart was aching with grief. She had cared for Darrell Holliman, had been held in his young strong arms, had been kissed by him. Even though he was only playing a game, she had been thrilled by his touch, moved deeply by his attention. Now he was gone. It was such a shock. It had all happened so suddenly. It wasn't fair. Darrell with his beautiful smile, his gentleness, and devil may care attitude and wit. If not for Richard, she might have cared deeply for Holliman. Of course he was in love with Dawn. She would never understand how Dawn could not love him. What more could a woman ask in a man? He was actually beautiful of countenance. He was a gentleman, and as she had recently learned, very well educated, being a graduate of West Point. And it was all wasted. It was strange that he had been content to work as a store clerk. He was a joy and a mystery. Suddenly her own tears were flowing.

"Where is my father? I need him," Dawn cried.

"He should be home soon," Debbie said. "He went to Fort Daily late last night so he could be with Darrell this morning."

"Why didn't he tell me he was going? I would have gone with him. Damn him!"

"You would have fallen apart. Darrell didn't need to witness that. Remember the way he looked the last time you saw him. It's easier that way."

"Father had no right to make that decision. I could have been with Darrell one last time. He would have wanted that. Now it's too late!" She lapsed into another fit of tears.

Dawn attacked Mac the moment he stepped inside the house.

"I wanted to go with you to see Darrell!" she wailed. "How could you do this to me? I'll never see him again."

Mac debated as to whether or not to tell her that Darrell was still alive. She had already suffered the shock of his death once. That he would die very soon was certain. What was the point of putting her through it a second time. His fate was irreversible. He tried to mentally block her cries of anguish.

"He needed me. I should have been there for him. It would have eased it for him."

Mac took her by the shoulders and shook her gently. "You have to understand that what I did was for the best."

"No! You had no right!"

"Oh, hell," he moaned. "He's still alive. The hanging was postponed because the Captain had an accident and wasn't able to witness the execution. But it's all the same. Can't you see that? It will happen tomorrow or the next day. There is absolutely no hope."

"You lied to me! There is still time. I'll go tomorrow. I don't care what you say. And don't you try to stop me!"

"Why can't you understand? He doesn't want you to see him behind bars. Think about his feelings. He wrote you a letter. Maybe you will listen to him."

Mac took the letter from his jacket pocket and held it out to her.

"Oh, Darrell!" She cried. "I don't want to lose you." She took the letter, her hands trembling, tears poured down her face. Clasping it to her heart, she ran from the room. Debbie looked at Mac, her eyes brimming. "She's suffering so. Maybe you shouldn't have given her the letter just yet."

"He asked me to, and I gave him my word. Maybe it will comfort her."

"It's a reminder that he's gone. What on earth could he say that would comfort her?"

"She's my daughter, but I do not understand her. She didn't grieve like this when Ned died."

"She didn't love Ned."

"She doesn't love Darrell either. He told me so himself. He knew she was in love with that Indian. He had known it from the start, and accepted it."

"Well, I haven't," Debbie said.

"It doesn't matter now. Light Eyes is all she has left."

Dawn took the folded sheet of paper from the envelope and unfolded it very carefully; she could hardly make out the words through the flood of tears.

"My Love,

I won't have to die of a broken heart after all. I have never been in love before, and having loved you, I could never love another. I wish you happiness with your Light Eyes; he must be someone very special. Don't be sad; don't grieve for me after I'm gone. It was just a matter of time from the start. God gave me the time to find you and love you. Thank you for liking me so much. In my heart I believe that you might have loved me just a little bit. It felt like it when I held you in my arms. You gave yourself to me, and I never expected that, nor did I deserve it. You made me happy. I will think about you until I cease to think. All my love—I love you!

Your faithful friend,

Chris Roman, known to you as, Darrell Holliman"

Dawn's wails of grief shattered the silence throughout the house. She was all alone. She would be alone the rest of her life without Darrell. She wanted to hold him in her arms and make everything all right again. She didn't want to live without him. She wanted to die too.

CHAPTER

Burman was infuriated by Henry McCloud's threat to expose him for accepting bribes. He knew of course that he was running a bluff. Burman had his movements documented in detail. He was a soldier and it was his duty to eliminate Indian aggression. McCloud had sought his help on numerous occasions, claiming the Indians had become hostile. He would not be intimidated by him. He would stand his ground. Henry McCloud did not give orders to the army. Burman would be glad when Henry was six feet under. New Mexico needed some breathing room.

Henry had returned to his ranch immediately following the delay of Darrell's execution. Rush had accepted his gift of a thousand dollars and took to his bed. The outcome of his injuries depended on Burman's actions. It was conceivable that Burman might send another officer to carry out the sentencing.

In the mean while Darrell's life rested in the hands of Henry McCloud and his power of persuasion. As he waited in his cell for the hangman, he knew nothing of what was going on around him. And his depression deepened with each passing hour.

He thought about the way Dawn had hung on to his hand and screamed as they put him on his horse and whisked him away, taking him to a cell and very shortly his death. He could still visualize tears streaming down her cheeks, her empty arms reaching out to him. He slumped on his cot and wept silently.

Brigadier General Burman, accompanied by a small detail of soldiers, arrived at the McCloud ranch two days after receiving the first wire from Captain Rush. The second wire came within hours of the first one. Rush was insulting his intelligence, and he wondered how much McCloud had paid Rush to fall off his horse. After he settled things with McCloud he planned to go to Fort Daily in person and see Lieutenant Colonel Chris Roman hanged. He would show McCloud who had the power. He held life and death in his two hands.

Burman was ushered into Henry's spacious bedroom by Princess Lake. She was introduced as his nurse, but Burman knew she was much more, in fact his bodyguard. She towered over the general, and he was reasonably tall. Her long, thick, arms hung at her sides, extending from shoulders that resembled those of an ape. Burman cringed reflexively when he looked up into her ugly face. The shades were drawn against the sun. The room was dim lit and stuffy. He glanced around; saw Henry lounging near the fireplace huddled in a blanket. He nodded his head and the nurse took her leave.

Burman drew a deep breath before addressing Henry. "Good afternoon, Henry." He moved toward him, bending slightly forward, gawking, deciding that Henry didn't look too healthy.

"I see that you got my message." Henry motioned to a chair in front of him. "Make yourself comfortable, if it's possible here under my roof."

"I am not your enemy, Henry."

"You'll have a hard time convincing me otherwise."

"Now, see here! I didn't come all this way to take your insults."

"How can the truth be an insult? I'm not one of your flunkies. You know what I want."

"I'm a bit confused, Henry."

"Don't play dumb with me, Stanley. You know all the facts. A friend of mine is behind bars at Fort Daily waiting to stretch a rope, and you're responsible."

"Chris Roman sealed his own fate."

"You sealed his fate when you had him court-martialled."

"He was guilty of insubordination, and that's a hanging offense."

"So is murder."

"We're at war, Henry. Have you ever stopped to consider how many dead Indians it cost for every acre of land you control? What right do you have to say a damned word about what happened at Sand Creek? Indians need killing. They get in the way of progress. You told me that once yourself, Henry."

"I'm not talking about dead Indians, Stanley. I'm talking about a young lieutenant. He's worth more than a dozen like you."

"I'll see to it that you eat those words, Henry."

"You don't fool me, you son of a bitch. Roman was on the rise. He has more common-sense and intelligence in his big toe than you have in your entire body. You're afraid of him, afraid he would root you out of your niche. Roman is an honest man and a gentleman, and you're a disgrace."

"You can have your say, Henry, but your opinion of me comes from a polluted mind. I'm not the one behind bars. That should prove to you who has the intelligence. Roman is where he belongs."

"It took one hell of a man to do what Roman did. It's men like him who should be giving the top orders and passing them along to stuff-shirts like you. You're a pissant, Stanley. When you arrested Roman, you arrested a United States Marshal. Even as a wanted man, he was on his way up. You're holding him down the only way possible. You conniving bastard!"

"He killed his commanding officer, and that makes him a traitor."

"Wheeler needed killing! He did the army a service."

"The order he gave Roman came directly from me. Roman refused to give that order, and I'll see him in Hell."

"You didn't have the right to arrest a U.S. Marshal. He's a peace officer, and you're a god damned chickenshit. You don't have enough sense to pour piss out of a boot. Roman has a conscience. Not all men do, and that includes me, but he doesn't deserve to die for disobeying one of your orders. You're not God! You're a puffed up idiot."

"I'm god where Roman is concerned. I still give the orders, McCloud. Roman is a dead man."

"I demand that Roman get a new trial. He attempted to save the lives of four hundred peaceable Indians, and that's no crime."

"My report states that they were hostile. I'm surprised by your sudden concern for Indians. I can recall, not too far in the past, when you encouraged the killing of 'Dirty Indians' because they got in your way. Now you suddenly expect an army officer to be exonerated for insubordination. He had his trial, and he was found guilty by his own confession. He might have been charged with murder if Captain Wheeler hadn't struck the first blow."

"Turn him loose, Stanley, and I'll make you a rich man."

"You won't win this tug of war, Henry. Roman will hang and there is absolutely nothing you can do to stop it."

"I can kill you!"

"I have thirteen armed men riding with me, McCloud. If you fire on me they have orders to kill you and anyone else who takes arms against us. What's it going to take to convince you?"

"You won't always be surrounded by your men."

"You're old, Henry, and you look sick. It's too bad that you're not well enough to watch Roman struggle, plead, and cry just before they put the black sack over his head."

"He'll face that hangman without so much as a whimper. He's a man, and you're jealous."

"I came here in good faith. Don't try to cause me any trouble because it will come back on you ten fold. Whatever happens can't possibly make any difference to you. You're dying, McCloud. You might as well climb down off your thrown, because you're ruling days are just about over."

"I'll still outlive you."

"Is that a threat, McCloud?"

"You can take it any way you like, but I swear to you, Chris Roman will not die in vain."

"Dead is dead. Vindication doesn't give back life."

"That's right, Burman, it only evens the score. That way, nobody wins."

Burman threw his hands up. "You're too accustomed to making demands and having people scramble to please you." Burman said stiffly. "You lose McCloud. I have you blocked, and I would imagine that you consider that a loss of face." He turned away from Henry and moved toward the door. Princess Lake showed him out, and he kept his eyes glued to the floor, he had no desire to look into her grim, ugly, face. Burman was escorted to the gate by thirteen of McCloud's men. By the time they were safely off his ranch he was wiping sweat from his brow. McCloud had him covered. He would be looking over his shoulder as long as Henry McCloud lived. He wished him a short and unhealthy life. His next stop was Fort Daily.

Henry had Princess bring him pen and paper. She waited while he scratched the message he wanted sent to Captain Rush. She gave Pine orders to have it sent immediately. McCloud did not expect an answer.

Rush scanned the message: "Burman headed your way to hang Roman. Darrell Holliman, worth ten thousand dollars, will never be free until Roman is dead and buried. Henry McCloud."

Rush read the message several times. He could make no sense of it. McCloud had made him a gift of a thousand dollars to delay the hanging, and now he wanted Roman dead and buried. If Burman was on his way to Fort Daily, he would absolutely carry out the punishment. So what was the point Henry was trying to make? He focused on the last sentence. It didn't make sense. Death set all men free. But Henry had said, "Dead and buried." The old man was talking in riddles. It was time he paid Lieutenant Roman a visit. Perhaps he might shed some light on it. He picked up the wire, folded it, and put it in his jacket pocket. Holding his back in frowning misery he walked across the parade ground toward the guard house. He had looked in on the lieutenant several times but they had not had any serious conversations. He had done so to show his respects. Though he outranked Roman he realized that he did not measure up to his intelligence. Roman was a West Point graduate, Rush had moved up through the ranks. He had Romans achievement file and it was outstanding. He certainly didn't deserve to be where he was. He considered General Burman a blind fool.

He ordered the guard to unlock Roman's cell. When the guard stood at attention beside the open door, Rush said, "At ease Sergeant. I take full responsibility. Wait outside."

Darrell's heart jumped like a frog inside his chest. He came to attention and saluted Rush. Rush returned his show of honor. "Relax," he said. "It's time we had a talk, off the record."

"I thought you might be here for another reason."

"Sorry, I didn't mean to alarm you."

"I'm getting used to the idea. I've even quit sleeping. It's such a waste of time."

"I hate the hell out of this, Roman. You don't belong in here. It's a miscarriage of justice. I wish I had the power to change it."

"Thank you, sir. I appreciate that."

"Are you all right? Is there anything I can do to help you through this?"

Roman smiled slightly. "I think I've painted myself into a corner."

"It would seem that way."

"I couldn't have done otherwise. I know I was right, and I was fully aware of the consequences. I don't intend to fret over it. How's your back, sir?"

"As you can see, I'm able to be up and around."

"I suppose my stay has come to an end."

"If I had my way, I would let you walk away from this. Carrying out the order for your execution is the last thing in the world I want to do. You're a fine officer and you had a brilliant future in the military. To have it end like this is an insult to the army. You had just cause to refuse that order. I feel that General Burman overstepped his authority and made a grave mistake. One that you attempted to correct. However, that star on his shoulder held more sway. He's as far up the ladder as he will ever climb and he knows it. You're young Roman, well educated and smart. He knew it was only a matter of time before you outranked him. It's a damned shame."

"When will my execution be carried out?"

"Burman is on his way here from New Mexico. He intends to carry out the order in person."

"He'll enjoy it."

"I think he will live to regret it. I received a wire from Henry McCloud today. It's confusing. Sounds like he's flipped his lid. I thought you might be able to help me decipher it." He took the wire from his pocket, unfolded it and read it. He saw a flash of understanding in Roman's eyes. "Can you make any sense of this?"

"It's self explanatory. He wants me dead and buried, and Burman will have the honor of springing the trap door."

"Yeah, that much I understand. It's the part about Marshal Darrell Holliman that's confusing."

"Holliman is worth ten thousand dollars to someone, after Roman is dead and buried. He's making you an offer."

"To do what?"

"Keep Darrell Holliman alive."

"Since you and Holliman are one and the same, how is that possible? Burman won't miss."

"Henry McCloud is grasping at straws. I'm surprised he hasn't given up on me. There are some things his money can't buy, but he doesn't understand that yet."

"Burman called his bluff."

"What has Henry done?"

"He threatened to report Burman for accepting his bribes. In the past McCloud called in the army to move the Indians out of his way so he could expand his cattle ranch. I didn't think Burman would knuckle under. He knows McCloud can't prove it."

"How do you happen to know about the bribes?"

"Henry McCloud told me when he came here to see me. He wants to have your execution stopped. He figured he could force Burman to his knees and change things for you. But he needed time. He gave me a thousand dollar gift to delay the hanging until he had time to work on Burman."

"He's fighting a losing battle, and you're treading on thin ice. You could end up in the cell next to me. Burman will stop at nothing. He's a crazed man. Out of control."

"Exactly! Henry McCloud has threatened to kill him."

"That won't help me. I've had my day in court."

"Yeah, and Burman is sticking to his guns. He has lost his fear of Henry McCloud. He's drunk on ambition. An appeal would be useless because you admitted your guilt. What exactly do you make of McCloud's wire?"

"Evidently he thinks I'm kill proof. You die when you're hanged."

"I wonder if there's a way to rig a hangman's knot so that it fails to break a man's neck?"

"That's impossible."

"Maybe not. I witnessed a hanging once where the guy's neck didn't snap. He hung there until he choked to death. It was sort of like double jeopardy. If a man can live through his execution, I think he should go free."

"The man didn't live through his execution. He just died the hard way." Darrell felt a chill crawl up his spine.

"If the man had been taken down immediately, he might have survived."

"Yeah, with his head laying on his own shoulder."

"What have you got to lose?"

"Are you suggesting what I think you are?"

"If I can get the hangman to rig the knot so it doesn't tighten, and you're cut down before you choke—"

Darrell laughed. "Forget it!"

"I could use ten thousand dollars, and you could use a break."

"I'm a cinch for the break. That would be quite a trick, especially in front of witnesses. What you're suggesting is utterly ridiculous. Burman will make damned sure I've stopped breathing before he nails the lid down."

"You don't deserve to die, Roman. It's Burman who should dance at the end of a rope. And I don't mind taking a bribe, if you benefit from it."

"I don't think you realize what you're saying. Even if what you suggest were possible, you would be risking your life. I can't allow you to take the chance."

"What's wrong with you? Do you relish the thought of dying?"

"I'm not going to live happily ever after even if by some miracle I might survive. My love life is on the rocks."

"The world is full of women."

"You saw McCloud's granddaughter. The world has only one like her."

"So what's the problem? Judging from the fits she was throwing, I don't think you have anything to worry about."

"The next full moon seals my fate."

Rush's head jerked up in surprise, and he wondered if Roman was flipping out. "What's the moon have to do with this?"

"That's when I turn into a werewolf."

"I've been told that you have a rare sense of humor. But how can you joke at a time like this?"

"Forget the whole thing. It won't work. I don't know how to stop breathing and stay alive."

"You breathe real shallow."

"You can't breathe at all with a rope around your neck. I think you're actually serious about this."

"I am."

"You really surprise me. I can't believe that you're willing to risk your neck for ten thousand dollars."

"It's more than just the money. Burman's mistake needs to be corrected. If you hang, he's wasting a good man."

"And I've wasted four years of my life at West Point. I've gone from a career in the military to a jail cell, now that's quite a leap backwards. What's your real reason for trying to help me?"

"Satisfaction. I hate Burman's guts. He's a pious bastard, and he's enjoying this."

"Do you have any idea what happens to a man's body when he's hanged?"

"You're the man with the West Point education. You tell me."

"The hangman's knot is placed behind the ear or under the chin. When the trap door opens he drops six or eight feet before the knot tightens. The head is snapped to one side and the spinal column is either fractured or dislocated. The rupture of the spinal column breaks the spinal cord and causes instant death. If by some freak of nature that doesn't occur, the man on the end of the rope dies from suffocation or the lack of blood supply to the brain. Not a pleasant thought. I prefer the quick version."

Rush looked a bit green. "I don't blame you."

"If we actually tried a stunt like that, what did you have in mind to bury? A man can't die without leaving leftovers."

"We have a body."

"Does it look like me?"

"It doesn't have to."

"Burman might decide to hold a wake with beer and peanuts just to celebrate."

"Once you drop through that trap door he'll nod and walk away. That's what he does every time."

"When do you expect Burman to arrive?"

"If he takes the train, by tomorrow."

"How long have you had the body?"

"Two days. We notified his brother and he said we should bury him. So he's all ours."

"And by the time Burman gets here he'll be stinking to high-heaven. You can't hold him above ground that long. I would imagine that he's already pretty ripe."

"We got him packed in salt."

"Who was it?"

"Lynch Young."

Darrell looked thunderstruck. "Now that's poetic justice. He thought he would get a promotion out of this and all he got was salted down and a pine box. What killed him? Did he choke to death on that gag?"

"He was drunk, got into a poker game, and he was a poor loser. He pulled a knife on the man with the ace up his sleeve, and the man shot him. It was self-defense."

"So he took a knife to a gun fight. Too bad it didn't happen sooner."

"Yeah, that's for sure. Every man on the post hates General Burman's guts."

"That doesn't help me."

"It might. Are you game to try this? Your life depends on it."

"You're putting your neck on the chopping block. Burman must realize how unpopular he is. He most likely knows about the hanging incident where the guy's neck didn't snap. He'll make sure that my body takes that quarter turn to the right."

"Well, mistakes happen. How can he prove it wasn't just another accident, if he happens to figures it out?"

"Another accident will cause him to be suspicious."

"I ate dirt, Roman. I have a dozen witnesses. I still hurt like hell. That fall I took turned out to be more truth than fiction."

"I didn't swallow the story about you being thrown by your own horse. I'm surprised Burman isn't already suspicious."

"Suspicions are one thing, proof is quite another."

"Yeah, you're right. Burman's in the gray area."

"Gray area?"

"Confusion. What do you want me to do?"

"Practice holding your breath and looking dead."

"Dead people turn blue. How will I manage that?"

"If you hold your breath long enough, you'll turn blue."

Rush was trying to make light of the dangers involved, but Roman realized that the chances of them pulling it off were mighty slim. Too many things could go wrong. Number one, the hanging knot. To get past a broken neck would be a miracle, and then he could hang there with his tongue lolled out until he choked to death. Now that was something to look forward to. He was beginning to think that it might be less painful to do it the conventional way.

The full moon would end all hope of his ever having Dawn. She would be with the man she loved soon, so what difference did it make if he lived or died. His future was at a dead end anyway, rope or not.

Rush cut through his painful thoughts. "I'm going to have a chat with the hangman and see what he comes up with."

"You had better go easy on that. He may be a dedicated friend of General Burman's."

"I know the man personally. I can tell you that he would get pleasure from black-sacking the general."

"Move slow."

"We don't have time to move slow."

"If you can pull this off it will be one hell of an accomplishment, like a little boy who just learned how to stand up and pee."

"You really amaze me, Roman. Most men in your shoes weep and moan. What is it that makes you so different?"

"I cried over spilled milk once and my mother rubbed my nose in it."

Rush looked at him and shook his head. "I'll be back in the morning. Maybe I'll have some good news. It's been a pleasure talking to you. I'll get the guard to lock your door. And it's nothing personal."

"You wouldn't happen to have a shot of whiskey laying around, would you?"

"I'll see to it." He walked away thinking, he's feeling it.

CHAPTER

53

Dawn had taken to her room much the same as she had at the Rowling Ranch after seeing Light Eyes again. She refused to open her door even when baby Henry cried for her. She lay on the bed clutching Darrell's letter to her breast as tears rolled down her cheeks onto her damp pillow. She had been taking him for granted, been mean to him, and she had refused to tell him that she loved him. Oh, why hadn't she told him? She was consumed with a powerful longing for him, to have him hold her and make her feel safe. She realized now that he had made her feel loved. He had been so gentle and caring, his every move as smooth as silk, and it wasn't pretense; she knew the difference. His love and concern came from his heart.

Debbie came to her door at intervals pleading to be let in, but she responded with, "Go away. Leave me alone." There was only one person who could comfort her, and he was about to lose his life.

"I'm sorry Richard," Debbie said regrettably. "She refuses to let me in. I can hear her sobbing."

Mac was pacing around in circles. He felt so helpless. He was worried about Dawn for many reasons. "If Light Eyes plans to come for her during the full moon, then she had better prepare herself for his visit. I don't know how to handle this. Will he come to the door like a gentleman and knock? Or will he come only part way and expect her to meet him? I know she's grieving, we all are, but she damned well needs to come down here and take care of her own business."

"She is in no shape to think straight. I think you should just tell the Indian that she's ill and he should come back later. She is ill, Richard."

"I'm going up there. She will either talk to me or I'll break her door in."

"Richard, please! You must not add to her grief."

"It won't be easy, but I'll control myself. I promise."

She looked after him with a worried frown as he slowly climbed the stairs, his hand sliding along the polished banister.

When he reached Dawn's room he tapped lightly. "We have to talk about this. You're not being fair, hiding and worrying Debbie and me. You have to face the situation. There is no other way. Now, open the door. Don't close us out of your life. You need us. We love you."

She rolled over in bed, still clutching Darrell's letter and got shakily to her feet. She wiped at her wet, tear stained, face with the back of her hand. She unlocked the door and opened it a crack. Then she threw it wide and rushed into Mac's arms. "Oh, Father! I don't want him to die! Please, do something before it's too late. Don't let them do this to him. Please!"

"Oh, God," he moaned. "There is no power on earth that can stop the hanging. I would give my own life in exchange for his if it were possible. It's killing me too!"

"There has to be a way! This can't be happening. Not to Darrell."

"Come downstairs. We have to talk." He put his arm around her shoulders and led her carefully down the stairs. He could feel her trembling. "You have to eat something. You've been up there all day. You're making yourself sick."

"I can't eat."

Mac saw how she was clutching the letter to her breast as if it were the shield of life, and he wondered what Darrell had said. She seemed more grieved than ever. He wanted to ask, but he dared not risk her erupting into another flood of hysterics.

He led her to the couch and sat down beside her. He put his hand beneath her chin and turned her face so he could look into her eyes. "You have to decide what to do about Light Eyes. If he promised to come for you during the full moon, then he will be here soon. Within a day or so. Perhaps even tonight. Have you made any plans?"

"When he made the decision, Darrell was safe. Everything is different now. He had not been arrested, and I didn't know he was wanted by the army. He told me about it on the train while we were on our way to New Mexico. Grandfather wanted him to stay there, because he would be safe as long as he was on McCloud land. Darrell had promised to take care of me, and he kept that promise. He would have even killed Captain Rush if he had denied him his freedom long enough to see me safely back home. I feel so guilty. If I had listened to you and stayed at home, Darrell wouldn't be about to die. I want to do something to save him, but I don't know how, and nobody will help me!"

"Your grandfather tried. He talked Captain Rush into delaying the hanging to give him time to bribe General Burman. It didn't work. If anyone could save him, it would be Henry McCloud. There is simply nothing else to be done. Burman is on his way to Fort Daily to carry out the execution himself. He's determined to kill Darrell. Actually, he's Chris Roman, but I can't get used to the idea."

Dawn was silently looking off into space, not actually focusing on anything. Without looking up, she said. "It's over. He's gone." She glanced down at the letter. "All I have left of him is this. I wonder, Father, what will he be thinking about when they put that rope around his neck? Will he think about me? Oh, God! Will he know that I love him? That I will always love him? If I had gone with you today, I could have told him. Now he will never know. That's all he ever wanted was to hear me say those three words, and I never did."

Debbie had been listening, and what Dawn said shocked her. She rose from her chair and moved to kneel in front of Dawn. She took her hands into both of hers. "Why, Dawn? Why didn't you tell him?"

She looked at her, blinking back tears. "I just couldn't, because I had promised myself to Light Eyes."

"But you just admitted that you love Darrell. Do you still love the Indian as well?"

"I do, but there is something missing. I had never been with anyone before he took me to his lodge. I would never have let Ned touch me after that, but I thought Light Eyes was dead. I tried to be a wife to Ned, but I hated it when he put his hands on me. Can you understand how I felt?"

"The Indian was unfair to you. He should have let you know he was alive. He allowed you to grieve over him needlessly."

"I don't think I would have ever seen him again if he hadn't chased Frost all the way to the Rowling Ranch. I told him I was married, but I couldn't explain because we were being watched. Ned was in the barn with Frost's horse. I think he would have shot Light Eyes again if I hadn't been standing there. Light Eyes was hurt because I had given myself to another man. He didn't mention anything about us being together after I told him about Ned. He just rode away. The next time I saw him he was lying in Doctor Keel's office, fighting for his life."

"In the meantime I met Darrell Holliman. I liked him at once. He was exciting and different, and most certainly a gentleman. He made me happy. I was able to endure Ned and my grief over losing Light Eyes because I had a friend. He is the best friend I have ever had, except for you, Debbie."

"I will never forget the first time I met him. He was wearing an apron and standing behind the counter at the trading post. When he smiled at me, I felt like melting. He always affected me that way. I think he could read my mind. He knew I wanted him to hold me in his arms and kiss me. And one day he did." She looked at Mac and flushed. "It happened the day you caught us alone together inside the store with the door locked."

"You didn't fool me. I could read you like two books. What went through my mind at the moment was: why couldn't she have met Darrell before she married Ned. If I could pick a son, he would be like Chris Roman. He was looking for a job and I was overjoyed to hire him. It's incredible. I had a man from West Point dusting my shelves. It was a terrible waste of his mental capacities and ability. But he didn't mind. He found what he wanted right here, and that's why he stayed. I told him today that I thought he made one hell of a good lawman."

Dawn put her face in her hands and began to sob again.

"You didn't tell him in words that you loved him." Mac said, "but you proved it in other ways."

"I did tell him once, and he kept it a secret for a while because I didn't realize I had said it. I told him I was sorry that I kept leading him on and that I didn't want to hurt him, but that one day I would have to break his heart."

"How could you do that?" Debbie said disapprovingly. "How could you hurt him like that?"

"Because I didn't want to give him the wrong impression. He knew about Light Eyes, not his name or that he was an Indian, but he knew there was another man that I loved very much."

"Why did you tell him you loved him if you didn't mean it?" Mac asked.

"It just happened once when we were—" She broke off, her face flaming.

"I know about your relationship. Darrell told me today."

"He told you?"

"It was more like I trapped him into a confession. I was telling him about your mother, that she was absolutely perfect in face and body. And he said, 'Just like Dawn.' I said to him, there is only one way you could know that. He didn't deny it. He's a truthful man. He wanted me to know that he never forced you, that you were a willing partner. I appreciated his honesty."

"You were in love with him, Dawn, or you would never have done that," Debbie said.

"He always left it up to me. I wanted him to make love to me. I would ask him to. It always made him happy."

Mac looked away from her beautiful face for a moment. He was recalling that Elizabeth used to ask him the same thing.

"You still haven't answered my question. What do you intend doing about the Indian when he comes here?"

"Don't you mean, if he comes here?"

"I thought he promised to come to you during the full moon." Debbie said. "Did I misunderstand?"

"No, but he treated me like a slut at first because I married Ned when I was already his wife. He told me to go away, that he didn't want me now."

Debbie became angry. "He had no right to say that, not when it was his fault. What did he expect you to do? The baby needed a father, a name. What kind of man is he?"

"I didn't tell him about his son."

"Why not? It would have explained everything."

"I don't want him that way. I waited for him four months.

I would never have seen him again if he hadn't tracked Frost to the Rowling's ranch. If he was well enough to chase Frost, he was well enough to come to me."

"What was his excuse?"

"He didn't have one. He said he was too weak. Well, he didn't look nor act weak. I think he got himself a fat squaw, and just forgot about me."

"A man can be weak in more ways than one, Dawn," Mac said. "You really don't know how badly he was injured. The man was shot in the back. Every nerve in our body passes through our spine. He could have some serious nerve damage."

"Are you looking to find excuses for him?"

"It's rare to find a Comanche who lies, especially one as honorable as Light Eyes. I think you should give him the benefit of the doubt. Tell him about his son, and then see what his attitude is. I can send him away, or I can make excuses if you're not up to dealing with him right now. You're not emotionally ready to take him on. I think you realize that. I will simply tell him that you're sick. And it's the truth. You don't have to go with him until you're ready."

"I'm too confused to sort it all out. I'm going to spend some time with my son. I haven't seen him all day."

"Laughing Eyes is tending him in the nursery."

Dawn held the letter to her lips for a moment, and then slid it into her pocket.

CHAPTER

54

Captain Rush was noticeably excited when he entered Roman's cell later that night. "I've talked to Cecil Putnam, the man with the rope, and he has devised a plan to hang you without breaking your neck."

"That's very amusing," Chris said.

"I'm absolutely serious," he said bluntly. "I can arrange it. Cecil's ready to do it. It's up to you."

"What are the pit-falls?"

"Burman's becoming wise."

"That's it? Is Cecil really all that confident?"

"Nothing is perfect. There is always the possibility that something might go wrong, but it's your only hope to walk away from this. Now, let me explain. What he can do is install a flexible cord inside the knot. When the trap door opens and you drop those eight feet, the shorter stretchy cord extends first before the rope tightens, and it will break your fall. In other words, the knot will not have time to snap. You will actually be hanging from the cord inside the hangman's knot that's attached to the rope. The cord will not be visible. Your head will be to one side, naturally. But you will not get the snap that breaks the spiral cord."

"So I hang there and choke."

"I'll have you cut down immediately. But you have to pretend to be dead. Don't struggle to breathe, because you won't be able to. You will have a tendency to fight the rope. If that should happen, it's all over, and we lose. So save your energy. Dead men don't move. You will need to take that quarter turn to the right that's customary when the neck is broken."

"That should give me one hell of a crick in the neck."

"That's certain."

"Maybe we should try it out first, in case it doesn't work."

"Always the joker."

"Now, let me get this straight in my mind. I will actually be hanged by a flexible cord inside the knot. When I drop, the cord will stop my fall before the knot tightens and snaps my spinal cord."

"That's right. The fall is what does the damage. If we eliminate the sudden stop, then all we have to worry about is getting you down before you choke to death."

"A small matter," Darrell said. "Then what happens?"

"You hang there and play dead until we cut you down. You will need to fill your lungs just before the trap door springs because you won't be able to breathe for a while."

"Cecil will tie your hands behind your back with a rotten rope. It will break with a minimum of pressure. If need be, you can free your hands. But I don't recommend it. If something goes wrong and we can't cut you down before you choke to death, you will be able to reach up, grasp the rope and get enough leverage to allow you some breathing room until the rope is removed. Actually it will be the cord that cuts off your air. The rope won't have tightened, and the knot will just be for effect. If that should happen, you'll still hang, but it will be the usual way. Because you're tall, you will be closer to the ground. If we could get something under your feet, it would give you some slack. I can't predict where Burman will be during your execution. He may watch from the platform, or he may stand or sit in front of the gallows. He's going to be our biggest problem. He will be watching for your body to take that quarter turn to the right. That proves the neck has been broken. You need to keep that in mind and propel yourself in that direction. I realize that's a hell of a thing to expect a dying man to perform. You may not remember, or you may lose your sense of direction while you're choking."

"It sounds to me like there are a lot of unexpected surprises in your little bag of tricks. I might be letting myself in for a mighty painful death.

JACKIE BARNES

I don't have much faith in my hanging there nonchalantly biding my time while I choke to death. And you might follow on my heels if this plan goes sour."

"You can always reconsider. Do you have a gut feeling about this?"

"I feel like I'm at the end of my rope. It's a funny thing; I've heard that expression many times as a response to a bad situation." He smiled. "It has merit."

"To minimize the damage to your neck, you're a cinch to get; I'll sew some padding inside your collar. When Cecil puts the sack over your head, he will flip it up. It's not to eliminate the rope burn, but to keep the cord from cutting so deep into your neck when you suddenly stop short. And who knows, it might even lessen the severity of the whip lash."

"Is there a possibility that I might get my throat cut?"

"God, I hope not! I hadn't thought of that."

"Don't worry about it. I won't complain. Like you said, nothing is perfect." And then he thought about Dawn.

"Now for the bad news. Burman will be here in the morning. Have faith, Roman. I still believe in miracles, and I think we have a fair chance of pulling this off."

"If we don't, I want you to know that I won't have any hard feelings."

Rush laughed. "You are really something. I'll miss having you around. I'll see you later. It's about eight hours to daybreak. What would you like to eat?"

"My insides feel a bit sensitive. I'll just have to die on an empty stomach."

"Could you drink some coffee?"

"I could use a bottle."

"I would gladly accommodate you, but you have to be stone sober to pull this trick off. After it's over, I'll get drunk with you."

"I'll hold you to that, if I'm still able to swallow."

"I suspect Burman will go by the book, so I'll say my good-byes now. I expect to see you after the hanging, alive." The two men shook hands. Rush started to leave, and then suddenly embraced Chris. "Good luck, Lieutenant."

"Thank you, sir."

Darrell didn't know exactly what he had wanted from life when he set out in search of his destiny. Certainly nothing grand. He had never desired wealth or power, but he had hoped to live to old age, to have children and grandchildren. And here he was without even the love of a woman. His short life was moving very swiftly toward its end. So much for twenty-three wasted years. He felt a grain of hope, and yet there was no hope. He had already lost the only thing in life he valued. He closed his eyes, and in his mind, conjured up Dawn's beautiful face, dark eyes bright and moist with desire, soft full lips parted slightly, eager to be kissed. His emotions were running high. Soon the shades of life would be drawn, and he would slide into that orbit of eternal darkness. He wanted his thoughts sealed inside his vision, to be unaware of the rope as it was dropped over his head and the knot placed behind his ear. The last thing he wanted to remember was the face of the woman he loved.

Darrell had no need of sleep. He would be put to sleep in a few short hours. A sleep without dreams. A sleep he would not awaken from. He stood before the bared window looking up at the big yellow full moon. It was ironic the way things had worked out. His life was to end on the full moon, the same moon that would mark the beginning of Dawn's life with the Indian.

Henry McCloud had one of his men stationed in Daily awaiting the outcome of Roman's fate. Henry was as good as his word. He had tried to reason with Burman, offering him money to reconsider Roman's fate, and he had all but laughed in his face. Burman would regret his decision. Henry didn't bluff. If Roman hanged, Burman would die. He would learn the hard way that Henry's power still outranked the General's.

Burman had never applied military discipline where his own actions were concerned. He was a man who sought to create his own book of rules if the customary ones failed to give him the desired results.

He was cold and unreasonable, instilling permanent terror in the minds of the young recruits. He was edging his way toward the commanding field of military tactics by attempting to remove his stumbling blocks. He had the incentive, however he lacked the education, and his deficiencies were becoming more and more apparent when compared to the keen mental capabilities of younger officers, namely Lieutenant Colonel Chris Roman.

Lieutenant Roman was loose and cool. He was not reaching for high places. He just automatically flowed effortlessly in that direction. Roman was both easy to look at and easy to like. Burman resented the smooth magnetism he projected; yet Roman seemed unaffected by his popularity. He was self-sustained, depending on no one, whereas Burman was a boot licker and rear kisser when it came to his superiors to make compensation for his lack of intelligence. He was scraping his way up the ladder. Taking Roman down, in his mind, proved him to be the superior.

He figured his performance in the matter would add another letter of recognition to his military accomplishment file, which was less than unimpressive.

CHAPTER

55

Brigadier General Stanley Burman was in full dress uniform to witness the execution. His boots were spit shined to perfection, the toes reflecting the light. He had attended to even the minutest details. The star on his shoulder was gleaming, as well as his medals that were insignificant and few. He was clearly flaunting his victory and superior position of control.

Rush saluted him in military fashion, his jaw flexing in displeasure. Burman glanced around him briefly, noting the room was in perfect order and spotlessly clean. He took the chair behind the desk. Rush remained standing.

"Are you fully prepared to carry out Lieutenant Roman's execution?"

"Yes, sir, everything is in order. We have arranged for his im-mediate burial."

Burman came to his feet. "I have not ordered an immediate burial. I have decided to make an example of Roman. I want his body left hanging for three days to be viewed by the recruits. I want them to see first hand the penalty for mutiny."

Rush was outraged. He glared speechlessly at Burman for a moment while marshaling his objections. He had not been prepared for this. "In all due respect, sir, might I remind you that Lieutenant Colonel Roman is an officer, and as such, deserves due respect."

"He is no longer an officer, but a traitor."

"It's true that he's guilty of insubordination, but his failure to carry out that order did no harm as far as loss of life, injury, or inflicting hardship. He was sentenced to hang, which is the maximum penalty. To punish his corpse would seem barbaric and opposed to human decency. You would be, in fact, punishing the recruits for something they took no part in."

"Roman deserves to be exploited!"

"And he will be, the moment the trap door swings open. It should end then and there."

"Then you refuse?"

"I disagree. Your suggestion is without merit. I am in full charge of the recruits on this post. I was appointed to this position by Lieutenant General Dean Mason, and as such, I will decide what is best for my men. I will never agree to force them to look at Roman's body until it rots. If you wish to take over here, then you will have to clear your request through Lieutenant General Mason, sir!"

Burman had no desire to buck Mason. Mason had him outranked by two stars. "Roman deserves to be dishonored," he chanted.

"Hanging, sir, is looked upon as the highest form of dishonor a man can suffer. I'm afraid you have me a bit confused. This is an execution, not a dishonor celebration."

"And I am the one who brought the charges. Roman is a disgrace to the army."

"There are those who disagree with the court's ruling. To some Lieutenant Roman is a hero. I personally think that Roman is considered a hero in the minds of many. I suggest we get this done quickly and be done with it. To prolong this, to leave his body on exposition may very easily work in reverse as to your intentions. To have Chris Roman remembered as a martyr is not complimentary to your image or that of the army. Let it be done with and forgotten."

"Yes, of course, you're right. That had slipped my mind. There are always those ignorant individuals who will disagree with capitol punishment. There are even those who are against ending Indian aggression by elimination. The only thing that will change their minds is to get scalped. I think that would be a most deserved cure."

"It's time to get Roman ready for his execution. Do you want to see him before he's taken from his cell?"

"I do not wish to be insulted. He has a glib tongue and he will attempt to use it on me. When he's ready to climb the steps, I'll put in an appearance. I want to see Roman fight the inevitable. He cried at Sand Creek, and now he can cry over his own death. It's a pity you have to cover his face with a hood. I would like to see his expression of anticipation seconds before his spinal cord is snapped."

Rush felt his stomach roll over. Burman was a craven, blood-thirsty, monster. Rush had to bite his tongue to stop the murderous words that were ready to explode from his lips. They were hanging the wrong man. More than ever he wanted Chris to survive. If there was any justice, God would not look the other way, but answer his prayer and spare the young Lieutenant.

Burman was actually smiling. He had Roman where he wanted him, at his mercy. He was anxious to witness the extermination of his rival. Very shortly, he would celebrate his long awaited victory.

"It's time to go Lieutenant Roman," Rush said in a desperate tone. "Everything is in order."

Roman came to his feet and saluted, Rush. "Thank you, sir. I'm ready." A slight smile touched his lips, and then his expression became set.

"Are you all right?"

"On the surface. Actually, sir, this is beginning to wear me down."

"You can't give up now. You have to hang in there and hope."

"I keep thinking about hanging there choking, and I don't have much hope."

"I'm not going to let you smother. If you're still alive on the end of that rope, I damned sure won't let you die. That's a promise. How long can you hold out?"

"As long as I have to. Until I die. It has to happen one way or the other. There's no escape if you can't get to me in time. I won't fight a losing battle."

When the guard appeared with the leg irons, Rush waved him away. "I won't allow this man to be shackled."

"Sir! Army regulation—"

"Damn the regulation," Rush stormed! "I won't allow it," he said flatly. "You trust an officer, you don't shackle him. For God's sake, hanging is more than enough punishment."

JACKIE BARNES

"I don't mind, sir," Roman said. "It's a small matter."

"I take full responsibility for this, Lieutenant." His voice was calmer now.

"I suppose General Burman will have the pleasure of springing the trap door."

"He would enjoy it, but it's against army regulations."

"Burman has his own twisted interpretation of army regulations. He seems to do just about anything he desires."

"Not on my post. He found that out today."

"Burman is absolutely unbending, ungiving, and unreasonable. If I had more time I would like to hear about this."

"I'll tell you later, after we get this damned hanging behind us."

"You sound confident about this, and it hasn't even been tested."

"We're going to test it in about ten minutes."

Chris felt the bottom fall out of his stomach. Ten minutes had never been important to him before.

"I'm going to walk you up the steps to the platform. I'll stay with you as long as I can."

"Thank you, sir. I can use the moral support."

They were making their way slowly across the parade ground; the gallows loomed up before them. Chris closed his eyes for a second, faltered for a heartbeat. Rush took his arm to steady him, felt tremors surging through him like quakes.

Burman waited until Roman was on the platform before he stepped onto the parade ground. The troops were in drill formation facing the gallows. All heads turned in the direction of the general. They snapped to attention and saluted him. The General gave them a limp salute in return without missing a step.

Burman was not satisfied to witness the execution from the position of the troops; he wanted direct involvement and moved up the steps to the platform. Rush saluted Burman, and the general flipped his hand at him, and then turned his attention to Roman. He stood directly in front of him, was forced to look up to meet his eyes. Roman stood tall and proud, reflecting his military training. General Burman slouched loosely, not quite reaching Roman's shoulders. Burman walked completely around Roman, saw his hands were bound behind him, his legs free.

"Why isn't this man shackled?" He blasted.

Rush stepped up to him. "It was my decision. If he tries to escape, I'll shoot him."

"If he tries to escape, I'll shoot both of you."

For a moment Burman's eyes locked with Roman's. He had expected to see panic in his expression, craved to hear him plead and cry. The two blue eyes that stared back at him sparked with fire. He could almost feel the heat of his antagonism. This man he could not break. There was no fear in him.

"Get on with it," Burman ordered. "Read the charges."

Roman closed his mind to what Rush was saying. He thought about Dawn, wanting to hold on to his mental image of her and blot everything else out of his mind. He thought about the way she had crawled into his lap on the train, curling up close to him, her soft hands caressing his face, lips soft and sweet pressing his. He wanted to see her again, hold her in his arms. God, how it hurt! He became aware of Rush standing in front of him. He saw the pain in his eyes, and the realization shot through him. He doesn't think it will work either. He felt an instant of emotional shock. Rush knew it was hopeless and was trying to comfort him with false hope. He wanted to throw up as bile rushed up bitter and hot into his throat. He swallowed hard.

"Do you have anything you would like to say before we carry out the sentence?" Rush asked.

Roman looked at the men standing at attention, their faces grim. He saw fear on some of their faces. He felt steadier now, his trembling guts had settled down. Death is beautiful, he told himself. Only the dying is ugly. It would all be over soon.

Shockingly, Roman smiled down at the recruits and said in a firm voice, "Don't let the reason for my execution poison your minds or turn your hearts to stone. Don't allow any man to sway your opinions concerning what you know to be right or wrong. Not all orders given by superior officers are for the benefit of humanity. General Burman was acting in the capacity of God when he decided the fate of the four hundred peaceable Indians at Sand Creek. He ordered their slaughter simply because he considered them in the way. They had far more right to the land than the greedy squatters who forced their way forward leaving a trail of death and blood behind them. They were stealing land that had belonged to the Indians for thousands of years."

"Shut him up!" Burman shouted. "Hang the sonofabitch and get this over with. I don't intend to listen to his goddamned sermon!"

Rush would stick to army regulations. He felt a great deal of satisfaction watching Burman sweat, his face red with anger, raving. He was out of control. "I'm sorry, sir. Lieutenant Roman has been condemned to death, and he has the right to speak out before he dies. It's regulations."

"Then he had better watch his accusations!"

Roman turned slightly to look at Burman, and continued to speak loud and clear. "If you disagree with what I am saying, if my actions go against your own warped book of rules, then tell me, what more can you do to me? I'm dying for what I believe in. That God put the Indians on this earth, and on this land. Further, he provided for them with wild game for food and skins for clothing, and with which to build their lodges. This is their land. They were here first. I believe the world is big enough to support all of mankind. The problem being, some men want more than their share. Greed is the culprit, and killing is not the answer. There is black and white, good and evil, truth and lies, right and wrong. And in the middle of these choices we find the gray area. Some of you will wonder, what is the gray area? It's confusion. So why are we confused? Do we not know the difference between right and wrong? God gave us minds to think and reason with. It's confusion that breeds mistakes. Know which way to jump. Know and do what your common-sense and conscience dictates, and you will seldom go wrong. I refused to be responsible for the deaths of four hundred human beings that were of no threat to anyone. Another officer gave that order and the Indians were slaughtered. Women and children butchered, infants with their heads bashed in, women raped, and the chief mutilated and scalped. His hair hung from the flag pole, flying in the wind beside the American flag, the symbol of Burman's shameful victory over the helpless."

"He's preached enough. Shut him up if you have to gag him!" Burman was screaming.

Rush ignored the General and Roman continued.

"I tried to prevent this miscarriage of justice, and I am to die for it while Burman dreams of a promotion. Another star to keep company with the one he wears so proudly on his stooped shoulders, making him a god with the power to choose life or death for whomever he desires. You have all heard that I killed Captain Wheeler. Wheeler became angry when I refused to take his order to murder the peaceable Indians. We were not at war with the Sand Creek tribe. There was no aggression whatsoever. Wheeler blew up and struck me. We fought. I was restrained and arrested for insubordination. Wheeler died later from the injuries I inflicted upon his body. I was not charged with the death of Captain Wheeler. General Burman can take the credit for Wheeler's death. The order Wheeler was carrying out came directly from Burman. I will be executed here today in the presence of Brigadier General Burman while he looks on with stars in his eyes. If justice had been served, Burman would be standing here instead of me. I refused to take an order. Burman took four hundred lives. Black or white? Right or wrong? You be the judge. Don't be caught in the gray area. Don't be confused. Since you are here to witness my execution, I want you to understand what I'm dying for. And may God have mercy on Burman's soul!"

Roman looked around. Burman had vacated the platform and was standing below him, glaring up at him with a killing expression.

Rush was looking at him with pride. "Well done," he said.

"Thank you, sir. I'm ready."

"Step forward, Lieutenant."

Roman moved to stand over the trap door. The hood was lowered over his head and he felt Cecil's fingers on the back of his neck lifting his padded collar. A shudder racked his insides as the rope was slipped over his head and dropped around his neck. The hangman's knot was adjusted slightly and placed behind his left ear. He experienced one instant of panic, and then he settled down. He took a deep breath, filling his lungs. Then came the swish of the trap door as it swung open.

CHAPTER

56

Darrell felt the floor drop from beneath his feet and he plunged down into an abyss of darkness followed by an abrupt jolt as the cord sliced through the padded collar and cut into his neck. He had propelled himself slightly as he fell and his body made the one-quarter turn to the right ever so slowly. He had remembered everything in that fraction of a second. He had experienced a thin thread of hope when he felt Cecil turn up his collar, realizing that the hangman was attempting to save his life. He felt the pull of the cord as it tightened around his neck holding him is suspension. He knew the oxygen he had inhaled before he dropped through the floor would be depleted in a matter of seconds. His neck was throbbing agony; his lungs were struggling to hold the air, to exhale slowly. How swiftly he began to smother. He wanted to gasp, to struggle, but he had to remain still. The hood was further constricting his air. He was beginning to panic; nothing seemed to matter except taking another breath. He was tempted to pull his hands free, grasp the rope and lift himself enough to loosen the cord that was choking him to death. But to what end? He would only suffer the horror of hanging all over again. He tried to swallow, but his throat was closed and on fire. His panic increased. His lungs felt ready to burst. Waves of dizziness swept over him, his ears roared, and then the darkness surrounding him came closer. He saw Dawn's face for an instant, and then it was consumed in the thickening blackness. He was dying, felt the loosening of his senses, the fading of strength, and he let himself go.

Burman had stood for a good thirty seconds staring at Roman's body as it hang like a sack of feed, turning slowly to the right to the creak of the protesting rope that held his weight, for Roman was a big man, tall and muscular. Burman's eyes were actually glittering with satisfaction.

Rush made a dash for the steps the instant Roman dropped out of sight through the opening in the floor. He watched Burman in a frenzy as he took his time enjoying the spoils of his victory. Rush dismissed the soldiers and ordered them to their barracks. "Stop gawking!" he said, more forceful than he had intended. His outburst got Burman's attention and his head snapped in Rush's direction. All the time, Rush was mentally counting the seconds, wondering why Burman kept standing there wasting time when every second brought Roman closer to death. Perhaps he was already dead judging from the appearance of his body. The one-quarter turn had been accomplished, and he was hanging there as still as death.

Burman turned away at last and started back across the parade ground toward the officers' quarters.

Rush moved very quickly under the gallows and caught hold of Roman's legs, straining to lift him, to give the rope slack. The rope would be either cut or untied from the platform where it was secured to a cross beam above the trap door.

Cecil had been watching Burman, anxious for him to leave so he could cut Roman down. He dared not make any moves that might cause the slightest shred of suspicion. He saw what Rush was doing through the drop door and quickly cut the rope. He saw Roman drop the rest of the way to the ground.

Roman was vaguely conscious of someone grasping his legs. He felt the slight loosening of the cord that was choking him. Suddenly he was dropped to the ground. Someone rolled him over and the hood was jerked from his head. He saw Rush's troubled face as he removed the rope and cord from around his neck.

"Thank God, you're alive," he said in a relieved tone. "Don't move. We're not out of the woods yet. Breath easy, we have to get you out of here."

Roman drew a shallow breath and a sharp pain tore through his lungs. He started to cough and Rush slapped his hand over his mouth.

"You have to hold it in until it's safe. Cecil's bringing the stretcher."

Cecil hurried back with the stretcher and threw Roman on it face down; his hands still tied behind his back, and dropped a blanket over him. If anyone happened to be watching they had to play it safe. You didn't handle a dead man with kid gloves. Under the protection of the blanket with his head turned to the side, Roman took his first full breath, and the tears that burned behind his eyes let go, and he cried silently as he was jostled and bumped hurriedly toward the building behind the guard house where the bodies were kept until burial. Once inside with the door closed, Rush jerked the blanked off, smiled down at Roman, and shouted, "By, God, we pulled it off!"

Cecil broke into pandemonium, dancing around, shaking Roman's hand and hugging him. "It feels damned good to be saving a life instead of taking one."

Roman found it impossible to talk; his throat felt like it had been scalded. Rush was coaxing him to drink water, while Cecil rubbed grease on his cut, rope burned, neck.

"Can you turn your head?" Rush asked.

Roman tried it out, cringing. "It's still tied together, but it's stiff and sore." He smiled broadly. "I will never complain. If not for you two, I'd be dead right now."

Rush turned his attention to Cecil. "You had better go get that rope before somebody figures out what we did."

Cecil nodded and hurried out the door. Rush locked it behind him. "We don't want Burman stumbling in here."

"How long will he be here?"

"He should be leaving anytime. You'll have to hide in here until after dark. We can't have a dead man walking around. I'll slip you into my quarters as soon as I feel it's safe. When you feel up to, I'm going to put you on your horse and get you out of here. The sooner, the better."

Roman glanced about the shed, saw several pine boxes. "I hope I don't have to hide in one of those."

Rush laughed. "You can stay right where you are. We'll take Lynch out of the salt box, nail him down in one of those coffins, and tag it with your name. Officially, Lieutenant Colonel Chris Roman is dead, soon to be buried. You're back to being Marshal Darrell Holliman again."

"How will I ever explain all this to the satisfaction of the people in Courgat?"

"Mistaken identity. It happens all the time."

"What if it doesn't work?"

"It has to work. Lieutenant Chris Roman was hanged in front of General Burman and a hundred and forty enlisted men. And we have a body. The only way you can be hanged again is in the name of Darrell Holliman. Chris Roman has paid his dues. All that's left is for Burman to sign the death certificate and close his files. And I know he's anxious to do that. It's over, Roman. You're a free man. Now relax. I'll sneak you out a tray of food and a bottle of whiskey. But don't get drunk."

"You can skip the whiskey. I don't think my throat can tolerate it. I can barely drink water. By the way, how did you talk Cecil into helping me."

"He hates Burman as much as we do, but he also likes money. I'm going to split the ten thousand with him. I couldn't have pulled it off without him. I have to send Henry a wire. Now that presents a problem. I have no idea how to ask for payment. Do you have a suggestion?"

"That's easy. Simply tell him that Chris Roman is dead and buried."

"He's probably already aware of the hanging. It's no secret. It's big news because the issue was controversial. He has no way of knowing that you're still alive. That secret rests with us three people."

"You wouldn't have any reason to send him a wire if it were true. Don't worry. He'll pay you."

"You know him pretty well."

"I know both our worlds revolve around the same woman."

"His granddaughter?"

"That's why he was desperate to save me, and it was only a gamble. He wanted me for Dawn, but Dawn didn't want me for herself."

"I saw that woman grieving over you. I'll never believe that."

"I didn't want to believe it either, but she's not operating from the gray zone."

"Your speech to my troops really amazed me. Your gray area, or zone, whatever you choose to call it, is one hell of a theory. And it makes perfect sense."

"It works for me."

"Have you ever considered becoming a preacher?"

"They're too many of those fools roaming around already. Their hell-fire doctrine is nothing but a scare tactic. They have no proof, and I deal in facts and common-sense. They're all in the gray zone, down to the last plate passer."

"You run deep, Roman."

It may seem that way. What it all boils down to is that I do what I consider is right. No one sways my thinking."

"While you rest, Cecil and I will dig the body out of the salt and make the transfer."

"Just like killing two soldiers with one stone."

"I never thought of that. I'm going to miss you, Roman."

"How does one thank a man for saving his life? Words are shallow, feelings run deep, but how does one put his emotions into words? I'll never forget you, Captain. Every time I open my eyes and see the light, I'll know that you put it there."

"My thanks is seeing you walk away from this. Justice has been served."

Darrell rode out of Fort Daily at midnight, headed for his little house in Courgat. He needed time to put what was left of his life back together. He would decide later which tree to light in. He had no reason to stick around now that Dawn was gone from his life forever. The life that Rush had saved was destined to be an empty one. He would have to grieve for a while, shed some tears, and then he would try to pull himself back together.

CHAPTER

57

Henry McCloud shook with anger when he read the wire from Karson confirming that Lieutenant Chris Roman had been hanged that morning at daybreak. Karson had followed Burman from the time he left McCloud's ranch until he reached Fort Daily. Burman had made the journey explicitly to witness the young officer's death. Henry wondered if Burman had the pleasure of tripping the latch on the trap door. So Burman had called his bluff. Henry had never made an empty threat in his life. He was a man of his word and he didn't eat crow. He had prepared before hand to even the score with Burman. Henry was confident and determined to see Burman deflated, and his unshakable certainty was bought solely by his own power and success.

Burman would die, and if it could be arranged, he would suffer a long and agonizing death. His mind was made up that Burman would not live to see another sunrise.

When General Burman left Fort Daily he was accompanied by two soldiers. Karson would have to wait until he caught Burman alone unless he was prepared to kill the two soldiers as well. The fact that he was flanked by the two men was proof that he had taken McCloud's threat seriously. Burman was watching his back. Killing Burman would be a little tricky because the job had to be done before the sun rose on another day. Henry had been explicit. He wanted the job done on the same day Roman was hanged. It was worth ten thousand dollars to Henry, and Karson would shoot his own brother for that kind of money. It was just a matter if time. Burman was a dead man.

Burman had suddenly become a happy man. Seeing Roman hanged had given him a new lease on life. But he still had McCloud to worry about. How much longer, he had no idea. McCloud was a sick man and Burman was aware of his worsening condition. He didn't like the situation. He was forced to be cautious until the old man died.

He was in the mood to celebrate and decided to stay the night in town, get drunk in the privacy of a rented room, and buy the company of a woman. An important man like himself had to be careful of his reputation. He had to consider his wife's feelings as well. She thought him to be faithful. If she should discover his secret fancy for strange women, it would be embarrassing. He couldn't afford a scandal.

Burman and his two watchdog companions had drinks at the Saddle Sore Saloon, seated at a table in the corner of the room. While they sipped their drinks, Burman was looking the whores over, deciding his choice. He pointed the one out that he fancied and told private Gill to bring her up to him after he got settled.

He paid for a room and a bottle. The other man, Private Terry, followed him up the stairs. He stationed himself outside Burman's door seated in a chair he had leaned back against the wall for comfort. He would take the first watch.

Gill waited around a few minutes before approaching the whore. "You want to make some money?"

She looked him up and down. "You privates never have any money. Get some stripes, and then come back."

"I'm not asking for me. How do you feel about generals?"

"A general! Well, why didn't you say so?" Her painted mouth spread in a wide smile. "I seen him looking us over. So he picked me. I consider that a real complement. Which room?"

"The one with the guard outside the door."

"He must be a real important man."

"And a horny one. Get your ass on up there." He watched her climb the stairs, then walked over to the bar and ordered a beer.

Karson was watching her too, a smile pulling at the corners of his mouth. He would wait for the woman to come out before he went in. As for his two guards—child's play. He didn't mind waiting. He wouldn't get bored. He ordered another drink.

Terry sat slouched in the chair, his hat brim covering his eyes that he was having a hard time keeping open. He wondered how much longer it would take Burman to finish with her. He was dozing when the door opened and the whore came out with a fist full of bills.

She looked at him and said, "Your general can't hold his liquor. He's dead drunk."

Terry opened the door a crack and looked in. He was hit with the foul odor first, and then the grizzling sound of Burman snoring. He closed the door and went downstairs in search of Gill. He was engaged in a card game with five other men. Terry walked over to him. "I need a break."

"Man, I can't leave now. I'm winning."

"I ain't sitting in that chair all night."

"What are you worried about? He'll sleep for hours. Pull up a chair and join us. I'll even buy you a beer. I'm loaded."

Karson watched the card game for a while. When he figured they were totally engrossed in the money changing hands and unconcerned about the welfare of the general, he made his way up the stairs.

The chair Terry had occupied was leaning against the wall outside Burman's room. The door was unlocked and Karson let himself in. The room stank of whiskey and sex. Burman was sprawled naked on the rumpled bed, his mouth wide open, snorting like a hog at intervals. Karson pulled the cover off a pillow, rolled it into a ball and stuffed it into Burman's mouth. His eyes popped open. He flailed his arms, kicked and bucked, struggling to sit up. Karson drew his gun and stuck it in his face. Burman's eyes bulged and he stared at Karson in stark fear. "I have a message for you, general, sir!" Karson said.

Burman mumbled around the gag in his mouth.

Karson slapped his face and his nose began to bleed. "Shut up and listen. Henry McCloud made you a promise and he always keeps his word. You hung a friend of his. That was a big mistake, and it will cost you your life. That's what Henry promised you. You wasted a brilliant officer, and you ain't good enough to shine his boots. You're a puffed-up piece of skunk shit!"

Karson had brought a black leather valise with him. He opened it and took out leg irons. "He even sent you some jewelry." He shook and rattled them in his face. "You ordered Lieutenant Roman to wear these, now you're fixing to try 'um on for size."

Burman slung his head from side to side, his eyes blaring. He looked like an owl. "Put 'um on." Burman continued to shake his head. "You can do it. I got the key right here." He dangled it in front of his face.

Burman didn't make a move to cooperate. Karson lowered the barrel of the gun and aimed at his crotch. "You know, I just love to fish," Karson said, with a real serious expression. "Your balls would make excellent bait. And that little worm will fit a hook perfectly."

Burman stopped resisting. He was shaking so hard that managing the shackles became a monumental chore. "Now you know how Chris Roman felt when you had him put in leg irons. Henry wants you to receive everything you dished out. Stand up you rotten bastard." Burman wallowed to his feet. "Put your hands behind your back." Karson tied them securely and shoved him back on the bed. Tears were pouring down his blanched face, his naked body sweat drenched and trembling.

Karson reached into the valise again and brought out a hangman's rope. "Henry figured you needed a necktie to go with your jewelry." Burman went wild, flouncing like a fish, wallowing himself clear off the bed.

Burman was a small man in comparison to Karson, who was almost as broad as he was tall. McCloud had hired him to do his more strenuous work, and he carried out Henry's orders to a hair.

Karson kicked him in the butt, yanked him up by his hair and shoved him back on the bed. Burman's panic stricken eyes followed every move he made. He dropped the hangman's rope back inside the valise and snapped it shut. He moved to the door, opened it a crack and glanced up and down the hall to make sure no one was there. He threw a blanket over Burman, slung him over his shoulder, and picked up the valise. He edged the door wide open with the toe of his boot and stepped into the hall. He reached back to close the door before moving cautiously toward the back stairs. At the bottom of the stairs was the door that led into the alley. He set the valise down and tried the knob. It was locked. He threw his shoulder against it and broke it open with a splintering of wood. He grabbed the valise and moved quickly down the alley, staying in the shadows. His horse was tied and waiting out of sight behind the building.

He threw Burman across the horses rump, mounted and rode a ways out of town. He stopped at the first tree that suited his purpose. He dismounted and dragged Burman to his feet. "End of the line, sir," he said mockingly. "Henry's throwing this little party for you in honor of Lieutenant Roman. I don't have a sack for your head, but I got everything else I need."

Deciding they were far enough away from town for privacy, Terry pulled the gag from his mouth. "You got any last words, asshole?"

"You won't get away with this! I'm a general. I'm due respect. Henry McCloud will die for this."

"Henry McCloud is already dying. He's a sick man. He would have made you rich for saving Roman, but you wanted to show Henry who had the power. It's a shame Henry ain't here to witness this."

Burman was screaming as Karson slipped the rope over his neck and placed the knot behind his right ear. "Henry told me to read you the charges, but I can't read, so I memorized what I was told to say. 'General Burman, guilty of murdering four hundred Indians and hanging Lieutenant Roman, is sentenced to hang by his neck until he be dead. May God have no mercy on your black soul." He hoisted Burman onto the horses back, straightened him up and slapped the horse on the rump. Burman was screaming when the horse ran out from under him. He hung there kicking and gagging. It took several minutes for Burman to choke to death. His face turned a peculiar shade of blue, even his lips.

Karson swung into the saddle and rode toward New Mexico to make his report to McCloud and collect his pay. He had done his job. Henry would be pleased.

CHAPTER

58

Morgan read the message over three times, not wanting to believe what he was seeing. Lieutenant Colonel Chris Roman had been hanged at sunrise. It came over the wire to all law enforcement offices as a closed case. The sender was Brigadier General Stanley Burman. The message came from Fort Daily. Morgan folded the message and put it in his pocket. Richard McCloud had to be told. If Darrell Holliman and the Lieutenant were the same person, then the McCloud house would be filled with grief. He hated to be the one to tell them, but it was best. They didn't need to find out from another source.

Mac knew immediately why Charles was there. His face was stamped with grief. He invited him in, and as was true of human nature, he didn't want to hear what he had to say, thinking, as long as I don't know for certain there's is still hope. Then he admonished himself for thinking that Henry might have intervened, and perhaps Roman was still alive. He couldn't bear to think of him as dead. It could have been an act of providence that Rush had been injured on the eve of Roman's scheduled execution that would have been carried out at daybreak the next morning, had Rush been able. "Care for a drink, Charles? You look like you could use it."

"Thank you kindly, Mac. But I don't think a drink will cure what ails me." Charles took his hat off and laid it carefully on the hall table. "I just got a wire from Fort Daily. I thought you should know." He looked absently about the room, stalling. He didn't have the courage to just blurt it out.

"For God's sake, tell me what it said."

"Roman was hung this morning," he heard himself saying.

Richard took a moment to collect himself. Hope was gone. Darrell was gone. A man who had never really existed. It was Chris Roman they had all learned to love, and his young life had been wasted. His heart suddenly sunk like a stone.

"Damn them to hell!" It was a cry of helplessness, pain, and grief.

His burst of anguish was heard throughout the house. There came the sound of running feet down the hall and on the stairs.

Then both Debbie and Dawn were standing before him.

Dawn was looking up at him with moist pleading eyes, saw the rage and shock in his expression. She took a shuddering breath. "Nooooo!" She collapsed into his arms.

"Lay her on the sofa," Debbie said. "I'll get a cool cloth."

She hurried from the room and returned with a pan and a wet rag just in time to hold the pan beneath her chin and the cloth to her head while she vomited. It took a few minutes for her convulsive heaving to stop, but her sobbing did not.

Charles Morgan was feeling their pain and pacing around aimlessly. "God, I'm sorry about this, Mac. I knew your girl loved Darrell. They always seemed so happy and content with each other. They was always smiling. This is a damned shame, I'll swear."

Dawn pushed herself up and leaned against the couch cushions while Debbie bathed her face. "Father," she said, her voice thick with grief, "are you positive this time?"

Before he could answer, Morgan took the folded slip of paper from his pocket. He held it out to her. "This wire came from Fort Daily about an hour ago."

She backed away from it as if it might bite her. "I don't want to see it. Please, let me go on thinking that Darrell Holliman is out there someplace, that Chris Roman was not Darrell."

Mac shook his head sadly. "You have to face it. Darrell's real name was Chris Roman. He told you himself, and he told me. He's gone, and you have to get on with your life."

"Oh, I feel so guilty. Why couldn't I have told him just once how much I loved him?"

"Dawn, listen to me. You couldn't tell him, because you didn't realize it yourself. I'm not sure that you actually know what you're feeling now. You have grief, love, and guilt all wound up in the same ball of yarn. Give yourself time to untangle your emotions."

"Listen to your father," Debbie said. "You have loved the Indian for a long time, and you still do. You're confused."

"I should have listened to Darrell. He was right; I am living in the gray zone. The place between Heaven and Hell where the Devil cracks his whip and leads us in the wrong direction. There is only black and white. There is nothing in the gray zone. Absolutely nothing!"

Mac looked at his daughter in absolute confusion. "What on earth are you talking about? What is this about a gray zone? What did Holliman tell you?"

"The truth!"

"About what?"

"Myself, you, my grandfather. You think he was shallow, making light of serious situations, his own misfortune, the way fate could take a person's dreams and turn them into nightmares. You really didn't know him at all. I wonder which tree he lit in."

Both Mac and Debbie were staring at her in amazement. She wasn't making sense. Darrell Holliman was indeed a mystery. It was Chris Roman who seemed to have an anchor.

Debbie wondered if he did in fact have a duel personality. He seemed to adapt to any situation or crisis with little or no effort. He was a graduate of West Point, an officer on his way up, and yet he seemed right at home behind the counter at the trading post, selling fussy women dresses and dry goods and making them smile with pleasure. Then suddenly he was the town's hero, out drawing and out thinking Buck Femmer. He made the sheriff's job look like child's play, and from there to becoming a United States Marshal. He was a miracle, and he had been hanged. It was all so unfair. If not for Richard, she could have fallen in love with Darrell so very easily. And what about Dawn's feelings for him? She had made love with him, yet she had denied her feelings. Where ever the gray zone might be, Debbie felt she might be another victim. Darrell was gone and he left them all in confusion. The gray zone. She knew immediately that Darrell's theory was worth giving a lot of thought to.

Dawn could not shake her strange feelings. Why had she refused to read the wire from Fort Daily that confirmed Roman's death? Why was she stubbornly holding on to hope when there was none? Where had they buried him? She wanted to kneel by his grave and weep, tell him that she loved and missed him. Who did he have? She knew exactly nothing about his past except that he had once been an officer in the army, and been court-martialed for insubordination. What about his parents? Who was grieving over his passing? Who else loved him? Which tree had he flown from? And why was he so different?

She could close her eyes and see his face. She would think about him when she entered the trading post. Seeing again the beautiful young man wearing a white apron standing behind the counter smiling at her, and the sudden passion and weakness she experienced the first time she heard his voice. Every time he touched her, a chill traveled up her spine. She would expect to see him when she passed by the jail. He had looked so brave and sure wearing the silver star on his shirt and the gun buckled across his slender hips. But most of all, the old Benson house would haunt her. For it was there that she discovered the magic of being loved.

She ached for him. She missed everything about him, and now that it was too late she realized how much she loved him, had loved him from the first time she looked into his warm blue eyes. She had let a man stand between them that, in fact, she now wondered if she had ever loved. He had betrayed her, yet he had accused her of betraying him. He would never know about his son. She was thankful now that she had not used the child's birth as an excuse to trap him. His words still rang in her ears, words of rejection. He had admitted that he no longer wanted her. But she knew that he had felt that way from almost the beginning, because he never came back to her after he had been shot, even though he had recovered. Darrell had protected her at the cost of his own life, and she had told him that one day she would have to break his heart. Now who's heart was breaking? She had in fact been destroyed by the gray zone, stupidly allowing the Devil to crack his whip and lead her astray.

CHAPTER

59

Dawn ran into Light Eye's arms and pressed herself against him, felt his lips against hers. He was not telling her to go away now and she reveled in triumph. She sensed the eyes of the other Indians glaring at her, heard cries of anguish, whispered objections, the shrill cry of a woman who was provoked to hysterics. In the shelter of Light Eye's arms she glanced tentatively about, caught a young Indian maiden scowling at her with a mixture of anger, jealousy, and rebellion. She was speaking in Comanche, her voice loud and threatening. Who was she? What did she mean to Light Eyes? He was ignoring her as though he had not heard her frenzied outburst.

Brave Horse was standing in front of them mumbling words she did not understand. Drums were beating; the fires were many, flaming high, sparks rising into the night sky. Braves in paint and headdress were dancing and chanting, passing in front of the great fire of celebration, throwing shadows across the dusty ground. She could smell the mingling odors of their sweat streaked bodies. The fire had grown in intensity, roasting hot, its high flames blown by the gusting wind, actually licking at the frenzied dancers. Sparks were lifted into the air, drifting like fireflies toward the dark sky, winking and twisting and disappearing. She could feel the heat against her face, blistering and painful.

The squaws were roasting meat over cook fires built near their lodges. The young children were gathered near their mothers watching the braves. She saw the faces of babies that were strapped to their mother's backs. Some of them were screaming in terror. She looked closer at the little faces, and the eyes that stared back at her were blue.

Light Eyes was drawing her into his lodge, his hold on her arm was like iron. And then the flap dropped into place and they were in total darkness. It was stifling hot inside and stank of dead animals and humanity. He was undressing her, caressing her, touching her in all the places of excitement. It had been such a long time that she had almost forgotten the feel of his flesh, his hard body, rough hands. And when he entered her, she cried from pain and disappointment. Her body had not prepared for him. He was taking her impatiently, hurriedly, cruelly, and she screamed, "Stop! Please, stop!" But he did not. He put his hand across her mouth to silence her. She couldn't breath. She tried to push him away and became tangled in the stinking skins of his bed.

She awoke with a start, struggling to escape the blanket that covered her. Debbie was there in the dark shaking her awake. She threw her arms around her and sobbed, "Help me, Debbie! Please!"

"What on earth is the matter? Why were you screaming?" Dawn looked about the suddenly lit room; saw that her father had touched a match to the wick of the lamp beside her bed. All the shadows passed away. She saw concern in his face, and love.

"I want to die," she sobbed. "I'm so miserable."

"It will get easier," he said.

"No, it will never get easier. He's dead! Darrell is dead! I'm afraid. I don't want Light Eyes to come for me. I had a dream. It was about Light Eyes. I'm not like him. I know that now. What will I do?"

"You will do what your heart tells you. You married one man you couldn't love. Don't make the same mistake a second time. Be sure you know what you're doing." Debbie said.

"Don't you understand? I can never have the one I truly love and want."

Debbie rocked her in her arms, speaking softly. "It is less painful to feel lonely than to be trapped in an impossible marriage. My daddy was lonely, and look where he is now. Give it some time. You're sick with grief."

"If only I could have told him how much I loved him."

"You're tormenting yourself. You have to stop this before you lose your mind."

"I just feel so helpless."

"It's all part of the healing process. Try not to think about it."

"I feel better now. You can go back to bed."

"We don't mind staying with you for a while, just until you fall asleep."

"I'm all right now." I know what I have to do."

Debbie tucked her in, kissed her, and she and Mac left the room. They left the light burning.

Outside her door Mac paused for a moment. "Do you think she's all right?"

"She's still in shock. She's lost. She has to find herself."

"I've been meaning to talk to you about something," Mac said. "This seems like a good time, if you're as wide awake as I am."

"I could make us some coffee."

"That sounds good. Let's go down to the kitchen."

They walked down the stairs holding hands. Mac looked down at her and smiled. "I'm the luckiest man on earth."

"I love you too," she said.

Mac waited until the coffee was made and two steaming cups set before them on the kitchen table before he broached the subject of Henry McCloud. "I can't put this off any longer. Darrell told me how sick Henry is. He amazed me with his understanding. I have never known a man like him before. He was too honest for his own good."

"And too tender hearted," Debbie said. "That's why he's where he is. He didn't gain a thing, and he gave his life. What does he think of Henry?"

"He pities him. Other then that he gave no clue. I don't know. He had a way of keeping his opinions to himself, but at the same time saw situations all the way to the core. He was one amazing young man."

"Oh, Richard, it grieves me to think about him being punished for his tender heart and honesty."

"I know. He encouraged me to set things right between Henry, and me. He said I didn't have much time that Henry is dying."

"How could he know that?"

"I don't know, but I believed him. If Dawn is serious about ending it with Light Eyes, then I certainly can't put this off. Darrell said Henry plans to kill Light Eyes to keep Dawn from ruining her life. I think Henry took a real liking to Darrell. It amazes me because I didn't think he was capable of caring for anyone except himself."

"It sounds like he loves Dawn."

"She stands to inherit his kingdom when he dies. Darrell was concerned about that."

"Why?"

"Because of her Indian blood she can never own land."

"But no one knows."

"Martha Rowling knows."

"Yes, but if Dawn gives up the Indian there is no reason for her to ever suspect that Henry isn't her grandson. The baby is only half Indian."

"And he can never own land either. Henry intended for me to have it all according to his letter. Darrell said I was his first choice, but when I didn't answer his letter, ignored him in fact, he became desperate. When Dawn showed up, she was the answer. The catch was, he knew she couldn't own land. That's where Darrell entered the picture. If Dawn married Darrell, he could hold on to the kingdom."

"Henry sounds like an amazing man."

"He doesn't want to see all his work go up in smoke. If he dies intestate, the state will take it all, unless I want it. The only way the land can be kept in the family is if I go to him and accept his offer. He will expect me to come home and take care of him until he dies."

"So you have decided to accept all his wealth and land?"

"That's not what I'm concerned about."

"Then what?"

"Dawn told Henry about her plans to marry an Indian, and that she was not in love with Darrell. That's why Henry said he would have the Indian killed as soon as he learns his identity. He threatened to have his entire village wiped out if it was the only way he could get the right Indian. He thinks he's protecting Dawn. Don't you see? If she has given the Indian up there is no reason for Henry to have him killed."

"Oh, I can't imagine Henry doing a horrible thing like that."

"He's ruthless, and he doesn't bluff. I know him."

"That means you will be forced to stay in New Mexico? What about your own affairs?"

"It all depends on how sick Henry is. He knows by now that Roman was hanged. He tried to stop it, but General Burman refused his offer of money."

"Have you told Dawn your plans?"

"I just made up my mind about it. I don't think this is a good time to discuss it with her. She's too torn up."

"She must be told before you go?"

"As soon as I'm certain that it's over between her and the Indian. If he should show up here, she might take one look at him and change her mind. She doesn't have Darrell anymore. It's sort of like, Light Eyes or nothing."

"How will you manage Henry's ranch and still take care of your own? What will you do with all that land? I know you don't really want it."

"It wasn't the land I objected to, but the underhanded methods he used to acquire it. I have decided to give the land back to the Indians. It belongs to them anyway. Henry doesn't have to know."

"Oh, Richard! That's wonderful! I'm so proud of you."

"I'm glad you approve. You know something? This coffee is making me sleepy. Are you ready to go back to bed?"

"Can I sleep in your arms?"

"Where else?"

CHAPTER

60

She saw Light Eyes standing beside his horse in the light of the full moon. He had come to her as promised, moving as close as he dared. She realized with a stab of pain that he could never be a part of her family, that the invisible line between them was stronger than a fortress. They were both half Indian and half white. But in their cores they were only one breed. The dominant blood that flowed in their bodies guided their thoughts and actions, and was in fact, what they truly were. His ways were too different from hers, and she could not adapt to his. What she was inside could never be changed. She was white. Light Eyes was Indian. All her romantic notions seemed foolish, if not impossible. Surely he must have felt it himself. The color of his skin had very nearly caused his death. To want her for his own had put his life in jeopardy. They were too far separated.

Light Eyes was as confused as Dawn. He had his dreams as did the white man, and the beauty of McCloud's daughter had fired his blood and clouded his thinking. The craving for a woman was the same in all men, it overshadowed common sense and rational thoughts, was ruled by the force within their loins. The mental image he held of her stalked his mind like a predator, coloring his thinking, and he had become weak of mind, losing direction. His passion for her had almost killed him. He feared the passions of the white man, their prejudice and greed. McCloud would object, as his own father objected, fearing for his people the repercussions of having the daughter of this powerful man living in his son's lodge. They would come for her, kill for her, and then she would be taken away, and many would die.

The old chief saw in a vision the blood of many warriors staining the earth in the path of the white man's determination to take back their own. The woman held power over his son, drew him to her, firing his spirit while dulling his mind. This marriage he would not allow. If Light Eyes wanted the woman then he must take her far away from their village. His people must not suffer because his son craved the fruit of the white man's loins.

Dawn moved reluctantly out the door and down the steps. Behind her in the square of light cast on the porch, Richard McCloud watched, the depth of his emotions cast on his face. Dawn was about to face her true feelings, and the Indian's life depended on her decision.

As she drew near to Light Eyes, she saw clearly his moonlit washed face, his head dress of many feathers, signifying his position as son of Chief Brave Horse. Their eyes locked for a moment, and then he opened the blanket and held out his arms.

She walked into his embrace and he folded the blanket around her. She felt the immediate press of his body, his warmth, and yet there remained a chill inside her.

Behind them, Richard McCloud watched the scene with sinking heart. She was wrapped in the Indian's arms. How quickly, it would seem, he had soothed her grief over the man she had claimed to have loved. He stepped back inside and closed the door behind him.

After a moment's silence, Light Eyes said softly, "You are even more beautiful in the moonlight."

She felt his trembling and asked, "Are you well?"

"Only the scar reminds me of my wound."

"I doubted you would come," she said. "I don't know what you feel for me. You said you didn't want me. Why are you here? I do not understand?"

"To take you with me."

"Why have you changed your mind? I can't change the fact that I married Ned Rowling, and you can't change the fact that you let me go on believing that you were dead. I waited and grieved for four months. If you had wanted me, why did you hide?"

"I was not ready to come to you."

"Why not? What was stopping you?"

"My father needed me. My people needed me."

"I needed you too. But that didn't matter. You didn't have time for me." She drew away from him. "Have you decided that you have time for me now?"

"I don't like what you did. You should have waited."

"How long?"

"Until I decided it was time."

"Until you decided! I didn't think there was anything to wait for. Dammit! I thought you were dead! Why can't you understand that?"

"Then why were you not in mourning? I am your husband. Squaws mourn their husbands for years."

"You wanted me to believe you were dead! If this is one of your Comanche laws, it stinks!"

"All that is passed. We do not think about it anymore."

"Speak for yourself."

"Come, we go now."

She stepped back, moving out of the folds of his blanket, out of his arms. "You're not my husband. Husbands don't desert their wives, play dead, and expect to be mourned. I'm not going with you. Now I don't want you." He was staring at her. She was shocked by the anguish in his expression.

"Next time," he said, "you will come to me."

"There will be no next time. I will never come to you."

"I will wait," he said stubbornly. "Will you mourn me?"

"Yes."

"Please, don't. Find you a nice fat squaw and have blue eyed babies with her. I just discovered that I don't love you. The man I truly loved is dead."

"The man, Ned?"

"No, I never loved him."

"You married him. I don't understand you."

"The man I loved only died a few days ago. I'm in mourning. Not for years, but for the rest of my life."

"Who was this man?"

"The man who was hanged for trying to save the lives of four hundred Indians at Sand Creek."

A light of understanding flashed across Light Eyes face. "I know of this man you speak of. A brave soldier. Lieutenant Chris Roman. It is right that you mourn him many years."

Dawn stared at him in shock and disbelief. "You have heard of him?"

"I will tell my people. We will mourn with you. I understand you now. Roman was great warrior. Tonight we light many fires in his honor. I will not return. It is best this way." He turned, mounted his stallion, and rode away.

She stood looking after him, her pent up tears breaking the surface in a flood of grief. Now she had nothing. Light Eyes was gone, Darrell was dead, and she would mourn him for the remainder of her miserable life.

Richard McCloud heard the door open and the tread of his daughter's feet as she came toward him where he sat grieved and silent with tears in his eyes. He came to his feet and she ran into his arms. "I thought Light Eyes took you with him. I thank God that you changed your mind."

"I didn't change my mind. I never intended to go with him. I'm not living in the gray area any longer. I have loved Darrell Holliman since the first time I saw him standing behind the counter at the trading post wearing an apron and smiling at me. I don't want to live without him. I'm lost and I will mourn him for the rest of my life."

"It will get easier in time—"

"No! It's killing me. Can't you understand? He gave his life protecting me, and died thinking I was going to take baby Henry and spend my life with Light Eye's. He will never know how much I loved him. He asked me why I couldn't love him, and I told him it was because I loved somebody else. I hurt him! Oh, God, how I hurt him! He's dead and it's my fault. I can't live with this grief and emptiness. I want to die too." She turned away and fled up the stairs. She needed to be alone to grieve, to read Darrel's letter and weep, for it was all she had.

Debbie had remained silent, allowing Richard to handle the situation. He had to be the one to deal with the Indian, and now he didn't have to because Dawn had ended it. It was Darrell Holliman she loved, had loved from the beginning.

"Oh, Richard, I was so afraid the Indian would take Dawn with him. She had thought for such a long time that she loved him, that she was his wife."

"She might have loved him and ruined her life if not for Chris Roman. He saved my daughter from throwing her life away. She had no future with Light Eyes. She has found her way out of the gray zone thanks to Chris. He still has a great deal of influence over her, even from his grave. It's such a tragic loss. We will always miss him. His passing has left an empty place in all our hearts. Knowing him for even so short a time has enriched our lives. He was indeed a miracle."

CHAPTER

61

Darrell rode all night, putting as many miles as possible between him and the place of tormenting memories and crushing pain. He had teetered on the edge of death, felt himself drifting into eternal darkness when Rush took hold of his legs and lifted him high enough to loosen the cord that was cutting off his air. That thin thread of oxygen had saved his life. At one point his brain had been so starved that he had stopped mentally fighting for survival. For a heartbeat he wanted to die, would have welcomed it. He had given up. His last thoughts were of Dawn, her precious face brightening the dark vacuum inside the impenetrable thick black hood. He saw her again the way she had looked when they pulled her from his arms and put him on his horse to take his last ride. She was screaming, tears falling down her cheeks like rain.

He fought back his tears, thinking about the first time he had made love to her. He had seen and held perfection in his arms for the first time in his life. He had know from the beginning that she wanted him the same way he wanted her, all they needed was the opportunity, and he had made the plans very carefully.

He looked up at the full moon with its soft orange hue, the lovely Indian Summer moon. It had been a year since that magic night. It was Indian Summer again. This year Dawn would be looking at the moon with her Indian lover beside her. A sharp pain of regret tore through him.

It was the perfect time for a honeymoon. He wondered how long it would last. The days would be comfortably warm and the night chilly. Snuggling temperature, he thought, just right for making love. The Indian had it all and had left him with nothing.

He wondered if Light Eyes realized how lucky he was. He thought about baby Henry. What kind of life would he have? Would he be pushed to the ends of the earth right along with his mother? He thought about his conversation with Mac. Would he accept Henry's kingdom? He owed Henry McCloud his life. He had made it all possible with his ten thousand dollar gift. He probably knew by now that Darrell Holliman was still alive. He made it his business to know all things of importance and of interest to him. And what about Mac? Did he know?

Darrell suddenly felt completely lost. He wasn't sure what he should do or where he should light. He had no reason to go back to Courgat now that Dawn had gone to live with the Indian. He had some money hidden in his little house. Money he had put away for a rainy day, and he had just been caught in a downpour. He was forced to go after it. He had to find a job or starve. What could he do? He was a soldier. Been trained for that job, and he was all washed up.

He didn't feel comfortable being Darrell Holliman, even though Chris Roman no longer existed. The realization came as a sudden shock. He was actually dead. He had been Chris Roman all his life, now he was mourning his own death. He missed his dreams of having a military career. He had planned his future very carefully, and now he was dead. He missed himself, crazy as it might seem. He thought it might be safer for him if he changed his name again and lit out for Oregon or California. He had to decide what was best. He was floating. He had to pull it together. He needed an anchor.

Rush had provided him with enough provisions to last him several days, so he decided to go back to his house for a while and work things out in his mind. His next stop would be New Mexico. From there, he knew not where. He was indebted to Henry McCloud and he wanted to thank him in person, if he could get past the gate keeper. He didn't have Dawn as an excuse now.

There was no way he could just pick up the pieces of his life and move forward as though Chris Roman had never existed. He didn't feel like lying, and he couldn't tell the truth. All he could do was disappear and try to make a new life for himself someplace else. Mac would know of course that he was still alive someplace. He would get the details either from Captain Rush or Henry, if he took Henry up on his offer to accept his kingdom. He would like to know how it all came out. Would Mac swallow his pride and forgive a dying man his mistakes? He was sorry he wouldn't be around to watch baby Henry grow up. At any rate, he was in one hell of a fix. He didn't know which way to jump.

He reached Courgat just before daybreak, rode through town and headed for home. He should be feeling something other than pain and loneliness. He was lucky to be alive. It had taken a miracle to save him, and he should be thanking God. There was something missing in his life now, something he had found, loved, and then lost. On day, perhaps, he might find a new reason for living.

Captain Rush wasn't surprised when Burman was found hanged, his body swinging from an oak tree about a mile outside the town of Daily. He had been taken from his room at the Saddle Sore Saloon while the two soldiers he was traveling with were down stairs playing poker. The whore he had employed had nothing to add to their story. Burman had been drunk and sleeping it off when she left him. The army was trying to keep that part of the case secret, not to save Burman's honor, because he had never had any, but to spare his widow.

Henry McCloud was known as a man who always kept his word. He had sent Henry the wire as Roman had instructed him. Cecil was already making plans to spend his share. As far as Burman was concerned, Cecil was sorry he hadn't had the pleasure of hanging him himself. Burman would, of course, have a military funeral with full honors, but if anyone grieved it would be just for show, out of respect for his widow.

His murder would be investigated fully, but Burman had so many enemies that it was impossible to settle down on one suspect. Everyone who knew him had wanted to slit his throat. Rush figured the investigation would be only for show also. The major in charge of the investigation had hated Burman for years, but that might be true of any man appointed to the job.

Rush wondered how Roman would take the news. He felt certain that he would feel no pity. Rush even had second thoughts about Burman's death. If Henry McCloud hadn't threatened to kill Burman if Roman hanged, he might even be suspicious of Roman.

Charles Morgan paid Mac another visit early the next morning. This time he didn't look quite so grim, as a matter of fact he was smiling. "I just got another wire from Fort Daily, from Captain Rush. I think he just used me as an excuse to pass the news along to you, so I'll let you read it." He held it out to Mac. Mac was smiling too after he read it. "I suppose you have this all figured out don't you Mac?"

"Probably, but I'll keep it to myself."

"I can understand that. That bastard, Burman, got just what he deserved. Who ever done it made the rotten snake suffer some. I sure wouldn't like to meet my maker that way. I got choked on honey one time, damned near died. I can tell you, it's a helpless feeling when you ain't able to draw a breath. I sooner be burned at the stake then to get choked to death."

Mac thought about Roman dying that way and a shudder racked his frame. "What makes it even worse is to die that way when you don't deserve it. Chris Roman should have been decorated for bravery, not punished for trying to save lives. God, I miss him!"

"So do I. I guess you know that I'm back to being just a sheriff. If there ain't no marshal, then I ain't no deputy marshal."

"Makes sense. Too bad."

"How's your daughter feeling?"

"She's having nightmares. I'm worried about her."

"I'll take some time for her to get over that man. I just can't believe what they done to him. Did you ever suspect he wasn't who he said he was?"

"Not for a moment. But I knew he wasn't an ordinary man."

"Did he ever talk to you about it after they arrested him?"

"It was Dawn he confided in. I never questioned him. I just trusted him. I knew instinctively that I could. It will take us all a long time to get over the shock and grief."

"Guess I better get on back to town."

"Before you go, I need to tell you my plans."

"You going to expand your business again?"

"In a way, I guess. I'm going to New Mexico to visit my father. Darrell took Dawn to visit him—I guess you know all about that. Anyway, Darrell said he's sick. He wants me to have his ranch when he dies. I don't want it, nor need it, but he wants it that way. According to Darrell, I don't have much time, or I should say, Henry don't have much time. So I'm leaving tomorrow. I would appreciate it if you would sort of keep an eye on Debbie and Dawn. I'll get Jack to take care of the ranch until I get back. You might keep an eye on him too. He's a hard worker, but you never know when a young man like him might get his mind on something else."

"He got a woman he's seeing?"

"Not that I'm aware of."

"I'll check on 'um all for you. Don't you worry none."

"Thanks Charlie, I knew I could depend on you."

"How long will you be gone?"

"That's something else I wanted to talk to you about. Henry is going to expect me to stay. He's all alone except for his hands, and they don't exactly please him."

"What about Debbie. Will she be going later?"

"I won't know the answer to that until I talk to Henry and find out how sick he is. If Darrell was right, Henry might die before I get there if I don't hurry. I'll talk to you again before you leave. Thanks for bringing the good news."

Charles laughed. "Not very often is it considered good news when a man dies. But I reckon Burman couldn't really be considered a man."

Mac was anxious to tell Dawn about Burman's death. He was hoping it might ease her suffering to know that the one responsible for Roman's death had reaped what he sowed. Sort of a rope for a rope. He waited until he could tell Dawn and Debbie at the same time.

"Charles was here this morning to see me. He got another wire from Fort Daily, from Captain Rush. General Burman was murdered last night."

Dawn asked excitedly, "Who killed him?"

"They haven't found that out yet."

"Was he shot?"

"No, he was hanged by the neck until he choked to death."

"Good! I hope they never catch the guilty person."

"He got what he deserved," Debbie said.

"I think Grandfather had him killed."

"You must not say that!" Debbie warned.

"Why not? He said he would, didn't he?"

"If the authorities get suspicious they might arrest that old man. You must not voice your opinions to anyone besides your father and me."

"You don't have to worry about that. I would have killed him myself if I could. He killed Darrell."

"He killed Chris Roman, who we knew as Darrell."

"He was Darrell Holliman to me. Forever!"

CHAPTER

62

Richard McCloud had never imagined himself entering Henry's domain again. He had been a disappointment to Henry, but no more of a disappoint than his father had been to him. He wiped away the droplets of sweat that popped out on his forehead and upper lip as he approached the entrance to Henry's kingdom. He had sent Henry a wire telling him when he would arrive. The gate was open and a rider wearing a white hat and leather fringed jacket was waiting. He noticed that his expression wasn't all that inviting. Mac rode through the gate and stopped, waiting for the rider to make a move. He spurred his horse and rode up beside Mac, looking him over carefully.

"Are you Richard McCloud?"

"Yeah. I'm here to see my father."

"He's expecting you." The cowboy drilled him with a piercing glare. "He's been waiting eighteen years. I'll show you to the house. It's about a mile from here."

"Who are you?" Mac said, gritting his teeth.

"Pine Kemp," he said with bloated pride. "Mr. McCloud's top hand. I'm in charge here."

"Of what?" Mac responded hotly.

"This ranch."

"Does Henry confide in you concerning his personal business, or do you eavesdrop?"

"I been with him for twelve years. Some things you just naturally understand. I met his granddaughter. She's real fond of Mr. McCloud. She gave him a reason for living."

"Did he tell you that, or do you read minds?"

"I know some things. Did you come to pick his bones?"

"It's none of your business, but I'm here because he wrote me a letter begging me to come home."

Pine looked up sharply. "Are you here to take over?"

"That's between Henry and me."

"It has something to do with me too. I been taking care of things around here just like he wants. He depends on me."

"What has he promised you for all your years of faithful service?"

"What do you mean?"

"I'm not an idiot. Stop hedging and tell me what you want."

"I think I'm due something."

"Don't you draw wages?"

"A man don't work without pay."

"Then you have been compensated. Or do you intend to pick his bones?" He shot back his insult.

"I expect a fair shake."

"I see you're concerned over who will take over here after Henry dies. I can assure you that it will not be you."

"Then who?"

"Let's just say that it's negotiable."

"You're already acting like you run things."

"I'm not running anything, and I suggest that you stop running your mouth."

They came into view of the house and Mac was astounded for a moment. The place didn't look the same as he remembered. Rooms had been added; the landscaping resembled a botanical rock garden. Mac could imagine how colorful and beautiful it must be in spring when all the shrubs and flowers were in bloom. He wondered what a lonely old man needed with so much space. It wasn't for Elizabeth; perhaps it was in memory of Elizabeth. He sudden felt moved by what he was seeing.

Kemp only went as far as the front door. There he turned sharply and started back down the stone steps of the huge gallery. The door was opened by a large woman in a white dress, her hair pulled severely back from her face and knotted at the back of her head. She looked to be over six feet tall and had the frame of a gorilla. She wasn't fat, she was brawny and muscular. She turned silently and led the way through the house to Henry's bedroom on the first floor. This wing had been added. The windows, dressed with heavy blue drapes that extended from floor to ceiling, were open and the scene was breathtaking. Mac saw clearly the river, trees, and brilliant blue sky. The room also doubled as a sitting room, and was equipped with a large oak desk where Henry conducted his business.

Henry was lounging in front of the fireplace, a lamp burned beside his chair; a book lay open in his lap. He motioned with one thin, veined, hand and the woman left the room. Mac felt nerves ticking in his stomach. Henry looked frail and helpless, hunched in the shoulders, his white hair wispy and thin, and was combed in such a way as to cover his balding head. His eyes were half closed, but he was not sleeping. His head moved slightly so that he brought Mac into focus.

Mac stood immobile for a long moment, shocked by Henry's fragile appearance. He was not at all the way he remembered. Neither of them spoke as they examined one another curiously.

Henry was pleased with Richard's appearance. He was a fine looking man. He was tall and wide in the shoulders with narrow hips, his hair still the same soft brown. He had matured exceptionally well. Had always been better looking than his brother Ralph.

Henry waved him forward, and he moved on his silent command, as he had done so many times in the past when he was summoned.

He experienced the familiar rush of nerves in his stomach. After so many years he still anticipated the sting of his tongue, the sharp rebuke as was customary when he was a boy.

Henry looked up at him with moist eyes. "I'm surprised that you came. It's been months since I wrote you. You could have written back."

"I apologize for that."

"How do you apologize for the eighteen past years of silence?"

"I suppose the same way you might apologize for waiting eighteen years to write me a letter. For some reason, I didn't think my response was urgent."

"How was I to know where you was?"

"I left a note."

"You should have left Elizabeth."

"Please, I didn't come here to duel with you over Elizabeth. We both loved her. She made her choice. I thought you understood that. I know you bought her, but you don't deal in human beings like a sack of flour. Let it drop. What's done is done."

Henry coughed and wheezed into a handkerchief, then took a sip of water before continuing. "Tell me, Richard, why did you finally come back? Was it to fill your purse?"

Mac could have argued with him then. Told him that he neither needed nor wanted his money, big house, and land, that he could not respect him for his methods of obtaining his wealth. He saw the weakness in his reamy filmed eyes, the trembling of his thin body, his hands shaking. To speak his mind now would only offend Henry. He was offering him an apology, the only way he knew, with money. To Henry, money was the cure for all things.

Let him die in peace, if it were possible, and Mac wondered how a man like Henry could find even a splinter of peace after all his years of cruelty and greed. He had made up his mind to accept Henry's offer, if it still stood. It was best for all those concerned for him to be gracious.

Henry broke Mac's chain of thought, asking, "I want to know why you came back. I know you don't need my money. Dawn told me you're a rich man. What changed your mind?"

"Lieutenant Chris Roman."

"Roman! Explain that."

"Roman was a special breed of man. He was wise and mature beyond his years. You met him. It would be impossible for you not to have sensed the wisdom in his thinking."

Henry smiled slyly. Richard was speaking of Roman in the past tense. He doesn't know Roman's alive, he thought. "I wanted Roman to stay here on the ranch so I could protect him. I needed a man like him to run things. I'm down to depending on idiots. Kemp is a good example of the mentality of my men. Roman's intelligence amazed me, not to speak of his outrageous theories. He actually belittled my raging success. He said things that made me feel like I had wasted my life, that I had nothing of any value, that in the final analyses that I would wind up with an empty purse. He said that after the success came the tears. Can you imagine him saying a thing like that?"

"Having associated with Roman, yes. Did you argue with him?"

"I tried to. But he made me feel foolish."

Mac was taken aback. He couldn't even imagine Henry taking that kind of putdown from anyone. "I'm surprised you didn't have him shot. What was his theory?"

"In short: That we never own anything, we just use it. That all things belong to God."

"He was right, you know. We can't take a thing with us when we die. We just use things while we're here on earth."

"How can a young man think up stuff like that?"

"Roman ran mighty deep."

"I thought about what he said later. It kept running through my mind. He was right. I found out a little more about Dawn's relationship with him later. I was thinking about what would happen to my ranch, my holdings, after I didn't get a response from you. I knew Dawn could never own a grain of sand because of her Indian blood. I figured Roman was the answer. If she married him he could hold on to it for her, and I trusted him, and I had never trusted another man in my life. He told me that Dawn could never depend on him, that he was facing a rope. And not only that, that Dawn was in love with another man. He didn't know the man's identity and Roman didn't press her for answers. However I did. Both Roman and I discovered quite by accident that the other man was an Indian. I was upset. When Roman told me the reason he was wanted by the army, I knew immediately who he was. I had been curious to meet him from the day I learned about the Sand Creek massacre. I knew who was responsible for his arrest."

"It's a shame that Roman's brilliant career ended at the end of a rope. He had a great future. It's a goddamned shame that all his knowledge was wasted."

Mac wasn't really surprised by what Henry was telling him. Nothing of any importance had ever gotten past Henry. He suddenly blurted, "Did you have Burman killed?"

Henry laughed. "What do you think about the way justice was served?"

"Necessary and most fitting."

"I'm happy to know that we are in agreement."

"Absolutely!"

"Tell me about that damned Indian Dawn thinks she loves."

"That's one of the things I need to discuss with you. Roman told me that you planned to kill him to protect Dawn from ruining her life."

"I suppose you disagree with me on that. Surely you don't want her to throw her life and little Henry's away slaving for a buck and living in misery the rest of her life, eating dogs, skunks, snails, and every other damned thing. Does she realize that a squaw doesn't get any further from camp than a walk to the river for a bucket of water—if she even has a bucket. I know she won't have a window to throw it out of. They have no privileges. All they do is slave and lay on their backs. It's not a life. It's a damned shame. You tell me who he is and where he can be found and I'll have him killed."

"There is no need for that. He came for Dawn and she refused to go with him. She finally came to her senses and discovered she didn't really love the Indian because she loved Darrell Holliman, the man we know was actually Lieutenant Chris Roman."

"Why do you keep referring to Roman in the past tense?"

Mac looked sharply at Henry, thinking, that's a curious statement. Didn't he realize that Roman was dead? He was supposed to know everything. "I thought you knew. I mean, you had Burman killed because he had Roman hanged. He's dead!"

"And buried," Henry said. "I know that. I'm the one who saw to it that he was dead and buried."

"What the hell are you talking about? The word came from Captain Rush. He ordered it."

"That's exactly right. Chris Roman was hanged. He's dead and buried—but Darrell Holliman is very much alive. Roman had to die to save Holliman. There was no other way."

Mac came to his feet with a start, grasping at last what Henry was saying. He took two steps and was on his knees in front of his father's chair. He put his head in his lap and gave way to his relief in a flood of tears. He felt Henry's hand stroking his back and smoothing his hair. "You saved him! How on earth could you save him from a hanging? There were witnesses—"

"I don't know how it was managed. I don't have the details yet. I have a man on the way to Fort Daily at this moment. All I know is that Darrell Holliman rode out of Fort Daily at midnight two days ago."

"You haven't heard from him? Where was he headed? Where is he? Dawn is on the verge of a nervous breakdown."

"We'll know more when my rider gets back. He's delivering ten thousand dollars to Captain Rush."

"Rush managed it?"

"It's really amazing what money can accomplish. Sometimes the impossible."

"I can tell you that Rush didn't do it just for the money. He knew Roman didn't deserve to be punished. And of course Darrell has a way with people. He's well liked and loved. I can't figure out where he went."

"He's someplace licking his wounds. He's been through pure hell, and he's suffering over his belief that Dawn's living with that goddamned stinking Indian."

"She didn't go with the Indian."

"Holliman doesn't know that. I couldn't understand why she was planning to live with the Indian when she wouldn't let Holliman out of her sight. She dragged him around by the hand every step she took. He had a lot of influence over her, but he couldn't get her mind off the Indian."

"When she lost Roman she finally came to her senses, but it came too late."

"They shared the same bed while they were under this roof. She certainly liked that about him."

"Roman confessed to me that they had been intimate."

"I supposed you slapped him around and accused him of taking advantage of your daughter. I can tell you, she was willing."

"He was behind bars when he told me."

"He was playing it safe. He probably expected you would shoot him."

"I sort of tricked him into telling me. I told him how perfect Elizabeth was in face and body, and he said, 'just like Dawn'"

Henry looked stricken for a moment and Mac was sorry he mentioned Elizabeth in that respect.

"How do you feel about what they were doing?"

"I was disappointed in my daughter, of course. But Darrell was in love with her, he was about to die, and I was glad that he at least had her that way."

"All that and she was still hanging on to that damned buck."

"I have to find him. He thinks Dawn is with the Indian. That's why we haven't heard from him. He's someplace grieving."

"Well, you can't set him straight until you find him. He may be in another state by now, using another name."

"He doesn't have to run anymore. The man the army was looking for is dead and buried," Mac said. "He can walk right back into Courgat and pick up where he left off."

"If I was him," Henry said, "I think I might get lost too. In the mean time, why don't you send Dawn a wire and let her know he's still alive so she can stop grieving."

"I can't let her find out that way. I have to tell her myself. I have to go home for a while, Henry, but I'll be back."

"Kind of like taking a bitter dose of medicine I would imagine, the prospect of staying here with me."

"I never hated you Henry. I just didn't approve of the way you did things."

"I don't suppose you can ever forgive me, can you?"

"I wish you had asked me that eighteen years ago, before you became so rich, before you needed me. I could have taken you seriously then."

"I wish you could take me seriously now. I'm not sorry for the things I've done, but I am sorry about the mistakes I made where you and Ralph were concerned. That's what I want your forgiveness for. Do you think you might be able to do that?"

"I don't know."

"I hope I live long enough to change your mind. It's all I have left to hope for. I want my son back, if only for a little while. I love you, Richard."

I never stopped loving you, Henry. I just didn't like you."

"That's what Dawn said about Roman. She said she didn't love him, but she liked him. Roman liked the way she liked him. If he could settle for liking, I guess I can do the same. Before you leave, I want you to explore the house that will soon be yours. Later it will be a house my granddaughter will live in with baby Henry. Dawn's a queen and she deserves a castle and my kingdom."

Mac took the ring of keys from Henry and started with the rooms on the first floor. The rooms of little use or no use were draped with dust sheets and the doors locked. Elizabeth's old room had remained untouched for all the years. Mac cried, thinking about the night they had run away together. The bed they had slept in last was still unmade. Their pillows lay side by side, so close that they overlapped. Her gown lay at the foot of the bed. He picked it up and held it to his face and wept. The past came rushing back, all the pain and sorrow, and the joys of loving Elizabeth as well. How he wished he had never left. Maybe Henry had been right in thinking that Elizabeth might still be alive. Thinking about how much Elizabeth wanted to live, and how she died so young, brought him visions of Chris Roman. If not for Henry, his life would have been wasted. And there was no son or daughter to carry on his spirit. It seemed as if Henry had produced a miracle. Elizabeth was gone, all he had was his memories, and they were slowly fading with the passage of time. He had even stopped dreaming about her. And now, standing in this room with her personal things, all the pain came rushing back. Her hairbrush lay on the dresser; several strands of her long black hair still clung to the bristles. He had Debbie, and he loved her, but his love for Elizabeth was still as strong as ever. He thanked God for Dawn. If not for her Elizabeth would have died in vain.

Mac prowled through the cold dusty rooms that lay behind the bolted doors. Thirty minutes later he returned to the spot where he had started. Henry's nurse was with him and Mac cringed at the sight of her.

How easily she handled Henry, as though he were a child and she the mother. She lifted him with ease from the chair he had been lounging in and put him back to bed on the freshly changed sheets. She straightened his nightshirt and covered him, tucking the blanket snuggly around his trembling body. She put three pillows beneath his head, bathed his face, and put oil on his parched dry lips. Finished, she stepped back. Henry nodded and she left the room. All during this time she had not uttered a sound, nor had she cast her eyes in Mac's direction. Henry noticed Mac's puzzled expression and laughed weakly. The sound rattled from his thin chest. "She is ugly. I have to admit that, but she's exactly what I need. She hovers over me like a setting hen on her eggs. She protects me, feeds me, bathes me, and guards me when I'm sleeping. She's the watchdog."

"She's very quiet. I haven't heard her utter a word."

"She can't speak."

"Why not?"

"A goddamned Indian cut her tongue out. I gave her a home. I hate them red bastards! I want her taken care of after I'm dead. She has no one."

Mac held his tongue, afraid he might ask the wrong question. He remembered how furious Henry would become if he or Ralph asked too many questions. What entered Mac's mind was whether or not the nurse went with the house. He shivered at his thoughts.

"I sent for my lawyer, Richard. He will draw up my will. To make this as simple as possible, I'm transferring my holdings into your name. There is a clause stating that Dawn is second beneficiary in case something happens to you, or you decide you don't want the estate or the headaches that go with it. It's not that I don't trust you, Richard, but fate has ugly claws. Things can happen. I want my granddaughter to have a part in this. I would feel a lot better about this if she had Holliman to guide her. I'm going to make an effort to find him. A man like Chris Roman can't hide too long."

"I don't know what to say. You have worked miracles. Saved a man from hanging, and now you're signing over your kingdom to me and my daughter. I appreciate it, Henry. And I hope I haven't offended you. I came here to make peace with you."

"Maybe you'll give some thought to forgiving me."

"I'm getting there, Henry. I love you. I want you to know that."

"You still can't say it, can you, son?"

"Say what?"

"Father."

"You are my father. Nothing can change that fact."

"And nothing can change the fact that you don't respect me."

"I respect you for what you've done for Dawn and Holliman."

"What about you?"

"Yes, and for me, Father."

Henry leaned back with a contented sigh. "You got on your knees to me today. I didn't deserve that. I love you, Richard, and I forgive you for taking Elizabeth away from me."

Like a bolt of lightning everything suddenly became clear to Mac. For all the years since he left home, Henry had grieved for Elizabeth, and Mac was responsible for his grief. Elizabeth had been dead for eighteen years while Henry hoped to see her again someday. If Henry could forgive him for breaking his heart, then he could forgive Henry for every mistake he ever made. He leaned over and embraced his father. "I forgive you too, Father." He kissed him on his thin, dry, lips. When he drew back and looked at the old man, he saw the beginning of tears sliding down his withered cheeks.

CHAPTER 63

Darrell finished chopping the stove wood and stacked it by the back door. It was a beautiful Indian Summer day, warm as Spring. He pulled off his shirt, spread it on the porch and lay down on it, looking up at the rich blue sky. The sun was shining dimly and softly, the horizon gentle and hazy. There was hardly any wind, the air smoky and still. He drifted off to sleep, making up for his sleepless night.

He was awakened by the chatter of squirrels in the pecan tree near the house. He watched them for a while, chasing each other, leaping from limb to limb. If only he could be as free as nature, but his mind refused to let go, to clear away the pain and loneliness. He had lost everything, his name, his career, and Dawn. He hadn't wanted to die, not like that, choking to death, but nothing really seemed to matter now. He was dead inside, empty. The walking dead, he thought cynically. Feeling sorry for himself wasn't helping matters. He had to make a move, leave the state, try to outrun his misery, and try to piece together his shattered life.

He had enough coffee grounds left to make one last pot of coffee. He carried an armload of wood into the kitchen and laid a fire in the cook stove. He took his one and only cup from the shelf that held his few dishes. He thought about how close Dawn had come to moving in with him. The house wasn't much, it was good enough for him, but he would have fixed it up for Dawn. He took the time to sweep the floor and make his bed.

He could make a fair bed. At West Point he had made his bed daily, and it had always passed inspection. His heart felt heavy when he reminded himself that he was dead. He was beginning to feel dead. It was official. If he wasn't dead, and Burman found out, he would kill him all over again.

He had a few biscuits left and three pieces of jerky. Not much for a man his size with a healthy appetite. He had to make a move. Sleeping on the back porch watching squirrels wasn't the answer. He hadn't had a bath in days, he had forgotten how many, and it was beginning to get his attention. He set the coffee pot on the stove and drew up two pails of water to heat for his bath. He carried the wash tub into the kitchen and set it by the stove. From his saddle bags he removed a change of clothes, razor, shaving soap, and his toothbrush. The rest of his clothes were back at the jail. By now the whole town would be aware of the fate of Chris Roman, and since he had been arrested and accused of being Roman, there was no way he could just ride into town like nothing ever happened. How would he explain?

He decided to wait until after dark to leave. He took his money from the hiding place and stuffed it in his pocket. He had three hundred dollars. That would see him through until he found work, but first he had to light some place. Maybe he could find another job as a store clerk. That's all the experience he had, unless he wanted to use his gun. He didn't like his choices. Chris Roman was dead, and Darrell Holliman was the man who shot Buck Femmer. He had to change his name again. That gave him something to think about. What would he call himself this time?"

He ate two biscuits, a strip of jerky and drank two cups of coffee. He left the pot on the stove to keep the remainder of the coffee hot. He tried to concentrate on his predicament, but his thoughts kept returning to Dawn, the Benson house, and Indian Summer. The day had been unseasonably warm, but as soon as the sun went down a chill crept into the smoky, still air. He noticed how much the moon had shrunk in the past few days, but It still had the soft orange hue.

He packed his saddle bags with the things he would need, put on his jacket and went to the barn to saddle his horse. He didn't bother to lock his door. He didn't figure on ever coming back.

He had gone about two miles when he decided to ride by the Benson house. His fondest memories were there and he wanted to be close to them.

Maybe it would help ease the pain inside him. He was tired, hadn't been able to sleep for days. He was still alive, but there was no joy in living unless a man had something to live for. As he rode away from Courgat he was taking his misery with him. There was no way he could run away from himself. He was leaving behind his dreams, his past, and Chris Roman. But his misery trailed him like a hound dog.

The house looked the same, dark and deserted. He felt a knot growing in his stomach, his head filled with memories.

His dreams had all begun here, the pure joy of having the woman he loved. The feel of her flesh had been intoxicating. The sight of her body, so perfect in every way had brought tears to his eyes. She didn't have a single flaw. He had been amazed, shocked in fact. How could any woman possess such absolute perfection? He had discovered a miracle in every respect. The way she gave over to him so totally. She enjoyed him and admitted it. He thought about the way she curled against him, throwing one beautiful leg across his middle, plastering herself against him, yet he had lost her to an Indian. He thought about Ned, how he had wanted to kill Light Eyes and failed. He wondered if things might have worked out for Dawn and himself if Ned had succeeded. He wished now, that he had. It would seem that the Indian had nine lives just like a cat. He seemed indestructible.

He dismounted and tied his horse to the clothes line so he could run up and down. He took his saddle bags and went inside. Moon light bathed the inside of the house, and he found his way to the room that held his memories, the room that had been Dawn's. The bed was rumpled, just as they had left it. He took off his boots and lay down. The house was cold and he pulled the blanket up to his chin. He felt a little more at ease, able to relax at last. He ached inside with a terrible emptiness he had no power to alter or change. He missed her, he would always miss her. He was closer to his memories here in this house. He saw her again in his mind, the way she looked and moved, her lips pressing his, tender and sweet. She was so beautiful, so willing, soft, and clinging. He recalled the expression in her dark yes when she asked him to make love to her. God it hurt. He cried, needed to cry to release all the pain and suffering, to cry over his own death and the helplessness of his situation. He couldn't leave tonight, just ride away and forget it all. He was tired; he had never realized that grief could sap a man so completely. He clutched her pillow in his arms and gave over to his exhaustion. When his tears were spent he drifted off to sleep on the damp pillow.

Dawn was crying when Debbie went into her room to tell her goodnight. She looked up, wiping at her eyes. "When will Father be home?"

"I don't know, he may have to stay. It all depends on Henry's state of health. Darrell told Mac that Henry was dying. That's why Richard didn't waste any time going to New Mexico. He was afraid he might die before he got there. Your grandfather is leaving Richard his estate. There will be papers to draw, provisions to make. All the legal matters will have to be taken care of. It takes time."

"What will he do with all that land?"

"He wants to give it back to the rightful owners, the Indians."

"Brave Horse?"

"He will certainly include Brave Horse. I don't know how much land is involved, but I would imagine there is enough there for several Indian villages and hunting grounds. He will be able to tell you more about it when he comes back."

"I should have gone with him."

"Perhaps you should have, but there was no way of knowing how long he will be gone. You would have been away from baby Henry, no telling how long."

"My son needs a father."

"He has a father."

"Not a real father. Light Eyes is just an Indian. He doesn't have time for a son. He has his father to take care of, and his people need him. He doesn't have time for anything else."

"How do you feel about him now?"

"Actually, I don't feel anything. I'm dead inside. But I never really loved him. I was just fooling myself. I was always in love with Darrell. The moment I saw him, my insides trembled." Her tears came again. Would she ever stop crying?

Mac rode to the telegraph office and sent a wire to Charles Morgan. It seemed important that he know Roman was still alive. Mac was concerned with finding him. He had no idea what his state of mind might be, or where he was headed when he rode out of Fort Daily.

Charles read the wire, his hands trembling. There had to be some mistake. He read it over again. The way it was worded had to mean something. "Concerned about Darrell Holliman. Check his house. He should be there by now. Mac"

Dead men don't just get up and head home. It was late and Charles had been sound asleep when Hank beat on the door to wake him. Wires that came that late at night had to be important.

Charles put his clothes on and went to the livery to get his horse. I must be out of my mind, he thought. Out looking for a dead man in the middle of the night.

The little cabin was dark and there was no sign of life. The door was unlocked and he let himself in. He felt the heat of the cook stove and was jolted by a fist of nerves. He struck a match and looked around for a lamp. A lantern hung from a rafter over the table. He lit the wick, took the lantern down and went through the three rooms. There were coals in the stove and a coffee pot on top. The bed had been made neatly. Some one had been there but was gone now. He took the lantern and went to the barn. He looked the ground over carefully, saw hoof prints and fresh horse droppings. He scratched his head in confusion. If Darrell Holliman was alive, then who did they hang? He wondered if he was losing his mind, or if Mac had. Maybe Darrell Holliman wasn't Chris Roman after all. But he hadn't denied it. He put the lantern back where he found it, blew out the flame, and left the house. He thought about it all the way back to town. What did he know? Exactly nothing. Someone had been in Holliman's cabin, that was certain, but he had no idea who that might have been. He decided to keep his mouth shut about the whole thing until he heard from Mac. Something wasn't adding up.

Dawn got out of bed, weary of tossing around trying to get comfortable so she could go to sleep. It was impossible. She wasn't in the least sleepy. Her tortured mind would not let her relax. She walked the floor in circles, her frustration mounting. She had to get out of the house. Walk, ride—do something before she lost her mind. She hurried to the barn, lit the lantern and saddled her horse. She had to be very quiet. Debbie was a light sleeper, and she didn't want to hear her sermon about the dangers that lurked out there in the darkness. Actually she felt safer at night. The Indians slept at night, so they wouldn't be out riding around, and she could better hide herself in the darkness if something or somebody started stalking her. She wasn't afraid of the dark. That was foolish. Without thinking about where she was going she headed for the Benson house. The memories of Indian Summer and Darrell in her arms drew her like a magnet. She couldn't sleep at home, maybe she could find peace there in her old bedroom with her memories of Darrell, and the magic of his lean muscular frame pressing against hers. Her thoughts sent a tingle of longing through her body. Her precious Darrell, loving and dependable, would never hold her again and make her feel safe and loved. If only she could dream of him, it would ease her agony for a short time.

She dismounted in front of the house and tied her horse to the hitching post. She didn't have to hide this time, there was no reason.

The front door protested with a squeal of rusty hinges when she pushed it open. She was greeted with the dank odor of desertion and dust. The lamp that had been on the table in the parlor had been moved, used to light their way when she and Darrell explored the house. It was left in her old bedroom where they had made love by it's dim light. She moved cautiously in that direction. She stopped suddenly, stood very still, sensing something, and she had no idea what she was feeling. The shock of memories combined with loneliness, grief, and pain, shifted inside her, bleeding together like a mixture of water colors, a swirl of confusion. Her intimate relationship with Darrell had begun in this room. And it had been a relief to finally stop fighting the fever of passion that burned through her, and she let him finish what they both wanted and needed. She moved toward the half open door and pushed it open. Her chest felt tight and she could scarcely breathe. The darkness yawned at her, and she froze for a moment. She heard a rustling sound. Could it be rats? It was coming from the direction of the bed. Her heart leaped in fear, for she heard the sound of breathing, soft and steady. She became paralyzed, panic stricken, unable to retreat, and too scared to move forward. She saw the covers move, a shadow raise up, and she screamed. The shadow, a man, was instantly on his feet closing the space between them, and she kept on screaming, her voice shrilling clear to the rafters.

Then a voice came out of the darkness, a cry of elation. Darrell's voice. "Dawn! Darling, don't be afraid. It's me, Darrell." She was there, she wasn't gone, and he didn't feel dead anymore.

"Oh!" she cried, and then she was in his warm strong arms, weeping hysterically, grasping him, straining to hold him closer, sobbing, gasping, her body quaking. "I thought you were dead!" she wailed. "I was told they had hanged you. I couldn't stand losing you! I wanted to die too."

"No, no, darling. I'm here. "I'm all right. I won't ever leave you again. Please, don't cry, sweetheart. I'm sorry, I'm so sorry for hurting you."

"Just hold me! Make me feel safe again."

He picked her up and laid her gently on the bed. He lay down beside her and pulled her against him. His lips were on her face, eyes, nose, and neck. He tasted their mingling tears as their lips melted together in a frenzy of passion.

When at last they came up for air, she said against his lips, "I thought I had lost you, that I would never hold you again. I have been going out of my mind."

"I'm very much alive; I just now realized it."

"I wanted to die too when they said you had been hanged—that you were dead. I was dying inside because I thought I would never get to tell you how much I love you. Oh, Darrell, I have always loved you, since the day I first saw you behind the counter at the trading post. I have never loved Light Eyes."

"Do you know how long I've waited to hear you say that? I thought you never would, that you only liked me."

"I never realized how much I loved you until you were gone. Oh, it was killing me. I have suffered ever moment of every day. Feeling guilty, lost, lonely, knowing I would grieve for you the rest of my life, and never love another man."

"I haven't been able to sleep for days. I came here to be near my memories of you. I was content lying in your bed holding your pillow. I was able to at last rest. I had decided to leave the state, change my name, and just disappear. If I hadn't come here tonight, I would have lost you forever. But I thought I already had."

"Who was hanged?"

"Chris Roman—me."

"But you're here. So they didn't really hang you."

"Oh, they hung me all right, but the rope was rigged so the knot wouldn't break my neck. I hung there choking until Captain Rush could cut me down."

"Oh, you suffered." She was holding him close, trembling against him.

"General Burman witnessed my execution, and he enjoyed it so much that he lingered almost long enough for me to choke. I will always have to watch my back where he's concerned."

"No you don't. My grandfather had him killed."

"What! When?"

"The same day you were hanged."

"How did he manage that?"

"He can do anything he likes. He had Burman hanged too. He was found still hanging from an oak tree."

"It was Henry who saved my life. And he even eliminated the man who was a threat to my freedom. I intend to thank him personally. I'm thankful to be alive. There was a time when I wished they had hanged me. I had nothing to live for. Now I do. You love me. I've been born again."

"I like you too. You are still my best friend, and I love the way you make me feel."

"I thought you were gone. I want to look at you. I have to prove I'm not dreaming." He drew away from her long enough to light the lamp, and then stood there looking at her. "God, you're beautiful!"

"So are you," she said, and then gasped when she saw the bruises on his neck, the rope burns, and deep cuts from the cord that had actually saved his life. "Oh, God! Your neck! They did hang you. They tried to kill you!"

"That was the general idea."

She touched his neck gingerly, caressing the bruises and kissing the cuts softly. "I'm so sorry." She looked up at him, fresh tears washing down her face. "I can't live without you. I know that now. I love you so, and I need you, always."

"I promise never to leave you. I even refuse to die."

"Please, don't tease me."

"I told you once that I never joke about my life. I've had too much trouble hanging on to it. My life belongs to you now, and I don't want to cheat you. I have to live a long time so I can take care of you and our babies."

"Can you even imagine how beautiful our children will be?"

"If you want us to have babies, then we had better get married first. I'm sure that little Henry would like to have a brother or sister, and I want a child, as long as it's yours."

"It will be a half-breed."

"No it won't, only one-fourth."

"Are you sure?"

"I don't care. Will you marry me?"

"Yes, today, right this minute. I want you so badly."

"We have a lot to talk about, but I don't want to talk. I just want to hold you and kiss you and make love to you." He tightened his arms around her, and he was trembling. "I want you as I have never wanted anything in my life." He began to remove her clothes. When she was naked he couldn't take his eyes off her. From her tiny feet to the top of her raven black hair she was perfection.

She watched as he undressed, touching him, caressing him, admiring him. She knew she was looking at a miracle. He had survived. This very special man she treasured and loved. To destroy him would be the most horrible waste she could imagine.

He shuddered as her soft lips and smooth hands slid over him, and he was thankful that he had taken the time and effort to bathe and shave. She wouldn't have liked him very much stinking.

They lay together beneath the blanket, and she plastered herself against him. She could not find the words to express her love, the relief of finding him again, and the promise of becoming his wife. In her mind he was already her husband. She felt safe again, loved and cherished. He took her ever so gently, slowly, and she moaned beneath him. "Oh, I love the way you make me feel." The magic of their love continued until the Indian Summer sun came sifting into the room and spread over them. Darrell got up, pulled the shade down, and then went back to bed. She threw one slender, beautiful leg across him and snuggled close. At last they slept contentedly.

CHAPTER

64

Debbie was crying, out of breath, and shaking when she stormed into the Sheriff's Office. Morgan looked up in surprise, wondering if her sudden visit had anything to do with Mac's wire.

"I can't find Dawn," she cried. "She's been gone all night. I'm afraid she might have ridden to the village of Brave Horse. Her horse is gone."

"I wish Mac was here. I don't know how friendly them Indians are when a stranger comes riding into their camp, but I'm fixing to find out."

"If Dawn decided to go to the village, it was a snap decision. The last time I spoke to her she was crying over Darrell."

"Funny that you should mention Darrell. I got a wire from Mac late last night, and I can't make no sense of it."

"If Mac sent you a wire, it has to be important. What did it say?"

"I got it right here. I'll let you read it."

She read it out loud: "'Concerned about Darrell Holliman. Check his house. He should be there by now? Mac.'"

"See what I mean? What do you think he's talking about?"

"You're right, it doesn't make any sense. We know that Chris Roman was hanged, and Roman and Holliman are one and the same. If Darrell Holliman is alive, so is Chris Roman."

"I been out to Darrell's little house. There's something strange about that too. I didn't find anybody, but somebody's been living there. There was a fire in the cook stove, and the bed was made, real neat like."

"Oh, my God!"

"What?"

"Men don't make neat beds. They don't make beds at all. Chris Roman is still alive. He made that bed. He went to West Point, Charles. The men are taught to be neat. They make their own beds. Darrell Holliman is in Courgat, or was. I understand why Mac worded his message like that. He was afraid the wrong person might read it."

"Then where is he?"

"Wherever he is, Dawn is with him. It makes sense."

"I sure hope that's right. What do you want me to do?"

"There is nothing we can do but wait for them to turn up."

"I wonder how Darrell kept from gettin' hung. Rush sent the wire hisself three days ago saying Roman got hung."

"I have a feeling Henry McCloud may have arranged it. He has enough money to buy anything he wants. I had better get back home just in case they show up. I left Laughing Eyes there with little Henry. Jack's out riding fence."

"I'll go out there with you. I promised Mac I'd see after you and Dawn, and I let Dawn get away from me."

"Don't blame yourself Charles. She left in the middle of the night."

"That does seem peculiar, don't it? I got my horse tied up out front. I'll see you home."

Dawn opened her eyes, felt the press of Darrell's body and reached out to him, and their bodies twined together. "You really are here."

"Right where I belong." He suddenly sat up. "My God, Mac is probably out searching for you."

"He's in New Mexico."

"What about Debbie? What did you tell her?"

"I didn't tell her anything. I wanted to be by myself to grieve, and I knew she would lecture me about nine kinds of danger. She acts like a mother hen."

"I've got to get you home."

"I won't go. I want to stay right here in your arms."

He smiled at her and settled back down. She took his face between her hands and kissed him. "I will never let you go. I'm afraid to let you out of my sight."

"I'm not going anyplace. I'll take you home and stay there with you."

"Will you sleep in my room?"

"You know I can't do that."

"Why not?"

"I just escaped the hangman. I won't be able to out run a bullet when Mac throws down on me."

"He wouldn't dare. He's not even home, and it's none of Debbie's business. Where's your gun?"

"In my saddle bag."

"They took your badge. I thought they might have taken your gun too."

"They did, but Rush gave it back to me. I'm not going to have a shoot-out with Mac, if that's what you're thinking."

"I was just curious. Will you get your badge back?"

"I might have a little problem with that. How do I explain being two different people? It might work if I had two heads."

"You don't have to explain anything. When have you ever cared what people think?"

"If they don't trust me, I might as well hang it up. Maybe Mac will give me my old job back."

"With your West Point education you're far above being a store clerk."

"I was trained to be an officer, but it didn't work out to my advantage. It about killed me. Are you forgetting that I'm dead? I'm not Darrell Holliman. That's a fictitious name. I was born Chris Roman."

"Do you realize how little I know about you?"

"I had to keep a low profile. There wasn't anything I could say about Darrell Holliman. He didn't exist. And I couldn't talk about Chris Roman without getting hanged. So instead of making up wild stories about myself, I kept my mouth shut."

"Where is your mother?"

"She died four years ago. I was an only child. It wasn't my mother's intention, she just couldn't have anymore. My father was a soldier. He got killed after I was appointed to West Point." He gave her his cute boyish smile. "They thought I was intelligent. I have a high IQ, but don't tell anyone. It's a curse."

"What kind of curse."

"You have to pretend the rest of your life."

"Pretend what?"

"That you have a high IQ. Truthfully I'm rather stupid."

"You're teasing me again."

"Do you know what you are?"

"A disgrace?"

"No, you're my doll baby."

"You are teasing me."

He pulled her close and kissed her. "I really should take you home, while I still have the courage."

"But you don't want to. You like being here with me, naked."

"It's handy, but I like you with clothes on too."

"Can we wait just a little longer?"

"Absolutely."

Mac had sent the wire to Morgan just before he boarded the train for home. Henry understood his urgency. He had gone to a lot of trouble and expense to save Chris Roman. He had big plans for him. He realized he was becoming weaker with each passing day, and he wanted to see Dawn safely married to Roman before he died. He still didn't feel too comfortable about leaving the Indian alive. What if Dawn should change her mind later? She couldn't go running to the Indian if he was dead.

Henry's Lawyer had made all the changes Henry requested, and Richard had come through for him. He had to admit that he was proud of him. He had made something of himself, and he hadn't asked anything from him. He expected him to return within the week. He had asked that he bring Dawn and Roman back with him. He realized that he could never address Chris by his real name, and it was a shame. The name Roman was never to be forgotten, where as, Holliman was known for outdrawing a fast gun. He was in as much danger as Holliman as he had been as Roman. He was still a target. He hoped to change all that in the future.

Mac reached home late in the evening the day after he sent the wire to Morgan. He knew he would get in touch with Debbie, and he could imagine her shock at learning Darrell had escaped the rope. He didn't know how it was managed as yet, but when he talked to Darrell he would hear it in his own words. He felt his tension building, along with his excitement.

The minute he walked through the door Debbie threw herself into his arms. "Is Darrell alive, Mac?"

"Yes!"

"Oh! Thank God! My prayers have been answered."

"It's hard to believe, but Henry said he rode out of Fort Daily around midnight the same day he was hanged. I don't understand how it happened. I was never so shocked in my life. For once, justice was served. Roman didn't deserve to die."

"Your wire to Morgan made me think he might be alive. When Charles checked his house he found that someone had been there. There was a fire in—"

"Hold on just a minute. Where's Dawn? I have to tell her, and I'm afraid of how she will react. It will be one hell of a shock. It actually brought me to my knees."

"She's not here, Mac. She left last night without telling me. She's not home yet."

"Surely she didn't go to the Indian village!"

"I don't know. That's the first thing that entered my mind.

If she did, you must go after her."

"I wish I knew where Darrell was going when he left Daily.

He had made up his mind that Dawn meant to go with Light Eyes when he came for her during the full moon. We know she didn't go with him, but Darrell doesn't."

"I was hoping that she might be with Darrell someplace. Perhaps he did come here, just hoping she might have changed her mind about going with the Indian."

"Then he would take her home with him."

"Well, somebody has been living there. Charles noticed that the bed had been made neatly."

"He was probably there by himself, and he's gone now. No telling where."

Mac was pacing the floor when he heard the sound of hoof beats on the drive in front of the house. He hurried to the front door, expecting the worst. His relief was so great that he almost went to his knees a second time. Darrell and Dawn were coming up the path arm in arm.

Darrell looked at him and smiled. "You can always expect the unexpected where I'm concerned," he said, and grasp Mac's hand. They shook vigorously, and then Mac grabbed him and hugged him.

"I never expected to see you again. When Henry told me you were alive, I don't mind telling you, I lost it! It was the biggest shock of my life, and the most welcome one."

"I'm sorry about all this, Mac. This is a shock to me too. Not the hanging part, but having Dawn back in my arms. I have something to live for now. There was a time when I didn't care if they hung me."

Dawn threw her arms around him. "I love you so much. I didn't have much to live for either. Now I feel safe and loved."

She turned to look at Mac. "And guess what? We're going to get married. Do you have any objections?"

"None whatsoever. Where have you two been?"

"Together," Dawn said bravely, before Darrell had a chance to respond.

"How? Where?"

"Darrell was out at the old Benson house. I found him there."

"How did you know where to find him?"

"I didn't."

"We both went out there for the same reason. That was where we fell in love last Indian Summer," Darrell said.

"Come inside. It's cold out here. I'm anxious to know how you escaped the hangman."

Darrell took off his coat, and Mac gasped, "My God, Darrell! Your neck!" And then he was shocked into silence.

Darrell looked at him and smiled slightly. "When a man gets hanged it's bound to leave traces."

"You were actually hanged?"

"Yeah, right on schedule."

"How did you manage—I mean didn't they notice that—"

"No, Rush cut me down before I choked to death."

"It usually breaks a man's neck."

"The hangman rigged the knot so it wouldn't. Henry McCloud is responsible for my survival. I intend to thank him in person. How is he?"

"Impatiently waiting for you and Dawn to pay him a visit."

"We have a little something to take care of first. We need a preacher."

"You needed a preacher last Indian Summer."

Debbie entered the room, saw Darrell, and flew into his arms. "You really are alive." She stepped back to look at him, then reached out and touched his neck. "They hurt you! Oh! You have been through so much. Are you all right?"

"I'm just fine, Debbie. How about yourself?"

"I've been very upset over you. I thank God that you're safe. Were you here last night?"

"This isn't the time for questions," Mac said, saving Darrell the trouble of explaining. "I think this calls for a drink. I feel like celebrating. How about you, Darrell?"

"I could use some coffee." He looked at Dawn. "How about you, sweetheart. Are you hungry?"

"Yes, I haven't eaten since yesterday, and I know you haven't either."

Debbie blushed. "I'll make sandwiches. The coffee is already made."

They followed her into the kitchen. Darrell ate three thick ham sandwiches and drank several cups of coffee while Dawn nibbled on one thin sandwich.

After they had eaten, Dawn took his hand and led him into the drawing room. She sat down and pulled him after her. She moved against him and leaned her head on his arm. Mac watched her, certain that she wasn't about to let Darrell out of her sight. Darrell looked contented, leaned down and kissed the top of her head. "Comfortable?" She shook her head.

Mac cleared his throat to get their attention. Darrell looked up and met his eyes. Dawn snuggled closer to him, sighed and closed her eyes. They hadn't gotten much sleep and she was tired.

"Have you made any plans?" Mac asked.

"It's a little soon for me to be making plans."

"I can understand that after the hell you've been through. I know Henry will entice you and Dawn to stay in New Mexico and run his ranch. He needs help. I met his top hand."

"Pine Kemp," Darrell laughed. "He's a vulture." Mac looked surprised. "He thinks Henry owes him."

"That figures. You're a threat to him too. Watch your back."

"Do you think he might be dangerous?"

"I think he would betray his own mother for the money in her sugar bowl. Henry needs help all right, and he's needed it for years. Actually it's a bit late for him to start worrying. You're going back— right?"

"I intend to stay until he dies. My visit was very productive. We laid our cards on the table, talked about where we both went wrong. I guess you could say that we finally woke up."

"You forgave him," Darrell stated, smiling. "I'm glad. He can die in peace now. It's hell to die in the gray zone. I know, because I almost did." Dawn stirred beside him and he looked down at her. "I could die happy now, knowing Dawn loves me. It's hard to die knowing no one cares. I appreciate life now because I'm loved and needed, and I have the most beautiful, perfect, loving woman in the world beside me, and I promise to always take care of her. I want us to be married as soon as possible, but first I have to find a job. I won't be dependent on anyone to put food on my table."

"As Roman you had a job for life, and now you're unemployed as Holliman."

"It's all the same. I still think like who I am, not who I pretend to be. Darrell Holliman is certainly no credit to me. But we must let the chips fall where they may. Too bad mine wound up stuck to the sole of somebody's boot."

"If you accept Henry's offer, you will have earned it. He feels the same as you. What he has acquired during his life time, he's earned. A bit underhanded at times, but he worked it out without anyone pointing the way for him."

"It doesn't matter which tree I light in, just as long as Dawn's there on the same limb with me and no one saws it off. She's my life."

"I always wanted a son."

Darrell looked at him, his eyes a little moist. "I appreciate that, Mac. I've made some mistakes, and you have every right to shoot me."

"Just make it right."

"All Dawn ever had to say was, yes. She did the right thing when she turned me down. I wasn't free to lead a normal life, and certainly not a long one. That rope wasn't about to go away like a bad dream. When I asked her to marry me the first time she was still married to Ned. I was being selfish instead of honorable. I can see that now."

"What about your Marshal's appointment? All you have to do is pin that badge on your shirt and you're back in business. You already have a job. Why look for another one?"

"I can't show myself in town yet."

"I don't see why not."

"What do you suggest I do about these rope burns and cuts?"

"You could wear a neckerchief for a while. Are you in pain?"

"Just a little stiff in the neck. I can handle it."

"When I go back to New Mexico do you want to go with me?"

"I owe Henry my life. I want to thank him."

"Then we might as well make plans to leave as soon as possible. Henry looks a bit worn out."

"I have to talk it over with Dawn."

"That's fine. I guess you realize that she's sleeping."

"I thought she was awfully quiet, but she doesn't snore," he said without thinking, and cringed from the look Mac shot him, thinking, I'm just asking to get shot. "I'll carry her up to her room if you'll point the way. I don't want to wake her up. She's worn out."

"You don't look too frisky either. We have plenty of room; you can spend the night if you're too tired to make it home."

"That would never work."

"I know what's going on with you two. Naturally I don't approve, but Dawn has a mind of her own. If it was anyone but you, it might be a different story."

"I'll respect your wishes, Mac. As soon as I get her settled I'll go on home. I'm happy now. I have what I want."

Darrell carried Dawn upstairs, pulled her shoes off and covered her with a blanket. As soon as he turned to leave the room she woke screaming. "No! Don't leave me!"

"I'll be back tomorrow," he said, holding her, rocking her. "I'm not about to disappear again. I promise."

"I'm going with you!"

Hearing the commotion, Debbie rushed into the room. "What on earth is wrong?"

"Darrell wants to leave," she wailed.

"He's going home. He's not leaving," Mac said.

She sprang out of bed and ran to stand in the door way to block him. "I won't let him go! I won't!"

"Dawn, will you be reasonable? He's safe now. You don't have to worry anymore."

Darrell looked stricken. He didn't want to leave her but he was in Mac's house. He had no choice. "He's right, darling. I'll see you first thing in the morning."

Debbie pulled on Mac's sleeve to get his attention. "She's been through so much, Mac. She's still in shock. She's been through the shock of losing him twice. She needs him."

"I won't allow them to commit fornication under my roof, and that's final."

Dawn glared at Mac. "All right!" She walked over to her bed and plopped down. "I won't say another word. You're the boss! Father!"

Darrell kissed her and hurriedly left the room before she threw another tantrum. He walked straight through the house and out the front door without another word.

Debbie glared at Mac. "You've hurt him. Why do you have to act so staunch? Why close the barn door after the horse is already loose?" Mac drew her out into the hall and closed the door behind them before he said anything. "What's the matter with you, woman? There's a time and place for everything?"

"She almost lost him. What she's feeling right now is natural. Darrell Holliman—Chris Roman, which ever, is a gentleman. He's in love with Dawn. He will walk through fire for her. He would have hanged before he would have let her travel to New Mexico unprotected. They have been intimate for a year. What are you worried about?"

"I don't have to stand here and listen to this." He spun around and stormed down the hall. Debbie followed on his heels.

Darrell felt bad all the way home. He didn't blame Mac for being upset, but he was damned well trying to leave. He felt a bit of relief when he got home. He couldn't get out of Mac's house fast enough. He put his horse in the barn and went to bed. He lay there for what seemed like hours, his emotions in a storm. He was in one hell of a fix. He had a good mind to take Dawn and leave the damned country. But thinking like that was crazy, and expensive. He heard the back door open, then close. He sat up and swung his legs over the side of the bed, his hand closing over the grips of his .45. He saw her small shadow in the light coming through his bedroom window. He lay back down, held his arms out, and Dawn crept into his bed and moved against him. She threw one leg over him, snuggled as close as she could get, and they both slept.

CHAPTER

65

Debbie shook Mac awake and he sat up with a start. "What's wrong?" "Dawn's not in her room!"

"Well, we know where she is this time. I should have guessed. She settled down too fast. She's acting like a spoiled brat! And Darrell certainly isn't helping matters."

"I hope you're not thinking about going after her."

"That's exactly what I'm going to do. She just defies me!"

"She's not a child anymore, Richard, that you can take by the ear and lead."

"What do you suggest I do? Holliman knows how I feel about their behavior. I told him."

"Are you blaming him? He was agreeable. Dawn was the one making the fuss. He left here alone to go home. He was tired. I felt so sorry for him when I saw the bruises and rope cuts on his neck. They hanged him, Richard! He actually went to the gallows expecting to die. Don't cause him anymore grief."

"He has a lot of influence over Dawn. Henry even noticed that, and commented on it. Why doesn't he reason with her?"

"He tried."

"Darrell knows I won't allow them to sleep together under my roof."

"He wasn't expecting to sleep with her. If he had lain down beside her she would have been content. He would have remained a gentleman. That's the way he is. What would be the harm if she slept in his arms? I thought you trusted him. You told me you did."

"He's in love with her, and she has him twisted around her little finger."

"Of course she does, in one respect." Debbie laughed softly. "That's the way it's supposed to be. A woman holds a certain power over a man."

Mac got up and started dressing. "I'll bet he took her with him."

"No he didn't. I checked on her an hour later, and she was sleeping."

"She was playing possum. She needs to learn a lesson. She can't trail Holliman every step he takes. Henry said that while they were there visiting with him that she dragged him around with her every step she took, wouldn't let him out of her sight. If any two people ever needed to get married, they certainly do. She will probably want to go to work with him."

Mac pulled his boots on and Debbie cried, "Don't do this, Richard. You can't go barging in there and demand that Dawn go home with you. She's under Darrell's roof now. And you need to understand something: you're not dealing with Darrell Holliman, the meek store clerk; you're dealing with Chris Roman, a very courageous young man, and he will protect Dawn, even from you, if need be. He knew the danger when he accompanied Dawn to New Mexico, but he didn't let that stop him. He was ready to die to protect her. Darrell would never take advantage of her. She invites his attention, she told me. She asks him to make love to her. What would you expect him to do? Refuse? He's in love with her, Richard, and when people are in love, they make love. It's the most natural thing in the world."

"Yes, for married people. I'm shocked that her morals are that loose. Holliman needs to control the situation before she has another child trailing after her that looks like him. I'm surprised it hasn't happened already."

"I'm going to ask you a question and I expect you to answer truthfully, even though I'm certain you will hedge."

He glared at her. "I'm not a liar."

"Of course not, but sometimes you forget to be human."

"I resent that remark."

"Tell me, while we were living in separate rooms under this roof before we were married, did you ever want to make love to me?"

He was astounded by her question. "Why are you asking? You know the answer."

"And you're hedging."

"All right! You know damned well I did."

"What would you have done if I had invited you into my room and asked you to make love to me?"

"That's different. You would never ask that."

"Still hedging, I see. Why don't you answer?"

"What's the point to all this?"

"I just want you to try on Darrell's shoes for a moment. Would you have turned me down?"

"No! I would have made mad love to you all night."

"See who holds the power?"

"Let's go back to bed. All these questions are making me tired."

"I'm not trying to make you tired. I'm trying to make you understand."

"You have. I'll back off, but I still don't like it."

"You might as well because your daughter won't give an inch. They should get married, but I'm not sure Darrell is up to it yet. He was hanged, an incomprehensible horror. I can't even imagine his suffering as he hanged there choking helpless and panic stricken waiting for death to swallow him up." She grew quiet for a moment. "He will make light of the whole thing to escape the agony of remembering or explaining. No man can walk through hell and not get branded, marked for life. I'm not talking about the scars on his neck either. It has to have affected him psychologically. Dawn has gone through the agony of suffering his death twice. She will never forget the grief, emptiness, total feeling of loss. They need each other, to be together, to heal. If you pull them apart now they will be lost again to all the pain and anguish. Stop interfering. Give them a chance. Trust Darrell. Don't punish him anymore."

"I do trust him."

"Then start acting like it before you drive him away."

"Wild horses couldn't drag him away. My daughter has him mesmerized."

"If he decides to move on, he will take Dawn with him."

"I'll ride out there first thing in the morning and apologize to them both."

"You might consider taking some groceries with you. You know Darrell didn't drop by the store to buy food. He was half starved. You saw

THE WARMTH OF INDIAN SUMMER

the way he ate. I feel sorry for him. He's at a cross-road right now. He is dead in one respect. He can never get his natural life back. Chris Roman is dead and buried, and it's a shame. All his training and knowledge is being wasted. He's starting all over as if he had just been born. There will always be a gap in his life."

"You're right and I'm acting like a blind fool. I need you to set me straight. From this point forward I promise to be more understanding. I can't even imagine the horror of what Darrell lived through. He has more courage than any man I have ever known. I'm a fortunate man to have him for a prospective son-in-law. I couldn't love the man any more if he was my own son. The last thing in the world I want to do is hurt him. He's already suffered the miseries of hell." He smiled sheepishly. "He would have to be crazy to reject Dawn. Like he said, "She's his life""

Darrell was awakened by pounding at his back door. He untangled himself from Dawn and got up, reaching for his pants. Dawn sat up and looked at him. "That's probably Father! Make him go away."

Darrell opened the door doing up his buttons, expecting to see Mac's angry face. He was surprised to find Charles Morgan on his door step. For a moment Morgan stood there staring at him.

"Well, I'll swear, you are alive. I heard you was, but I had to see you with my own eyes." He stuck out his hand and Darrell shook it. Darrell wasn't wearing his shirt and Morgan was shocked when he saw his neck. "Them sorry bastards damned sure did hang you."

"Come on in. I'd offer you a cup of coffee but I don't happen to have any."

Charles tossed his hat on the kitchen table. "I never been so glad to see anybody in my life. I brought you your badge. You need to pin it back on, even if you ain't able to go back to work yet. The whole town is anxious for you to come back. They understand that they arrested the wrong man. The folks was fightin' mad about it. The mayor plans to have a celebration to welcome you back."

"They will have to celebrate without me."

Dawn got up, wrapped up in a sheet and stood in the doorway to the bedroom. "Good morning, Charlie."

Charles' face turned red. He looked stricken. "Oh, I didn't realize you was here. I apologize for horning in like this." He picked up his hat. "I'll

619

be running along. I just dropped by to see how Darrell is doing. I'll bring you out some coffee and grub. I know you can't be seen in town yet, not 'till your neck heals. I'm curious as to how a man can hang and not break his neck, though it appears you choked some." He headed for the door. "I'll be back later, if you don't mind."

"You're welcome here anytime. I appreciate your bringing me my badge. I'm here if you need me."

"That sure is a relief to me."

Darrell closed the door, and felt Dawn arms circle him from behind. He turned around and she took his hand, dragging him back to bed. "It's too early to get up."

"I expect Mac will turn up at my door next. I think we had better get dressed."

"And do what?"

"Sit around and starve?"

"I'll go to the trading post today and get everything we need. We could use some new dishes."

"Are you planning to move in? You wanted to once. I think we had better make it legal before Mac shoots me."

"We can think about it later. Come back to bed. I want to hold you. I know you're safe when you're in my arms."

She dropped the sheet, Darrell pulled off his pants, and they went back to bed where they became twined together again. "Now I feel safe," she said.

"It's too early to go out there, Richard. Give them time to get up. They were both worn out."

"I don't think they will get their strength back lying in bed. They need these groceries, besides I plan to leave for New Mexico in the morning. Henry wants them to come with me. I don't have time to wait around. Henry's getting weaker. We have some important legal business to take care of."

"If you'll wait around for a while, they will come to you, and don't you dare find fault. Leave them alone."

Mac was careful to hold his tongue when Darrell and Dawn showed up around noon. He had to admit they looked more rested.

"You're just in time for dinner. Go on in the dining room. Debbie was expecting you. She set you a place. What have you had to eat today?"

"Nothing," Dawn said.

"Charlie Morgan paid us a visit this morning. He brought me my badge. He's coming back with some grub later."

"I was about to go out there myself with groceries. I know you can't go shopping. Somebody is bound to notice your neck. If that happens you'll wind up right back at Fort Daily in a cage. Debbie suggested that you wear a scarf to hide your neck injury. We can't take any chances on the train either."

Mac realized how they had all been profoundly affected by Darrell's narrow escape with his life and had taken upon themselves to look after him. No one must ever cause him to suffer again.

Darrell appeared indifferent on the surface, as was his nature. However, he was aware of their sharing his burden and was deeply touched.

"My coat hides it when I turn the collar up, and it's cold enough for me to wear one."

"If it makes you nervous, you don't have to go."

"I owe Henry McCloud my life. I think saving me must have become an obsession with him."

"He has been obsessed with success all his life, and he considers you as an important asset in his determination to give Dawn the keys to his kingdom. If you've made up your mind, then you may as well get packed."

"Most of my clothes are back at the jail. I was staying there to be close to work in case of trouble."

"I'll go get your clothes. If you will make me a list, I'll pick up the things you need at the trading post. I have to talk to Zeek. Looks like he'll be taking over until I get back, and I don't know how soon that will be."

When bedtime came, Mac held his tongue when Dawn took Darrell's hand and pulled him toward her bedroom. She was content to have him lie on top of the covers with his clothes on, just as long as he was near enough for her to touch. He laid his head on her pillow and she put her face close to his, her hand caressing his injured neck. The door was left open.

Mac and Debbie looked in later and found them sleeping peacefully. "Now wasn't that easy, Richard. You didn't have to make a fuss. I told you Darrell would remain a gentleman."

"I should listen to you more. I wouldn't make near as many mistakes."

Their journey to New Mexico was uneventful. Since Dawn would draw attention to Darrell, Debbie loaned her one of her bonnets that tied beneath her chin. It helped hide her face. Darrell wore his coat, and added a scarf to cover his neck. Mac was a nervous wreck by the time they reached their destination. Darrell had his Marshal's badge in his saddle bag; however, he wore his gun. Mac knew he wouldn't hesitate to use it if it became necessary. But if he wore his badge he might as well wave a red flag.

Henry was overjoyed by their visit. He shook both Mac's and Darrell's hand. From Dawn, he got a kiss. "I'm glad Rush and that hangman had enough initiative to rig that rope and knot so it didn't break your neck, but it sure did do some harm. It will leave a thin scar since it was the cord and not the rope that did the damage. It will never be noticed unless somebody is looking close for it. When the bruises clear up, you can go about your usual business."

"I owe you my life, Mr. McCloud. I don't have the words to thank you. I hope I can prove worthy of your faith in me."

"I have all the faith in the world in Chris Roman, and no matter what you choose to call yourself, you are Chris Roman, and don't you change one iota. I'm leaving my ranch and all I own to Richard and Dawn as joint beneficiaries in case Mac changes his mind or dies. She can never own land, as you know. We discussed all that when you were here the first time. I know Richard doesn't want nor need anything from me, but he was understanding enough to make things safe for Dawn. And now it's up to you, Chris. You can own land, and you'll have to take care of it for Dawn if Richard decides to sign over his holdings to her. If not, when he dies his widow will have the right to an interest, if that's the way Mac wants it. There is one stipulation though."

"What's that?"

"You will have to be married to Dawn. As her husband you will handle the reins. What do you say? I have the papers all in order. If what I'm doing meets with your approval I'll sign them, and my attorney will see to the filing. What about you, Roman? Do you agree?"

"Dawn and I plan to be married, irregardless of any plans you may have made. I will do whatever she asks as long as it's in her best interest and makes her happy. I can and will take care of her without any outside help or interference. I personally have no material interest in your estate, Mr. McCloud. Dawn will either accept it or she will not. What ever she chooses to do, I will respect her wishes."

Henry smiled. "According to your theory, as I recall, I have planned and worked all my life and wound up with nothing. And in the end, the shedding of tears. I assume that you were referring to this last stage of my life as the time for tears. Am I right?"

Henry had gotten Mac's attention, and he waited for Darrell's response with much interest.

"You have had the full use and benefit of power and success, and you certainly deserved it. In the final analysis it evaporates like dew on a mid-summer's morning. So much time, careful planning, and sweat, and if you don't give it away, it will be taken away, and that's not much to look forward to. But dying, like birth, is part of God's plan, and we are helpless to change the order of things. In the end, God takes it all back. We never own anything, we only use it. Death has no happy endings. You're a poor man, Mr. McCloud. Every thing belongs to God, and we can't lease to own. What good are riches when we are all headed for the same judgment? We all live to die. And you can't bribe God with what already belongs to him."

"You have a cryptic point of view, Chris. But we must live our lives as best we can."

"That's true. In fact, I'm already dead, and what I had, I lost. Even my name is history."

"You're grieving over Chris Roman."

"That I am. Not many men live to walk across their own grave."

"I'm sorry to hear that, but you're an honest man to have admitted it. If I had more time, Chris, I swear I would have that judgment reversed.

I feel that my life has been worth something, though I'm now a poor man. I feel rich when I look at you. I see the rewards brought by my power and wealth. But you're right. I'm losing it all. Maybe Richard can take up your fight after I'm gone. I will leave him my tools." He looked at Mac, searching his face. "Promise me that you will do your best to right this terrible injustice that's been done to Chris."

"Officially Lieutenant Colonel Chris Roman is dead. Why would they bother to reverse the judgment?"

"It's always after a man's death that the leaders of this country seem to want to clear a hero's name. Once he's cleared he can come out of hiding."

"I'll do my best," Mac replied.

"I have asked you this before, but it was before Chris Roman was dead and buried. What is it you want out of life now?"

"The answer is basically the same; to have the love of a good woman, to live comfortably, and go to my grave with a clear conscience."

"Then you have no objections to my final plans?"

"If there are any objections, then Dawn will be the one to make them."

"Then it's settled?" Henry said.

"As far as I'm concerned, it is," Mac agreed.

"What about you, Roman. Do you agree?"

"If that's what Dawn wants. I leave it up to her."

She had been holding his hand, and she squeezed it. "I want you to take care of me for the rest of my life."

"Then we're all in agreement," Henry said. He rang a bell and Princess Lake came into the room. "Tell Pine to fetch my lawyer, and be quick about it. And tell him I want a preacher out here before sundown. I intend to see these two young people tie the knot before I die."

"That kind of knot I can live with," Darrell said, absently rubbing at his neck. "This is about to become the happiest day of my life."

"And mine," Dawn said, throwing her arms around him.

"It's too bad Debbie has to miss the wedding, but she'll understand." Mac said.

Princess took charge of all the preparations. And for the first time since their arrival, the ugly woman actually had a smile on her face, and she became pleasant to look at. She even helped Dawn dress for her wedding, taking up the hairbrush to brush her long black hair.

Darrell was decidedly nervous. He had wanted Dawn from the moment he saw her, and that dream was about to become reality. He thought about his uniform as he dressed in jeans and a white shirt. He should be having a military wedding with all the honors. He had planned his future that way. He had little to offer his bride except for his love and devotion. She should have been the wife of an officer, a man she could be proud of; however, she had accepted his proposal knowing he could never be Lieutenant Colonel Chris Roman again. The thought grieved him.

When the Reverend Armstrong arrived, Darrell went downstairs to meet him. He was short and bald with a fat face. Judging from his expression, Darrell knew he enjoyed his work and considered Darrell to be a fortunate man. Darrell was anxious to have the ceremony over with, take his bride and search for some privacy. What he was feeling at the moment was sensuous and demanding. He longed to lock the world outside their bedroom door and throw the key away.

They would be married in Henry's magnificent library. Princess Lake cradled Henry in her arms and carried him to the couch and made him as comfortable as possible with the aid of several feather pillows. One wall was lined with shelves from floor to ceiling, and contained hundreds of books and maps. Darrell took the time to glance at some of the titles, impressed by Henry's collection. Henry watched him proudly. "I see you're a man who appreciates literature."

"Without the works of great writers, we would lose sight of history and silence the mind's of great philosophers. I noticed you have the translation of the Dialogues of Plato."

"Have you read them?"

"Yes, but I must disagree with Socrates argument concerning the soul's immortality."

"I collect more books than I read. Most of them are over my head."

"That's what makes life interesting, as are the Meditations of Marcus Aurslius. I have come to understand the hope of my own destiny. Before my release from Chris Roman, I had no future. I had to die before I could live."

"Do you read the Bible, Chris?"

"The Bible is nothing more than a collection of history. It is, in part, written in circles and riddles. Not meant to be understood or it would have been written calling an eye an eye. Great scholars have yet to figure it out. That the world is evil is a fact, and there is no way to correct the ever gaining problems of mankind, who move forward without caution, marching toward their inevitable collision with death, for life opposes us no matter which way we turn."

Henry was staring at Chris. "You really amaze me. I've never met a man like you. You can be very misleading in character."

"I actually died, Mr. McCloud. I don't like it. I miss all the things I stood for as Lieutenant Colonel Chris Roman."

"Will you be content as Darrell Holliman?"

"No, but it's something I must learn to live with. I have the woman I love, and I'm content with that phase of my life. Had I lost her, I might have turned into a drunk or some other worthless shred of humanity. Dawn's my life, my reason for existing, no matter what I call myself. But I will always be Chris Roman. Nothing will ever change that fact."

Dawn and Darrell repeated their vows with sincerity and tears in their eyes. The events that had finally led them to this conclusion were astronomical. Darrell had risen from the dead to claim the woman he loved, a woman who had fought her way back to reality and the man she had loved from the beginning. Chris Roman filled her heart with love, joy, and promise. And according to God's holy ordinance, they were now one flesh.

Mac's eyes were moist when he hugged his daughter and shook Darrell's hand. "I don't have to ask you to take care of my daughter. I know you will, as you have in the past. Welcome to the McCloud family. I couldn't be more pleased."

"I don't have much to offer my wife. I'm a poor man."

"You're all she wants."

Dawn held on to her new husband's arm, looking up at him with love and desire dancing in her dark eyes. "I will be very happy living in your little house, and so will baby Henry."

"I think you two should live in the house I built for Dawn."

"That's Debbie's house, and yours. I don't belong there anymore. I belong with my husband, wherever he chooses."

Darrell swooped his bride into his arms and carried her up the stairs to their bedroom.

Mac watched them go with an audible sigh of relief. "You can't imagine what a load this marriage has lifted from my shoulders. They've been acting married for a year."

"Well, it's all legal now, so stop fretting, Richard. When did their moral breakdown start?' Henry asked.

"Last Indian Summer."

"Then they couldn't help themselves. Haven't you heard that Indian Summer is a time of magic spells? A special god is smiling down on young lovers and they can't contain their passion."

"No, I never heard that."

"If you don't believe me, look at all that's happened. They fell in love last Indian Summer. Roman cheated the hangman, now they're married, and it all happened within the short span of this Indian Summer."

"I hadn't given that any thought, much less credit, but you may be right. I think you and I need one more drink to celebrate." Henry waved to Princess and she filled their glasses.

"Why don't you have a drink with us, Princess?" Henry said. Her smile broadened. She filled another glass and sat down to sip with them.

Upstairs, Dawn was safe and secure, wrapped in her husband's loving arms.

"Forever, my love," he whispered.

"I love you too," she whispered back, and threw one slender, beautiful leg across his middle.

He sighed contentedly.

The End

Or is it?

Printed in the USA
CPSIA information can be obtained
at www.ICGtesting.com
LVHW091237051023
760079LV00006B/741